The Last Days of Mankind

The Last Days of Mankind

KARL KRAUS

THE COMPLETE TEXT

TRANSLATED BY FRED BRIDGHAM AND EDWARD TIMMS

WITH A GLOSSARY AND INDEX

Yale UNIVERSITY PRESS NEW HAVEN AND LONDON

A MARGELLOS
WORLD REPUBLIC OF LETTERS BOOK

The Margellos World Republic of Letters is dedicated to making literary works from around the globe available in English through translation. It brings to the English-speaking world the work of leading poets, novelists, essayists, philosophers, and playwrights from Europe, Latin America, Africa, Asia, and the Middle East to stimulate international discourse and creative exchange.

The translation of this book was supported by the Austrian Federal Chancellery—Division for the Arts.

Yale University Press books may be purchased in quantity for educational, business, or promotional use. For information, please e-mail sales.press@yale.edu (U.S. office) or sales@yaleup.co.uk (U.K. office).

Set in Electra type by Tseng Information Systems, Inc. Printed in the United States of America.

Frontispiece: The execution of Cesare Battisti, 12 July 1916

Library of Congress Control Number: 2015939015
ISBN 978-0-300-20767-5 (cloth : alk. paper)
ISBN 978-0-300-27117-1 (paperback)

A catalogue record for this book is available from the British Library.

10 9 8 7 6 5 4 3 2 1

CONTENTS

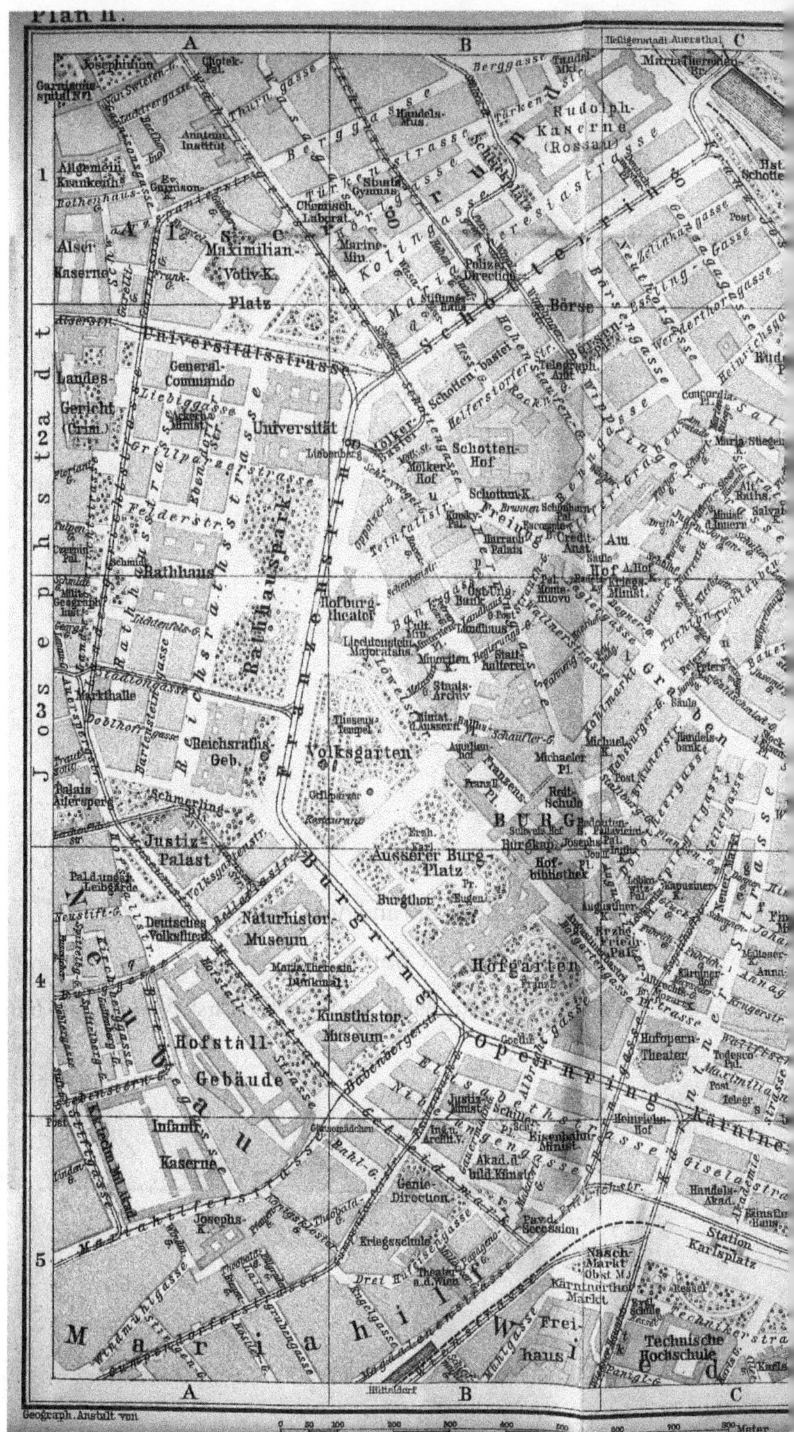

Plan of Vienna City Centre, 1905

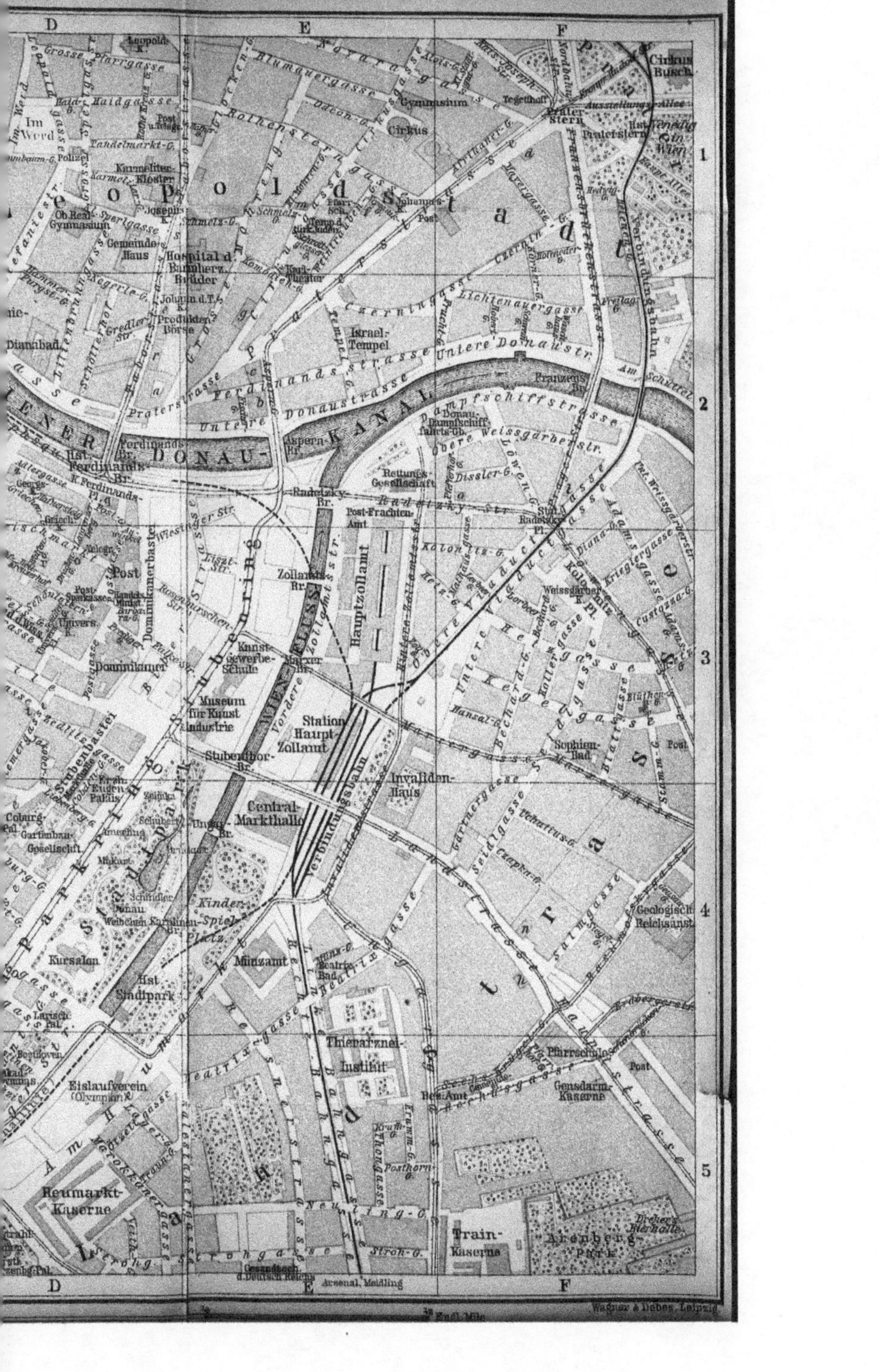

D
E
F
1
2
3
4
5
Leopold-K.
Grosse Pfarrgasse
Haidgasse
Im Werd
Tandelmarkt-G.
Polizei
Karmeliter-Kloster
Ob. Real-Gymnasium
Gemeinde-Haus
Hospital d. Barmherz. Brüder
Produkten Börse
Dianabad
Blumauergasse
Rothensterngasse
Gymnasium
Cirkus
Tegetthoff
Prater Stern
Praterstern
Cirkus Busch
Ausstellungs-Allee
Venedig in Wien
Czerningasse
Lichtenauergasse
Israel. Tempel
Ferdinandsstrasse
Untere Donaustr.
Praterstrasse
Franzens Br.
Dampfschiffstrasse
Untere Donaustrasse
Donau-Kanal
Aspern-Br.
Ferdinands-Br.
Obere Weissgärberstr.
Dissler-G.
Rettungs-Gesellschaft
Radetzky-Br.
Radetzky-Str.
Post-Frachten-Amt
Kolonitz-G.
Zollamts-Br.
Hauptzollamt
Dominikanerbastei
Post
Rosenbursengasse
Univers.
Dominikaner
Kunst-gewerbe-Schule
Museum für Kunst und Industrie
Station Haupt-Zollamt
Stubenbastei
Stubenthor-Br.
Invaliden-Haus
Central-Markthalle
Verbindungsbahn
Weissgärber K.
Kriegergasse
Custozza-G.
Sophien-Bad
Post
Coburg-Pal.
Gartenbau-Gesellschft.
Stadtpark
Kursalon
Hst. Stadtpark
Münzamt
Beatrix-Bad
Beatrixgasse
Geologisch. Reichsanst.
Salmgasse
Landstrasse
Thierarznei-Institut
Pfarrschule
Gensdarm.-Kaserne
Post
Eislaufverein (Olympion)
Heumarkt-Kaserne
Am Heumarkt
Neulinggasse
Strohgasse
Train-Kaserne
Arenberg-Park
Dreher's Bierhalle
Arsenal, Meidling
Wagner & Debes, Leipzig

INTRODUCTION: FALSEHOOD IN WARTIME

Edward Timms and *Fred Bridgham*

The early twentieth century was the great age of the newspaper press, as mass literacy endowed the printed word with unprecedented power. Newspaper production was revolutionized by rotary presses and linotype compositing machines, while modern roads and railways, together with the telephone, telegraph, and teleprinter, were transforming communications. In Western Europe and North America democratic institutions, social reforms, and scientific discoveries seemed to be laying the foundations for a new era in the history of mankind. But it was also a period of intense imperial rivalries, backed by highly trained forces and sophisticated armaments industries. Given the precarious international situation, it was possible at moments of crisis for journalists to tip the balance between peace and war. Liberal papers such as the *Manchester Guardian* (edited by C. P. Scott) and the *New York Times* (under Adolph Ochs) may have been committed to the peaceful resolution of conflicts, but wars were good for newspaper sales. Moreover, wealthy proprietors like Hearst and Northcliffe, Hugenberg and Benedikt, were imperialists capable of pressurizing governments into declarations of war.

Almost alone in the period before the First World War, the Viennese satirist Karl Kraus saw the press as an apocalyptic threat. In his magazine *Die Fackel* (The Torch), founded in April 1899, he would reprint prize examples of newspaper propaganda and expose their falsification of reality.[1] His witty diatribes attracted a large readership, and with a print run of over 10,000 copies the magazine proved viable without having to rely on commercial advertising. To protect his independence Kraus created his own imprint, Verlag Die Fackel, which published book editions of his writings.

Where the editorials of the leading Austrian daily, the *Neue Freie Presse*, were celebrating the advances of German culture and the triumphs of European civilization, Kraus would expose the realities of conflict and suffering. He had a gift for dissecting the cliché-ridden language of his contemporaries. Sonorous metaphors like "standing shoulder to shoulder" evolved into satirical leitmotifs, culminating in his indictment of the anachronistic ideals that sustained the Central Powers during the First World War. His own style, by contrast, was enlivened by an aphoristic wit and moral fervour that left his readers uncertain whether to laugh or cry.

The apocalyptic tone of Kraus's bleakest visions appeared to leave little hope for mankind. Borrowing from the Bible in a prophetic essay entitled "Apocalypse", published in October 1908, he identified Kaiser Wilhelm II as an "apocalyptic horseman" with the power to destroy the peace of the earth.[2] Moreover, the dangers arising from autocratic power were intensified by a technology that was running out of control: "ultimately, mankind lies dead beside the machines it has created, incapable of putting them to constructive use because so much intelligence has been expended on inventing them" (F 261–62, 1–5). This foreshadows the critique of mechanized warfare in *Die Fackel* of 1914–18, but it would be wrong to see Kraus's satire as exclusively negative. It drew on a conception of human dignity shaped by the moral vision of Kant and the cultural ideals of Goethe. The satire of *Die Fackel*, which Kraus wrote single-handed from 1912 onwards, combined analyses of impending disaster with the advocacy of a better world.

Kraus was born on 28 April 1874 as the son of a prosperous Jewish paper manufacturer. Growing up in Vienna, he had to contend with the pressures of a deeply conservative and stridently anti-Semitic environment. A recent study by Paul Reitter has identified undertones of Jewish self-hatred in Kraus's "anti-journalism."[3] His writings are certainly shaped by the impulse to construct an identity free of allegedly negative "Jewish" characteristics, but this is by no means the whole story. A further apparent constraint arises from the fact that Kraus's satire is basically a collage of quotations, framed by his own ironic commentaries. This means that much of *Die Fackel* consists of reports clipped and reprinted from the newspapers of his day. This quotation technique gives his writings their historical density, but it would be wrong to see them as parochial. His satire certainly emerged from a specifically Austrian Jewish milieu, but—like the work of Freud and Herzl, Mahler and Wittgenstein—it has far-reaching implications.

How Is the World Governed and Made to Fight Wars?

During the years 1908–14 Kraus's critique of the press acquired a new urgency as he highlighted the threat of war. The Austrian annexation of Bosnia-Herzegovina precipitated a crisis in the Balkans, provoking a fierce reaction in the Serbian capital, Belgrade. By March 1909 the Austro-Hungarian army was poised to invade Serbia, hoping by this means to crush the political aspirations of the South Slavs within the borders of the Habsburg Empire. However, the government needed to find a moral justification for war and thus to ensure that the conflict remained localized. The Austrian Foreign Ministry accordingly orchestrated an anti-Serbian campaign, finding a willing ally in the patriotic historian Heinrich Friedjung. On 25 March 1909 the *Neue Freie Presse* published an article by Friedjung which purported to justify military action. Drawing on documents supplied to him by the Foreign Ministry, he accused members of the Croatian Diet (the administration of one of the Hapsburg provinces) of a treasonable conspiracy with the government in Belgrade.

This article was intended as a fanfare for war, but at the last moment, under pressure from Russia, the government of Serbia backed down. The threat of war receded, and in place of the intended humiliation of Serbia it was Austrian foreign policy that was put on trial. Members of the Croatian Diet brought a libel action against Friedjung, which Kraus regarded as so important that he attended in person. The trial, which lasted fourteen days, was fulsomely reported in the *Neue Freie Presse*. It began with patriotic bluster as Friedjung produced copies of his documents, which identified the alleged conspirators by name. One of those named, Bozo Markovitch, a university professor in Belgrade, was surprised to discover from reports of the trial that he had held secret meetings with the Croatian conspirators and induced them to accept treasonable payments. Risking arrest, Markovitch travelled to Vienna to testify that at the time of the alleged meetings in Belgrade he had actually been in Berlin, attending lectures on jurisprudence. This testimony was greeted by judge and jury with incredulity—until the Prussian police, famous for their meticulous record keeping, confirmed that Markovitch had indeed been in Berlin at the time of the alleged conspiracy. The documents were exposed as forgeries and Friedjung was humiliated.

Kraus responded with a trenchant analysis of the Friedjung trial, exposing the irresponsibility of the Foreign Ministry and the susceptibility of public opinion. "In a deluded world", he wrote, "Austria is the last to lose its credulity. It is the most willing victim of publicity in that it not only believes what it sees in print, but also believes the opposite, if it sees that in print too" (F 293, 1). The case provided him with a model of political mystification, showing that the patriotic fervour whipped up by the press by no means lost its hold when its fraudulence was exposed. In other contexts Kraus may understate the role of governments as instigators of political mystification, treating the press in isolation, as if it were an independent force for evil. Here he does justice to all the main factors: the government as instigator, the press as its willing agency, the collusion of intellectuals, the gullibility of readers, and the impact of jingoistic slogans. He makes the probable consequences equally clear: a war in which thousands of lives will be lost.

Kraus's article has a paradigmatic value with applications for our own day. In 1909, when Friedjung claimed that Austria was "in danger", citing forged documents in an attempt to stage a war, his lies were exposed in court. Sadly, the political lesson was not learnt, and the warmongers ultimately had their way. Moreover Kraus's analysis has a prophetic resonance. Almost a hundred years later, the evidence used to justify the invasion of Iraq in 2003 proved to be just as flawed as that cited by Friedjung. The photographs of Iraqi bases allegedly equipped with weapons of mass destruction, displayed by the U.S. Secretary of State at the United Nations in order to win support for the invasion, owed more to slick public relations than to reliable intelligence. It was now America that was "in danger" and Britain that was standing "shoulder to shoulder" with the dominant military power.

Far from resolving the Balkan crisis, the Austrian annexation of Bosnia was followed by a series of further conflicts, accompanied by equally irresponsible press coverage. Through a close focus on journalistic style, Kraus showed that the language of politics had lost its clarity and flexibility, becoming overloaded with anachronistic metaphors. Hence the increasingly prophetic tone of his critique of Austrian affairs: "On occasion", he wrote in December 1912, "an operetta culture will start parading its enthusiasm for war. Its mercenaries are writers. Totally irresponsible types, who launch a première one day and a war the next" (F 363–65, 71). The example Kraus cites on the following page highlights the irresponsibility of cartoonists, notably Fritz Schönpflug, co-founder of the humorous weekly *Die Muskete* (The Musket). Schönpflug was famous for his facetious images of the Austro-Hungarian army, such as his drawing of General Staff officers from the Autumn Manoeuvres (Herbstmanöver) series, reproduced here.

Even the adjutants of the portly army commander are equipped with anachronistic sabres and implausibly elegant uniforms, as if they were characters from an operetta. Austrian officers were permitted to wear this paraphernalia when off-duty, and the Schönpflug drawing cited by Kraus in December 1912 portrays them in an urban context: on the Ringstrasse in Vienna. Pleasure-seeking officers are planning a supper party with their friends at a favourite Viennese restaurant. The jocular dialogue with which Schönpflug embellishes his design reveals that it is actually a disguised advertisement—for the Hopfner restaurant chain. These casual exchanges may sound harmless, but for the satirist they epitomize the mindless hedonism of Austrian public life under the shadow of war. Hence the paradox with which his commentary concludes: "An advert for a restaurant? No, a report from the battlefront!" (F 363–65, 72).

In the following issue, still echoing with the threat of war, Kraus laments

Drawing of General Staff officers from the Autumn Manoeuvres (Herbstmanöver) series

that Austrian affairs now resemble a botched Schönpflug drawing (F 366–67, 13). He treats the cartoons as a prism through which the tensions destabilizing the Habsburg Empire can be seen in lurid colours. To understand this reaction we need to take account of the cultural politics of the period. Schönpflug and his fellow cartoonists did not merely create figures of fun to distract their readers from an impending crisis. During the years 1908–14 *Die Muskete* contributed to international tensions by repeatedly publishing xenophobic caricatures of Austria's potential adversaries, especially the political and military leadership of Serbia. Set against patriotic images of the Austrian armed forces would be caricatures of conniving and despicable Serbs. Thus on 15 April 1909, after the government in Belgrade was compelled to accept the annexation of Bosnia-Herzegovina, Schönpflug's cover design for *Die Muskete*, ironically entitled "Peace!", portrayed a humiliated Serbia being comforted by Britain and Russia. The Serbs, the cartoon implies, are still hoping for a war against Austria. Hence the caption: "Something postponed may still be condoned."

Historically even more significant was Schönpflug's cover design for the issue of *Die Muskete* published on 16 July 1914, shortly after the assassination of Archduke Franz Ferdinand, when the peace of Europe hung in the balance. Under the title "Sarajevo" the cartoon depicts the smirking figures of King Peter of Serbia and Tsar Nicholas of Russia self-righteously washing their hands—in a bowl of blood! The King of Montenegro can be seen gloating in the background. Like Friedjung's forged documents, this inflammatory cartoon seems designed to criminalize Austria's adversaries, providing a pretext for launching a war against Serbia and its allies.

Such cartoons, backed by cynical official communiqués and tendentious editorials, shaped a public response to the assassination of the Archduke that filled Kraus with foreboding. In *Die Fackel* of 10 July 1914 he compiled a panorama of press clippings to portray an irredeemably dysfunctional society. The prime minister, nominally in charge of national policy, is observed relaxing with members of the cabinet in the Café Pucher, while nightclubs continue to churn out popular entertainment as if no catastrophe has occurred. *Die Muskete* is again identified as a symptom of Austrian decay—through its blurring of the boundaries between military professionalism and journalistic frivolity (serving officers are writing for the magazine under pseudonyms). This endemic confusion of spheres provokes apocalyptic conclusions. Austria, Kraus warns while paying tribute to Franz Ferdinand, is an "experimental station for the destruction of the world" (F 400–403, 2). The publication of this article was followed three weeks later by the declaration of war on Serbia.

During the First World War, despite the constraints of censorship, Kraus was able to publish 19 substantial issues of *Die Fackel.* His was virtually the only journal in any of the belligerent nations to adopt a critical view of the war from the start and sustain it with increasing vehemence until the bitter end. In 1911 he had been received into the Catholic Church, and his opposition to war was nourished by an underlying religiosity. Resisting the politically orchestrated euphoria that swept through Europe, he launched his antiwar campaign in November 1914 by reading in public a critique entitled "In dieser großen Zeit" (In This Age of Grandeur).[4]

Despite the censorship, Kraus succeeded in publishing "In dieser großen Zeit" the following month. His argument deconstructs the idea that the World War has ushered in a heroic era, as proclaimed by the propaganda apparatus set up in every belligerent country. The telegram, Kraus observes in this critique, is "an instrument of war like the grenade" (F 404, 12). In order to make the thousands of casualties acceptable, the public was saturated with poems and articles celebrating the ethical value of war and the glory of laying down your life for your country. When Kraus argued that people's minds had been numbed by clichés, he had one slogan especially in mind: "dying a hero's death." Through decades of practice, he argued, "the newspaper reporter has so impoverished our imagination that it becomes possible to fight a war of annihilation against ourselves." A more truthful use of language would reveal the "hero's death as cruel destiny" (F 404, 9–10). During the years 1915–18 he intensified his campaign against the insanity of modern warfare, publishing incisive articles, pithy aphorisms, and plangent poems. Being exempt from army service (due to curvature of the spine), he frequently travelled from his home in Vienna to Berlin and other cities to give further readings criticizing the war. His subversive satire led him to be denounced to the authorities as a traitor.

"When war is declared, Truth is the first casualty", according to the motto chosen by Arthur Ponsonby in 1928 for his book *Falsehood in War-Time.*[5] Kraus had arrived at this insight twenty years earlier. His targets, from the very first number of *Die Fackel,* were "Phrasen" (clichés and slogans) and "Lügen" (deceptions and lies). His analysis of patriotic propaganda acquired an even sharper edge in autumn 1915 when he wrote: "How is the world governed and made to fight wars? Diplomats tell lies to journalists and believe them when they see them in print" (F 406–12, 106). This introduced a subtle conception of media-induced false memory: the hypnotic power of repetition leads politicians to believe the falsehoods they have themselves put into circulation. The result was a self-generating system of mendacity with disastrous consequences for the future of mankind.

The Last Days of Mankind

Kraus's most effective technique was to reprint propagandistic statements from the press, highlighting their fatuousness and barbarity. A similar documentary method is deployed with even greater versatility in his masterpiece, *The Last Days of Mankind*, conceived in the summer of 1915 and largely composed during the war. In this grandiose satirical panorama journalists and military commanders, politicians and profiteers, are re-created as dramatic characters, mouthing the dehumanizing slogans of the day. The claim that Germany and Austria have "drawn the sword" is ridiculed as a prime example of the way newspaper language disguises the horrors of a war that in reality involves trenches, shrapnel, and poison gas. Kraus's play, which could not be published until after the collapse of the Central Powers, concludes with an apocalyptic vision of the destruction of the earth.

Publication began immediately after the lifting of censorship. The first edition, enhanced by a number of photographs, filled four special issues of *Die Fackel*, dated November 1918 and April, June, and August 1919. This was followed in 1922 by the expanded book edition, framed by two even more expressive photographs, which also accompany our translation. These photos have both documentary and symbolic value. The frontispiece, which records the scene after the Italian dissident Cesare Battisti was hanged as a traitor by the Austrian authorities, was circulated as a warning against disloyalty to the Habsburg crown. For Kraus, who highlights the complicity between cruelty and the camera, this epitomizes the sadistic attitude towards persecuted minorities.

The subject of Kraus's play is the tragedy of mankind, bent on self-destruction by the methods of modern warfare, while still clinging to outdated ideals of military heroism and national glory. Interwoven with the cataclysmic action are a multitude of satirical strands, each embedded in its cultural matrix: bungled Austrian diplomacy, aggressive German expansionism, brutal military leadership, the greed of war profiteers, the complicity of international big business, the injustices of martial law, the gullibility of newspaper readers, and above all the sloganizing of the press. The cult of war as an "age of grandeur" is satirized in scene after scene, following the approach defined in the Preface: "The document takes human shape; reports come alive as characters and characters expire as editorials; the newspaper column has acquired a mouth that spouts monologues."

There are numerous scenes that reproduce—as dramatic monologue or tragicomic dialogue—the purple prose that some fanatical patriot or propagandist has perpetrated during the war. Political speeches, military bulletins, newspaper editorials, commercial adverts, interviews with public figures, snippets from the gossip columns, chauvinistic sermons, and patriotic songs—the range of sources is remarkable. But this documentary technique is enlivened by an irrepressible satirical imagination. The Preface may suggest that the "most improbable conversations conducted here were spoken word for word; the most lurid fantasies are quotations." But the impact is intensified by scenes that blend documentary transcription with comic invention, punctuated by satirical verse. The play concludes with visionary images projected in cinematic style, followed by a verse Epilogue entitled *Die letzte Nacht* (The Final Night).

This mixing of modes is evident from the Prologue, set in June 1914 as news of the assassination of Archduke Franz Ferdinand in Sarajevo hits the streets of Vienna. Almost the first figures we encounter are a group of officers on the Ringstrasse planning a supper party at their favourite restaurant—they decide on Hopfner's. "D'ya see the latest Schönpflug cartoon?" one of them asks. The underlying irony is that these officers, who reappear in the opening scene of each Act, are themselves modeled on Schönpflug cartoon characters, reshaped in accordance with the "restaurant/battlefront" paradox formulated by Kraus in December 1912. Their fatuous exchanges now hint at something far more sinister. The Schönpflug drawing they admire might well be that venomous cartoon portraying King Peter of Serbia and Tsar Nicholas of Russia as blood-stained criminals. It is left to our imagination whether the officers are chuckling about that prototype of visual hate speech or some harmless humoresque.

Trivial local responses to cataclysmic events generate a pervasive black humour. As the scene shifts to the Café Pucher, the prime minister, while preparing to issue a communiqué, asks the waiter for a humorous magazine—not *Die Muskete* but *Die Bombe*! The tragedy of mankind is indeed being played out by "operetta figures" (as the Preface suggests). Kraus shows an exceptional ear for the rhythms of Austrian vernacular, interspersed with patriotic rant and journalistic verbiage. Each of the five Acts opens in similar style, with crowds convulsed by the cries of news vendors announcing the latest sensation: the euphoria in August 1914 after the ultimatum to Serbia has precipitated world war (Act I); reactions after the Italian declaration of war on Austria in May 1915 (Act II); the Romanian declaration of war on the Central Powers in July 1916 (Act III); and the ultimatum by President Wilson leading to the American entry into the war in April 1917 (Act IV). Within this framework the handling of chronology is flexible (there are already references to Italian treachery in Act I). For Kraus, as he observed in 1917, operates "not with mathematical but with apocalyptic precision" (F 462-71, 171).

The fluctuating fortunes of war on the Southern and Eastern Fronts are most vividly reflected in Act V. Gloating over the rout of Italian forces at Caporetto in autumn 1917 followed by the capitulation of Soviet Russia at Brest-Litovsk, an Austrian parliamentarian declares: "We are the victors, and we demand the spoils" (V, 3). Attitudes in Berlin are even more euphoric as Pan-Germans demand vast territorial annexations at a mass rally (V, 7). But growing pessimism on the streets of Vienna is reflected in rumours that a desperately weakened Austria-Hungary may be seeking a separate peace (V, 17). Finally, the collapse of the Central Powers in October 1918 is dramatized by a grandiose drunken banqueting scene at army headquarters (V, 55).

Kraus's underlying humanism is reflected in the prominence given to the word "Menschheit" ("mankind" or "humanity"), both in the title and in the dramatic chorus, the scenes in which a naively patriotic Optimist discusses the war with the Grumbler, Kraus's raisonneur. One of their most striking dialogues, which deals with attempts to legitimize air raids that kill civilians, offers a further instructive parallel between then and now. Although the aerial destruction of urban areas was a rare occurrence when Kraus wrote this play, his analysis has proved paradigmatic. Experience, the Grumbler observes, should have taught the perpetrators of "murder from the air" that "when they intend to hit an arms dump they infallibly hit a bedroom, and instead of an armaments factory a school for girls." When the Optimist objects that this is not "deliberate", the Grumbler replies: "No, worse than that: fortuitous!" (I, 29). They can't help it happening, so they express regret and do it again.

This analysis has a prophetic ring. On 30 July 2014, at the height of the Israeli-Gaza conflict, the Jabaliya School for Girls was hit by shells that killed refugees sheltering inside. The justification offered by the Israeli Defence Force was that militants had fired mortars earlier that day "from the vicinity of the school."[6] Clearly, the issues raised by *The Last Days of Mankind* are with us still. Since Kraus's day there has been an exponential increase in the bombing of urban areas and the casuistry used to justify it. The truth identified by the phrase "murder from the air" is now shrouded in euphemisms like "collateral damage." But even Kraus never imagined a global conflict in which democratically elected governments would *intentionally* bomb civilian targets like Dresden and Nagasaki, incinerating hundreds of thousands of defenceless people. British politicians of the Second World War spoke of "obliteration bombing" as they set about the task of destroying Germany "city by city", a policy condemned by one of Winston Churchill's most principled critics, Bishop George Bell.[7]

In defending the cause of humanity, Kraus was repudiating nationalistic loyalties and aligning himself with the moral philosophy of the Enlightenment. The overwhelming majority of his countrymen, not least the German-speaking

Jews, identified themselves with the Habsburg Monarchy and the German Reich. Leading authors like Richard Dehmel and Hugo von Hofmannsthal eloquently endorsed the German and Austrian cause, but Kraus took a very different line. If patriotism meant supporting the use of poison gas, and if it was treason to repudiate victories gained by this means, then he declared himself to be "one of the greatest traitors of all times" (F 474–83, 43). As his opposition to the war became increasingly vocal, Kraus was denounced as "the leader of defeatism in Austria" (F 501–7, 91).

During one of his wartime public readings in Berlin, Kraus contrasted the fanaticism of Kaiser Wilhelm II with the idealism of Immanuel Kant (F 474–83, 155–56). While German nationalists associated the Categorical Imperative with patriotic duty, the satirist endorsed the programme of international reconciliation set out in Kant's essay "On Perpetual Peace." Kant recognized the importance of creating new international institutions. In "Perpetual Peace" he associated war with the state of nature "where no court of justice is available to judge with legal authority." After arguing for a republican constitution guaranteeing equality for all citizens, he suggested that peace could be secured by "a pacific federation."[8] Implicit in these arguments are the concepts of a League of Nations (with the power to regulate disputes) and an International Court of Justice (to punish breaches of the peace). For over a century after Kant's death such ideas remained utopian, but in 1918, in the new climate created by President Wilson's Fourteen Points, it was finally possible to put these proposals into practice. For Kraus, there was hope for humanity, after all. He greeted Wilson's "immortal deed", the liberation of Europe from military tyranny, as the fulfilment of Kant's "immortal idea" (F 501–7, 113).

Journalistic Spin and Humanistic Education

Even after the trauma of defeat, the German nationalist press was unwilling to acknowledge that militarism was discredited. European politics of the interwar period were dominated by the ideological struggle between conflicting myths of the First World War, designed not simply to recall the past but to shape the future. The pacifist movement interpreted the conflict as "the war to end wars", while reactionaries cultivated myths of military prowess as the inspiration for a conservative revolution. They remembered the war as they wished it to have been (and as they intended it to be next time round): as a triumph for German military power.

Kraus repeatedly denounced the chauvinistic postwar mentality that threatened to produce further wars. As early as January 1921 he prophetically identified Germany as the country "where the swastika rises above the ruins of the global conflagration" (F 557–60, 59). Against this, he defended the independence of the Austrian Republic. Responding in May 1926 to the agitation in favour of "Anschluss" (German annexation), Kraus argued that the hypnotic power of newsprint was creating a "counterfeit reality" in which "nothing is real except for lies." Newspapers in Berlin and Vienna, by appealing to racist conceptions of "Volkstum", were generating a circular discourse that had no basis in any actual political event. To fill the vacuum, the press was recycling slogans deriving from "the latest beer-hall conversations of the two realms." By confusing political identity with biological homogeneity, the media created a frame of reference that was essentially fictitious. But this gigantic apparatus had the capacity to turn "non-events" into "action and death" (F 726–29, 59–61).

In his campaign against mystification Kraus found a kindred spirit in Bertrand Russell, an outspoken critic of British militarism. In July 1931 he quoted in *Die Fackel* a passage from Russell's *Sceptical Essays* about the need for teachers to encourage critical thinking:

> For example, the art of reading the newspapers should be taught. The schoolmaster should select some incident which happened a good many years ago, and roused political passions in its day. He should then read to the schoolchildren what was said by the newspapers on the one side, and what was said by those on the other, and some impartial account of what really happened. He should show how, from the biased account of either side, a practised reader could infer what really happened, and he should make them understand *that everything in the newspapers is more or less untrue*. (quoted F 857–63, 71–72)

To counteract these tendencies Kraus transformed political memory into performative art. He excelled at mocking the chauvinists from the public stage, especially by reading scenes from *The Last Days of Mankind*. Only the Epilogue was staged during his lifetime, but the message of the play was conveyed in condensed form through antiwar poems such as "The Ravens" (from Act V, scene 55) and "The Dying Soldier" (from the Epilogue), which Kraus recited in public on numerous occasions. Another excerpt repeatedly featured in his programmes showed how false memories are constructed. A staff officer on the telephone is dictating a press release about the Austrian fortress of Przemysl, which has been captured by the Russians. The loss of the fortress, the pride of the Austro-Hungarian army, is now to be played down as insignificant. When this is queried by the journalist at the other end of the line, the Staff Officer replies: "My dear fellow, you can make people forget anything!" The corresponding scene in the following Act takes place after the recapture of Przemysl. This time the press release reverses the argument, reaffirming the fortress's strategic importance. When this blatant deception is queried, the Staff Officer's rejoinder shows the same contempt for the public: "You can make people forget anything!" (Act II, scene 16, and Act III, scene 22). In these ludicrous scenes the Staff Officer may appear to be a character from an operetta, but his technique of rewriting history anticipates that of the Ministry of Truth in Orwell's *Nineteen Eighty-Four.*

Kraus excelled in analyses of specific journalistic devices, some of which retain their exemplary character long after the occasion faded into history. In a further example dating from January 1921 he analysed the dangers of journalistic "spin." In German this idea was commonly applied to devious arguments thought to be derived from Rabbinic Judaism—"der jüdische Dreh." Kraus turned the tables by using the title "Ein christlicher Dreh" ("Christian Spin") to introduce his analysis of the coverage of a debate at the League of Nations by the Catholic *Reichspost.* A report in this right-wing daily had attributed Austria's enhanced international reputation to the electoral victory of the Christian Social Party. Citing the full text of the debate, Kraus exposed this tendentious report as a "disgraceful forgery" (F 557–60, 63–72).

During the mid-1920s the tone of Kraus's writings became more hopeful as he supported the reforms of the Social Democrats, who were constructing a more egalitarian community in Vienna. Recognizing that the war had left a legacy of nationalist resentment and social deprivation, he actively engaged in the political struggle. It was in the sphere of culture that he became most directly involved, for he shared the Austro-Marxist view of "Bildung" (culture and education) as a force for social renewal. His recitals made a significant contribution to socialist cultural politics, as members accustomed to the tedium of party meetings were roused from their slumbers by his captivating performances. His gift for composing and reciting topical verses, inserted into works by Nestroy or Offenbach, revived one of the most potent of popular traditions, using hard-hitting epigrams to clinch the connections between culture and politics.

One of the primary aims of the educational reforms was to remove chauvinistic literature from libraries, and in 1922 a purge was undertaken of books that glamorized militarism, the Habsburg dynasty, and the Catholic Church. Kraus proposed radical new texts for inclusion in school textbooks. In place of the cult of military valour, children should learn about the debilitating effects of war on the civilian population. The need to educate the next generation in an antimilitarist spirit led him to wonder why the reformers had not included any poems from *The Last Days of Mankind* in their school anthology (F 588–94, 86). This would help to ensure that "little Aryans, when they grow up, would not develop into such big Aryans that they can't wait for a World War" (F 668–75, 58).

Kraus responded to Hitler's seizure of power in Germany by composing *Die Dritte Walpurgisnacht* (*The Third Walpurgis Night*), an incisive analysis of Nazi atrocities compiled during the summer of 1933. It could not be published until after the defeat of Hitler's Germany, and in 2020 an English translation was published by Yale University Press. Kraus did not live long enough to witness the annexation of Austria, followed by an even more apocalyptic Second World War. He died in Vienna of natural causes on 12 June 1936 and lies buried in a Grave of Honour. His most eloquent memorial is *The Last Days of Mankind*. To mark the play's centenary we now present the complete text in English for the first time, incorporating translation strategies that are summarized in our Afterword and elucidated in the Glossary.

Notes

1. References to *Die Fackel*, ed. Karl Kraus (Vienna, 1899–1936), are identified by the abbreviation F followed by the issue and page number.

2. For a comprehensive account of the apocalyptic themes that shaped Kraus's career, see Edward Timms, *Karl Kraus—Apocalyptic Satirist*, Part 1: *Culture and Catastrophe in Habsburg Vienna* (New Haven and London: Yale University Press, 1986), and Part 2: *The Post-War Crisis and the Rise of the Swastika* (New Haven and London: Yale University Press, 2005).

3. See Paul Reitter, *The Anti-Journalist: Karl Kraus and Jewish Self-Fashioning in Fin-de-Siècle Europe* (Chicago and London: University of Chicago Press, 2008).

4. For an English translation of "In dieser großen Zeit", see *In These Great Times: A Karl Kraus Reader*, ed. Harry Zohn (Montreal: Engendra Press, 1976; repr. Manchester: Carcanet, 1984), 70–83. Much as we admire the pioneering translations of Harry Zohn, we feel that "In This Age of Grandeur" comes closer to capturing the resonance of Kraus's title.

5. Arthur Ponsonby, *Falsehood in War-Time: Containing an Assortment of the Lies Circulated Throughout the Nations During the Great War* (London: Garland, 1928), 11; for an update, see Phillip Knightley, *The First Casualty: The War Correspondent as Hero, Propagandist and Myth-Maker from the Crimea to Iraq* (Baltimore: Johns Hopkins University Press, 2004).

6. www.newyorker.com/news/amy-davidson/shattered-school-in-gaza-2 (*New Yorker*, July 30, 2014; viewed August 2014).

7. G. K. A. Bell, "Obliteration Bombing", in Bell, *The Church and Humanity 1939–1946* (London and New York: Longmans, 1946), 129–41.

8. *Kant's Schriften* (Akademieausgabe), vol. 8 (Berlin, 1912), 346 and 356; cf. Kant's *Political Writings*, ed. Hans Reiss, tr. H. B. Nisbet (Cambridge: Cambridge University Press, 1970), 96 and 104.

PREFACE

by Karl Kraus

The performance of this drama, which would take some ten evenings in terrestrial time, is intended for a theatre on Mars. Theatregoers on planet earth would find it unendurable. For it is blood of their blood and its content derives from the contents of those unreal unthinkable years, out of sight and out of mind, inaccessible to memory and preserved only in bloodstained dreams, when operetta figures played out the tragedy of mankind. The action is likewise without heroes, fractured and improbable, as it picks its way through a hundred scenes and hells. The humour is no more than the self-reproach of an author who did not lose his mind at the thought of surviving, with his faculties intact, to bear witness to such profane events. He alone, compromised for posterity by his involvement, has a right to this humour. As for those contemporaries who allowed the things transcribed here to happen, let them subordinate the right to laugh to the duty to weep.

The most improbable actions reported here really occurred. Going beyond the realm of Schillerian tragedy, I have portrayed the deeds they merely performed.* The most improbable conversations conducted here were spoken word for word; the most lurid fantasies are quotations. Sentences whose insanity is indelibly imprinted on the ear have grown into the music of time. The document takes human shape; reports come alive as characters and characters expire as editorials; the newspaper column has acquired a mouth that spouts monologues; platitudes stand on two legs—unlike men left with only one. An unending cacophony of sound bites engulfs a whole era and swells to a final chorale of calamitous action. Those who have lived among men, and outlived them—as actors and mouthpieces of an age that has exchanged flesh for blood and blood for ink—have been transformed into shadows and puppets and re-created as dynamic nonentities.

Spectres and wraiths, masks of the tragic carnival, necessarily have real-life names, for nothing is fortuitous in an age conditioned by chance. This gives no

*See "Glossary and Index" for information about historical individuals mentioned in the play, place names, titles of books and journals, composers of operettas and songs, and sources of significant literary allusions (here: Schillerian tragedy).

one the right to regard the action as a local affair. Even what occurs at the corner where Vienna's Ringstrasse meets the Kärntnerstrasse is controlled from some point in the cosmos. Let those who have weak nerves, even if strong enough to endure those times, turn their backs on our play. One should not expect the age when such events could occur to treat this conversion of horror into words as other than a joke, especially when the most gruesome dialects resound from the depths of the homely territory it plumbs, or to think of what has just been lived through and outlived as other than an invention. An invention whose contents they despise.

Far greater than the infamy of war is that of men who want to forget that it ever took place, although they exulted in it at the time. War is no longer a live issue for those who have outlived it, and while the masks parade on Ash Wednesday, they do not want to be reminded of one another. It's all too easy to understand the disenchantment of an epoch forever incapable of experiencing such events, or grasping what's been experienced, compounded by the failure to be convulsed by its collapse. It is an age whose actions exclude the impulse for atonement, but it has an instinct for self-preservation that enables it to close its ears to the gramophone record of its heroic melodies, and a readiness for self-sacrifice that will enable it to strike them up again should the occasion arise. For the continuing existence of war appears least inconceivable to people whom the slogan "Now we are at war" enables to commit and endorse every possible infamy; but the reminder "Now we were at war!" disturbs the well-earned rest of the survivors.

They fancied they could conquer the world market—the goal that was their birthright—as knights in shining armour; they have to make do with a less glorious trade and sell their gear in the flea market. No wonder they can't stop saying "Don't mention the war"! And it is to be feared that some future age, sprung from the loins of this desolate generation, will have no greater power of understanding, despite being at a greater distance. Yet an unqualified admission of guilt at belonging to mankind, as it currently exists, must at some place and time be welcomed and valued. And "even while men's minds are wild", let us (echoing Shakespeare) deliver Horatio's message to the forces of renewal as a judgment arising out of the ruins:

And let me speak to th'yet unknowing world
Of carnal, bloody, and unnatural acts,
Of accidental judgements, casual slaughters,
Of deaths put on by cunning and forced cause,
And, in this upshot, purposes mistook
Fallen on th'inventors' heads. All this can I
Truly deliver.

DRAMATIS PERSONAE

Prologue

Scene 1 (p. 29)

(Vienna. At the corner where the Kärntnerstrasse meets the Ring and people take their evening stroll.)
Newspaper vendors. A passerby. His wife. Four officers. Two sales reps. Fischl. A Viennese. His wife. Regular subscriber to the *Neue Freie Presse.* Oldest subscriber to the *Neue Freie Presse.* Some drunks. Four young men arm in arm with their girls. The crowd. Fritz Werner. Fräulein Löwenstamm. Fräulein Körmendy. An intellectual. His wife. Poldi Fesch. Policeman. Two petty bourgeois. Two reporters. Cabby.

Scene 2 (p. 34)

(Café Pucher.)
Eduard, headwaiter. A banker. A stranger. Franz, a waiter. Prime minister. Minister of the interior. Head of the cabinet office.

Scene 3 (p. 36)

(Office in the Comptroller of the Imperial Household's chambers.)
Nepalleck.

Scene 4 (p. 39)

(Same.)
Usher. Nepalleck.

Scene 5 (p. 39)

(Same.)
Nepalleck. Old manservant.

Scene 6 (p. 40)

(Same.)
Nepalleck. Montenuovo. Old manservant.

Scene 7 (p. 40)

(Same.)
Montenuovo. Nepalleck.

Scene 8 (p. 40)

(Same.)
Usher. Prince Weikersheim. Nepalleck.

Scene 9 (p. 41)

(Same.)
Nepalleck.

Scene 10 (p. 41)
(Southern Railway terminal.)
Nepalleck.
The following marionettes:
Angelo Eisner v. Eisenhof. Spielvogel and Zawadil. Hofrat and Hofrätin Schwarz-Gelber. Dobner v. Dobenau. Count Lippay. Riedl, café proprietor. Dr. Charas. Stukart, head of security. Wilhelm Exner, section head. Sieghart, Land-bank governor. Landesberger, Anglobank president. Herzberg-Fränkel. Stein and Hein, progressive-liberal municipal councillors. Stiassny and Stiassny, consuls. Three honorary counsellors. Sukfüll. Birinski and Glücksmann. Hugo Heller, bookseller. Flora Dub. The Grumbler. Journalist.

Prologue Extras:
Promenaders, passersby, coffeehouse staff, the public, policemen, dignitaries, court society, ladies of the higher nobility, clergy, municipal councillors, notabilities, lackeys, journalists.

Act I

Scene 1 (p. 47)

(Vienna. At the corner where the Kärntnerstrasse meets the Ring and people take their evening stroll.)
Newspaper vendors. Demonstrator. An intellectual. Ruffian. Prostitute. Several passersby. The crowd. Two reporters. Two army suppliers. Four officers. A Viennese. Voices from the crowd. Beggar boy. Two girls. A policeman. Another intellectual. His girlfriend. A fare. Cabby. House-porter. Two Americans from the Red Cross. Two Turks. Two Chinese. Lady with just the hint of a moustache. A circumspect person. The voice of a cabby. A voice. Passerby. His wife. Troop of boys in military peaked caps and with wooden sabres. Group of singers. Bag

snatcher. His victim. A female voice. Poldi Fesch. His companion. Two devotees of the *Reichspost*. Enlisted soldiers singing. A regular subscriber to the *Neue Freie Presse*. The oldest subscriber. Fritz Werner. Fräulein Körmendy. Fräulein Löwenstamm. Three ruffians. Two sales reps.

Scene 2 (p. 59)

(South Tyrol. The approach to a bridge.)
Member of the Tyrolean territorial reserve. The Grumbler.

Scene 3 (p. 60)

(The other side of the bridge.)
Soldier. The Grumbler. Captain.

Scene 4 (p. 60)

The Optimist and the Grumbler.

Scene 5 (p. 62)

(The Foreign Office.)
Count Leopold Franz Rudolf Ernest Vinzenz Innocenz Maria. Baron Eduard Alois Josef Ottokar Ignazius Eusebius Maria. The voice of Berchtold.

Scene 6 (p. 65)

(In front of a hairdressing salon in the Habsburgergasse.)
The crowd. Violin shop owner. Hairdresser. Friedjung, a historian. Brockhausen, a historian.

Scene 7 (p. 67)

(Kohlmarkt. Outside the revolving door at the entrance to Café Pucher.)
Old Biach. Honorary Counsellor. Businessman. Intellectual. The Grumbler. Haberdasher.

Scene 8 (p. 69)

(Suburban street.)
Four young men. The proprietor of Café Westminster.

Scene 9 (p. 72)

(A primary school.)
Teacher Zehetbauer.
The boys: Anderle, Braunshör, Czeczowiczka, Fleischanderl, Gasselseder, Habetswallner, Kotzlik, Merores, Praxmarer, Sukfüll, Süssmandl, Wottawa, Karl Wunderer, Rudolf Wunderer, Zitterer.

Scene 10 (p. 76)

(Café Pucher.)
Eduard, headwaiter. Old Biach. Honorary Counsellor. Intellectual. Businessman. Haberdasher. Prime minister.

Scene 11 (p. 81)

Two who have "wangled it." The Subscriber. The Patriot. Newspaper vendor.

Scene 12 (p. 94)

A giant in civilian dress and a dwarf in uniform. Newspaper vendor.

Scene 13 (p. 95)

(The electrified railway Baden–Vienna.)
A drunk. A couple. The conductor. Galician refugee couple. Consumption tax inspector. A Viennese.

Scene 14 (p. 96)

(The apartment of the actress Elfriede Ritter.)
Elfriede Ritter. Füchsl, a reporter. Feigl, a reporter. Halberstam, a reporter.

Scene 15 (p. 100)

The Optimist and the Grumbler.

Scene 16 (p. 101)

(Army headquarters.)
Army commanders: Auffenberg. Brudermann. Dankl. Pflanzer-Baltin. Aide-de-camp.

Scene 17 (p. 103)

(Vienna. Premises of the Association of Café Proprietors.)
Riedl. Three café proprietors. Waiter.

Scene 18 (p. 106)

(Vienna's Deutschmeister barracks.)
Gentleman. Sergeant Weiguny. Cadet Wögerer.

Scene 19 (p. 107)

(War Welfare Office.)
Hugo v. Hofmannsthal. A cynic. Poldi.

Scene 20 (p. 109)

(A military unit on the Bukovinian front.)
Lieutenant Fallota. Lieutenant Beinsteller.

Scene 21 (p. 114)

(A battlefield.)
Two war correspondents. Alice Schalek. The painter Hollitzer.

Scene 22 (p. 119)

(In front of the War Ministry.)
The Optimist and the Grumbler. Newspaper vendor. Two refugees. Nepalleck. Eisner v. Eisenhof.

Scene 23 (p. 124)

(Beside the pond in Janov, Galicia.)
Ganghofer. Aide-de-camp of Wilhelm II. Wilhelm II. Orderly.

Scene 24 (p. 129)

(Chief of the General Staff's room.)
Conrad v. Hötzendorf. A major. Skolik, a photographer.

Scene 25 (p. 132)

(Vienna, on the Ring.)
Profiteer. Landlord. Sergeant Wagenknecht. Sergeant Sedlatschek. Hans Müller. Voice of a cabby. Voice of a prostitute. Mendel Singer (passing by). Sieghart (passing by). A man picking up a cigar end. Female newspaper vendor.

Scene 26 (p. 139)

(South-west Front. Military post at a height of over 2,500 metres)
A lookout. Alice Schalek. Soldier. Officer. Orderly.

Scene 27 (p. 141)

(The Vatican.)
The voice of Benedict praying.

Scene 28 (p. 142)

(Newspaper office.)
The voice of Benedikt dictating.

Scene 29 (p. 142)

The Optimist and the Grumbler.

Scene 30 (p. 167)

(On the Graben at night.)
Two commercial middlemen with their lady companions. Newspaper vendor.

Act I Extras:
Promenaders, passersby, beggars, black-marketeers, prostitutes, officers, soldiers, demonstrators, customers, coffeehouse staff, ministers, passengers, German nationalist students, Galician refugees, entourage of Wilhelm II.

Act II

Scene 1 (p. 168)

(Vienna. At the corner where the Kärntnerstrasse meets the Ring and people take their evening stroll.)
Newspaper vendor. Jewish Refugee. Viennese loan shark. Sales rep. A badly wounded casualty on crutches. Bermann. A well-dressed lady. Weiss. Four officers. A soldier on crutches. An intellectual. Poldi Fesch. His companion. Enlisted soldiers singing. Three black-marketeers. Three German grenadiers. Three Viennese municipal officials. Two reporters. Berlin black-marketeer. Porter. Cries from the crowd.

Scene 2 (p. 174)

The Optimist and the Grumbler.

Scene 3 (p. 175)

The Subscriber and the Patriot.

Scene 4 (p. 177)

(Military Headquarters. A street.)
A journalist and an old general. Another journalist and another old general.

Scene 5 (p. 178)

(South-west Front.)
Two voices from the background. An old general and a Sicilian soldier. Member of the War Press Bureau.

Scene 6 (p. 179)

(An infantry regiment 300 paces from the enemy.)
Infantry officer. Padre Anton Allmer.

Scene 7 (p. 179)

(Beside the battery.)
Artillery officer. Padre Anton Allmer. Alice Schalek.

Scene 8 (p. 180)

(The Prater amusement park.)
Impresario responsible for the trench in the Prater. Representative of the Wilhelm press agency. His colleague. The voice of Archduke Karl Franz Josef. Hofrätin Schwarz-Gelber. Lieutenant who wants to remain incognito. Professor Kunze. The Patriot. The Subscriber.

Scene 9 (p. 182)

(Semmering. Terrace of the Southern Railway Hotel.)
Youngsters and oldies. Fatties and shorties. Lady who has just recited Heine. Dangl. Babble of voices. Semmering regular. Chairman of the board.

Scene 10 (p. 183)

The Optimist and the Grumbler. A file of grey-bearded recruits. Young men singing.

Scene 11 (p. 194)

(A suburban street.)
Two policemen. Women and men queuing. Grocer. A well-dressed woman.

Scene 12 (p. 195)

(Kärntnerstrasse.)
A big eater. A normal eater. A starving man.

Scene 13 (p. 196)

(Florianigasse.)
Hofrat Dlauhobetzky v. Dlauhobetz (rtd). Hofrat Tibetanzl (rtd).

Scene 14 (p. 198)

(A hunting party.)
v. Dreckwitz. The hunting party.

Scene 15 (p. 200)

(Office at a command post.)
Hirsch. Roda Roda.

Scene 16 (p. 203)

(Another office.)
A General Staff officer on the phone.

Scene 17 (p. 204)

(Restaurant Anton Grüsser.)

Anton Grüsser, restaurateur. Four waiters. Two young waiters. The headwaiter. A gentleman and a lady. A midget newspaper vendor. Two girls with picture postcards. Two women with picture postcards. Man selling flowers. Woman selling flowers. Woman hawking newspapers. Three customers. A regular. Bambula von Feldsturm. The Grumbler.

Scene 18 (p. 209)

(Vienna. Schottenring.)

Frau Pollatschek of the IAAH. Frau Rosenberg of the IAAH. Frau Bachstelz of the CACKV. Frau Funk-Feigl of the CACKV. A disabled veteran on crutches. Beggar woman. A boy. An infant. A pregnant woman. The Grumbler.

Scene 19 (p. 214)

(Belgrade.)

Alice Schalek. Serbian women laughing. An interpreter.

Scene 20 (p. 215)

(A suburban street.)

An old woman. A lieutenant. The crowd.

Scene 21 (p. 215)

(A suburban apartment.)

The Liebal family: father, mother, boy. Frau Sikora, a neighbour.

Scene 22 (p. 216)

(Headquarters garrison. A street.)

A captain from the War Press Bureau. A journalist. A corpulent, elderly gentleman with side-whiskers and pince-nez, a marshal's baton in each hand.

Scene 23 (p. 218)

(City centre.)

A disabled veteran with a blind soldier. A hack from the gutter press. A sales rep.

Scene 24 (p. 218)

(During a performance in a theatre in the suburbs.)

Hansi Niese. Her partner. The audience.

Scene 25 (p. 219)

(The restaurant Wolf in Gersthof.)

Wolf in Gersthof. The inspector general of the Red Cross, Archduke Franz Salvator, his chamberlain, two aristocrats, and little Putzi. A customer. Folksingers.

Scene 26 (p. 220)

The Subscriber and the Patriot.

Scene 27 (p. 221)

(Position near the Uzsock Pass.)

An Austrian general. A Prussian second-lieutenant.

Scene 28 (p. 222)

(Military headquarters. Cinema.)

The commander in chief of the army, Archduke Friedrich. King Ferdinand of Bulgaria. A voice calling "Ka-boom!"

Scene 29 (p. 222)

The Optimist and the Grumbler.

Scene 30 (p. 227)

(Somewhere on the shores of the Adriatic. In the hangar of a seaplane squadron.)

Alice Schalek. The sub-lieutenant of a frigate.

Scene 31 (p. 228)

(In a U-boat that has just surfaced.)

A mate. U-boat officer. Members of the War Press Bureau. Alice Schalek.

Scene 32 (p. 229)

(A factory requisitioned under the emergency regulations of the War Powers Act.)

Military supervisor of the factory. Factory owner.

Scene 33 (p. 232)

(A room in Hofrat Schwarz-Gelber's house.)

Hofrat and Hofrätin Schwarz-Gelber.

Act II Extras:

Galician refugees, black-marketeers, promenaders, beggars, regular officers, hospital commandants, those in reserved occupations, civilians who have "wangled it", the wounded, soldiers, provincial actors, audience, visitors to Semmering, army suppliers, officers, prostitutes, journalists, customers.

Act III

Scene 1 (p. 240)

(Vienna. At the corner where the Kärntnerstrasse meets the Ring and people take their evening stroll.)

Newspaper vendors. Two army profiteers. Four officers. A young girl. A girl. A woman. Two devotees of the *Reichspost.* Regular subscriber to the *Neue Freie Presse.* The oldest subscriber. A cripple. Poldi Fesch. His companion. Two disabled veterans. The singing of conscripts. Voice of a cabby.

Scene 2 (p. 242)

(In front of our artillery positions.)

Alice Schalek. The gunner.

Scene 3 (p. 243)

(On the Isonzo front. A command post.)

Lieutenant Fallota. Lieutenant Beinsteller.

Scene 4 (p. 247)

(In Jena.)

Two philosophy students.

Scene 5 (p. 248)

(Hermannstadt in Transylvania. In front of a closed German bookshop.)

A Prussian infantryman. A German bookseller.

Scene 6 (p. 249)

(In Vinzenz Chramosta's grocery shop.)

Vincenz Chramosta. Customers. The inspector.

Scene 7 (p. 250)

(Two Commercial Counsellors leaving the Imperial Hotel.)

Commercial Counsellors. Disabled veteran. Cabby. Beggar woman.

Scene 8 (p. 251)

Old Biach.

Scene 9 (p. 252)

(War Archive.)

Captain. Dörmann. Hans Müller. Men of letters. Two orderlies.

Scene 10 (p. 258)

(A chemical laboratory in Berlin.)
Privy Councillor Professor Delbrück.

Scene 11 (p. 258)

(Meeting of the Cheruscan Society in Krems.)
Pogatschnigg. Frau Pogatschnigg. Winfried Hromatka. Kasmader. Übelhör. Holomatsch.

Scene 12 (p. 261)

(At a dance in Hasenpoth in Lithuania.)
Baltic gentleman and Baltic lady.

Scene 13 (p. 261)

(Appeal hearing in the district court of Heilbronn)
Public prosecutor. The lady accused. Two persons in the courtroom.

Scene 14 (p. 262)

The Optimist and the Grumbler.

Scene 15 (p. 265)

(A Protestant church.)
Church superintendent Falke.

Scene 16 (p. 265)

(Another Protestant church.)
Consistory Councillor Rabe.

Scene 17 (p. 266)

(Another Protestant church.)
Pastor Geier.

Scene 18 (p. 267)

(Pilgrimage church.)
Sexton. A visitor.

Scene 19 (p. 268)

(Constantinople. A mosque.)
Two young Berliners. An imam. A lady.

Scene 20 (p. 270)

(Editorial office in Berlin.)
Alfred Kerr.

Scene 21 (p. 271)

(Consultation room in Berlin.)
Professor Molenaar. A patient.

Scene 22 (p. 271)

(Office at a command post.)
General Staff officer on the telephone. Two old generals. Journalist.

Scene 23 (p. 272)

(Headquarters.)
Archduke Friedrich. The two Buquoys. Adjutant.

Scene 24 (p. 273)

Two devotees of the *Reichspost*.

Scene 25 (p. 277)

(In front of the War Ministry.)
Two young men.

Scene 26 (p. 277)

(Ringstrasse.)
Fifty draft dodgers.

Scene 27 (p. 277)

(In front of the War Ministry.)
Another two young men.

Scene 28 (p. 278)

(Ministry of Defence.)
Captain. A civilian.

Scene 29 (p. 279)

(Innsbruck. A restaurant.)
Colonel. Colonel's wife.

Scene 30 (p. 279)

(Market square in Grodno, Belarus.)
Town hall official. Curtseying girls. Dignitaries. German officials. German officers.

Scene 31 (p. 279)

(Censorship at a German front unit.)
Officer in charge of censorship. Captain. Airman. Senior NCO. Sergeant. Territorial reserve. Gun crew. Sixteen drivers. Lieutenant. Reconnaissance airman. Second-lieutenant. Military bandsman. Lance-corporal. Soldier. Captain in the medical corps. Gunner. Junior company commander. Acting officer. Sapper. Volunteer. Major-general.

Scene 32 (p. 282)

(A quiet poet's retreat in the Styrian Woods.)
Kernstock. Two admirers.

Scene 33 (p. 283)

(At a sector control post.)
Alice Schalek.

Scene 34 (p. 284)

(Berlin, Tiergarten.)
Exchange Professor. National-Liberal Reichstag deputy.

Scene 35 (p. 286)

(Lecture hall in Berlin.)
The poet. The audience.

Scene 36 (p. 287)

(Lecture hall in Vienna.)
The Grumbler. A member of the audience and his wife.

Scene 37 (p. 288)

The Subscriber to the *Neue Freie Presse* and the Patriot.

Scene 38 (p. 290)

(In a railway compartment.)
Two sales reps.

Scene 39 (p. 292)

The Optimist and the Grumbler.

Scene 40 (p. 293)

(The German spa Gross-Salze.)
Kommerzienrat Ottomar Wilhelm Wahnschaffe. Frau Kommerzienrat Auguste Wahnschaffe. Little Willy and Little Marie. An invisible choir, representing laughter from abroad. Two wounded soldiers. Two nursemaids.
Children: Hänschen and Trudchen. Hans Adalbert and Annemarie. August and Guste. Mieze. Klaus and Dolly. Walter and Marga. Little Paul and Little Pauline. Jochen and Suse. Elsbeth.
A mother. A gentleman. Two fathers. Two little sons.

Scene 41 (p. 306)

The Optimist and the Grumbler.

Scene 42 (p. 310)

(During the Battle of the Somme. Gateway to a park in front of a villa.)
The German Crown Prince. A company marching past.

Scene 43 (p. 310)

(War Ministry.)
Captain. A civilian.

Scene 44 (p. 311)

(Kastelruth, South Tyrol.)
Second-lieutenant Helwig. Another second-lieutenant. Waitress. Duty officer.

Scene 45 (p. 311)

(A Viennese nightspot.)
Rolf, the impromptu poet. Two officers. Frieda Morelli, chanteuse. A voice. Hungarian cattle dealer. Proprietor of the nightspot. Cloakroom staff and washroom attendant. Grain merchant. A regular. Drunken Red Cross official. His colleague. Army doctor. His colleague. Drunken customer.

Scene 46 (p. 316)

(Night. The Graben in Vienna.)
The Grumbler. A drunkard answering the call of nature.

Act III Extras:
Masked figures and lemurs, promenaders, wounded veterans, the blind, beggars, customers, literary figures, Cheruskans in Krems, dancers in Hasenpoth,

law-court officials, persons in the courtroom, churchgoers, officers, restaurant customers, soldiers, audience at a lecture, barmaids, nightspot hostesses, men-about-town, gentlemen from the Red Cross, Polish legionaries, nightclub staff, the Nechwatal salon orchestra, the Miskolczy Jancsi gypsy band.

Act IV

Scene 1 (p. 138)

(Vienna. At the corner where the Kärntnerstrasse meets the Ring and people take their evening stroll.)
Newspaper vendors. Four officers. Countess. Her lady companion. Blind soldier in a wheelchair. An intellectual. His companion. Poldi Fesch. Baby Fanto. Black hotel porter. Singing conscripts. Berlin exporter. His companion. A passerby with hands raised. Another passerby. An officer's wife. Her companion. Two walkers. Two devotees of the *Reichspost*. An oddball. His companion. Lenzer v. Lenzbruck. Frau Back v. Brünnerherz. Woman selling flowers. Two gentlemen. Storm. Fräulein Löwenstamm. Fräulein Körmendy. A fare. Cabby.

Scene 2 (p. 322)

The Optimist and the Grumbler.

Scene 3 (p. 323)

(A railway station near Vienna.)
A porter. Six Viennese. The Grumbler. The Austrian Face. Someone in the know.

Scene 4 (p. 325)

(Vienna, Kohlmarkt. In front of the window display of a picture gallery.)
Margosches. Wolffsohn.

Scene 5 (p. 326)

The poets: Strobl. Ertl.

Scene 6 (p. 326)

(Student drinking fraternity.)
An alumnus. The members. A recruit.

Scene 7 (p. 328)

(Medical convention in Berlin.)
Psychiatrist. Psychiatric patient. Professor Boas. Professor Zuntz. Professor Rosenfeld (Breslau). President of the Medical Board. Constable Büddicke.

Scene 8 (p. 333)

(Weimar. Gynaecological clinic.)
Professor Henkel. Professor Busse. Female patient. Assistant. Prince of Lippe. Nurse.

Scene 9 (p. 334)

(A German Reserve Division.)
A colonel.

Scene 10 (p. 334)

(The Isonzo front. Brigade headquarters.)
Alice Schalek. Chorus of officers.

Scene 11 (p. 338)

(Divisional headquarters.)
Commanding officer. Kaiserjägertod. Major.

Scene 12 (p. 339)

(Regiment on the retreat. In a village.)
Kaiserjägertod. Starving soldier. Colonel. Lieutenant Gerl.

Scene 13 (p. 339)

(Hospital near a divisional headquarters.)
Seriously wounded patient. Warden. Singing from nearby.

Scene 14 (p. 340)

(A German Reserve Division.)
A colonel.

Scene 15 (p. 340)

The Optimist and the Grumbler.

Scene 16 (p. 341)

(Goods station in Debrecen, Hungary.)
Sentry. Lieutenant Beinsteller. Second-lieutenant Sekira.

Scene 17 (p. 341)

(Vienna. Town Hall.)
Official. An applicant.

Scene 18 (p. 343)

(The Durchhalter family apartment.)
Father, mother, and children.

Scene 19 (p. 343)

The Subscriber to the *Neue Freie Presse* and the Patriot.

Scene 20 (p. 343)

(Sofia. A banquet of German and Bulgarian newspaper editors.)
Count Oberndorff, the German ambassador. German and Bulgarian editors. Kleinecke (Berlin). Steinecke (Hanover).

Scene 21 (p. 345)

(Foreign Ministry.)
Haymerle. Newspaper editor.

Scene 22 (p. 347)

(In the Wahnschaffes' sitting room.)
Frau Pogatschnigg. Frau Wahnschaffe.

Scene 23 (p. 349)

Three fashionable German ladies.

Scene 24 (p. 350)

The Subscriber to the *Neue Freie Presse* and the Patriot.

Scene 25 (p. 351)

(Hindenburg and Ludendorff at lunch.)
Hindenburg and Ludendorff. Paul Goldmann.

Scene 26 (p. 353)

(Semmering. Ridgeway walk.)
The Honorary Counsellor. Old Biach.

Scene 27 (p. 369)
(Berlin, Tiergarten.)
Padde and Kladde.

Scene 28 (p. 372)

The cinema manager. A female voice.

Scene 29 (p. 373)

The Optimist and the Grumbler.

Scene 30 (p. 386)

(Court-martial.)
Captain-Advocate Stanislaus v. Zagorski. The eleven offenders. Officers.

Scene 31 (p. 390)

(Schönbrunn. The Emperor's study.)
Franz Joseph. The valet on the right. The valet on the left.

Scene 32 (p. 398)

(Kragujevac. Court-martial.)
Lieutenant-Advocate. Clerk.

Scene 33 (p. 398)

(Promenade in Bad Ischl.)
Julius Korngold. Four visitors to the spa. Fräulein Löwenstamm. Fräulein Körmendy. Bob Schlesinger. Baby Fanto. Regular subscriber to the *Neue Freie Presse*. The oldest subscriber.

Scene 34 (p. 400)

(Police station.)
Inspector. Policeman. Seventeen-year-old girl.

Scene 35 (p. 400)

(Berlin all-night bar.)
A raucous voice. Frieda Gutzke. Katzenellenbogen. Krotoschiner II.

Scene 36 (p. 401)

The Optimist and the Grumbler.

Scene 37 (p. 404)

(German headquarters.)
Wilhelm II. Generals. Adjutant v. Seckendorff. Three officers. v. Hahnke. v. Duncker. v. Krickwitz. v. Flottwitz. v. Martius.

Scene 38 (p. 406)

(Winter in the Carpathians.)
Company commander Hiller. Fusilier Helmhake. Two soldiers.

Scene 39 (p. 407)

(Same location. Hiller's dugout.)
Junior doctor Müller. Company commander Hiller.

Scene 40 (p. 408)

The Optimist and the Grumbler.

Scene 41 (p. 408)

(A military hospital.)
General staff physician. Lieutenant-colonel Demmer v. Drahtverhau. Medical officer. Sergeant. Padre.

Scene 42 (p. 411)

The Optimist and the Grumbler.

Scene 43 (p. 414)

(War press quarters.)
Captain. A journalist.

Scene 44 (p. 416)

(Army training unit. Vladimir-Volinski, Ukraine.)
Captain. A clerk.

Scene 45 (p. 416)

(Count Dohna-Schlodien, at home.)
Count Dohna-Schlodien. Twelve reporters.

Act IV Extras:
Masked figures and lemurs, promenaders, wounded veterans, cripples, the blind, beggars, doctors, officers, troops, hospital patients, sentries, cinema audience, visitors to a spa, nightspot customers, demimondaines, convalescents, the wounded, the dying, members of the War Press Bureau.

Act V

Scene 1 (p. 418)

(Evening. At the corner where the Kärntnerstrasse meets the Ring.)
Newspaper vendors. Four officers. Singing conscripts. Poldi Fesch. His companion. Turi and Ludi. Fallota. Woman selling flowers. Two leg stumps in a ragged uniform. A whispering voice. An enormous roar.

Scene 2 (p. 420)

The Optimist and the Grumbler.

Scene 3 (p. 422)

(In front of the Parliament building.)
A woman who has collapsed from hunger. Pattai the patriot.

Scene 4 (p. 422)

(Foreign Ministry.)
Count Leopold Franz Rudolf Ernest Vinzenz Innocenz Maria. Baron Eduard Alois Josef Ottokar Ignazius Eusebius Maria.

Scene 5 (p. 424)

(Near Udine.)
Two generals. An infantryman.

Scene 6 (p. 425)

(The base at Fourmies.)
Territorial reservist Lüdecke.

Scene 7 (p. 426)

(Circus Busch.)
Pastor Brüstlein. Editor in chief Maschke. A dissenting voice. Professor Puppe.

Scene 8 (p. 427)

The Optimist and the Grumbler.

Scene 9 (p. 428)

(The esplanade at Bad Ischl.)
The Subscriber to the *Neue Freie Presse*. The Patriot. Old Biach. Visitors.

Scene 10 (p. 435)

(Berlin. A wine restaurant in Kaiserpassage.)
Zulauf, a liberal politician. Ablauf, a liberal politician.

Scene 11 (p. 437)

(General meeting of the Social Democratic wartime election campaign for the mega-constituency of Teltow-Beskow-Storkow-Charlottenburg.)
Comrade Schliefke (Teltow). A heckler.

Scene 12 (p. 437)

(Bad Gastein.)
Subscriber to the *Neue Freie Presse*. The Patriot.

Scene 13 (p. 438)

(Office in a command post.)
General Staff officer on the telephone.

Scene 14 (p. 439)

(Battlefield near Saarburg.)
Captain Niedermacher. Major Metzler. Wounded French soldier. German soldier.

Scene 15 (p. 439)

(Near Verdun.)
General Gloirefaisant. Captain Massacré. Colonel Meurtrier.

Scene 16 (p. 440)

(War Press Bureau in Rodaun.)
Alice Schalek. Fellow reporter.

Scene 17 (p. 446)

The Subscriber to the *Neue Freie Presse* and the Patriot.

Scene 18 (p. 447)

The Optimist and the Grumbler.

Scene 19 (p. 448)

(Vienna. Michaelerplatz.)
Chorus of riffraff.

Scene 20 (p. 448)

(Military command post.)
Captain. Clerk.

Scene 21 (p. 449)

(War Ministry.)
Captain. Clerk. Officer cadet.

Scene 22 (p. 453)

(Provincial government in Brno.)
The governor. A clerk.

Scene 23 (p. 454)

(In a primary school.)
Teacher Zehetbauer.
The boys: Anderle, Gasselseder, Kotzlik, Merores, Sukfüll, Zitterer.

Scene 24 (p. 456)

(National Tourist Association.)
Reporter. Official.

Scene 25 (p. 457)

(Café on the Ring.)
Mammut. A waiter. Zieselmaus. Walross. Hamster. Nashorn. Tapir. Schakal. Leguan. Kaiman. Pavian. Kondor. Löw. Hirsch. Wolf. Posamentier. Spitzbauch. Schlechtigkeit. People rushing in. Gollerstepper. Tugendhat. Mastodon. Raubitschek. Vortrefflich. Gutwillig. Aufrichtig. Beständig. Brauchbar. Toilet attendant. Pollatschek. Lustig. Disabled war veteran. Bernhard Moldauer. Two of his friends. His wife. His daughter. The uncle. Young profiteer. Restaurant manager.

Scene 26 (p. 461)

(Berlin. Friedrichstrasse.)
Chorus of voices. A youth. A girl. Policeman. Berlin profiteer and Viennese profiteer, shoulder to shoulder. Newspaper vendor.

Scene 27 (p. 462)

(High Command garrison. A cabaret.)
Marionettes:
Drunken General Staff officer. Chorus of waiters. Girl on the right. Kohn. Fritzi-Spritzi. Proprietor. Toilet attendant and cloakroom staff. Fettköter. Girl on the left. General Staff officer. Other General Staff officers.

Scene 28 (p. 466)

(Viennese lecture hall.)
The Grumbler. A member of the audience and his wife.

Scene 29 (p. 468)

The Subscriber to the *Neue Freie Presse* and the Patriot.

Scene 30 (p. 468)

(Two Commercial Counsellors emerging from the Imperial Hotel.)
Two Commercial Counsellors. One-armed beggar woman. Cabby. Woman collapsing from hunger. Disabled war veteran.

Scene 31 (p. 470)

The Optimist and the Grumbler.

Scene 32 (p. 472)

(Reporting to battalion.)
A major. Four soldiers. Lance-corporal.

Scene 33 (p. 473)

The Optimist and the Grumbler.

Scene 34 (p. 476)

(In the Bohemian village Postabitz.)
A woman.

Scene 35 (p. 476)

(Hospital in Leitmeritz in northern Bohemia.)
Disabled prisoner of war on Red Cross exchange. His neighbour in the next bed.

Scene 36 (p. 476)

(Transit camp in Galicia for repatriated prisoners of war.)
The friend.

Scene 37 (p. 479)

(After the winter offensive in the Sette Communi on the Italian Front.)
Two war correspondents. Two soldiers. Captain. Plump figures emerging from motorcars. The Emperor, wrapped in heavy furs. Colonel. Major.

Scene 38 (p. 481)

(Hofburg Palace. Press office.)
Captain Werkmann. Clerk.

Scene 39 (p. 481)

(Kärntnerstrasse.)
Archduke Max. Lackey. The tenor. The crowd. Newspaper vendor.

Scene 40 (p. 482)

(A side street.)
A blind soldier and his little daughter. Disabled veteran with a hurdy-gurdy. Second-lieutenant.

Scene 41 (p. 482)

(Army High Command.)
A major. Another major.

Scene 42 (p. 483)

The Optimist and the Grumbler.

Scene 43 (p. 489)

(Vienna. Stadtpark.)
An enormous crowd. Newspaper vendors. Two ladies. Gentleman. Husband and his beloved spouse. Fat black-marketeer. His girl. A companion. Voice of a sceptic. Fräulein Körmendy. Fräulein Löwenstamm. A man about town and a snooty lady. Three speakers. Two groups. Someone who arrives panting. Elderly gentleman. Young man in belted coat. His friend. Steffi. Agitator. Representative of the film company. Restaurant proprietor.

Scene 44 (p. 492)

The Optimist and the Grumbler.

Scene 45 (p. 495)

(Innsbruck. Maria Theresienstrasse.)
Butcher's boy. Girl with sabre. Officer without sabre. Two other officers. Two policemen. Military inspector.

Scene 46 (p. 496)

Two devotees of the *Reichspost,* asleep.

Scene 47 (p. 498)

(First-class compartment.)
Lieutenant-colonel Maderer von Mullatschak.

Scene 48 (p. 499)

(At 3,000 metres.)
Officer cadet. Alice Schalek.

Scene 49 (p. 499)

The Optimist and the Grumbler.

Scene 50 (p. 500)

(Swiss mountain railway.)

Gog & Magog. Trudchen.

Scene 51 (p. 505)

(A barracks in Siberia.)

Siberian prisoners of war. Austrian captain.

Scene 52 (p. 505)

(Vienna. Northern Railway Station.)

Wounded soldiers on a prisoner-of-war exchange. Various voices. Spielvogel and Zawadil. Eisner v. Eisenhof. Hofrat and Hofrätin Schwarz-Gelber. Wilhelm Exner. Dobner v. Dobenau. Riedl. Stukart. Sieghart. Landesberger. A mother. Her daughter. Dr. Charas. Flora Dub. Stiassny and Stiassny. Three Honorary Counsellors. Sukfüll. Birinski and Glücksmann. Hans Müller. Putzker. Hugo Heller. Newspaper editor.

Scene 53 (p. 508)

(A deserted street.)

Corybants and maenads.

Scene 54 (p. 508)

The Grumbler at his desk.

Scene 55 (p. 517)

(Ceremonial banquet at the headquarters of an army corps.)

Austrian general. Prussian colonel. Orderly. Major-general. Colonel. Lieutenant-colonel. Major. Captain of Horse. Duty officer. Telephone officer. Captains. Lieutenants. Second-lieutenants. Chief supply officer. Senior medical officer. Regimental doctor. Senior military prosecutor. Field chaplain and field rabbi. Artillery officer. Intelligence officer. Géza von Lakkati de Némesfalva et Kutjafelegfaluszég. Romuald Kurzbauer. Stanislaus von Zakrychiewicz. Petričič. Iwaschko. Koudjela. Baggage officer Felix Bellak. Wowes. German General Staff officer. German captain. Two Prussian captains. Two Prussian lieutenants. Prussian second-lieutenant. Two war correspondents. Sister Paula and Sister Ludmilla. Orderly. The band.

Act V Extras:
Rows of the wounded and the dead, playboys, beggars, members of the Upper House, rucksacks, knapsacks and bodies crammed in a tram, troops, participants in an enormous rally, passersby in Berlin's Kaiserpassage, constituency election campaign members, German and French soldiers and officers, German prisoners of war, the wounded, coffeehouse customers, armadillos, girls in insect-like costume, waiters and waitresses, race-card vendors, a procession of ruffians, middlemen, operetta singers, bohemians, faith healers, ponces, rent-boys, prostitutes, swindlers, pimps, black-marketeers, street-walkers, General Staff officers, war profiteers, nightspot hostesses, audience at a lecture, promenaders, hospital patients, remnants of a regiment, travellers amidst their luggage, passengers on a Swiss mountain railway, members of the society Laurels for Our Heroes, officials, those serving refreshments to the wounded, journalists, Austrian and German officers, military supplies staff, apparitions.
Speaking apparitions:
The boy Lobodan Ljubinkovits (d. 1915); A war correspondent; The 19-year-old and the 21-year-old; Two military judges; A senior military judge; Captain Prasch; An Uhlan lieutenant; The gas masks; The soldiers who have frozen to death; The old Serbian peasant; The flames; The 1,200 horses; Leonardo da Vinci; The children from the *Lusitania*; The dogs of war; The dying forest; The mothers; The Austrian Face; The Ravens; Women auxiliaries; The unborn son.

Epilogue: The Final Night (p. 553)

Dying soldier. Male gas masks. Female gas masks. General. First war correspondent. Second war correspondent. The dying man. A sergeant. A blinded man. Female war correspondent. Wounded soldier. The Death's Head hussar. Nowotny von Eichensieg. Dr. Ing. Abendrot. Fressak, a hyena. Naschkatz, a hyena. Chorus of the hyenas. Lord of the Hyenas. Three gossip columnists. Voices from above. Voices from below. Two orderlies. Film cameramen. A voice from above. The voice of God.

PROLOGUE

Scene 1

Vienna. At the corner where the Kärntnerstrasse meets the Ring and people take their evening stroll. The evening of a summer public holiday. A throng of people, all wanting to be part of the action.

NEWS VENDOR Ex-tra-aaedi-shun! Arsh-duke ass-ass-inated! Mur-draar-rested!

SECOND NEWS VENDOR Ex-tra-aaedi-shun—! *Neue Freie Presse!* Sarajevo blood-bath! Mur-dra a Serb!

PASSERBY (*to his wife*) Not a Jew, God be praised.

WIFE Let's go home! (*She pulls him away.*)

FIRST OFFICER Evening, Powolny! Well, what d'ya say? Supper at the Gartenbau?

SECOND OFFICER (*with walking stick*) Don't-ya know it's closed?

FIRST OFFICER (*taken aback*) Closed?

THIRD OFFICER Well, I'll be blowed!

SECOND OFFICER Closed, I'm tellin-ya.

FIRST OFFICER So what d'ya say then?

SECOND OFFICER We'll just have to eat at Hopfner's.

FIRST OFFICER Of course—but I meant, what d'ya say about the political situation. You're the expert—

SECOND OFFICER Well, it'll shake things up a bit (*brandishes his cane*)—no bad thing—can do no harm—about time too—

FIRST OFFICER What a dashing fellow you are! But y'know who'll really go wild—Fallota, he's always saying—

FOURTH OFFICER (*joins them, laughing*) Evening Nowotny, evening Pokorny, evening Powolny—the very man! You know all about politics. Come on, tell us, what d'ya think?

SECOND OFFICER Well, that rabble has simply got out of hand.

THIRD OFFICER Y'know what?—That's spot on.

FOURTH OFFICER Absolutely—I was at a bash in the mess last night—! D'ya see the latest Schönpflug cartoon? Fantabulous!

SECOND OFFICER Fallota—now there's a patriot for you, never stops saying it's not enough just doing your duty, at times you've actually got to *be* patriotic. When he gets something into his head there's no stopping him. Know what I think? We might just have to sweat it out for a bit. Suits me!

THIRD OFFICER So, let's go along to Hopfner's, shall we?

FOURTH OFFICER Look, d'ya recognize those broads there?

SECOND OFFICER Know Schlepitschka von Schlachtentreu? What an intellect! Reads every word of the *Presse* and knows it all back to front. Says we should read it too. We're for peace, apparently, but not for peace at all costs. Think that's true? (*A barmaid passes by.*) Look, that's the one I told you about—had her the other night—for free. (*The actor Fritz Werner goes past.*) My compliments!

THIRD OFFICER I don't think I know him.

SECOND OFFICER Get away! You don't know him? Werner?!

THIRD OFFICER Oh, fantastic! Know what I thought? I thought it was Treumann!

FIRST OFFICER Get away! How can you mix up Treumann with Werner?!

SECOND OFFICER You've obviously never studied logic—it was the other way round—he mixed up Werner with Treumann.

THIRD OFFICER Y'know what I—no, hang on (*ponders*)—know what I really think? *Husarenblut* is a cut above *Herbstmanöver*!

SECOND OFFICER Get away!

FIRST OFFICER You're the intellectual, so tell me—

FOURTH OFFICER Of course it was Werner!

FIRST OFFICER You're the intellectual, so—

SECOND OFFICER So?

FIRST OFFICER Ever see *Der lachende Ehemann*? Know Marischka?

SECOND OFFICER Afraid not.

FIRST OFFICER Know Storm?

SECOND OFFICER Of course!

FOURTH OFFICER Let's go, no point hanging round here with all the high and mighty. Let's go to Hopfner's since the Gartenbau is—

THIRD OFFICER Know Glawatsch too? (*Exeunt, in conversation.*)

NEWS VENDOR (*comes running*) *Tagblatt*—Heir to throne and wife assassinated—read all about it!

SALES REPRESENTATIVE What are we going to do with the rest of the evening?

SECOND SALES REPRESENTATIVE They say the Venedig is still open.

FIRST Right, so we take a tram down to the Venedig.

SECOND I'm not sure, I'm all on edge until we hear the results—

FIRST We'll hear down there! Over in the Imperial the racing tip was Melpomene, all day yesterday, nothing but Melpomene. But what a bunch, you know as well as I do—it's taught me a lesson and cost me a packet—there's Fischl! (*He calls across the boulevard.*) Fischl!—Melpomene?

FISCHL Not a hope!

FIRST Oh, go to hell!

FISCHL After you! Glaukopis first, Melpomene second.

A VIENNESE (*to his wife*) But I'm telling you, nobody liked the Archduke—

HIS WIFE Mary and Joseph! Why ever not?

THE VIENNESE Because he wasn't popular. Riedl himself told me—(*Exeunt.*)

REGULAR SUBSCRIBER TO *NEUE FREIE PRESSE* (*in conversation with its oldest subscriber*) Now we're in for it!

OLDEST SUBSCRIBER In for what? (*Looks around.*) Things can only get better. It'll be like it was under the Empress Maria Theresa. Mark my words!

REGULAR SUBSCRIBER So *you* say!

OLDEST SUBSCRIBER That's what I'm telling you!

REGULAR SUBSCRIBER I hope you're right! But—for heaven's sake—Serbia! My youngest boy!

OLDEST SUBSCRIBER In the first place, war is unthinkable in this day and age—and secondly, why would it be your son they call up? Aren't there plenty of others? (*Murmurs*) God, Thou art just! I can't wait for tomorrow's editorial. Benedikt will find words he's never found before, even his editorial when Mayor Lueger died will pale in comparison. At long last he'll be able to say what he really thinks—with caution, of course. But he'll speak from the heart, to everyone, even the goys—you'll see—, even the higher goys, even the highest goys—especially the highest! He knows what's at stake, always did.

REGULAR SUBSCRIBER We shouldn't tempt providence. Maybe there's no risk of war.

OLDEST SUBSCRIBER You pessimist! (*Exeunt.*)

SOME DRUNKS (*force their way through the throng*) Haaalooo! Down with Serbia! Let 'em have it! Smash 'em to pieces! Long live Habsburg!

FOUR YOUNG MEN ARM IN ARM WITH THEIR GIRLS (*sing*) "Prince Eugene made a bridge, a bridge he made, So they crossed the river and took Belgrade—"

CROWD Three cheers! (*Fritz Werner returns, waving in acknowledgment.*) Three cheers for Werner!

FRÄULEIN LÖWENSTAMM Go on, ask him now.

FRÄULEIN KÖRMENDY (*approaching*) I'm a great admirer, and I wonder if I could ask you for your—

(*Werner takes out a note pad, signs, and hands her the sheet. Exit.*)

He was so sweet.

FRÄULEIN LÖWENSTAMM Did he look at you? Let's get out of this crowd—and all because of the assassination. Storm is the only one I really fancy. (*Exeunt.*)

NEWSPAPER VENDOR Ex-tra-aaedi-shun—! Arsh-duke Franz Ferdinand—

INTELLECTUAL It'll be a tremendous loss for the theatres. The Volkstheater was completely sold out—

HIS WIFE That's an evening ruined, and no mistake. We should have stayed in, but no, you always have to go out—

INTELLECTUAL I'm amazed at your egoism, I'd never have thought you could be so totally lacking in social awareness.

HIS WIFE You think I'm not interested? Of course I'm interested. There's no point eating in the Volksgarten if there's to be no music anyway. We might as well go straight to Hartmann's—

INTELLECTUAL All you think of is food! At a time like this, who cares—they'll pull out all the stops—wait and see.

HIS WIFE As long as we get a place where we *can* see.

INTELLECTUAL It'll be a funeral there's never been the like of before! I still remember Crown Prince Rudolph's—(*Exeunt.*)

POLDI FESCH (*to his companion*) We're out on the town tonight—yesterday I was out partying with the Sascha Film people, tomorrow I'm bingeing with—(*Exeunt.*)

POLICEMAN Keep to the left, please! To the left!

NEWSPAPER VENDOR *Reichspost!* Second edi-shun! Heir to the throne and his wife assassinated!

PETTY BOURGEOIS Live and let live! Of course, for the man in the street the Archduke wasn't the right type. And I'll tell you why. Your ordinary Viennese is used to doing things his own way, that's why. But He, on the other hand—Hadrawa spotted Him once—incognito, of course—paying a taxi fare and tipping, just like you or me, but—here's the thing—not a groschen more.

SECOND PETTY BOURGEOIS Go on!

PETTY BOURGEOIS And even in the posh stores he never paid over the odds. Not him! Do you think he would let the likes of us put one over on him? He'd have sorted us out! After all, how are we to survive? He didn't miss a trick. You can bet your life! It's all a matter of temperament. Live and let live, I say, or die in the attempt. And for why? The man in the street—

NEWS VENDOR Ex-tra-aaedi-shun—!

PETTY BOURGEOIS Let's have one. How much?

NEWS VENDOR Ten cents.

PETTY BOURGEOIS For this bilge! Extortionate! And nothing but empty waffle. Hey—look at that girl, neat, eh? Look at the curves! Leaves my old lady standing—no comparison!

SECOND PETTY BOURGEOIS Get a grip! She's a protestute!

PETTY BOURGEOIS Look, there's a crowd outside the Hotel Bristol, let's go and see. Must be some celebrity. (*Exeunt.*)

POLICEMAN Keep to the left, please, to the left!

REPORTER (*to companion*) Here we can really put our finger on the pulse of public opinion. Look, the news had spread like wildfire across the boulevard, wave upon wave. All at once the merry hustle and bustle which ordinarily fills the air at this hour was silenced. On every face one read despondency, a sense of utter shock, above all a numb sadness. Complete strangers addressing one another, people forming little groups and scrambling for the extra editions—

SECOND REPORTER Here's how I would put it: Under the trees lining the Ringstrasse you could see groups of people who wanted to be part of the action, discussing what had happened. Policemen dispersed the groups, declaring they would not permit any further gatherings. Whereupon groups began to converge, and became a dense and impressive mass—look, over there!

(An altercation between a cabby and his passenger in front of the Hotel Bristol, passersby take sides, boos, and cries of "Shame!")

NEWSPAPER VENDOR Ex-tra-aaedi-shun—! Heir to throne and consort murdered by conspirators!

CABBY But surely, on a day like this, your honour—!

(Change of scene.)

Scene 2

Café Pucher. The same evening shortly before midnight. The coffeehouse is almost empty; only two tables occupied. At one, a senior Bankverein official has just sat down. At the other, two bald-headed gentlemen, each smoking a cigar with card mouthpiece, immersed in the comic magazines. The girl at the till is asleep. A waiter waves his napkin in front of her face as a joke. Another is being chased out of the kitchen by the coffee-chef brandishing a dishcloth, at which the cook and headwaiter start to laugh.

HEADWAITER EDUARD Where d'you think you are—in some corner café? Shame on you! The ministers are reading, shame on you, and Fräulein Paula's trying to sleep!

BANKER Hey, you!

EDUARD Herr von Geiringer?

BANKER A Trabucco and the extra edition!

EDUARD *(takes a box of cigars and the paper from his inside coat pocket and says)* A nice Trabucco and something to raise the spirits!

BANKER Was nobody in tonight? Why's it so dead? Not even Dr. Gomperz?

EDUARD No one, Herr von Geiringer.

BANKER Nobody telephoned?

EDUARD No, nobody yet. At least, with this fine weather—it may be that over the holiday the gentlemen are out of town—

BANKER What holiday is it today?

EDUARD Peter and Paul, Herr von Geiringer.

(While the two continue their conversation, a stranger has come in. He sits at a table facing the two older gentlemen. A waiter brings coffee.)

STRANGER Waiter, who are the two gentlemen there, they look very familiar—

FRANZ *(bending over)* That's the ministers' regular table. The gentleman with the pince-nez, the one reading the *Kleine Witzblatt*, that's His Excellency the

Minister of the Interior, and the gentleman with the pince-nez studying *Pschütt*, that's His Excellency the Prime Minister.

STRANGER Really! And are they only here on account of what's happened, or are they regulars?

FRANZ Almost every evening. Their Excellencies are—essentially—bachelors, you see.

STRANGER Really! And who is the gentleman who's just joined them?

FRANZ Ah, is he there already—that's His Excellency the Head of the Cabinet Office.

STRANGER Really!

(Franz rushes off and brings the Head of the Cabinet Office a lemonade and the Interessante Blatt. *After a pause:)*

PRIME MINISTER *(putting down the caricatures in* Pschütt*)* Nothing special today.

MINISTER OF THE INTERIOR *(yawns and says)* Boring!

PRIME MINISTER Days like this really drag on!

HEAD OF CABINET OFFICE The dog days are on us.

PRIME MINISTER *(after a reflective pause)* I think we might need to issue a communiqué after all. Given the measures the government envisages in light of the situation created by recent events, and after exhaustive discussion by the assembled cabinet members etcetera, etcetera.

MINISTER OF THE INTERIOR Where feasible.

PRIME MINISTER Eduard!

MINISTER OF THE INTERIOR So what measures shall we take?

PRIME MINISTER That will depend on the communiqué. Eduard!

EDUARD Excellency?

PRIME MINISTER Aren't there any new ones today? Bring the—what's it called?

EDUARD *(searching among the comic magazines on the table)* Is something missing, Excellency? You're right!

(He goes to the newspaper shelves. Meanwhile the Banker crosses to the Ministers' table, where the Minister of the Interior has stood up, and engages him in conversation. Eduard beckons to the waiter Franz, who has just been chased from the kitchen with a dishcloth and is starting to wave his napkin in the sleeping till-girl's face.)

EDUARD Are you still at it? Like you're in some corner café? Shame on you! (*He continues searching on the newspaper shelves.*) What have you done with the illustrateds—yet again! The *Bombe* for the ministers' table!
(Change of scene.)

Scene 3

Office of the Imperial Chamberlain, Prince Montenuovo. At a desk sits Hofrat Nepalleck, reporting on the telephone to the Cabinet Office about the measures taken to restrict attendance at the Royal Funeral. He is continuously bowing to the instrument, almost crawling into it.

NEPALLECK Funeral Third Class—of course, Your Excellency—Your Excellency can rest assured—Prince Montenuovo seized the initiative at once—Pardon? Pardon, Your Excellency, what was that? This is such a bad line again today—Damnation, operator! This is an official call—it's scandalous!—Pardon, Your Excellency, we were interrupted—yes—yes—yes—at your service—it will be seen to—but of course—put them off—all of them—naturally—the Prince seized the initiative at once—of course—the Prince will be delighted—the Prince's sentiments entirely—Your Excellency can rely on that—no, no, none of the monarchs are coming to pay their respects—nor any of the Royal families' members—no, no, nor any relatives either—naturally—Pardon?—No, they all wanted to come—but no one will now—a Grand Duke was all set to, but fortunately we managed to prevent it in time—that would be the last straw—if they started offering explanations so as to avoid war at all costs—Pardon?—not cut off again! Damnation, what a shambles!—yes, the English too—no, no one—no courtiers at all—only ambassadors and so on—and only a select few, of course—those we can't say no to—it's all in hand—all nicely screened and sifted—as far as was feasible—a question of the available space—tiny chapel—Lord, how we laughed!—the wording?—Just a moment. (*Takes a piece of paper from his pocket.*) "Restrictions on number of delegates representing foreign courts and military delegates, owing to considerations of the available space—" Pardon?—naturally, of course it will be a most bitter disappointment, no participation of the military, neither official nor in general—Pardon, Your Excellency? In Belgrade? Oh well, they'll find it very odd—absolutely, so if it makes them even more insolent—we've no objections, have we, Your Excellency?—Just so!

Ah, spot on, Your Excellency, splendid, Funeral Third Class, No Smoking—marvellous idea, I must tell the Prince, the Prince will split his sides—as it is, the anointing of the bodies has given us nothing but trouble—yes, the Bohemian nobility, making rather too many demands, those gentlemen—His old cronies and all the relatives—how did we respond?—Prince Montenuovo seized the initiative at once. Quite simple: apart from His Majesty's entourage and officials, at most only the children's guardian to be admitted—Pardon? The children?—no, the Prince is against that on account of the seating arrangements—Pardon? Yes, they want to process on foot—naturally, not to the Prince's liking at all—almost a demonstration—Exactly, like the unemployed! I must tell the Prince, he'll split his sides—How do you mean, Your Excellency? Couldn't care a hoot? Oh absolutely, or two hoots!—But of course, not a word!—all the formalities will have been observed—*His Majesty's need of rest, pure and simple*—Let them say what they like and be damned!—of course—Funeral of Heir to Throne to be Third Class, basta!—no need to put ourselves out—*à propos*, Excellency hasn't heard the latest impertinence from His office?—They claim that according to Spanish ceremonial we should be responsible for the burial in Artstetten, not only for the transport to the Western Railway Station—the cheek of it! According to protocol we are only responsible for the Habsburg Tomb, the Capuchin Crypt—end of story!—But of course the Prince seized the initiative at once and told them they should be grateful we're even bringing the body to the Western Station. Everything else is up to the Municipal Funeral Service—or the Society for Life Eternal, just so—of course, at any rate doing it on the cheap—or as He would have liked, out of piety, exactly! I must tell the Prince, the Prince will split his sides—no, informal, small intimate reception—Need we engage any extra help? None at all, we get rid of the lot—That's true, sweated labour—of course if it had been up to me, I was against it from the start, bringing that Chotek woman's corpse back in the same train—I always say, in cases like that, if you hadn't climbed up, you wouldn't have fallen down—but alas—yes, quite, the Prince's good heart—and in addition, as Your Excellency is aware, His Imperial Majesty intervened, so there was nothing to be done—anyhow, at least we managed to rectify matters to the extent of having her coffin displayed at a lower level than his—To be sure, it won't be pleasant tomorrow at the Southern Railway Station—but no crowd at least—Pardon? Oh quite, not like catching an excursion train on a Sunday, exactly, I must tell the Prince, the Prince will—Sorry? Sorry?

Ah yes, the newspapers? They've had their instructions, all of them, play it low key. Watchword: No ostentation but silent mourning or whatever—I couldn't care less—Pardon, Your Excellency? As silent as the—excellent, I must tell the Prince, the Prince will—Pardon? Yes, delighted that the Cabinet Office is just as deeply grieved as the Office of the Imperial Chamberlain—the Prince will split his sides—Some of the variety theatres wanted to know if they should cancel their performances. Answer: the Court has not yet decreed any official period of mourning, so it's left to the discretion of each establishment—nice, eh?—one can imagine their discretion!—certainly friend Wolf in

Gersthof needn't shed any more tears than we do. But Venedig in Wien, that'll be of interest to the Prince, they had the sense not to ask and simply decided the show must go on. Good Lord, in these hard times who's to begrudge them their bit of business and fun—live and let live, of course—Oh quite, certainly, not just us alone but the whole Empire—the whole Empire—just so, everyone shares the same feeling, very true, the show must go on—What? Damnation, not again—more interference!—very true, people want to relax and enjoy themselves—that's exactly right, the Grim Reaper will appear soon enough—live and let live—people want to see happy, smiling faces, otherwise *they'll* start making faces—yes indeed, anyone who can't put on a friendly face doesn't deserve to hold high office!—of course, in that respect we need have no fears for the future, thank goodness.—Pardon? What of the Prince, the new one? Or rather, the former future Imperial Chamberlain? The late favourite has passed on, gone to meet his Maker, may God bless Him, the Devil take him, well, it was a very singular bereavement, at any rate the only one deeply afflicted by it is—no, he won't be honouring us with a visit any more—Pardon?

Those who were with him in Sarajevo? Harrach? Might have been. Didn't they say "he protected him with his own body"?—they certainly pulled rank down there—Morsey apparently had a go at a policeman, why hadn't he arrested one of the perpetrators, but he simply replied, cool as you like, "Attend to your own affairs, Lieutenant!"—The police in Sarajevo simply did their duty, no more, no less—The gendarmerie—how many were there? Prince Montenuovo seized the initiative with Tisza at the time, but all the necessary precautionary measures were already in hand. Six for his personal protection—surely more than enough!—Exactly, a quite reasonable compromise for the two hundred he was granted for Konopiste, to stop honourable members of the public from walking on the grass—That certainly pleased him, waste of money though it was—Pardon? The Foreign Office are already on the rampage? But of course, it's the best pretext imaginable for declaring war, of course—At last, at last!—It'll be interesting to see how long their investigations last in that nest of vipers—another fair compromise, six gendarmes for Sarajevo, so we just need a few more for Belgrade!—absolute rabble!—But of course, we're as pure as the driven snow in comparison—True, he had premonitions of danger, but we bolstered his courage, an officer is not afraid!—just so, he was in God's hand until the day he died—there was no avoiding it, I know, I know, but we must exact retribution now it's happened!—exactly, afterwards one simply has to do one's stuff, yes, yes, it has its good side too, at home and abroad—a settling of accounts—Oh yes, Conrad can now seize—but of course they'll love it! We must demand satisfaction, any child can see that, it's the last straw!—a question of prestige if ever there was one—we'll carry it through—but of course—Pardon? But of course, that's where the Germans will come to our rescue—namely, we are for peace, though not for peace at all costs—no, Your Excellency, no chance of getting away on leave, how could I?—that's how it is, nothing to be done, I'm spared nothing—once again, of course, you can put your mind at rest—I shall pass it on—profound thanks, Your humble servant, Your Excellency!

Scene 4

As before.

USHER Beg pardon, Hofrat—a visitor.

NEPALLECK Who?

USHER (*timidly*) Ah, one of the—ah—other—

NEPALLECK (*imperiously*) There are no others! Those times are past! Didn't I tell you that if anyone comes—

USHER Beg pardon—he says it's only an inquiry.

NEPALLECK I'd like to know what there still is to inquire about. Let's have him in then. (*Exit usher.*)

Scene 5

Enter an old manservant of the late Archduke.

NEPALLECK (*between clenched teeth*) What do you want?

OLD MANSERVANT Your humble servant, Hofrat, sir,—ah—in the circumstances, I'm not sure if—that is to say—in other circumstances—

NEPALLECK Out with it, what is it you want?

MANSERVANT Well, the calamity, the dreadful calamity—is it not, Hofrat, sir?—and I who was already in service under His Imperial Highness—as was—Archduke Ludwig, God rest his soul—

NEPALLECK Aha, to put it in a nutshell, you're an itinerant valet—well, my dear fellow, put the notion right out of your head, there are no jobs going here!

MANSERVANT (*in tears*) No no, Hofrat—no no, Hofrat—

NEPALLECK What? The cheek of it!

MANSERVANT But no, Hofrat—I don't want—I don't want—

NEPALLECK What do you want then?

MANSERVANT But no—the Archduke was a strict master, it's true—but His Highness was—strict—and—good—but so—

NEPALLECK My dear chap, let's have none of your cock-and-bull stories here—tell us what you want from us!

MANSERVANT I want nothing, Hofrat, nothing, nothing, nothing at all—just to speak—just to speak—just to speak—before his corpse, one last time—

NEPALLECK (*raising his voice*) I've no time to speak to you, capito?

(Disturbed by the noise, Prince Montenuovo rushes in from the right, his face distorted with rage.)

Scene 6

MONTENUOVO What's going on? Ah ha, one of them here! You there, clear off! None of you lot will find a job here. Out, quick!

MANSERVANT (*astonished*) I—oh, sweet Jesus—I only want to—to be of service, Your Serene Highness—(*Exit.*)

Scene 7

MONTENUOVO You know very well this isn't a refuge for the homeless, Hofrat—and now that I have seized the initiative—I just want some peace!

NEPALLECK Your Highness can rest assured, it won't happen again, the fellow only wanted—

MONTENUOVO I don't give a damn. Just don't let me see any of that Belvedere crew taken on here!—How many invitations?

NEPALLECK Forty-eight.

MONTENUOVO What did you say?

NEPALLECK Oh, a thousand pardons, I was thinking of tomorrow evening. Twenty-six.

MONTENUOVO Strike off the six. (*Exit.*)

NEPALLECK Very good. (*Sits down again at his desk.*)

Scene 8

Prince Weikersheim, closely followed by usher.

USHER Please, Your Serene Highness, I'm under the strictest instructions not to admit any officials from the Belvedere—

PRINCE WEIKERSHEIM What's that? Instructions? What? Does one need an appointment here? (*Exit usher. Nepalleck remains sitting at his desk without looking up. The Prince, after an interval*) You there! (*After a further interval, louder*) You there! What—what's the meaning of this? (*Shouting*) You there, on your feet!

NEPALLECK (*casually turns his head*) Good day, good day.

PRINCE WEIKERSHEIM (*flabbergasted, after an interval*) What—what's that? So—quickly—(*pointedly*) you there, you know who I am?

NEPALLECK Is something the matter? Of course, I know. You are the former Baron Bronn, now elevated to Prince von Weikersheim.

PRINCE WEIKERSHEIM And you, you are a—*And* him in there, your superior! (*Exit, slamming the door behind him.*)

Scene 9

NEPALLECK (*laughs convulsively. The telephone rings.*) Your humble servant, Your Excellency, just a moment ago one of them—(*Montenuovo puts his head round the door, quick as a flash Nepalleck turns round.*) At your service, Your Highness—

(*Change of scene.*)

Scene 10

Southern Railway terminal. In the pale morning light, a lobby from which one can see, through a wide doorway, the hall-cum-waiting room reserved for members of the court. Black drapes everywhere. In the middle, initially just visible for those outside, two sarcophagi, one placed somewhat lower than the other, surrounded by tall candlesticks with burning candles. Wreaths. Prie-dieux. Black-liveried footmen are lighting the last candles and preparing for the reception of the mourners. The throng in the foreground and the just visible part of the staircase is being held back by policemen. Dignitaries, officials in various uniforms appear, remain in the foreground or disappear towards the waiting room, exchanging silent or whispered greetings. A continuous coming and going. A delegation of municipal councillors in full evening dress appears. Hofrat Nepalleck enters, to all appearances very downcast, and receives numerous condolences from those present. This and the following events take place in the half-light. The conversations are those of shadows.

NEPALLECK It's the most terrible thing, Prince Montenuovo is quite disconsolate that his indisposition prevents him from personally attending this illustrious memorial ceremony. Count Orsini-Rosenberg is also confined to his bed. What a catastrophe has befallen us! Here on the right, the most resplendent wreath with chrysanthemums on the coffin of Her Most Serene Highness, the late archduchess, is from the Prince.

(A tall gentleman, his attire and demeanour reflecting deep mourning, approaches Nepalleck and sympathetically presses his hand.)

ANGELO EISNER V. EISENHOF He was my friend. I was close to him. For instance, at the opening of the Adriatic Exhibition. But what is my grief compared with yours, my dear Hofrat! What you must have gone through these past few days!

NEPALLECK I am spared nothing.

(In the meantime the door opposite has opened and one can see the hall filling up with preeminent representatives of the court, the government, and the church. A master of ceremonies shows each to his allotted place. In the foreground, continuing up to the commencement of the religious ceremony, more participants and would-be observers keep streaming in, presenting their invitations and being either admitted or turned away. Several ladies of the higher nobility are escorted out by a steward. Ten gentlemen, in frock coats, are led with due deference and without having to show their credentials past the waiting crowd as far as the door of the waiting room, where they remain lined up in such a way that they can observe all that happens while almost completely blocking the view of those outside. From the moment of their appearance, the sarcophagi are hidden from sight. While each of the ten takes out a notepad, two officials approach the group and introduce themselves as follows.)

ZAWADIL Spielvogel.

SPIELVOGEL Zawadil.

BOTH *(speaking together)* A dismal morning. We've been here since six to make the arrangements.

ANGELO EISNER V. EISENHOF *(joins them and speaks intently with one of the ten. They all begin to write. He points to various figures who crane their necks and try to push forward through the rows of people. He motions to each in reassurance, gesturing towards the ten and miming the act of writing, as if to signal that their presence has been duly noted. Meanwhile Hofrat Schwarz-Gelber and his wife have managed to get close to those writing and to tap one of them on the shoulder.)*

HOFRAT SCHWARZ-GELBER & HOFRÄTIN SCHWARZ-GELBER No power on earth could have kept us from being here in person.

ANGELO EISNER V. EISENHOF *(turning away with an indignant look, to Dobner v. Dobenau standing beside him)* People like that are out of place at a religious ceremony. Probably their first time. What will my friend Lobkowitz think—there, he's just looking across. (*He gestures repeatedly in greeting.*) Ah, he's spotted me but he didn't recognize me.

DOBNER V. DOBENAU (*his expression glacial, slowly*) As Lord High Steward I should rightly be in there with the pillars of society.

COUNT LIPPAY After my artistic triumph with my portrait of the Pope, as Count Palatine I had frequent opportunity to draw His Holiness's attention to the piety of the illustrious deceased, while as Papal Chamberlain pointing out that his piety remained unshakeable in spite of all such events, which His Holiness was pleased to acknowledge and approve.

EISNER V. EISENHOF Well, well, Lipschitz, *you* here too? Our fathers in Pilsen would never have imagined in their wildest dreams—

COUNT LIPPAY Not a word, Baron, not a word, all water under the bridge. You know as well as I do: a prophet in his own country . . . and all roads lead to Rome. But have you not seen my sons, Count Franz and Count Erwein?

DOBNER V. DOBENAU As Lord High Steward I should rightly be—

CAFÉ PROPRIETOR RIEDL At the Adriatic Exhibition I had dealings with His Imperial Highness—as a patriot and simple business man I served him his coffee in person, and why not?—that's not beneath me, even if people do know who I am—his noble endeavours to promote expansion of the fleet always had my warm support, as chairman of the committee and in the spirit of Tegetthoff, to continue undaunted along the path on which we had already embarked.

DR. CHARAS Under my direction the First Aid Service has also turned out for this occasion, though there have not yet been many opportunities to assist.

HEAD OF SECURITY STUKART As head of the Security Service my presence is required as a matter of course. Quite apart from my social prestige, my attention was inevitably drawn to the purely criminalistic aspect of the case, which I can approach quite objectively since it concerns a murder which no one can accuse me of using to boost my own reputation. In Vienna such a thing would be impossible. I cannot deny that my esteemed colleague in Sarajevo, up to the time of the assassination itself, employed tactics similar to those which have repeatedly worked well for us here, namely, either to remain ignorant of a planned crime or to allow it to come to full maturity in order the better to expose it after the event. But my respected colleague in Sarajevo regrettably failed to implement this proper criminalistic objective, even assuming he had aimed to do so. I, on the other hand, would have made it my personal business far beyond the call of duty, after the deed had been committed and our Security Service was working feverishly on the case, to gather all the threads together in my own hand until I had succeeded in making the perpetrator break down and confess under the weight of the evidence, which my respected colleague in Sarajevo regrettably failed to do owing to the fact that the perpetrator was caught at the scene of the crime. I can only put this disastrous turn of events down to clumsiness, perhaps to the excessive zeal of the assassin who did not resist arrest, or to an unlucky chance which in this particularly deplorable case completely paralysed any police action. However, since the victim of the perpetrator bears no responsibility for this catastrophic outcome, my presence here, albeit among others, will be noted and understood.

SECTION HEAD WILHELM EXNER I am here to represent technological interests.

LAND-BANK GOVERNOR SIEGHART I have been appointed governor. In full expectation that governmental authority shall henceforth be exercised uninterruptedly along lines conforming to my worldview, I take my rightful place here today.

ANGLOBANK PRESIDENT LANDESBERGER Even though they call me a banking magnate, I do not consider it beneath my dignity to claim a modest though proud place before the coffin of one of the mighty, albeit one who pursued ideals different from my own.

HERZBERG-FRÄNKEL My name is Herzberg-Fränkel. I know that while alive he had no particular sympathy for people of my kind, but with death comes reconciliation.

STEIN & HEIN, PROGRESSIVE-LIBERAL MUNICIPAL COUNCILLORS I don't honestly know what business I have being here, but since here I am, here I stay.

TWO CONSULS (*speaking together, introduce themselves*) Stiassny. It's true we had no connection with the deceased to speak of, but we have nevertheless hastened to do our duty.

THREE HONORARY COUNSELLORS (*appear side by side*) We come as a delegation in the belief that we owe it to the shades of the deceased, in the hope of better times to come, not to be diverted from the conviction that he wanted the Good, but was badly informed.

SUKFÜLL As a delegate commissioned by the committee to convey its grief, we are facing an uncertain future and are not yet in a position to assess whether what happened will impede or advance the planned promotion of tourism. Be that as it may, allow me to pay my respects to the deceased.

BIRINSKI & GLÜCKSMANN As representatives of art, we have been commissioned by art to renew its pledge, here at the bier of His late Royal Highness, to strive towards the ideal, while others will have come as representatives of industry.

HUGO HELLER, BOOKSELLER Thanks to my extensive cultural contacts it would surely have been easy for me to have established a lasting attachment to the eminent deceased, had it not been for the fact already noted that death intervened.

(During this speech a lady in deepest mourning has entered. Everyone makes way for her.)

HOFRÄTIN SCHWARZ-GELBER *(thunderstruck, elbows her husband in the ribs and says)* What did I tell you! She turns up everywhere she isn't wanted. Can't one ever be among one's own kind!

FLORA DUB How peaceful they look, lying there! If she were still alive, she would remember me once, throwing flowers at her. He wasn't particularly fond of floral parades, of course. If I've come, it's to show them I've no hard feelings.

GRUMBLER *(in foreground)*

Almighty God, Lord over great and small,
You use small-minded men to test the great,
used this great man to test their pettiness.
Through that which he demanded and endured
he failed the test. Now You have called him home.
Was this Your purpose when you first devised
the blissful counterpoint of life and death?
And can the mortal foe, that rabid mob,
now storm the uplands of eternity?
Can grief no longer be a spark divine
when murderers proclaim it as their own,
making the blood they've shed a crimson jewel,
the tears of heartfelt grief a worthless paste,
a sham that Judas flaunts to hide his sneers?
If so, then we have reached the end of time
and face Your judgment. Let them pay the price
and everywhere the misbegotten feel
that it is finished! Let their blood be shed,
while mourning their demise with God's own tears.

(Meanwhile the religious ceremony has begun with extreme solemnity. All the royal household assembled in the hall can be seen kneeling in prayer, the three

children of the murder victims sobbing at the front. From time to time the priest's voice can be heard. The organ begins to play. One of the ten, who have by now worked their way completely into the hall, suddenly turns to his neighbour and says in a loud voice)

JOURNALIST Where's Szomory? We need atmosphere!

(The organ ceases to play. People pray silently, interrupted only by the sobbing of the three children.)

JOURNALIST *(to his neighbour)* DESCRIBE HOW THEY PRAY!

ACT I

Scene 1

Vienna, at the corner where the Kärntnerstrasse meets the Ring. Flags flying from windows. Soldiers march past to cheers. General euphoria in August 1914 after the ultimatum to Serbia has precipitated world war. Everyone wants to be part of the action.

NEWS VENDOR Ex-tra-aa edi-shun—!

SECOND NEWS VENDOR Ex-tra-aa edi-shun! Both communiqués!

DEMONSTRATOR (*who has broken away from a group singing the Prince Eugene March. His face flushed and already quite hoarse, shouts uninterruptedly*) Serbia—we'll murder 'er! Serbia stinks! Up Habsburg! Hooray! Up Serbia!

INTELLECTUAL (*spots the mistake, gives him a dig in the ribs*) Eh? What do you think you're—

DEMONSTRATOR (*confused at first, thinks for a moment*) Serbia—we'll murder 'er! Serbia stinks! Up! Down with Habsburg! Serbia!

(*A second group mills around, a prostitute among them, directly behind her a disreputable character trying to snatch her handbag.*)

RUFFIAN (*shouts continuously*) Hurrah, hurrah!

PROSTITUTE Hands off! You scoundrel! Let go or I'll—

RUFFIAN (*lets go of her handbag*) Why aren't you cheering? Call yourself a patriot? A whore, that's what you are, and don't you forget it!

PROSTITUTE A bag-snatcher, that's what you are!

RUFFIAN You slut! We're at war, in case you didn't know! A whore, that's what you are!

FIRST PASSERBY United we stand, please! United we stand!

CROWD (*beginning to take notice*) She's a whore! What did she say?

SECOND PASSERBY Blow me if she ain't said summat against the House of Habsburg!

CROWD Grab her! Give her a thrashing! (*The girl has managed to duck into a passageway and disappear.*) Ah, let 'er go! That's not our style. Up Habsburg!

FIRST REPORTER (*to his companion*) Quite an atmosphere! What's going on?

SECOND REPORTER You ain't seen nothing yet.

FIRST ARMY SUPPLIER (*together with another, standing on a Ringstrasse bench*) We can see them better from here. Don't they look splendid marching past, our brave soldiers!

SECOND ARMY SUPPLIER Wasn't it Bismarck who said—it's in today's paper—our boys, don't you just want to kiss them?

FIRST ARMY SUPPLIER You know they've even called up Eisler's eldest?

SECOND ARMY SUPPLIER Get away! Have you ever heard the like of it! And them so rich! Was there nothing they could do?

FIRST ARMY SUPPLIER Apparently they're trying now. He'll probably go up and wangle it.

SECOND ARMY SUPPLIER And if the worst comes to the worst—you wait and see, he'll end up buying him that motorcar he's always dreamt of.

FIRST ARMY SUPPLIER Though that can turn out badly, too.

FIRST PASSERBY How do you do, Director General!

THIRD PASSERBY (*to his companion*) Did you hear? Know who that is? A director general in plainclothes. He's in charge of the generals, so watch what you say.

FIRST OFFICER (*to three others*) Evening Nowotny, evening Pokorny, evening Powolny—the very man! You know all about politics. Come on, tell us, what do you think?

SECOND OFFICER (*with walking stick*) Well, I put it all down to the encirclement.

THIRD OFFICER Y'know what?—That's spot on.

FOURTH OFFICER Absolutely—I was at a bash in the mess last night—! D'you see the latest Schönpflug cartoon? Fantabulous!

THIRD OFFICER Y'know, the paper says war was unacceptable.

SECOND OFFICER Unpreventable, it said.

THIRD OFFICER Unpreventable, of course. I just misread it. Anyhow, what are your plans?

FOURTH OFFICER Well, with any luck I'll get attached to the War Ministry.

FIRST OFFICER You're a great one for the girls, you should join us. I went to hear Mela Mars at the Apollo last night—Novak of the 59th was telling me he'd heard I'd been put forward for a silver medal.

NEWS VENDOR *Tagblatt*! Great victory at Chabatz!

FOURTH OFFICER My congratulations—did you see her? Very tasty, and no mistake!—Hang on, I'll just—(*exit*.)

THE OTHERS (*calling after him*) See you later at Hopfner's, then!

A VIENNESE (*holds forth, standing on a bench*)—and so we had to avenge the Archduke's ashes—no bullshitting!—and so, my fellow citizens, I say unto you—let us rise up as one, with banners fleeing, and unite with the Fatherland in its hour of destiny! Encircled as we are by enemies on all sides! We're fighting a war of self-potence, I tell you, a lowly whore—I mean holy war! Behold our brave boys boldly confronting the enemy, regardless, behold them out in the field facing the foe head-on, answering the call of the Fatherland—and that means defying the vagaries of the weather—just look! And so I also say—if you count yourself a citizen, it's your duty to chip in, however little—right away! Shoulder to shoulder, on the spot! And that means, follow their example, yes sir! And so I also say—stand together as one man! Let the enemy hear it loud and clear: it's a lowly whore of self-potence! Like a phoenix we stand—that means, they can't penetrate! We're on top and Austria will arise like a phalanx from the all-consuming flames—if you ask me! We've been marched off to war in a just cause, no two ways about it, and that's why I also say: Serbia—we'll murder 'er!

VOICES FROM THE CROWD Bravo! Hear, hear! Serbia—we'll murder 'er!—Like it or not!—Every one shot!

VOICE FROM THE CROWD And Russia too—

SECOND VOICE (*bellows*)—what a crew!

THIRD VOICE Not a clue! (*Laughter*.)

FOURTH VOICE Give 'em their due!

ALL Bang bang! Yahoo!

SECOND VOICE And then to France?

THIRD VOICE Just watch 'em prance! (*Laughter*.)

FOURTH VOICE At the end of our lance!

ALL Will they fight? No chance!

THIRD VOICE Who else do we hit? Every Brit!

FOURTH VOICE The Brit we'll hit!

ALL Bravo! A Brit with every hit! Bravo!

BEGGAR BOY *Gott strafe England!*

VOICES Strafe them all! England stinks!

FIRST GIRL Poldi promised me a Serb's guts. I wrote about it to the *Reichspost.*

VOICES Hurrah for the *Reichspost*! Our Christian daily!

SECOND GIRL I wrote to them too. Ferdie's going to bring me back a Russian's kidneys!

CROWD Bring 'em on!

POLICEMAN Keep to the left, please, to the left.

INTELLECTUAL (*to his girl*) This is where we could plumb the soul of the people, if we had the time—what is the time? According to today's editorial, it's a joy to be alive. Isn't Benedikt brilliant, the way he says the glory of classical antiquity illuminates our own age.

FIRST GIRL It's half past now. Ma said I'm in for it if I don't get home by half past.

INTELLECTUAL Ah, don't go, stay. Just look at the people, in a state of ferment! Look, they're uplifted!

FIRST GIRL Where?

INTELLECTUAL I mean, spiritually, as if they'd been transformed, purified—like it says in the editorial, pure heroism. Who would have thought it possible, how the times have changed, and how they've changed us.
(A cab draws up outside a house.)

FARE How much?

CABBY Your honour surely knows.

FARE I don't know. How much?

CABBY The normal fare.

FARE And what is the fare?

CABBY Same as you pay everyone else.

FARE Have you any change? (*Hands him a gold 10-crown piece.*)

CABBY Change? I can't take a coin that size, it might be French gold!

HOUSE-PORTER (*approaches*) What's that? A Froggy? Well, well, what have we here! A spy, I shouldn't wonder—let's show 'im! Where's he come from?

CABBY The Eastern Station.

HOUSE-PORTER Aha, from Petersburg!

CROWD (*which has collected around the cab*) A spy! A spy! (*The fare has disappeared through a doorway.*)

CABBY (*calls after him*) Stingy bastard!

CROWD Ah, let 'im go! No reprisals, they've no place here—that's not our style.

AMERICAN FROM THE RED CROSS (*to another*) *Look at the people how enthusiastic they are!*

CROWD They're English, those two! Speak German! *Gott strafe England*! Let them have it! You're in Vienna! (*The Americans escape through the doorway.*) Ah, let 'em go. That's not our style.

TURK (*to another*) *Regardez l'enthousiasme de tout le monde!*

CROWD Two Frogs! Speak German! Let 'em have it! You're in Vienna! (*The Turks escape through the doorway.*) Ah, let 'em go. That's not our style. Hey, they're Turks! Didn't you see, they had a fez? They're allies! Get them back here and sing the "Prince Eugene March"!

(*Enter two Chinese in silence.*)

CROWD Japs! Japs in Vienna, what next! They want hanging by their pigtails, the rascals!

FIRST VOICE Let 'em go! They're Chinese!

SECOND VOICE You're one too!

FIRST VOICE Speak for yourself!

THIRD VOICE All Chinks are Japs!

FOURTH VOICE Are you a Jap then?

THIRD VOICE No.

FOURTH VOICE A Chink—or the missing link! (*Laughter.*)

FIFTH VOICE Half a mo, half a mo, that's going too far, get an eyeful of this, in the paper it says (*he takes a sheet of newspaper from his pocket*) "Such patriotic excesses cannot be tolerated under any circumstances, and are moreover likely to damage tourism." So how can we develop tourism afterwards, tell me that?

SIXTH VOICE Bravo! He's right. Tourism, to push it up, that's no easy task, it's not as if—

SEVENTH VOICE Belt up! War is war and when someone comes along jabbering in American or Turkish or—

EIGHTH VOICE That's right. We're at war, no doubt about it! (*Enter a lady with just the hint of a moustache.*)

CROWD Look at that! A spy in disguise, spotted it straight away! Arrest 'er! Lock 'er up, on the spot!

CIRCUMSPECT PERSON But gentlemen—think about it—surely she would have had it shaved off!

FIRST VOICE Who?

CIRCUMSPECT PERSON If she were a spy.

SECOND VOICE He forgot! Gave himself away!

VOICES Who?—Him!—No, her!

THIRD VOICE That's how cunning them spies are!

FOURTH VOICE So we can't spot 'em as spies, they grow a moustache!

FIFTH VOICE Don't talk tosh, she's a female spy, and so we can't spot it she's stuck on a moustache.

SIXTH VOICE She's a female spy disguised as a man!

SEVENTH VOICE No, a man disguised as a female spy!

CROWD At any rate, a suspicious character, needs questioning by the police! Grab 'im!

(The lady is led off by a policeman. Singing can be heard—"Staunch stands and true/the Watch on the Rhine.")

FIRST REPORTER *(holding a notebook)* That was no flash in the pan, no sudden drunken rapture, no feverish roar of mass hysteria. Vienna has accepted, with manly fortitude, the decision that will determine its manifold destiny. Know how I'll summarize the atmosphere? The atmosphere can be summarized in the phrase: far from being high-handed or fainthearted. Far from being high-handed or fainthearted, that's the slogan we've coined for the prevailing atmosphere in Vienna, and it cannot be said often enough. Far from being high-handed or fainthearted! What do you say?

SECOND REPORTER What can I say? Brilliant!

FIRST REPORTER Far from being high-handed or fainthearted. Thousands, nay, tens of thousands surged through the streets today, arm in arm, rich and poor, young and old, high and low. The bearing of each and every one showed he is fully aware of the gravity of the situation, but also proud to feel throbbing in his own veins the pulse of this dawning age of grandeur.

VOICE FROM THE CROWD Kiss my arse!

FIRST REPORTER Listen to them striking up the "Prince Eugene March" and the national anthem, over and over, and of course the "Watch on the Rhine", that goes without saying, signalling our good faith towards our allies. Work finished earlier than usual this evening in Vienna. And before I forget, we must make a point of describing the crowd massing in front of the War Ministry. But above all, the one thing we mustn't forget to mention—guess what?

SECOND REPORTER I know! We mustn't forget to mention the crowd massing in their hundreds, nay, in their thousands in Fichtegasse, in front of the offices of the *Neue Freie Presse.*

FIRST REPORTER Clever boy! Yes, that's what the boss likes. But why hundreds and thousands? Figure it out. Why not thousands, nay, tens of thousands, what does it matter since they're already massing?

SECOND REPORTER All right, as long as it's not taken to be some hostile demonstration. Remember last Sunday—after all, the age of grandeur was already dawning—the paper still had all those ads for masseuses.

FIRST REPORTER In this age of grandeur such a petty thought is out of the question. Leave that to Kraus in the *Fackel.* They were all cheering our paper and shouting: Read it out to us! Read it out!—obviously the article on Belgrade—followed by thunderous ovations—

SECOND REPORTER Thunderous, nay, tens of thunderous ovations—

FIRST REPORTER —ovations for Austria, for Germany, and for the *Neue Freie Presse.* The sequence wasn't exactly flattering for us, but what a tribute from the rapturous crowd! All evening long, whenever they weren't busy in front of the War Ministry or the Foreign Office, they stood packed together in Fichtegasse, shoulder to shoulder, massing.

SECOND REPORTER Where do they get the time for it, I'm always amazed.

FIRST REPORTER Simple, in an age of grandeur there's time to spare! The news in the evening edition was cited and discussed again and again. The word Auffenberg flew from mouth to mouth.

SECOND REPORTER How's that?

FIRST REPORTER I can tell you, it's an editorial secret, so don't mention it until after the war. Here's what happened. Roda Roda telegraphed the paper yesterday about the battle of Lemberg, and at the end of the telegram were the words: Beat the drum for Auffenberg. The words had already been set. At the last minute someone noticed and they took them out, but they did beat the drum for the exploits of Auffenberg!

SECOND REPORTER Street scenes are now the boss's big thing. He wants evocations of every cornerstone a dog has left its manifesto on. He called me in yesterday and said I should observe typical street scenes as if they were genre pictures. But that's just what worries me, I don't like crowds, yesterday I had to join in singing the "Staunch stands and true/the Watch on the Rhine"—let's get away, it's starting up again, just look at these people, I know this atmosphere, all of a sudden you're swept up and singing "God Preserve the Emperor."

FIRST REPORTER God forbid! You're right, I don't see why you have to be there in person either, it's lost time, you should be writing about it instead of just standing around. Before I forget, it's very important to describe how resolute they all are, with here and there some individual tearing himself away, wanting to do his bit at all costs. You can bring that out very vividly. The boss called me in yesterday and said you have to whet the public's appetite for the war, and for our paper too—they go hand in hand. The particulars are very important, the details, in a word the nuances, and especially the distinctive Viennese tone. For instance, you must mention that as a matter of course all class distinctions have been set aside with immediate effect—people wave from their automobiles, even from their carriages. I myself have seen one lady in her lace finery get out of her car and fling her arms round the neck of a woman in a shabby headscarf. It's been that way since the ultimatum, everyone united, heart and soul.

VOICE OF A CABBY Get outta my way, ya dorty scum!

SECOND REPORTER Know what I've observed? I've observed people gathering in groups so as to be part of the action.

FIRST REPORTER Yes, and then—?

SECOND REPORTER A student made a speech, about everyone having to do his duty, and someone stepped out from a group and said "High time!"

FIRST REPORTER Not bad. I can only confirm that a great solemnity has enveloped the city, and such solemnity, tempered by a sense of exaltation and consciousness of this historical moment in world history, can be read in every face, in those of men who have already been called up, in those of men still left behind—

VOICE FROM CROWD Kiss my arse!

FIRST REPORTER —and in the faces of men entrusted with high office. Idle comfort and thoughtless hedonism are a thing of the past; the rallying cry is now sanguine sobriety and proud dignity. The physiognomy of our city has been transformed at a stroke.

PASSERBY *(to his wife)* Who cares!—You can go to the Josephstadt if you want, I'm going to the Theater an der Wien.

NEWSPAPER VENDOR Austrian advance! All positions captured!

WIFE I'm sick of seeing *Husarenblut.*

FIRST REPORTER No trace anywhere of anxiety or dejection, no one on edge or sicklied o'er with the pale cast of thought. But equally, no blithe underestimation of the event or foolish thoughtless chauvinism.

CROWD Hurrah, a German! Serbia—we'll murder 'er!

FIRST REPORTER Just look at that, the enthusiasm of the south guided and governed by German gravity. That's what I see in the financial centre. For the Jewish quarter you might want to focus more on feverish excitement.

SECOND REPORTER Not my line, I'm all for elevated moods myself. Here and there, I'll say, you can see some white-haired old fellow fondly recalling the distant days of his youth, or some elderly motherly figure, stooped and trembling as she waves farewell and bestows her blessing. There's a woman clearly worried about her son or her husband. Turn around, and you can see them waving—they really are waving.

(A troop of boys in military peaked caps and with wooden sabres passes by, singing: "Who will choose the soldier's trade—Prince Eugene made a bridge, a bridge he made—")

FIRST REPORTER Make a note: a pretty genre picture. In any case we must aim to say as much about the common people as we can: the boss wrote only today that it is the source from which spiritual refreshment springs.

GROUP *(singing)*

> Those Serbs and Russian shits,
> We'll hack them all to bits!

Hurrah! Down with 'em! Hey, look at them two Jews!

SECOND REPORTER I don't know about you, but I don't feel like observing any more genre scenes. Let the boss come and refresh his spirits at the source, if he dares. I'd rather be far from—

FIRST REPORTER Far from being high-handed or fainthearted, this phrase we've coined for the prevailing atmosphere in Vienna—*(both leave quickly.)*

A commotion occurs. A young man has stolen an elderly woman's handbag. The crowd sides against the woman.

FEMALE VOICE Well, my dear, now we're at war, it's not like peacetime, everyone has to contribute a little something, this is Vienna!

POLDI FESCH *(to his companion)* Yesterday I was out partying with the Sascha Film people, today—*(exeunt.)*

(Enter two devoted readers of the Reichspost.*)*

FIRST DEVOTEE OF THE *REICHSPOST* Wars are processes that reform people's character and purify them, they're seedbeds of virtue and inspiration for heroes. Now guns speak—straight from the shoulder!

SECOND DEVOTEE OF THE *REICHSPOST* At last! At last!

FIRST DEVOTEE Wars are a blessing, not only on account of the ideals for which they are fought, but also for the purification they bestow on the people who wage them in the name of the highest good. Times of peace are dangerous times. All too easily people become soft and shallow.

SECOND DEVOTEE After all, the individual needs a bit of a scrap to shake him up.

FIRST DEVOTEE Possessions, peace of mind, pleasure—they all count for nothing when the country's honour is at stake. So may the war in which our country has been caught up—

SECOND DEVOTEE —so may the war, which seeks to punish an outrage and to guarantee order and peace of mind, be wholeheartedly embraced and blessed.

FIRST DEVOTEE Let us sweep all before us with an iron fist!

SECOND DEVOTEE In Prague, in Brno, in Budweis—everywhere they are rejoicing at the Emperor's decisions.

FIRST DEVOTEE In Sarajevo they sang "God Preserve the Emperor."

SECOND DEVOTEE Loyal Italy stands side by side with Austria.

FIRST DEVOTEE Prince Alfred Windischgrätz has volunteered for military service.

SECOND DEVOTEE His Majesty has been straining every nerve and sinew all day long.

FIRST DEVOTEE On the 27 July, between 12 and 1 pm, the financial arrangements for the war were finalized at the Post Office Savings Bank.

SECOND DEVOTEE The supply of provisions to Vienna for the duration of the war was settled by the Mayor in collaboration with the Prime Minister and the Minister of Agriculture.

FIRST DEVOTEE Did you see what they said in the paper? No price rises because of the war.

SECOND DEVOTEE That makes sense.

FIRST DEVOTEE In unswerving loyalty—

SECOND DEVOTEE —we pay homage to our venerable and beloved Emperor.

FIRST DEVOTEE Mayor Weiskirchner said: My beloved Viennese, we are all living through an age of grandeur.

SECOND DEVOTEE Well, it's no small matter.

FIRST DEVOTEE We also remember and honour our ally in shining armour, he said.

SECOND DEVOTEE His loyal people have already laid their homage on the steps of the imperial throne.

FIRST DEVOTEE At the Emperor's summer residence in Bad Ischl.

SECOND DEVOTEE You'll see, the war will conjure up a renaissance of Austrian thought and action, just you wait. A clean sweep!

FIRST DEVOTEE High time the inner life had a new stimulus. Rat-a-tat-tat—and that's that!

SECOND DEVOTEE We need to be cleansed by a storm of steel, that's what we need! A storm of steel!

FIRST DEVOTEE Have you been mobilized yet?

SECOND DEVOTEE No way! Exempt! And you?

FIRST DEVOTEE Unfit.

SECOND DEVOTEE A sigh of relief runs through the whole population. This war—*(exeunt.)*

(Soldiers marching past can be heard singing "In der Heimat, in der Heimat da gibt's ein Wiedersehn" [equivalent of "Keep the home fires burning/Till the boys come home"].)

REGULAR SUBSCRIBER TO THE *NEUE FREIE PRESSE* *(in conversation with its oldest subscriber)* Interesting what today's editorial says—that the Serbian court and all the rest of them are having to get out of Belgrade. *(He reads out.)* "This evening it was not Vienna which was isolated and provided no safe refuge for court, government and troops. It was Belgrade."

OLDEST SUBSCRIBER Golden words! That sort of thing is good to hear, and one feels just a trace of glee.

REGULAR SUBSCRIBER Although one might object that Vienna is currently further away from the Serbs than Belgrade is from the Austrians, since Belgrade lies directly opposite Zemun, while Vienna does not lie directly opposite Belgrade, and that they have already started firing from Zemun on Belgrade, while they cannot, thank God, fire from Belgrade on Vienna.

OLDEST SUBSCRIBER I can follow your train of thought, but where does it lead? However you look at the situation, you have to conclude that what he says in the editorial is true. Namely, that in Vienna the court and everything else can stay where it is, but not in Belgrade. Or isn't that true? You strike me as something of a sceptic.

REGULAR SUBSCRIBER What does "true" mean? It's simply undeniable, and I've never felt more strongly that he was right than when he wrote that. For when he's right, he's right. (*Exeunt.*)

NEWSPAPER VENDOR —In Lemberg we're still holding on!

FOUR YOUNG MEN ARM IN ARM WITH THEIR GIRLS "He made a bridge, a bridge he made, So they crossed the river and took Belgrade—"

CROWD Three cheers! (*Enter Fritz Werner, waving in acknowledgment.*)

FRÄULEIN KÖRMENDY Go on, ask him now.

FRÄULEIN LÖWENSTAMM (*approaching*) I'm a great admirer, and I wonder if I could ask you for your—
(*Werner takes out a notepad, signs, and hands her the sheet. Exit.*)
He was so sweet.

FRÄULEIN KÖRMENDY Did he look at you? Let's get out of this crowd—and all because of the war. Storm is the only one I really fancy. (*Exeunt.*)

FIRST RUFFIAN Hi, Franz, where are you off to?

SECOND RUFFIAN *Auxtrois Franzois.*

FIRST RUFFIAN Where?

SECOND RUFFIAN *Auxtrois Franzois.* The hat shop. To smash in his window display if he doesn't take the sign away. It's got me hopping mad!

FIRST RUFFIAN Quite right too. It's a scandal, so it is.

SECOND RUFFIAN If I see a sign for French *Modes*, I'll smash it to bits. (*Exit in a rage.*)

FIRST RUFFIAN Hi Pepi, where are you off to?

THIRD RUFFIAN I'm off to make my little contribution.

FIRST RUFFIAN Go on! What a philanthropist!

THIRD RUFFIAN Eh? A what pissed? Say that again, you—(*slaps him in the face.*)

CRIES FROM THE CROWD Did you see that? Shame on you! Who does he think he is? Take yourself for Nikolaïevitch?

VOICE FROM THE CROWD Getting pissed in the middle of a war—that beggars belief!

(Enter two sales representatives.)

FIRST SALES REP So today for the first time: *I Gave Gold for Iron.*

SECOND SALES REP You? Pull the other one! The thought of you giving—someone brought up in—

FIRST SALES REP Who says I gave? Use your head! Look at the playbill over there: *I Gave Gold for Iron,* opens tonight. I fancy going.

SECOND SALES REP Good idea, me too. Fascinating, what's happening right now! Yesterday, at the *Gipsy Princess,* Gerda Walde read out from the Extra edition of the paper about the 40,000 Russians caught in the barbed-wire entanglements—you should have heard the cheers, they called her back at least 10 times.

FIRST SALES REP Were there any wounded soldiers in the theatre??

SECOND SALES REP There were, too! That's what makes everything so interesting. There was a wounded soldier sitting beside me recently. Now, what was the name of the show? Oh yes—*Ich hatt einen Kameraden.*

FIRST SALES REP *You* had a loyal comrade??

SECOND SALES REP Who said I had? It's a show by Viktor Léon!

FIRST SALES REP Any good?

SECOND SALES REP Smash hit!

NEWSPAPER VENDOR Belgrade bombarded—!

(Change of scene.)

Scene 2

South Tyrol. The approach to a bridge. A car is stopped. The chauffeur shows his travel document.

MEMBER OF TERRITORIAL RESERVE Good-day t'ya, gents! May I ask for yer—

GRUMBLER At last a civil greeting! The others are all hopping mad, ready to shoot first and—

RESERVIST Lookin fur a Rushun orto-mobeel, fulla French gold, y'see—

GRUMBLER But you can't stop a car dead, it takes a few yards to pull up—that could lead to a dreadful accident!

RESERVIST *(enraged)* Dammit—if it doan't stop—we blast 'em all to bits—blast 'em all to bits—blast 'em all to bits!—*(The car drives on.)*

(Change of scene.)

Scene 3

The other side of the bridge. Soldiers surround the car. The chauffeur shows his travel document.

SOLDIER (*with levelled gun*) Halt!

GRUMBLER The car has already stopped. Why is the man hopping mad?

CAPTAIN (*enraged*) He's doing his duty. If he's just as mad with the enemy at the front, so much the better!

GRUMBLER Yes, but we're not at the—

CAPTAIN There's a war on! Basta! (*The car drives on.*)
(*Change of scene.*)

Scene 4

Optimist and Grumbler in conversation.

OPTIMIST You can think yourself lucky. In Styria they shot a Red Cross nurse when her car didn't stop for a couple of yards.

GRUMBLER Power has been given to pigmies. It goes against their nature.

OPTIMIST Unfortunately, there will always be unavoidable overreactions by subordinate elements in wartime. But at such times everything must be subordinated to a single goal: victory.

GRUMBLER The power conferred on pigmies will not be sufficient to finish off the enemy, but it will be enough to finish off this country.

OPTIMIST Militarism signifies more power for the state through armed force—

GRUMBLER —which leads to the final dissolution of the state by the same means. In wartime, everyone pulls rank on everyone else. The military pulls rank on the government, which sees no way to escape such unnatural coercion except through becoming corrupt. If the statesman allows himself to be ruled by the military, he has succumbed to a fairytale fascination with heroes whose time is long past. To allow such fantasies to determine matters of life and death in modern times will be disastrous. Letting the military rule is like setting the fox to keep the geese, or turning the gamekeeper into the poacher.

OPTIMIST I don't know how you can justify such a gloomy prognosis. You seem to be doing what you always did in peacetime, generalizing from unavoidable side effects. You take some minor irritations and treat them as symptoms. This is an age of grandeur, yet all you do is quibble about trifles.

GRUMBLER But such trifles will grow with the times!

OPTIMIST Living at a time when such momentous things are happening will inspire even the least of us.

GRUMBLER The little thieves that have not yet been hanged will become big thieves and go scot-free.

OPTIMIST What even the least of us will gain from the war is—

GRUMBLER —his cut. He'll hold up his hand and point to scars he doesn't have.

OPTIMIST Just as the state gains honour by taking up this unavoidable, defensive war to uphold its prestige, so too does every individual, and the blood now shed will bring forth—

GRUMBLER —filth.

OPTIMIST Yes, you have always seen filth everywhere, but now you sense that your time is past. Stay in your corner, carp and cavil away like you always did—the rest of us are entering an era of spiritual awakening! Do you not see that a new era has dawned, an age of grandeur?

GRUMBLER I knew it when it was *this* small, and it will become small again.

OPTIMIST How can you still deny it? Don't you hear the jubilation? Don't you see the rapture? How can any sentient heart be immune to it? Yours is the only one! Can you really believe that this great surge of emotion in the masses will not bear fruit, that this glorious overture will have no sequel? Those who rejoice today—

GRUMBLER —will lament tomorrow.

OPTIMIST Who cares about individual suffering? Or even individual life? At last man's sights are raised again. He lives not only for material gain, but also—

GRUMBLER —for medals.

OPTIMIST Man does not live by bread alone.

GRUMBLER But waging war will mean running out of bread.

OPTIMIST There will always be bread! But we live in hope of final victory, of which there can be no doubt, and before which we—

GRUMBLER —shall starve to death.

OPTIMIST What loss of nerve! What a sorry figure you will cut one day! Don't isolate yourself from such celebrations! The gates of the soul are thrown wide open. Memories of the days when we on the home front participated in the deeds and sufferings of the glorious fighting front, if only by reading the daily reports, will leave on the soul—

GRUMBLER —no scars.

OPTIMIST The nations will learn from this war only—

GRUMBLER —how to wage more wars in the future.

OPTIMIST The bullet has left the barrel, and mankind will—

GRUMBLER —feel it go in through one ear and out the other!

(Change of scene.)

Scene 5

At the Foreign Office.

COUNT LEOPOLD FRANZ RUDOLPH ERNEST VINCENZ INNOCENZ MARIA The ultimatum was tremendous! At last, at last!

BARON EDUARD ALOIS JOSEF OTTOKAR IGNAZIUS EUSEBIUS MARIA Stunning! To think they were that close to accepting it!

COUNT I'd have been livid! Fortunately we had those two little clauses, our right to conduct investigations on Serbian soil, and so on—and they couldn't swallow that. So now they've only themselves to blame, the Serbs.

BARON If you think about it—because of two little clauses, over a trifle like that—the World War broke out—Hilarious, really!

COUNT We couldn't possibly have omitted those two clauses. Why were they so dead set on not accepting those two clauses, the Serbs?

BARON Oh well, it was clear from the start that they wouldn't accept.

COUNT We knew that in advance! Good old Poldi Berchtold, say what you like. Add to that, all of society now speaks with one voice. Tremendous! I ask you—what a feeling of elation! At last, at last! It was beyond endurance. Handicapped every step of the way. Well, life is going to be different now! This winter, the minute peace is declared, I'll be whizzing along the Riviera.

BARON I'll be happy if we can just whizz along the Adriatic.

COUNT You're joking! The Adriatic is ours. Italy won't lift a finger. So I tell you, the minute peace is declared—

BARON And when d'you think we'll have peace?

COUNT Two weeks, three at the very most, I reckon.

BARON Don't make me laugh!

COUNT What d'you mean? We'll make short work of Serbia, my friend, very short work indeed. You'll see how well our boys fight. Look no further than our dashing Sixth Dragoons! And they say a few society people are already at the front, think of that! Then there's our artillery, first-rate! All working away in unison like crazy!

BARON But what about Russia?

COUNT The Russkis will be glad to be left in peace. Trust Conrad—he knows why he allowed them to take Lemberg. As soon as we're in Belgrade, it'll be a different story. Potiorek is terrific! I tell you, the Serbs are being torn apart! The rest will follow automatically.

BARON So when d'you really think—seriously—

COUNT In three, four weeks we'll have peace.

BARON You were always a tremendous optimist.

COUNT So when d'you think, then?

BARON Nothing doing under two, three months! You'll see. If all goes well, two. But my dear chap, it will have to go very, very well!

COUNT Well, excuse me, but lasting that long would be such a dreadful bore! Really charming! It couldn't last that long, though, if only because of the food situation. Only the other day Frau Sacher was saying to me—You don't think the food regulations will work, do you? Even at Demel they're already worried if they can keep going. Charming, eh?—We're already tightening our belts where we can, but in the long run—Ludicrous, can't be done! Or d'you really think—?

BARON You know my opinion. I don't put much faith in the hinterland. After all, we're no Prussians, even if we are obliged to accept them as—only yesterday I was talking to Putzo Wurmbrand—y'know, the fellow who's got little Marie Pallfy in tow—he's Krobatin's right-hand man, y'know, so super-patriotic—well, he says, when you start a defensive war—and he's the one who persists in calling it a defensive war—

COUNT Wait a minute—are you saying it isn't a defensive war then? Do leave off, you're such a monumental defeatist! Have you already forgotten the predicament we were in? That we were, so to speak, compelled to strike back since our prestige was at stake *et cetera*—well, it seems to me—forgive me—but haven't you forgotten the encirclement?—only yesterday I was talking to Fipsi Schaffgotsch, maybe he is a bit affected, being with that Bellgarde woman, but a really nice fellow—anyway, what was I going to say?—oh yes—isn't it true we were forced to allow the Serbs to attack us at Temes-Kubin, so we could—

BARON What d'you mean?

COUNT What do I mean? Come off it! Don't you know better than anyone that a Serbian attack at Temes-Kubin was essential—I mean, for us to be compelled to strike back—

BARON That goes without saying.

COUNT Well then, it wouldn't have been essential otherwise, would it? Just like the German response when the French dropped bombs near Nuremberg! Well then—I mean to say—if that isn't a defensive war!

BARON Well forgive me, but what did I say? As you know, I was the one who was for a trial of strength from the start, providing it proves decisive, so I couldn't care less what you call it. A defensive war—that sounds as if you're having to apologize. All's fair in love and war, that's what I say.

COUNT Well yes, you're right. But that Poldi Berchtold, eh! What a dashing fellow, always is, always was, say what you like. You have to look and act the part in our business—and you've got to hand it to him! The way he gave them all the slip and stole off to Ischl to get the Emperor's signature—they'd probably have tried to prevent the ultimatum! But he—well, tremendous! One coup after the other!

BARON Stunning! Never thought he'd bring it off like that. He doesn't suffer fools gladly. The way he cut down attendance at the funeral and excluded the Russian Grand Duke, that was Poldi Berchtold all over.

COUNT Of course. It wasn't his fault that Russia then interfered after all. If he'd had his way, the World War would have been confined to Serbia. Know what Poldi Berchtold has? Poldi Berchtold has what a diplomat in a world war needs above all else: *savoir vivre*! I was tremendously impressed the way he simply stuck those English idiots' proposal inside his race-card—giving their gracious approval to our occupying Belgrade—what a mercenary bunch of hypocrites—and the way he comes up to the club afterwards—remember?—gives us that look and says: Let the army's will be done! Came up trumps again, eh! You must admit that wasn't easy, at such a momentous moment—
(A bell rings in an adjacent room, followed by)

BERCHTOLD'S VOICE Iced-coffee! (*Sound of door closing.*)

BARON I ask you—half past eleven! I ask you—half past eleven and he's already ordering his iced-coffee! I must say, I'm tempted for once to—I confess I might just—iced-coffee, that's really his strong point!

COUNT It's maybe his only weakness! He adores iced-coffee! But you must admit, Demel's iced-coffee—sheer perfection!

BARON Sunshine today—look outside—isn't that great!

COUNT (*opens and reads the text of a dispatch*)—Reports that in Lemberg we're still holding on—

BARON You see!

COUNT Our own Poldi Berchtold—you know what I mean (*drops his voice and continues reading dispatch*)—Reports that in Lemberg we're still holding on—retracted—oh, what the heck, it's always the same thing—what a bore—I'm sick and tired of it—(*crumples the paper up*)—what was I going to say?—the more I think about the situation—all in all—I think a little intimate supper out of town with Steffi might be just the thing tonight.

(*Change of scene.*)

Scene 6

In front of a hairdressing salon in the Habsburgergasse. A crowd of people, very agitated.

CROWD Down with 'im! Smash everything!

FIRST INDIVIDUAL FROM THE CROWD (*trying to appease crowd*) But my good people, the man had done nothing! The violin shop owner next door is his enemy—

VIOLIN SHOP OWNER (*harangues the crowd*) He's a Serb! He's guilty of an offence—a comment he made against an eminent personage! I heard it myself in person!

HAIRDRESSER (*wringing his hands*) I'm innocent—I'm a court hairdresser—why on earth would I want to—

SECOND INDIVIDUAL You can see from his name he's a Serb, take his shaving mugs and bash 'im over the head—

THIRD INDIVIDUAL Lather his face! Down with 'im! Down with the Serb cutthroat!

CROWD Down with 'im—! (*They wreck the salon.*)

(*The historians Friedjung and Brockhausen appear at the corner in conversation.*)

BROCKHAUSEN Only today I contributed a fitting comment to the press on this very theme—with compelling logic I refuted a priori any comparison of our people with the French or English rabble. You might want to use the passage in your own work, my dear Friedjung, I place it at your disposal. Here it is: "The conviction which inspired and brought comfort and encouragement to those well versed in history as being the quintessence of historical wisdom, namely that barbarism shall never achieve final victory—that conviction was instinctively assimilated by the population at large. Certainly, the cheap and unsavoury patriotism of the howling mob has never made itself heard on the streets of Vienna. There was no outburst of mass hysteria, however short-lived.

Since the war began, this ancient German state has made the most attractive virtues of the German people its own: unwavering self-confidence and deep-rooted faith in the victory of a good and just cause." (*He hands him the extract.*)

FRIEDJUNG A truly excellent appraisal, my dear Brockhausen, one that hits the bull on the head and takes the nail by the horns. I shall make a note and mark it well. And by Jove, here we have an example straight away! A patriotically inspired crowd giving expression to their feelings with due moderation, a velvet hand in an iron glove, as befits the Viennese tradition. The immediate cause may well be found in the name Habsburgergasse. Evidently the gathering in its artless way wanted to pay homage to the name, just as they would have had every reason to demonstrate in the Babenbergerstrasse in Leopold's time.

BROCKHAUSEN (*uncertainly*) But all the same, it appears to me—

FRIEDJUNG (*uncertainly*) All the same, it is somewhat strange—

BROCKHAUSEN The good people are making quite a noise.

FRIEDJUNG At any rate, more than what is traditionally right and proper.

BROCKHAUSEN One mustn't forget, the reason for their excitement is justified. Who was it said—

FRIEDJUNG Since the day our august monarch called thousands, nay, tens of thousands of our sons and brothers to the colours, the merry throng here by the mighty river of the Nibelungs does indeed seem to be in a state of ferment and turmoil. And yet, "though the juice bubbles madly in fermentation—"

BROCKHAUSEN The days when they called themselves Phaeaceans are past. "Time's humming loom—"

FRIEDJUNG Oh look, presumably they all want to go into that hairdressing salon. He's an official court hairdresser and the innocent spirit of the people doubtless thinks—

CRIES FROM THE CROWD "That's him seen to!" "Rat-a-tat-tat—and that's that" "Damned Serb—bastard!" "Shave those Serb shits with the broken bits!" "The sponge'll do my old woman!" "I've saved all the bottles of perfume!" "Let's have some!" "Jesus, look at the beautiful white coat!" "Go on, lend me one of the sprays!" "Gott strafe England!" "The bastard's got away!"

VIOLIN SHOP PROPRIETOR Didn't I tell you he's a traitor! It's high treason!

BROCKHAUSEN The crowd is agitated and rightly thinks it is once again on the trail of Serb traitors.

FRIEDJUNG Isn't it remarkable what a good nose the people have when they get wind of a plot against the inalienable territories represented in the Reichsrat. Unless I'm very much mistaken, documents relating to the Slovensky Jug plot for a Greater Serbia will be found in this hairdresser's—the plot I started to uncover back in 1908.

BROCKHAUSEN It's only the way it's been done I find somewhat problematic.

CROWD Get him! Smash 'im to a pulp! Serbia—we'll murder 'er!

FRIEDJUNG Perhaps it would be advisable, my dear Brockhausen, faced with this justifiably agitated violin shop proprietor, to make a wide detour around an obvious divergence from the historically proven fact that the Viennese population rejects the cheap and unsavoury patriotism of the howling mob.

CRIES FROM THE CROWD "What are those two Jews doing here?" "They look like they came from the Balkans!" "All they need is a kaftan!" "They're Serbs!" "Serbs, both of them!" "Traitors!" "Give 'em a hiding!"

(The two historians duck into a doorway.)

(Change of scene.)

Scene 7

Kohlmarkt. Outside the revolving door at the entrance to Café Pucher.

OLD MAN BIACH (*very agitated*) The simplest thing would be to throw five divisions against Russia, that would soon settle it.

HONORARY COUNSELLOR Obviously. Attack is the best defence. Look what the Germans have achieved. What drive! Their breakthrough in Belgium was unparalleled! That's what we need.

BUSINESSMAN Tell me, what's happening about your son?

HONORARY COUNSELLOR Exempt—that's one worry less. But the way things are—the war situation—take it from me, it doesn't look good out there. Something like that breakthrough in Belgium—some fresh offensive spirit—I'm telling you, that's what we need—

BUSINESSMAN Give us Belgium down here and we'll break through too.

INTELLECTUAL We need a Bismarck—

BIACH What good is diplomacy now? Let weapons talk! Can we expose ourselves to the risk of failure? If we don't break through now—

GRUMBLER (*wants to enter the café*) Excuse me—

INTELLECTUAL I can see that. But doesn't the flank attack take precedence as a strategic factor in open warfare—

HABERDASHER Oh you needn't worry about that, they're surrounded. Soffi Pollak told me herself.

BIACH Come off it! How can *she* know, tell me that!

HABERDASHER How? Hasn't her husband been mobilized with the medical reserves in the Gartenbau?

HONORARY COUNSELLOR I thought he was exempt? Surrounded, that would be marvellous: you know it means we have them in a stranglehold.

BIACH (*avidly*) They should strangle them till they choke! I'd love to be there when they do!

HABERDASHER Klein will be—he's in the War Press Bureau. Yesterday he wrote that they'll bleed them white. He won't loosen his grip until they do.

BUSINESSMAN What luck to be right in the thick of it! Tell me about this War Press Bureau, sir. Do you only get in if you're unfit for active service, or if you're fit?

GRUMBLER Excuse me—(*They make way.*)

HABERDASHER What do you mean, fit? Anyone who can write can get in if he doesn't want to shoot, but wants the shooting done by others.

HONORARY COUNSELLOR How d'you mean? Why doesn't he want to shoot, softhearted?

HABERDASHER No, hardheaded. You can't be softhearted in the army, and being in the War Press Bureau is as good as being in the army.

BIACH This War Press Bureau must be wonderful! You can see everything. It's right up close to the front, and the front is where the battle is, so Klein will be almost in the battle and see everything without being in danger.

BUSINESSMAN They always say you see nothing at all on a modern battlefield. So in the War Press Bureau you actually see more than if you're in the battle itself.

INTELLECTUAL Yes, up to a point, and you can even report on several fronts at once.

HONORARY COUNSELLOR It was Klein who wrote that fascinating press report about how most wounds on our side were superficial ones to hands and feet, from which he deduced that the Russians prefer flank attacks—

HABERDASHER He's no Roda Roda, that's for sure! A lot of water will flow under the Dnieper's bridges before he can write like Roda Roda!

HONORARY COUNSELLOR The thing I like most about Roda Roda is that he's so full of dash. Says he's going to observe the battle on the Drina next day, and observe it he does. Class act!

BIACH No two ways about it, once an officer, always an officer—unmistakable, the *esprit de corps*! My son may be exempt, but is still very interested, he even wants to subscribe to the *Streffleur*.

HONORARY COUNSELLOR I can't help but feel very pessimistic.

BIACH What do you mean, pessimistic? In Lemberg we're still holding on, can you ask for more than that?!

BUSINESSMAN Proves my point!

INTELLECTUAL There's no cause for pessimism. If it were to be decided right now, at worst it would be a draw.

HABERDASHER And I can tell you—I even have it from a man in the Ministry—it's virtually all over. We move in from the right, the Germans from the left—a pincer movement, till they choke to death.

HONORARY COUNSELLOR Sounds fine—but what about Serbia?

BIACH (*savagely*) Serbia? What about Serbia? We'll brush it aside!

HONORARY COUNSELLOR I don't know—I can't help feeling—today's bulletin—you have to read between the lines, and if you look at the map—even as a mere layman—I can prove to you that Serbia—

BIACH (*irritated*) Let Serbia go hang, Serbia is a sideshow. Enough already! Let's go in, I'll be interested to see what the Ministers have to say today—I suggest, gentlemen, we sit at the table next to theirs. (*They go in.*)
(*Change of scene.*)

Scene 8

Suburban street. A milliner's shop, a Pathéphone record shop, the Café Westminster, and a branch of the cleaners Söldner & Chini. Enter four young men, one of them carrying a ladder, strips of paper, and paste.

FIRST Here's another one! What does that say? *Salon Stern, Modes et Robes*. Paper the whole thing over!

SECOND Yes, but we could leave the name, and what kind of shop it is. Here, let me. Watch. (*He pastes and reads*) "Sal Stern Mode." That'll do—it's German now. On to the next.

FIRST Patephon, look, what's that ? Is that French?

SECOND No, it's Latin, that can stay. But what's that there: "German, French, English, Italian, Russian, Hebrew music"?

THIRD What should we do?

FIRST It has to go, all of it!

SECOND No, let's try this (*He pastes and reads*): "German—Hebrew music." That'll do.

THIRD But what have we here? Look at that! Café Westminster. That's surely English, isn't it!

FIRST Yes, but we'd better check with them first. It's a coffeehouse, the owner might be some celebrity and we'd be in trouble. Let's get him out here. Wait a minute. (*He goes in and returns at once with the proprietor, who is visibly alarmed.*) You see the point, don't you?—a patriotic sacrifice—

PROPRIETOR What an imbroglio, but if you gentlemen are from the Voluntary Committee—

FOURTH Look, why did you call your coffeehouse that in the first place? That was shortsighted.

PROPRIETOR But gentlemen, how could I have known? I feel bad about it myself now. Look, the reason I called it that is because we're right beside the Western Station, and that's where the English milords arrive during the season—so they should feel at home straight away—

FIRST So, did you ever have an English lord in your coffeehouse?

PROPRIETOR I'll say! Those were the days! Heavens, yes!

FIRST Congratulations! But look, none of them can come now anyway.

PROPRIETOR Thank God for that!—Gott strafe England!—but look, people have got used to the name, and after the war, when, God willing, the English customers come back—look, give me a break!

FIRST Sorry, mister, the voice of the people can't make allowances for things like that, and the voice of the people, as you will know only too well—

PROPRIETOR Of course, we entrepreneurs are aware—aren't we more or less a people's café—but—what am I going to call it then?

SECOND Don't worry about that, we won't hurt you—it'll only take a second—and quite painless. (*He scratches out the "i."*)

PROPRIETOR Eh?—what's that going to turn it into, then?

SECOND There. Now you get a painter to put in a *ü*.

PROPRIETOR A *ü*? Café Westmünster—?

SECOND A *ü*! It means just the same, and it's German. Kosher! Not a soul will notice any change, but everyone will be aware it's something quite different. So, what do you say?

PROPRIETOR Genius, pure genius! I'll have the painter come right away. Thank you for your indulgence, gentlemen. It'll stay that way for the duration. It's fine for as long as the war lasts. Afterwards, of course, I'll probably—what do you think the lords would say if they came back and saw the *ü*? They wouldn't believe their eyes!

(Two customers are just leaving the coffeehouse and saying good-bye to each other. One says: "Adieu!" The other: "Adio!")

FIRST What was that? You've got French and Italian customers? One says "Adieu" and the other even says "Adio"? You seem to have an international clientele—something suspicious there—

PROPRIETOR Look here, just because somebody says "Adieu"—

SECOND But didn't you hear the first one say "Adio"? That's the language of the archenemy!

THIRD —those cunning basturds!

FOURTH —the perfidious double-crosser on the River Po!

FIRST Exactly! The traitor who was our archenemy!

SECOND Our archenemy, who double-crossed us!

THIRD On the Po!

FOURTH On the Popo! And don't you forget it!

(The proprietor has retreated, step by step, into the café.)

FIRST *(calling after him)* English Dago! A wop on the popo!

SECOND That'll larn him t'use furren words. On to the next!

THIRD Well, look at that, we've struck it lucky today: Söldner & Chini! That's the same mélange as at the coffeehouse. Söldner—everyone knows the English are mercenaries—and Chini—that's an Italian!

FIRST May God punish England and destroy Italy—paper over the whole thing! Chemical dry cleaners? We'll make a clean sweep of them! That gets my goat! By tomorrow the whole district must be purged of un-German words. If I find one more, I'll have his guts for garters! *(The second man pastes over the sign.)*

THIRD We'd better separate, you two stay here on the boulevard, we'll go across vis-à-vis.

FIRST Beg pardon, but I can't come today, I've got to get off, pronto—I have a rendezvous.

SECOND That creates an impasse. Without you we risk a contretemps. As for me, I'm blasé about any imbroglio, but people are on the qui vive, and if we get into a fracas—

FOURTH As far as I'm concerned it's a mere bagatelle—but we could end up in a mêlée. It hasn't eventuated yet, but—

SECOND Yes, I know, we must avoid a debacle. Savoir faire, I always say, harmonize with people! Don't submit to force majeure! We must be resolute and persevere in our patriotic operation. Atupri!

THIRD Absolutely, but what if someone argues—as people do—that we're destroying his raison d'etre—and starts some brouhaha, or even gets furioso, then—

FIRST O, come on! Complete no-brainer! Or just riposte, stante pede, that there are higher interests at stake now! Then he'll accept force majeure. After all, people have plenty of savvy. No need for long discussions. You'll get nowhere by entering into parpourlers with all and sundry.

SECOND But what if he gets enraged—people get etepetete so quickly—

FIRST Then you just call him an agent provocateur, basta! So, nil desperandum! Let's rendezvous tomorrow, and I'll act as your aide again. Heavens, it's a quarter to five, I've got to go, pronto—or by jingo I'll be late—so, bonne chance tonight!—Adieu—!

THIRD Ciao!

FOURTH Servitore!

SECOND Orevar!

FIRST (*turning back*) Apropos, if anyone protests, you can simply legitimize yourselves as interim volunteers from the Provisional Central Committee of the Executive Commission of the League for Language Purification and a General Boycott of Foreign Words. Adio!
(Change of scene.)

Scene 9

A primary school.

TEACHER ZEHETBAUER —But higher ideals have now descended upon us, so promoting the tourist trade has to be put on hold and can occupy only a fall-back position. Nevertheless, we must not lose heart since it is our duty—after each of us has made a start and done his bit for the Fatherland—to keep right on to the end of the road, unswerving and undaunted. The tender shoots of tourism which we have planted far and wide, and which have also taken root in your young hearts as nurtured by our highly esteemed national school inspector and our esteemed district school inspector—these shoots, I say, must not be crushed under the iron heel of our battalions, indispensable as they may be in this age of grandeur, but on the contrary must be forever tended with loving care. It is certainly essential at this time that each and every one of us should stand our ground like a man—and that means you, too. You too must go into action, go to your parents or guardians and request the splendid children's game "Let's Play World War" as a surprise birthday present, or, since Christmas is almost upon us, "Death to the Russians" I can also tell you that, as a reward for your good work and behaviour, and of course subject to the approval of your esteemed parents or guardians, each of you shall be permitted this Sunday to drive a nail into the emblematic Iron Warrior, each nail signifying—

CLASS Oh, great!
(A boy raises his hand.)

TEACHER What is it, Gasselseder?

GASSELSEDER Please, sir, I already did drive in a nail with my father. May I drive in another one?

TEACHER If your esteemed parents or guardians permit, the school authorities will raise no objection to your patriotic desire to drive in another nail.
(A boy raises his hand.)
What is it, Czeczowiczka?

SECOND BOY Please, sir, I have to go.

TEACHER Go? You're too young to go, hang on until you're a bit older.

BOY Please, sir, I have to.

TEACHER I cannot grant your request at this time. Shame on you! Why do you want to go?

BOY Please, sir, I need to, it's urgent.

TEACHER Wait for better times. You would set a bad example to your classmates. The Fatherland is in urgent need, too. Let that be an example, now is the time to hold out.
(Two boys raise their hands.)

TEACHER What is it, Wunderer major and Wunderer minor, Karl and Rudolf?

BOTH Please, sir, we would rather drive our nails into the Iron Post.

TEACHER Sit down! Shame on you! There is no more room for nails on the emblematic Iron Post. But if you work hard, the Iron Warrior shall become such an emblem, a landmark and talking point for your children and your children's children.

KOTZLIK Please, sir, Merores keeps pushing me!

MERORES That's not true, he called me a Jew, I'm going to tell my dad, he'll write to the *Tagblatt,* then you'll be for it!

TEACHER That's enough, Kotzlik and Merores, don't forget: United we stand! Turn to the text in our reader: "Hymn of Hate Against England." Merores, stay on your feet and answer my question: what's the name of the poet who wrote this poem?

MERORES I know, it's Frischauer.

TEACHER Wrong. Sit down.

BOY (*whispers*) Lissauer.

TEACHER Praxmarer, if you prompt again, I'll make you write out Hofmannsthal's *Prince Eugene.* Now I've lost the thread.

Some boys rush to the teacher's lectern and search under it.

TEACHER What are you looking for?

BOYS The thread, sir. Sir said he had lost the thread.

TEACHER Don't be ridiculous. I don't mean figuratively, but literally.

BOY Perhaps you'd like my guideline, sir—

TEACHER Wottawa, you haven't understood me either. I can see none of you are up to it. I wanted to test you on the "Hymn of Hate", but I'll let you off that for today. By tomorrow I want you to have prepared the ideals required by the grandeur of the age, for I won't be able to make any more allowances. What would the district school inspector think if he pays us a visit and you go on like this? Now that you should be out promoting the second war loan, it's even more of a duty not to fall short of expectations. So, be sure you have the "Hymn of Hate" off by heart by tomorrow! I can only repeat and repeat again: Hold out, do your bit, promote the war loan, collect scrap metal, bring out your gold lying idle in your treasure chests! But I'll be lenient with you today, so back to the tourist trade. It must be promoted! I've already explained to you why now, of all times, tourism must not be neglected. Although the stormy blast of war is sweeping over our country, while our august monarch has called thousands and tens of thousands of our sons and brothers to arms, nevertheless the first stirrings of a growth in the tourist trade can be observed. So let us never lose sight of this lofty ideal. There is a beautiful story in your reader entitled *A River of Gold.* No, we won't do it now, rather let us strike up the old song you learnt in the days of peace, do you remember?

(A boy raises his hand.)

TEACHER Well, Habetswallner?

BOY Please, sir, I know: "In a Wondrous Country Inn."

TEACHER Wrong!

(A boy raises his hand.)

TEACHER Well, Braunshör?

BOY "True and Honest Ever Be."

TEACHER No! Shame on you!

(A boy raises his hand.)

TEACHER Well, Fleischanderl?

BOY "To Wander Is the Miller's Joy."

TEACHER Sit down!

(A boy raises his hand.)

TEACHER Well, Zitterer?

BOY "Off We Go to Far-off Places."

TEACHER Sit down! We can't go to far-off places right now, people there should come to us!

(A boy raises his hand.)

TEACHER Süssmandel, do you know?

BOY Please, sir, may I go out?

TEACHER What are you thinking of, didn't I tell you we can't do that now, neither in the classroom nor when you go out into life. So, none of you knows the song?

(A boy raises his hand.)

TEACHER Anderle, do you?

BOY "What Need Have I of Goods or Gold."

TEACHER Go and sit at the back! Where did you learn that? Shame on you, Anderle! I see you've forgotten it in this age of steel. Isn't it the dear old song you all sang when you were learning your vowels? Shame on you! Let me take up my fiddle and you'll all soon be singing along.

(A boy raises his hand.)

TEACHER Well, Sukfüll, are you going to put the class to shame?

SUKFÜLL "Promote the Tourist Trade!"

TEACHER Good boy, Sukfüll, you've put the whole class to shame. I'll tell your father so he can congratulate you.

(He takes up his fiddle and the class joins in singing.)

A a, Ha ha! Here come tourists, hallelujah!
We're not broke, we're up and running,
Now we see the tourists coming,
A-a, Ha ha! Here come tourists, hallelujah!

E e, He-he! Don't your lordships all agree?
Classy cabs and classy lassies,
Come and see their classy chassis.
E e, He-he! Don't your lordships all agree?

I i, Aye-aye, our love of loot we'll gratify.
Don't be stingy, for your pleasure
Pay through the nose, though at your leisure.
I i, Aye aye, our love of loot we'll gratify.

O o, Oh ho, waltz away, quick, quick, slow,
Happy city, now we've found you,
"Wiener Blut" flows all around you.
O o, Oh ho, waltz away, quick, quick, slow.

U u u, our hearts will welcome you.
To Vienna, land of song
For evermore, so come along,
U u u, our hearts will welcome you.

(Change of scene.)

Scene 10

Café Pucher. The ministers are gathered together.

EDUARD *(to Franz)* We're still missing the *Muskete*, the *Floh* and the *Interessante*—

(Enter five others; they sit down at a neighbouring table. The Prime Minister turns to the Minister of the Interior.)

OLD MAN BIACH As I live and breathe, he said something about a bomb—

EDUARD *(brings the illustrated magazines)* Beg pardon, Excellency, have you finished with the *Bombe*?

BIACH Ah—

THE OTHERS *(among themselves)* What did he say?

BIACH Nothing—I was wrong.

HONORARY COUNSELLOR (*to his neighbour*) Interesting—in today's *Tagblatt* it says—

(The waiter Franz comes to their table. In turn, cries of "Double cream for me!" "With skin for me, and more milk!" "Weak and milky and the six o'clock edition!" "Filtered cappuccino!")

HONORARY COUNSELLOR And a Mélange for me, no wait, I think I'll have a small Gold for a change, and the *Presse.*

BIACH (*picks up the* Neue Freie Presse) Magnificent!

THE OTHERS What's up?

BIACH Look, I find that impressive! For the past 14 days he's been celebrating the fiftieth anniversary of the *Presse*, it's always the headline, then come accounts of the Battle of Lemberg with eyewitness impressions. That tells you at least that there are still some happy events in Austria. After all, it is an event there's never been the likes of before. The bulwark of liberal German mentality, morality, and culture, no less, and all the prestigious names offering congratulations—just look at that—hold on—three, four, no five full sides. Everyone vying with each other to congratulate, even the highest in the land are not hanging back.

HONORARY COUNSELLOR I wrote in today—it'll appear tomorrow, you'll see!

BIACH (*excitedly*) If you've written in, I will too. It's no small honour to appear in such company—

INTELLECTUAL Only one thing I find odd, now I think of it—every time, with all the thousands and tens of thousands of people conveying their congratulations, every time he publishes the address as well: The Honourable Moriz Benedikt, Editor of the *Neue Freie Presse*, 11 Fichtegasse, Vienna I. I can't help thinking that's rather vain! He could have left out the "Honourable", and giving the address, say, 20 times would surely have been enough.

BUSINESSMAN Don't say that. One can't hear it too often.

HONORARY COUNSELLOR (*almost simultaneously*) I don't see that, he doesn't want to change a thing, that's what they wrote and that's what should appear, he's right!

BIACH What's he saying? What's he saying?

BUSINESSMAN (*trying to placate them*) But—oh, forget it—in Lemberg we are still holding on!

HABERDASHER Above all, it shows you that all the letters are genuine, look, Admiral Montecuccoli, no less, and nothing but Excellencies—

HONORARY COUNSELLOR Montecuccoli and Excellencies, so what? Is Berchtold a nobody? Sent in his congratulations yesterday in his own hand!

BIACH Berchtold? That's nothing! Weiskirchner! See with your own eyes, what do you say to that! Can you believe it? Weiskirchner, the most rabid anti-Semite! Congratulating him "In all sincerity"! What does that say there? That's nice, who wrote that, I wonder: "The *Neue Freie Presse* is the prayer-book of the intelligentsia."

BUSINESSMAN But it's true! What's that there? Ah, interesting, the Dukes Agency takes great pleasure in the close relationship it enjoys with the *Neue Freie Presse*. The biggest advertising agency in Vienna, that's saying something!

INTELLECTUAL Look at that! Even Harden—the most brilliant stylist, as we know—Harden calls him—listen to what he calls him, that's brilliant!—"Chief of the Intellectual General Staff"!

HABERDASHER Ingenious, but not original. A few dozen of the letters have already used it; besides, it's the obvious thing to say.

BIACH Of course, especially when the talk of Lemberg comes right next. And the speeches at the banquet were tremendous, too.

BUSINESSMAN It can't have been at the banquet—the banquet was cancelled because of the World War, wasn't it?

HONORARY COUNSELLOR Modesty forbids—

HABERDASHER That's carrying respect too far!

BIACH Of course it is! Anyhow, even if it wasn't a banquet, it was still tremendously impressive. If it hadn't been for the war, you would have really seen something. But they refused to give up. The way they all acclaimed him was a sight to behold, the Head of Accounts and even the top delivery-woman. A press party like that is like a family get-together. I have it that the speeches were all taken down in shorthand at the time.

HONORARY COUNSELLOR But wasn't the stenographer one of those acclaiming him too?

BIACH Yes, but all the while he was taking it down.

BUSINESSMAN Look at the list, I ask you—there's no end to it—

INTELLECTUAL Yes, sad indeed.

BUSINESSMAN How do you mean, sad?

INTELLECTUAL Oh sorry, I was looking at the list of casualties further down—it just happens to come next, after the list of those conveying their congratulations.

BIACH So what?—what else could they do?—yes, to be sure, it's an event our children's children will still be talking about.

HONORARY COUNSELLOR That's true. It's not every day a paper is 50 years old.

BIACH Quite right, but I meant—Lemberg.

HONORARY COUNSELLOR Who's talking about Lemberg?

INTELLECTUAL (*looking around apprehensively*) Unfortunately there's no denying, it wasn't our finest hour.

BIACH What?—Not our finest hour? Say that again, out loud!

INTELLECTUAL (*softly*) Look, I only meant, Lemberg—

BIACH Who's talking about Lemberg? Even if that dents our courage and our hopes, still we take heart from the front pages—the anniversary!

HONORARY COUNSELLOR You know what impresses me most? It's not what's on the front page that impresses me, it's not what's in the middle that impresses me, what impresses me is what's at the back! Do you remember, on the day of the anniversary, the 100 pages of bank advertisements, all full-page! They had to shell out for those—in the middle of the moratorium, too—till they were bled dry! Ah, the press—its power is unshakable, but when it does the shaking, it soon strips the plum tree.

BIACH There you are, then, there's no one in Austria with more chutzpah. He's got imagination and temperament and intellect and convictions *and* is banking on God Almighty.

HONORARY COUNSELLOR You know who that reminds me of, Herr Biach, the language you just used there?

BIACH Who it reminds you of? Who should it remind you of?

HONORARY COUNSELLOR Of the Editor himself, with all those "ands."

BIACH And what if it does? Is it any wonder? You can't help but be spellbound. Did you read the "Questions and Answers for the Layman" in the Evening Edition the other day? Good stuff, eh? In the Evening Edition he can really be himself. He repeats everything over again. After the proclamation "In Lemberg we are still holding on", he said it was the word "still" that strikes you, it catches your eye and demands attention and enables you to imagine it. He's covered everything with just the word "still"! "Yesterday it was reported—today it is reported", you can't get that out of your head. He talks just like the rest of us talk, only more clearly. You couldn't say whether he talks like us, or we talk like him.

HONORARY COUNSELLOR Yes, and the editorial, wasn't that the cat's breakfast! From the very first sentence—inimitable! "The Brodsky family is one of the richest in Kiev." And that's it! You're right in the middle of it all. Then he jumps from that to Talleyrand, what he said at dinner, and then you're right in the middle of the Hungarian Compromise.

BIACH What impresses me most is when he says "Just visualize it." Or when he evokes the power of imagination, which he does thrillingly, and you can imagine him straight away in the middle of all the gun smoke—God forbid!—and the rest of us along with him. But the most important thing for him seems to be the atmosphere, the impressions, the details, and it's gripping when he describes how they've stirred up the passions. I must say what I personally like best, though, is when he imagines them tossing and turning in their beds, especially Poincaré and Grey and even the Tsar, gnawed at by worry, because things are beginning to fall apart. And maybe at this very minute, and maybe they have already, and maybe, and maybe—it's tremendously dramatic! I've been told he dictates what he writes. You can imagine him dictating an editorial. I tell you, the mind boggles at the thought of the candelabra quivering in the editorial office when he dictates!

INTELLECTUAL But I happen to know, since I once went in person to complain about "The Refuse Collector and the Horsefly"—

BIACH What do you know?

INTELLECTUAL That they don't have any candelabra there!

BIACH (*getting worked up*) So what do they have, then? Enough already, my dear sir—you're a notorious killjoy, always finding fault. So they've got standard lamps, no matter!—the candelabra still quiver! Some of us hold on to our illusions. Waiter, bring me *Bloch's Weekly* and *Danzer's Army Journal*.

BUSINESSMAN Wait! Now—if we could just hear what the ministers are talking about!—(*They all listen. Biach pulls his chair up close to the ministers' table.*)

PRIME MINISTER Look at the *Pschütt*, what a mess it's in again today, the state of it!—really irritating—instead of suspending the illustrated magazines in their frames, the waiters just hang them up anyhow—the liberties they take! The state the paper is in when I get it is just awful—I'll see to it they're put to one side for me, that's simplest.

BIACH (*very worked up*) Do you know what I've just heard? Heaven's above, I heard it with my own ears—the state's in a mess, liberty's at stake, they're going to take people aside and hang them—

BUSINESSMAN Shh . . . !

BIACH Suspension of all liberties, state of emergency to be declared!

HONORARY COUNSELLOR Well, now we know!

INTELLECTUAL A political sensation *par excellence,* that's what it is, and literally direct from the horse's mouth!

BIACH (*proudly*) So what do you say to me now?!

HABERDASHER It's your duty to leak it to the press straight away!

BIACH Yes, the situation is grave—

HONORARY COUNSELLOR —and who can know what tomorrow might bring—

HABERDASHER —and the state is duty-bound to put a brake on all such passions that have been stirred up—

BUSINESSMAN —and the mood of the people is important—

INTELLECTUAL —amid mounting anxiety—

BIACH —and it's gone 10 o'clock and my Rosa is sitting at home and doesn't like it when I come home late, so I propose we pay and go.
(The headwaiter comes, they depart, all turning once more with timid curiosity to look at the ministers' table.)

BIACH (*leaving*) We have experienced an historical moment. I shall never forget the grave expression on the face of Prime Minister Count Stürgkh for as long as I live!
(Change of scene.)

Scene 11

Meeting between two of those who have "wangled it."

FIRST Hi there, you still in Vienna? So they exempted you after all?

SECOND I went up and wangled it. But why are you still in Vienna? Did they exempt you after all?

FIRST I went up and wangled it.

SECOND Of course.

FIRST Of course.

SECOND Don't know what happened to Edi Wagner, think he managed to wangle it? He was called up in October, then the story was, his old man had bought him a Daimler since his major—you know, Tschibulka von Welschwehr—had promised to get him into the Automobile Corps, then I heard he was either to go to Officers' Training at Klosterneuburg or to work in a munitions factory—office work, of course—then someone said he would be declared indispensable to the family business, and his uncle—you know, the fellow who was talked into funding the military reserve hospital in the Fillgradergasse—I ran into him at the time and he told me that if push comes to shove he'd find a place for him in the Red Cross, no one knows for sure, and I really would like to know where the poor devil landed up.

FIRST I can tell you. His old man, mean bugger that he is, thought twice about the Daimler, and got him into that Danish company that makes paper tablecloths, but he got fed up with that and said he'd rather join up, and he got assigned to the Blumau munitions factory, but that was a bore, and now he sits night after night in the Chapeau, sometimes in uniform, sometimes in civvies, how he managed is a mystery to me, I can only think that when all the protection didn't work, he went up and wangled it himself. Could be, of course, he really was exempted, or even found medically unfit. Anyhow, so long, I have an appointment with a certain somebody who might have a consignment for me, and boy, what a consignment . . . I've hit the jackpot—

SECOND You lucky swine. Heard the latest? Pepi Seiffert was killed—in action at Rawa Ruska—so long—must go—I've got a meeting in the War Welfare Office, they're having a Tea Dance tomorrow and I promised I'd bring little Fritzi-Sprizi along, Sasha will be there, be a sport and come too, and bring your bit of fluff with you! See you!—

FIRST My dear chap, I've other things on my mind, if they come off I'll give you a ring, so long—oh, that reminds me—I must tell you—
(Enter a newspaper subscriber and a patriot.)

PATRIOT Healthy young people, did you see? You could put together a whole army corps on the Ringstrasse!

SUBSCRIBER Truly revolting. French malingerers, the shame of it!

FIRST *(turns round)* Are you talking about me?

SUBSCRIBER You? I don't know you, leave me alone—

SECOND Then take that back!—There's no way you can know—

PATRIOT But please, please, gentlemen, this gentleman was talking about malingerers in France, so there's no need for you to get worked up, after all, you're not French.

FIRST Oh, I see, sorry, if you didn't mean Austria I was mistaken, my respects.
(Both leave.)

SUBSCRIBER You see—cheeky into the bargain! He actually thought we meant him when we mentioned malingerers in France.

PATRIOT Probably a French malingerer skulking here, up to no good, there's no way of knowing, is there? I'll be hanged if he's not a deserter, or even a spy!

SUBSCRIBER That's my impression, too, no doubt about it!

PATRIOT Not to mention what's happening in every enemy country!

SUBSCRIBER Don't I know it! While we're on the subject, look at France—hasn't their draft board just announced a second review? Just imagine, recalling those who have been already declared unfit for service!

PATRIOT But not only recalling—those they take are then sent to the front! "Enrolment of those already discharged in France" is what I read.

SUBSCRIBER Or take the wretched state of the French Army Supply Corps.

PATRIOT War supplies contracted out at exorbitant rates!

SUBSCRIBER They say differences in the price of preserved food and munitions consignments are definitely fishy.

PATRIOT Extortionate prices have been paid for cloth, linen, and flour.

SUBSCRIBER Some middlemen have made huge profits from the sales contracts. Using middlemen, imagine!

PATRIOT Where?

SUBSCRIBER In France, of course.

PATRIOT Scandalous!

SUBSCRIBER To allege something like that openly in parliament!

PATRIOT It would be unthinkable here! Fortunately we have—

SUBSCRIBER No parliament, eh?—

PATRIOT A clear conscience, is what I meant.

SUBSCRIBER Millerand himself admitted everything. It's impossible to avoid mistakes, he said, but we will proceed regardless with all severity.

PATRIOT I see no sign of that!

SUBSCRIBER And what about Russia? Very telling that they've had to convene the duma and the government has had to put up with some frank speaking.

PATRIOT No chance of that happening here! Fortunately we have—

SUBSCRIBER A clear conscience, eh?

PATRIOT No parliament, is what I meant.

SUBSCRIBER And what do you say about the harvest?

PATRIOT Quite simply this: Bad harvest in Italy. Crop failure in England. Poor prospects for the Russian harvest. Concern about the harvest in France. And what do you say about the exchange rate, eh?

SUBSCRIBER What do you want me to say? The fall of the rouble speaks for itself.

PATRIOT God knows, if you compare it with our crown, for instance—!

SUBSCRIBER The lira has crashed as well—by 30 percent!

PATRIOT And our crown fortunately only double that.

SUBSCRIBER Apropos of Italy, did you read this morning about the chaos down there already? The *Messagero* complains about inadequate refuse collections in Rome. What a characteristic light that throws on conditions there—

PATRIOT Just compare that with our streets in Vienna! As if they're any dirtier in wartime than in peace! Have you ever read a single word of complaint on that subject in any of our papers? Well, at most the occasional feature in the *Presse*—about "The Refuse Collector and the Horsefly", say—but even that is interesting!

SUBSCRIBER And those are grievances already remedied in part. Didn't you read where it said "Some Refuse Collectors Laid Off"? There you are!

PATRIOT And what do you say about England, then?

SUBSCRIBER Their potato prices have shot up dramatically.

PATRIOT Yes, and it even turns out they're still lower there now than ours were before the war. Just imagine!

SUBSCRIBER And what about the way our civilian detainees are treated in Russian camps? Did you read about how they're made to suffer? While it's common knowledge how we pamper our Russian prisoners of war!

PATRIOT And how do they thank us? By taking the most flagrant liberties, of course! I heard they were put to digging trenches in Tyrol on the Brenner, just to keep them occupied. And what do you think they did? They refuse! Well, they got short shrift for that, of course. A detachment is sent from Innsbruck, they're asked again if they'll dig the trenches. "No!" they say. Guns are levelled. Well, what did they expect? Did they think we'd have any scruples? Forget international law. There's a war on. But mugs that they are, our men, they still show restraint and ask them again, the rebels. "No!" they say. We take aim. Then, of course—you should have seen it, all at once everyone is volunteering, yes, they'll dig the trenches. In a flash they're scrambling to start digging—and that's that. All of them except for four, that is. Who are shot, of course. Naturally. Among them an officer cadet—just listen to this—

SUBSCRIBER I'm listening.

PATRIOT Probably their ringleader. Had the cheek to launch into a harangue against Austria, up there in the mountain. Probably an anti-Semite. Just listen—

SUBSCRIBER I'm listening.

PATRIOT The men—our men, I mean, those with their heart in the right place—were too worked up when they fired, they simply couldn't hit their target, so the captain had to help out in person and shot all four with his service revolver. So what do you say now about the liberties the Russians take with us?

SUBSCRIBER They take with us? The liberties they take with Austrian prisoners of war back home, would be more like it. In case you haven't read what it says today, here, I've got it with me, listen: Russian troops misappropriate prisoners of war to participate in hostilities. The War Press Bureau writes: Since the Russians were driven out of Galicia, scarcely a day passes without the discovery of a further hitherto unreported infringement of international law by Russian troops, with the result that it is now certain there is hardly a single article of the rules of war which has not been trampled underfoot by the Russians.

PATRIOT A nice state of affairs!

SUBSCRIBER Just listen to this—

PATRIOT I'm listening.

SUBSCRIBER Thus, it has now been ascertained through investigations by the rural constabulary in formerly occupied parts of Galicia, that following a directive of the Russian army commanders, for the entire duration of the occupation, all men and women fit for any kind of work—except when needed for other tasks—were forcibly enlisted, specifically, to dig ditches—

PATRIOT Is that what it says?!

SUBSCRIBER —and were deported for that purpose as far away as the Carpathians. The fact that the enemy were expressly forbidden by the Hague Conventions to demand services from the peaceful inhabitants of an occupied territory—labour which is tantamount to fighting against their own country—naturally didn't trouble the Russians in the slightest.

PATRIOT Didn't trouble them! Scum!

SUBSCRIBER But listen to this—

PATRIOT I'm listening.

SUBSCRIBER Consequently, it is no wonder—as has now been likewise established—that the Russians also misappropriate members of the Austro-

Hungarian army who find themselves their prisoners of war to do construction work that can be used against us.

PATRIOT Outrageous! Exactly the same case!

SUBSCRIBER —although this equally contravenes the Hague accords, according to which prisoners of war may not be used for work in any way connected with military operations. By curious coincidence, the 82nd Austro-Hungarian Infantry Regiment recently took a Russian base that members of the same regiment had been forced to build as prisoners of war. The following inscription in Hungarian was found there on a wooden panel: "This base was built by Hungarian Transylvanians of the 82nd Infantry Regiment." To the recently reported forcible expulsion of Austrian citizens from their homeland can now be added this forcible involvement of Austro-Hungarian citizens in the hostilities against their fatherland—not as a riposte but as a strategic reinforcement on the part of the Russians. Well, what do you say to that?

PATRIOT Typically Russian! Unheard of! And certainly not a riposte, but a strategic reinforcement, no two ways about it! And our poor Austrian soldiers—it's unlikely a single one dared refuse.

SUBSCRIBER Do you think everyone has the chutzpah of that Russian officer cadet?

PATRIOT To launch into a harangue against the state, right at the top of the mountain!

SUBSCRIBER Slap bang in the Carpathians!

PATRIOT What do you mean, the Carpathians? At the top of the Brenner!

SUBSCRIBER At the top of the Brenner! You really have to admit, not a day passes without such dizzy contrasts. Poles apart!

PATRIOT That was an excellent article of Professor Brockhausen's, where he writes that defenceless prisoners have never been harassed here, even with words.

SUBSCRIBER He was right. Wasn't it in the same issue of the *Presse* where the commandant of Lemberg disclosed that Russian prisoners being transported through the streets were abused and beaten with sticks by some members of the public? He stated emphatically that such behaviour was unworthy of a civilized nation.

PATRIOT So he acknowledged that we are a civilized nation, a cultured people, and not just the Jews.

SUBSCRIBER Just so. But really, there's not a single issue on which we wouldn't act differently to our enemies, who are after all the very dregs of mankind.

PATRIOT For example, the civilized language we use, even when speaking of the enemy, who are after all the greatest scum on God's earth.

SUBSCRIBER And above all, unlike them we are always humane. For example, an editorial in the *Presse* even talked about good times ahead for the fish and crustacea in the Adriatic, with so many Italian corpses to feed on. Is that not the very height of humanity, to be mindful of the fish and crustacea in the Adriatic in these bitterly hard times, when even human beings are starving!

PATRIOT Yes, exaggerated perhaps, as he often is. But—there are no half-measures with him! And it's not only our humanity in war that they lack, but something far more valuable—endurance! Look at them: despondency already reigns supreme. They'd be glad if it was all over. As for us—?

SUBSCRIBER That struck me as well. For instance, the defeatism in France!

PATRIOT Dejection in England!

SUBSCRIBER Despair in Russia!

PATRIOT Disillusionment in Italy!

SUBSCRIBER The overall mood of the Entente!

PATRIOT The edifice is crumbling.

SUBSCRIBER Poincaré is consumed by worries.

PATRIOT Grey is disgruntled.

SUBSCRIBER The Tsar tosses and turns in his bed.

PATRIOT Belgium oppressed by fear.

SUBSCRIBER That's a relief! Demoralisation in Serbia.

PATRIOT How refreshing! Despair in Montenegro.

SUBSCRIBER Hope so! Consternation in the Quadruple Alliance.

PATRIOT Invigorating! London, Paris, and Rome irresolute. Just look at the headlines, there's really no need to read any further, you already know what's coming. You see how badly it's going for them and how well for us. We have our moods too, but rather different ones, thank God!

SUBSCRIBER Yes, here joy reigns supreme, confidence, exultation, hope, contentment. We're always in good spirits, and why not? We've every reason to be.

PATRIOT Holding out till the end, for instance, we're passionate about that.

SUBSCRIBER No one else manages that as well as we do.

PATRIOT Your Viennese, in particular, is a real diehard when it comes to holding out till the end. He can endure all hardships as if they were pleasures.

SUBSCRIBER Hardships? What hardships?

PATRIOT I mean, if there happened to be hardships—

SUBSCRIBER Luckily, there aren't any.

PATRIOT Quite right. There aren't. But then—if there aren't any hardships—why do we have to hold out?

SUBSCRIBER I can explain that. It's true there are no hardships, but we *would* easily endure them—there's an art in that and we've always had the knack.

PATRIOT Just so. Queueing, for instance, is fun—people queue just for the sake of it.

SUBSCRIBER The only difference to before is that it's wartime now. If there wasn't a war on, quite frankly you'd think it was peace. But war is war, so some things you've got to do now that you only wanted to do before.

PATRIOT Exactly. Nothing's changed here at all. And if, once in a blue moon, those exempted first time round are recalled and enlisted, whatever way you look at it, our young people under 50 just can't wait to get to the front.

SUBSCRIBER And the older age groups haven't been mustered yet at all.

PATRIOT "Nineteen-year-olds conscripted in Italy"—did you read that? There you have it—the whole terrible truth in the headline.

SUBSCRIBER No, I must have missed that. Just imagine, so young! Ours certainly have to be more mature. Unless I'm mistaken, now it's still the turn of 50-year-olds, though of course only behind the lines—there are still enough 49-year-olds at the front.

PATRIOT In France they're already recalling the exempted 48-year-olds!

SUBSCRIBER Greybeards! The younger ones are seemingly all used up already. We're dispatching our 17-year-olds in March, that'll please them.

PATRIOT Naturally, the best years of their lives! You know the other difference? Equipment. That's crucial. Here, it's taken for granted, we don't make a fuss about it. Did you read today: Italians worried about warm mountain attire for their soldiers?

SUBSCRIBER The things they have to worry about!

PATRIOT We don't give such things a second thought. A mere bagatelle! An order is placed for supplies, and that's an end to it. You must know the story about the wool blankets? No?

SUBSCRIBER No.

PATRIOT It's a brilliant illustration of how we just take everything in our stride, as it comes. Feiner & Co. sign a contract for a million and a half wool blankets from Germany. Our War Ministry thought that was roughly how many were needed for the Carpathians in winter. But they didn't take it too seriously since they reckoned on final victory before then. Well, when it gets serious after all, there's a sudden change of heart and they say: "Fine, but first the customs formalities must be observed." There's no way the Finance Minister can be prevailed upon to release the goods before that happens, and the War Minister reiterates: we need them. Then—how can I put it?—for six months this goes back and forth between the War Ministry and the Finance Ministry. Throughout the whole battle for the Carpathians. Then the firm takes a stand, and Katzenellenbogen from Berlin intervenes in person—as you know, he's virtually our War Minister's right hand. He goes off to the Finance Minister and tells him to his face: "That's not on!" The Finance Minister says he can't sort the matter out straightaway. So Katzenellenbogen tells him—and you know his sheer effrontery and how forceful he can be—he tells him, in the first place, it will bankrupt the firm, in the second place, the wool blankets will have had it. They're out there in the wet and cold and almost all of them are already done for—

SUBSCRIBER Who?

PATRIOT The wool blankets, of course! They're lying out in the open.

SUBSCRIBER Who?

PATRIOT The wool blankets, of course! What a question! Anyhow, he declares categorically: "In the first place, the firm goes bankrupt, in the second place, the wool blankets will have had it, and after all, in the third place, the soldiers do need them." The Finance Minister shrugs and says it can't be done, the procedure must be followed. First the customs, then the blankets—

SUBSCRIBER But why didn't the War Ministry pay?

PATRIOT Why, you ask? Because the War Minister took the view that he couldn't, the formalities had to be settled first.

SUBSCRIBER The customs formalities? But wasn't that what the Finance Minister wanted?

PATRIOT On the contrary, the formalities about the Finance Ministry releasing funds to pay the customs duty.

SUBSCRIBER Ah, I see. And what happened then? I'm dying to hear—

PATRIOT What happened? Katzenellenbogen goes off again and tells him to his face: "Excellency", he says, "the War Ministry is digging its heels in. Now let me make a suggestion", he says. "In business, if a client can't pay right away, one takes soundings, and if they show the client is reputable, it's normal to give him time to pay. Excellency, let me make a suggestion. Take soundings about the War Ministry. They'll tell you it's reputable. What good will blocking it do you? Give it time to pay!" Well, he saw the sense of that, granted the delay, and the wool blankets were released and distributed.

SUBSCRIBER So, it all ended happily after all.

PATRIOT Up to a point. But it was already March. When they got the blankets they were—how shall I put it—totally ruined. So now they got refugees to stitch them together, two blankets at a time, and by now it's April and everything has proceeded to plan, even if at double the cost—well, the little matter of stitching together a million and a half wool blankets had to be paid for, of course—well, now everything is ready and waiting, what do you think they discover?

SUBSCRIBER Well—?

PATRIOT They discover the soldiers don't need the wool blankets anymore. For in the first place, it's not so cold in the Carpathians anymore, and in the second place, most of them had in any case already lost their feet through frostbite.—So now I ask you, man to man: are woollen blankets something for us to worry about?

SUBSCRIBER But the Italians do! Serves them right! What do you say about "Price rises for food in Italy"?

PATRIOT I didn't see anything about that, I only read about the "Bad harvest in Italy."

SUBSCRIBER Aren't you mixing that up with "Crop failure in England"?

PATRIOT That's another story, just as you have to distinguish it from "Food shortages in Russia."

SUBSCRIBER Look, it's everywhere the same. For example, they've already introduced casualty lists everywhere.

PATRIOT Yes, just like here, they copy everything we do—

SUBSCRIBER Excuse me, what do you mean by that? Do we have—

PATRIOT On the contrary, we've just introduced a Daily British Casualty List.

SUBSCRIBER I noticed that as well, while our casualty list only appears once in a blue moon.

PATRIOT Do they expect us to forge it and invent false names? At the very outside, we've had maybe 800 wounded this year.

SUBSCRIBER In Italy no list has appeared at all. That's more than suspicious. They daren't admit all the huge losses they've suffered already.

PATRIOT Apropos of Italy, did you see: "Dismissal of Italian general"? For proven incompetence at the front! Further dismissals are expected!

SUBSCRIBER Shhh . . . ! Hardly seems possible. Have you ever heard of one of our generals being—

PATRIOT Well, yes.

SUBSCRIBER For incompetence?

PATRIOT That as well.

SUBSCRIBER But at least he didn't have an opportunity to prove it at the front!

PATRIOT You're right about that, sure enough. Incidentally, did you know there were already draft dodgers in Italy?

SUBSCRIBER What did you expect? And it's scarcely entered the war! But do you know what else they've already introduced? Censorship! Freedom of expression seems to be in a bad way in all the enemy countries. No free speech at all, I've heard.

PATRIOT At best, the papers there are allowed to write that our military situation is much better than theirs. Well, truth will out. English critics of the war describe the situation of the Entente Powers as hopeless.

SUBSCRIBER That's a fine state of affairs, allowing them to write that! If anyone here said anything like that, just imagine what would happen to him!

PATRIOT If he were to say the situation of the Entente Powers was hopeless?

SUBSCRIBER No, if he were to say the situation of the Central Powers was hopeless. He would be strung up, and quite right too! No one here would take such a liberty.

PATRIOT And why should he? He'd have to lie! Look, even in England they tell the truth when they have to admit they're in a bad way.

SUBSCRIBER Some patriots they must be! The other day one of them wrote that England deserves to be wiped out by Germany. Well, he got what was coming to him. Know what sentence they handed out? Fourteen days!

PATRIOT (*shakes his head in disbelief*) Prison for criticism in England. That's a fine state of affairs! Fourteen days!

SUBSCRIBER Yes, those fine gentlemen don't like hearing things like that, they can't stand the truth. That said, no journalist here would take such a liberty.

PATRIOT And is it any better in France? Not a jot. Didn't you read in the *Presse* today: "Prison for spreading the truth in France"? I ask you, just for telling the truth! It was a woman, and she said Germany was prepared for war but France wasn't. So if for once you tell them the truth to their faces—

SUBSCRIBER Yes, they can't take it, the powers-that-be in France! They're all for waging war and attacking Germany, their peace-loving neighbour, out of the blue, that's their style—

PATRIOT Golden words! Germany is waging a defensive war. Not a soul in Germany was prepared for this war. Heavy industry was taken completely unawares.

SUBSCRIBER Absolutely. And when this poor woman in France utters this simple truth in simple words that even the man in the street understands—

PATRIOT No, you're mistaken there, the woman was sentenced because she—

SUBSCRIBER Because she told the truth!

PATRIOT But she said Germany was prepared for war—

SUBSCRIBER But the truth is, Germany was *not* prepared for war—

PATRIOT But she said Germany *was* prepared for war!

SUBSCRIBER But that's a lie!

PATRIOT But she was sentenced for telling the truth—

SUBSCRIBER But why was she sentenced then?

PATRIOT Because she said Germany was prepared for war!

SUBSCRIBER But how can she be sentenced for that in France? She should have been sentenced for that in Germany!

PATRIOT How come?—Wait a minute—no—maybe . . . Look, the way I see it is: of course, she told the truth, but it being France and the way the French are, she was sentenced for lying.

SUBSCRIBER Wait a minute—you're muddling things up. I think what happened is: she lied, and they sentenced her because they can't face the truth in France.

PATRIOT That's surely it! It's in their blood, don't you think? People there get carried away and take liberties.

SUBSCRIBER Exactly. From what we read, the newspapers there tell their own government a few home truths, but spread nothing but lies about us. It's perverse! If you believed everything the London papers say about us, you'd believe England was finished.

PATRIOT But I ask you, who believes that! We simply react differently. Our whole journalistic mentality is different, I'm told. Thank heavens! You could say our editors are even more enthusiastic than our soldiers. Especially in the cultural section.

SUBSCRIBER Talking of which—I meant to tell you, you know who's coming here today? Go on, guess. The greatest living writer, Hans Müller!

PATRIOT Well, you can tell him from me, I heartily agree with every word he writes! What's he like, as a person? I'd be interested to know. There's only one way to describe his style: cheerful and charming. Wasn't it more than charming when he went up to a soldier in his field-grey uniform in the middle of the street in Berlin and gave him a big kiss, not to mention his blessing on our combined weapons in the church at the end of his article. He's my favourite by far! None of the rest of them with their personal style, not even Roda Roda or Salten, has captured the "shoulder to shoulder" feeling so well, in fact, you might say he literally writes shoulder to shoulder—for instance, with Ganghofer. He's as good as that! At first, when he was writing his features from the field as "Cassian at the Front", they were so authentic, so enthusiastic, you really believed he was at the front. Later, by pure chance, I found out he was in Vienna all along, it was in Vienna he wrote them! How he captured the front! What talent! I'd just be interested to know, what's he like as a person?

SUBSCRIBER As a person—hard to say. Just at the moment pretty worried, but so what—the day after tomorrow—who'd believe it!—he's got to appear before the recruiting board.

PATRIOT Well, well, and what's he worried about?

SUBSCRIBER About recruitment, of course!

PATRIOT He's worried? That they won't take him?

SUBSCRIBER What do you mean? He's worried, of course, because he's afraid they *will* take him!

PATRIOT You're joking! Hans Müller? The same Hans Müller who's sweating blood for the Fatherland? Really! I could have sworn no one embodied the Special Relationship better than Hans Müller—and that he would live and die for it! Indeed, I thought he had returned from Germany, after embracing our brave field-grey soldiers, specifically because he couldn't wait to enlist voluntarily! He'll be happy and cheerful, I thought to myself, if they take him—and he'll do himself a mischief if they don't take him!

SUBSCRIBER How come? Didn't you hear yourself that the features from the front were from Vienna, and wasn't it that that impressed you—the way he captured the front while writing from Vienna?

PATRIOT The features from the front—I thought he had written them because he was offended they hadn't taken him along yet—just to show them! He wanted to show them what he would be capable of writing about the front once he was actually at the front! I simply can't believe what you've just told me. You'll have mixed him up with someone else.

SUBSCRIBER He'd be happy if they mixed him up with someone else at the recruiting board the day after tomorrow.

PATRIOT Listen, that really annoys me! I can only assume you aren't well enough informed. If someone has written the way Hans Müller has written, so authentically, so enthusiastically, he's bound to be happy they'll take him—

SUBSCRIBER (*worked up*) So—so they have to take everyone? Everyone has to be happy? No one can have the slightest worry anymore about anything else? It's not enough that he's enthusiastic? No, he has to do military service? Him, of all people? You're a dreamer! As if you can't wait to see him doing drill! But your worries are unfounded, and his too, I hope. And if they do take him—luckily Hans Müller is already a name to conjure with. They'll employ him according to his talents!

PATRIOT You know that I agree with you about everything—but on that point our views diverge. I believed in Hans Müller and what I've just heard disappoints me. Of course, your point of view is that of a newspaper subscriber. For you, such a collaborator is indispensable—

SUBSCRIBER And you see everything through the eyes of a patriot—I hope you see far enough! Adieu, I must find an extra edition. What about you?

PATRIOT I'm going to do my bit. (*Exeunt in different directions.*)

NEWSPAPER VENDOR Ex-tra-aa edi-shun—! Both communiqués!
(*Change of scene.*)

Scene 12

Enter a giant in civilian dress and a dwarf in uniform.

GIANT It's all right for you, you can be of use to the community. I was immediately turned down by the regimental doctor.

DWARF For what reason?

GIANT Too weak. According to the same old findings of fifteen years ago. Then I looked like you.

DWARF If that's the case, I'm surprised they didn't accept you. The regimental doctor hardly looked at me, and I was accepted like a shot. Mama was very unhappy.

GIANT Mummy's boy!

DWARF But I'm satisfied. Man grows to match his higher goals, as Schiller says.

At first I had doubts whether I was fitted for the grandeur of the age and able to fight shoulder to shoulder. But in civilian life one is only mocked, while I'll come back from the army a hero, after many a bullet has whistled over my head. When the others throw themselves to the ground, I stay on my feet!

GIANT Lucky you!

DWARF Don't let it worry you. There's nothing you can do about it. It's up to the board.

GIANT I slipped through the net.

DWARF I caught the doctor's attention.

GIANT Let's get some food. I've a huge appetite.

DWARF I might have a little something.

NEWSPAPER VENDOR Ex-tra-aa edi-shun—! Both communiqués—!

(Change of scene.)

Scene 13

The electrified railway Baden–Vienna.

A giant of a man, bushy moustache, dead drunk, in civilian life possibly a removal man, check trousers bearing traces of overindulgence in wine and recent forced ejection from source of same. Beside him a bag from which, at intervals, he takes a bottle. He enters into a dispute with a couple after knocking against the girl, threatens her companion, and shouts throughout the whole journey.

DRUNK What a waster—getting his dander up—what have you ever done for the Fatherland? Where are your papers? Let me see!—Look me in the eye—I've got sons like you at the front—and with more beard than you have—they're out there doing things—for the Fatherland—D'you know where I'm from?—from Baden, that's where—what a waster—let's see your papers, then—who do you think you—you—getting your dander up—just because you've your sweetie with you—what have you ever done for the Fatherland?—look at me—I do things—for the Fatherland—if they all got their dander up like him there—what are you looking at me like that for?—Maybe I offended you?—what a waster—I do things—show me your papers—here, look at that—know what that is?—a postcard from the front from my nephew—for the Fatherland—what a waster—I want to see his papers—he's done nothing—for the Fatherland—(*When he has calmed down a bit after being talked to by the frail-looking conductor, he slumps against others sitting near him, offering them his bottle, one after the other.*) Friends and neighbours, help yourselves—as fellow Austrians!

A GALICIAN REFUGEE COUPLE God forbid! (*They escape by changing seats, but leave their umbrella behind.*)

DRUNK (*now slurring all his words*) Waster—for the Fatherland—show your papers—

CONSUMPTION TAX INSPECTOR (*appears*) What have you got in your bag there?

DRUNK (*faintly*) Waster—for the Fatherland—show papers—(*after a long talking-to is prevailed upon to open his bag and pay a tax of 20 cents. Meanwhile, the train halts.*)

A VIENNESE (*who has meanwhile occupied the place where the refugees were sitting*) So we all have to wait because of some piddling triviality! Nothing but bother on this line! It's all too much!

(*He leaves the train, with the umbrella. It is raining. The drunk does likewise. The train pulls out.*)

DRUNK (*outside, more animated again*) For the Fatherland—he should—he should show his papers—waster—done nothing—for the Fatherland—

REFUGEE COUPLE (*breathe a sigh of relief and occupy their former seats. A moment later they jump up.*) Where's the umbrella? God, where's the umbrella? Conductor, where's the umbrella?

(*Change of scene.*)

Scene 14

The apartment of the actress Elfriede Ritter, recently returned from Russia. Luggage partly unpacked. The reporters Füchsl, Feigl, and Halberstam are holding her by the arms and plying her with questions.

ALL THREE (*talking at once*): Has the knout left any marks? Show us! We need the particulars, every detail. How was Muscovy? Your impressions of the capital of the Slav empire? You must have suffered dreadfully, didn't you? You *must* have!

FÜCHSL Describe how they treated you like a prisoner!

FEIGL Let the Evening Edition have your impressions of your stay!

HALBERSTAM What was your frame of mind during the journey back? Tell the *Morgenblatt*!

ELFRIEDE RITTER (*smiles; her accent is north German*) Gentlemen, I thank you for your keen interest. I'm really touched that my beloved Viennese still take me to their hearts. And for troubling yourselves to come in person, my heartfelt thanks! I'll happily put off my unpacking, gentlemen, but with the best will in the world I can only say that it was very, very interesting, that nothing happened to me at all, what else? . . . hmm, that the return journey, though a little tedious, was not in the slightest onerous, and (*with a twinkle in her eye*) that I am pleased to be back in my beloved Vienna.

HALBERSTAM Interesting—so it was a tedious journey, so she admits—

FEIGL Onerous was what she said—

FÜCHSL Hang on, I wrote the intro back in the office—wait a second—(*writes*) Released from her sufferings in Russian captivity, and having finally reached her destination after an onerous and tedious journey, the artiste wept tears of joy at the realization she was once more in her beloved city of Vienna—

ELFRIEDE RITTER (*waving a finger threateningly*) My dear sir, that's not what I said! On the contrary, did I not say I could not complain about a thing, not the slightest thing—

FÜCHSL Aha! (*writes*) The artiste can today look back on her ordeal with a certain ironical detachment.

ELFRIEDE RITTER Yes, but really—I really must say—no, no, gentlemen, I'm shocked—

FÜCHSL (*writes*) But when one jogs her memory, the state of shock once again returns. Frau Ritter movingly describes how she was deprived of any possibility of complaining about the treatment she suffered.

ELFRIEDE RITTER But gentlemen, what are you trying to do—I really can't say—

FÜCHSL She is simply unable to say what—

ELFRIEDE RITTER But really—I really can't say—

HALBERSTAM Oh go on, you've no idea of all the things you can say! Look, my dear, the public wants something to read, geddit? I'm telling you, you *can* say—here, you can, though perhaps not in Russia, here we have freedom of speech, thank God, not like in Russia—here, praise be, one can say whatever one wants about conditions in Russia! Did any of the Russian newspapers pay you the attention we're paying you here? Well then!

FEIGL Be reasonable, Ritter; do you think a little bit of publicity will do you any harm, now you're about to tread the boards again? Well then!

ELFRIEDE RITTER But gentlemen—I can't just—the way you've twisted it is hair-raising—if you'd seen it with your own eyes—on the streets or in meetings with officials—if I'd had occasion for the slightest complaint—of being harassed or whatever—do you think I would remain silent?

FÜCHSL (*writes*) Still trembling with emotion, Frau Ritter gives an account of the mob pulling and twisting her hair, how she was harassed by officials for making the slightest complaint and obliged to remain silent throughout.

ELFRIEDE RITTER But my dear sir, are you pulling my leg? I'm telling you the police officers, on the contrary, were very approachable, they received me with open arms and provided support at every opportunity. I could go out wherever I wanted and come home whenever I wanted. I assure you, if I had felt for a moment like a prisoner—

FÜCHSL (*writes*) The artiste tells of once attempting to go out, when the police immediately approached her and, seizing her by the arms, dragged her home, so that she literally led the life of a prisoner—

ELFRIEDE RITTER Now you're making me really angry—it's not true, gentlemen, I protest—

FÜCHSL (*writes*) She becomes really angry when reminded of these experiences and her unavailing protests—

ELFRIEDE RITTER It's not true, gentlemen!

FÜCHSL (*looks up*) Not—true? What do you mean, not true, when I've written down your every word?

FEIGL When we publish something, are you saying it isn't true?

HALBERSTAM You know, I've never come across that before. Interesting!

FEIGL She'll be sending in a correction next!

FÜCHSL Listen, don't start inventing fairytales! You'll regret it!

FEIGL You'll only do yourself harm!

HALBERSTAM What's her next role going to be?

FÜCHSL If I tell the director at the casting meeting on Saturday, Berger will get to play Gretchen, that I can guarantee!

FEIGL That's the thanks you get, when Fuchs always treated you so well? You don't know Fuchs! If he finds out, look out when you've your next première!

HALBERSTAM And in any case, Wolf has it in for you since that time you acted in his play, just so you know. In addition, Wolf is very anti-Russian, if he were now to hear you've no complaints about Russia—he would tear you to shreds on the spot!

FÜCHSL That's nothing, what about Löw? For heaven's sake, don't take on Löw, an actress simply has to make concessions, no two ways about it!

FEIGL On the other hand I can tell you, in confidence, that it would be hugely beneficial to you, not only with the public but even with the press itself, if you had been ill-treated in Russia.

HALBERSTAM Think it over. You're from Berlin and you've quickly adapted to Viennese conditions. You've been well received from the start, with open arms—

FÜCHSL I can only say, this is no joking matter. Someone who's been in Russia and has no tales to tell of the suffering endured, that's laughable, and you a first-class artiste! I tell you, your whole career is at stake!

ELFRIEDE RITTER (*wrings her hands*) But—but—but—my dear sir—I, thought I was—please, my dear sir—I only wanted to—to tell the truth—forgive me—please, please—

FEIGL (*enraged*) You call that the truth? So we are lying?

ELFRIEDE RITTER I mean—forgive me—I, I, I believed it was the truth—but if you—gentlemen—believe that it—wasn't the truth—After all—you—gentlemen of the press—must have a—better grasp. I can see that—as a woman—I can't really have a proper—understanding, can I? For heaven's sake—you understand, don't you—after all, we are at war—we women are panic-stricken—I'm so happy simply to have escaped from enemy territory in one piece—

HALBERSTAM There you are! Now it's all coming back to you—

ELFRIEDE RITTER Ah, dear sir, of course. You understand, don't you—that first flush of joy at being back in your beloved Vienna—you see everything you've escaped from and survived in a more rosy light—just for a moment, of course—but then you're seized again with rage and resentment—

HALBERSTAM What did I tell you? We knew from the start that you would see—

FÜCHSL (*writes*) The artiste is still seized with rage and resentment when she remembers the torments she endured, and as soon as the first flush of joy at being back in the metropolis has given way to her gruesome memories—(*turns to her*) So, is that the truth now?

ELFRIEDE RITTER Yes, gentlemen, that's the truth—look, I was still overcome by—one is so panic-stricken, so—

FÜCHSL Wait—(*writes*) Still feeling panic-stricken, she doesn't dare speak of it. In the land of freedom she is at times still prey to the notion she is back in Russia, experiencing its shameful disregard for individual human rights, freedom of opinion and free speech. (*Turns to her.*) So, is that the truth now?

ELFRIEDE RITTER Really, my dear sir, I don't know how you can plumb the deepest—

FÜCHSL Well, there you are!

HALBERSTAM What did I tell you? She admits she suffered—

FEIGL Endured!

FÜCHSL Endured? Was literally tormented!

HALBERSTAM Well then, that's all we need. Let's go, after all, we're not just here for the fun of it—

FÜCHSL Obviously. I'll finish it off in the office. So—we need not fear a correction? That would be the last straw!

ELFRIEDE RITTER Oh, but dear sir!—It was really charming of you to come. Do come again soon—Adieu, adieu. (*Calls upstairs*) Grete! Gre—te!

FEIGL She is a very sensible woman. Grüss Gott, Fräulein. (*Leaving, to the others*) She has survived the ordeal and is too panic-stricken to say what she has undergone—big deal!

(*Elfriede Ritter sinks into a chair, then gets up to finish unpacking.*)

(*Change of scene.*)

Scene 15

Optimist and Grumbler in conversation.

OPTIMIST It's both uplifting and touching the way even trade names bring out the importance of patriotism at this time, it could even reconcile you to the rise in prices.

GRUMBLER Well then you won't be able to forgive the Hotel Bristol, which has retained its name, although there was no Hotel St. Pölten in London, even in peacetime.

OPTIMIST Nevertheless, by turning its "Rôtisserie" into a "Carvery", the Bristol showed it had the courage and the determination to do some soul-searching. And look at this—"The Fleet." Pure and simple! It's a gentlemen's outfitters, and a short time ago everyone knew it was called "The English Fleet." (*The shopkeeper appears in the doorway.*)

GRUMBLER Yes, but we don't know—wait a minute, I'll ask him *what* fleet his present sign represents. Given the confusion, perhaps he'll lower the price of shirts a bit. (*The owner retreats.*) It's the Austrian fleet!

(*Change of scene.*)

Scene 16

Headquarters. Enter four army commanders.

AUFFENBERG No, gentlemen, it's out of the question! I've no intention of being made a scapegoat for defeat, like Benedek, I simply won't put up with that—

BRUDERMANN Oh, go on, don't be difficult, what should the rest of us say? I only lost 80,000 men, and they're already muttering against me.

DANKL They're totting up my 70,000.

PFLANZER-BALTIN Just ignore them! I'm launching an attack tomorrow, regardless! We attack tomorrow, otherwise we're up to our neck in it! Attack, is my advice, what are they born for if not a hero's death—tell me, what else our lot are good for! Attack, attack—(*he has a seizure.*)

AUFFENBERG Stop right there—I couldn't agree more. I've always said our gallant soldiers should grin and bear it and die fighting. I'm in the middle of drawing my plans up, too. Even if it doesn't do any good, it won't do any harm either, is what I say. Oh yes, before I forget—the adjutant forgot to remind me yet again, you have to think of everything yourself—

BRUDERMANN Why, what's up?

AUFFENBERG Nothing—stupid, really—it's just that I must send him a card, that's all. Ever since Lublin I've been meaning to, but in all the chaos of the retreat I completely forgot. Just a moment! (*He sits at a table and writes.*) There, that'll please him.

DANKL What are you writing?

AUFFENBERG Listen: "At this moment in history"—

PFLANZER-BALTIN Ah, bolstering up the men's morale—that's not my line. We've got machine guns and padres! Tomorrow we attack, and then—

AUFFENBERG "At this moment in history—"

BRUDERMANN Are you writing the battle orders?

AUFFENBERG No, a postcard.

DANKL And who are you writing these world-historical words to?

AUFFENBERG Listen: "At this moment in history, when I would normally be sitting in those cosy rooms of yours which I know so well, my thoughts turn to you and your staff, and from our distant quarters out here in the field I send you cordial greetings. Auffenberg."

BRUDERMANN Who's it to? Krobatin?

AUFFENBERG Are you joking! Ludwig Riedl of the Café Europa!

ALL Ah, Riedl!

BRUDERMANN A man of feeling, our tenderhearted Auffenberg! You know, I'm pleased for you. They won't be able to drag you through the mud now on account of those 90,000 Tyrolese and Salzburgers that you sacrificed. Sacrificed, they called it!

PFLANZER-BALTIN Just ignore them! I'm up to 100,000.

DANKL You know what? Let's all write to Riedl!

BRUDERMANN Well, yes, but I'm more at home in the Opera Café—I'd rather write to—(*sits and writes.*)

PFLANZER-BALTIN The Café Heinrichshof is like a second home to me, I'll drop a line to—(*sits and writes.*)

DANKL Yes, you're right—I've been a regular in the Café Stadtpark for 29 years—I used to read the reports of the General Staff there every day with Höfer—(*sits and writes.*)

AUFFENBERG (*aside*) They're all copying me. First the strategy, and now keeping in touch with back home. Pity Potierek isn't here, but he wrote me a postcard to the front from the Café Kremser, and Liborius Frank is sitting together with Puhallo v. Brlog at Scheidl's. Conrad is about to get married, so that's an end to our coffeehouse existence. They're all copying me. I was the first to send in my photo to the *Humorist.* I was a trailblazer. Something different for a change—not just always theatre people. Now they're all at it, nothing but generals, it's getting tiresome, high time some females appeared again. I was the first to get the press involved a bit more, now each of them is in league with some slimy hack just to provide publicity. I'll be interested to see if Riedl has the gumption to submit my card to the *Extrablatt.* But wait, I mustn't forget, the attack's in a week's time and I've got to—Hey, Pflanzer, what do you think: should I attack right away or wait a week?

PFLANZER-BALTIN I don't want to interfere on that score, but if I was in your shoes, I would launch an attack the like of which—

BRUDERMANN Now that your men are on their last legs anyhow, I agree. There'll be time enough for them to pick themselves up. Attack, I say!

DANKL That would be stupid. He should save it for the 18th of August, if he really can't wait until the second of December. That would always be a nice surprise for the Emperor on his anniversaries.

PFLANZER-BALTIN That's just flattery, and I want nothing to do with it. I'm launching an attack tomorrow, I know my onions!
(Enter an aide-de-camp of Pflanzer-Baltin.)

AIDE-DE-CAMP Beg to report, Excellency, the professors have arrived and want to present the honorary doctorate.

PFLANZER-BALTIN Aha. Let them wait. If it's heavy, tell them to put it down while they catch their breath. *(Exit aide-de-camp.)*

AUFFENBERG Congratulations seem to be in order. Which faculty is it from?

PFLANZER-BALTIN Czernowitz.

BRUDERMANN Is that all? It's not even a faculty, it's only a chair. What subject?

PFLANZER-BALTIN Philosophy, of course.

DANKL And your rehabilitation, where's that?

PFLANZER-BALTIN Czernowitz. It's no great shakes, but after all—

BRUDERMANN I had expectations from Graz since the students there were fighting under my command. But that came to nothing, unfortunately, since they're having to close down for the same reason.

DANKL You can congratulate me soon on an honorary doctorate from Innsbruck.

AUFFENBERG Those are all provincial fleapits. I wouldn't accept one from any of them! I say: Vienna or nothing. Apropos of Vienna, Riedl'll be tickled pink! I mustn't forget to remind the aide-de-camp not to forget to remind the courier, or he'll end up forgetting my card for Riedl!

DANKL, BRUDERMANN, PFLANZER-BALTIN That's a good idea, let's do that too, by courier is always the safest way.

AUFFENBERG *(aside)* They're all copying me. First the strategy, and now keeping in touch with back home!
(Change of scene.)

Scene 17

Vienna. Premises of the Association of Café Proprietors. Enter four café proprietors, including Riedl. All address him heatedly.

FIRST It's not on, Riedl. You're a patriot and simple tradesman, you've no right to keep all those trinkets—look, it's only for as long as the war lasts anyway, afterwards you'll get them back.

SECOND Don't make me see red, Riedl, you'll compromise the whole profession, and you its leading light—you have to, whether you want to or not, you have to!

THIRD Let him be, he'll listen to me. Riedl, don't be such a bore! Are you a Viennese? Well then! Are you a German? Well then!

RIEDL But see here, how is it going to look in the next edition of the *Lehmann Gazetteer*—I was always the one who had the most decorations in the whole of Vienna, no one else had as many lines devoted to him—

FIRST I feel your pain, Riedl, it must be hard for you, but you have to make the sacrifice. It would be a disgrace, it would be tantamount to treason, when so many of the top brass are your regular patrons, and one even has his own table!

SECOND Look, we all have to make sacrifices in this age of grandeur, I only put the price of a small black coffee up to 4.44 instead of 4.50—the widow's mite, and all that—

THIRD Ridiculous, I can't believe the famous patriot Riedl, the president of our association, the commandant of the Navy Veterans—it's not possible, Admiral Tegethoff would be turning in his grave if he found out. I don't believe it! You, Riedl, the only one of us with his own monument while still alive—

RIEDL True, and one I erected myself! A self-made man is what I am, through and through—built my own house, and I thank God heart and soul for it, every time I come home I love to see that beautiful bas-relief!

FIRST Well then, what need have you for baubles from our enemies? You must give them all up, Riedl, all of them, including the one from Montenegro, and even the Order of the Liberation of the Republic of Liberia!

RIEDL Oh no, not that one too? It was always my special pride and joy. And listen, I was thinking of retiring at the end of the year anyway—so no, it's impossible.

SECOND Riedl, you must.

THIRD Riedl, you've no choice.

RIEDL And the Order of Franz Joseph as well, I suppose?

FIRST On the contrary, that one you can now have printed in bold in *Lehmann.*

RIEDL (*after an inner struggle, takes the great decision*) All right, then, I'll do it! I know what I owe the Fatherland. I renounce the honours bestowed on me by the enemy governments, the swine! I wouldn't even accept money back for what the trinkets cost me!

ALL (*all at once*) Three cheers for Riedl! – That's the Riedl we know! – Long live the city of Vienna and our own Riedl! – Long live St. Stephen's Cathedral and Riedl's beside it! – Gott strafe England! – Punish it! – Down with Montenegro! – Throw them all away! – Riedl, our greatest patriot!

RIEDL (*wiping his brow*) I thank you – I thank you – I must just ring home so they can take them to the Red Cross. You'll read about it in tomorrow's paper – (*becoming pensive*) Here I stand, a lifeless trunk.

SECOND Listen to him, that's culture for you! Now Riedl talks like a classic!

RIEDL It's not from a classic, it's what the editor of the *Extrablatt* always says when he loses at cards. And now – (*choking with emotion*) – it's me – that's losing – !

THIRD Don't be sad, Riedl! Don't be sad! What you give up now you will get back twofold and threefold. And that perhaps sooner than you think.
(*A waiter rushes into the room.*)

WAITER Herr von Riedl, Herr von Riedl, a card has arrived, Fräulein Anna told me I should bring it quick – it's great news – the whole place is in an uproar.

RIEDL Let me have it, what is it – (*reads, trembling with shock and joy*) Gentlemen – at this hour – this is an historic moment – as a patriot and a simple tradesman, honoured by my fellow citizens with countless proofs of their affection – as president of our association – but never – no, never have I – take a look –

ALL Well, what is it?

RIEDL My most illustrious patron – our preeminent warlord – has – during the battle – thought – of me! Hold me! I must inform – the *Extrablatt* –
(*They all support him and read.*)

FIRST Is that all? What a letdown! And there was me thinking – Yesterday I got a card from Brudermann – (*pulls it out of his pocket.*)

RIEDL Oh stop it, you're embarrassing me.

SECOND Come on, there's no harm in it, you're being stupid – something like that wouldn't affect me. Look, the day before yesterday I got a card from Pflanzer-Baltin – (*pulls it out of his pocket.*)

THIRD You're all getting too big-headed, by chance last week I received from Dankl – (*pulls it out of his pocket.*)

ALL THREE (*read out loud at same time*) At this historic moment, when I would normally be sitting in those cosy rooms of yours which I know so well, my thoughts turn to you and your staff, and from our distant quarters out here in the field I send you cordial greetings – Dankl – Pflanzer – Brudermann.

RIEDL (*erupting*) I don't believe it! That's plagiarism! Plagiarism, I tell you! A hoax! Compared with me, you're like fleas on a dog's back! I'm not having it! I haven't given back any decorations yet, and I've no intention of doing so, and if Auffenberg doesn't give me an explanation at once—I'll keep the lot!

(Change of scene.)

Scene 18

In Vienna's Deutschmeister barracks.

An elegantly dressed gentleman of about 40 is waiting in a dingy room without any chairs. Enter Sergeant Weiguny.

GENTLEMAN Excuse me—sergeant—I wonder if you could—tell me perhaps—I've been standing here for three hours, you see—and nobody has appeared—I've been declared unfit for active service, you see—I've reported voluntarily before the call-up deadline to be allocated clerical work—and they told me to—stay put—but I must say—

SERGEANT Shut your trap!

GENTLEMAN Yes—certainly—but I would like to—I must—at least, could I just—notify my family—I can't just—dressed as I am—I need—my toilet things—a toothbrush, a blanket and—

SERGEANT Shut your trap!

GENTLEMAN But—I beg you—forgive me—I came to report—I didn't know—I must—

SERGEANT You fat bastard, if you say another word I'll thump you so hard, you'll—

(The gentleman takes a 10-crown note from his waistcoat and offers it to the sergeant.)

SERGEANT Well, well—look, squire—I really can't let you go home, no way, but if it's a blanket you want, leave it to me. (*He leaves the room.*)

(Enter a cadet from the adjoining room.)

CADET What's up? Are you the one who was arguing with the sergeant? Hi! Don't you remember me? Wögerer, from the athletics club—

GENTLEMAN Yes, of course!

CADET Unfit for active service, eh?—Listen, an intelligent fellow like you, what are you doing bandying words with a sergeant?

GENTLEMAN But what can I do? I've been standing here for three hours. I've got to get home—my people have no idea—I came to register voluntarily—

CADET Well, you've really landed yourself in it. Who was it gave you that advice? But if you want to go home, of course you can.

GENTLEMAN Yes, but how do I go about it?

CADET Don't make me laugh, a distinguished gent like you—I'll help you—this is what you do—you go to the captain—

GENTLEMAN And he'll let me go home?

CADET Normally he wouldn't, of course, he's very strict, but you simply tell him, and tell him straight out, man to man, don't be shy (*he salutes*): "Beg respectfully to report, captain, there's a girl I need to see."—Then, just you wait and see, the captain will say—I bet you anything he says: "What, you need to see a girl? Push off then, you filthy swine!" And after that, you can go!
(*Change of scene.*)

Scene 19

War Welfare Office.

HUGO VON HOFMANNSTHAL (*glances at a newspaper*) Ah, an open letter to me?—That's decent of Bahr, not to have forgotten me in these terrible times! (*He reads aloud.*) "Greetings, Hofmannsthal. All I know is that you are under arms, dear Hugo, but no one can tell me where. And so I write to you via this newspaper. Perhaps some friendly wind will waft it to the campfire outside your tent and convey my best wishes—" (*He stops.*)

CYNIC Go on—read on! Doesn't he write well, Bahr!

HOFMANNSTHAL (*crumples the paper*) Bahr is unbearable—

CYNIC What's the matter? (*Takes the paper and reads out extracts.*) "Every German, at home or in the field, now wears a uniform. That is the immense joy of this moment. May God ever preserve it for us!—It is the age-old path already taken by the *Nibelungenlied*, and the minnesang troubadours and the mastersingers, our mystics and our German baroque, Klopstock and Herder, Goethe and Schiller, Kant and Fichte, Bach, Beethoven, Wagner.—Good luck, my dear lieutenant—"

HOFMANNSTHAL Stop it!

CYNIC (*reads*) "I know you are happy. You feel the joy of taking part. There is none greater."

HOFMANNSTHAL Listen, if you don't stop now—

CYNIC (*reads*) "And let us remember that, now and for all time: taking part is what counts. And let us ensure that from this day forward we shall always have something in which we can take part. If so, Germany's destiny will have been fulfilled, and minnesang troubadours and mastersingers, Herr Walter von der Vogelweide and Hans Sachs, Eckhart and Tauler, the mystics and the baroque, Klopstock and Herder, Goethe and Schiller, Kant and Fichte, Beethoven and Wagner—all shall have found their fulfilment.—" What connection do they have with you? Ah, perhaps he means that they have all been exempted. "And that is the gift of the All-powerful One to the pitiful race of men!" Thank God!—(*reads*) "Now you must surely soon be in Warsaw!"

HOFMANNSTHAL Stop it!!

CYNIC "Go at once to our consulate and ask if the Austro-Hungarian consul general is still there: Leopold Andrian." (*He has a fit of laughter.*)

HOFMANNSTHAL Why are you laughing?

CYNIC He probably stayed in Warsaw after the outbreak of war to issue visas to the troops when they arrive—that's indispensable in wartime—otherwise they won't be able to enter Russia! (*reads*) "And as you celebrate your joyful reunion, while the drums beat outside and Poldi paces up and down the room, declaiming Baudelaire in his ardent, sonorous tones, do not forget me, you are in my mind! You are so lucky—"

HOFMANNSTHAL Stop it!

CYNIC "—and what a flood of ideas just being there must inspire, does it not?" The things he thinks of!

HOFMANNSTHAL Leave me in peace!

CYNIC But you will soon be in Warsaw anyhow, won't you? For propaganda purposes, I take it, or something along those lines—Will you give your Hindenburg lecture again?

HOFMANNSTHAL Leave me in peace, I tell you—

CYNIC Brr, hasn't it turned cold again today—let me ring for someone to come and put some more wood on the camp fire outside your tent.

HOFMANNSTHAL That's really mean—go off and torment someone else and let me work!

(*Enter Poldi.*)

POLDI (*ardent sonorous dialect*) Hello there, Hugo my boy, what's the latest from Bahr?

(*Hofmannsthal puts his hands over his ears.*)

CYNIC How do you do, Baron, you've come at just the right moment.

POLDI Tell me, Hugo my boy, is it true Bahr hasn't been here all year, or could he really have enlisted?

CYNIC What, him too?

HOFMANNSTHAL Look, he's simply unbearable—come on, let's go in—

POLDI Hugo my boy, Baudelaire has got what it takes, let me recite a few pieces.

HOFMANNSTHAL And I'll show you my *Prince Eugene*!

POLDI Wunderbahr!

(Change of scene.)

Scene 20

A military unit on the Bukovinian front. Enter Lieutenant Fallota and Lieutenant Beinsteller.

FALLOTA Know what? I picked up a pretty Pole yesterday—very tasty! Pity we can't include her in that group photo we're sending in to the *Muskete*.

BEINSTELLER Ah, a pretty Polski!—Did you know the padre is having his photo taken for the *Interessante*, on horseback, giving the last rites to a dying soldier. Should be easy enough to arrange, if need be it can be mocked up—y'know, someone lying on the ground—then the editor asked for a prayer at the soldier's grave—no problem there.

FALLOTA Listen, I took a picture yesterday, a really interesting one. A dying Russian—like a genre scene—with a bullet wound to the head, completely drawn from life—y'know, he could even still stare into the lens. What a look!—y'know—as if I'd deliberately set it up, terrific, d'you think that would be something for the *Interessante*? Would they take it?

BEINSTELLER You bet! *And* they'll pay.

FALLOTA You think so? By the way, here's something you missed—the corporal fainted yesterday when he had to hold the spy—y'know, the Ukrainian priest—while he was being executed for the Sasha film. Pity you weren't there.

BEINSTELLER And what did you do with the fellow?

FALLOTA Tied him to a tree, of course. I'm not going to put him in the clink, am I? This isn't peacetime—clink, that's just what they'd like, that lot.

BEINSTELLER Y'know, I don't understand the Russians. The prisoners say they don't go in for that sort of punishment at all!

FALLOTA Don't talk to me about that nation of slaves! Did you read that poem by Kappus? In verse, rhyming verse even!

BEINSTELLER Everything in the *Muskete* these days is hilarious—Schönpflug—

FALLOTA A different kettle of fish altogether! I've a funny story I'm going to send in—Listen, you know what, I've started to keep a diary, everything I've lived through will be in it. Starting with the bash in the mess the day before yesterday. A tasty Polish girl, say no more, but very tasty—(*gestures.*)

BEINSTELLER Aha, gorgeous curves! Well, good for you. Me, I'm more interested in culture. I read a lot. I've almost got through all those Engelhorn novels. Before, when I was back at the base, we'd a pretty wild time of it as well. A bit of music, too. We have a gramophone now we got from the castle. You might lend me your Pole, then she could dance to it.

FALLOTA You know who else must have lived through a lot out in the field? Novak of the Fourteenth, he was a hell of a fellow. If he doesn't chalk up his 60 shots a day, he gets mad and takes it out on his own men. The other day Pühringer sent me a card: Novak sees some old Serb peasant fetching water on the far bank of the Drina. It happened to be during a lull in the fighting. He says to Pühringer: See him over there? Takes aim, bang, got him! Hell of a fellow, Nowak. Mows down anything that moves. They've already put him up for the Order of the Iron Crown.

BEINSTELLER Fantastic! Of course those idiotic peaceniks don't understand that sort of thing. You know, I'm curious to see how Scharinger is going to extricate himself from that stupid affair. You haven't heard, have you?

FALLOTA For making himself scarce during the attack?

BEINSTELLER Forgive me, but you're surely not going to accuse a professional soldier of—

FALLOTA Oh no, of course, you mean the story about the cook burning some dish, and Scharinger sending him into the front line—

BEINSTELLER No, no, it was on account of the coat—didn't you know? He had moved into where the colonel, Kratochwila von Schlachtentreu, had previously been billeted, then when he moved out again he took with him a coat of the colonel's that had been left hanging there. Didn't you know? Well, here's what happened. The colonel meets him and sees the coat, packed up ready to go. Scharinger finds a pretext, says he thought it belonged to the enemy who had taken it from the castle, and that he was just about to give it back. And the upshot was—well, you can imagine the furore. Anyway, he'll extricate himself somehow.

FALLOTA I really don't understand—it's always the same damned stupid things. I've never had any bother with that sort of thing. Of course, if it's plunder, then fair enough. Especially then! Even Joseph Ferdinand took a lovely carriage and horses, and clerical robes, and some bits of jewellery, too—well, he's knowledgeable about art, as we know. You know, I got a few nice bits and pieces as well then—I've got an eye for it—some really good stuff—there was even a piano, fantastic!

BEINSTELLER Hats off—gotta hand it to you!

FALLOTA Oh, that's nothing, the general's wife helped herself to lingerie and clothes from the quarters allocated to her husband, only for her own use, of course, in any case her daughter is provided for by the War Ministry. Those were the days! We just nabbed the grain and the livestock and anything else we needed. It was great fun the whole time—bastinado and all the rest of it. And champagne with everything. But now it's all gone dead. I can't say I'm really enjoying myself out here, except for the girls.

BEINSTELLER It seems to me, they're hankering after another offensive, at least that would make a change.

FALLOTA The last one was such a cock-up. Two thousand wounded and 600 dead—I'm not sentimental, as you know, and I'm all for putting in an effort—

BEINSTELLER It's a mystery to me as well.

FALLOTA It was all just to be able to report an advance, though we hardly advanced an inch. The men just lay there for four weeks—

BEINSTELLER Exactly. So they consulted their tarot cards again up there, and the cards say: Time to attack! When the men start grumbling about the dried vegetables, it's time to attack! If only to keep them in practice. Afterwards the idiot Archduke Friedrich says: are you happy with the outcome? And they say: well, the men had nothing else to do anyway. But I must say, high strategy that ain't, even though no one could ever call me squeamish! But what I say is, if it's not absolutely necessary—then go easy on the human raw material. As it is, first they squander the fully trained troops, then they send in the ones who've just been called up. For instance, the crocks and weaklings who can't tell a hand grenade from a dung heap. Is that hunky-dory?

FALLOTA They'll ingratiate themselves with big chief Pflanzer, at any rate.

BEINSTELLER You think?! The colonel sees red if there are too many still alive after a retreat. He once swore at a company: What's this, why haven't you all copped it yet? That's the Pflanzer Baldhin system, say Böhm-Ermolli's men.

FALLOTA There was a real stink with the wounded the other day. Who'd have thought it would have been such a big issue, there simply weren't enough ambulances. They'd all gone into town with the generals, to the theatre and so on.

They rang through to the town, but not one of them came back. Chaos, I need hardly tell you!

BEINSTELLER They're nothing but trouble, the wounded.

FALLOTA All the same, they should pay more attention to our men. Give the population a hard time, by all means, that I can understand, but after all we need the troops. This month there were 240 death sentences against civilians, carried out on the spot, it runs like clockwork now.

BEINSTELLER Political suspects?

FALLOTA Politically unreliable, half of them.

BEINSTELLER What did they do?

FALLOTA Oh, subversive activities and the like.

BEINSTELLER No!

FALLOTA I don't approve of martial law, you know, all that obsessive legal quibbling—and the endless paperwork, so stupid: Sentence passed! Sentence carried out! Have you ever read a legal submission? I haven't. Once I've strapped on my sabre, I've no need of that.

BEINSTELLER And you're meant to be present at executions, too.

FALLOTA Yes, well, at the start I even found that interesting. But now, if I'm in the middle of a game of cards, I just send the ensign. In any case, the sound carries into the room. We've a couple of good lawyers from Vienna right now. But still, it's a hell of a drag. I've been put up for the Distinguished Service Cross.

BEINSTELLER Congratulations. By the way, what's Floderer up to these days? Is he still shooting at his own men?

FALLOTA And how! A year ago they diagnosed general paralysis of the brain—all to no avail. They keep sending him away, and he keeps coming back. How he manages it is a mystery to me. The other day he shot a sergeant the lieutenant had sent to get ammunition, apparently he thought the fellow was beating a retreat. Didn't ask, just bang—stone dead.

BEINSTELLER One more or one less. In any case, let me tell you, when you've been at this game for a year, one more dead is nothing. But the wounded, they're a real pain. A year from now, when peace comes, there'll be nothing but one-legged organ-grinders—have your earplugs at the ready! What will we do with them all? Wounded—it's neither one thing nor the other. What I say is: a hero's death or nothing, otherwise those fellows have only themselves to blame.

FALLOTA And the blind ones are really repulsive. The ludicrous way they go tap tap tap. The other day I had just arrived at a station coming back from leave, and there were some other ranks laughing and pushing one of them around and driving him up the wall.

BEINSTELLER That's nothing—you should have seen the division commander the other day, taunting some fellow who had the jitters.

FALLOTA Yes, well, that sort of thing drives you to distraction if you've a sensitive nature, but you know what I think in cases like that? War is war, that's what I think in cases like that.

BEINSTELLER Say, how's your orderly doing? What age is he now?

FALLOTA Just turned 48. Got a clip round the ear for his birthday yesterday.

BEINSTELLER What is he in civilian life?

FALLOTA Oh, a composer or a philosopher or something like that.

BEINSTELLER Oh, did I tell you, Mayerhofer was in Teschen last week. Big white chief Friedrich has taken to walking round the streets, you know how? With his marshal's baton!

FALLOTA Does he take it with him when he goes to the privy?

BEINSTELLER Kaiser Willi has just given him another one. Perhaps he takes both.

FALLOTA Ha! It'll look like he's on crutches!

BEINSTELLER You know that big Jewess from Vienna, she's traipsing around down there again, peddling influence like the sainted Egeria—if she were open to negotiations, I'd be up for it—

FALLOTA You're a glutton for punishment! But yes, me too, I'd be happy to be back spending my evenings in the Gartenbau after mixing with the high and mighty on the Ring.

BEINSTELLER The Gartenbau, eh? I fear that's not going to work out!

FALLOTA Why's that?

BEINSTELLER You've just been in Vienna and don't know it's a hospital now?

FALLOTA Yes, you're right! (*Lost in thought*) Of course—but all the same, I'm not badly off here either. I've got a piano again, and a table lamp, so no stress—

BEINSTELLER You don't miss stress, mistress, mistress—

FALLOTA Say, I think it's going to rain.

BEINSTELLER (*looks up*) Ah, it is raining kittens and puppies. Let's go.

FALLOTA Heard anything of Doderer? There's one lucky bugger.

BEINSTELLER Yes, he always was a man-about-town.

FALLOTA About town, you're telling me—and as far from the front as possible! *(Change of scene.)*

Scene 21

A battlefield. Nothing visible. In the distant background occasional puffs of smoke. Two war correspondents in breeches, with field glasses and Kodak cameras.

FIRST WAR CORRESPONDENT You should be ashamed of yourself. You're no man of action. Look at me, I was in the Balkan War and nothing happened to me! *(Ducks.)*

SECOND WAR CORRESPONDENT What's happening? I'm not going a step further.

FIRST It's nothing. The impact made by the shells. *(Ducks.)*

SECOND Great God, what was that? *(Ducks.)*

FIRST A dud, it didn't explode, so not worth wasting your breath on it.

SECOND God almighty, a dud! Bloody hell, I didn't think it would be like this!

FIRST Take cover.

SECOND Take what?

FIRST Cover! Give me the field glasses.

SECOND What can you see?

FIRST Autumn crocuses. Reminds me of the Balkan War. Same atmosphere. *(He pricks up his ears.)*

SECOND What can you hear?

FIRST Ravens. They're croaking as if they'd got wind of their prey. Same as in the Balkan War. Danger beckons!

SECOND Let's go.

FIRST Coward! When danger beckons. *(A shot.)* Good God! Isn't that our lot over there?

SECOND From the Press Bureau?

FIRST No, our soldiers.

SECOND I thought it was.

FIRST Brave lads. None of them thinking of their nearest and dearest, all of them thinking only of the enemy. What's that lying there?

SECOND It's nothing, Italian corpses on the ground in front of our positions.

FIRST Wait! (*He takes a photo.*) Nothing reminds you that you're in a war. Nothing you see evokes its misery and hardships, its tribulations and horrors.

SECOND Wait! I got a whiff of the war just now. (*A shot.*) Let's go.

FIRST That was nothing. Just some outpost engagement, it seems.

SECOND I wish we'd stayed in Villach—good God, to think I was out partying with the Sascha Film people yesterday—I told you I wasn't ambitious. The enemy has this spot under observation, you'll see.

FIRST If you can't put up with mere skirmishes, I pity you.

SECOND Do you take me for a hero? Am I an Alexander Roda Roda?

FIRST I'm no Ganghofer either, but all I can say is, you should be ashamed of yourself in the presence of Alice Schalek—and here she comes! You can hide over there—

SECOND All right. (*He hides. A shot.*)

FIRST Actually, I don't want her to see me either. (*He crouches down.*)

ALICE SCHALEK (*appears, fully equipped with all necessary accoutrements, and says*) I want to go out to where the common soldiers are, the nameless ones! (*Exit.*)

FIRST Well now, there's someone who can set you a good example. (*They rise.*) She's off to the front line, itching to see the enemy trenches being mopped up—impressive, eh!

SECOND Well, that's women's work, isn't it? But what about us?

FIRST And the way she describes being in a hail of bullets—formidable! Don't you feel ashamed as a man?

SECOND Yes, I know she's courageous. But my field is the theatre.

FIRST The way she describes the corpses—and the stink of decomposition is no joke!

SECOND That's not my line.

FIRST Who was mad keen to experience a flank attack in the first place? You! And now you want to turn tail at the sight of a patrol. Before, you never shut up bragging about it—

SECOND We were all carried away at first. But now, a year later—

FIRST You wrote that you wanted to observe the war on the south-west front. Well, observe away, there it is. (*Ducks.*)

SECOND (*ducks*) Against Russia it was totally different, we never left the hotel,

I've no experience in this sort of thing, go ahead and call me a coward, but I tell you I'm going no further!

FIRST But the captain will be here in a minute, he guaranteed nothing will happen.

SECOND But I don't want to. I'll send off the article as it stands, you can give me the odd technical term or two.

FIRST You weren't schooled in the Balkan War, I don't know how you can't respond when danger beckons. (*Ducks.*)

SECOND Do you mind, I *do* know! I've described the intoxication, the blessed waters of oblivion in the jaws of death. You know how satisfied the boss was, the readers' letters arriving by the lorry load, don't you remember? After all, I was put up for the Distinguished Service Cross! (*Ducks.*)

FIRST But I don't understand how you don't find it satisfying to convince yourself in person—(*a shot.*) Good God, what was that?

SECOND You see—if only we were back in the Press Bureau. At least the enemy doesn't have us in his sights there.

FIRST I've the distinct impression that this is the counterattack! Well, so what. Now it's a matter of standing our ground like soldiers, duty-bound to stay at our post. It was specifically for us the captain arranged for the bridge that had been destroyed to be repaired—now we're here, we must buck up and make the best of it. C'est la guerre! (*Ducks.*) I'm all for providing atmosphere and colour, but when it gets serious—*only* providing atmosphere and colour is no good! In peacetime it was nothing but first nights, now you're paying for it. Why did you volunteer to be a war correspondent in the first place?

SECOND What d'you mean, are you saying I should have been a soldier?

FIRST Well, at least you owe it to your paper to show the right attitude. There's a war on.

SECOND I never pretended to be a hero.

FIRST That was the distinct impression anyone reading your last article would have had.

SECOND An article is an article. Please don't pretend you don't know that—my God, what was that this time?

FIRST Nothing, a small-calibre, old-system mortar from the IVb flak ammunition supply column.

SECOND Amazing how you know all those technical terms! Isn't it the one that always goes tsi-tsi?

FIRST You really haven't a clue. It's the one that always goes tiu-tiu!

SECOND Then I'll have to change my text a bit—you know what, I'll go back now so it goes off sooner. It has to be authorized, too.

FIRST Stay where you are, I tell you. I'm not staying by myself.

SECOND What sense is there in that?

FIRST Look, we mustn't let ourselves down. The officers are already laughing at us as it is. They're friendly enough to your face, of course, since they want their name in the papers during an offensive, but I often feel they're making fun of us during a retreat. I just want to show them for once that I can hold my own. Look, it's so dull in the Press Bureau—

SECOND Better dull than dangerous.

FIRST Look, is that really what you want in the long run? It's been going on for a year now. We're eating out of their hand. They soft-soap us, and all we have to do is put our name under what they tell us. They lie, we sign. I ask you, what sort life is that?

SECOND To my mind, it's pretty ludicrous in any case. What do I care about any of it? One article a month—what a relief! You can depict what their lives are like. But what point is there in me signing reports when the enemy has been pushed back or when he hasn't been pushed back? Am I General Höfer, the man who issues the military bulletins? Am I responsible for editing the World War?

FIRST What do you mean, Höfer? I've been out in the field longer than Höfer!

SECOND I'm not suited for any of this. I'm going to have a word with the division commander about a front theatre.

FIRST A front theatre? What do you mean? Ah, I see.

SECOND He was very taken with the idea, and it is my field. I'll remind him at dinner tonight. I'll tell him to his face that what I'm doing now isn't my line.

FIRST Yes, well, we can't all have the successes Ganghofer manages. We can't have a battle laid on for us.

SECOND How come? I'm not in the picture.

FIRST Hadn't you heard? It was on his last visit to the Tyrolean front. Seventeen of our men were even killed by ejected shell-bases, or at least wounded, it was the greatest recognition the press has been accorded in the World War so far!

SECOND Go on, surely that was a joke in *Simplicissimus*—that they had to wait until Ganghofer arrived before they could start the battle.

FIRST Yes, first it was a joke in *Simplicissimus*, then it became true. Count

Walterskirchen, the major in charge, stormed off in a fury. He was no friend of the press, but he was never mentioned by name. I heard he was killed two days ago.

SECOND You see, people like us are never accorded such honours. I'll mention the front theatre to him today! Even if we're not giants like Ganghofer. What do you want me to do? Look at Haubitzer—I mean Hollitzer, the painter—there he stands and paints. A giant compared to me. He sang "Prince Eugene" in the Kaiser Bar, and you would have thought he could win a battle on his own. Look at him now, though! Trembling as he paints, you wouldn't believe it! He's more afraid than any of us!

FIRST More than you, perhaps! Me, no! In any case, leave Hollitzer alone. He's brave enough to paint the battle out in the open, even though he's caught a cold. Did you see his picture? I mean his photo in the *Das Interessante Blatt*? "The painter Hollitzer on the battlefield."

SECOND You do what you want—I'm going no further, not at any price.

FIRST Take a leaf from Ludwig Bauer's book, in the Balkan War!

SECOND In the World War Bauer is in Switzerland—wish I was too!

FIRST Take a leaf from Szomory's book, or think of the courage of the soldiers, for that matter. They bite the bullet, they don't let themselves be ground down—(*ducks.*) So you want us to go back?

SECOND Yes, to Vienna! I've got to capture some atmosphere and colour. I don't mind putting my name to that! If it appears in the paper beside hers, Irma von Höfer's, that's fine. But beside his—I think not! Quite frankly, I'd be ashamed.

FIRST Not me! I committed myself to this, and I've got to see it through. (*He throws himself to the ground.*)

SECOND You always did have a marked weakness for the strategic moment. (*An explosion is heard.*) Great God!

FIRST Why are you so terrified?

SECOND Just now—I thought—it was almost—like the voice of—the Editor himself!

FIRST What a hero!—it was only the heavy artillery! (*Both run off, behind them, also running, the painter Hollitzer with his portfolio, waving a white handkerchief.*)

(*Change of scene.*)

Scene 22

In front of the War Ministry.
Optimist and Grumbler in conversation.

OPTIMIST You're wearing blinkers, so you can't see how the war brings out people's intrinsic nobility of character and kindles a spirit of self-sacrifice.

GRUMBLER No, I merely refuse to overlook the degree of inhumanity and infamy necessary to achieve that result. If it takes a case of arson to find out whether two decent residents are prepared to carry 10 innocent fellow occupants out of a burning building, while 88 despicable occupants see it as an opportunity for looting, it would still be a mistake to delay calling the fire brigade and the police while praising the magnanimity of human nature. There's no point in proving the virtue of the virtuous and thereby creating an opportunity for evildoers to become more evil. War is, at best, an object lesson since it accentuates contrasts. It may be valuable if it leads to no more war in future. The only contrast that war does not accentuate is that between the healthy and the sick.

OPTIMIST Because the healthy remain healthy and the sick remain sick?

GRUMBLER No, because the healthy become sick.

OPTIMIST And the sick, on the other hand, become healthy.

GRUMBLER You're thinking of the famous steel bath theory? Or the established fact that grenades in this war have provided a radical cure for millions of cripples? Saved hundreds of thousands of consumptives and restored as many syphilitics to society?

OPTIMIST No! It's thanks to the achievements of modern hygiene that so many of those who have fallen ill or been injured in the war have been cured—

GRUMBLER —and sent to convalesce at the front. But they're not cured by the war but in spite of the war, and with the aim of exposing them once more to the war.

OPTIMIST Well, war is war. But above all, our advanced medicine has succeeded in preventing the spread of typhus, cholera, and plague.

GRUMBLER Though that is not so much thanks to war as to a power diametrically opposed to war. But it would have had an easier task if there were no war. Or is it to war's credit that it offers an opportunity to deal in some small measure with its attendant symptoms? Those who defend war should treat these with greater respect. Shame on the pioneering science that prides itself on artificial limbs instead of on the power to prevent shattered bones once and for all. Morally, the current science of dressing wounds is no better than that which invented grenades. War has a moral power when compared with a science which is not merely content to patch up the damage war causes, but which does so with the aim of making its victims capable of fighting again. True, such ancient scourges of God as cholera and plague—the horrors of wars from the year dot—have succumbed to science and have deserted the colours. But syphilis and tuberculosis are faithful allies in this war, and a humanity contaminated by lies will be unable to conclude a separate peace with them. They keep pace with universal conscription and a technology that advances in tanks and clouds of gas. It will become clear that every epoch has the epidemic it deserves. To each, it's plague!

OPTIMIST Well, we seem to have reached the War Ministry. Today everyone is full of expectations—

(A gang of black-marketeers can be seen coming out of the main entrance.)

NEWSPAPER VENDOR Ex-tra-aa edi-shun—World news!

REFUGEE *(with fellow refugee)* Let me have that! (*Snatches a copy from the newspaper vendor's hand, reads aloud.*) "All well! War Press Bureau, 30 August 10.30 am. The mammoth battle continues this Sunday. Good atmosphere in headquarters, since all goes well. Weather splendid. Kohlfürst."

SECOND REFUGEE Must be some general or other. (*Exeunt.*)

GRUMBLER The faces carved on the façade of this sink of iniquity—eyes right!—eyes left!—look particularly austere today. If I have to look at one of those frightful heads a moment longer, I'll throw up!

OPTIMIST What have they ever done to you, those old martial types?

GRUMBLER Nothing, except for being martial yet incapable of refusing entry to Mercury's messengers. Wallowing in blood and muddling up myths to boot! Since when has Mars been the god of commerce and Mercury the god of war?

OPTIMIST Each age wages war in its own way!

GRUMBLER True. But this age lacks the courage to invent emblems for its decline. Do you know what the Ares of this war looks like? Look over there. A fat Jew from the Automobile Corps. His belly: Moloch! His nose: a sickle dripping blood. His eyes agleam, red as carbuncles. He drives up to Demel's in two Mercedes, each fully equipped with wire cutters. He waddles in as if wrapped in a sleeping bag. He seems to radiate life, but ruin attends every step he takes.

OPTIMIST Do tell me, what have you got against Oppenheimer?

(Meanwhile, the crowd has grown in front of the War Ministry, consisting mainly of German nationalist students and Galician refugees. There are many instances

of both types going arm in arm, and suddenly everyone starts discordantly singing: "Staunch stands and true/The Watch on the Rhine.")
(Nepalleck and Angelo Eisner v. Eisenhof meet.)

V. EISNER My dear Hofrat, your humble servant, how are we? And Prince Montenuovo? We haven't spoken since that—

NEPALLECK Greetings. Thank you, can't complain. The Prince is in top form.

V. EISNER The letter of commendation from His Majesty, that was something the Prince fully deserved, must have done his nerves a world of good! Everyone in society thinks the same now—

NEPALLECK Yes, of course—and you, Baron, are you heavily involved? Bending over backwards in your charity work, I imagine—

V. EISNER No, there you overestimate me, my dear Hofrat. I'm beating the retreat, rather. There's a pack of ambitious young fellows pushing their way forward right now, and I'm happy to leave the field to them. People like that are not to everyone's taste—so no, I've not the slightest intention of—of—

NEPALLECK But in a good cause, Baron, a good cause! If I know you, you won't want to neglect the whole range of operations entirely, even if—and I understand completely, why—you've no desire to sit on all the committees yourself—

V. EISNER No, at the moment I'm only presiding over the Upper House—no, what am I saying? I mean the Landlords' Association—rushed off my feet, there's so much to do—Riedl, for instance, he's not the man he was, as you well know, must have been let down or something, the war just seems to have treated him a bit unkindly—alas, even those most in the public eye have rather lost their bearings, others are pushing to the front—

NEPALLECK Yes, well, it will all settle down again—it's the same with us—

V. EISNER Yes, we must all be patient. For my part, I've had some very bitter experiences. As for charity, thereby hangs a tale, I can tell you. Oh yes, I could certainly feed some stories to the *Fackel*—*if* he was the sort of person you would want to be mixed up with, that is. You know, Hofrat, if you sacrifice yourself and do nothing but sacrifice yourself and then not get the slightest bit of thanks—Of course I'm not going to shirk my responsibilities, God forbid—my friends Harrach, Schönborn, and the others still give their parties, they still send me invitations—why, only yesterday Pipsi Starhemberg—you know Pipsi who's with Maritschl Wurmbrand now—

NEPALLECK Go on, I thought he was with Mädi Kinsky—

V. EISNER No, no, what are you thinking of, Bubi Windischgrätz has the field to himself there—you know, Bubi who's a major in the Guards now—anyhow, as I was saying, they come at you from all sides, it was only yesterday that Mappl Hohenlohe said to me at mass—you know Mappl whose girl is a Schaffgotsch—Why do we see you so rarely these days, he said. My dear Mappl, I said, the times they are changing, look at who's calling the shots these days, I don't understand how you can all play along with people like that. For my part, I like nothing better than peace and quiet. In a word, somewhere you're not recognized. Do you know what he said to that, Hofrat? You're right, he said! There I entirely agree with Montschi. Of course I regularly do my bit, but do I need to put myself about? No, that's not me at all. I've never sought public recognition. But you know, you can find yourself innocently at a *Te Deum* one day, and the next you're listed in the paper among those present!

NEPALLECK It's maddening, I know. At least I've now managed to insist that if they must print my name, it should be my full name. Not just always Hofrat Nepalleck, or Hofrat Wilhelm Nepalleck, but—since my name is actually Wilhelm Friedrich—Hofrat Friedrich Wilhelm Nepalleck. Just the thing at the moment, eh? I might as well move to Potsdam—

V. EISNER That's splendid! But—move to Potsdam? Would you really want to?

NEPALLECK Of course not, I only mean because of the Special Relationship. Me—leave the Prince! To this day the Prince is full of gratitude for my arranging Franz Ferdinand's funeral.

V. EISNER And very fine it was, too!

NEPALLECK Fine but restrictive—as befits a Funeral Third Class—

V. EISNER But another first-class triumph for you. It was really frightfully nice, over there at the Southern Railway Station. (*He greets a passerby.*) Was that not one of the Lobkowitzes? He'll be complaining again that I never recognize him—of course out in Artstetten—well, alas, it was a bit obvious that you had no hand in that, it was all rather vulgar.

NEPALLECK Of course—because they made it impossible for us! The Belvedere people couldn't be talked out of it. Oh, it wasn't for lack of trying. I insisted: according to Spanish ceremonial, let's make no bones about it! But at Artstetten, alas, they did start picking bones about it because those gentlemen were so stubborn.

V. EISNER What happened?

NEPALLECK Well, there was a storm, and the fire-brigade people ate their lunch beside their Highnesses' coffins in the main hall of the freight depot—

where the coffins had been put—and they smoked their cigars, it was a real scandal—anyhow, as you know, it wasn't our fault, it was all so beautifully solemn at the Railway Station.

V. EISNER I can see it now, I was standing between Cary Auersperg and Poldi. Haven't seen either of them since that historic moment.

NEPALLECK Yes, we did everything possible. But His Majesty's letter of commendation will have stuck in certain unmentionable gentlemen's throats: "In constant accord with my intentions." And above all the recognition that the Prince—in other words, we—went to such enormous trouble with the funeral. I know it off by heart: "In recent days the passing of My beloved Nephew, Archduke Franz Ferdinand, to whom you were so staunchly and loyally bound—"

V. EISNER That kills two birds with one stone.

NEPALLECK Exactly. "—has confronted you, my dear Prince, with the most exceptional demands and presented you once again with the opportunity—"

V. EISNER The Prince must certainly be happy that the passing presented him with the opportunity. One understands only too well.

NEPALLECK Just so. "—to give abundant proof of your selfless dedication to My Person and My House." There you have it! Plus effusive thanks and deep gratitude for outstanding loyal service, what more can you want, certain gentlemen will surely have been green with envy.

V. EISNER His Majesty's letter of commendation will surely not have been entirely unexpected by the Prince.

NEPALLECK Not in the slightest. The Prince seized the initiative immediately after the funeral—that is to say, I mean—

V. EISNER Yes, of course, you mean there was a precipitate rush of events. And behold, my dear Hofrat, now we even have a world war.

NEPALLECK Yes, in just atonement! In edifying expiation! Yes indeed. If the Prince had not seized the initiative—

V. EISNER What? For the World War?

NEPALLECK No, what am I saying? I meant, to meet His Majesty's need for peace and quiet.

V. EISNER What? In view of the World War?

NEPALLECK No—forgive me—I was thinking of something different. I meant to say, things couldn't go on the way they were, they simply couldn't. You know, since the annexation of Bosnia—

V. EISNER I predicted that to Aehrenthal. I still think the same, it was in the year of Aline Pallfy's coming out. I even went with Aehrenthal to the Foreign Ministry—

NEPALLECK Well, each of us has his own burden to bear, but—

V. EISNER How true, who hasn't, I've had some losses myself—

NEPALLECK What? You too, Baron?

V. EISNER Yes, yes, just as I had barely managed to keep going with a few consignments. I'm on the way over there right now—I might still meet Tutu Trauttmansdorff—yes, bite the bullet and keep going, keep going—our men have to keep up the good fight, today, tomorrow, and the next day, that's the main thing, everything else will take care of itself—good day to you and my humble compliments to the Prince—

NEPALLECK Thank you, thank you. I'll pass them on. Good day to you, bye—
(Singing can be heard: "Staunch stands and true—")
(Change of scene.)

Scene 23

Beside the pond in Janov. Enter Ganghofer, yodelling. Traditional loden jacket, black-velvet-faced waistcoat, knee breeches, rucksack, alpenstock, Iron Cross first class. Tyrolean hat with tuft of chamois hair, below that a shock of slightly greying blond hair. On his somewhat bent nose a golden pince-nez.

GANGHOFER

Halli halloo,
I'm at the front,
Halli halloo,
As is my wont.
A one-off child of nature
They'd all love to deploy,
But one who's grown too old, alas,
To be a soldier boy—

Though not to hold his own, for you
Can see I'm up to scratch.
I served on Szeps's *Tagblatt*
And there's no one I can't match.
With hunters' spirit, brave and bold,
Halli, halloo, the huntsmen blow,

And there's no need to tell the world
I write quite well, you know.

Those schmucks back in Vienna
Were too much competition,
A failure in my prime, I could
Not fulfil my mission.
So I got a loden outfit
And dressed to look the part,
And out into the forest
I swiftly did depart.

So the schmuck once on the *Tagblatt*
Is now the woodland schmuck.
I'm raking in the shekels and
I can't believe my luck.
Bavarians don't realize
Just what a schmuck I am,
They only see my blond hair,
At least that's not a sham.

Berliners simply can't resist
My thickly nasal twang,
And when the soil gives out a smell,
It's your Prussian's favourite tang.
When he sees a loden jacket
And a Tyrolean hat,
His heart melts and he tells himself:
What can compete with that?
I speak straight from the shoulder
To the highest in the land,
That charms even the Kaiser,
Who thinks I'm simply grand.
Thank goodness that I was a shmuck
Like the others in the pack,
For now the *Presse* wants me
At the front as a hack.

Roda Roda grovels,
But he's also missed a few,

For I'm the one who's landed
The top-level interview.
As one hunter to another
Men talk freely as men can,
Wilhelm talks to me so nicely,
Such a splendid Gentleman!

Then he'll read the schmuck for pleasure,
For the laughter I provide,
That's why I lie in waiting,
Like a hunter in his hide.
Halli halloo, Halli halloo (*the distant sound of a car approaching*)
Toot toot—toot toot—it's coming true,
The world awaits
Our interview.

AIDE-DE-CAMP (*enters running*) Ah, there you are, Ganghofer. His Majesty will be here in a moment. You can hear his car tooting. Just be free and easy, you know that's what Majesty likes, don't make a fuss, act perfectly naturally, as if you were meeting an old hunting comrade. As you know, in Majesty's view there are only three instances of perfection in art: in painting, Knackfuss, in music *The Trumpeter of Säckingen* and maybe also *Puppchen, du mein Augenstern*, and in literature you, my dear Ganghofer, and maybe, at a stretch, Lauff, Höcker, and Anny Wothe. Otto Ernst has some good bits too. So—no stage fright, Ganghofer, no call for that at all, Heavens no—just stand up straight as befits a hunter and a good down-to-earth fellow, Majesty is bound to stretch out his hand with a hearty laugh. (*Car horn sounds: toot toot—toot toot—*) Here is His Majesty. The photographer from *Die Woche* is with him. It's going to be one of the most enthralling scenes, "as Emperor and Poet walk side by side, for the heights of mankind they both bestride." And I'm not thinking of your mountains, my dear Ganghofer—oh, no!—but of the spiritual heights. So, chin up. (*Car horn sounds close by: toot toot—toot toot—*) Once more into the breach, dear Ganghofer! Go to it!
(*HM with entourage. In background the photographer from* Die Woche. *HM goes over to the poet and stretches out his hand with a hearty laugh.*)

KAISER Well, Ganghofer, you're everywhere! You know what, Ganghofer, you're good!

GANGHOFER (*broad dialect*) Your Majesty, my bleeding heart's on the trail of our victorious armies. Dammit all, that was a mountain to climb! (*He gives a hop.*)

KAISER (*laughing*) Very good, Ganghofer, very good. Ah—have you had any lunch yet?

GANGHOFER No, Majesty, who could think of such a thing in an age of grandeur like today?

KAISER Heavens above, you must eat, at once! (*The Kaiser beckons, a pot of tea is brought, together with two slices of heavy cake. The Kaiser himself puts his hand in a tin and stuffs Ganghofer's pockets full of biscuits while repeating:*) Eat, Ganghofer, go on, eat! (*The photographer takes photos.*)

KAISER Were you ever in Przemísel, Ganghofer? Eat, for Heaven's sake, go on, eat! (*Ganghofer eats.*)

GANGHOFER My most humble thanks, Majesty. Pschemisl, absolutely.

KAISER Well, satisfied? I mean, with Przemísel. But do eat, eat, Ganghofer!

GANGHOFER (*eating*) Forsooth. It was grand in Pschemisl.

KAISER Did you see Sven Hedin? Go on, eat, Ganghofer—

GANGHOFER (*eating*) Him too, forsooth, I saw.

KAISER (*his eyes light up*) I'm pleased you've met the man. That Swede is a capital fellow. If you see him again—but go on, eat, Ganghofer—give him my very best regards.

(*A Russian plane approaches from the east, gleaming gold in the evening sun like a golden beetle. Puffs of shrapnel follow it. The Kaiser stands still, looks up and says:*)

Too short!

(*Further shots at some distance behind the plane. The Kaiser nods, pondering.*)

Yes, when you have wings, the others always arrive too late. Go on, eat, Ganghofer.

(*Pause, while Ganghofer eats. Suddenly the Kaiser turns to the poet and says to him in a hushed voice, firmly and slowly, stressing every word:*)

Ganghofer—what—do you—say—to—Italy?

(*Ganghofer only manages to reply after a pause, when he has finished eating.*)

GANGHOFER Your Majesty, since it has happened, it's better for Austria and for us. Tabula rasa—always the best furniture in an honest household—makes a clean sweep of it.

(*The Kaiser nods. Breathes a sigh of relief and straightens up.*)

AIDE-DE-CAMP (*under his breath, to Ganghofer*) Dialect! Dialect!

KAISER Well, Ganghofer, have you got another nice article ready? Let's hear it—eh!

GANGHOFER At your service, Majesty, but unfortunately it's partly in High German—

AIDE-DE-CAMP (*under his breath*) Dialect!

KAISER Doesn't matter. Don't worry, read it out.

GANGHOFER The introduction is in the Swabian dialect, Majesty.

KAISER So much the better, delightful, read.

GANGHOFER (*takes a manuscript from his pocket and reads*) "Halfway there we hear that the first enemy trench in front of the ring of fortifications around Rozan has already been taken. It was a real coup, delivered by the Swabians. A fellow from Stuttgart coming along the road towards us, his arm in a white sling, says to me laughing (*broad dialect*): We've taken the first trench. The going really got tough. We were sweating like oxen. The Russians fairly pelted us with grenades. But so what! We've taken the trench! That's all that matters!"

KAISER Capital, Ganghofer.

GANGHOFER (*continues reading*) "I avail myself of the early morning to visit a well-developed little cousin of our hardworking Big Bertha. (*The Kaiser laughs.*) Still a young girl! And yet already bursting with astonishing energy! Her little mouth lies some four metres above my hairline. (*The Kaiser laughs heartily.*) And what a voice! You'd need to stuff your ears with cotton wool if you don't want your eardrums to burst. When she starts to boom out her thunderous song—a song to the inventive talent and power of the Germans—she spits a jet of flame long as a ship's mast from her throat, and if you're standing behind our little musical cousin (*the Kaiser roars with laughter*), you'd see a black disk getting smaller and smaller as it flies straight up in the air to a height 100 church spires piled one on top of the other wouldn't reach. And many seconds later all hell breaks loose in the Russian fortress of Rozan, belching smoke and fire. Quite a performer, our German iron maiden! (*The Kaiser slaps his thigh with his left hand, laughing.*) I take my leave of her with a feeling of enhanced confidence and supreme satisfaction, take the cotton wool from my ears after 400 paces, and find that the splendid girl's voice now sounds wonderfully melodious. (*The Kaiser gives a wolfish laugh.*) I acknowledge that this is a decidedly subjective judgment. I suspect that if I were commandant of the fortress of Rozan, I would think very differently."

KAISER (*who by the end has been listening and beaming, with eyes ablaze, now slaps his thigh repeatedly with his left hand*) Priceless! Bravo, Ganghofer, you've hit the bull's eye. Lauff serenaded Big Bertha and you pay court to her little cousin, hilarious! Killingly funny! But eat, Ganghofer, you're not eating—

(Ganghofer eats. The Kaiser, on impulse, goes to him and whispers something in his ear. Ganghofer gives a start, a piece of biscuit falls from his mouth, his face is suffused with rapture and an expression of confidentiality. He puts a finger to his lips, as if to intimate silence. The Kaiser does likewise.)

GANGHOFER Another bond to unite us, forged in the steel bath!

KAISER But to be revealed only on the day of fulfilment!

GANGHOFER And that day shall come!

KAISER Eat, Ganghofer!

(Ganghofer eats. An orderly brings him a message.)

GANGHOFER From Mackensen! (*He reads in joyous excitement.*) "Come as soon as possible. We have taken the Russian positions at Tarnów—"

AIDE-DE-CAMP (*under his breath*) Dialect!

GANGHOFER —"Tomorrow Lemberg falls." Yippy! (*He begins a Bavarian harvesters' dance. Then, collecting himself, earnestly, eyes upturned heavenward.*) Majesty!

KAISER Well, what is it Ganghofer? Go on, dance away!

GANGHOFER Must I still keep it secret?

KAISER Why, what's up?

GANGHOFER What Your Majesty has just confided to me—my heart can hold back no longer—that Majesty (*bursting out*) has promised three waggons of Bavarian beer for our brave Austrian troops!

KAISER All right, go ahead, tell the world! Let them hear there'll be something good to drink coming from that bounteous Bavaria of yours! But you yourself—eat, Ganghofer, do eat!

GANGHOFER (*eats and dances about at the same time, the Kaiser pats his aide-de-camp on the bottom, the photographer takes photos. The entourage prepares to leave. As the Kaiser is getting into the car, waving good-bye to Ganghofer once more, the horn sounds: toot toot—toot toot—. While this continues to be heard from a distance, Ganghofer dances on. Then he stops, and says in a completely changed tone of voice:*) That'll make a good editorial!

(Change of scene.)

Scene 24

Chief of the General Staff's room.

Conrad v. Hötzendorf alone. Attitude: arms crossed, weight on one foot, dangling the other, pensive.

CONRAD (*eyes raised heavenward*) If only Skolik were here now!

MAJOR (*enters*) Beg pardon, Your Excellency, Skolik has arrived.

CONRAD Skolik? Who's Skolik?

MAJOR Skolik, the court photographer from Vienna, the one who took that nice shot during the Balkan War—of Your Excellency poring over the map of the Balkans.

CONRAD Oh yes, I've some dark recollection.

MAJOR No, it was very clear, Excellency, very well lit.

CONRAD Yes, yes, I remember, it was glorious.

MAJOR He claims Your Excellency had made an appointment for him to come back.

CONRAD Well, hardly an appointment, I simply dropped a hint, since the fellow really does take nice pictures. From what he wrote, he's been plagued by the illustrateds, that picture of me was apparently a great success, in short—

MAJOR He also asked if he could take a photo of the generals while he's here.

CONRAD I don't much care for that! Let them get their own photographers.

MAJOR He says their faces are of no interest, it would only be of their uniforms and medals.

CONRAD Ah, that's different. Show him in, then, this Skolik fellow. Wait a minute—should I be immersed in the map of the Balkans again?—That was extraordinarily impressive—or maybe Italy for a change?—

MAJOR That's certainly more appropriate at this time.
(Conrad spreads out the map and tries out various poses. When the photographer enters with the major, he is already immersed in the map of the Italian front. The photographer gives a deep bow. The major comes and stands beside the table. He and Conrad stare fixedly at the map.)

CONRAD What is it now? Can I not have a minute's peace—I'm in the middle of—
(The major winks at the photographer.)

SKOLIK Just a quick photo, a one-off, Your Excellency, if I may be so bold.

CONRAD Here I am, busy making world history, and you come—

SKOLIK It's for *Das Interessante Blatt*, you see, they want—

CONRAD Aha, a memento for posterity—

SKOLIK Yes, and for *Die Woche* too.

CONRAD But if one winds up stuck between the generals in the same picture, I've been through all that before. I'd sooner—

SKOLIK No, Excellency, Your Excellency can rest totally assured—in view of Your Excellency's immortal name, it goes without saying that Your Excellency will appear as a totally separate picture. The others will all be lumped together as "Our glorious military leaders" or under some such label, and individually on picture postcards at best.

CONRAD Is that so? All right, then. Incidentally, don't forget Höfer, there's the clever one—gets his extra 20,000 crowns active service allowance for the pleasure of reading his name every time he buys an extra edition on the Ring.

SKOLIK Duly noted, Your Excellency. Of course. He'll be right at the front.

CONRAD What, at the front? Let's not get carried away! Where would you fit me in, then? Not too conspicuous, my dear fellow, not too conspicuous, and not with the others, you follow me, keep it discreet! Discreet!

SKOLIK A space has already been specifically reserved for Your Excellency. The cover picture in *Die Woche*. A very interesting number. I've still got to do the mannequins from the *Wiener Werkstätte* and one of Treumann, but I've been told there'll also definitely be one of His Majesty, the German Emperor, on a boar hunt, one never shown before, and right beside that a sensational one of His Majesty in conversation with the poet Ganghofer. So, I can assure Your Excellency—

CONRAD All right, not bad, not bad—but just at the moment, my dear friend, I'm rather tied up—couldn't you come back a bit later—you see, and I'm telling you this in strict confidence, you mustn't repeat it, I'm studying the map of the Balkans right now—ah, what am I saying, I mean of Italy—
(The major winks at the photographer, who is about to withdraw.)

SKOLIK What perfect timing!—A moment of profound deliberation that I must surely attempt to capture. I can already see the inscription: Chief of Staff Conrad v. Hötzendorf, with his adjutant Major Rudolf Kundmann, study the map of the Balkans—ah, what am I saying, I mean of the Italian front. Will that do, Excellency?

CONRAD Go ahead, I don't mind—since Kundmann can hardly wait—
(He stares fixedly at the map, as does the major who has not moved an inch. Both stroke their moustaches.)
Will it take long?

SKOLIK Just one historical moment, if I may be so bold—

CONRAD So should I go on studying the map of the—the map of Italy?

SKOLIK Please feel quite free, Excellency, just go on studying the maps—that's it—at your ease—unforced—let's see, now—no, that was a little bit unnatural, people might just think it was posed—Major, if you'd be so good, a little bit further back—the head—that's fine—no, Excellency, more casual—and more staunch, please, staunch!—The look of a Field Marshal, if you'd be so kind!—after all, it's meant to be—yes, that's it—it's meant to be a lasting histrio—a lasting historical memento of this age of grandeur—yes, perfect—except—just a teeny bit—yes, exactly—Your Excellency, scowl please! So—now—that's it, thank you!
(Change of scene.)

Scene 25

Vienna, on the Ring

PROFITEER You know who's completely disappeared?

LANDLORD I know, Kraus and his *Fackel*.

PROFITEER How did you guess! I often think to myself: no more of those flimsy little red mags, no more public readings—and I haven't seen the man himself for ages.

LANDLORD Don't mention Kraus to me—that man has no ideals, it's common knowledge. You forget I know his brother-in-law.

PROFITEER I know him in person.

LANDLORD You know him in person?

PROFITEER Certainly! I see him go past every day.

LANDLORD That's no association to be proud of. Mudslinger—scoffer—never anything constructive—wants to rewrite the world, full of himself!—Look, I know what it's like, I used to criticize everything myself when I was younger, I was impossible to please. Till my horns were clipped. His horns will be blunted soon.

PROFITEER His spirits do seem dampened.

LANDLORD There, you see! I've heard he's ready to retire.

PROFITEER And why not? I'm sure he's lined his pocket nicely.

LANDLORD Lined his pocket—! He's slumped to *this* size! He's washed up, I tell you. Depend upon it. It's obvious. Harden didn't stop when the war came. The things he writes about are more important, that's why—(*stops.*) They cut a dash, those German officers, more than ours do.

PROFITEER Of course, now when he really should be writing, he stops writing!

LANDLORD But how can he write?

PROFITEER You mean, because of the censorship? Oh, come on! A skilful pen like his—and you have to admit he does wield a skilful pen—he should be able to—

LANDLORD Not because of the censorship—he's simply not up to it. He's written himself out. Depend upon it. And besides—he must realize people have other worries these days. Sure, it was quite amusing in peacetime—but now people aren't in a mood to see everything picked to pieces. Wait and see, he'll soon lower his sights. You know what would serve him right—if they conscripted him! Off to the front! Let him show his stuff there! All he can do is grumble. (*The Grumbler passes by. They both greet him.*)

PROFITEER What a coincidence! So *you* know him in person too? How is that?

LANDLORD Only slightly, from a reading, I'm happy if I don't have to see him. One doesn't want any dealings with people like that. (*Fanto passes by. They both greet him.*)

BOTH (*simultaneously, awestruck*) Fanto.

LANDLORD (*wrapt in thought*) Great man!

PROFITEER Why doesn't he give readings? That would bring in a pretty penny.

LANDLORD (*as if jolted awake*) Who?—Oh yes—of course—Marcell Salzer is even touring around Belgium, I read only today, he's going from there to the army in France, and after that to headquarters and Hindenburg's troops.

PROFITEER Yes, and Hindenburg even wrote to him. He'll have a tale to tell! Did you read today about the incendiary shells that self-ignite in the air that they've been lobbing into Reims for the last 10 months? They don't let up! Working away! I can well imagine, can't you, that, come evening, they'll want to listen to Salzer.

LANDLORD Pity about Reims—that cathedral business!

PROFITEER Listen, don't take that line with me! When it's been established that we were dealing with a strategic military stronghold, then, excuse me, but it's pure hypocrisy on the part of the French. Sheltering behind a cathedral, what next! Don't talk to me about those scoundrels!

LANDLORD No need to bite my head off, you know! What did I say? You seem to think I don't know as well as you who the barbarians are. You can still feel sorry about the cathedral, though! As a property developer—

PROFITEER Ah, that's different. It's just that I can't stand it when people get sentimental in wartime, especially when it's all a notorious ruse! War is war, and that's all there is to it.

LANDLORD You're right there!

PROFITEER Where would it lead to? Can we risk a military setback? Attack is the best defence! Look over there—that's how you get respect!

LANDLORD Wait, I'm going to give them a cheer—Long live our brave boys in field-grey!

(Enter a German and an Austrian soldier, shoulder to shoulder.)

SERGEANT WAGENKNECHT So there we were all assembled, and our Lance-Bombardier says: If you're in the mood, lads, once more into the breach!

SERGEANT SEDLATSCHEK (*close beside him, looks up, startled*) No—!

WAGENKNECHT Do you mind, you're leaning on my shoulder.

SEDLATSCHEK Oh, sorry—(*steps back.*)

WAGENKNECHT All right, that's better. So, just imagine, the Lance-Bombardier left it to us—

SEDLATSCHEK Look at that department store: "You can't beat our loss leaders!"—(*points to a shop window.*)

WAGENKNECHT Lost leaders?—oh, I see—I thought you meant—now listen—(*he presses against Sedlatschek, who staggers back.*)

SEDLATSCHEK Oh, you're hurting my shoulder!

WAGENKNECHT Sorry. Now listen, the Lance-Bombardier—

SEDLATSCHEK Sorry to interrupt, but I don't quite follow.

WAGENKNECHT What?

SEDLATSCHEK Sorry—but you said the Lance-Bombardier gave the order. But surely you were all bombarding with lances, so who gave the order?

WAGENKNECHT I don't understand why you're confused, listen—and pay close attention—the Lance-Bombardier—

SEDLATSCHEK Yes, but—don't *you* "bombard with lances" too? Doesn't that make you a Lance-Bombardier as well?

WAGENKNECHT How come? Now listen—

SEDLATSCHEK No, you listen—the Lance-Bombardier is—someone who—throws lances over—isn't he?

WAGENKNECHT Throws lances over? What do you mean?

SEDLATSCHEK (*mimes throwing*) Look—don't you understand—throws lances—from here—look—on to the people over there.

WAGENKNECHT Ah, now I understand—no, no, my lad, that's priceless—a real hoot—killingly funny!—No, that's not what I meant. We're using not lances but bombs!

SEDLATSCHEK (*stares at him blankly*) What?—So is that a—Bomb-Lancer?

WAGENKNECHT No, no—there's no such thing! Heavens above! Now listen closely. What I mean is: the Bombardier throws the bomb at the target. But the Lance-Bombardier—

SEDLATSCHEK But the Lance-Bombardier—does what?

WAGENKNECHT He's in charge of the trainee Bombardiers, of course, that's why he's called Lance-Bombardier—how can I make you understand, for example—ah yes, of course—in a restaurant you talk about the Master Chef or the Headwaiter, don't you—

SEDLATSCHEK Ah, now I understand you. So: just as the Headwaiter is in charge of the kitchen—no, wait—just as the Master Chef is in charge of the waiters—no, hang on—

WAGENKNECHT Look, in that case we simply say Chef—You there, Chef, come over here a minute.

SEDLATSCHEK (*startled, turns and salutes*) Did you just call the Sergeant-Major?

WAGENKNECHT Good Lord, no! If I had, I wouldn't say Chef, would I? Look, if you're in a restaurant, you simply leave out their rank, and just say Waiter, thus: "Wai-ter!"—

SEDLATSCHEK Wait 'ere? But I am waiting 'ere!

WAGENKNECHT You're missing the point again. I was only trying to say: over-familiarity isn't acceptable with anyone else in charge, for instance, you can't say: You there, Sub! to a sub-lieutenant—that would be an insult. And it's the same with a Lance-Bombardier.

SEDLATSCHEK I understand—so you have to say: Dear Mr. Lance-Bombardier, please bring me a bomb—to throw over now?

WAGENKNECHT Why not, if it makes you happy—you Austrians are a bunch of weirdos! Excuse me for a minute, I must just make a call. (*He goes towards a public convenience. As he is about to enter, Hans Müller comes out, goes up to the German sergeant, and kisses him.*)

WAGENKNECHT Well, blow me down! Look here, it's very kind of you—what a charming breed you are, you Viennese—but still—

HANS MÜLLER Hurray! Not a day passes but I'm reminded of Bismarck's words: "Our boys, don't you just want to kiss them!" And so I do! My goodness, yes! I can do no other, when I catch sight of such a brave lad. I was proceeding on my melancholy way, meditating on those valiant sons now occupying so many an honest mother's heart, when you crossed my path—it was a sign, a corroboration of the most sublime alliance ever forged between two peoples—and if you don't find it irksome, cousin, I would gladly crack a bottle in your august company. Behold yonder, at no great distance, a hostelry known as the Bristol, since we love things foreign, where a fine table is set for us and enticing victuals beckon. There, though the gravity of the hour must remain foremost in our thoughts, time shall fly past in lively conversation. With this trusty walking stick, look, I can keep up with the best. So let us repair thither and make merry, will you come? I have a not inconsiderable desire to imbibe, comrade, so let us each raise a red rummer in a toast to the sun, what do you say? Or could you do more justice to a flagon of barley beer, that most wholesome Bohemian brew? It won't cost you a penny! And you shall sample the finest Virginia that an uncle of mine, who fairly reeks of the weed, has sent from over the ocean. Yes indeed, the two of us shall puff away, and as the wisps of smoke curl up, it may be that many a fraternal greeting shall likewise waft its way to those brave souls defending our hearths by showing the evil enemy a bold face, far away though they be since Italy picked a quarrel with us. And you yourself—were you in hospital, too? Are you an invalid? Or even wounded? So be it! So come, drink and refresh yourself to your heart's content! But we must also attend to our edification, that through contemplation we may savour this hour of reflection so fortuitously bestowed upon us, as truly befits a horrific conflict that holds out the promise of radiant, verdant happiness! But I see you hesitate? You're unwilling? You're a defeatist even? Stuff and nonsense! Cast off this morose display, discard it in the darkest corner, with the other piles of junk, useless when it's time to celebrate! Agreed? Shake on it! Take hold of a brotherly hand and let all the good spirits of your zest for life make merry! What's this? Still sulking and turning your back on a blue sky? Begone, such foolish thoughts! Growling morosely like a bear with a sore head, only a fool would cast doubt on the word of a friend, only a rascal would start rumours about his comrades. The devil take all scandalmongers! Everyone knows this is no time to be pulling a long face. You're no fool. You may not be a deep thinker either, but the two of us would get along well enough. Come on, stop being such a boor! (*A cab pulls up in front of the Hotel Bristol. A voice can be heard: "In wartime the fare is double!"*) What, are you surprised? Don't take it amiss, it's the custom here, the waggoner shows no respect, and he's an arch-villain into the bargain—

WAGENKNECHT Do you mean me?

HANS MÜLLER Don't hold it against him, he's eager to secure his monetary reward, for his reward in heaven counts for little. There's no limit to what travelling journeymen of that ilk can demand, their guiding principle is egoism pure and simple. It's just an everyday altercation, not a serious dispute, praise be—he claims the other should know the right fare anyway, the foreigner replies that he doesn't but would like the cabby to be so kind as to inform him, he declares that he is only asking for the going rate according to statute, the foreigner innocently asks what that is, he cheekily suggests the other pay what he usually pays, and gives fulsome expression to the hard times, for at feeding time he's as restless as his horse. The lively exchanges continue for some time, but the cabby won't yield and rejects any appeal to an officer of the law. And behold, the blunt exchange is brought to a peaceful conclusion, the other pays double, the cabby, still riled, extracts a further 10 percent tip for good measure, the other pays, the cabby spurs his speedy steed and departs, cursing his fare as a miserable skinflint. So be it! We must each seize the opportunity when it presents itself on a plate, and clever Prudence is the best guide. We are fools to Dame Fortune, and simpletons if we do not follow the wise ways of the world. That holds for you, too. If you had an ounce of common sense and a ready tongue, then slowly but surely everything would turn out to your advantage. (*A prostitute passes by and says: "Come with me, professor, let me give you a good time."*) Nay, I don't have time for that. (*To Wagenknecht*) Oh, you're surprised? Why don't you step in then, and let her gratify your every whim? She's a comely wench who will keep you entertained, for her free-lance profession is devoted to giving pleasure. The devil take all moaning minnies, and of course you must use your own discretion, yet I cannot but feel that associating with that sort of person is unworthy of the gravity of the times. Have the courage to be yourself, even if you are unskilled in courtly speech, unversed in the arts and sciences of the law, ignorant of all erudite treatises, don't worry, for a good honest trade pays dividends, and with me there is no need for you to watch your tongue. If it's a matter of some trinket you promised to bring back for your beloved, some winsome little cousin or pretty little thing you don't necessarily want to tie the knot with—you can speak quite frankly. You shall have it, even if it were a golden ring for her finger, it won't be the end of the world. Never fear! I know just the man for you, a merchant who from the goodness of his heart has seen many a valiant German warrior march off home to the flatlands, laden with precious gifts. Be not anxious on that account! Gold is a truly devilish substance that needs looking after, and there my good friend Traugott Feitel will bend over backwards to help you. (*Mendel Singer passes by. Müller greets him.*) What, you didn't recognize him? Ye gods! That was Meister Mendel of the venerable Singer family, and genial counsellor to the Emperor! But now it is surely time for you and me to repair forthwith to the hostelry. Mine host will welcome you with open arms and you shall relish the food and drink provided to tickle your palate. Come, my fainthearted friend, abandon the bane of doubt, put those melancholy blue devils to flight! They're after you with every trap and snare imaginable and will even saddle you with the gout. They wear all sorts of disguises and they'll catch you unawares and torment you. So, still at a loss, are you, standing there gawping? Do I look like a crank? Nay, you surmise my purse is empty? The theatre has brought me many a pretty penny, and I have earned an honest crust with songs about the war! I'm no killjoy, I only wish you well and was anxious to see you entertained, lest you were feeling down in broad daylight. Do you, a warrior, scorn the company of a poor wretch who has stayed behind? But that doesn't signify, for I'm no skulking malingerer! I can regale you with many a rousing refrain to stiffen the sinews, straining for the start. (*Sieghart passes by. Müller greets him.*) What, you didn't recognize him? Ye gods! That was Meister Sieghart, one of the best, supplies armaments and takes his cut—but say no more! So be it! Only a rogue gives more than he has, but I've dozens of juicy stories like that in my old kit bag. Hmm. Do you think I've some plot or intrigue in mind? Or that I'm a down-and-out villain up to some monkey business, a worthless coxcomb only good for idle chatter and gossip, who'll end up deceiving you? Pshaw! What a monstrous accusation! Completely untrue! I've never in all my life been hypocritical or mealy mouthed, and never mischievous. I'm neither a callow youth exactly, nor a pauper, but someone with his heart in the right place, someone who makes the most of life and lets tomorrow take care of itself. For I am valiant, I can change horses in midstream, and I'm a bright young lad! (*A man bends down to pick up a cigar end.*) Hello there, old fellow, hope you enjoy your smoke. (*Continuing*) Moreover, "Loyal and upright is ever my course", to the last breath of man and horse. Don't contradict me, there's no point! Let me but get a word in, and I shall sing you an air of my own making that you'll swear was set for a fiddle. Behold, the sun is already sinking o'er the fields, its last rays greeting the toil-worn reapers plodding their weary way, or many a happy homebound hunter with his bloodied kill, each and every one with eyes fixed on his tranquil goal, the peace of home and his own fireside, where waits his faithful loving spouse and swarm of happy children. Many a wife has sat there sewing till her fingers bled, piously pondering the while on her warrior's woes as the cold wind blows, and relieved of the duty of setting a richly laden table for him, she lovingly provides for the wider clan of his compatriots. Women and maidens of Vienna, on the banks of the ancestral river of the Nibelungs, I salute you!

WAGENKNECHT (*as if waking from a daze, to Sedlatschek*) Sedlatschek, listen—

SEDLATSCHEK (*approaches*) Say, you've taken your time—

WAGENKNECHT No, no, I wanted to go, but then this Jew boy comes up and starts blathering away—

HANS MÜLLER (*suddenly transformed*) So is it a crime now to invite you to the Bristol purely out of sympathy for our brotherhood in arms? Who d'you think you are? D'you think I'm impressed? Getting on your high horse! As if! Don't expect me to salute you, not a chance! I wanted to talk to you for an article I have to write for next Sunday on the Special Relationship—now, you can go whistle for it! (*Exit.*)

WAGENKNECHT (*following him with his eyes in astonishment*) Well, the types you meet in this wonderful Vienna of yours! The fellow looks like a Jew and babbles gibberish from the age of chivalry before there were any Jews. He's a journalist, and he kissed me! Instead of being taken care of by some Viennese lovely, I have to put up with that! For heaven's sake, I'm beginning to wonder if the price we paid for taking Warsaw wasn't too high!

FEMALE NEWSPAPER VENDOR Ex-tra-aa edi-shun—! Dscherman claims! All lied fictory!

SEDLATSCHEK You 'eard 'er, you seez 'er, there's yer Viennese lovely! (*Change of scene.*)

Scene 26

South-western front. Military post at a height of over 2,500 metres. The table is decorated with flowers and trophies.

LOOKOUT They're here already!

ALICE SCHALEK (*leading a group of war correspondents*) I see they've prepared a ceremonial reception for us. Flowers! Doubtless intended for my gentlemen colleagues, while the trophies are for me! My brave warriors, I thank you! We've advanced as far as this post, which is not saying much, but still. It's something to have been at least observed by the enemy. My dearest wish—to have visited an exposed position—the commandant could not fulfil, alas, since it might have alarmed the enemy, he said.

SOLDIER (*spits and says*) G'day.

ALICE SCHALEK Goodness, how fascinating! There he sits, like a painting, if he didn't give any sign of life you'd say it was a Defregger, no, what am I saying, an Egger-Lienz! I do believe he's even giving us a sly sidelong glance. The common man, as he lives and breathes! Let me tell you of our adventures, my brave warriors, before we made it through to you. The valley road, normally so full of activity, is indisputably in the hands of the War Press Bureau. Up on the pass, for the first time I felt something like satisfaction seeing the way a Dolomite hotel had been transformed into military quarters. Where are they now, those signoras with their painted faces and clouds of lace, and where has the Italian hotelier gone off to? Disappeared without trace. Ah, how that raises the spirits! The officer who was guiding us gave some thought to which peak would be the most convenient for us. He suggested the one that was least under fire, and my gentlemen colleagues were of course in agreement, but I said: no, you can count me out; so that's why we eventually came up here. That's the least we could do. But now answer me just this one question: Why did I never see any of the splendid characters before the war that I now meet daily? The common man is quite simply a sight for sore eyes! In the city—God, how boring! Here, each one is unforgettable. Where is the officer?

OFFICER (*from within*) Busy.

ALICE SCHALEK Drop whatever you're doing. (*He appears. She begins, almost literally, to extract details from his tightly sealed lips. Then she asks:*) Where's the lookout hole? You must have a lookout, surely? Everywhere I've been I've been able to use a five-centimetre lookout in the moss camouflage of the observation trench. Ah, here it is! (*She positions herself at the lookout hole.*)

OFFICER (*yells*) Duck! (*Alice Schalek ducks.*) They don't know over there where we're observing them from, poking your nose out could give us away. (*The male members of the War Press Bureau reach for their handkerchiefs and hold them in front of their faces.*)

ALICE SCHALEK (*aside*) Cowards! (*The battery opens up.*) Thank God, we've come just in time. Now the show begins—so tell me, Lieutenant, could any artist in his art produce a more thrilling, a more rousing show? Let those who stay at home call war the crime of the century to their heart's content—after all, I did, too, while I was on the home front—but those who experience it firsthand are in the grip of a passion. Am I right, Lieutenant, as someone right in the middle of it, that many of you don't want this thrilling life to end!

OFFICER No, no one wants their life to end. That's why everyone wants the war to stop.

(*The whistling of shells can be heard: Ssss—*)

ALICE SCHALEK Sss—! That was a shell.

OFFICER No, it was shrapnel. Can't you tell?

ALICE SCHALEK You obviously find it hard to grasp that the various timbres don't yet sound different to me. But in the time I've been at the front, I've learnt a lot, and I'll learn that too. — It seems the performance is over. What a shame! It was first-rate.

OFFICER Are you satisfied?

ALICE SCHALEK What do you mean, satisfied? That's not the word! Call it patriotism, you idealists; hatred of the enemy, you nationalists; call it sport, you modernists; adventure, you romantics; call it the thrill of power, you connoisseurs of the soul — I call it liberated humanity.

OFFICER What do you call it?

ALICE SCHALEK Liberated humanity.

OFFICER Listen, if only we got some leave once in a blue moon!

ALICE SCHALEK But the constant deadly danger surely makes up for that, doesn't that feel like real living? You know what interests me most? What are you thinking, what feelings do you have? It's amazing how easily men at 2,500 metres manage, not only without us women to help them, but without women in general.

ORDERLY *(enters)* Beg to report, Lieutenant, Sergeant Hofer is dead.

ALICE SCHALEK How simply the common man makes his report! He's pale as a sheet. Call it patriotism, hatred of the enemy, sport, adventure, or the thrill of power — I call it liberated humanity. I'm gripped by the fever for new experiences! Tell me now, Lieutenant, what are you thinking, what feelings do you have?

(Change of scene.)

Scene 27

In the Vatican.

The voice of Benedict praying.

— In the sacred name of God, our heavenly Father and Lord, and for love of the sacred blood of Jesus, which was the price of man's redemption, we appeal to you, who are ordained by divine Providence to govern the belligerent nations, to put an end to this terrible slaughter which has now been dishonouring Europe for a whole year. It is the blood of our brothers which is being spilt on land and at sea. The most beautiful regions of Europe, this earthly Eden, are sown with corpses and ruins. In the sight of God and man, you bear the dreadful responsibility for peace and war. Pay heed to our plea, to the fatherly voice of the vicar of the eternal and supreme Judge, to whom you will have to answer. The abun-

dance of riches which God the Creator has bestowed on the lands under your command doubtless enables you to continue the struggle. But at what a price? Let the thousands of young lives which are daily extinguished on the battlefields give answer—
(Change of scene.)

Scene 28

Newspaper office.
The voice of Benedikt dictating.
—And the fish, the lobsters and the spider crabs of the Adriatic have seldom enjoyed such good times as at this moment. In the southern Adriatic they had almost the entire crew of the *Leon Gambetta* for dinner. In the central Adriatic they subsisted on those Italians we were unable to save from the *Turbine*, while in the northern Adriatic the denizens of the deep devour ever more opulent fare. The battle cruiser *Amalfi* now joins the U-boat *Medusa* and two torpedo boats at the bottom of the sea. The assortment of marine spoils, hitherto limited to "maritime small fry", has been significantly augmented. The Adriatic, its floor increasingly bedecked with the shattered hulks of Italian ships, must taste more bitter than ever; over its blue waters wafts the stench of putrefaction arising from the late liberators of the karst plateau—
(Change of scene.)

Scene 29

Optimist and Grumbler in conversation.

OPTIMIST You can't deny that the war, apart from positively transforming those who must daily look death in the eye, has also raised people to a higher spiritual level.

GRUMBLER I don't envy death having to let so many poor devils look it in the eye these days. They're only hoisted to that metaphysical level by the gallows of universal conscription—irrespective of the fact that it fails to do even that in most cases.

OPTIMIST Good people become better, and the bad ones good. War purifies.

GRUMBLER It deprives the good of their faith, if not of their life, and it makes the bad worse. The contrasts were great enough in peacetime.

OPTIMIST But haven't you noticed how the war has raised people's spirits on the home front?

GRUMBLER As far as raising spirits on the home front goes, it seems to me no different from the dust thrown up by the brushes on the road sweeper, only to fall back to the ground.

OPTIMIST So nothing changes, then?

GRUMBLER On the contrary, the dust turns into slime, for it's the sprinkler's turn next.

OPTIMIST So you don't think anything has got better since the men marched away at the beginning of August?

GRUMBLER The beginning of August, yes, when they were given notice to leave, the day mankind's honour was terminated. Mankind should have contested that decision till the Last Judgment.

OPTIMIST But can you deny the enthusiasm of our brave soldiers as they march off to war, or the pride in the eyes of those who stand and watch them as they go?

GRUMBLER Certainly not; I merely point out that the brave soldiers would rather change places with the proud watchers than the proud watchers with the brave soldiers.

OPTIMIST But can you deny the great surge of solidarity the war has produced, as if by magic?

GRUMBLER The solidarity would be even greater if no one had to march off, and everyone could be a proud watcher.

OPTIMIST The German Kaiser has said: For me there are no Parties any longer, there are only Patriots.

GRUMBLER That may apply to Germany, elsewhere people perhaps have higher ambitions.

OPTIMIST In what way?

GRUMBLER Given the different nationalities elsewhere, they can't all be patriotic Germans.

OPTIMIST But you were the one who denounced the depravity of mankind in peacetime!

GRUMBLER Mankind carries its depravity over into the war, it infects the war with it so that the war becomes corrupted, and that depravity will continue, unscathed and magnified, when peace returns. Before the doctor can cure the plague, it will kill both him and his patient.

OPTIMIST Yes, but if mankind really is like that, is not war better than peace?

GRUMBLER When all is said and done, peace returns.

OPTIMIST But I should have thought war would put an end to the evil.

GRUMBLER It perpetuates it.

OPTIMIST All war?

GRUMBLER All this war. It feeds on the degeneracy of our age, whose bacilli replenish its bombs.

OPTIMIST But at least idealism has returned, has it not? Does that not signify the end of the evil?

GRUMBLER Evil flourishes best in the shadow of the ideal.

OPTIMIST But the inspirational examples of sacrificial courage must surely outlive the war.

GRUMBLER The evil lives by the war and outlives it, it gorges upon its victims.

OPTIMIST You underestimate the moral energy the war has unleashed.

GRUMBLER Far from it. It's true that many who now must die may also kill, but at least they are exempted from the opportunity to profiteer. Except that the others who proudly stand and watch make up for the loss. The sinners are those who have been exempted from service, not the new recruits.

OPTIMIST You're confusing a mere surface phenomenon, the distinctive feature of a corrupt metropolis, with its healthy core.

GRUMBLER The fate of the healthy core is to become a surface phenomenon. Civilization is moving towards a single global metropolis. You can turn a Westphalian peasant into a petty Berlin crook at the drop of a hat, but not the other way round, and there's no going back.

OPTIMIST But surely the great idea we are fighting for means recovery is possible, precisely because there is once more such an idea, and even one people can die for.

GRUMBLER Even if people die for it, that doesn't mean they recover. For they're not dying for that idea, but from it. And they die from it, whether they live or die for it, in war and peace. For they live by it.

OPTIMIST That's playing with words. What idea are you thinking of?

GRUMBLER The idea for which our people are dying, without having it, without profiting from it, and from which they are dying without knowing it. The idea of the capitalist, namely Judeo-Christian global destruction, which inspires those who are not fighting. Those people thrive by living off the idea and, assuming they're not immortal, will die of obesity or diabetes.

OPTIMIST Well, if that's the only idea which is being fought over, who will emerge as victor?

GRUMBLER Not the culture which has devoted itself most readily to the idea, I would hope—an idea which depends for implementation on precisely the power complex which this idea, and this idea alone, was capable of creating.

OPTIMIST If I understand you right, the others, the enemy, are fighting for a different idea?

GRUMBLER Let us hope so. For a more humane idea. For an idea that would liberate European culture from that power complex. To liberate themselves and bring about a moral transformation, having sensed the direction from which danger comes.

OPTIMIST And you believe the statesmen of the enemy powers are conscious of such things, even though they blatantly defend their trading interests and have been stigmatized in global headlines for their commercial envy?

GRUMBLER Global headlines appear twice daily here, and that's too often to create the authority necessary in dealings with the Entente. No, statesmen are never conscious of an idea, but it does remain dormant in the instinct of the peoples until, one day, a statesman puts it into practice. Then it takes on a quite different complexion, arising from a different motive. We should slowly be getting used to the fact that what they call British envy, French revanchism, and Russian rapacity is, rather, an aversion to tramping columns of sweaty feet in their hobnail German boots.

OPTIMIST So you don't believe it was simply a premeditated attack?

GRUMBLER No, I do.

OPTIMIST But then how—?

GRUMBLER As a rule, an attack is launched against the victim rather than against the aggressor. Or let us call it an attack that came as something of a surprise to the aggressor, and an act of self-defence which caught the victim somewhat unprepared.

OPTIMIST You are joking, aren't you?

GRUMBLER Seriously, I believe this European coalition against Central Europe to be the ultimate deed of which Christian civilization was capable.

OPTIMIST So you are obviously of the opinion that it was not Central Europe but the Entente which acted in self-defence. But what if the Entente is not capable of carrying through this defensive attack to a successful conclusion, as now seems to be the case?

GRUMBLER Then this trade war would provisionally be decided in favour of those who had less religion, before turning into an openly religious war 100 years hence.

OPTIMIST What do you mean?

GRUMBLER I mean that Europe's Judaized Christianity would then capitulate before the dictates of the Asiatic spirit.

OPTIMIST And with what weapons would the Asiatic spirit enforce that?

GRUMBLER Simply with weapons. With precisely that idea of quantity and advanced technology to which alone the idea of Central Europe, its infernal spirit, is vulnerable. Quantity China already has, next it will add the weapon of technology. In good time it will proceed to Japanization. It will proceed as England does today on a smaller scale, being obliged to introduce militarism in order finally to get rid of it.

OPTIMIST But England is not managing to get rid of it.

GRUMBLER I hope it will. And that, in the process, it will not get rid of what makes it England, if it were to become militarized; that it will not gain material victory at the cost of spiritual impoverishment. Otherwise Europe would become germanized. Militarism is perhaps a condition by which a European people is vanquished, after having vanquished with it. The Germans were the first to give up what they had been in order to become the top military nation on earth. May that not befall the others, especially not the English, whom a nobler instinct for self-preservation has up to now kept from introducing conscription. The present state of self-defence which calls universally and inexorably for conscription is born of despair, but it is also a gamble. England could defeat itself at the same time as Germany. The only race strong enough to survive technology does so outside Europe. At times that's how I see it. May the Christian God grant a different outcome!

OPTIMIST Aha, your Chinese! Militarily, the most inept race!

GRUMBLER Indeed! They lack all the achievements of modernity, for they may have passed through those stages in some earlier time unknown to us, and thereby ensured their survival. It will be child's play for them to regain them, once they need them, in order to make the Europeans give them up. The sparks will fly, too, but for a moral purpose. That's what I call a religious war worthy of the name.

OPTIMIST What idea will it help emerge victorious?

GRUMBLER The idea that God created neither man the consumer nor man the producer, but simply human beings. That the means of subsistence are not the purpose of existence. That one's belly should not outwit one's brains. That life is not founded exclusively on commercial interests. That time is a gift to be savoured, a goal to be attained not by swiftness of foot but by abundance of heart.

OPTIMIST That is primal Christianity.

GRUMBLER Not Christianity, for Christianity was incapable of resisting the vengeance of Jehovah. Its promise of salvation was too weak to assuage men's ravenous hunger for things of this world, seeking compensation here and now in place of eternal rewards. For such people do not eat to live, but live to eat, and even die for that cause. They want the brothel and the slaughterhouse, with the chapel in the background where a pope forlornly wrings his hands.

OPTIMIST So, in a word, the idea is the battle against materialism.

GRUMBLER So, in a word, the idea.

OPTIMIST But isn't German militarism precisely the conservative institution which opposes those trends of the modern world that you despise? I'm surprised a conservative thinker should speak against militarism.

GRUMBLER I'm not at all surprised that someone with progressive views should speak in support of militarism. You are quite right: for militarism is not what I mean, it's what you mean. It is the instrument which the dominant ideology of the day employs to enforce its power. Today it serves, just as the press serves, the idea of Judeo-capitalist global destruction.

OPTIMIST But in the declarations of the enemy powers, the talk is of nothing but their desire to defend freedom against autocracy.

GRUMBLER It's the same thing. The instinct of mankind, even of its least free representatives, is an inextinguishable desire to protect freedom of the mind against the dictatorship of money, human dignity against mercantile autocracy. Militarism is the instrument which enforces that dictatorship, instead of being internally employed against it, the role for which nature intended it. Since lethal weapons became industrial products, they have been turned against mankind, and the professional soldier no longer knows what interests he serves. Even Russia is fighting against autocracy. Through a last-ditch civilized instinct it is defending itself against the power most threatening to the mind and human dignity, namely the seductive power to which the Christian idea, with its intrinsic submissiveness, most readily, and in the most disastrous pact, succumbs.

OPTIMIST But can the heterogeneous peoples that have been drummed together for this war really have this single desire in common? Russian autocracy and Western democracy?

GRUMBLER Precisely this antithesis is proof of a deeper convergence, one which reaches out beyond the political goal. And the fact that even these contrasts can unite shows that Germany's misguided politicking, its incapacity to follow the basic rules of diplomacy, was the catalyst for a progressive convergence.

OPTIMIST But the Allies are such a hotch-potch, what a motley crew they are!

GRUMBLER The heterogeneity proves how authentic the hatred is.

OPTIMIST But hatred employs the most fallacious arguments.

GRUMBLER Hatred always does, but its fallacious arguments are proof of the authenticity of its instincts.

OPTIMIST So you're saying the Germans could have derived cultural regeneration from the realms of lies.

GRUMBLER Could have, yes, but a victory would make it seem redundant in their eyes. They could no longer be cured of their most dubious truths. For you surely have to ask whether the "lies from abroad"—provided they, too, are not *made in Germany*—do not contain more lifeblood than a "true" communiqué from the official German news agency. Abroad, you can distinguish between a lie born of national temperament and a truth based on rational insight. Here, even the truth is propaganda, and it is all paper-thin. If lying in the Latin countries is an intoxication, here it's a science, which endangers the organism accordingly. They're artists at lying, down there, they don't believe it themselves, but they want to hear it since the lie tells them more clearly what they feel: their truth. Here, when they lie, they don't use a word more than is absolutely necessary to achieve their purpose; they are the engineers of lying, they build lies which enable them to live and to wage war.

OPTIMIST Accusations of German barbarity in their conduct of the war are really too absurd.

GRUMBLER Let us assume that, God willing, the German conduct of the war is no more barbaric than that of the others—except for some measures taken solely as reprisals and which, by chance, always affect the civilian population, and except for some cases simply, if ingenuously, dubbed "incidents", such as the sinking of the *Lusitania.* But when the others say the German conduct of the war is barbaric, they feel, and are surely right to feel, the German conduct of the peace to have been barbaric. It must have been, otherwise it would not have been based for generations on the thought of preparing for the German conduct of the war.

OPTIMIST But when all is said and done, the Germans are also the nation of poets and thinkers, are they not? Does not German culture contradict the materialism you accuse it of?

GRUMBLER German culture is without content, a show house with which the nation of judges and hangmen ornaments the emptiness within.

OPTIMIST A nation of judges and hangmen? You call the Germans that? The nation of Goethe and Schopenhauer?

GRUMBLER It can call itself that, given its level of education, but by rights, according to the most popular article of its penal code, namely public nuisance, it should be condemned in the court of world opinion for doing so.

OPTIMIST Why's that?

GRUMBLER Because Goethe and Schopenhauer might more justly apply everything they alleged against in their German contemporaries to the current condition of the German people, and with more sting than *Le Matin*. As undesirable German nationals, they could count themselves lucky today if they managed to escape across the border. During the Wars of Liberation, all Goethe derived from the state of exaltation of his fellow countrymen was a feeling of emptiness, and today's vernacular German and newspaper language would be blessed if it had retained the level Schopenhauer found despicable in his day. No people lives more remote from its language, which is its life source, than the Germans. A Neapolitan beggar is closer to his language than any German professor to his! Yet this people is better educated than any other, and since its academics without exception—those who don't end up in a press bureau, that is—are busy perfecting gas bombs, it promptly turns its generals into academics. What would Schopenhauer have said about a faculty of philosophy that bestowed its highest honour on someone who organizes mechanized death? Educated they are, as even British envy is obliged to concede, they are instructed about everything. Their language fulfils the sole function of giving instructions. This is a people that today writes the truncated jargon of global commerce. Goethe's Iphigenie may not yet have escaped into Esperanto, but the Germans still abandon the language of their classics to the merciless barbarism of unscrupulous pirate printers. In an age when no one any longer senses, or actually experiences, the fate of language, it will make up for that by resorting to luxury editions, rare book collections, and other debauched manifestations of an aestheticism that is just as genuine a stigma of barbarism as the bombardment of a cathedral.

OPTIMIST Aha, but Reims cathedral was a military observation post!

GRUMBLER I don't care. Mankind itself is a military observation post—I wish cathedrals could bombard it.

OPTIMIST But I don't quite follow what you were saying about the German language. You've always seemed so engaged with—positively engaged to—the

German language, and in your pamphlet against Heine's influence you gave it preference over Latin languages. You've obviously changed your mind.

GRUMBLER Only a German could say I've changed my mind. It's precisely because of my engagement that I think as I do. Moreover, I am faithful. And I know that this war will bear me out, and that victory, which God forbid, would be a total betrayal of the spirit.

OPTIMIST But you do see the German language as the more profound?

GRUMBLER But far below it, the German who speaks it.

OPTIMIST But the other languages, in your view, are far below German?

GRUMBLER But the other speakers above it.

OPTIMIST Are you really in a position to establish a tangible connection between language and war?

GRUMBLER For example, the language which is most frozen in stock clichés also tends most readily, and in a voice ringing with conviction, to find itself totally blameless of what it blames in others.

OPTIMIST And you think that is a quality of the German language?

GRUMBLER Preeminently, yes. It has itself become a ready-made article, and finding a buyer for it gives those who speak it today a purpose in life. Its soul is like that of some petty bourgeois too busy to put a foot wrong because his life is absorbed by business affairs, and if it was too short to wind them up, well then, it's unfinished business.

OPTIMIST Aren't such thoughts rather far-fetched?

GRUMBLER Fetched from the most distant source, namely from language.

OPTIMIST Aren't the others on the lookout for business, then?

GRUMBLER But they don't live entirely for it.

OPTIMIST The English wage war as a business, and always let mercenaries fight it for them.

GRUMBLER That's because the English are no idealists, they don't want to risk their lives for their business.

OPTIMIST "Mercenary" comes directly from *merces*, pay—there's your language for you!

GRUMBLER Obviously. But "soldier" comes even more directly from the *solidus* the soldiers got paid. The difference, it's true, is that the soldier gets less pay and more honour when he goes off to die for his country.

OPTIMIST But our soldiers surely are fighting for the Fatherland.

GRUMBLER Yes, they really are. Fortunately, they're fired with enthusiasm, since otherwise they would be forced to do so. The English are no idealists. They're straightforward in their business dealings, and don't talk of their "Vaterland" – it seems they don't even have a word for it in their language; they leave ideals alone when their exports are threatened.

OPTIMIST They are merchants.

GRUMBLER We are heroes.

OPTIMIST Yes, but on the other hand you say that the English, along with all the rest of them, are fighting for an ideal?

GRUMBLER I say that they are capable of doing so under the most realistic pretexts, whereas we find the most idealistic pretexts for doing business.

OPTIMIST Preventing the Germans from doing business, is that what you call an ideal?

GRUMBLER Certainly, it's what we call commercial envy. In reality, it's knowing who benefits culturally from the expansion of a business, and who doesn't. There are peoples who should not overindulge themselves, since their cultural digestion is poor. Their neighbours immediately notice the bad smell and are more embarrassed than they are themselves. Global trade would once and for all isolate the German spirit, with which German culture has long lost all connection. But for that spirit to retain its connection with the outside world, a growth in exports is by no means beneficial. The English are entitled to a growth in exports, without detriment to what we think of as their barren soul. They can safely undertake whatever is necessary while indulging in the luxury of ornament and they go along with business dealings as readily as with their monarchy. In the German character, which aims to set the world to rights, all heterogeneous elements immediately produce some disastrous compound. The English are a cultured people because they know how to keep what little there is of their inner lives strictly separate from the problems of consumption. They don't want to be forced by some penny-pinching competitor to work more than six hours a day, so they can devote the rest of the time to those occupations for which God intended them: God or sport. As for their commerce with God, it would still be an internal matter, even if mere hypocrisy, to the extent that the mere thought of God distances them from their daily toil. And that's the important point. Meanwhile, the German works 24 hours a day, and it is at work that he fulfils the spiritual, intellectual, artistic, and other obligations he would otherwise neglect, given how he organizes his time, by turning the content of these obligations directly into fancy packaging and brand names and presentation. Nothing must be omitted. And this mingling of affairs of the spirit with the necessities of life, this focus on the means of life as the ends of life, as if groceries were its goal, and the simultaneous exploitation of life's higher purpose to promote foodstuffs, such as "Art in the service of commerce"—it is in this inauspicious element that German genius flourishes—and withers. This and this alone, this cursed tendency to be forever making such connections, dressing things up or turning them upside down, is the problem in this World War. We are merchants and heroes combined.

OPTIMIST Everyone knows the problem of the World War is that Germany wanted its place in the sun.

GRUMBLER Everyone knows that, but does not yet know that if Germany did win that place, the sun would set. To which the *Norddeutsche Allgemeine* would naturally reply that we would then fight in the dark. And fight, moreover, until finally victorious, and beyond.

OPTIMIST You are a grumbler.

GRUMBLER I am, though I gladly concede that you are an optimist.

OPTIMIST Were you not once one of those who used to sing the praises of German organization, at least in comparison with Latin muddle?

GRUMBLER Used to, and still do. German organization—even assuming it withstands unrestricted warfare—is a talent, and like all talents subject to historical variables. It is practical and instrumental, serving whichever personality puts it to good use, by contrast with the muddle in Austria, where even servile types are credited with personality. But how completely the German people must have relinquished their inner identity to be capable of coping so smoothly with externals! To acknowledge as much was never a compliment. Making the choice between different sets of human values that is urgently required, now there's a war on, the individual must subordinate his psychological needs to the general good. In peacetime, when condemned to lead a miserable life amid Austrian chaos, I yearned for Germanic order. Technology provided a pontoon bridge for explorations of the individual personality, so why concede any rights to those who only stand and wait? Now, in wartime, what matters is the personality of nations.

OPTIMIST And which one will be victorious?

GRUMBLER As a grumbler, I am obliged to take a pessimistic view, and to fear that the personality which has retained its individuality least will be victorious, namely, the Germans. Within the spiritual framework of European Christianity, that is what, in my darkest hours, I see happening. Spiritual starvation comes next.

OPTIMIST As a result of the World War?

GRUMBLER Of the European war, up to the decisive victory which in the true World War would be achieved over a spiritually united Europe. The Slav-cum-Latin insurrection, reinforced by auxiliary nationalities, will remain an episode until all of Europe possesses enough German morality, stink bombs, and obligatory conscription for Asia to teach it a lesson. That is what I sometimes fear. But mostly I am an optimist, and one of a very different stripe to you. At such times I confidently hope for a favourable outcome, and see that all this triumphalism is nothing but a criminal loss of time and blood to prolong the delay before the inevitable defeat.

OPTIMIST Be careful!

GRUMBLER I'm only saying it to you, and openly. You won't repeat it, and the hangman does not understand my style. I would like to speak more clearly. But I let the Prussians go for broke and keep my thoughts to myself.

OPTIMIST But you contradict yourself even in what you keep to yourself.

GRUMBLER But it is no contradiction to fear our victory and hope for our defeat.

OPTIMIST So there is no contradiction either between your praise of German character and your censure?

GRUMBLER No, there is no contradiction between my praise for a civilization which allows public life to function smoothly, replaces muddy streets with asphalt, and provides a thirsty imagination with systematic plans rather than some worthless notion of existential authenticity; and my censure for a culture that has become eclipsed by virtue of this self-same smoothness, efficiency, and know-how. It's not a contradiction, it's a tautology. In a generally deplorable world, I feel most comfortable where order reigns and society is sufficiently thinned out to provide me with a cast of supernumeraries who all look alike, and whose physiognomies therefore put no great strain on the memory. But I don't want that to be the condition of humanity at large; I am far from putting my personal convenience above a nation's communal desire for happiness, and think it misguided of the nation to allow itself to be lined up like a battalion of bread rolls.

OPTIMIST So can you also please explain the contradiction that you considered the military type as relatively the most decent servant of the state.

GRUMBLER That's no more a contradiction than the other. Among all the available types of mediocrity, the military type was the most adapted to the chaotic peacetime world. Service is a barrier against unbridled insignificance. Discipline, doing one's duty for its own sake, earns respect even for banality.

Judged by the eye of the moneyed bourgeoisie, it serves as a benchmark. Even the speculator, obliged for once to obey rather than command, comes back in better shape, trimmer and less tedious.

OPTIMIST As I live and breathe, that sounds almost like praise for war.

GRUMBLER No, only for enduring hardship—and only as long as you live and breathe! Death cancels out any gain.

OPTIMIST That's true. But when the speculators die, that's all right with you, I imagine.

GRUMBLER The speculators don't die. And anyway, claiming a glamorous death cancels out the benefits of physical fitness. The heroism of those who have no right to it is the most horrifying prospect of this war. It will serve some day as a backdrop, against which the increased or unaltered baseness of others will stand out more picturesquely and to better effect.

OPTIMIST But people really are dying. Look under the heading "Heroic Death" in the papers every day.

GRUMBLER Certainly, it's the same section that used to announce who had been awarded the title commercial counsellor. But sadly, a random shell splinter will create a nimbus of reflected glory around the surviving representatives of those commercial interests for which the others died.

OPTIMIST You mean, the representatives who stayed at home.

GRUMBLER Yes, they will be indemnified for the coercion to which the others were subjected, their mandatory death sentence in service of an alien idea called universal conscription.

OPTIMIST The warriors returning home will know how to react to such arrogance.

GRUMBLER The returning warriors will break through into the home front and launch the real war. They will grab for themselves the successes they had been denied, and the impact of war—murder, pillage, rape—will be child's play compared with the peace that will then break out. May the god of battles protect us from this coming offensive! A terrible agitation, liberated from the trenches and no longer constrained by any system of command, will start wielding weapons and seeking sensual gratifications in every sphere of life, and more death and disease will come into the world than could ever be contrived by the war itself. May heaven protect the children from the sabres that will serve as canes for spanking, and from the grenades brought back for them as toys.

OPTIMIST It's certainly dangerous for children to play with grenades.

GRUMBLER And the adults who do such things do not even shrink from praying with grenades! I've seen a cross constructed from one.

OPTIMIST Those are merely by-products. There was a time when you didn't despise war so completely.

GRUMBLER There was a time when you didn't misunderstand me so completely. War was once a tournament for the few, and every instance was compelling. Now, it's a mechanized lottery for everyone, and you are still an optimist.

OPTIMIST But it is impossible for the development of weapons to lag behind the technical achievements of modern times.

GRUMBLER True, but the imagination in modern times has lagged behind man's technical achievements.

OPTIMIST So, one wages war with imagination, then?

GRUMBLER No, for if one still had imagination, one would no longer wage war.

OPTIMIST Why not?

GRUMBLER Because then the suggestive power of a phraseology which lingers on after an ideal has become obsolete would not have enough scope to befuddle men's brains; because men could themselves imagine the most unimaginable horrors, and would know in advance how short a step it is from the colourful slogans and all the flag-waving enthusiasm to the field-grey misery; because the prospect of dying from dysentery for their country, or having their feet frozen off, would no longer have any emotional appeal; because they would march off in the sure knowledge that they would catch lice for their country. For they would know that man invented the machine only to be overpowered by it, and they would not trump the madness of having invented it with the even greater madness of allowing themselves to be killed by it. Moreover, they would realize they must defend themselves against an enemy of whom they see no more than columns of rising smoke, and sense that acting as agents for an armaments factory offers inadequate protection against the products of the enemy's armaments factories. So if men had imagination, they would know it is a crime to expose their lives to chance, a sin to debase death to mere chance, that it is madness to build armoured warships and at the same time torpedo boats to outwit them, to build mortars and at the same time trenches to take cover in, where you're only done for if you stick your head out too soon, so that foxholes offer the only escape from weapons and peace can then only be found under the earth. If, instead of newspapers, men had imagination, technology would not be a means of making life more difficult, and science would not aim to destroy it altogether.

Alas, heroic death hovers in a cloud of gas, and we experience only the choked wording of a communiqué! The bodies of 40,000 Russians twitching on the barbed wire were simply a special bulletin, read aloud in the interval by a soubrette to the dregs of humanity, so that the librettist who turned the slogan "I Gave Gold for Iron" into a shameful operetta might receive a curtain call. The numbers involved, so huge as to be unimaginable, mean that only one's own experiences and perhaps those of one's immediate neighbours retain any emotional force—things one can see, grasp, touch directly. Is it not noticeable how everyone dodges the collective whole, where for want of a hero everyone is a hero, and takes refuge in his own little world? Things open up more than ever before, yet there was never less community spirit than now. As never before, the format of the world is that of a gigantic triviality. Reality does not extend beyond the communiqué from the front, which breathlessly strains to reproduce its distinctive gasping and panting. The report of the action is, at one and the same time, a report of the action as imagined, the reporter having interposed himself and rendered the action unimaginable. And such is the sinister effect of his mediation that I would indict each and every one of those wretched figures, who plague us now with that interminable violation of the human ear, their inescapable cry of "Ex-tra-aa edi-shun!", as responsible for instigating this global catastrophe. Isn't the messenger equally guilty? The printed word has enabled a humanity with its shrunken soul to commit atrocities it can no longer imagine, and the terrible curse of mass circulation means that the word, propagating itself, brings forth yet more evil. All that happens, happens only for those who describe it, and for those who do not experience it. A spy being led to the gallows must take that long, final walk to provide some diversion for the cinema audience, and has to stare into the camera lens yet again before the viewers are satisfied with his expression. Don't let me pursue this train of thought as far as the gallows of mankind—and yet I must, for I am its spy and endure its death throes. My heartrending experience is horror at the vacuum which this unprecedented plethora of events presupposes in people's souls, before the crimes are recorded on camera!

OPTIMIST Such grubby by-products are an unavoidable consequence of great events. After all, it's possible the world didn't change overnight on the first of August 1914. Nor am I at all convinced that imagination is one of the human qualities activated in wartime. But if I understand you correctly, you want to deny that modern war leaves any scope whatever for human qualities.

GRUMBLER You do understand me correctly. It leaves them no scope, simply because modern war subsists on the negation of human qualities. There are none.

OPTIMIST What are there, then?

GRUMBLER There are quantities which are mutually self-destructive in equal measure, as they attempt to prove that they are no match for quantities transformed into mechanical energies. In other words, that massed troops can be obliterated by mortars. It was only the lack of imagination remaining after the transformation of mankind into mechanical energy that made this experiment possible and provided the proof.

OPTIMIST If the quantities are diminished in equal measure, one against the other, then where does it all stop?

GRUMBLER When all that remains of two lions is their tails. Or if, exceptionally, it were actually to happen that the greater quantity retains an advantage. I shudder at the thought of having to hope that will be the case. But I shudder even more at the fearful thought that the more principled quantity retains an advantage.

OPTIMIST Which would that be?

GRUMBLER The lesser of the two, of course. The greater might become weaker by virtue of the remnants of humanity it has retained. But the lesser fights with the fanatical belief in a god that has wanted this development.

OPTIMIST A Bismarck is what we need. He would soon put an end to all this.

GRUMBLER That cannot be.

OPTIMIST Why not?

GRUMBLER If the world keeps on totting up its balance sheets by the number of bombs dropped, no Bismarcks can be born.

OPTIMIST How else can we defend ourselves against the Entente's infernal plot to starve us to death?

GRUMBLER The infernal plot to starve us to death, in a war which revolves around the highest goods of the nation, namely making money and eating, is the infinitely more moral tactic, because it is more fitting than the use of flamethrowers, mines, and gases. The Entente's tactics reflect the pragmatism of modern warfare. But the Central Powers turn trading areas into battlefields and vice versa—as a result of a culture so confused it builds temples from tallow candles and puts art in the service of commerce. But it is not for industry to employ artists or to produce cripples. The wrong principle for living extends to the wrong principle for killing, so again means and ends diverge. When two consumer cooperatives are tearing each other's hair out, the more moral one is the one that reestablishes order, not by the consumers themselves but by means of a police force they have hired for that purpose, and if it doesn't mind losing its customers, or even losing its wares, then it is the more moral. Quite apart from the fact that the blockade is merely a warning to the Central Powers to protect their subjects from it by ending an insane war. If the accountant has not reined in the heroes on horseback, he should do so now, since even they clearly recognize that war is not a tournament, but an attempt to corner the textile market.

OPTIMIST The business of this war is—

GRUMBLER Precisely. The business of this war is business! But the difference is: one side thinks export and says ideal, the other says export, and this honesty alone, separating the two, makes the ideal possible, even if there were no trace of it before.

OPTIMIST You're not telling me they can be bothered with an ideal!

GRUMBLER Not at all, they merely want to deprive us of ours, and win it back by curing the German race of its uncivilized tendency to flaunt *Made in Germany* on its manufactured goods. For the Germans, ideals are "value added" to their goods when the others have them shipped in. They don't believe they can build an underground railway without God and Art. That's the cancer. In a Berlin stationer's I spotted a block of toilet paper with quotations from Shakespeare illustrating the purpose of each sheet and the humour of the situation. Shakespeare is, after all, an enemy author. But Goethe and Schiller were called up, too, the block contained the whole of German classical culture. Never before had I had such a strong impression that Germany was the nation of poets and thinkers.

OPTIMIST All right then, so you see a cultural instinct at work in the war the others are waging, and a demand for economic expansion in that of the Germans. But the effect of economic prosperity on the spiritual life of the Germans, would that not be precisely—

GRUMBLER No, it wouldn't, just the opposite. The total absence of a spiritual life was the prerequisite for these aspirations. Spiritual self-starvation, with its promise of success, would be beyond the range of any imagination, even supposing such a thing were still available.

OPTIMIST But are you not yourself convinced of the necessity of such a war, when you speak of a war of quantities? For it would bring the problem of overpopulation under control for a time, you would have to admit that.

GRUMBLER Radically so. Overpopulation worries would make way for depopulation worries. The legalization of abortion would have been a less painful remedy for that than a world war, and war would have been avoided.

OPTIMIST The prevailing conception of morality would never give its consent!

GRUMBLER Nor did I ever imagine it would, since the prevailing conception of morality only approves of fathers, fortuitously delivered from the random killing, dragging themselves along the pavement as penniless cripples, and mothers giving birth to babies to be torn to pieces by having bombs dropped on them.

OPTIMIST You're surely not suggesting that such things are deliberate?

GRUMBLER No, worse than that: fortuitous! One can't help it happening, but it happens with forethought. Regrettable, but still it happens. Fairly extensive experience in this area might have brought it home to those who organize murder from the air, and those entrusted with carrying it out, that when they intend to hit an arms dump they infallibly hit a bedroom, and instead of an armaments factory a school for girls. Repeated experience should have taught them that that is what the success of those raids means when they subsequently boast of having bombed the target.

OPTIMIST Be that as it may, it is a permitted weapon of war, and since mastery of the air has been achieved—

GRUMBLER —man, that scoundrel, seizes the opportunity to make the earth equally unsafe. Read Jean Paul's account of the ascent of a Montgolfier balloon. No one could write those five pages today, for those making incursions into the upper air have no respect for the heavens above, but as aerial invaders use their safe distance from the earth to launch attacks upon it. Men are incapable of enjoying the fruits of progress without paying the price. They promptly employ the very things that should improve life to destroy it. They struggle with what should make life easier. To ascend in a Montgolfier balloon is an act of reverence, the ascent of an aeroplane is a danger to those left below.

OPTIMIST But surely also for the airman himself who drops the bombs.

GRUMBLER Certainly, but not the danger of being killed by those he is going to kill, and he avoids the lurking machine guns more easily than the defenceless ones below avoid him. He also more easily avoids a fair fight between two equally armed murderers—fair, insofar as the violation of the element in which it takes place permits of such values. But even if it is the "intrepid" aviator who wields it, the aerial bomb signifies armed cowardice, it is as ruthless as the U-boat which signifies the principle of armed guile, the same guile which allows the dwarf to triumph over the armed giant. But the infants killed by the aviator are not armed, and even if they were, they would hardly manage to hit the aviator as surely as he will hit them. Of all the ignominies of war, the most shameful is that the only invention to bring man closer to the stars has served merely to provide confirmation of his baseness, as if he had not sufficient scope for it on earth.

OPTIMIST What of the infants who are being starved to death?

GRUMBLER The governments of the Central Powers are free to spare their infants this fate by weaning their adults off what they were spoon-fed from early childhood. But even supposing the enemy powers-that-be are as guilty of the blockade as our own, the bombing of enemy infants as a reprisal is the sort of thinking that does German ideology proud, the sort of intellectual position in which—by the God of the Germans!—I have no wish to take refuge.

OPTIMIST You're trying to find fault with the way the Germans wage war, without taking account of the fact that the others are using the same means.

GRUMBLER I freely acknowledge that, and I've no intention of making an exception of the French aeroplanes that use much the same heroic villainies in their violation of humanity. However, apart from the fact that we started it, the distinction seems to me to lie, on the one side, in a disposition which participates in the horror, knowingly or absentmindedly forgetful of what it involves, and on the other, a cast of mind which, not content with dropping bombs, accompanies them with jokes and even with "Christmas greetings" specially got up for the inhabitants of Nancy. Here we have once again the pernicious mixing of things made to be used, in this case, bombs, and the inner life, namely jokes, and even the fusion of the joke with the sacred—that mixture which is the greatest abomination of all, the height of debauchery, which a life impoverished by rules and regulations receives as a perk permitting mindless brutality in compensation for all that discipline, drill, and morality. It is the humour of the hangman, the licence of a morality that even takes legal action against love.

OPTIMIST Compensation for discipline? But did you not welcome discipline as a check on disorderly behaviour?

GRUMBLER But not as a lever of power! Rather chaos than order at the expense of humanity! Militarism as a workout and militarism as a state of mind—there is surely a distinction. Militarism is essentially a tool. But it becomes a law unto itself, an irreconcilable enemy of the human spirit, when transformed into the unwitting tool of antagonistic forces—forces hostile to humane values. Its code of honour, allied to the cowardice of technology, has become a farce, its self-imposed duty within a framework of general compulsion has degenerated into a lie. It is nothing but pretence, and it compensates for its slave status by hiding behind its machines to demonstrate its miserable power. The means has become an end in itself, to the extent that in peacetime we can still only think militarily, and war is merely a means to obtain new weapons. A war to the greater glory of the armaments industry. We do not merely want more exports and therefore more guns, we also want more guns for their own sake, and that's why they have to be fired. Our lives and our thinking are subjected to the interests of heavy industry; it's a heavy burden. We live under the sign of the gun. And since heavy industry has allied itself with God, we are lost. That is now the human condition.

OPTIMIST But we might also see our position from the perspective of a Nietzschean ideal, and come to a very different view of things.

GRUMBLER Yes, you might well do that, and you would then experience Nietzsche's astonishment that the "will to power" manifested itself after Sedan not as a triumph of the spirit, but as an increase in the number of factory chimneys. Nietzsche was a thinker who "imagined it would turn out differently." Namely, the spiritual uplift of the year 1870. That of 1914 he would have scarcely found credible for a moment, nor would he have been any longer astonished by the victory of his own thoughts. Yet perhaps, after all, he would have rejected the conqueror marching off to war with *The Will to Power* and other edifying intellectual ammunition in his kit bag.

OPTIMIST If war offers no cultural benefit, that holds for all of the belligerent nations. That is, unless you are determined on principle to admit of cultural possibilities only whenever franc-tireurs murder sleeping soldiers.

GRUMBLER Certainly not when our official press bureau exists for the sole purpose of making such allegations. But even in the present state of mankind, it would be unique for aviators who bomb infants to have internationally sanctioned licence to do so, and for franc-tireurs who commit murder to avenge murder not to be allowed to do so because they have no such licence. They are not killing under orders but under a different form of irresistible compulsion, not out of duty but in a frenzy of rage, that is to say, with the only possible motive that halfway excuses the killing; they are unauthorized killers, who cannot identify themselves by the appropriate costume, or by membership of some regional backup squad or reserve unit or special detachment or whatever shameful name they give it. Don't ask me to judge the moral difference between an aviator who kills a sleeping child and a civilian who kills a sleeping soldier. Decide yourself which is the more courageous choice—taking into account only the danger and not the responsibility—to attack a sleeping soldier or a wide-awake child?

OPTIMIST You may be right on that score, but you'd need a magnifying glass to find signs of humanity on the other side.

GRUMBLER If I were to look for them in our newspapers, indeed I would.

OPTIMIST Just think of the headline "Russians wreak havoc in Galicia."

GRUMBLER Though I couldn't make out from that whether the Galician castles were plundered by Polish peasants or Hungarian territorials. What did often appear under that headline, as if they had slipped through the grip of the compulsion to lie, were tales of noble action on the part of the Russians.

OPTIMIST You surely don't mean that story about a rape?

GRUMBLER Well, whether Hungarian territorials or an elite Viennese regiment have doffed their caps and asked the women of their own country, let alone those of the enemy, for a glass of water—I leave the decision, one way or the other, to your optimism, unshakeably grounded as it seems to be in the reporting of our War Press Bureau.

OPTIMIST Don't you find that, after all, we too give the enemy his due?

GRUMBLER Yes, we are sometimes content with the humour of idiotic picture postcards.

OPTIMIST No, I mean we really sometimes do him justice.

GRUMBLER If it makes people laugh, then yes. As when they related the curious fact—for the central European intelligentsia won't be caught telling the truth about the most maligned people in Europe—the curious fact, then, that the Russians stopped shooting over the Catholic Christmas, and instead left behind in their trenches a seasonal greeting to the enemy and hopes for peace.

OPTIMIST And the Austrians, I'm sure, responded in kind.

GRUMBLER Certainly, for instance a Doctor Fischl, an articled clerk until 1 August, then mobilized when the age of grandeur arrived, had a field postcard printed for the troops, inscribed: "Tomorrow the Russians celebrate their Christmas—time to tickle their fancy good and proper."

OPTIMIST That was a joke.

GRUMBLER Quite right, it was a joke.

OPTIMIST One mustn't generalize.

GRUMBLER I do. You can depend upon my unfairness. If militarism served to combat the despicable conditions at home, I would be a patriot. If it accepted those unfit for military service, if it waged war in order to deliver these human dregs to the enemy, I would be a militarist! But it sacrifices what is valuable and procures haloes for the dregs, even, when things go wrong in the field, crowning them victors over their own side. Only this way of looking at things can explain the patience with which the majority of mankind put up with an insult to nature such as universal conscription. Soldiers treated as trash know that the idea they are fighting for is their own survival, and in that sense they even fight for the Fatherland, which they know at heart to be an alien idea, though it is drummed into them day after day by an infantile ideology. Would they not otherwise come at last to resent this coercion to die for an alien idea, a form of serfdom a thousand times more oppressive than the worst excesses of despised reactionary tsarism? But the final outcome is that they make the idea of the Fatherland their own. Would people who have never enjoyed the privileges of a military career otherwise submit under duress to sharing its dangers? Allow themselves to be torn from their profession, their livelihood, their family, to be abused in barracks before dying to retain Bukovina? The fact that they would be shot beforehand if they refused to die for Bukovina is, of course, an immediate motive, and one which in itself provides a complete explanation. But conscription could not have been introduced if the great majority had not known that they themselves, though seeming victims of autocratic cravings, would finally vanquish their oppressors. You see, I too am an optimist. I cannot bring myself to think of mankind as a totally impotent rabble, willing to mire itself in mud and misery and mortal peril—just to please an alien elite.

OPTIMIST But surely the exaltation which the call of the Fatherland creates is a better explanation than coercion or personal advantage.

GRUMBLER The Fatherland? It's true that, of all those who instigate such spectacles, the voice of the Fatherland still retains the greatest hypnotic power. But the intoxication which lulls all suspicion of how totally defenceless they are would fail to work on the intelligent ones who are more alert, were it not for their underlying feeling that a victory would make them masters of the realm.

OPTIMIST But the war hasn't provided that yet.

GRUMBLER They merely avoid thinking about that, so they can relax for once. They don't need to knock their brains out until the enemy does it for them, something they no longer have sufficient power to imagine. For war turns life into a nursery, where it is always the other side that started it, where the one always boasts of the crimes he accuses the other of, and where the scuffles turn into war games. When war comes, one learns to be less appreciative of children playing soldiers. It is much too early a preparation for the childishness of grown-ups.

OPTIMIST On the contrary, the children's game of playing soldiers has received a new impetus. Do you know the game "Let's Play World War"?

GRUMBLER It's the other side of the coin, and every bit as squalid as the real-life "Let's Play Potty Training." Given this humanity, one might wish their infants to have their first successes starving each other or bombing each other to death, in any case, liquidating their nurses' clientele.

OPTIMIST If you had your way, mankind would be in line for extermination even before a world war. But, thanks be to God, it is up-and-coming—

GRUMBLER Up in arms, you mean.

OPTIMIST Marching onward and upward from generation to generation. You mentioned five pages of Jean Paul that could not be written today, but I'd say the invention of Graf Zeppelin has by no means deprived Germany of the possibility of producing poets. There are poets today who are not to be despised.

GRUMBLER And yet I despise them.

OPTIMIST And now, above all, now that it's wartime, German poetry has received an impulse which has revived it.

GRUMBLER A pity it didn't receive a box on the ears.

OPTIMIST What you say is rude, but not true. Whatever you might think of the war, the work produced by our poets breathes fire in much the same way this age of grandeur has engulfed our daily life, setting it alight.

GRUMBLER The poet's fiery mouth has one immediate point of contact with daily life: the hackneyed phraseology that our poets, adaptable as they are, adopted at once. They latched on promptly, before their bewildered clients could start to make demands. German poets! You are an inveterate optimist, but your optimism would soon turn to mockery if you tried to pass off those works as proof of the grandeur of the age. I can still differentiate between the poor philistines compelled to swap their office desks for the trenches, and—several levels lower on the moral scale—the miserable scribblers at home, their horrified scrawls worse than mockery, namely editorials or rhymes, who strike tenth-hand attitudes that were already false when first concocted, and who shamelessly turn the enthusiasm of those people breathing fire into a fabricated call for action. In all those works, I haven't found a single line that I would not have turned away from in peacetime, with an expression more indicative of nausea than of participating in a revelation. The only worthy line I've set eyes on is in the Emperor's Manifesto, which some sensitive stylist must have brought off after soaking up what it must feel like to have a lifetime's experience. "I have weighed everything in the balance." Times to come, even more than the times we have already endured, will show that weighing things even more carefully would have averted this unspeakable horror. But taken by itself, in isolation, the line has the power of a poem, above all perhaps if you sense the train of thought behind it. Look, over there—on that advertising pillar you can still feel its impact.

OPTIMIST Where?

GRUMBLER —Oh, what a shame, the very part of the manifesto containing that line is obscured by Wolf in Gersthof's face. Behold, like Tyrtaios spurring the Spartans on with his martial elegies, the true face of this war. And only now a poem!

OPTIMIST I know your exaggerated way of looking at things. You don't think there is such a thing as chance. But still, Wolf in Gersthof, someone I personally don't particularly like—

GRUMBLER Really?

OPTIMIST —after all, it's only an advertisement like any other, and an old one at that, note, from before the war. The space for the poster was already booked, maybe the place is still open for business, I've no idea, things don't change overnight, these are mere outer trappings anyhow, but I'm convinced—

GRUMBLER Of course you're convinced—

OPTIMIST —yes I am, I'm convinced that the Viennese, who really have been transformed overnight into a serious people, "neither high-handed nor faint-hearted", as the *Presse* so rightly said, have realized the gravity of the situation. I'm convinced that a year from now they won't want to be implicated in such mindless hedonism, whether the war is over by then or not. I'm convinced of that, yes!

GRUMBLER For my part, I have no convictions, and I think it makes no difference whether things turn out like that or not, or whether one approves or, in your case, finds it reprehensible if the mindless hedonism continues. Unlike you, I would be inclined to approve.

OPTIMIST Then I don't understand you.

GRUMBLER Look, I am convinced of one thing and one thing only: that people don't care. But I'll say this: a year from now Wolf in Gersthof, by then not so much a music hall as a symbol, will have expanded to meet the challenges of this age of grandeur, and its posters will be plastered over every street corner, over the line "I have weighed everything in the balance" and over everything else for which there was once still room beside it and below it. It will depict a false life in its true perspective. And a year after that, when a million men have been buried at the front, the survivors' dependants will look Wolf in Gersthof in the eye, at a face staring bloodily out like a laceration running through the world, and will read of hard times—and "Don't miss today's Grand Matinée and Evening Concert"!

OPTIMIST It makes my heart bleed to hear you talk like that—it's tantamount to taking an epoch that must surely appear momentous to even the most benighted, and deliberately talking it down. If the times have taught us anything, it is to disregard your way of looking at things.

GRUMBLER That is devoutly to be wished!

OPTIMIST May God grant you more elevated thoughts. Perhaps they will occur to you tomorrow at Mozart's *Requiem*—let's go together, the profits go to the welfare fund for war victims—

GRUMBLER No, the poster is enough for me—there, right beside Wolf in Gersthof! But what is that strange illustration? A church window? If my shortsightedness doesn't deceive me—a mortar! Is it possible? Whoever managed to combine both worlds in a single image, do you think? Mozart and mortar! What concert programming! Who could find such a happy combination? No, there is no point shedding tears. Just tell me if in the culture of the Senegalese, whose aid the enemy has enlisted against us, such blasphemy would be possible! There you see it, that is the World War against us.

OPTIMIST *(after a pause)* I think you are right. But, God knows, you alone see it. It eludes the rest of us, and so we see the future in a rosy light. You see it, so it exists. Your eye conjures it up and makes it visible.

GRUMBLER Because it is shortsighted. It perceives the contours, and imagination does the rest. And my ear hears noises that others don't hear, and they disturb the music of the spheres for me, which others don't hear either. Think about it, and if you don't reach a conclusion about it yourself, call me. I enjoy our conversations. You are a prompter for my monologues. I would like to appear with you in public. For the moment, I can only tell the public I am keeping silent, and if possible, what I am keeping silent.

OPTIMIST What, for example?

GRUMBLER For example, that this war, if it does not kill those who are good, may well create a moral island for the good, who were already good without it. But it will transform the whole surrounding world into an enormous backdrop of deceit, degeneracy, and the most barbarous blasphemy, as the evil it produced continues to have its effect, growing fat on its victims under cover of its phoney ideals. That in this war, the war of today, culture will not undergo a renewal, but will take refuge from the hangman in suicide. That it was more than sin—that it was a lie, a daily lie out of which printer's ink flowed like blood, the one feeding the other, pouring out like a delta into the great ocean of insanity. That this war of today is nothing but an outbreak of peace, and that it cannot be ended by peace, but by the war of the cosmos against this rabid planet! That innumerable human beings had to be sacrificed, not to be lamented simply because an alien will drove them to the slaughterhouse, but as tragic victims compelled to atone for an unknown guilt. That for someone who experiences as personal torture the unparalleled injustice that this worst of all worlds inflicts on itself—that for such a one there remains but one final moral task: to sleep imperturbably through this anxious period of waiting until redeemed by the Word or the impatience of God.

OPTIMIST You are an optimist. You believe and hope that the world is coming to an end.

GRUMBLER No, it is simply unfolding like my nightmare, and when I die, that will be the end. Sleep well! (*Exeunt.*)
(*Change of scene.*)

Scene 30

On the Graben. It is night.

TWO COMMERCIAL MIDDLEMEN (*arm in arm with their female companions, all tipsy, warbling*) Stargazer—stargazer—beware and take care—

NEWSPAPER VENDOR Ex-tra-aa edi-shun!—40,000 Russians dead at Przemysl!

FIRST COMMERCIAL MIDDLEMAN Stargazer—stargazer—

SECOND COMMERCIAL MIDDLEMAN —beware and take care—(*Exeunt.*)

ACT II

Scene 1

Vienna, several months after Italy's entry into the war. People gathering at the corner where the Kärntnerstrasse meets the Ring. The great majority are refugees from Galicia, black-marketeers, regular officers on leave, others posted to hospitals or allocated lighter duties on the home front, and those fit for military service who have "wangled it."

JEWISH REFUGEE Extro-oo edi-shoon. Buy a copy, loidies and gents—

VIENNESE LOAN SHARK That's all we need, the riffraff have arrived—wherever you look, nothing but Jews. What'll they be up to next? They'll stay put and steal *our* business!

COMMERCIAL AGENT For the moment I can't complain. But I can't say I'm doing anywhere near as well as Ornstein.

LOAN SHARK Which Ornstein? The one who was exempted from the draft?

AGENT Of course. Last Saturday he made eight and a half thousand out of kit bags with a single telephone call. Impressive!

LOAN SHARK So I heard. What did he do before the war?

AGENT Before the war? Didn't you know—matches! He was an agent for Lauser & Löw. Now he's set up on his own. Said he'd put some business my way. He's in the know with some major or other.
(A badly wounded soldier on crutches, limbs trembling, drags himself past.)

LOAN SHARK Yes, indeed, we must just hold out to the bitter end.

NEWSPAPER VENDOR Ex-tra-aa edi-shun—! *Neue Freie Presse*! Clawrious Jur-man fig-tree in Galicia! Ene-mee repulsed! Bloody 'and-to-'and foitin!

LOAN SHARK Knöpflmacher must be in the money, too. Did you hear, Eisig Rubel takes himself off to the spirits warehouse every day, what d'ya say to that, has it made, eh! Which reminds me—that was a first-rate article yesterday on the spiritual uplift.

AGENT Know what I heard today, they're going to put leather up by 50 percent.

LOAN SHARK Is that a fact. You'll see Katz rising in the world, then. He won't know what to turn his hand to next. Wait and see, he'll end up ennobled yet. The likes of us are content with less. You know what I'd like? I'd like to drive a nail into the Iron Warrior beside the Imperial Hotel, just for fun. Why don't we, what are you afraid of? We'd be in good company, so why not, you pay a crown and you get a certificate with your name on it for future generations, for the historical record!

AGENT Spare me such idiocies.

LOAN SHARK There's Bermann! Exempted!

BERMANN Hi there!

LOAN SHARK Come with us and drive a nail into the Iron Warrior, Bermann!

BERMANN I've nailed it already. (*Exit.*)

LOAN SHARK All right, I'll go by myself, then.

AGENT I don't hold with such fatuous nonsense.

LOAN SHARK What d'you mean, nonsense? Look at the sort of people—that was some idea! It'll rake it in for our brave soldiers, and you get a memento to the grandeur of the age, don't you see—(*A well-dressed lady passes by, they both stand rooted to the spot.*)

BOTH Between ourselves—

AGENT Did you hear that Raubitschek and Barber are giving themselves airs with their Red Cross medals?

LOAN SHARK There's something going on there. Wonder how much they had to pay?

AGENT Chicken feed. Though they'd have paid for the Grand Cross too, if they could have. Except it's only for services rendered and costs a bomb!

LOAN SHARK Well, I ask you, who can afford that, and those that can would sooner have a title. Eduard Feigl, the canned food king, is going to be a baron, they say. As soon as there's peace.

AGENT Who can think of peace right now? We've other things to worry about.

LOAN SHARK So all at once you're a warmonger, eh? Looks to me as if you've got something big brewing? Have I guessed right?

AGENT Something big, spot on, newshound that you are, something big! A man's got to live.

LOAN SHARK You're right. I always say: war is war. Look, whether the young people break their necks driving their cars or directly for the Fatherland—I can't go along with that sort of sentimentality.

AGENT Very true. This constant moaning about the war—I'm sick and tired of it. Sure, some things cost more—but that's what happens in wartime! You can rest assured, a lot of people taking that line at present will soon change their tune when they hear peace is on the way.

LOAN SHARK Absolutely, we're right behind it today, body and soul—

AGENT And in the middle of it all, just when they're beginning to reap the benefits, the war is suddenly called off!

LOAN SHARK A crying shame—for our poor soldiers!

AGENT (*gives a loud guffaw*) That's a good one—What did you think I meant? I was talking about business, and you—(*he chokes, laughing.*) The dust in the air today, it's scandalous—I'm going to write a letter to the paper about it—headline "The Iron Refuse Collector"—what am I saying, I mean "The Iron Warrior and the Horsefly"—no, that's not it—

LOAN SHARK I've already done my bit, right outside our house for all of three months there's been—

AGENT Look who's coming along there, Weiss in uniform! Of all things wonderful—! (*Weiss stops, out of sorts.*) So, then—you've been called up?

WEISS Ages ago, so long I've had time to forget. (*Exit.*)

LOAN SHARK How people change! Who'd have thought a year ago—if someone had told me—that they'd take Weiss! A man who earned the odd crust working for me!

AGENT So what, at any rate, he's very out of sorts.

LOAN SHARK He couldn't even afford a pair of trousers. Now he's wearing the Emperor's uniform. This is truly an age of grandeur.

AGENT Listen, here's something I wouldn't have believed possible, just listen to this: for eight days now I've been phoning Kehlendorfer about tickets for *Husarenblut*. Sold out for the next four weeks. I tell you, the war will be over and we still won't have seen the blood of the hussars! My wife keeps nagging me—

NEWSPAPER VENDOR —Attack repulsed—All positions captured!

LOAN SHARK I tell you, it doesn't compare with *Herbstmanöver*. And the *Csardasfürstin*, what do you say to that extravaganza! Have you been to the *Fürstenkind* yet?

AGENT *Fürstenkind*, of course we've been! That's where—wait a minute—that tremendous joke occurs—it had the whole place in fits. Remember celebrating the battle of the Masurian Swamps, where a whole Russian regiment was slaughtered? The joke turned this into "a bottle of Masurian schnapps." The house roared when he said it, Marischka—(*exeunt.*)

FIRST OFFICER (*to three others*) Evening Nowotny, evening Pokorny, evening Powolny—the very man! You know all about politics. Come on, tell us, what d'ya think of Italy?

SECOND OFFICER (*with walking stick*) If you ask me, I'd say treachery, pure and simple.

THIRD OFFICER Yep—spot on—what d'ya expect from them dagoes.

FOURTH OFFICER Absolutely!—I was at a bash in the mess yesterday—d'ya see the Schönpflug cartoon ? Fantabulous!

FIRST OFFICER You know what I've been wanting to do for ages, I'd like to go to the Gartenbau again.

SECOND OFFICER Go on, are you wounded then?

THIRD OFFICER What d'ya mean, wounded?

FOURTH OFFICER He's not wounded.

FIRST OFFICER I'm not wounded.

SECOND OFFICER Don't you know the Gartenbau is a hospital now! (*All laugh.*)

FIRST OFFICER Oh that's right, a hospital—(*ponders a while.*) Y'know, I couldn't remember that for the life of me—the war has been going on for so long—(*a soldier on crutches passes by.*)

SECOND OFFICER Shall I give him a dressing-down, after that sloppy salute he gave—

FIRST OFFICER Don't make a scene. Apropos, what about that Distinguished Service Cross?

NEWSPAPER VENDOR Ene-mee repulsed! Bloody 'and-to-'and foitin! Come and geddit—!

SECOND OFFICER I've been put up for it—scandalous how long it takes.

THIRD OFFICER What a shambles!

FOURTH OFFICER What d'ya expect, there's a war on. Not a tart in sight today.

FIRST OFFICER Y'know what? Let's go along to Hopfner's! (*Exeunt.*)

INTELLECTUAL (*to his companion*) I can assure you, as long as the mentality of our enemies—(*Exeunt.*)

POLDI FESCH *(to his companion)* I'm meant to be out partying with the Sascha Film people tonight—*(exeunt.)*

(Passing soldiers can be heard singing: "In der Heimat, in der Heimat da gibt's ein Wiedersehn—")

(Three black-marketeers, chewing toothpicks, emerge from the grillroom of the Hotel Bristol.)

FIRST BLACK-MARKETEER Listen, I went to a performance by Marcel Salzer yesterday. I tell you, gentlemen, that's something you shouldn't miss.

SECOND BLACK-MARKETEER As good as that?

FIRST BLACK-MARKETEER Yes! He recites a poem out loud, by some famous poet, what's he called?—wait a minute—yes—Ginzkey!

THIRD BLACK-MARKETEER Ginzkey, the carpet people?

FIRST BLACK-MARKETEER Apparently they're even related. Anyhow, there's a bit about Tannenberg, and how Hindenburg drives them into the swamps—you must have read about it in the papers at the time, the enthralling description—

SECOND BLACK-MARKETEER I still remember the heading: Encirclement of Russian troops by German army: Russians driven into Masurian swamps.

FIRST BLACK-MARKETEER Yes, well that's exactly what you get, only it's funnier—he goes glug-glug, glug-glug as they choke to death. I tell you—that charming face he pulls, Salzer, with those little piggy eyes of his—it's worth every penny.

THIRD BLACK-MARKETEER Shh—look out—here come the Field Greys. *(They stand motionless.)*

SECOND BLACK-MARKETEER *(devoutly)* In their shining armour.

FIRST BLACK-MARKETEER Ah yes, the Germans!

(Enter three German grenadiers, one behind the other, each accompanied by a Viennese municipal official in tails and top hat.)

FIRST MUNICIPAL OFFICIAL *(Viennese accent)* That's the opera house, now we're entering the Kärntnerstrasse, where I'll point out the Iron Post, the most notable landmark in Vienna that we have, erected to remind us that journeymen passing through each used to hammer in a nail, just as you've seen people doing at the Iron Warrior. Then comes the so-called Plague Column, because the plague was raging in the city of Vienna at that time, and he made a solemn vow to erect a great monument on the site.

FIRST GRENADIER By Jove, that's quite something!

SECOND MUNICIPAL OFFICIAL (*Viennese accent*) That's the opera house, now we'll go along the Kärntnerstrasse to the so-called Iron Post, a landmark because journeymen passing through each hammered in a nail. Then I'll show you the Plague Column, that was when he made a solemn vow, because the plague was raging in the city at that time, just like with the Iron Warrior, and that's why a monument was erected on the site.

SECOND GRENADIER By Jove, fantastic!

THIRD MUNICIPAL OFFICIAL (*Viennese accent*) There you've got the opera. But here's Kärntnerstrasse coming up, we'll go along to the Iron Post, that's where the journeymen passing through used to hammer in a nail, just like they do now with the Warrior. Then I'll take you to a monument on the Graben, the greatest landmark we have, for that's where the plague raged on the site, and he made a solemn vow, so that's the famous story of how the Iron Post came about.

THIRD GRENADIER By Jove, that's really amazing!

FIRST REPORTER (*to another*) Look, there you can really see what it means to stand shoulder to shoulder.

SECOND REPORTER They seem to understand each other well, but you can't hear what they're saying.

FIRST REPORTER He's explaining it to them.

BERLIN BLACK-MARKETEER (*speaking very fast in Berlin slang to a porter*) You there, come here and run across to that restaurant and see if there's a gentleman waiting there, or go and ask the pageboy or the waiter after Section Head Swoboda, one of the most influential people you have in Vienna right now, he has an appointment with a Mr. Zadikower from Berlin, ask him to be so kind as to wait a bit longer and to indicate what table he's at, the reservations book is probably at the reception desk, in case I'm held up, then I'll have dinner with him, but I've still one bit of business to do, but—d'you hear—in case I'm still held up, could he please come later to the Moulin Rouge or whatever the establishment is called now, you know, don't you, the place Mizzi dances, one of the prettiest girls you have in Vienna right now, I'll be there at a quarter to twelve, so quick now, did you understand? (*The porter stares at the stranger in amazement and says nothing.*) Heavens above! Don't you understand German?

PORTER Kum-agen-wot-was-it-ya-sed-ya-wonted?—

BERLIN BLACK-MARKETEER (*enraged, turning to the passersby, who gather in a group*) It's unheard of, listen to me, how dare he, it's absolutely scandalous, the things that go on in your beloved Vienna, I've had many a surprise, as a German from the Reich, we're well used to your laid-back Viennese slovenliness after all, charming little people that you are, but that really takes the biscuit, that's only possible in Vienna, to think that a population we are fighting shoulder to shoulder with can put up with such stupidity, it's staggeringly mind-boggling, you Viennese have simply no conception of being at war, that's why after a year you've hit rock bottom, whereas in Germany, one can certainly say, people take things seriously but are nonetheless confident, you, on the other hand—well, Hindenburg should be told, and I'm the man to do it, I'll give him a full account—

CROWD But what happened?

BERLIN BLACK-MARKETEER What happened? What a question! Funny little people! That man there, he was standing there like a proper Viennese porter, I wanted to send him over to the restaurant with an important message for a Section Head I had a rendezvous with, and he—I ask you, in wartime—

CROWD What's this all about, what did he do?

BERLIN BLACK-MARKETEER —he answered me in a foreign language!
(He goes off in high dudgeon. The crowd looks at the porter questioningly. He has stood as if frozen the whole time, and now walks off proudly.)

CROWD Gott strafe England!

NEWSPAPER VENDOR Ex-tra-aa edi-shun—! Clawrious fig-tree for our boys!
(Change of scene.)

Scene 2

Optimist and Grumbler in conversation.

GRUMBLER Do you think it's humanly possible for an Eskimo and a negro from the Congo to communicate with one another for any length of time, or even to fight together shoulder to shoulder? In my opinion, only if it's in an alliance against Prussia. An alliance between brash Berliners from Schöneberg and sentimental Viennese from Grinzing seems to me impractical.

OPTIMIST Why's that?

GRUMBLER In tales of old, of wonders much is told—as when the Nibelungs first swore their blood oath. But what are such tales in comparison with the wondrous, fabulous special relationships of our own bloodcurdling times? Think of a city like ours where you can't even make a telephone call, and a city like theirs where they do nothing but make telephone calls—two different worlds, surely. Can there really be a spiritual bond between them when there's scarcely a telephone connection? Think of two creatures shoulder to shoulder, one of them having made disorder the substance of his life, surviving through ingrained slovenliness, and the other whose sole purpose consists of being well organized?

OPTIMIST That being the model exemplified by our comrades-in-arms, whose organization in peacetime, tried and tested—

GRUMBLER —would soon slacken after contact with the model of slovenliness, if it were not already doomed to self-destruct in this war. The outer and the inner order of the German world is a shell that will soon crack open. Let it shatter then, shoulder to shoulder with us.

OPTIMIST Do you believe that German officialdom, for example, with its proven sense of duty, could ever slacken or even become corrupted?

GRUMBLER Recently, on the German-Swiss border, a railway official in uniform provided a symbol of the way things are going in Germany. He came up to me beside the ticket office and, under his breath, offered me a better exchange rate than the official railway one.

OPTIMIST Where you see moral degeneration, I see—

GRUMBLER —spiritual rebirth. It's a vision which will end up helping to change reality. Under the influence of the self-deluding war propaganda, chaos will become endemic. As the German war effort gains momentum, who'll be in charge of the clattering train?

OPTIMIST And what of us, in Austria?

GRUMBLER No further decline is necessary, surely. Here, it was war already in peacetime, with audiences after a concert fighting to reach the exit as if it was a chaotic retreat. We have a track record.

OPTIMIST In our special relationship there can be no rivalry. Our alliance has stood the test of time, and we shall fight together unto the bitter end.

GRUMBLER I think so, too. Except that the general confusion will be increased as we struggle to speak the same language.

OPTIMIST We are united by the language of the sword. Indissolubly linked to the Germans through thick and thin, through triumph and—

GRUMBLER —disaster!

(Change of scene.)

Scene 3

Subscriber to the Neue Freie Presse *and Patriot are excitedly discussing latest news.*

SUBSCRIBER Did you see in the paper, the Mayor, Dr. Weiskirchner, sent

Admiral Haus a congratulatory telegram after U-boat 5's brilliant exploit, and he has already replied?

PATRIOT And what was his response?

SUBSCRIBER "Please accept my heartfelt thanks for your extremely kind good wishes."

PATRIOT But did you know that the Israelite director of military pastoral care, Rabbi Dr. Frankfurter, delivered a patriotic address at Easter?

SUBSCRIBER You don't say! I missed that. And what then?

PATRIOT The text was submitted to Archduke Friedrich and Archduke Karl by the military commandant of Vienna.

SUBSCRIBER And then?

PATRIOT Both archdukes conveyed their thanks to the rabbi.

SUBSCRIBER Now that's great news. But here's something I can tell you. King Ludwig of Bavaria conveyed his heartfelt thanks by telegram to Benzion Katz, district rabbi of Borszcow, currently visiting Franzensbad, in response to his congratulatory telegram after the capture of Warsaw.

PATRIOT I know that, but you've left one bit out.

SUBSCRIBER I'm all ears.

PATRIOT Benzion Katz, district rabbi of Borszcow, currently visiting Franzensbad, in response to the capture of Warsaw and Ivangorod—

SUBSCRIBER Ah, also in response to Ivangorod?

PATRIOT Yes, also in response to Ivangorod—sent a congratulatory telegram to the commander in chief of the army, Field Marshal Archduke Friedrich—

SUBSCRIBER And then?

PATRIOT —to which the following response arrived: His Royal and Imperial Highness, the Most Serene commander in chief of the army, Field Marshal Archduke Friedrich—

SUBSCRIBER Aha, I know the rest: conveys his heartfelt thanks for the patriotic declaration. Signed, on behalf of His Highness, by His aide-de-camp Col. v. Lorz.

PATRIOT How did you know?

SUBSCRIBER Ah, I can tell you even more. Namely, the text of King Ludwig of Bavaria's response, which I only read later, you see, namely: King Ludwig of Bavaria conveyed the following response to Benzion Katz, district rabbi of Borszcow, currently visiting Franzensbad, in response to his congratulatory telegram after the capture of Warsaw: "My heartfelt thanks to you and your compatriots currently visiting Franzensbad for your congratulations at the capture of Warsaw. Ludwig."

PATRIOT Pity you only ever hear the responses, and never what Benzion Katz said in his telegram.

SUBSCRIBER Heavens, there are so many interesting things these days, you simply don't know which way to turn first. Oh, of course, did you know who's been entertaining wounded soldiers at reserve hospital no. 9 (the former regional governor's hospital) under theatre director Franz Brunner?

PATRIOT The wife of Section Head Jarzebecka, Rosa Kunze, Helene Gad, Marta Seeböck, Elsa v. Konrad, Larta Land, Professor Felsen, Gusti Schlesak, Henriette Weiss, Mizzi Ohmann, Christine Werner, and the two gentlemen, Ernst Salzberger and Viktor Springer.

SUBSCRIBER Marvellous, what an impressive list! In the cooperative reserve hospital no. 8 (the Rothschild hospital), as far as I know, the only cooperatives were: Mrs. Anna Kastinger, Miss Finni Kaufmann (accompanied on the piano by Hela Lang), Miss Ila Tessa, Adolf Raab, Miss Karla Porjes, the Uhl clarinet and accordion quartet for light music, and the Edelweiss Quartet under choirmaster E. Bochdansky, together with the gentlemen I. Michl, G. Steinweiss, and I. Zohner.

PATRIOT Just so. But did you know that in the hospital in the Apostelgasse, at the instigation of district school inspector Homolatsch, they're performing "German songs in words and images for choir and orchestra"?

SUBSCRIBER No, I'm amazed, but I do know one thing, namely that E. Koritschoner of Prague and Minna Husserl of Märisch-Trübau got engaged on the 15th of this month.

PATRIOT Just so. Yes, indeed, our people are doing great things. But did you see in the paper: "The Entente Despairs of Victory"?

SUBSCRIBER Yes, indeed, it all seems to be coming true, I do believe there will be an outbreak of despair about the Entente's victory such as the world has never seen.

PATRIOT We ain't seen nothing yet. (*Exeunt.*)

(*Change of scene.*)

Scene 4

A street near Military Headquarters. A journalist and an elderly general enter.

JOURNALIST Your Excellency is perhaps in a position to give me some indication of the present situation?

GENERAL (*after some reflection*) We lovingly—remember—our loved ones—back home—who lovingly bestow upon us—gift parcels—and who faithfully—remember us.

JOURNALIST Heartfelt thanks, Your Excellency. I shall not fail to ensure that this significant comment by one of our illustrious army commanders will be immediately conveyed to—(*Exeunt.*)
(Another journalist and another elderly general enter.)

JOURNALIST Your Excellency is perhaps in a position to provide my paper, as far as the relevant reporting restrictions permit, with an authentic account of what has just taken place?

GENERAL Dunno—all I heard was—the Prussians are coming—the Prussians—after that—then after that—we're—we're—in it up to here, yet again—those—those—damned Prussians—

JOURNALIST Interesting. Perhaps Your Excellency might know something of the fate of the Third Thoroughbred Artillery Brigade—something especially close to our hearts?

GENERAL You mean—dur—turd—dunder—head—distil—lery—trade—

JOURNALIST Many thanks, Your Excellency, I won't fail to convey this highly significant announcement by one of our victorious military leaders to—(*Exeunt.*)
(Change of scene.)

Scene 5

South-west Front.

VOICE FROM BACKGROUND Don't go too far forward, your Excellency, not too far!

SECOND VOICE Don't go on, Excellency, the enemy has us in his sights, don't you understand, no further!
(Enter an elderly general, deep in thought. A Sicilian soldier approaches and captures him with a lasso. The soldier leads the general off.)

MEMBER OF WAR PRESS BUREAU (*notices, exclaims*) It's not true!—I saw it with my own eyes!—That's just what they're waiting for!—Italian war correspondents' fairy tales!—No further comment necessary.
(Change of scene.)

Scene 6

An infantry regiment 300 paces from the enemy.
Heavy exchange of fire.

INFANTRY OFFICER Look back there, our good padre is joining us. That's nice of him.

PADRE ANTON ALLMER Good day to you, brave soldiers! God's blessing on your weapons! Are you giving the enemy a bloody nose?

OFFICER Honoured to meet you, Father—we're proud to have such a fearless padre coming up to our gun emplacements, in spite of enemy fire and heedless of the threat of danger.

PADRE Come on then, let me have a potshot or two.

OFFICER We're all delighted to have such an intrepid padre! (*He hands him a gun. The padre fires a couple of shots.*)

PADRE Kaboom!

SHOUTS Bravo! What a noble priest! Long live our beloved padre!

(*Change of scene.*)

Scene 7

Beside the battery.

ARTILLERY OFFICER Look, there's our good padre coming over from the infantry position. That's nice of him.

PADRE ANTON ALLMER Good day to you, brave soldiers! God's blessing on your weapons! Are you giving the enemy a bloody nose?

OFFICER It's going great guns, Father.

PADRE God be with you, I'd love to have a go.

OFFICER Certainly, Father, I hope you hit a few Russians.

(*The padre fires.*)

PADRE Kaboom!

SHOUTS Bravo!

OFFICER (*to his men*) What a splendid priest, a noble priest! A son of our beautiful Styria, too. I must write to the *Grazer Volksblatt*! (*To padre*) Our home regiment is happy and proud of its padre and plucky comrade-in-arms, who sets a fine example of leading from the front.

SHOUTS Hurrah!

OFFICER Our weapons are sanctified, now that the Reverend Father has fired. His Reverence has let fire!
(Alice Schalek approaches.)

SCHALEK What sort of position is this? You call this a position? I've seen better!

OFFICER Please, you must make allowances—time was short—

SCHALEK You know what, Lieutenant, I'd like to have a shot or two.

OFFICER Most willingly, miss, but it's unfortunately impossible at the moment as the enemy might become agitated. There's a lull in the fighting right now, and we're happy to—

SCHALEK Don't be a fool, man—you're saying the padre can have a go and I can't?—When I've come out here specifically—as you know, I only describe what I've experienced in person—remember, it's imperative I round off the description—and it appears on Sunday!

OFFICER Yes—well—I can't accept responsibility—

SCHALEK But I can! Give it here. So, how do you shoot this thing?

OFFICER Like this—
(Schalek fires. The enemy responds.)

OFFICER There, I told you so!

SCHALEK What do you expect? But for me it's so interesting!
(Change of scene.)

Scene 8

A stage in the Prater amusement park. The setting is a trench in which provincial actors practise shooting, telephone, sleep, eat, and read newspapers. The trench is decorated with flags. Some thousand spectators are standing in front of it, row upon tightly packed row, numerous officials, dignitaries, and reporters in the foreground.

IMPRESARIO —and I herewith dedicate this trench, designed to conjure up life in a real-life trench before the eyes of the honourable public, to the noble purpose of supporting the patriotic War Welfare Fund, and I most humbly beg His Imperial Highness to declare the trench open.

REPRESENTATIVE OF THE WILHELM PRESS AGENCY *(to his colleague)* Among the notable military and civilian figures, one spotted—

COLLEAGUE *(writing)* Angelo Eisner v. Eisenhof, Flora Dub, Hofrat and Frau Schwarz-Gelber—

REPRESENTATIVE But I don't see them—

COLLEAGUE Yes, but I know.

REPRESENTATIVE Shush! It's the inauguration. Write: began at six o'clock on the dot.

VOICE OF ARCHDUKE KARL FRANZ JOSEF Coming to see the trench has been a pleasure. As a soldier myself—

AUDIENCE Hip! Hip! Hurrah!

FRAU SCHWARZ-GELBER *(to her husband)* You can see nothing here, come on, we'll be more visible over there.

(There follow presentations. The audience gathers around, then disperses. Everyone wants to be part of the action.)

LIEUTENANT WHO, HAVING DISBURSED THE SUM OF ONE CROWN AS A DONATION TO THE RED CROSS AT SCHAUMANN'S THE CHEMIST IN STOCKERAU, WANTS TO REMAIN INCOGNITO *(to a gentleman)* Let us hope that this event, instigated no doubt by some suggestion from high places, will raise a not inconsiderable sum for the charity. I'm interested in all such endeavours on behalf of War Welfare, for the person you see before you is none other than the donor at Schaumann's the chemist in Stockerau of a contribution of one crown in aid of the Red Cross, by a lieutenant who wished to remain anonymous, yielding a sum total of 1,091 crowns in cash and 2,000 crowns annuity, in addition the previous return of 679,253 cash, which makes 680,344 crowns cash and—

PROFESSOR KUNZE What, as much as that?

LIEUTENANT Yes, indeed, it all adds up. I was long undecided whether or not to make my name public, but since I'm a sworn enemy of any kind of publicity when it's a question of doing good, I decided to keep my identity hidden. To remain half-anonymous—that halves the value of the charitable act. Look at this: Otto Ni. from Leitmeritz and Robert Bi. from Theresienstadt congratulate Rusi Ni. in Vienna on the happy family event: "All went well, no problems!"—2 crowns 7 heller, but if you add the previous return, that only makes 576,209 crowns 52 heller. My position is quite different, quite apart from the fact that I was the lone contributor, and that I had absolutely no need of a happy event to—

PROFESSOR KUNZE I envy you. I've done more, but all in all it really didn't add up to much. The person you see before you is none other than the man who suggested to his hunting party that every member should make a contribution of 2 crowns to War Welfare. I was the first to do so, of course, and the others soon followed my lead, so that I was in a position to make it known. I long hesitated whether or not I should keep my identity hidden, but since I'm a sworn enemy of any kind of anonymity when it's a question of setting an example, I decided to go public. You see, I hold very different views to yours. In total, then, it came to 26 crowns, for there were 13 of us. After all, that's a not inconsiderable sum, but of course, compared with the result—*(they leave, still conversing.)*

PATRIOT In London there's an amusing novelty, a trench in the park. I read in the paper recently: "The Prince of Wales in the trenches." That's where he spends his time fooling around, of course, he hasn't been to the front yet!

SUBSCRIBER They're only playing at war.
(Change of scene.)

Scene 9

Semmering, Alpine holiday spa. Terrace of the Southern Railway Hotel. The Alps aglow. Gathering of Youngsters and Oldies, Fatties and Shorties. Jackals and Hyenas can be seen. A lady has just recited a poem by Heine with deep emotion and earned rich applause. Semmering regulars are sunk in quiet contemplation.

YOUNGSTER Weiss is the best tourist. He goes at walking pace, or he goes at a trot, or if he's running out of time, he goes at a gallop. He's never been late for our regular card game yet.

OLDIE A first-class Alpine sunset. Look at the director general in the window, his face is aglow.

DANGL *(arrives, out of breath)* My dear guests, they've just telephoned from Vienna, Durazzo has fallen—great successes at Verdun!

ALL Long live Dangl!

FATTY I have a hunch that the skies are illuminated because of Durazzo.

SHORTY Today it's such a joy! Today all are gathered together, those unconditionally devoted to Semmering and all the usual suspects.

BABBLE OF VOICES Where's Weiss?—Please don't shout, Stukart will hear—Did you hear about Durazzo, easy-peasy—I'll be curious to see if he comes in good time today—Say what you like, Heine is the greatest German poet and always will be, even if they blow their top—I greeted the Section Head and he greeted back—You'll see, he'll live on in the annals of history—He wants to climb the Sonnwendstein, he said—They won't take Verdun!—Are you a big eater? Take me, I'm a big eater—The panorama was fabulous—I'm telling you, he'll make it, even at walking pace—The losses have to be taken with a pinch of salt!—He must earn a pretty penny—The way she recited it, it really bowled me over—Bet you he comes at a trot today—The professor said the position down there is looking very good—I could come up with three more truckloads—when he got himself baptized she demanded a divorce—But I'm telling you, today he's going to miss out—If you want a good laugh, go down to the theatre in the Josefstadt, it'll have you rolling in the aisles—What do you mean, troop transports? The Semmering train won't stop running!—The panorama was fabulous—Look, there he comes running, what did I tell you, Weiss at a gallop! (*The company retires.*)

SEMMERING REGULAR (*as he leaves*) Let him sleep, he's worried about his scrap metal deliveries.

CHAIRMAN OF THE BOARD (*sleeping, with a gesture of sudden inspiration*) Melt down! (*He wakes up.*)

(*Change of scene.*)

Scene 10

Optimist and Grumbler in conversation.

OPTIMIST One thing I can say with conviction and a clear conscience: since war was declared, I haven't met a single young person still in Vienna, and any still here will be feverishly impatient to be up and away.

GRUMBLER I get out so little. But I do have a shared telephone line. Even when it was peacetime, it was child's play to listen in to all the conversations of the neighbourhood even without banging on the button: people planning a game of poker, a business speculation or hoped-for copulation. My only connections with the outside world are wrong numbers. Since the World War broke out and utterly failed to bring any improvement to the nation's telephone service, conversations revolve around a new problem. Day in, day out, every time I'm called to the telephone to hear other people talking to each other—so, at least 10 times a day—here's what I hear them say: "Gustl went up and wangled it." "How's Rudi doing?" "Rudi went up and wangled it, too." "And Pepi? Hasn't he finally gone to the front?" "Pepi's got lumbago, but as soon as he's back on his feet he'll go up and wangle it."

OPTIMIST Be careful what you say.

GRUMBLER Why? I could prove it. There are still judges in Austria.

OPTIMIST Given your view of things, I'd have thought you'd welcome every dispensation.

GRUMBLER Indeed I do, every one. I stand by my standpoint. But my country does not stand by my standpoint, and those who want to be exempted take my country's standpoint and not mine. While I think it a disgrace that one is forcibly obliged to die, I think pulling strings to avoid death aggravates that disgrace, so much so that, in this country, you would need to be suicidal to continue living. And that's the ultimate right of free men faced with obligatory conscription.

OPTIMIST But surely there must be exceptions. Take literature. The country not only needs soldiers—

GRUMBLER —but also poets, to instil in soldiers the courage poets don't themselves possess.

OPTIMIST But writers have certainly risen to meet the challenge of the noble cause. You surely can't deny that the war has put them on their mettle.

GRUMBLER In most cases it has mobilized their mercenary instincts, or in those few with character, only their stupidity.

OPTIMIST Someone like Richard Dehmel, someone who joined up voluntarily after all, set an example—

GRUMBLER —which he debased with his war poems. He called the sound of machine guns "the music of the spheres" and said animals were capable of patriotism. He enlisted "the German horse" in a disastrous cause—a creature even more defenceless than man against compulsory military service.

OPTIMIST Well yes, in times like these all poets get carried away—

GRUMBLER —to celebrate in words the deeds of those who are desecrating creation.

OPTIMIST Take Kernstock—

GRUMBLER I'd rather not.

OPTIMIST A poet, gentle as a lamb, what's more a man of God by calling.

GRUMBLER Yes, his mettle has certainly hardened with a vengeance, I grant you. I'm thinking especially of those lines where he calls on his young Styrian boyos to crush the fruits of Italian manhood into blood-red wine.

OPTIMIST Or think of Brother Willram—

GRUMBLER Sad to say, there my memory doesn't fail me. Isn't he the Christian poet who thinks blood blooms red and dreams bloody dreams of spring? Perhaps you are alluding to the injunction of this saviour of souls, and I quote: "To slay the dragon you must lure it on to your bayonet, then skewer it." Or: "Take pleasure in that high-pitched whine as you riddle with bullets the enemy line."

OPTIMIST No, I meant his proclamation: "The craven coward, that Italian villain, is fair game now, so ripe for killing." Or the verse where his steed, snorting nobly with courage sublime, crossed o'er rivers of blood and through the red flood smashed the enemy line.

GRUMBLER But wasn't the cavalry already out of action? Even a one-horse carriage home from a late-night bar costs a fortune.

OPTIMIST Don't underestimate the power of poetic illusion, especially that poem where he begs the Good Lord to bestow such a benediction on the enemy that even the Devil is horror-struck as we wade in the bloodbath.

GRUMBLER The Devil? He's all the more horror-struck, the less horror-struck the priest is.

OPTIMIST Or take Dörmann.

GRUMBLER He's no priest.

OPTIMIST But he is a poet! Remember how we were entranced by his words: "I love those languid beauties—"! Twenty-five years on he's got over that anaemic taste—as have we all, thank goodness—and embraced a more full-blooded conception—

GRUMBLER You forget that those languid beauties already had blood-red mouths.

OPTIMIST So what! How does that compare with those verses of his which are now all the rage: "Serbs and Russians, who's that shot ya? All together now, we gotcha!" See how the decadent poet of yore has grown resolute and invigorating! Has he not summoned up the blood?! How tremendous the impact of this moment in time—to have so transformed the amorous darling of the Graces and made him capable of such relentless feeling, such a dynamic pursuit of perfection!

GRUMBLER It just came over him.

OPTIMIST Can you deny that the adaptation of literary production to the needs of the country has benefitted, not just the country, but not least the individual artist? Moreover, at a time when everyone is doing his duty to his country, his country also has the opportunity to recall its duty towards its foremost sons. I'm thinking especially of a man like Lehár. It's obvious that the composer of the Nechledil March should be exempted from all military service.

GRUMBLER Beethoven would have been certified unfit on account of his deafness, so confined to piano-playing for bashes in the officers' mess. What representatives of painting and literature would you say deserved similar consideration?

OPTIMIST I'd say Schönpflug, for all his drawings of comic military types, and

Hans Müller for his sunny articles—so heartening and uplifting, they really help us to hold out until the end.

GRUMBLER I, too, would be most surprised if a poet received by Wilhelm II in Vienna's Imperial residence—a scandal which, incidentally, hasn't yet led to its closure—should not one day be exempted from gruelling service in the Austro-Hungarian War Archives.

OPTIMIST You are quite right. After all, such men provide the most welcome proof of their indispensability by what they create. But apart from them, we do need war columnists and war correspondents; they are exempt from service at the front in order to—

GRUMBLER —whet other people's appetite for it.

OPTIMIST In their own way they prove their worth as well as the military doctors who—

GRUMBLER —prove all the more unfit, the more people they declare fit for service, hence the more sure they are to save their own lives—

OPTIMIST —the more wounded they restore to life—

GRUMBLER —so that they can lose it again. While military assessors can count on saving their own lives by depriving healthy people of theirs.

OPTIMIST One shouldn't generalize.

GRUMBLER You are allowed to do anything except generalize.

OPTIMIST The country needs soldiers, but it needs war correspondents too. After all, we're at war, so they have to tell us about it.

GRUMBLER

So there's a war on? That's what we are told
by those revolting hacks who write reports
on what they're feeling when they view the conflict.
Those nosey scribblers wouldn't half deserve
a kicking from a warhorse thrashing out
with its hind legs. But those riding on top
invite the scum to join them at their table
and talk their tactics through. Was war too weak
to overcome the enemy within?
Scoops for his paper, cooked up at the front,
conceal war's miseries behind his bland façade.
He's indestructible—lives on—he'll never serve.
Is there no arms drill for the rank and vile?

When there's a war on, they can live in peace?
Good people go to war, the scum sit tight.
No need to lose their lives, for they can write.

(A file of grey-bearded recruits goes past.)

OPTIMIST Look, they're enlisting.

GRUMBLER Not quite.

OPTIMIST What do you mean?

GRUMBLER Properly speaking, they've been compulsorily enlisted. The present participle "enlisting" would indicate that they're doing it of their own free will, that's why it has to be a past participle. So they are compulsorily enlisted. Soon they'll be in the front line.

OPTIMIST Very well. So they are forced to go and fight.

GRUMBLER Quite right, they are forced. Universal conscription has turned mankind into a passive noun. Once men joined the forces, now they're forced to join. Only in Germany have they gone a stage further.

OPTIMIST In what way?

GRUMBLER I saw a big poster in Karlsruhe which said: Let Soldiers Go! What's more, it was over the entrance to the High Command.

OPTIMIST How is that possible, that's revolution! How can the High Command in Karlsruhe—

GRUMBLER Well, they need clerks for their office and want civilians to apply, so that soldiers who still work in the office are freed up to go to the front. Hence "Let Soldiers Go!" Here we would say "Let Soldiers Join the Forces", which conveys just enough free will. But I think the German poster achieves its goal in any case. For even if it doesn't achieve its goal, the German military authorities know how to ensure the vacant clerical posts will be filled. There could only be a lack of applicants if all the possible candidates had already become soldiers of their own free will.

OPTIMIST Even an official announcement from the High Command in Karlsruhe doesn't stop your eternal grumbling.

GRUMBLER As it happens, I saw another poster when I was over there, in a police station. Its text is still ringing in my ears:

Thrash the villains, drive them south,
Chase them into Etna's mouth,
Let Vesuvius make them yell,

Sizzling in the jaws of hell!
Thrash them till they know they're sunk,
Squeeze their guts out in a funk!
Have no mercy in your heart,
Traitors must be torn apart!
Dynamite each valley there,
Purge the perfidious perjurer.
Smash their skulls in, to a man,
Proud of the name "barbarian"!

OPTIMIST Other nations might do that sort of thing too.

GRUMBLER One shouldn't generalize. But perhaps you're right. Even the English might do it after they've had a few more years of conscription. Soon all nations will realize every valley is there to be dynamited. Except for one line: "Squeeze their guts out in a funk"—that has a certain local colour, don't you think?

OPTIMIST A bit crude, that's all. One shouldn't generalize.

GRUMBLER One certainly shouldn't. It wouldn't occur to an Englishman, whether white or coloured.

OPTIMIST It's only an isolated instance in Germany, too.

GRUMBLER But one only possible in Germany. And the fellow who coined it is sitting in some office and would jump if you burst a paper bag.

OPTIMIST Well, there you are—

GRUMBLER But the same fellow, when he gets to the front, is a passionate killer, twists his bayonet in a dying man, proudly tells the tale back home, and still jumps if you burst a paper bag.

OPTIMIST I don't understand you. In war there are both good people and evil. You say yourself that the war has merely heightened the contrasts.

GRUMBLER Exactly, including that between you and me. In peacetime you were already an optimist, and now—

OPTIMIST In peacetime you were already a grumbler, and now—

GRUMBLER Now I even accuse clichés of murder.

OPTIMIST Well, why should the war have cured you of your *idée fixe?*

GRUMBLER Just so. It has even reinforced it. The great cause has made me more narrow-minded. I see those who are "compulsorily enlisted", and feel that is an offence against language. There are bloodstained scraps of nature hanging from the barbed-wire entanglements.

OPTIMIST So you really want to enlist grammar in this war?

GRUMBLER No, that's not it. I'm not interested in rules for their own sake, only in the meaning of the living whole. War makes language a matter of life and death. Look at what has happened. A commercial logo and a coat of arms are now indistinguishable. The pursuit of profit under a shop sign ends up as the pursuit of merit under insignia. It's a mingling of the spheres, and the new world is a crueller one than the old, since its horrific new meaning is rendered even more horrific by the old forms it hasn't been able to outgrow mentally. From nursery rhymes to flamethrowers! Paper to banner! Having once unsheathed the sword, we must now unleash mustard gas. And this *is* a cutthroat war, a war to the death.

OPTIMIST That's beyond me. Let's keep our feet on the ground. We mean business in this—

GRUMBLER Exactly, we mean—business!

OPTIMIST If the combatants were not pursuing an ideal, they would not go to war. It's not a question of words. It's because the peoples are pursuing ideals that they put themselves—

GRUMBLER Under the hammer!

OPTIMIST But you must surely acknowledge that the language of our military leaders is quite at variance with the trivial prose you despise in the world of business.

GRUMBLER Certainly, for the only connection their language reveals is with the world of show business. For instance, I read one divisional commander's review of ". . . those who exhibited in the highest degree the heroism, death-defying bravery and self-sacrifice of which *first-class troops* are capable. . . ." I'm sure the divisional commander had in mind the music-hall revues with those *first-class troupes* in which he frequently took such pleasure in peacetime. Business pure and simple comes into play more in the continuing confusion of signs and insignia.

OPTIMIST You mean literally?

GRUMBLER Materially, and literally, so—literally.

OPTIMIST Language is indeed a cross we have to bear.

GRUMBLER That one wears on one's chest. Or in my case, as a burden on my back.

OPTIMIST Isn't that rather an exaggeration?

GRUMBLER Take an example: I maintain that a people is finished when it clings to its clichés at a stage of its evolution when it is once again experiencing their content. That is proof that it is no longer experiencing that content.

OPTIMIST Explain!

GRUMBLER A U-boat commander keeps the flag flying, plans for an air raid are watered down. And it becomes even more vacuous if the metaphor is materially appropriate. If, for instance, instead of an onshore troop manoeuvre, a maritime operation is scuppered. Or if success in our present positions is "bombproof", while the bombardment of an enemy position is a "smash hit."

OPTIMIST Yes, every one of these expressions comes from the context of war, which is precisely the context in which we now live.

GRUMBLER No, we don't. Otherwise the scab that has formed over language would have dropped off of its own accord. I recently read that news of a fire in Hietzing had spread like wildfire. The same applies to the global conflagration.

OPTIMIST But surely the fire is no less real?

GRUMBLER Precisely! Paper burns, and has set the world on fire. Pages of newsprint have served to kindle global conflagration. What we are experiencing is that our final hour has struck. For the church bells are being turned into guns.

OPTIMIST The churches themselves don't seem to be taking it so tragically, since in many cases they are voluntarily making their bells available.

GRUMBLER After the war they'll toll no more. So the connection between a requiem and a mortar gradually comes to light after all.

OPTIMIST In every country the Church is invoking God's blessing on its national armaments—

GRUMBLER —and aiming for an even greater arms buildup. Agreed, the Church cannot be expected to invoke God's blessing on the enemy's armaments, but it still might have managed to pronounce a curse on its own. Then the Churches in the belligerent countries would have understood each other better. As it is, the Pope can condemn the war but still speak of "legitimate national aspirations", while on the same day the Prince Archbishop of Vienna gives his blessing to a defensive war against "ruthless national aspirations." Well, if the inspirations had been stronger than the aspirations, the latter would not exist, and nor would the war.

OPTIMIST So the Black International has failed even more than the Red.

GRUMBLER Only the Press has survived by showing in black and white how bloodshed becomes newsprint—

OPTIMIST It's gratifying to hear you recognize its power—

GRUMBLER —although I exaggerate its influence. What power has Benedict against—

OPTIMIST What have you against Benedikt—

GRUMBLER No, I mean the Pope. What power has a sermon for peace compared with a leading article for war? And since all the sermons are for war—

OPTIMIST That I admit. The salvation of the world was proclaimed differently in Bethlehem.

GRUMBLER Bethlehem in America will correct the mistake made nineteen centuries ago.

OPTIMIST In America? How so?

GRUMBLER Bethlehem is the name of the biggest armaments foundry in the United States. Here, every church provides material for our Bethlehem, each contributes its mite.

OPTIMIST The name is just a coincidence.

GRUMBLER You're sceptical. As a nonbeliever, you probably don't know what a paternoster is?

OPTIMIST A prayer!

GRUMBLER A lift, an elevator! You optimist!

OPTIMIST Ah yes, of course. But Bethlehem—? That really is the name of the place where armaments are made and supplied to Germany's enemies?

GRUMBLER By Germans.

OPTIMIST You're joking. Carnegie is head of the Steel Trust.

GRUMBLER Schwab is.

OPTIMIST So, German-Americans are now supplying the enemy—?

GRUMBLER Citizens of the German Reich!

OPTIMIST Says who?

GRUMBLER Anyone in the know. The *Wall Street Journal*, rated at least as authoritative as our *Stock Exchange Gazette* in financial affairs, has established that 20 percent of the shares of the Steel Trust are in German hands, not German-American but Reichs-German. And more than that. You can read there what a German Socialist paper says: "While one has learnt that several authentically Anglo-American manufacturers have rejected orders from the French and English governments, the Socialist *Leader*, published in Milwaukee, has named several German-Americans who are expressing their public support for the German cause loud and clear—

(A group of young men with Chinese lanterns go past singing "Dear Fatherland, sleep easy now.")

—while the production lines they run are turning out cartridges, rifles and other war material for England and France. It gets even worse: in the United States there are subsidiaries of Reichs-German firms involved in this business! Does one still have any right to protest against America's conspicuous neutrality, when, all things considered, it has no reason to relinquish such massive profits just to please us, as if we were its blue-eyed boys?"

OPTIMIST Unbelievable—but you must admit, the Germans do have beautiful blue eyes.

GRUMBLER Blue eyes and an honest face, and in whatever land their heart may be, it's in the right place. Did you know it was Germany that produced those Italian maps of Austria that depict their irredentist aspirations as already achieved—maps that are displayed in our bookshops as proof of enemy effrontery? And that the French postcards illustrating the origins of the "Marseillaise" were printed in Dresden? I saw an advertisement for a film with the arresting title: *Germans are men of iron and steel—Foreigners are full of guile!*

OPTIMIST Well, isn't that so?

GRUMBLER You wouldn't say so if you had seen it. Some gremlin had misspelt one word: *Germans are men of iron and steal—*

OPTIMIST Germans stealing!

GRUMBLER Exactly: what a steal! Fortunately the offending letters had been conscientiously corrected, if only by hand, and the truth honourably reestablished.

OPTIMIST So you remain faithful to your practice of taking misprints—

GRUMBLER —for the authentic text.

OPTIMIST Men of steel—

GRUMBLER Men who steal—what guile!

OPTIMIST Well, as far as the Italian maps and the French postcards are concerned, you might say it shows how proficient the Germans are—

GRUMBLER That the enemy have to import their hatred from Germany, even if it chokes them! Which is not so much a humiliation for the Germans as for the enemy, is it not?

OPTIMIST No, I wouldn't say that, but I do say that you are seizing on aberrations.

GRUMBLER A healthy body has no aberrations.

OPTIMIST But remember that the Germans in America have erected bastions of traditional Germanness.

GRUMBLER I remember that in these bastions they are producing munitions to use against those of their own breed.

OPTIMIST Yes, business is business.

GRUMBLER No, German business is German business.

OPTIMIST In politics I always say: Nothing succeeds like success. So the sinking of the *Lusitania* will certainly make waves.

GRUMBLER It already has. Throughout the world, in so far as it is still capable of experiencing abhorrence. But also in Berlin.

OPTIMIST Even in Berlin?

GRUMBLER Once again, one must cite the evidence to prove it (*he reads out*): "As the liner was sinking, hundreds of passengers jumped into the water. Most were swept away in its wake. Many held on to pieces of wood blown off the ship after the explosion . . . in Queenstown there were tragic scenes: women searching for their menfolk, mothers calling for their children, elderly women in a daze, their hair dripping wet and dishevelled, young women wandering aimlessly about with their infants clutched to their breast. There was already a pile of 126 bodies: men, women and children of all ages. Two poor little mites clasped in each other's arms in death. It was a heartbreaking, unforgettable sight." That's it.

OPTIMIST Yes, but what about Berlin?

GRUMBLER In Berlin? In one of its music halls, the day directly after the catastrophe, a film was shown depicting all this, and the advertisement for it read: "The sinking of the *Lusitania*. Live footage. Smoking permitted during this item."

OPTIMIST That's certainly tasteless.

GRUMBLER No, it has a style all its own!

OPTIMIST Well, I can't pass a sentimental judgment on the case of the *Lusitania.*

GRUMBLER Nor can I, only a criminal one!

OPTIMIST They were warned.

GRUMBLER They were warned of danger by the threat of a crime, so the murder was preceded by blackmail. A blackmailer can never plead by way of exoneration that he had given prior warning of the crime he then committed. Were I to threaten you with death if you were either to do or to fail to do something to which I have no entitlement, then it is blackmail and not a caution, and after the deed I am a murderer and not a legal executor. Smoking permitted. But when you think of those children's corpses, do try, dear Fatherland, to sleep easy!

OPTIMIST The U-boat could do no other—

GRUMBLER —than take the place of the iceberg that a few years earlier had rammed the *Titanic*, like the wrath of God visited upon the utter madness of technological excess, to teach man, no longer awe, but the shock of terror. Now technology itself administers the punishment, and all is for the best. But on that occasion God, who committed the act, was still called upon by name. About this U-boat hero, world history remains silent. The official report does not give his name. The enemy claim that the man had received a medal is dismissed by the official German news agency as a lie. And, moreover, with a show of outrage which, coming after all its smugly wholesome phraseology, finally exposes the deed.

OPTIMIST Compared with heroes like Commander Weddingen, he certainly has no claim—

GRUMBLER But why not? After all, the deed is being celebrated. Why is it not being hushed up like the doer?

OPTIMIST The deed was not noble, but expedient. The *Lusitania* was carrying weapons intended for use against the lives of German soldiers.

GRUMBLER German weapons!

(Change of scene.)

Scene 11

Suburban street. A proletarian crowd in front of a grocer's shop. Policemen keeping order. A large notice is put up saying "Bread sold out." The crowd stays put.

FIRST POLICEMAN Ain't you seen it's all sold out?

FIRST WOMAN IN THE CROWD I've been here since two in the morning!

SECOND POLICEMAN Move along there, please!

SECOND WOMAN Is that fair? We've been standing 'ere for eight hours and now they sed it's sold out!!

FIRST MAN Smash his shack to bits!

SECOND MAN Just try! Ask him now if he's any bread and he'll box your ears so hard you'll think the spire of St. Stephan's is sugar candy.

THIRD WOMAN We pay taxes as well as them Jews, we wanna eat as well!

FOURTH WOMAN It's all the fault of them Jews!

SHOUTS Hand over the bread!

SECOND POLICEMAN If you don't move along, you'll have to face the consequences.

FIRST POLICEMAN For resisting the law! You risk being arrested!

SHOUTS Phooey! Bread!

SECOND POLICEMAN We'll lock you up!

SHOUTS Make 'im open up!

SECOND POLICEMAN You'll get your coupons next week anyway.

FOURTH WOMAN Blimey, by then we'll have kicked the bucket!

FIRST POLICEMAN You'll just have to bite the bullet!

OLD WOMAN (*leaves, shaking her head*) Jesus, it's pitiful! The menfolk they shoot and the women they starve!

FIRST POLICEMAN There's only one thing for it—crowd disperse!

THIRD MAN All right, then, we'll wait for the coupons. What chance of bread—

FOURTH MAN —when the baker's cupboard is bare?

FIFTH MAN Too right, the baker's cupboard is bare! (*Scornful laughter. The crowd departs muttering angrily.*)

GROCER (*opens his door to a better-dressed woman, who has remained behind*) Sneak in 'ere, lively like—

(*Change of scene.*)

Scene 12

Kärntnerstrasse. A big eater and a normal eater meet.

NORMAL EATER Well, how goes it, how have you survived the World War?

BIG EATER Please don't talk about it, I beg you. Give me some of your bread coupons instead, I'm collecting them wherever I can.

NORMAL EATER Not likely! I haven't enough for myself, even though I'm just a normal eater! But I can imagine you must be furious. I was saying to my wife only yesterday, this won't suit Tugendhat at all, everyone knows Tugendhat is a big eater. We had just been reading an interesting analysis in the paper about how big eaters need more than normal eaters, just as normal eaters need more than little eaters.

BIG EATER Are you a little eater?

NORMAL EATER I wouldn't say that exactly—middling—I'm a normal eater. But I'm not managing either. If it goes on like this, you can stuff your bloody war!

BIG EATER It can't possibly go on like this. I'm known to be a big eater, I should have informed the authorities what I need every day.

NORMAL EATER But you must admit, that first day of bread coupons was a sensation. As an individual you can only go by your own impressions, of course, but you get a fuller idea of what it was like from the papers.

BIG EATER Yes, they went into detail. Sent a hundred reporters to all the restaurants. But in each one it was different. For instance, while the regulars at Leber's got used to the new arrangement—

NORMAL EATER —the waiters at the Weingartl out in Grinzing had their work cut out—

BIG EATER —dealing with people curious to know—But in all the restaurants it was apparently the same in one respect: as soon as the head waiter pulled out his scissors to snip off a coupon—

NORMAL EATER —people wanted to be part of the action. No wonder, can you imagine a greater upheaval?

BIG EATER Yes, it's terrible what we have to go through here.

NORMAL EATER Well, at least those in the trenches needn't envy us.

BIG EATER I must actually admit, on the first day of bread rationing—it felt like the baptism of fire. The only difference being, with the baptism of fire you can wangle it. But with the bread coupons? Did you say you were a big eater—?

NORMAL EATER Middling. I'm a normal eater.

BIG EATER Yes, but me, I'm known to be a big eater, I really must say—you know—everyone I meet in Vienna asks me, they're all curious what I'll do—

NORMAL EATER I really sympathize, a big eater like you, when even a normal eater like me—

STARVING MAN (*approaches them, stretches out his hand*) Please, I've nothing to eat—

BIG EATER —and since I'm known to be a big eater—(*they leave, deep in conversation.*)

(*Change of scene.*)

Scene 13

Florianigasse. Enter Hofrat Dlauhobetzky v. Dlauhobetz (rtd.) and Hofrat Tibetanzl (rtd.)

DLAUHOBETZKY V. DLAUHOBETZ I'm curious to know whether tomorrow's *Mittagszeitung*—that's my favourite paper, you know—whether it will print my poem, I sent it in yesterday. Like to hear it? Wait a minute—(*takes out a piece of paper.*)

TIBETANZL You've done another poem? What about?

DLAUHOBETZKY V. DLAUHOBETZ You'll soon see what about. "The Warrior's Song." That's instead of "The Wanderer's Song", get it?

> I wandered lonely as a cloud
> That floats on high o'er vales and hills

TIBETANZL But—that's really fantastic!—that's by me!

DLAUHOBETZKY V. DLAUHOBETZ What? By you? That's a classic! It's by our most famous romantic poet! But listen to this, you'll soon see the difference. Now I'll have to start all over again.

> I wandered lonely as a cloud
> That floats on high o'er vales and hills
> When all at once they called out loud
> Hindenburg, a name that thrills.
> And Warsaw soon our troops will seize
> With banners dancing in the breeze.

Isn't that classic, it all fits, only instead of daffodils I put Hindenburg, and then of course Warsaw at the end. If they print it, say what you like, I'll send it to Hindenburg, I'm a great admirer of his.

TIBETANZL That's really fantastic! Yesterday I did the self-same poem. I wanted to send it in to the *Muskete*, but—

DLAUHOBETZKY V. DLAUHOBETZ You did the same poem? You're not going to—

TIBETANZL But I changed a lot more than you. It's called "The Baker's Song":

> I wandered lonely as a cloud
> Towards a scene that made me stop,
> For all at once I saw a crowd
> Queuing at the baker's shop.

DLAUHOBETZKY V. DLAUHOBETZ Oh, that's quite different, very droll!

TIBETANZL

> The baker's gone to sleep, they say,
> There won't be any bread today.

DLAUHOBETZKY V. DLAUHOBETZ That's telepathy, that is!

TIBETANZL Yes, but all to no avail. Now I'll have to wait to see if yours appears.

If yours appears, I can't send mine to the *Muskete*. Otherwise they'll think I'm parodizing! (*Exeunt.*)
(*Change of scene.*)

Scene 14

A *hunting party.*

V. DRECKWITZ Oh, do stop bragging about your hunting exploits! My single year in Russia was worth three of yours with your sloppy peace. There was no end of good hunting in the land of the enemy. Glorious days, hunting down the vanquished foe, right on his heels until, done to death, he submits to his conqueror. War is surely the most natural occupation of real men. But then there was also a balm for every wound in those days, one I scarcely dared dream of—the Iron Cross without ribbon! There were certainly times you had to take a sip from the old flask out in the field to warm yourself up, at least inwardly. It's at such moments that you fall into a trance. I thought about our splendid French war, what fun it was, chasing the enemy cavalry into the mud whenever they showed as much as a hoof, and we ended up giving our horses their head in the sunny Champagne. You got an odd lump in your throat just thinking about all the good bubbly that had trickled over your palate back then! Give your memory a little prod, and you're in another enemy country: Belgium! Fertile fields, rich cities thronged with people, just waiting for us. I chalked up one sky-blue Gurkha and two Belgian bicyclists to add to my tally. And then—sweeping aside all frontier posts—into the land of the Poles! And, by Jupiter, our muskets and lances were not going to rust there either!

At first there was nothing to shoot at. Enemy still missing—lack of participation. On horseback it's hard enough to get at the wretches, but they're in a blue funk when it comes to shooting. After an interminable march, when it was already pitch-black, we reached our billets. Oh dear, that was quite incredible! If you've never seen a Russki hovel, you wouldn't believe such things exist. Indescribable, you really have to see it, to feel it. The Cossacks had finally managed to pull themselves together and blocked our advance over a bridge. But they had heavy infantry as well. One of our squadrons was about to attack when it came under hellishly heavy fire which rang out spookily through the inky darkness. At dawn the whole regiment attacked and put the rascals to flight. One of ours had his head grazed by a glancing bullet, so there were splinters of bone flying around. We had sneaked up quietly and already knocked off the outpost. Bang, goes a shot, bang, bang, a second and a third! Then the place erupts with constant, unbridled firing! Boom, boom! our big guns thunder; crash! bang! wallop! go the hand grenades the stupid Russians were tossing out of the windows, thinking that was a good idea. Everyone imaginable is running back and forth across the street, but in the dark no one can make out which side they're on. Anyway, we flatten ourselves against a big house, waiting to see which side Lady Luck is on today. But the uproar just went on, there was no sign of the military situation being settled one way or the other. Anyone who got in the way just got a kick in the backside. I'd be a shameless liar if I were to call the little skirmish particularly nice and pleasant, but we got through it, and it paid off later. A hundred and fifty paces beyond the town we quickly dug ourselves in, right up to our collar studs. Keyed up with excitement we waited for things to happen—and for the Russians who were sure to come. For the moment, we were the only ones—our little group of eight—capable of singing "The Watch on the Rhine." So—there we lay, not a peep out of us, our fingers on the trigger. As for my merry men, I was pretty confident. None would fire without my order. There was a young volunteer beside me, couldn't stop his teeth chattering 10 to the dozen. I gave him another quick dig in the ribs. Then I gave the order "Open fire!" yelling at the top of my voice to let the rascals on the other side hear the dulcet tones of a Prussian giving an order. And I had to yell loudly, for after the first salvo there was a great howl from the other side, so terrible, so blood-curdling, it made my hair stand on end, and as our rifles banged away merrily into the dense throng of moujiks, they streamed back, tripping over the dead and wounded—amid the constant screams of those in their death agony! And us right on their tails, yelling and cheering!

Just like animals, a whole group of them herded together in the nearest doorway. We could easily have brought them all down at our leisure. They were completely stunned, ready for the kill, too scared to utter a sound. Everything seemed to calm down. All we needed was a nice dram of schnapps.

But I had a feeling they were still planning some devilish trick or other. Now I wanted to check out the enemy reserves. A few well-aimed bullets was the only way. I shouldered my rifle, squeezed the hair trigger: bumps-a-daisy, down falls the first fellow! Quickly repeat—another kill. Numbers two and three fell like a sack of potatoes before they'd recovered from their initial shock. That put some life back into the group, only they seemed not to know which way to run. The next Russian, number four, took the bullet a bit too low. That was perhaps a good thing for me, for the fellow yelled blue murder. I'd quickly taken the carbine from the chap beside me and fired off the next five shots into the dense cluster at the garden fence. A few yells showed those bullets hadn't been discharged in vain either. I couldn't really stomach these last shots, it's true, especially since I'd no feeling of being in danger, for the Russians had clearly no intention of shooting. But what can you do? It's each man for himself, after all, I didn't start this war! We'd mopped up the flank, I went back satisfied to my boys. The Russian officers pulled a wry face when they saw our little group of six standing there. But my charming manner put their minds at rest. We shook hands warmly, with me smiling the patronizing smile of the victor. But it really was a nice moment, and the military success exceptionally gratifying. Together we all went off to the marketplace which was full of Russians. I thanked the captain of artillery for the precision of his shrapnel fire, then I had to go back to my division and report. All-round satisfaction. My six men were immediately awarded the Iron Cross, just as they stood. I was put up for Iron Cross First Class, but it took almost a year for that to come through.—And now, judge for yourselves my lads, if you can impress me with your ludicrous fisherman's tales. What I experienced on the Russian trail—you'll have to admit—that was a humdinger! Our hunting journal, *Hare and Hound*, did me the honour of requesting me to write a report on my hunting achievements in Russia. I intend to do so. And then off to the happy hunting grounds in France! But before that, let's sit back and crack open a few more bottles of bubbly! Here's mud in your eye!

ALL Your health, Dreckwitz! Good hunting!

(Change of scene.)

Scene 15

Office at a command post.

HIRSCH *(enters singing to the melody of the "Carpenter's Song" from Raimund's* Der Verschwender)

Hurray! The war is splendid fun,
And happy is the song I sing,
Tomorrow's column's almost done,
War reporting's just the thing.
I might have grown up tall and strong,
And still not graced the field of glory.
[Exempted, you can earn a bomb,
You just write and file your story.]

Secondly, life's much too boring
On the home front for a hero,
So I choose to do my warring
In the army's posh Press Bureau.
By the trenches I'm not tempted,
That is such a mundane caper!

[So us hacks can get exempted,
Now I'm serving on the paper.]

Third and fourth, I'll soon report
News of how the battle went.
How our valiant heroes fought
Is written from the rear, then sent.
Till victory is assured I'll stay,
For that you have my word, we'll win!
[As soon as I have had my say,
The enemy promptly packs it in.]

Fifthly, I can safely write
That we live in clouds of glory.
The way our valiant soldiers fight
Gives our guys their cover story.
Sixth and seventh and still counting,
Watching as the bullets pass,
[The cash I earn will still keep mounting,
As long as this great war shall last.]

(*Calling into the next room*) Major, if you see the general, tell him I'm going to interview him and all his staff! There'll be no shirking today! (*Exit.*)

RODA RODA (*enters singing, to the tune "O Tannenbaum"*)

O Rosenbaum.
O Rosenbaum,
Writes for each classy paper,
He frets at base,
The front's the place,
For an opinion shaper.

I have to see
With my own eyes,
Till I know all I need to.
If shrapnel burst
Should do its worst,
Then I'll know how to bleed, too.

What do I care
For wife or child?
Or for my own protection?

With sons of toil,
'neath tons of soil,
My trench is just perfection.

Faced with the foe,
Cut out the talk,
Get in the right position.
No interviews,
They'd just confuse
My latest composition.

I once was under
Arms myself,
So I know who's who here now.
I get around,
Cover the ground,
A source to make things clear now.

Though long ago
I had to quit,
The scandal drew attention.
They want to know
If I'm still fit,
For they all want a mention.

The military
Is home to me,
My battle news conclusive.
I scan each front,
As is my wont,
Then send my world-exclusive.

The Vistula's
The place today,
Tomorrow the Isonzo,
And every day
I'm in the fray
As it goes on and on so.

The brigadier
Now says it's clear,
The foe's in total disarray.

But should it be
Their victory,
I'll still just say we won the day.

I scarcely ever
Get back home,
I like it out here—oh ja!
A Rose may be
In my family tree,
But my name's Roda Roda.

(*Calling into the next room*) Major, if you see the general, tell him the colonel needs to be transferred—he refused me a pass for Fort 5 in Przemysl. He doesn't seem to know who I am. That's no excuse, just the opposite. I'll soon show those fine gentlemen what discipline is—got that? (*Exit.*)
(*Change of scene.*)

Scene 16

Another office.

GENERAL STAFF OFFICER (*enters and goes to telephone*)—Hello there, have you got the report on Przemysl ready?—Not yet? Ah, still sleeping it off—Go and see to it, otherwise you'll be late again for the bash in the mess. Now look here—What, forgotten everything again?—Ye gods—Listen, and get it into your head this time—Main points: First, the fortress was absolutely worthless in any case. That's the key point—How's that? you can't—What, you can't get people to forget the fortress has always been the pride and joy of—My dear fellow, you can make people forget anything! So listen, the fortress was a dilapidated old ruin—What's that? All the latest artillery? I'm telling you, a dilapidated old ruin, got that? All right, then. Secondly, do you hear, the loss was not due to enemy action, but to hunger, OK? And don't put too much emphasis on inadequate provisions as a factor, you know, a botched job, everything in a mess, etc., play all that down if you possibly can. I know these factors will seem all too obvious, but you'll find a way. Hunger is the main thing. Proud of suffering hunger, you understand! Not by hunger but by enemy action—damn, what am I saying—not by enemy action but by hunger! So, that'll do—What do you mean, it won't do? Because people will notice there were no provisions—what?—and will demand to know why there weren't enough provisions? All right, then, you tackle that and say: impossible to pile up all the necessary provisions because then the enemy would get hold of them when he takes the fortress. How would he have got hold of them? By hunger? No by force of course in that case, don't ask such

stupid questions. Don't you understand, when he takes the fortress by force, and we have provisions, then he'll take the provisions. That's why we mustn't have any provisions, then afterwards he can't take any provisions, instead he takes the fortress by hunger, but not by force. Go on, you'll find a way, cheerio, I must get to the mess—I've no intention of surrendering to hunger—finito!
(Change of scene.)

Scene 17

Restaurant Anton Grüsser. In the foreground a gentleman with a lady. A man goes from table to table, continually bowing without speaking. In the foreground, left, at a table, the Grumbler.

FIRST WAITER Have you ordered yet, sir?

GENTLEMAN No, may I see the menu? (*Exit waiter.*)

SECOND WAITER Have you ordered yet, sir?

GENTLEMAN No, the menu, please. (*Exit waiter.*)

FIRST YOUNG WAITER Anything to drink, sir? Beer, wine—

GENTLEMAN No. (*Exit young waiter.*)

THIRD WAITER Have you ordered yet, sir?

GENTLEMAN No, the menu, please. (*To a waiter hurrying past*) The menu!

SECOND YOUNG WAITER Beer, wine—

GENTLEMAN No.

FOURTH WAITER (*brings the menu*) Have you ordered yet?

GENTLEMAN No. You've only just brought the menu. What's ready?

WAITER What's on the menu.

GENTLEMAN On the menu it says "May God punish England!" I can't eat that.

WAITER Perhaps something freshly made? The gentleman might perhaps like—

GENTLEMAN Have you roast beef?

WAITER I'm sorry, today's a red-meat-free day. I could conjure up a nice schnitzel for the lady, or a pork fillet, or perhaps roast goose—

GENTLEMAN First the hors d'oeuvres. What's that—Choice Morsel?

WAITER It's an appetizer.

GENTLEMAN I've already lost my appetite. Well, maybe—whatever's that: fishy egg-oil sauce?

WAITER That's a fish mayonnaise.

GENTLEMAN And what's a Hollowed-out Puff-pastry?

WAITER That's a vol-au-vong.

GENTLEMAN And a Mixed Dish: what's that?

WAITER That's a ragout fin.

GENTLEMAN Oh for goodness sake—bring that then—and afterwards, wait a minute—whatever is that: double rib of beef, stewed in its own juice, military style with manoeuvres, and a Dutch dip?

WAITER That's an Entercut with Hollandaise sauce.

GENTLEMAN 52 crowns, that's a bit steep, isn't it!

WAITER Yes, but the gentleman shouldn't forget we're at war, and today's a red-meat-free day.

GENTLEMAN All right, you might as well bring that. (*Exit waiter.*)

LADY You see, we should have gone to Sacher after all, that would only cost 50 there.

WAITER Have you ordered yet, sir?

GENTLEMAN Yes.

SECOND WAITER Have you ordered yet, sir?

GENTLEMAN Yes.

FIRST YOUNG WAITER Beer, wine?

GENTLEMAN No.

THIRD WAITER Have you ordered yet, sir?

GENTLEMAN Yes.

FOURTH WAITER (*returning*) I'm sorry, it's off. (*Crosses out almost all the dishes.*)

GENTLEMAN But you only just—

WAITER Yes, but today being a red-meat-free day, it's no wonder. Still, the gentleman could have two Lost Eggs, perhaps with a piquant sauce, that's still on the menu—

GENTLEMAN Lost Eggs, what's that? Who's lost them?

WAITER (*in a low voice*) Oeufs pochés—that's what they were called before the war.

GENTLEMAN Aha, and you think that renaming food is the way to win it?—No, wait—Turn-coat Noodles—what are they?

WAITER Italian Macaroni, of course.

GENTLEMAN Oh, of course—and Gangster Salad, what's that then?

WAITER Salade Niçoise.

GENTLEMAN Ah yes, stands to reason. So—bring us: homemade offal with mashed potatoes and poached eggs, with spicy mixed vegetables, and afterwards, a fruit purée and two slices of Grüsser whipped-cream cake. What was that called before?

WAITER Grüsser tarte à la crème.

GENTLEMAN And why Grüsser?

WAITER After the boss. (*Grüsser comes to the table, greets, and leaves.*)

GENTLEMAN Who was that gentleman?

WAITER That's the boss! (*Exit.*)

HEADWAITER Have you ordered yet, sir?

GENTLEMAN Yes.

MIDGET NEWSPAPER VENDOR (*dashes from table to table*) Fig-tree after fig-tree! Ex-tra-aa edi-shun! Italions heavily defeated! Fig-tree after fig-tree!

TWO GIRLS (*with picture postcards and wearing War Welfare insignia, move from table to table*) Please make your contribution to War Welfare—

FIRST YOUNG WAITER Bread, anyone? May I have the menu?

GENTLEMAN (*looks about for menu*)—ah, I don't appear to have one.

TWO WOMEN (*with picture postcards move from table to table*) Contributions to War Welfare please—

MAN SELLING FLOWERS (*hurries up to table*) Would you like some flars?

WOMAN SELLING FLOWERS (*from behind*) Yellow—lovely yellow flars—for the lady?

WOMAN HAWKING NEWSPAPERS Ex-tra-aa edi-shun!

SECOND CUSTOMER (*summons headwaiter*) Hey, Finance Minister—!

HEADWAITER (*bends over towards customer*) Heard the latest, sir? What's the difference between a Galician refugee and—(*says the rest into his ear.*)

SECOND CUSTOMER (*his smile broadens until he breaks out laughing*) Brilliant! But do you know the difference between a Red Cross nurse and—(*says the rest into his ear.*)

FIRST WAITER (*with 18 plates*) The sauce is for—? (*He spills some over the lady.*) Oh, my fault, paton!

THIRD CUSTOMER Who just said Pardon? You've a waiter saying Pardon in your good German establishment, Herr Grüsser!

GRÜSSER Herr von Wossitschek, you wouldn't believe how difficult it is with these people today. If you say the least thing to them, they just quit, there are more than enough jobs going, they say. It's a real cross I have to bear, the better ones are in the field, and these ill-bred ones left behind—

THIRD CUSTOMER Oh quite, quite, but—

GRÜSSER Pardon, Herr von Wossitschek, I must go and greet my customers. (*Does so.*)

THIRD CUSTOMER Pardon, pardon, don't let me keep you.

REGULAR Evening, Grüsser, how's it going? Hey, did you hear about Leberl, they've really landed him in it—

GRÜSSER But look at the prices he's charging! And he's not at all popular, either. But take me, I'm a celebrity here and I've never had the slightest difficulty.

REGULAR Come and join us, Grüsser.

GRÜSSER Gladly, in a moment, but I still have to do some greeting—(*does so.*)

REGULAR Yes, of course, off you go.

BAMBULA VON FELDSTURM (*bellowing and thumping the table*) Damnation, will I never get served today? You, over here!

WAITER Be with you in a moment, Major.

GRÜSSER What can I do for you, Major?

BAMBULA VON FELDSTURM What's going on, landlord? Will I never get served today? The service here is not what it was, I've noticed that for the last year, where are all the waiters?

GRÜSSER Called up, Major.

BAMBULA VON FELDSTURM What? Called up? And why have they all been called up?

GRÜSSER Because there's a war on, Major.

BAMBULA VON FELDSTURM But I've noticed it for a whole year, apart from those four, you've no waiters left. For an establishment this size! I've noticed it for a whole year.

GRÜSSER Since the war began, actually, Major.

BAMBULA VON FELDSTURM What? That's scandalous! Just so you know, the other officers are all complaining, too, they'll stop coming if it goes on like this. They're all getting hot under the collar. Captain Tronner, Fiebiger von

Feldwehr, Kreibich, Kuderna, Colonel Hasenörl, they're all getting hot under the collar, only yesterday Husserl von Schlachtentreu of the 66th said, if it goes on like this—

GRÜSSER Yes, Major, wouldn't we all like it to be over and for peace to come—

BAMBULA VON FELDSTURM What's that, peace?—that's enough of your pacifist whingeing—I was on the Emperor's Manoeuvres—what if our commander in chief could hear you!—We've got to bite the bullet and hold on to the bitter end, my friend—there is no alternative! (*A waiter hurries past.*) Eyes right, you! Damned fellow, just wait, I'll have him called up—See, what sort of service is that?!

GRÜSSER What did you order, Major?

BAMBULA VON FELDSTURM Nothing, just a sirloin, but with a nice bit of fat—

GRÜSSER I'm sorry, today is red-meat-free day.

BAMBULA VON FELDSTURM What? Red-meat-free? What newfangled nonsense is that?

GRÜSSER Well, we're at war, Major, and so—

BAMBULA VON FELDSTURM Don't talk gibberish. What's the war got to do with you running out of meat, tell me that! It wasn't like that before!

GRÜSSER Yes, but now there's a war on, Major!

BAMBULA VON FELDSTURM (*jumps up in a rage*) You don't have to keep rubbing my nose in it—you and your bloody war, I've had a bellyful! You won't see any more of me and the other officers in your establishment—we'll go to Leberl! (*Storms out.*)

GRÜSSER But—Major—(*shakes his head*) Bizarre!

THIRD CUSTOMER (*to a waiter*) There's nothing at all? Not even a dessert?

FIRST WAITER Viennese turnover, cinnamon cookies, English custard tarts—

FIRST CUSTOMER What? English—now we're at war?!

FIRST WAITER Left over from peacetime.

FIRST CUSTOMER Pull the other one! The bill!

FIRST WAITER The bill!

SECOND WAITER The bill!

THIRD WAITER The bill!

FOURTH WAITER The bill!

YOUNG WAITER (*under his breath*) The bill!

GRÜSSER (*has gone to Grumbler's table, greets him, bends over him with the dead man's glassy stare, like the angel of death, only slowly becoming more animated, and says*) According to the latest mineralogical reports the weather seems to be clearing, so custom should pick up again—you've been out of town, I'm sure, quite right, quite right—we're all kept busy these days, aren't we, good Lord this war, the misery, business is suffering, the middle classes, wherever you look—it's still impossible to predict the consequences—even one of the gentlemen of the press, the minister's right-hand man, said himself—bizarre—hm—but you seem to have lost your appetite today, what a shame, the very day we've got some nice brisket, all the gentlemen were saying how good it was, ah well, make up for it next time with a real delicacy, the merest sliver of the Grüsser special I keep for regulars—Leopold, clear the table—asleep again, the scallywag!—well good-bye, good-bye—

(*The gentleman and lady in the foreground have fallen asleep.*)

FIRST WAITER (*rushes in*) I'm sorry, I'm not serving anymore.

GENTLEMAN (*waking with a start*) Super—exempted?—Oh, I see. All right then, we'll go. (*Rises with lady.*) Adieu.

FIRST WAITER Paton, permit me to point out, on your next visit, we are a German restaurang, so speaking French is not allowed—(*wipes his brow with his napkin.*)

GENTLEMAN Well, well—

GRÜSSER (*behind them*) Honoured-g'day-good-bye-and-thankyou-your humbleservant-myrespectsandcompliments-untilnexttime.

(*Change of scene*)

Scene 18

Vienna, Schottenring. Enter Frau Pollatschek and Frau Rosenberg.

FRAU ROSENBERG My dear Frau Pollatschek, the behaviour of our women is inexcusable! We who have set such a shining example of discipline expect our fellow housewives of Austria to keep it up, and limit the purchase of pork to Thursdays and Saturdays only. Our local groups will assuredly keep the flag flying. And that goes for lard, too!

FRAU POLLATSCHEK The Imperial Association of Austrian Housewives permits the sale of pork and lard on Thursdays and Saturdays.

FRAU ROSENBERG Exactly! We housewives of Austria were duty-bound to speak our mind in a question which touches on our vital interests. We of the

IAAH could not stand idly by with folded arms and watch the machinations of the market as it set prices, especially the price of pork belly!

FRAU POLLATSCHEK What we need, above all now, is unity. Through unity to purity, that's my slogan, especially for boiled topside of beef!

FRAU ROSENBERG And I would add, if my opinion in the matter could tip the scales, that we shall not be deterred by any terrorism. *Per aspera ad astra,* is what I say, at least as far as sirloin is concerned. We of the IAAH—

FRAU POLLATSCHEK See who's coming, do you know them? Bachstelz and Funk-Feigl of the Central Association of Communal Kitchens in Vienna. They'd happily poison me with a spoonful of soup, the two of them.
(Greeting.)

FRAU BACHSTELZ My respects, ladies, we've come straight from the market hall, I wish you could have seen what's going on there, especially with the delicacies!

FRAU FUNK-FEIGL In the communal interest, since we all must do our bit now the men are away, we took a deep breath and dashed down there, for we know when battle must be joined, unlike certain other persons, of whom I will say only this: If they do these things in our salad days, well then, venerable ladies, I can only say—

FRAU ROSENBERG My dear friend, I very much regret—

FRAU FUNK-FEIGL I'm not your dear friend, I'm on the committee of the CACKV and have just as much right as anyone on the IAAH! It's easy to concoct regulations for our salad days, but afterwards? Wasn't it Schiller who said: Life's for the living, so plunge right inside—

FRAU ROSENBERG I merely wanted to say, I very much regret you've let yourself get carried away and become personal. I know very well your letter in the *Neue Freie Presse* today was pointedly directed against the IAAH, unmistakably, and written, moreover, at a time you still belonged to the IAAH—

FRAU FUNK-FEIGL That's not true, I'll tell my husband, he'll take you to court!

FRAU ROSENBERG Go ahead! I can prove what I said is true. I'll prove in open court that you're a crank! At least you'll hear the truth for once! You intrigued against the IAAH when you were still in it!

FRAU BACHSTELZ You'll have to prove that!

FRAU POLLATSCHEK I tell you to your face, so just listen, this is not a time to indulge in personal vanity, and don't you forget it! We're not the ones addicted to a separatist tendency. If someone belongs to the IAAH, she must belong to it body and soul, our paper is the *Morgen*, and—do I really have to spell it out—the situation is much too grave, today when solidarity is half the battle!

FRAU FUNK-FEIGL *You* want to teach *us* solidarity! Someone who grew up in the back of beyond—

FRAU BACHSTELZ Typical IAAH! Slandering people behind their backs! We pinch and scrape in order to set a good example!

FRAU FUNK-FEIGL If you hadn't intrigued, we'd still be in the IAAH. We had a knife held to our throats until we were forced to found the CACKV. I ran from pillar to post. Now I can guarantee that we'll have some order, and I'm telling you today, if you start claiming our successes as your own, you'll be knocking your head against a brick wall!

FRAU BACHSTELZ We pinch and scrape—

FRAU POLLATSCHEK Yes, so you can buy osprey feathers.

FRAU BACHSTELZ Prove that!

FRAU POLLATSCHEK Last Saturday, you were seen at the Volkstheater première in osprey feathers.

FRAU BACHSTELZ That's infamous! You're just singing the Agriculture Minister's latest tune, you should be ashamed of yourself!

FRAU ROSENBERG Prove! What do you mean, prove? The proof is on your hat!

FRAU BACHSTELZ That's from last year, as you well know!

FRAU ROSENBERG You're behaving just like an ostrich, burying your head in the sand!

FRAU FUNK-FEIGL So what! You're wearing a bit of ostrich on your head yourself!

FRAU ROSENBERG That's from last year, as you well know! I'm wearing a war blouse!

FRAU FUNK-FEIGL So what!

FRAU BACHSTELZ You can't compare my blouse with your blouse—that's pure fantasy! We were the ones who took the plunge and created a new Viennese fashion!

FRAU POLLATSCHEK You, with your figure! That's a laugh! My taste compared with your taste!

FRAU BACHSTELZ (*screeching*) You're one to talk! If it weren't for the grandeur of the age, I'd soon lay hands on you!

FRAU ROSENBERG Just ignore these noisy publicity seekers, fortunately more vital interests call at this critical time, and if we form a phalanx we can simply dismiss this despicable and impotent yapping. We know what's making them so furious, don't we?

FRAU BACHSTELZ You—! If you repeat that slander one more time!

FRAU ROSENBERG What do you mean? Was it something I said? Just because the inspector spoke to us longer yesterday in the communal kitchen than with you, that's no reason to get worked up, my dear—!

FRAU BACHSTELZ (*in a paroxysm*) That's an infamous insinuation, you'll regret—just wait—I'll put my husband on to you—wait and see, the whole of the Central Austrian Imports Board will be on to you!

FRAU ROSENBERG My husband will soon see him off, and the rest of them, you can rest assured! He has the whole of the Milk Marketing Board behind him! Just a word from him and the UFA studios and the Viennese Car Manufacturers will be on to you, too—he's on the executive board!

FRAU BACHSTELZ Well, *my* husband can call on the Department of Arms and Munitions Supply! My husband is an Honorary Counsellor! How your husband got exempted is well known!

FRAU ROSENBERG Yes, he was able to pull strings—what of it? You're furious because he has connections. He's well in with Sascha Publicity Films. Just wait, I'll bring this all up at the committee meeting, that means a vote of no confidence at the AGM, that I guarantee!

FRAU FUNK-FEIGL You're the one who's utter rubbish, you'll get thrown out of the IAAH, that I guarantee, the CACKV will show you—I've got connections, I'll take it to the *Neue Freie Presse*—

FRAU POLLATSCHEK In the next edition of the *Morgen* you'll be able to read—let me see, we of the IAAH—

FRAU FUNK-FEIGL Don't mess with us, we of the CACKV—

(*All four screech away, only the words IAAH and CACKV being audible through the noise, and leave, gesticulating vehemently. A disabled person on crutches hobbles past. Enter a beggar woman holding a boy by the hand and an infant in her arm.*)

BEGGAR WOMAN Ex-tra-aa edi-shun—*Neue Freie Presse*—

BOY New Vile Pressure—!

INFANT Vile—lying—liars—

(A pregnant woman passes by.)

GRUMBLER

A touching prospect when the multitude are dying!
Yet better for us to be spared this interlude,
though it reminds us of a final natural order
to which debased humanity still clings,
which ends in natural death—without negating life.
But rarely is what follows an advance. So look away,
for such remnants of humanity in a race
now pledged to other goals is painful to behold.
Uncanny is the thought that this same woman,
revealed to us as she placidly comes walking by,
bearer of life and hope, full of her sacred mission,
with pain accompanying the blessed gift,
could give birth to an army profiteer!
The pride of motherhood, glorious since the dawn of time
Keeping profoundest sympathy within its natural bounds,
used rightly to be proud to keep from prying eyes
the harmony of creation known to mothers alone.
But faced with man's deformity, such pride
loses its former sanction. So turn your gaze away
and let pride veil its face once more. Look away, mother,
alone, you are too weak and lacking modesty.
This is well-meant advice, but also an appeal
a hundred thousand mothers may hear and understand
that they have suffered greater pain than that
which you alone are due to bear. Go home,
why do you bear your burden to the marketplace,
as if what you can offer the world were better far
than what it's lost, no, more than that, as if now
finally, the new longed-for redeemer could be born,
as if a Socrates were the least of the gifts
you could conceive. We've learnt our lesson from a weight
of harsh experience. We are in any case no longer curious,
no longer wish to know, however good the news,
we wish that what awaits you should be your own affair,
chastely maternal, as is fitting, till one day fulfilment

merits the world's attention. Go home, mother, we shall come
when the time's ripe, enduring until then no deeper suffering
for you than for the newborn life soon to be mobilized,
claimed from the thrall of motherhood by death's domain,
the greatest of the sacrifices birth brings. Go, make yourself
fit for service. Wait for your age group's time. You're a volunteer,
what have you to offer? Stay at home, one day is like the next,
death always looks like death. Go home! Surprise us!

(Change of scene.)

Scene 19

Belgrade. Destroyed houses. Enter Alice Schalek.

SCHALEK I've fought my way through. What appeals to me above all, here as so often, is the human interest story. Is this place supposed to be civilized? These houses are as bad as the most ramshackle offices and shops in our teeming suburbs, that's why they deserve to be bombarded. The desolation of the place is so great that a photographic reproduction is simply out of the question. But what I never cease to find shocking is that the town wasn't even paved. That may have contributed to the decision to raze it to the ground. Even the royal palace has nothing to offer. The souvenirs we took are not worth mentioning. What sort of monarch buys his china dinner service from a provincial manufacturer in Bohemia! There is such a thing as poetic justice. It's a thought that haunts me wherever I go in Belgrade. If only one knew whether these are the houses of the people who invented their national fanaticism? I've finally become convinced that no person of character could live in such a city.

(Some Serbian women appear and laugh as they encounter her. One runs a hand caressingly over Schalek's cheek. Then a rapid conversation bubbles up among them, again they all laugh happily, loud and clear. Schalek, aside:)

This laughter is getting on my nerves and I can't find out what's causing it. It could conceivably come anywhere on the scale of human feelings, but the fact that Belgrade has been shot to pieces is scarcely a cause for laughter.

(One of the Serbian women offers Schalek a jar of preserves and laughs.)

A baffling mystery.

(Enter an interpreter.)

INTERPRETER *(after speaking to the women)* They say it's just a matter of holding out for a few terrible days. The people of Belgrade think the conquest of their city is just an interlude. They think we Austrians will soon be driven out again, that's why they're laughing with malicious glee.

SCHALEK That can't be the only reason. Ask her what they feel, and why she gave me a jar of preserves.

INTERPRETER (*after speaking to the woman*) She says nothing can affect Serbian hospitality.

SCHALEK But why specifically a jar of preserves?

INTERPRETER (*after speaking to the woman*) She says they wanted to show they were women, and preserves are women's domain.

SCHALEK (*takes the jar of preserves*) I don't want to see these women again, don't want to witness their frightful disappointment, for worse than any collapsed houses and bombed streets, worse than the rout of their army and the storming of the city—the worst is still to come for the Serbs. (*The Serbian women laugh. Schalek, as she leaves:*) I shudder as I leave, for it will take a long time to get their laughter out of my mind.

(The Serbian women leave in the opposite direction, their laughter can still be heard.)

(Change of scene.)

Scene 20

Suburban street. A heavily laden handcart, drawn by two feeble, emaciated dogs on war service.

OLD WOMAN (*shouts*) Scandalous! That should be reported to the authorities!

LIEUTENANT Halt! Show your papers! You've just insulted the army!

CROWD (*collects*) What a ninny!—Clear orf!—What's up?—Nothing much, just high treason!—Serve her right, standing up for dumb animals when she's nothing to eat herself!

(Change of scene.)

Scene 21

Suburban apartment. A boy, about 10 years old, half-dressed, his body covered with welts, blood blisters, and bruises, is hanging from a strap. He is in a state of complete neglect, seemingly half-starved. He is howling. A neighbour stands in the doorway, wringing her hands. The father (in uniform) is lying on the sofa.

NEIGHBOUR (*to the mother, who is putting a saucepan on the hob*) But Frau Liebal, how can you beat the boy like that? If I report it, you'll get a formal reprimand!

MOTHER Listen, Frau Sikora, he's such a stubborn brat, you can't imagine! He wants hot breakfasts!

FATHER Feeling sorry for the little bastard, eh? He's fit as a fiddle again now, but the other day I gave him such hell with my bayonet, I thought he was done for. And now look, he's none the worse for it!

NEIGHBOUR But Herr Liebal, Herr Liebal, it's no laughing matter. Look out, or one of these days you'll get a reprimand!

(Change of scene.)

Scene 22

Headquarters garrison. A street. Army suppliers, officers, prostitutes, journalists. Enter a captain from the War Press Bureau and a journalist.

CAPTAIN So, here's the draft for the brochure *Our Glorious Military Commanders*—are you listening, my little scribbler, don't keep ogling the tarts all the time, there's a war on—so, this is the draft I've done, and it's up to you to improve it if there's the odd mistake. (*He reads it out.*) "When the time comes that the raging tides of war have subsided, when the consolations of time have healed the wounds and dried the tears, then we shall look back with unclouded gaze on the glorious days when a rod of iron forged the destiny of the world!" Then a new line, don't forget—"And above all else there shall rise up the figures of those men who at that time shaped our destiny and that of our Fatherland." In bold! *(In the background, crossing the stage from right to left, can be seen a corpulent elderly gentleman with side-whiskers and pince-nez, a marshal's baton in each hand.)*

"Full of veneration and love we behold them, who like those heroes in the very front line, in unflagging, ardent struggle, were called upon to guide the fortunes of battle—"

JOURNALIST Just a moment, so the commanders are in the very front line just as much as the heroes who guide the fortunes of battle, how can that be?

CAPTAIN Don't try any of your tricks on me, otherwise I'll send you to the front yourself.

JOURNALIST You—me?

CAPTAIN Do you want to commit suicide?! If the brochure turns out well, I'm out of the firing line. Are you listening, little scribbler? "Our ardent appreciation of these heroes and heartfelt gratitude should be paid—"

JOURNALIST To those who guide the fortunes of battle in the very front line? Ah, I see, you mean the commanders again.

CAPTAIN Who do you think you're kidding? So—"should raise a monument in our hearts, wherein they can live forever as exemplifying the highest fulfilment of duty and self-sacrifice for the good of the Fatherland." In bold—even bolder!

(In the background, crossing the stage from left to right, can be seen the corpulent elderly gentleman with side-whiskers and pince-nez, a marshal's baton in each hand.)

Are you listening, little scribbler, and don't keep ogling the tarts! "The painter Oskar Brüch has given this monument noble and tangible form. With veracity his etching needle has captured their characteristic features, creating a work of historic significance, *Our Glorious Military Commanders*, destined to convey to posterity not only the names and images of the great figures of our time—" In bold—boldest of all!

(In the background, crossing the stage from right to left, can be seen the corpulent elderly gentleman with side-whiskers and pince-nez, a marshal's baton in each hand.)

"—but also an adornment for every library and every home—" Now we have to add something about the historic significance of each of those portrayed—my God, ogling again—my dear fellow, you're in army headquarters here, not in some brothel, got it?

JOURNALIST Hey, wasn't that the colonel's girl, Camilla?

CAPTAIN If that's your cup of tea, I'll send her to you to check her out, but I need you to check the brochure first—

JOURNALIST Done.

CAPTAIN And then comes something about the cover, extremely distinguished, in the best possible taste, attractively priced, signed by the Imperial and Royal War Ministry. And that's that! Well, what do you say, scribbler?

JOURNALIST My compliments, captain, your mastery of the language, no professional journalist could have done a more effective job.

CAPTAIN Hah! And, oh yes, on the front of the brochure, so that people get an immediate impression of global destiny and supreme self-sacrifice, we'll put as an illustration the image of the man who incorporates all that in the most exemplary fashion—our revered Commander in Chief, Archduke Friedrich!

(In the background, crossing the stage from left to right, can be seen the corpulent elderly gentleman with side-whiskers and pince-nez, a marshal's baton in each hand.)

(Change of scene.)

Scene 23

City centre. A blind soldier, without arms and legs, in a cart pushed by another disabled veteran. They wait, for the narrow footpath is blocked by a hack from the gutter press in conversation with a sales rep.

DISABLED VETERAN Excuse me—

HACK I ask you, what do they think they're at, last Monday they cut 80 lines on me.

SALES REP From the article criticizing Budischovsky & Co for that faulty shipment?

HACK Yes—it used to be that when something was set and then didn't appear, you got paid. And if you didn't get paid, you still let it appear and were sure to be paid next time. Now, a hatchet job simply doesn't appear, *and* you don't get a thing out of it.

SALES REP Did Budischovsky know?

HACK Yes—but these days the people rely on the censor. Next time I'll really cook their goose, just wait till the weather changes. For now, let the censor play around with us. Just you watch, though, the next thing I fire off will be really something—dynamite!

SALES REP I look forward to it.

HACK First I'll submit it to the censor. I'll explain how senseless the government line is, it protects the suppliers from us, but the government needs us more than it needs the suppliers. We're being squeezed out of existence. I'll describe how the press has carried out its duty throughout the war in quite exemplary fashion. I'll depict how we have served every bit as responsibly as the soldiers, how we've stood our ground like the men in the trenches, *and* without being paid for it!

DISABLED VETERAN Excuse me—

(Change of scene.)

Scene 24

During a performance in a theatre in the suburbs. On the stage, Hansi Niese and a partner.

NIESE (*playing her part*) What, you want a juicy kiss? You, a simple soldier? How dare you! All of you together, though, all you brave soldiers, then I'd gladly kiss you all—but just the one? O no! Either all at once (*thinks for a moment*) or—why not, one for all!—let me give a single soldier a big kiss! Let me plant a big smacker on him that'll make old Vienna quake and St. Stephen's spire tremble. And this one, single soldier—is—*(goes to front of stage, deeply moved)* our beloved—our Dear Old Gentleman in Schönbrunn! But he, alas—our Emperor—is the very one who is out of our reach!

(Tumultuous applause. A stagehand appears on the stage and hands the actress a special edition.)

NIESE Let me see! If Gerda Walde can do it, so can I!

AUDIENCE Bravo Hansi!

NIESE *(atmosphere of total suspense; she reads out to audience)*—by the incomparable bravura of our brave troops, Czernowitz has been recaptured! *(Tremendous applause.)*

AUDIENCE Bravo! Bravo! Bravo Hansi!

(Scene changes.)

Scene 25

The restaurant Wolf in Gersthof. The evening of the day on which Czernowitz was retaken by the Russians. At one table: the inspector general of the Red Cross, Archduke Franz Salvator, his chamberlain, two aristocrats, and little Putzi. Music and singing: "Happy, happy folk are we, it's all in our heredity."

CUSTOMER *(to Wolf)*—is that really Salvator, or just someone very like him?

WOLF No, no. The gentleman can rest assured, that's him all right.

CUSTOMER But surely it can't be—and today of all days? The Emperor's son-in-law?

WOLF But it is!

CUSTOMER The one who's with Valerie?

WOLF The very one.

CUSTOMER Tell me, have the gentlemen just dropped in by chance?

WOLF No, they're often here, they telephoned this afternoon already to reserve a table. Excuse me, I must—

(Wolf and two other folksingers line up beside the VIP table, the music strikes up the melody of "The Dear Old Gentleman." The folk-singers sing into the archduke's ear:)

Out there in Schönbrunner Park,
Brooding since this war began,
Sits a dear old gentleman,
Sick at heart—

(Change of scene.)

Scene 26

Subscriber to the Neue Freie Presse *and Patriot in conversation.*

PATRIOT Well, what do you say now?

SUBSCRIBER What do you want me to say? If you're referring to Sir Edward Grey's failing eyesight, then I say: the whole crew has it coming to them!

PATRIOT That too, but what do you say to the muzzling of public opinion in England?

SUBSCRIBER Yes, I heard. The editor of the *Labour Leader* was summoned before the magistrate because some things the paper published contravened the Defence of the Realm Act. They're running scared!

PATRIOT But is it any better in France? What do you say about France? You know what they've introduced there?

SUBSCRIBER Prison sentences in France for disseminating the truth. I suppose you mean the lady who said—

PATRIOT That too, but now some gentleman said—

SUBSCRIBER Of course, the gentleman who said France has no munitions, for which he was sentenced to 20 days! For saying the Allies are in a bad way and Germany was prepared for war—

PATRIOT Can you explain that to me, please, it's one of those things I don't understand: is it false to say Germany was prepared, then, or is it true to say Germany wasn't prepared—

SUBSCRIBER Are you saying Germany was prepared?

PATRIOT Well then, how—?

SUBSCRIBER Once and for all, listen! Germany, as is well known, was attacked. In March 1914 there were already Siberian regiments—

PATRIOT Of course.

SUBSCRIBER So Germany was fully prepared for a defensive war that it had long wanted to wage, and the Entente had long wanted to wage an offensive war, but wasn't prepared for it.

PATRIOT Ah, now what seemed to be a contradiction is becoming clear to me. Sometimes you think something is true, and yet it's false.

SUBSCRIBER In the *Presse* that often sticks out a mile, where you've two columns one beside the other, and it has the advantage that you can see the difference between us and them clear as day.

PATRIOT Did you read about the Italian soldiers looting and causing havoc?!

They took a good 500,000 crowns from an armour-plated safe in Gradisca and 12,000 from another safe into the bargain!

SUBSCRIBER So I read. Bandits! What do you say to the colossal German victory?

PATRIOT I didn't see that, where was it?

SUBSCRIBER What a question! In the next column! It seems to me you don't read thoroughly enough—

PATRIOT The next column? I must have missed that completely. Where was the victory?

SUBSCRIBER In Novogeorgievsk. "Gold in the spoils of Novogeorgievsk" was the title.

PATRIOT And what did it say?

SUBSCRIBER It said: Among the spoils of victory from Novogeorgievsk there were also two million gold roubles.

PATRIOT Brilliant! The things they lay their hands on—!

(Change of scene.)

Scene 27

Position near the Uzsock Pass.

AUSTRIAN GENERAL *(surrounded by his officers)*—The war, gentlemen, has left its mark on each and every one of us, and I must say it's been instructive. But we haven't finished the business yet, gentlemen, not by a long chalk—much remains to be done, dear me, yes! We have won battle honours to emblazon on our colours, splendid victories, as the envious must concede, but it is imperative that, for the next war, we introduce some organization. It's true we have talents in abundance, what we lack is organization. That must be your ambition, each and every one of you, to introduce organization. Look gentlemen, say what you like against the Germans, but they've got organization, you can't begrudge them that—I've said it before and I'll say it again, if only we had a tiny bit of organization, the rest would take care of itself—but as it is, organization is what we lack. There the Germans are ahead of us, you've got to give them that. Certainly there are some things where we're ahead of them—that certain something, for instance, our style, that easy-going, devil-may-care *je ne sais quoi*, no one can begrudge us that—but when we get ourselves into the soup, the Germans come along with their organization and—

PRUSSIAN LIEUTENANT *(appears in the doorway and calls back over his shoulder)* The Russkis can just hold their horses, they'll know soon enough what's hit 'em! (*Storms into the room without saluting, goes straight up to the general, looking him hard in the eye:*) So tell me, Excellency, why you Austrians couldn't getta grip on this crummy little pass on your own? (*Exit.*)

GENERAL (*stands for some time in a daze*) Well, what was—what was all that about? (*Turns to those around him.*) You see, gentlemen—what bravado, and more importantly—what organization!
(*Change of scene.*)

Scene 28

Headquarters. Cinema. In the front row, the commander in chief, Archduke Friedrich. Beside him his guest, King Ferdinand of Bulgaria. A Sasha film is being shown, every image depicting the effect produced by mortars. Smoke can be seen rising and soldiers falling. The sequence is repeated 14 times over an hour and a half. The military viewers are giving it their professional attention. Not a sound can be heard. Only every time the image shows the mortar producing its effect, there can be heard from the front row the word:
Ka-boom!
(*Change of scene.*)

Scene 29

Optimist and Grumbler in conversation.

OPTIMIST So, in your opinion, what would constitute a hero's death?

GRUMBLER A chance misfortune.

OPTIMIST That would be a fine thing, if the Fatherland thought like you do!

GRUMBLER That's what the Fatherland does think.

OPTIMIST What, it calls a hero's death a misfortune? Pure chance?

GRUMBLER Almost. It calls it a grievous stroke of fate.

OPTIMIST Who does? Where? No list of military casualties ever omits to speak of soldiers being privileged to die for the Fatherland, and even the humblest private individual, who otherwise might well have spoken of a grievous stroke of fate, will invariably take a certain pride in announcing in simple words that his son died a hero's death. Look, here's an example for instance, in today's *Neue Freie Presse*.

GRUMBLER So I see. But turn back a few pages. Yes, there. The Chief of the General Staff Conrad von Hötzendorf thanks the mayor for his condolences following "the grievous stroke of fate" inflicted on him by the death of his son, killed in action. That's how he put it in the obituary as well. You're quite right, every little shopkeeper whose son has been killed in action poses as a hero's father—as officially prescribed. But the Chief of the General Staff drops the mask and reverts to the traditional simple sentiment—one justified in this, of all deaths—using the conventional yet enduring formula. A Bavarian princess congratulates a relative on his son's heroic death—on that elevated social plane, one is almost expected to play the virago. The Chief of our General Staff not only accepts condolences, but repeatedly bewails the cruelty of fate. The man who is, after all, rather more closely connected to this fate than all the rest of them—more than the soldiers who may be on the receiving end, more than the fathers of the soldiers who can only lament it—the man who may not be its author, perhaps, but at least its director, and if that's too much, then let's say its stage manager or prompter—this is the man who talks of a grievous stroke of fate. He speaks the truth, all the others must tell lies. His personal pain helped him escape from obligatory heroism. The others remain its prisoner. They must tell lies.

OPTIMIST No, they don't tell lies. People are passionately moved by the hero's death, and the nation's sons feel intoxicated by the prospect of dying on the field of honour.

GRUMBLER The mothers too, alas, who might have saved this generation from such infamy, but have renounced their right to do so.

OPTIMIST Because they were not yet ready for your subversive ideas. And the Fatherland itself even less so. It's self-evident that those in charge must think as patriots. The instance you mentioned is fortuitous. Baron Conrad simply wrote the conventional phrase. He let something slip—

GRUMBLER Yes, a real feeling.

OPTIMIST In any case, that instance proves nothing. There's something different I want to show you that is more persuasive, and totally supportive of my view. Even you will have to acknowledge the evidence—

GRUMBLER For what?

OPTIMIST For the well-nigh miraculous unity, for this solidarity in our communal suffering, with all the social classes competing to—

GRUMBLER Get to the point!

OPTIMIST Here—wait, I must read it out to you, I want to be sure you don't miss a word: "An announcement by the War Ministry. The Telegraphic Communications Bureau reports: The Royal and Imperial War Ministry has declared the 18th August of the current year a special holiday for all personnel employed in concerns charged with the production and development of munitions and other essential equipment. The War Ministry takes this opportunity to pay tribute to

the exceptional devotion to duty and the untiring efforts of all those workers who, by the fruits of their labour, have helped our incomparably brave troops to win the sublime victor's laurels with death-defying courage." Well?
(The Grumbler remains silent.)

You're at a loss for words, it seems. The Social-Democratic press prints it under the proud headline: "Recognition for the achievements of the workforce." How many of these workers may be unhappy that they only get one day off as a reward, even if it is the Emperor's birthday—

GRUMBLER If you say so.

OPTIMIST —instead of having the satisfaction granted them of being relieved of factory work altogether—

GRUMBLER Just so.

OPTIMIST —and at long last offered the opportunity to take the munitions they merely produce in the factory and try them out at the front! The stout fellows must be inconsolable that they merely support their fellow countrymen and class comrades with the fruits of their labour and are not permitted to join them with their own death-defying courage. The chance to get to the front, the highest distinction a mortal man can—

GRUMBLER Mortality seems to be the quality most in demand. So it's your opinion that being drafted to the front is felt to be the highest reward—felt by the person so drafted, that is?

OPTIMIST Yes, I do think that.

GRUMBLER That may well be. But do you also think it is bestowed as the highest reward?

OPTIMIST I'm sure of it! You seem to be at a loss for words.

GRUMBLER Just so. That's why I must resort to the text of a public announcement, rather than respond in my own words. I shall read it out to you, I want to be sure you don't miss a word.

OPTIMIST From a newspaper?

GRUMBLER No, it's unlikely it could be published. All you would see would be a blanked-out space. But it's been posted in those factories that benefit from being under government protection, and have consequently managed to dispel any unrest in the workforce.

OPTIMIST But you've heard how passionately committed the workforce is to the war effort, and restless at most because it cannot participate in some other way. When even the War Ministry itself recognizes its dedication—

GRUMBLER You seem to want to spell out what left me speechless. Rather let the War Ministry speak for itself: "14th June 1915. It has been brought to the attention of the War Ministry that the behaviour of workers in a great number of factories operating under the War Production Law is extremely unsatisfactory in respect of discipline and morale. Insubordination, insolence, disobedience towards works managers and foremen, passive resistance, malicious damage of machinery, unauthorized absenteeism, *et cetera*, are offences against which even the instigation of penal proceedings have in many instances proved ineffective—"

OPTIMIST These people are manifestly impatient to get to the front. This privilege is being withheld from them—

GRUMBLER No, it is being offered to them: "Consequently the War Ministry is compelled to decree that such cases shall be prosecuted with the full rigour of the law. The prescribed penalties are severe, and can be made even more so through appropriate sanctions; moreover the offender, once convicted, shall draw no wages while incarcerated, so that conviction in such cases may be taken to constitute a highly effective deterrent and corrective—"

OPTIMIST Those are indeed severe penalties, and such characters have also forfeited any prospect of being sent to the front.

GRUMBLER Not quite. "Workers liable for military service who are investigated and identified by due legal process as the *ringleaders* of such outrages are no longer to be returned to their workplace after completing their sentence, but are to be transferred by the military controllers of the factories in question to the nearest reserve unit with a view to their being *drafted* to the appropriate troop formation. On arrival, these persons are to undergo immediate training and to be assigned to the nearest battalion scheduled for the front. If any worker thus *compulsorily enlisted* is classified as suitable only for sentry duties, arrangements are to be made for him, after the completion of his training, to be assigned to a sentry squad in or adjacent to the combat zone. Signed, for the War Minister, by General Schleyer with his own hand."
(The Optimist is speechless.)
You seem to be at a loss for words. As you see, people who long for the good fortune of getting to the front end up instead being sent to the front as punishment.

OPTIMIST Yes—even as a specially severe punishment!

GRUMBLER Yes, indeed—the Fatherland conceives of the opportunity to die for the Fatherland as punishment, and the most grievous punishment to boot. For the citizen, it is the highest honour. He wants to die a hero's death. Instead of which he is sent for training and assigned to the next battalion scheduled for the front. He wants to enlist, instead of which he is compulsorily enlisted.

OPTIMIST I can't believe it—a punishment!

GRUMBLER There are various degrees. First, a disciplinary measure, secondly, a tribunal hearing, thirdly, imprisonment, and fourthly, the most severe form of penalty: the front. The repeat offenders are sent to the field of honour. The ringleaders! Those with a criminal record are sentenced to a hero's death. A hero's death, for the Chief of the General Staff, namely when it is his son who dies, is a grievous blow of fate; the War Minister calls it a punishment. Both are right—the one and the other—the first true words spoken in this war.

OPTIMIST Yes, you make it difficult to be an optimist.

GRUMBLER No, that's not so. After all, I admit that true words are also uttered in wartime. Especially regarding the main point at issue. I'd almost forgotten the truest of all.

OPTIMIST Which is?

GRUMBLER Something that could almost reconcile you to "being compulsorily enlisted", or vengeance for debasing mankind as "human raw material": namely, "being activated", for as long as mobilisation lasts, as a MOB! After FLAK and KAG and RAG and all the other abominations, one almost welcomes these amputations of language—and of life. For as long as mobilisation lasts, we are truly activated as a MOB!

OPTIMIST Your approach drains the colour from every patriotic flag. Is everything a lie, everything prostitution? Where can truth be found?

GRUMBLER With the prostitutes!

Let no one dare deride the memory
of those so often spurned as Fallen Women!
They stood their ground against a greater foe,
the Monstrous Regiment of Men. They fell,
each one alone, the mistress of her fate,
not facing random threats from mere machines
from which you might escape, for they defied
the stormtroops of implacable repression.
They are the Fallen. So let's honour those
heroic victims of the field of honour
who served the greater motherland of Nature!

(Change of scene.)

Scene 30

Somewhere on the shores of the Adriatic. In the hangar of a seaplane squadron.

ALICE SCHALEK (*enters and looks around*) Of all the problems of this war, that of individual bravery interests me most. Even before the war began I often pondered the nature of heroism, for I had met men aplenty who put their lives on the line—American cowboys, pioneering explorers in the jungles and primeval forests, missionaries in the desert. But they usually looked like you imagine heroes look, every muscle taut as if forged of steel. How different the heroes you are faced with now in the World War. They're people with a liking for the most harmless jokes, who secretly dream of hot chocolate with cream on top, and then tell you now and again of their experiences, which are among the most amazing the world has ever seen. And yet!—The War Press Bureau is now quartered on an empty steamship lying at anchor in a bay. In the evening a big dinner, music and wild goings-on; shut your eyes, and you could imagine yourself back in the old days at some jolly revel in the mess. Well, I'm dying to find out how the sub-lieutenant of this frigate—ah, here he is! (*The sub-lieutenant of the frigate has entered.*) I haven't much time, so keep it brief. You are a bombardier, so, what do you feel when you're dropping bombs?

SUB-LIEUTENANT OF FRIGATE Usually we circle the enemy coast for half an hour or so, drop a few bombs on the military targets, watch them explode, photograph the fireworks, and then return to base.

SCHALEK Have you ever been in mortal danger?

SUB-LIEUTENANT Yes.

SCHALEK What did you feel?

SUB-LIEUTENANT What did I feel?

SCHALEK (*aside*) He looks at me closely and somewhat askance, weighing up subconsciously how I can be expected to understand what is still in a state of turmoil in his mind. (*To him*) We noncombatants labour under such stereotyped concepts as courage and cowardice that the frontline officer must always suspect we have no ear for the infinite multitude of nuances continually changing and shaping his feelings. That's my guess—am I right?

SUB-LIEUTENANT What? You're a noncombatant?

SCHALEK Don't take offence at that. You are a combatant and I would like to know how it feels. And above all, what it feels like afterwards.

SUB-LIEUTENANT Well, it's strange—it's like being a king who suddenly turns into a beggar. You know, you almost do feel like a king, soaring at such an inaccessible height, high above an enemy town. There they are, down below, defenceless—at our mercy. No one can run away, no one can save himself or take cover. You've got power over everything and everyone. There's something majestic in that, it puts everything else in the shade, Nero must have felt something similar.

SCHALEK I can understand your feelings. Have you ever bombed Venice? What's this, you've got scruples? Let me tell you something. The problem of Venice is one that needs pondering long and hard. When we entered this war, we were full of romantic ideas—

SUB-LIEUTENANT Who was?

SCHALEK We were. Our intention was to wage war chivalrously. Slowly and after painful object lessons we've cured ourselves of that habit. Which of us, only a year ago, would not have been horrified at the possibility of bombs being dropped on Venice! But now? Just the opposite! When they shoot at our soldiers from Venice, then our soldiers have to shoot back at Venice, calmly, openly and without sentiment. The problem will only become an acute one when England—

SUB-LIEUTENANT Do I need telling? Put your mind at rest, I've bombed Venice.

SCHALEK Bravo!

SUB-LIEUTENANT In peacetime I used to head for Venice all the time, I loved it dearly. But when I bombed it from above—no, I didn't feel the slightest flicker of false sentimentality. And then we all flew happily back to base. It was our finest hour—a day to be proud of!

SCHALEK That's all I need to hear. Now your comrade is waiting for me in his submarine. I hope he proves as valiant as you! (*Exit.*)

(Change of scene.)

Scene 31

In a U-boat that has just surfaced.

MATE Here they come!

OFFICER Submerge again fast!—No, too late.

(Enter the journalists of the War Press Bureau, led by Alice Schalek.)

Gentlemen, yours are the first faces we've seen. It's a strange feeling being back in daylight.

JOURNALISTS Well, tell us, what's it like down there—?

OFFICER Terrible. But up here—

JOURNALISTS Give us details.

OFFICER He'll give you them, the mate—

JOURNALISTS The maid? Schalek? Why only her? What about us? (*After clearing up this misunderstanding, the journalists descend on the mate.*) So, are those the torpedo tubes?

MATE No, they're the potash cartridges for breathing through in emergencies.

JOURNALISTS Aren't those the diesel motors?

MATE No, they're water tanks.

OFFICER (*turns to Alice Schalek*) You haven't said a word yet?

ALICE SCHALEK I feel as if I'd lost the power of speech. Permit me to touch on something that's puzzling me. What I'd like to know is what you felt when you plunged this colossus with so many men in its belly down towards a silent watery grave.

OFFICER At first I felt over the moon—

SCHALEK That's all I need. Now I'm quite sure of one thing: The Adriatic is ours forever!
(*Change of scene.*)

Scene 32

A factory requisitioned under the emergency regulations of the War Powers Act.

MILITARY SUPERVISOR Put 'em in chains, flog 'em, lock 'em up, and if all else fails, compulsory enlistment for front-line service—there's nothing else we can do, that's the lot. Our hands are tied.

FACTORY OWNER (*with a dog whip dangling from his wrist*) As far as possible, I try kindness. (*He points to the dog whip.*) But I'm at a loss to know what to do if these snivelling trades unionists keep on stirring up trouble—agitating for negotiations about the workers' terms of employment, complaining about the food—how are we expected to keep going with all their claims about legal status and working conditions and the changes to workers' rights in wartime—

MILITARY SUPERVISOR You're telling me! Compulsory enlistment for 'em, and if possible for their union representatives too. As it is, we've wrung all we can from the War Production Act and the Army Reserve Act. No one can reproach us of negligence on that score. Best of all was the business in August 1914 with the blacksmiths and mechanics. In the morning they were still earning their 6 crowns for piecework, at midday the recruiting sergeant told them straight out: you're in the army now, and behold, without a hitch, by the afternoon they were doing the same work at the same workplace—for soldiers' pay. Complaints? Not a dicky-bird. But if you ask me, there's no need for any recruiting sergeant—

FACTORY OWNER Oh ho!

MILITARY SUPERVISOR I mean, what we did at the Service Corps Depot in Klosterneuburg should have been done everywhere. I simply told 'em, you're in the army now, so you're only entitled to soldiers' pay.

FACTORY OWNER Ah ha!

MILITARY SUPERVISOR One day they complained about rough treatment or what have you. I had them report to me and asked them who'd put them up to it. The fellow replies: "We're organized workers and we asked our unions for advice, and they sent us two representatives"! All right, then, I say, let's send for these gentlemen and they can join you and do some work instead of stirring up trouble. At that the fellow says: "We're organized workers doing our duty for the Fatherland, but we also look to our union for protection." I—

FACTORY OWNER The dog whip—nothing else works! So, Lieutenant, what did you—

MILITARY SUPERVISOR What did I do? Traitors, the lot of you, I told 'em, and in case you feel like complaining again in future, 30 days confined to barracks, and that's final! Case dismissed!

FACTORY OWNER So lenient! I'm amazed! It was high treason!

MILITARY SUPERVISOR Well, you know, one mustn't overdo it. The sad thing is, the civil courts still support the blighters.

FACTORY OWNER I know of such a case. At Lenz's steelworks, in Traisen, where the fellows were getting paid 25 crowns a week as it is, two of them sued to get that overturned because the rate had originally been 44. The district court found against Lenz. You should have seen the smile on the faces of those two rascals as they left the courtroom!—

MILITARY SUPERVISOR I know the case—two policemen carted them back to the factory. The military supervisor there, a mate of mine, lands them with 10 days confined to quarters—and back to work. What a shining pillar of the state those courts are, I must say! Fortunately Lenz is the mayor, so he can have people detained on his say-so. That's what he did with those women workers, had patrols pick 'em up on Christmas Day, off to the workplace and then into detention.

FACTORY OWNER They complained about me once to the union because of "ill-treatment" and inadequate wages. I ask you—38 to 60 cents an hour!

Well, I sent for one of the ringleaders and said: You put in a complaint, but you know what this dog whip is for? And I brandish it. Up chirps the fellow: "We aren't dogs." So I just point to my gun holster and say: "For you, I've a revolver too." He starts banging on about—"human dignity" or something. Anyway, the fellow really did manage in the end to get the complaints board to say the pay was too low!

MILITARY SUPERVISOR But of course he was immediately—

FACTORY OWNER Of course, compulsorily enlisted. Your predecessor was very obliging in that respect. There was another one who complained about too low pay, I had 'im flogged and your predecessor slapped on three weeks in the cooler.

MILITARY SUPERVISOR I'll give you no cause for complaint either, you'll see. Those fellows should be glad they're not working in a mine, that's all I say.

FACTORY OWNER I know. The military command in Leitmeritz made it a lot easier for the mine owners. The workers are simply reminded they took their oath on the articles of war, so complaining can in certain circumstances be interpreted as mutiny, in which case the instigators and ringleaders can be summarily court-martialled and condemned to death. Ah yes, the mine owners—

MILITARY SUPERVISOR At the anthracite cooperative in Eibiswald in Styria they have to work Sunday shifts, there's no restaurant or café open after 8 pm. What's more, during five days in detention they have to serve three on bread and water. They're taken under escort from the pit straight to the communal detention centre, and that's a fair distance. In Ostrava they started flogging right from the start of the war, systematically! On a bench in the police station, held down by two soldiers. The fellow got another thrashing after he squealed to his union rep. Anyone who complains—compulsorily enlisted, even if they've no military training. That's how to treat 'em!

FACTORY OWNER (*sighing*) The mine owners have it made! They can keep going!

MILITARY SUPERVISOR Yes, but nowadays you other employers aren't exactly unprotected either. The foremen see to that! They know how to give a good clip round the ear. Six hours daily in handcuffs, that's what I always hand out to those in detention. And when they're marched straight from the factory through the streets at the point of a bayonet—that sets the right example! No shower beforehand, their head shaved once they're brought in, even if it's only a 24-hour stretch, the cost of food deducted from their wages—even if they only have to go from Floridsdorf to Josefstadt to report, that's half a day's pay gone, without even counting the lost wages when they're detained, and such like, and then, to top it all—if only for the more serious cases—compulsorily enlisted! So you see, none of the employers ever had anything to complain about!

FACTORY OWNER Listen, you won't find me complaining. It's well known I don't bother the military authorities except in an emergency. I prefer to take care of things myself. What I say is: as long as kindness does the trick—(*he points to his dog whip.*)

(*Change of scene.*)

Scene 33

Room in Hofrat Schwarz-Gelber's house. Late evening. Enter Hofrat and Hofrätin Schwarz-Gelber.

HIM (*breathing heavily*) Thank God, sound the trumpets, made it—aah—

HER What a drama, playing the martyr.

HIM That's the last time—rest assured—the last time!

HER And the last time for me, too—with you! You can bet your life on that! (*She begins to get undressed. He sinks into an armchair, rests his head in his hands, jumps up again and paces around the room.*)

HIM Why—please tell me—the one thing I want to know: why oh why did God curse me with you—why did it have to be me that has to live this life?—why couldn't it have been someone else?!—I've strained every sinew from dawn to dusk—for you—you're killing me with your war welfare—your charity committees and branch offices and all the rest of it, concerts and sewing-bees and tea salons and twiddling your thumbs at meetings, and hospitals, day after day hospitals—God, what sort of life is that!—(*going over to her aggressively*) what—what more do you want from me—isn't it ever enough—I—I—I'm not a well man—I'm not—in good health—

HER (*screeching*) Why are you kvetching at me? Me force you? It's you who are forcing me! If only I'd a single day's rest from you!—I—didn't I have to schlep you up and down till they said: give us a break—and made you vice president! You think they're queuing up for you? It's me you have to thank for it—if I hadn't been hanging on to Professor Exner's coattails the whole time—God, how I had to twist his arm—I'll tell you what you are! An idealist, that's what you are! You think you'd have got where you are today any other way! Which what way? Your handsome mug, eh? Your oily smarm, perhaps? Just so you know, it's me you have to thank for your whole career, me, me, me—Liharzik is dead—you could be today where he was, you could be anywhere—but you're a dishrag!

You, of all people, you're handed things on a plate—I give you a push and you don't budge an inch—you dream your pipe dreams but you haven't got the chutzpah to nail it!

HIM For God's sake, lay off—shut your gob—with my social status—I'm risking enough—

HER Don't give me that shtick about status, we've gotta get moving. Your status-matus! Who d'ya think you are? I made all the running for your status! I did the legwork! Was it for my own sake? Was it for my sake I ran from pillar to post? Get real!

HIM What else?

HER Oh, stop kvetching I can't stand the sight of you! You know it's all baloney. My God, you hounded me to be in one place one day and somewhere else the next—always hassling me—if Grünfeld was giving a piano recital, I had to make a speech—the things I had to put up with—I didn't know whether I was coming or going, was it a meeting at Countess Berchtold's or tea with Countess Bienerth; I thought the flower parade was for promoting sponsorship rather than in aid of the refugees, then there was that Korngold première, and a constant stream of funerals and prize races, the Iron Warrior and his Shield, and when they suggested a presentation war goblet, you were thrilled right away, in all these years I've never seen you like that before, you insisted on being involved from the start, said it wouldn't work without you, I said leave me out of it, but no, you hounded me, you literally pushed me to go to all those teas and committees, you tortured me over laurels for our heroes, so I went chasing all round the shop, nothing but charity events, in aid of this, in aid of that, in aid of who else, I ask you, but you? Give me a break! And when I think back on today—God—traipsing from one hospital to the next—all for what? All for what? Ingratitude!

HIM For Heaven's sake, now you stop kvetching! To hear you talk, anyone would wonder if you know what it means to love thy neighbour. It makes me puke—

HER It makes *you* puke! Can I help it if they overlooked you today? I swear to you, I schmoozed the War Welfare commissioner, I told him, when they come, he should see to it that we get places right at the front, since we were unlucky last time, at the last minute I gave him another nudge, he knows I've got some pull with Hirsch—he hasn't mentioned him in the *Neue Freie Presse* for some time—I did everything possible, I was standing almost next to Princess Blanka when she told the blind man it was for the Fatherland—and you want to take your rage out on me! Is it my fault Angelo Eisner plonked himself in front of us at the last minute and we couldn't see a thing for his bulk? You're out of luck because he's bigger, but I'm the one who has to carry the can! You blame me—

me—but I—I—you know what you are—you know what you are—me—a Bardach, from one of the best families (*screeching*)—I'm far too good for a creature like you (*she throws her corset at him*)—you—you nobody—you wally!

HIM (*rushes at her and grabs her*) You—you—don't get me worked up—don't get me worked up, I tell you—I won't answer for myself—if I lay my hands on you—what—what—what do you want from me—you scumbag—you want nothing for yourself?—Your ambition will be the death of me! If you'd had children you'd have had something else to think about—look at me—the grey hairs are because of you (*sobbing*)—I—I—I went to see Hochsinger—it's my heart—it's no longer—what it should be—that's your fault—(*bellowing*) now you'll hear the truth—for you can't even claim to be—another Flora Dub!—the fortune I'd need to keep you in hats—where am I—supposed to get the readies—what more do you want from me—

HER (*in a paroxysm of rage*) Flora—Dub!—You have the nerve—me, in the same breath—with Flora—me and Dub!—me—a Bardach by birth! You know what you are—a pushy, ambitious little creep! Risen from the gutter! Green with envy! And a face black as thunder if you happen to be overlooked! Whenever you think of Eisner, you toss and turn in your sleep! Is it my fault he's an aristocrat? Why don't you go to Fürstenberg and get him to adopt you!

HIM (*softening*) Ida—what have I done to you—look—let me speak—seriously—look—what am I—Hofrat—me—ludicrous—a Jew is what I am!—(*He sinks, sobbing, into the armchair.*)—How do I put up with it!—Is that—is that—a way to live—always at the back—right at the back—behind all the others—having to depend on Hirsch—the last time we—the last price-raising—I mean prize-racing—they didn't—even—notice us—(*becoming calmer*)—I even pushed you forward—Countess Wydenbruck noticed—commented on it—and today—scandal!—people talking—I'm finished—Spitzy laughed—

HER Let Spitzy go hang! What's he got to laugh about! Spitzy only got where he is because of the World War. Before that, his name never appeared in the papers. But now? Every page, day in, day out, they *fawn* on Spitzy—it makes you puke!

HIM *Von* Spitzy! Surely he hasn't been enobled—that'd be the last straw!

HER It's enough to make you spit!

HIM He wants to be one of those twits.

HER Waiting for Spitzy! My gut feeling is he fancies he's Spitzer.

HIM Give the man a medal—if it fits!

HER I said as much to the commissioner. Can't do a thing, he says, that's typical

Vienna for you, he says. Look, he says, Spitzy—scuse me!—has got the press in his pocket, and besides, he helps with the provision of artificial limbs.

HIM That commissioner—I could tell you a thing or two about him!

HER For me he's a pain in the neck.

HIM The contrast between the Gartenbau today, a military hospital, and when the war began—what a change of tune! When I think back to the Battle of Lemberg, you remember, when the *Neue Freie Presse* celebrated its jubilee, Mayor Weiskirchner sent his congratulations, only the other day I was telling Professor Sieghart—

HER You, telling Sieghart?

HIM You—you don't remember—me talking to Sieghart? No one in the world would believe you!—Everyone saw it!—You don't remember? How he came over to ask us to go on the subcommittee for support groups—you must remember, he had the idea of fund-raising for "Caviar for the People", actually the idea came from that poet Kulka—anyway, I said to Sieghart, Excellency, I said, I don't much care for the commissioner, I don't care for the head of the clinic, and I don't care for all that worthless crew. He doesn't reply, but I can see he's thinking it over. I say to him, Excellency, the situation is much too grave. Well, all I can tell you is, he didn't say no. What's behind it, I ask. He shrugs and says, "There's a war on." That told me all I needed to know. Now all I need—

HER If you hadn't just stood there like a wally at the constituent assembly for the Valhalla Association, the whole thing would have been settled already.

HIM Excuse me, but that's just the sort of occasion where I try to avoid being conspicuous. Everyone was sticking their neck out when the fellow from the Wilhelm Press Agency turned up—

HER And I was signalling to you to do the same!

HIM No, I tell you. You should know me better than that! It can't be done in the public eye, so pin your ears back. Eisner, you wait and see, is capable of going up to see them one fine day and wangling it. But I've made up my mind—I'm just waiting for—the next opportunity—I could really get him into hot water—don't tell anyone, but he let drop a derogatory remark about Hirsch!

HER Hold on, don't stir up trouble! Don't get mixed up in anything! I could do the same, but I've always held back, Flora Dub said things about Alice Schalek—said she throws her weight around during the battle, and things like that—I could drop a hint to General Odelga's wife, I reckon she'll be at the tea in aid of the invalids on Sunday—listen to me, Sigmund—don't be so neurotic—you're overstressed—I tell you, we'll get there in the end! Pull yourself together—I bet you Friday is our big chance—surely you remember, the afternoon tea for our prisoners in Eastern Siberia. No listen, wait, even better—Saturday, the one for the German warriors! You'll see, you'll hit the jackpot! If not at one, at the other. Guaranteed! There's no way we're putting it off until the cabaret for the Navy League! Go and show them what you're made of! Take a leaf from Haas's book—*Baron* Haas!—him, not her—he's only a goy, but what chutzpah!—I'm telling you! Now it's make or break. Just don't go acting the dummy on me again, do you hear! All they're waiting for is for you to open your mouth. As I live and breathe—I can't help feeling we're already on the list as it is—

HIM You really think so—wouldn't that be—it's been a long, hard slog—too long—but what makes you think—?

HER Not just think—I know! You think it's hopeless. I say, nothing's hopeless! You've always been a pessimist about this war. I can't tell you the whole story, but as you know, that Frankl-Singer woman on the *Sonn-und Montagszeitung* is a close friend of Frau Lubomirska, my lips are sealed. You should have seen Dub's face when she saw me talking to her. How shall I put it, she was throwing a fit. Even Siegfried Löwy was nodding his head, so it was all as clear as daylight to me. It could be one of my greatest achievements if it comes off. Only, the sponsors of the soup kitchens mustn't hear about it or the good ladies will blow their top—according to Polacco. Even today I had a feeling, it can't be long now. You remember the commotion—when they all descended on that soldier on his deathbed—you know, the one who was kicking up a fuss because he thought his mother was downstairs but they wouldn't let her come up, against the regulations, Hirsch even said his heroism will live on in the annals of history, he'll headline it in the press—that's when I had the feeling—when they were all gathered there—I was paying particular attention, I looked and quite distinctly saw the Lady-in-Waiting looking over at us, believe me, everyone was pointing us out—I wanted to catch your eye—but I had to keep watching that tall gentleman, in case he comes by—and then they started discussing again—just as Hirsch was making notes on the atmosphere, they were discussing the concert for the widows and orphans—that's when I had the feeling again—I can't help it—(*close to him, hissing*) if only you don't become a shrinking violet!—now's not the time!—any other time, fine, but for God's sake, not now!

HIM (*ponders a while, then resolutely*) What's on tomorrow?

HER (*hurriedly sorts out invitations*) Vienna aids Ortelsburg—that's a drag, we'd better go, but we don't really have to. Afternoon tea for the Injured at Thury's, pointless, but can do no harm. Constituent assembly of the executive committee for the Sausage Day in aid of convalescent Tyrolean Chasseurs—I have to do that one, I'm their patroness. But wait a minute, here we are, War Welfare Bureau, musical tea, Fritz Werner will sing, I'm sure to get to talk to him, he really has influence—

HIM Says you!

HER I'm telling you, he has!

HIM Influence, ludicrous—

HER Oh yeah? Well, the big chief has just asked for his portrait. He's a great admirer. He's been to see *Blood of the Hussars* at least 50 times.

HIM He's just a nodding acquaintance, no more.

HER So you know better! All right, then, let's assume Fritz Werner has no influence, what about—listen—what about Spitzer? Even if I don't set great store by people in general, I do rate Spitzer! Just look at the way they all show off when he turns up! Spitzer is the one who counts these days, people talk of nothing but Spitzer's career! I tell you, we must strike while the iron's hot, while we can still turn it into gold! No dithering now! Listen to what I'm saying—what's this all for otherwise—pull yourself together, be a man! Make people like you! What is there to think about? You've always managed it before, why not now? So, grit your teeth and see it through to the end!

HIM (*holding his head in his hands*) It all flitted past so quickly today. Couldn't cope—not a hope! I wasn't in good fettle today. I felt something was wrong straight away. From the very start I noticed they took no notice of us, and at the end when they did notice us, I was too distracted to notice. I tell you, it's my heart—Hochsinger insists I should take it easy. Take it easy, he says, take it really easy. But how can I—my God—go on, tell me, what were they all actually saying to Spitzer when he—

HER To Spitzer? But that wasn't today! That was Sunday!

HIM For Heaven's sake—the cross I have to bear—Sunday—my head's swimming—all right, then—it would have been worse if I'd forgotten to speak to Sieghart, God forbid! So how, or what—anyway, tell me—about Spitzer, I want to know—

HER Sunday? Well, they were within a hair's breadth of the commissioner—I was quite sure—how could you doubt it? Listen, it was staring you in the face! If that beanstalk of a nurse hadn't poked her nose in, you know, the one with the weird idea of nursing all day long, everyone knows how unbalanced she is, just as I was about to go over to the bed, damn it, she shows up, I was only a step away—

HIM Wait a second! That was—wait—where were they standing? Wasn't that when they were talking about launching a new appeal—I remember, a Gardenia Day or something along those lines, and they decided in aid of Viennese Fashion in the Home, or—

HER Exactly, Trebitsch even said he'd given 1,000 crowns anonymously—

HIM Pompous ass, everyone says so, now he's posing as an intimate friend of Reitzes—you see, I've got it now, wait a second, of course I know! Don't interrupt me, there was also, it's coming back to me, there was also talk of taking shots in the hospital for the Sascha Film Company, that too makes me want to puke, so you see, I do remember! But one thing—where were they standing? The situation—we didn't get through, that I know—we were forced back—

HER You don't remember? I can see it now! At the bedside of the soldier—

HIM At his bedside—the one with his mother?

HER Come on, that was today!

HIM Wait a minute—the blind one!

HER Princess Blanka's blind soldier? That was today!

HIM But when Archduke Salvator—

HER Salvator's blind one—that was on Tuesday in the Polyclinic! The blind soldier, I can see the whole scene now! You remember—Hirsch had his notebook out—

HIM Excuse me, but that was while they were serving refreshments at the railway reception! When that divorcée, Löbl-Speiser, pushed in front of us—

HER Just the opposite, things were looking really good, if you'd only followed my advice and latched on to Stiassny.

HIM Stiassny? But that was at the Iron Warrior! You see, now you're mixing things up!

HER (*raising her voice*) Me, mix things up! You're mixing things up! The Iron Warrior? Who's interested in the Iron Warrior these days?

HIM Wait a minute, then—at the bed of—why all these riddles, tell me the soldier's name and be done with it.

HER Not after all that! Now you see how far you'd get if it wasn't for me and my memory—

HIM You and your memory! What good is your memory to me! Bah—it's a dog's breakfast!

HER You're tormenting me—here's me run off my feet—and I have to help you remember as well!

HIM Stop shouting—I'll throw it all up—I'm not going tomorrow—you can go to your soup kitchen by yourself—I've had it up to here—to hell with the whole war!—that's all we needed—as if there wasn't enough running around as it is—get out of my sight!—my patience is snapping!—as far as I'm concerned, you can go—

HER (*screeching*) You're kvetching because you've no memory! You don't remember who you say good-day to! You say good-day to people you don't need to, and when you do need to, you don't! Every time we walk along the Graben I have to keep prodding you! The work I've done for you—you—you know what you are without me? Without me, you're a social nobody—you're a nerd!

HIM (*covering his ears, eyes raised to the ceiling*) Don't be so vulgar—! (*After a pause, during which he walks up and down.*) So would you now be so kind?—Have you calmed down? So tell me then—

HER No, why should I—Sunday—they're all gathered round the bed—I go forward—they're all—

HIM Wait! Let me finish—they're all in the staff room—

HER (*screeching*) You're tearing my heart out—as if you can't count up to three—I'm run off my feet—from pillar to post—

HIM And I am grateful. I know it's not easy.

HER Enough already! Don't keep nagging me—you've got the message at last and can stop asking me questions—I'm the one who's right, not you—I've already told you, they noticed us on Sunday—when they were gathered around the bed—

HIM Wot-d'ya-mean! Around the bed?—surely you're imagining that—

HER As I live and breathe! At the bed of the soldier when the head doctor showed us everything—

HIM Ah—now I remember! Why didn't you say so right away? The one who'd lost his feet from frostbite?

HER Yeah—and won a medal for bravery!

ACT III

Scene 1

Vienna. At the corner where the Kärntnerstrasse meets the Ring and people take their evening stroll. Masked figures and spectral apparitions all want to be part of the action. Romania has just entered the war on the side of the Entente.

FIRST NEWSPAPER VENDOR Ex-tra-aa edi-shun—! Venice bombarded! Eye-talians routed!

FIRST ARMY PROFITEER You should've read the Evening Edition, it leaves no room for doubt.

SECOND ARMY PROFITEER It was an authentic report?

SECOND NEWSPAPER VENDOR Ex-tra-aa edi-shun—! 100,000 Eye-talians killed!

FIRST ARMY PROFITEER I'm telling you: Kramer is to give guest performances in Marienbad from the first of the month—verbatim.

THIRD NEWSPAPER VENDOR Kragujevac conquered!

SECOND ARMY PROFITEER Thank God for that. Means my wife will be staying away a bit longer.

FIRST ARMY PROFITEER Your lovely lady?

FOURTH NEWSPAPER VENDOR *Tagblatt*, second edi-shun! German communiqué!

FIRST OFFICER (*to three others*) Evening Nowotny, evening Pokorny, evening Powolny—the very man! You know all about politics. Come on, tell us, what d'ya say to Romania?

SECOND OFFICER (*with walking stick*) Y'know, I say it's just the same as with Italy—treachery!

THIRD OFFICER Yep—that's spot-on.

FOURTH OFFICER Absolutely—I was at a bash in the mess last night—! D'ya see the latest Schönpflug cartoon? Fantabulous!

YOUNG GIRL Eight thousand Russians for 10 cents!

GIRL (*waggling her hips, under her breath*) Great Eye-talian fig-tree!

WOMAN (*face bright red, comes running*) Venice bombasted!

THIRD OFFICER What's she shouting? Venice—?

SECOND OFFICER Gave me a shock, that—did it give you a shock too?—but it's not our Venice in the Prater, it's only the other one.

THIRD OFFICER Ah.

FOURTH OFFICER Go on, did you think our own lot—

SECOND OFFICER No, I thought maybe Italian planes, well, why not—

FIRST OFFICER Don't be so lily-livered! Yesterday I got a postcard from the front, what d'ya say to that!

SECOND OFFICER From Fallota, I bet!

THIRD OFFICER What's friend Fallota up to, d'ya know? Still the philosopher? Or has he seen a bit of real life by now? I must say, I see a lot of life these days in the War Ministry.
(*Enter two devotees of the* Reichspost.)

FIRST DEVOTEE OF THE *REICHSPOST* We've already come to terms with the demands made on us by the God of War. We've managed to bear those burdens so far, and are firmly resolved to go on bearing them, with a will, through to a successful conclusion.

SECOND DEVOTEE OF THE *REICHSPOST* The war also bestows blessings. It inculcates its lessons with vigour, licking the nations into shape with an iron rod.

FIRST DEVOTEE The war dispenses benefits too, it awakens man's noblest virtues, wresting Promethean energies of light and fire from the heavens.

SECOND DEVOTEE The war truly bestows life and light, it is mighty in its admonishments, a harbinger of truth and well of knowledge.

FIRST DEVOTEE What a wealth of virtues this war has already revived, virtues we thought sunk in the mire of materialism and egoism that defines our age.

SECOND DEVOTEE Have you already signed the war-loan pledge?

FIRST DEVOTEE Have you?

BOTH TOGETHER We've already come to terms with the demands made on us by the God of War. (*Exeunt.*)

REGULAR SUBSCRIBER TO THE *NEUE FREIE PRESSE* (*in conversation with the oldest subscriber*) That's interesting: today's *Presse* says tomorrow's edition of the official Hungarian *Gazette* will announce the conferment of the title royal counsellor on the chief clerk of Ignaz & Son in Budapest, Emil Morgenstern.

OLDEST SUBSCRIBER Amazing news! (*Exeunt.*)

CRIPPLE (*two stumps and open-mouthed, one hand holding shoelaces, the other newspapers, in a hollow staccato*) Ex-tra-aa edi-shun—! Half of Serrbia totally conquered!

THIRD OFFICER Serbia totally—?

POLDI FESCH (*to a companion*) I was planning to go out partying with the Sascha Film people tonight, but—(*exit.*)

FOURTH OFFICER That's nothing, didn't you hear, 100,000 dead Eyeties taken prisoner! (*Two disabled war veterans hobble past.*)

SECOND OFFICER Nothing but draft dodgers wherever you look. Makes you almost ashamed to be in Vienna.

(*Older age group of conscripts march past, singing "In der Heimat, in der Heimat da gibt's ein Wiedersehn"*—)

THIRD OFFICER Know what, let's go along to Hopfner's!

FOURTH OFFICER It's dead today. Always the same tarts—

FIRST OFFICER (*leaving*) Romania, y'know—that's no joke—know what I think, though, we can count on the Germans to—(*exit.*)

FIFTH NEWSPAPER VENDOR Ex-tra-aa edi-shun—! Fig-tree on all fronts! Romanians advancing!

CABBY'S VOICE "There's a war on, it'll cost you 10 times that!"

(*Change of scene.*)

Scene 2

In front of our artillery positions.

ALICE SCHALEK Isn't that one of our unsung heroes, the common man at the front? He'll be able to tell me in simple words what the psychology of war is. His job is to pull the string that ignites the fuse on the firing pin of the mortar—ostensibly a simple task, and yet, what incalculable consequences for the arrogant enemy *and* for the Fatherland are attached to this crucial moment! Is he conscious of that? And can he rise to the occasion, spiritually? Admittedly, all those sitting comfortably back home know about fuses is that they sometimes blow out, nor do they have any conception of what heroic possibilities the common man at the front, the very one who ignites the fuse on a mortar—(*she turns to a gunner.*) So tell me, what do you feel when you pull that string?

(The gunner looks puzzled.)
Well, what insights does it give you? Look, as an example of the common man, one of our unsung heroes, you surely must—
(The gunner is struck dumb.)
I mean, what are you thinking when you fire the mortar, you must be thinking something, so what is it you're thinking?

GUNNER *(after a pause, during which he sizes Schalek up)* Damn all!

ALICE SCHALEK *(turning away in disappointment)* Call that an example of the common man! He will remain unsung! *(She continues along the front.)*
(Change of scene.)

Scene 3

On the Isonzo front. A command post.
Enter Lieutenants Fallota and Beinsteller.

FALLOTA *(eating)* Y'know, I just picked up this crumpet, wanna share?

BEINSTELLER *(takes it)* Hump it, eh? Good for you. Still up for it!

FALLOTA Y'know, say what you like, but our lot really do look after art—make sure nothing happens to things worth seeing—monuments and curiosities and what have you. I was just reading in the *Deutsches Volksblatt*—look, here it is—a report from the War Press Bureau: The Italian and French papers are spreading the tendentious falsehood that our troops and the German troops in the occupied parts of Russia are turning Greek-orthox—ordox sanctuaries, such as churches and monasteries, into restaurants, cafés, and cinemas. This assertion is a wilful fictitious libel. It is a truth universally acknowledged that our troops—and the same holds true for our allies—always treat churches and monasteries on enemy territory with the greatest piety. In our army, the respect due to places devoted to religion is an irrefutable fact, one that none of our soldiers has violated, even in this war.—So there you have it, in black and white.

BEINSTELLER Just shows you, the lies people tell in wartime.

FALLOTA Y'know, I can vouch for that, I was once myself in a cinema in Russia that had previously been a church—and I tell you, you couldn't see the slightest trace of any devastation—impleccable!

BEINSTELLER Sure, there were a few Jewish cemeteries—I saw them myself—all a bit of a shambles, and the gravestones they'd helped themselves to. But what we did in Greece to the orthodox sanctuaries, I wasn't there, so I can't say.

FALLOTA Y'know, it would be a fine thing if everyone were as crapulous when it comes to works of art. I read in the paper, look, here it is, in the *Journal de Genève*, the lead article—

BEINSTELLER Farticle. (*Laughter.*)

FALLOTA —calls for all Swiss citizens to sign a petition to His Majesty, appealing to his benevolence and magnanimity, to vouchsafe protection for works of—

BEINSTELLER arty farty. (*Laughter.*)

FALLOTA —works of art in Italian territory occupied by the Central Powers. Then comes an editorial comment—look at this, superb!—: "Such petitions may be justified when the Entente occupies territory. When we do, they are superfluous. For we are a civilized people."

BEINSTELLER Of course we're a civilized people, but what good does it do—we tell them a hundred times, but still they moan that we're the barbarians.

FALLOTA Y'know, we'll soon knock it into their heads. When we stroll into Venice!

BEINSTELLER (*sings*)

> As victors into Venice we go,
> The statues and pictures make quite a show.
> The pretty pictures we'll use for ignition,
> When it rains we'll sit under a Titian.
> Wham! Bang! Kaboom! Grenades! Perdition!

FALLOTA Where d' ya dig that up?! That's quite a song—

BEINSTELLER Don't you know it? That's the battle song the volunteers sing in the Imperial Rifles. There are lots more verses, they get better and better, I have it somewhere, I'll write it out for you.

FALLOTA I've one for you, too. The *Macaroni March*—know it?

BEINSTELLER I've heard of it, in the Austro-Hungarian 10th Army's *War Journal*, including the music—but unfortunately that issue's out of print.

FALLOTA No problem, I know it by heart, listen. Y'know what "tzing" and "pang pang" signify?

BEINSTELLER Sure, those are the sounds a repeating rifle makes—

FALLOTA OK, and "takka takka"?

BEINSTELLER That's the report from a Mannlicher M95.

FALLOTA All right, I see you're in the picture—so listen:

Takka takka, pang pang, tzing, how we made those bullets sing!
Takka takka, pang pang, tzing, how we made those bullets sing!
The cowardly wops we shot stone dead,
The others turned around and fled.
Takka takka, pang pang, tzing, how we made those bullets sing!
Macaroni's off the menu,
The battlefield's our only venue.
Takka takka—

D'Annunzio and friend Sonnino,
Drown 'em in a vat of vino.
Takka takka—

Emmanuel, no Victor he,
His number's up, for treachery.
Takka takka—
We'll thrash you till you howl and shriek
To punish your infernal cheek.
Takka takka—
Trieste's ours, hands off! or you
Will end up beaten black and blue.
Takka takka—

The Tyrolean mountainside
Is also where we'll tan your hide.
Takka takka—
Through Villach think you to advance?
You cheeky monkeys, not a chance!
Takka takka—

Your harbours are all overflowing
With ships we've sunk, the number's growing.
Takka takka—

So there they lie, those dirty rats
Have had their noses all squashed flat.
Takka takka, pang pang, tzing, how we made those bullets sing!

BEINSTELLER (*who has accompanied each verse with gestures and exclamations, enchanted*) Takka takka, pang pang, tzing! I love it! Yes—yes—y'know, humour like that is only possible in German, it doesn't work in their idiotic languages, it's beyond them!

FALLOTA Not to mention the humour at the front—in the same issue—you simply must read it for yourself!

BEINSTELLER Hang on a minute, d'ya know this one?—I collect them, you know. (*Produces a notebook.*) Look, it's in the *War Journal* of General Linsingen's Army Group in the Carpathians: "A Happy Man." Field Grey (whose adored one has accepted his proposal of marriage): Believe me, beloved, I've never felt so happy since the day I was deloused.

FALLOTA (*doubles up*) Say, have you come across the latest collection, *The Louseleum*?

BEINSTELLER Of course.

FALLOTA Hang on—d'ya know this one? I collect them, y'know. (*Produces a notebook.*) Look, it's in the *War Journal* of the 2nd Army: "Carry on!" A recruit who's only been at the front for a few weeks has to answer a call of nature—

BEINSTELLER In a hurry, couldn't wait, the son of a bitch.

FALLOTA Hang on, wait for the punch line. So, he has to relieve himself and goes to the latrines, right up against the main village street. Two second-lieutenants pass by. Our recruit is in two minds what to do. Finally he gets up, stands to attention and salutes as per regulations. The first officer laughs and says: "As you were, carry on!" What d'ya think, that's one for the folks back home!

BEINSTELLER (*doubles up*) Hang on—d'ya know this one? It's from the 10th Army *War Journal*, more delicate, innocent-like, y'know, but funny with it. Hence the headline: "Out of the mouths of babes and sucklings." I have a full beard. One day I'm going for a bit of a walk and run into this really sweet little nipper of three or four. I look at the young gent—he looks at me. Suddenly he sticks his hand out: "Mister", he says, "why have you so much hair on your face?" Signed Zois.

FALLOTA (*doubles up*) That's Zois for you, he's a sense of humour all right!

BEINSTELLER The way he edits the *War Journal*, it's a real pleasure to read. Even his name is funny—Baron Michelangelo Zois—Michelangelo—

FALLOTA Y'know, that's a painter, some Italian or other, but Zois is not related, take it from me.

BEINSTELLER The very thought—related to an Eyetie!

(Change of scene)

Scene 4

In Jena. Two philosophy students meet.

FIRST PHILOSOPHY STUDENT I tell you, laddie, it's a wonderful life! The victor of Jutland has been made an honorary doctor of our university!

SECOND PHILOSOPHY STUDENT Doubtless for what he said about that great romantic poem.

FIRST Eh?

SECOND What, you mean you didn't know? His comment on that submarine poem!

FIRST What, you mean the poet prophesied that—?

SECOND No, no, not the original poet, I mean, the famous lines:

I wandered lonely o'er a sub
That lurks beneath the tranquil seas,
When all at once I heard a thud,
A crash to make your pulses freeze.
No trace now of the English fleet:
We're doomed to slumber in the deep.

FIRST Divine!

SECOND The sort of thing some English captain might say, but it's actually by our greatest romantic poet, isn't it?

FIRST What about Admiral Scheer, then?

SECOND Scheer said he was bowled over, thought it was terrific, and hopes the English captain's fears will soon be realized.

FIRST Amen to that! I can see now why a university as illustrious as our beloved Jena would want to make such an award—and wouldn't Schiller have been pleased! It was just after our vice chancellor had summoned one of those odious pacifist boobies and read out the ban issued by the General Command on any such activities. And did you read our vice chancellor's speech at the *Philosophy Week* conference in Bad Lauterberg? Very nice it was! I'll tell you this, things are looking up. What was it General Kluck said? "Let us blow the enemy's brains out with a bullet to the heart!" His very words, and now Scheer is an honorary doctor of the University of Jena.

SECOND Schiller was a field surgeon. On the other hand, alas, there's Hindenburg's sheer philistinism.

FIRST True. Since Königsberg awarded him an honorary doctorate after he taught those Pan-Slav scum a lesson—well, of course, they had to, for appearances' sake—but apart from that? Not a peep from him—

SECOND Yes, well, the occasional catchword, perhaps—"Give 'em a good kicking!" or "Once more into the breach!"

FIRST Though maybe that's not one of his.

SECOND Ah, but here's a phrase he's just coined: "Be on your guard against wimps!"

FIRST Only the University of Berlin could have—put like that, it's totally lacking in your typical German vigour.

SECOND Well, how should he have put it, then?

FIRST How? Simple enough: Bugger off, you defeatist turds!

SECOND Yes, well—only the navy, it seems, is firmly anchored in philosophy.

FIRST Or vice versa.

SECOND How d'you mean?

FIRST Well—look at this (*he reads out a newspaper item.*) The Schopenhauer Society met in Kiel at Whitsun, its aim being to disseminate the ideas of this great and popular, though also misunderstood, philosopher, and to deepen knowledge of his thought in popular consciousness. A visit to the naval docks rounded off the conference, at which the Imperial Navy, in the person of Corvette Captain Schaper, instructed participants in the mysteries of a top-class submarine with a lecture, followed by a viewing, including repeated dives.

SECOND Schaper seems to go even deeper than Schopenhauer.

(Change of scene.)

Scene 5

Hermannstadt in Transylvania. In front of a closed German bookshop.

PRUSSIAN INFANTRYMAN (*hammers on the door*) Open up, or we'll smash your shop to smithereens—we Germans are starving for a good read!

GERMAN BOOKSELLER (*opens*) I obey, not out of fear but out of delight at your threat. My ambition as a German bookseller is to be able to supply as many of my German brothers as possible with German books. For nothing is too good for us Germans. I see you are amazed, my German brothers, to find a bookshop full of good German books so far from the German Fatherland! Go ahead and satisfy your truly German cultural thirst among them, while I sit right down and write a report for the German book trade's *Börsenblatt* about this typically German occurrence.

(Change of scene.)

Scene 6

In Vinzenz Chramosta's grocery shop.

CHRAMOSTA *(to a woman)* The cottage cheese? Four crowns the quarta-pound—Wot, too much? It'll cost yer 6 by the weekend, sniff at it and yer can go round the corner and buy the crap there, it's cheaper, g'day to you!—*(To a man)* Wot yer want? Wanna taste? Are yer crazy? There's a war on! Try that crap too, see if it tastes better!—*(To a woman)* Stop pushing, wait yer turn! Wot yer want? A cucumber? They go by weight, but I'm tellin yer, the smallest is 2 crowns!—*(To a man)* Wot? A sausage? Get lost, where d'yer think we can get hold of sausages these days, cretin—the things people get into their head, amazing!—*(To a woman)* Wot yer staring at? That's the right weight, including the paper—it weighs too. There's a war on! If yer doan like it, give it 'ere, but doan let me catch sight of yer again, stupid old bag, and that's final!—*(To a man)* You back there, that's enough muttering, think I'm deaf? There's zilch for ya 'ere today—I've 'ad a bellyful of customers like you, clear orff!—*(To a woman)* The lettuce is 12 crowns!—Wot? It sez 8? Yes, it may say 8 crowns, but 12 is what it costs. That's my top price, no way do I knock even a cent off! If yer doan wannit today, come back tamorra and it'll be 14, g'day t'ya, silly old trout—still there?—that's it, finito, capito? *(The customers mutter.)* Wot's that I 'ear? Mutiny in the ranks? If I hear another squeak out of you, I'll have the lot of yer locked up! Serve yer right! For today, just clear orff. I've 'ad just about enough. Such a shower of down-and-outs, how can I sell anything to that lot! *(Those present disperse, grumbling. Enter a price inspector.)*

INSPECTOR Spot check!

CHRAMOSTA *(taken aback)* What the heck—?

INSPECTOR May I see the invoice for the lettuce, please?

CHRAMOSTA *(takes a long time before he finds it and hands it over)* Okay—but it—it doesn't really—signify. I 'ad to pay extra, just to get it in the first place!

INSPECTOR *(makes a note)* Wholesale price 4 crowns, 50 heller. What's the retail price?

CHRAMOSTA It's 8, innit? Can't yer read? D'yer think us shopkeepers get the food for free? And anyway—we're the ones that fix the prices, and doan yer fergettit! It's my sphere of incompetence! If it's all right by my customers, I doan give a shit for the authorities! There's a war on!

INSPECTOR You don't want to adopt that tone! I'm going to report you for inflated prices and profiteering!

CHRAMOSTA Wot? Yer sunnavabitch! Yer wanna murder me? I'll murder you! *(He throws a porcelain bowl of cottage cheese that had been standing on the counter, weighing some 12 kilos, at the official, without hitting him.)*

INSPECTOR You'll answer for your actions!

CHRAMOSTA Wot? Dinna 'urt yer feelings, did I? Well then! Think yer can put one over on me? Who d'y'think you are? I'll soon show yer the difference! If yer fancy yer can pin summat on me, yu've another think coming! I signed up to the War Loan, know wot that means? In any case—wot'yer doing coming in 'ere? I pay my taxes, an doan yer forgettit! It's none of yer shit bizniz, an I've 'ad a bellyful! Barging in 'ere and snooping around—yer bastard, the cheek of it,—if yer doan geddorff my patch this minnit, I'll slaughter yer, that's my style! *(He seizes two knives.)*

INSPECTOR I'm warning you!

CHRAMOSTA Wot, ye're warning me? Yer stuffed shirt! Yer scavenger! I could kill yer! *(Throws a basket of hazelnuts after him.)* What a pest!
(Change of scene.)

Scene 7

Two commercial counsellors leaving the Imperial Hotel. A disabled soldier hobbles past.

FIRST COMMERCIAL COUNSELLOR *(looking around)* Aren't there any taxis? Scandalous!

BOTH *(waving their walking sticks at a passing taxi)* Hey—!

FIRST *(calling after a cabby)* Hey, you—are you free?

CABBY *(shrugging)* I'm booked.

SECOND At least you can still get something to eat, that's the only thing left to us *(they are surrounded by all kinds of beggars)*—young Louis Rothschild's showing his age—he can only be, at most—wait a minute, how long ago was it that he took over—

FIRST Doesn't Vienna have a funny feel to it—the atmosphere? You know what it is with the people? I'll tell you what it is with the people. They're war-weary! A blind man can see that! *(A blind soldier stops in front of them.)* Look, quick, who's that woman just coming in?

SECOND Don't you know?—wait—that's—that's—her from the ballet, what's her name—Speisinger! You know, the one who's with that red-haired Polish bloke!—Oh yes, and old Biach has war psychosis, what do say to that?

FIRST Is that a fact! What are the signs?

SECOND Every other word he utters is from a *Neue Freie Presse* editorial—he's overwrought.

FIRST But he always was overwrought. Works himself into a lather over our Special Relationship with Germany. Crazy!

SECOND Yes, but look what it's come to now. He gets in a state if you don't have immediate recall. He's convinced himself the gibes from the Entente are aimed at him personally. Besides, it's been established he's showing signs of megalomania.

FIRST And what are the signs?

SECOND He imagines he's the editor in chief.

FIRST How pathetic.

SECOND Anyway, tell me, did you get your boy into the what's-it-called—the War Archive?

FIRST Yes, but he's got a hernia, so I hope they let him go again soon. He's aiming for higher things, as you know, Ben Tiber at the Apollo Theatre wants to take him on as a literary adviser. He has a hernia.

SECOND My youngest has talent. I have hopes, too—But I'm in a bit of a state right now, I have an audience with Leopold Salvator tomorrow, if I pull it off—I'll buy my wife a fur coat.

(A beggar woman with a wooden leg and one of her arms a stump stops in front of them.)

BOTH *(waving their walking sticks at a passing taxi)* Hey—!

(Change of scene.)

Scene 8

Enter Old Man Biach, deep in thought about the latest editorials.

OLD MAN BIACH Cleopatra's nose was one of her most beautiful features. Sybil, the Greek prophetess, was a worker's daughter. *(Looking around cautiously)* Schiller's Tell says, every man is intent on his own business—and mine is murder. *(After a pause, with sudden resolve and a vehement gesture)* Today's top priority: the commercial traveller must put out feelers and sound out the market. *(With satisfaction)* Ivangorod already in its death throes. *(With malicious glee,*

barely concealed) Poincaré shaken and Lloyd George humiliated. (*Forcefully*) English and Germans scheduled to meet in Stockholm. (*Exit.*)
(*Change of scene.*)

Scene 9

War Archive.
A captain. Men of letters.

CAPTAIN You there, I want you to draft the military commendation applications, as the theatre critic of the *Fremdenblatt* that shouldn't be too hard for you.—Right, and you, your feature on that French sculptress, Auguste what's-her-name, sounds a bit like Rodaun, very neat, with your turn of phrase you'll have no difficulty doing a preface for what will be our definitive treatise *Under the Habsburg Banner*, but it's got to have real oomph, remember, something that speaks straight to the heart, and naturally you mustn't forget to mention Her Most Serene Imperial Highness, the Archduchess Maria Josefa!—And you, Müller, Robert, what are you up to, nothing escapes my notice, y'know, that article of yours about Roosevelt, very colourful, a bit too flattering, see to it you let me have that essay "What do we expect from our Crown Prince?" and don't keep me waiting! You came on a bit too strong for the Amerigans, but no harm done.—And you, what about the Double-headed Eagle, still not finished? Time to freshen up the steely pinions of our beloved Habsburg eagle!—But what's the matter with you, my dear Wildgans? Since you got back from headquarters, you've just been lazing around! You've picked up their habits out there! But let me tell you something. His Most Serene Imperial Highness, Archduke Friedrich, may be enchanted by your war poems, that may be enough for you but it's not enough for me, not by a long chalk! So see to it that your hymn of consecration for the allied armies lands on my desk pronto, otherwise you're on a charge!—Well, Werfel, what about that appeal for Gorizia? Not too much bombast, d'you hear. Moderation in all things! Too much schmaltz, you're not dancing a waltz.—You there, of course! You may be an Expressionist or whatever, and expect an extra portion of everything. But you can forget about that, the one thing I want from you is the sketch I commissioned, "To the Last Breath of Man and Horse", so fire away, jumping Jehoshaphat! Your "Breakthrough at Gorlice" turned out quite well.—(*To an orderly who has just entered*) What is it now? Ah yes, right. (*He takes the photographs handed to him.*) Very graphic! These are the photographs of Battisti's execution. Ah, look, our hangman Lang, amazingly lifelike! So, there it is for you lot to insert! Add a description and file it with the others, the photos of executed Czech legionnaires and Ukrainians and so on.—Now here's something—how would you categorize it? The splendid poem on the feast thrown by His Most Serene Imperial Highness, Archduke Max, at Monte Faë on the Piave, a juicy morsel for our poets, listen:

On the Faë the commandant,
His Highness, ever the gallant,
Smiles and greets the happy crowd,
The while his table does them proud
With food and drink—how much?—no matter,
As every man surveys his platter.

But oh dear, things soon start to go wrong. There's the funny bit as they keep guzzling till one of them of course has had enough—

He loosens his tie, the merry carouser's
No option but to unbutton his trousers.

Well, finally, of course, he's no option but to throw up. What a laugh! And then what happens?!

He looks at the orderly—fascinating!—
And takes him for a lady-in-waiting—!
He pinches arms, then cheeks—all four—
The amorous swain is after more!
But over the rest let us draw a veil,
For modesty must in the end prevail.

Very good! Next day it's back to the carousing, of course.

The barrel's down to the last drop,
But finally, before they stop,
On bits of bread they smear the lees,
And stuff their bellies, full of grease—

Well, it goes without saying, as you can imagine, it's only natural, the cooks were really cheesed off, but His Imperial Highness thought it was great fun. And when they all get back to base, oh dear, oh dear—

The morning after makes them think
With heads still spinning from the drink.

What a sight!—and, yes, a suitable poem for the War Archive, naturally not only on account of its frontline humour and celebration of His Imperial Highness's hospitality, but because it's a rarity! And that's because it was printed by the frontline press under a constant heavy barrage—Hats off, respect!—and you must admit, its typography is very tasteful.—And you, Corporal Dörmann, let that be an example to you, spur on your Pegasus, you've gone quiet since you took on the Serb and Russki shits, and cut and hacked 'em all to bits! What's up? That was good stuff:

> Come French monsieur and English gent,
> And take that up your fundament!

That really was Dörmann, the Iron Warrior!

> Just wait, you'll catch it now,
> We'll make you squirm, and how!
> And since your big mouth never closes,
> You need a fist right where your nose is.

So—go make 'em squirm! Why so melancollic? Well, I feel your pain—of course, you'd rather be out there, active in the field, than in here. It really is a pain.

DÖRMANN

> I envy the fallen their glorious role,
> But duty denies me that ultimate goal.

CAPTAIN Sturdy fellow, setting a fine example!—Now you, Müller, Hans, no need to cheer you up, eh, you're hard at it all the time. Are you working overtime? Let's have a look, "Three Falcons Above Lovcen"! That's the stuff, I won't forget to mention you to the major-general.

HANS MÜLLER We have grasped how sweet and seemly it is to do our duty. Like soldiers on parade we hammer out rhythms to drown out empty lives, lived closer to the gaudy show than to the reality beneath.

CAPTAIN Quite, quite. But y'know what would interest me? To hear from your own mouth an authentic account of how you showed what a man you are when war was declared. That wonderful article from "Cassian at War", the one where you pressed your ear to the ground on the vast Russian plain, well it's common knowledge you wrote that in Vienna, naturally, and we were all gobsmacked how well you captured it. But when the war broke out—you were in Berlin then, weren't you, in person? So, naturally enough, that's where you kissed the Allied soldiers, wasn't it?—but y'know, some folk say you smooched with them in Vienna too, on the Ring—Kraus and his *Fackel*, y'know, such types have a wicked tongue. So tell me the truth of the matter, were you in Berlin then, or only in Vienna—naturally that's something the War Archive should know!

HANS MÜLLER Beg to report, Captain, sir, it's common knowledge I was effectively active in Berlin when the war broke out, and that was exactly what I depicted in my article "Germany Arises" on the 25th August 1914. We were standing in the Neustädtische Kirchstrasse, unaware of any imminent onslaught, a Russian spy had just been swallowed up in the jaws of the crowd, I can see it now—and at that moment I spot a procession of ordinary folk bearing our good old black-and-yellow flag before them, moving straight towards the Brandenburg Gate. They're singing our beloved national anthem. I, nothing loath, sing along with them, "God preserve, God protect", right through to the next verse. At this, a fellow marcher by my side shoots me a heartfelt glance, then slips his arm under mine and gives it a comradely squeeze—

CAPTAIN Aha, shoulder to shoulder.

HANS MÜLLER —and, reading my lips, sings the same text I'm singing myself. It was this honest fellow—he'd a moustache and wasn't exactly handsome, nor what you could call very elegant—he was the one I kissed on the mouth, in front of the Austro-Hungarian Embassy.

CAPTAIN Well, that beats everything! If Ambassador Szögyeny had seen that from his window, it would have made him a happy man.

HANS MÜLLER Probably telling it like that makes it sound too emotional—

CAPTAIN Nonsense, not a bit of it—

HANS MÜLLER —and perchance I shall not succeed in reaping the plaudits of the ultra-aesthetes—(*muttering among the literati, cries of Oho!*)

CAPTAIN Silence!

HANS MÜLLER But I know that even if the Mona Lisa herself were to step down from her frame and bestow the unique smile of her lips upon me, her embrace would not make me as happy and deeply stirred in my innermost being as the brotherly kiss on the lips of this wonderful German man.

CAPTAIN (*moved*) That was well done! And apart from that, what else did you see and do at the dawning of this age of grandeur?

HANS MÜLLER Beg to report, Captain, sir, that summer day at noon when men and women in the royal cathedral trooped up to the altar to invoke the God of German armaments—that shall remain in my memory forever. In the gallery of the cathedral sits the Kaiser, upright, his helmet in his hand. At his feet, the congregation formed a surging black sea—

CAPTAIN Aha, so he was already in Constantinople.

HANS MÜLLER —a black sea of the faithful. The organ thunders down from above, the sun breaks through the windows and there arises as if in clamorous worship—

CAPTAIN Yes, yes, fine, but y'know, I'm less interested in the colour than in what you did yourself, personally, at the time.

HANS MÜLLER Woman and men clasp each others' hands, the organ thunders—

CAPTAIN Get to the point!

HANS MÜLLER Aye, aye, sir! I feel a hot lump rising in my throat, with firm resolve I can still manage to restrain myself, for I'm surrounded by brave, disciplined men, one and all, and at such times one must not show weakness. But now I look up at Kaiser Wilhelm, immersed in what seems an unutterable extremity of emotion, as he sinks his ashen head, lower and lower, and lets the shattering tones furrow his brow—

CAPTAIN You're making my flesh creep!

HANS MÜLLER —in a fervent gesture he presses the helmet to his breast. Nothing can save me now—

CAPTAIN Why, what happened to you?

HANS MÜLLER —I sob out loud—

CAPTAIN You never!

HANS MÜLLER —and lo and behold, the brave men beside me, with their grey hairs and iron will, they're all sobbing with me, and not ashamed to do so. And y'know what churned up the heart of this poor unmilitary guest in their midst? Through the veil of streaming tears I see standing beside their noble ruler another, my own Emperor, that chivalrous, kindly old gentleman—

CAPTAIN Don't blub, Müller!

HANS MÜLLER —and from the bottom of my heart I add my fraternal prayer to theirs: "O God beyond the stars, give thy blessing at this time also to Franz Joseph the First, bless my beloved and venerable Fatherland, let it remain strong and thrive—for ever and ever—bless my brothers in this hour of need, honour bound to march off to mortal danger, bless us all, our future, our fighting strength, our destiny—Lord God, thou who holdest the destinies of men and of nations in thy hands, in our most ardent and fervent love of our native land, we all, all, call out unto thee . . ."—beg to report, Captain, that's the end of the article.

CAPTAIN Not without some genuine feeling there. Tell me, what's the *Presse* paying for a prayer these days—ah—I mean, for an article?

HANS MÜLLER Beg to report, Captain, sir, 200 crowns, but in truth I'd have done it for the love of God—I would!

CAPTAIN No, for you received more than that, the highest honour open to a gentleman of the press was bestowed upon you—the German Kaiser received you in the Viennese Hofburg, he's an admirer of your muse, it's no secret if I tell you there's even some talk that you've supplanted Lauff. Let me take this opportunity to congratulate you. Tell me, what was it His Majesty said by way of greeting, you described it so well—

HANS MÜLLER The Kaiser comes towards me right up to the door and holds out his hand, looks at me, beaming with eyes aglitter, and with the most gracious of smiles says: "You have presented us with such poetic inspiration in wartime—what may we expect from you in time of peace?"

CAPTAIN A smutty farce—is what you should have said.

HANS MÜLLER Beg to report, Captain, sir, your inhibitions just melt away when you hear his voice—but I just couldn't get the courage up, Captain!

CAPTAIN Yes, of course it is a tricky situation. But just tell me, what was it impressed you most about the German Kaiser?

HANS MÜLLER Beg to report, Captain, sir—everything!

CAPTAIN Is that all?

HANS MÜLLER I'm still so deeply stirred, I'd be incapable of conveying the magic power of his personality, his unforced dignity, the luminous power of his gaze that compels your attention, as if mirroring a transparent and profoundly moral nature—

CAPTAIN That's enough! Y'know—it's naturally no wonder that the German Kaiser can be taken in by a Jew from the back of beyond. But for a Jew from the back of beyond to be taken in by the German Kaiser—that's incredible! (*Enter an orderly delivering a letter.*) Not again—what is it? (*He reads.*) Strewth! This concerns you, Müller. (*Müller gives a start.*) On the major-general's orders, you are to be released from the War Archive at once. (*Müller turns pale.*) A handwritten note from his Majesty the German Kaiser has arrived with the request that the author of that magnificent patriotic drama *Kings* should not be held back from his own creative writing through employment in the Austro-Hungarian War Archive. (*Muttering among the literati.*) Silence!—Farewell, Müller! But y'know what? (*Moved*) The "Three Falcons Above Lovcen"—finish that off for us! And when you're able to work again on your own account, and naturally turn to peace-time production—you'll be able to think back occasionally on your hours of military service, and then you'll be able to say: happy times!—and I hope you'll still have a soft spot for the War Archive.

HANS MÜLLER For better or for worse!
(Change of scene.)

Scene 10

A chemical laboratory in Berlin.

PRIVY COUNCILLOR PROFESSOR DELBRÜCK (*muses*) For some time now the English papers have been at it yet again, spreading all sorts of disinformation about the German population's allegedly poor level of nutrition. It doesn't exactly reflect any enthusiasm for war among the English people if their spirits have to be repeatedly raised by spreading such news, all of which is flagrantly contradicted by the facts. Medical opinion has made it explicitly clear that current wartime diet is beneficially wholesome, to which can be attributed the steady decline in the incidence of illness among both men and women. Not to mention nursing infants, who are provided with perfectly adequate and exemplary care. Even the Official German News Agency has to acknowledge that our hospitals are much less full in wartime than in times of peace, and that the simplified style of living has had directly beneficial effects on the health of many. It is now my intention, in the 66th general meeting of the Association of German Spirits Manufacturers, to explain that we owe this success primarily to mineral nutritive yeast. (*Adopts an orator's stance.*) The protein content of mineral nutritive yeast, which determines its nutritional value, is mostly obtained from urea. Gentlemen! We are witnessing here a triumph of pure intellect over base matter. It is chemistry which has made this miracle possible! A development already initiated in 1915 was taken up afresh with great success: the substitution of urea for sulphated ammonia in the production of yeast. Gentlemen! If urea can be used in this fashion, the further possibility presents itself that urine and liquid manure might point in the same direction. (*Exit.*)
(Change of scene.)

Scene 11

Meeting of the Cheruscan Society in Krems.

POGATSCHNIGG, KNOWN AS TEUT As Wotan is my sworn witness, the days are fast approaching when food and drink shall again be in plenteous supply, when we shall savour once more a succulent fillet of pork, rich in fatty crackling, breathe in the aroma of roast potatoes nicely browned to a turn in genuine butter, the real thing, with tasty little gherkins sweetly sprung from the elysian fields of Znaim, washed down with a draught of John Barleycorn's dark nectar from Kulmbach country in bounteous Bavaria (*shouts of Hear! It sounds like "Ear! Ear!"*)—a wholesome rye loaf, kneaded and baked to melt in your mouth, and a toothsome salad! Proud-hearted Vindobona, home of the Nibelungs on our great, ancestral river, Vienna will hold out till the end, that's our slogan! (*Shouts of Yes we can!*) Our glorious attack on the Eyeties has been crowned with success, we can be confident those villainous Abruzzi have been expelled for ever from Tyrol's imperishable peaks! (*Shouts of Ear! Ear!*) We are equally confident that the Muscovite bear shall slink home wounded, licking its bleeding paws! Followed by the Jewish rabble, reeking of garlic, that claim to be our compatriots! Yes, indeed! (*Shouts of Bravo! Hail Teut! Hail Pogatschnigg!*)

A VOICE The dirty yids! (*Laughter.*)

FRAU THERESA POGATSCHNIGG (*takes the floor*) Never hasting, never wasting—as the fine old German saying goes. Wasn't it Barbara Waschatko, that most German of Germans, who said in the *Ostdeutsche Post*: Sewing socks for soldiers, we saw the old year out. Sewing socks for soldiers, we'll see the New Year in! Never have our thoughts been closer to those out in the field than now, when snow vies with rain and ice and we ask ourselves what is hardest for our valiant warriors: the red globe of the sun suspended in a cold February sky, or the water trickling into the trenches, ceaselessly, dismally—drip, drip, drip. (*Shouts of Ear! Ear! Splendid!!*) But as women we cannot help smiling amidst the tears, and even in pain, we still make no secret of our need to be beautiful. Did not Cleopatra, too, put on all her finery to die? (*Shouts of How true! Splendid! Good old Aunt Tracy!*)

WINFRIED HROMATKA (*junior member*) Honourable brother and sister Cheruskians! As a representative of the Young Cheruskians, it is not only my duty to renew our oath of loyalty, pledging to continue the struggle forced upon us to its victorious conclusion, that is to say, to the last breath of man and mount. (*Shouts of Ear! Ear!*) For, honourable Cheruskians, a German peace, as our past master Hindenburg so aptly said, is not a soft peace. (*Cries of Hurrah!*) No, it also our duty to honour our Valkyries who bring comfort and consolation to our heroes, as whose noblest representative I would like to salute my honourable colleague, the previous speaker. (*Ear! Ear!*) Defy the enemy to the end, but the fair sex we must defend! Long live Frau Pogatschnigg! (*Shouts of Hurrah! Good old Aunt Tracy!*)

KASMADER (*rises*) Honourable brothers and sisters, fellow Cheruskians! We have heard German words today that truly speak straight to the heart. As a representative of the German postal workers I would like to make a suggestion concerning self-restraint, given that the German household, encircled by British envy, French hatred, and Slav malice, is now more than ever reliant on self-satisfaction. (*Shouts of Splendid!*) In this connection I would like to suggest that female domestic staff in German households should be released from service in order to free up more German combatants for the army. They would, moreover, acquire new ways to do their bit for the Fatherland. All German women, old and young, will naturally, when peace comes, hand back the posts they have occupied all the more willingly to the returning heroes, since they are greatly indebted to them for the protection of German hearths and homes. (*Shouts of Splendid! Ear! Ear!*) Only when there are insufficient numbers of the latter are female resources to be engaged for this purpose. But these would be richly repaid by the uplifting feeling of having added their little contribution on the home front to what has already been achieved. For in truth, each and every one of us here on the home front participates in the struggle, ready and willing to make the greatest sacrifice. And so I conclude with the exhortation: See it through to the bitter end! In the words of a poem of my own making: (*shouts of Quiet! Listen!*)

Save on soap! No, I'm not joking,

(*Shouts of "Quite right!" "Bravo Kasmader!"*)

Even better: no more smoking! (*Laughter.*)
Heavy overcoats I'd ban, (*Shouts of "Boo!"*)
With collars made of Astrakhan,
Knee-length leather boots are out, (*Shouts of "Boo!" "Eyetie fad!"*)
That's a fashion you can flout. (*Shouts of "Quite right!"*)
Each coin you spend is one too many,
The Fatherland needs every penny!

(*Shouts of "Ear! Ear!" The speaker is congratulated.*)

ÜBELHÖR (*rises and reads from a sheet of paper*)

You ask me what's my heart's desire?
The only thing that I'd require
Is made of breadcrumbs, fine and white—
A dumpling, that's my heart's delight!

(*Laughter. Shouts of "Me too!" "Ear! Ear!"*)

HOMOLATSCH (*rises, stares straight ahead through his gold-rimmed spectacles, and says with index finger raised*)

My wife—my child—my home—all three—
Earth's finest—thank you, Germany!

(Sits down quickly. Shouts of "Ear! Ear!" "Bravo Homolatsch!")
(Change of scene.)

Scene 12

At a dance in Hasenpoth in Latvia. Baltic gentleman and Baltic lady in conversation.

GENTLEMAN My dear.

LADY What d'ya mean?

GENTLEMAN You're not dancing.

LADY Naa.

GENTLEMAN Why?

LADY If I dance, I sweat. If I sweat, I stink. So: don't dance, don't sweat, don't stink.

(Change of scene.)

Scene 13

Appeal hearing in the district court of Heilbronn

PUBLIC PROSECUTOR —In June of this year the accused gave birth to a child whose father is a French prisoner of war. The Frenchman, who is a waiter, has been in custody since 1914. From the end of 1914 until 1917 he was on the castle estate. Here he was employed in many different tasks, especially work in the fields and gardens. The accused Baroness was herself a regular participant in these activities. In the case before the court, the accused attempted to charge the French father of her child with rape. However, the court lent no credence to the charge. It was conspicuous that this was the first time the accused had put forward this defence. The fact that, for a full six months after the inception of the pregnancy, the French prisoner remained in employment on the estate itself rendered the submission invalid. Consequently, the court found the accused Baroness guilty. She was sentenced to five months' imprisonment. Her incarceration took place immediately as there was reason to suspect she might abscond. The grounds for the judgment emphasized as aggravating circumstances the defence commonly advanced, also in this case, of charging the prisoner with having committed a crime, as well as the social position and upbringing of the accused, while her previous, totally unblemished, reputation and inexperience in sexual matters were adduced as mitigating factors.—My lords, if it please the court, in view of the outrageous leniency of this sentence, I need not waste words. The facts of the case, namely unnatural intercourse with a prisoner of war, have been adequately clarified in material terms. There is no need to spell out the immoral effect of such a shocking example. I have no doubt but that the court will share my feeling that we are on the brink of an abyss from which offended morality can only be saved if we bear one thing in mind: what would become of the Fatherland were every German housewife to sink so low! (*General agitation.*) With this in mind, I respectfully ask the court to reject the defence's action for annulment, and instead to increase the sentence to two years. *(The court adjourns for deliberation.)*

SOMEONE IN THE COURTROOM (*hands a newspaper to his neighbour*) Tremendous successes of our bombers north-west of Arras and behind the Champagne front. Over the last three days and nights some 50,000 pounds of bombs were dropped.

NEIGHBOUR The moral effect was certainly no less than the material effect. *(Change of scene.)*

Scene 14

Optimist and Grumbler in conversation.

OPTIMIST The development of weapons thus far, with poison gas, the tank, the submarine, and the cannon with a range of 75 miles, has brought about a situation—

GRUMBLER —in which the army should be dishonourably discharged from the Combined Services for cowardice in the face of the enemy. According to the military conception of honour, the world would then finally attain eternal peace. For the one thing that remains inconceivable is what possible connection exists between some chemist's inspiration, in itself a disgrace to science, and heroism. How fame in battle can be attributed to a "chlorious" offensive without choking in shame on its own poison gas?

OPTIMIST But surely it's immaterial what weapon does the killing? How far do you go along with technical arms development?

GRUMBLER Not an inch, but if you forced me, I'd say as far as the crossbow. Naturally, since men cannot live without killing each other, it's immaterial how they do so, and mass murder is the more practical way. But technical developments thwart man's romantic impulse. As we know, this is satisfied only by personal confrontation, man to man. The courage of the man with a weapon may match up to a growing mass of enemies; but courage degenerates into cowardice when the mass obscures the soldier behind it. And it becomes quite pitiful when the soldier himself has no overview of mass warfare. We've reached that stage now. But worse is to come, hatched in laboratories according to the Devil's all too scrutable ways. Tanks and poison gases, developed to the point of perfection by the competing nations, eventually quit the field in favour of bacteria. There will be no resistance to the redemptive idea that epidemics, once merely the consequences of war, should now become the primary weapons. But since man will be unable to dispense with a romantic pretext for his evil-doing, the commander whose plans the bacteriologist will implement will still be wearing military uniform, just as the chemist does today. Should the Germans be credited with the glory of inventing, the others with the villainy of perfecting these weapons, or else the other way round?—You decide which is the more hopeful scenario.

OPTIMIST All the same, with their highly developed military technology, the Germans have surely proved—

GRUMBLER —that Hindenburg's conquests and triumphs surpass those of Joshua. Modern methods are better adapted to the objective of destroying and exterminating the enemy, and a breakthrough after gassing three Italian brigades trumps any coup produced by Jehovah's miracle weapons.

OPTIMIST So you see a similarity between the modern German thirst for conquest and that of the ancient Hebrews?

GRUMBLER Up to and including the similarity of their gods! Among the peoples who have played a world-historical role, they are the only two who think themselves worthy of the honour of possessing a national God. While all the other peoples confronting each other on this crazy planet merely share the delusion of aspiring to victory in the name of the same God, the Germans follow the ancient Hebrews by adopting a separate God of their own, one to whom the most horrific sacrifices are offered up in battle. The privilege of being the chosen people seems to have passed straight down to them, and of all the nations whose minds have been turned by the idea of nationality, they are the one which has most frequently identified itself as such, incessantly addressing itself as the German nation, and even seeing the word "German" as an adjective capable of comparative and superlative inflection. But the connection between the pan-German and the Hebraic life-form and their expansionary drive at the expense of others deserves a broader and deeper analysis. Except that the ancient Hebrews always paid lip service to the commandment "Thou shalt not kill", thereby finding themselves again and again—to the greater glory of God—in dreadful, though always genuinely felt and conscience-stricken, divergence from the laws of Moses, while the modern Germans make no bones about claiming Kant's categorical imperative as a philosophical justification for "Give 'em a good kicking!" It is also true, of course, that in Prussian ideology, by virtue of the country's familiar confusion of concepts, even the Lord of Hosts has degenerated into the commander in chief and the Kaiser's superior officer.

OPTIMIST Only his ally, surely. Who but you would have come up with the bizarre notion that there existed some spiritual link between Hindenburg and Joshua?

GRUMBLER Schopenhauer: who thought the institution of a separate God, one who makes a "covenant" pledging to His people the lands of their neighbours which must then be won through plunder and murder, went hand in hand with that of a national God to whom everything that sustains the life of other peoples must be sacrificed. Kant: who deplored the victor's invocation of the Lord of Hosts as a typically Israelite custom, and whose warnings anticipated the Kaiser's fondness for invoking the philosopher and the Lord of Hosts in the same breath. What an antithesis: on the one hand the royal Prussian Kantian, with his bulletproof faith in his ally in Königsberg; and on the other the warning by Kant himself to respect the moral laws decreed by the Father of mankind and beg the heavens to forgive the grievous sins committed through the barbarity of war. When I next appear on the public platform in Berlin, I shall test out this devastating and all but annihilating contrast under the title "A Kantian and Kant."

OPTIMIST That could lead to your deportation as an undesirable alien.

GRUMBLER Which I already am in my own country. Yet I remain convinced, after all we have been through, that "our Lord still has great things in store for the German people." And I still believe that the affinity between both of "God's chosen peoples" is revealed even in the most insignificant acts and facts of life, as radiated by the spirit which truly links the two cultures as a worldview: money-minded romanticism. As it were, unto the third and fourth generation. For in both cases a philosophy of life is being constructed, like a total work of art, in which things of this world are determined by things of the spirit, so that wars are handled like balance sheets, according to the principle "In God we trust." It could be shown that the Old Testament rule of "An eye for an eye, a tooth for a tooth" is the maxim—even quite literally so—by which the new Germans wage war, and it is certainly no coincidence that a recent official communiqué from our War Press Bureau (as quick on the uptake as the clown chasing a horse in the circus) could use this formula to justify air attacks. It truly brings out the importance of the notion of "reprisals." And who, apart from you, could fail to sense the truly biblical tedium with which this urge to retaliate and annihilate is expressed in daily reports from the Battle of Jericho?

OPTIMIST From the Jericho front? When do we read anything about that?

GRUMBLER Every day—in the Extra Editions!

(Change of scene.)

Scene 15

A Protestant church.

CHURCH SUPERINTENDENT FALKE —This war is a punishment visited by God upon the nations for their sins, and we Germans, together with our allies, are the instruments of divine retribution. There can be no doubt that the Kingdom of God will be hugely advanced and profoundly enhanced by this war. At this point, it must be freely and unequivocally acknowledged that Jesus's commandment "Love your enemies!" applies only to relationships between individuals, not nations. In the conflict between nations there is no room for loving one's enemies. Here the individual soldier need have no moral scruples. As long as the battle rages, the Christian precept of love is totally irrelevant! It does not apply to the heat of battle. The commandment to love our enemies has no longer any meaning for us on the field of battle. There, killing is no sin, but a service to the Fatherland, a Christian duty, indeed a service to God! It is a service to God and a sacred duty to punish all our enemies by overwhelming force, by shock and awe, and if needs be, to annihilate them! And so I repeat unto you, while the cannons thunder in this World War: Jesus's commandment "Love your enemies!" no longer applies! Away with all scruples of conscience! But why then, the question arises, have so many thousands been shot and crippled? Why so many hundreds blinded? Because that was God's way of saving their souls! Look around you, behold the miracles of the Lord, and pray: "Deliver us, O Lord, to Paradise!"

(Change of scene.)

Scene 16

Another Protestant church.

CONSISTORY COUNCILLOR RABE —So, more steel in the blood! And to the fainthearted I say: once war has begun, it is not only our right, but sometimes even our patriotic duty, to regard treaties and the like as scraps of paper to be torn up and tossed into the fire, if by so doing the Fatherland can be saved. For war is the last resort, the long-term strategy by which God brings the nations to their senses, by force if they will not be guided along the God-given path in any other way. Wars are trial by ordeal and divine judgment made manifest in world history. That is why it is also God's will that nations at war should make full use of all the forces and weapons He has bestowed upon them in order to impose His judgment on the nations. So, more steel in the blood! German women too, and the mothers of fallen heroes, no longer take a sentimental view of war. They too, when their loved ones are in the field or have died in combat, are averse to pity and lamentation. God wants us to make the greatest possible impact through an iron will and intensification of energy! And so I say unto you again: more steel in the blood!

(Change of scene.)

Scene 17

Another Protestant church.

PASTOR GEIER —Look about you: the brilliant achievements of German genius in action are strung together like pearls on a sparkling necklace. German genius has created the miracle of the U-boat. It has produced the legendary gun that shoots shells into the ethereal regions, visiting destruction on the enemy some 80 miles away! But German genius not only furnishes us with weapons; it is no less indefatigable in supplying ideas, both defensive and offensive. As I can reveal to you today, Schulze in Hamburg has been commissioned by our Foreign Office to prepare a scientific study of fundamental importance on *The desecration of corpses and graves by the English and the French.* This work is to be disseminated for international propaganda purposes to win us the sympathy of neutral nations, and we hope it will be welcomed by those neighbours who still remain sceptical. Over the length and breadth of our German lands spirits awaken, ready to proclaim our just cause, to invigorate the idle, to convert the backsliders, and to win us new friends. Our farsighted government has recognized that Switzerland not only is a potential transit route for armaments, but also may be grateful for an insight into our military strategy through words and images. Films of our U-boats sinking countless tons of food have a huge impact on any neutral public; people faint, especially women, who are of course particularly sensitive to the loss of such priceless goods, and gradually the realization dawns that the damage we are inflicting on our enemies is simply incalculable! Nor does the German language lag behind. *The Battle of Champagne* is the title of a brochure published in Stuttgart by the Secretariat for Student Social Work, aimed primarily at Swiss intellectuals. Take to heart the words of the magnificent poem, "A Soldier's Prayer", which I found in this excellent piece of propaganda, and which our government has already distributed in neutral countries to enlighten them as to our true nature, to kindle an understanding of the German character, and so gradually help dismantle the hatred with which we have been persecuted:

Soldiers praying for salvation,
Hear them pray to God above:
Duty is our inclination,
Cannon's roar our pledge of love.
Rifles splutter out Our Father,
And with bayonets raised on high
We advance against the Other,
Whom we mean to crucify!

Comrades, shrapnel from your mortar
Sprinkles incense on the field,
Use grenades as holy water,
And your sins will soon be healed.
Sing a heartfelt psalm to Jesus,
If a mine fails to ignite.
Once the foe is blown to pieces
You'll be holy in His sight.

Take your hand grenades and string them
Round your neck: a rosary!
At the enemy then fling them,
Sap their spirit, watch them flee!
"Watch on the Rhine", our fervent prayer,
Will strike a wrathful chord.
Those praying hands, now claws, shall tear
In shreds the Gurkha horde,
For we are the Chosen People,
Hangmen's henchmen for the Lord!

So look around you and pray, as witnesses to the wonders of the Lord: Deliver us, O Lord, to Paradise!
(Change of scene.)

Scene 18

Pilgrimage church.

SEXTON Here you see an interesting devotional gift, presented to our church by two soldiers who fought at Col di Lana: a rosary with beads made of Italian shrapnel bullets. What they are strung on is barbed wire. The cross is cut from the rotating ring of a burst Italian grenade and has three Italian rifle bullets as pendants. The Christ figure has been made from a shrapnel bullet. On the back of the cross are engraved the words: "In gratitude. In memory of the war in Italy. Cima d'Oro, 25.7.1917. A. St. and K. P. from Lana." The rosary weighs some two and a half pounds, so for prolonged prayer it needs a strong hand. Would you would care to try, ladies and gentlemen?

VISITOR *(trying)* Whew!—Can't do, far too heavy.

(A church bell rings)

SEXTON Listen! It's ringing for the last time. It's about to be taken down. Shrapnel bullets are being turned into rosaries, and church bells into cannons. We render unto God what is Caesar's, and unto Caesar what is God's. That's what I call give and take—everyone doing his bit.

(Change of scene.)

Scene 19

Constantinople. A mosque. From behind the curtain can be heard raucous laughter.

FIRST VOICE What, they expect us to put on these big straw slippers? Well I never! Divine!

SECOND VOICE Hey, look at that beardy-weirdy with the Quran there—

(Enter, noisily, two young men, representing Berlin business interests. They keep their hats on. Behind them, silently, head lowered and hands hidden in his wide sleeves, the Imam.)

FIRST Y'see, that's what a mosque looks like—so behave yourself, my dear Fritz, and respect the customs! *(Laughter.)*

SECOND So, here we are in a mosque, with a fully functioning Imam, too—divine!

FIRST Tip-top!

SECOND Weird and wonderful! *(Hands in pockets, they slide around in their straw slippers, losing them continually and each time breaking out in raucous laughter.)*

FIRST Y'know, when we gain a firm foothold here, they'll soon see their feeble economy put in order—and how! *(He bumps against the other.)* Fritz, watch out—

SECOND Not exactly overrun, this place, is it? You see more people in the Metro. Only the one in this whole vast space, and even then it's a female—*(he points to a lady and gives the other a nudge)*—missed out there, eh!—You likka Zuleika?—*(Laughter.)*

FIRST (*warbles*) Sailing down the Bosphorus, d'ya think she—gives a toss for us?—

SECOND (*about to burst out laughing*) You're telling me!—If only we could, God Almighty!—Behave yourself!

FIRST Do you think of a full moon or a half moon when you look at her? (*Both burst out laughing.*)

SECOND They're a good-natured, easy-going little people—maybe just a bit too easy-going, yes, altogether too easy-going—well, we'll soon lend them a helping hand, show 'em what discipline is. It's not a lost cause yet. We'll swing it somehow. (*Loud laughter. He makes a parody of greeting the Imam, who is standing some way off.*) G'day!

FIRST Morning! (*The Imam makes several attempts in mime to draw attention to their headwear.*) Look at that—what's he getting at, the buffoon?

SECOND The man's deaf and dumb—(*they laugh and give each other a shove.*)

IMAM (*to the lady*) Tell them they are in a house of prayer.

LADY (*going up to them*) The Imam asks me to tell you that you are in a house of prayer, so would you be so kind as to take your hats off?

FIRST Why, of course, if that would give him a kick—Morning! (*they greet and laugh.*)

LADY May I suggest you keep your voices down a little; you surely wouldn't laugh out loud in a church either.

SECOND (*laughing loudly*) No, but what's this place got to do with a church?

LADY This is a house of God, after all.

FIRST Ye gods—this grotesque pile?!

LADY At least don't offend the feelings of those for whom it represents all that is sacred!

SECOND Huh, these kismet cranks couldn't care less about all that. Fine, we're off. Morning! (*They leave, ranting away and laughing loudly.*)

IMAM (*to the lady*) Don't let their childish foolishness upset you; as surely as God smiles at them, let us do likewise.

LADY They mean no harm.

IMAM God gave the Europeans science, the Orientals majesty. But these young men have not attained the spiritual state of those who walk in the shadow of the Most High.

(*Change of scene.*)

Scene 20

Editorial office in Berlin.

ALFRED KERR (*at his desk, composing a Romanian song*) I'm f . . . finished. I mean, my R . . . Romanian song. (*He reads aloud*)

In remotest hamletescus
Tinkle Russian baksheeshescus,
Greasing palms of glad turncoatskis
And our leaders with banknoteskis.

Breaking all the normal groundrules
Means we're branded rotten scoundruls,
Set to swallow Hungarescu,
Win back Saxon Transylvescu.

Cry Triumphul!—an eruption
Fills this cesspit of corruption.
Its capitul is Bucharescu,
Its women dirty and grotescu.

But, alas, we get a thrashing,
Germans, Bulgars, both come dashing
Through Dobrudja, won it backul,
Tutrakan, too, woe! alackul!

We fell for it, so more fools we,
God knows if that was meant to be,
From sitting on our high horsescu,
We're for a kicking, or worsescu!

A . . . art is my m . . . muse and it b . . . butters my bread. In its p . . . pursuit I risk the r . . . risible with r . . . rotten r . . . rhymes. My fame and f . . . fortune to prolong, this was my R . . . Romanian song.

In wartime Alfred Kerr insists
On writing for the Nationalists.
But Kerr's no idiotic hack,
The Liberals will take him back.

Bingo!
(Change of scene.)

Scene 21

Consultation room in Berlin.

PROFESSOR MOLENAAR (*to patient*) Yes, it's heart disease. You've little hope of being passed fit for active service—a nice state of affairs. You see what comes from smoking! In spite of the High Command's orders, people are still smoking throughout the land. There can be little doubt that immoderate smoking in general, and specifically that of young people puffing away prematurely, has so far cost the country at least two army corps in this war. It's shocking how many comparatively young men have heart disease and are consequently cut off from military service, marriage, and procreation. In the interests of our Army Reserve, a ban on smoking is urgently needed. Leaving aside the issue of whether tobacco is more beneficial or harmful in war itself—say, when going over the top—it's certain that hundreds if not thousands of nonsmokers have endured the strains and rigors of service in the field just as well as smokers. After all, war was waged for millennia before the discovery of tobacco. So how did people manage then? The quantity of fumes on battlefields today is incalculable! Is it really necessary? It is well known that outstanding army commanders such as Count v. Haeseler, Conrad v. Hötzendorf, and Mackensen are declared opponents of tobacco. And have they not endured the strains of service in the field just as well as the smokers? I'm thinking especially of Falkenhayn, Boroevic, and Hindenburg. As we know, death for the Fatherland deprives the army of the services of many young people. That's why the vice of smoking is so deplorable: it prevents people from being killed in battle or even procreating new recruits. You, young man, have contracted heart disease, so you have little hope of being found fit for active service. Don't take it to heart. It may get better. There'll always be wars. That said, your lungs seem to be affected as well. Take a deep breath. (*He listens.*) You can breathe again—it's out of the question. A desk job at best. That'll be 20 marks.

Scene 22

Office at a command post.

GENERAL STAFF OFFICER (*on the telephone*)—Hello, have you got the report on Przemysl ready?—Not yet? Ah, still sleeping it off—Go and see to it, otherwise you'll be late again for the bash in the mess—yes, it *is* on—Now look here—What, forgotten everything again?—Listen, here are the main points: Everyone knows we lost Przemysl because our garrison was at starvation point, remember?—now the situation is quite diffic—different—the enemy succumbed to our superior strength, no way did he succumb to hunger, the enemy was never starving! Only we were! The Russians always had plenty of provisions—but they couldn't withstand the vigorous assault of our brave troops, stands to reason—the force of our attack—Moreover: the fortress is completely undamaged, we took possession of it intact—and all the latest artillery—What? We can't make people forget—just old junk? No, no, of course we don't say that anymore! My dear fellow, you can make people forget anything! Just listen, and don't mess it up—a modern fortress, the very latest—old Austria's pride and joy—retaken in perfect condition. Not by force but by hunger—dammit, what am I saying! Not by hunger but by force! Go on, you'll find a way—as long as you make people believe it—you won't have any trouble this time—so, 'bye! End of story!

(Enter two old generals.)

FIRST Ah yes, the Germans! Now they've made Falkenhayn a Doctor of Philosophy! That doesn't happen to the likes of us, though.

SECOND But excuse me, there's Boroevic—

FIRST Yes, yes, but it doesn't happen to the likes of us.

(A journalist passes by.)

FIRST Honoured, my dear sir!

JOURNALIST Excellency! Good to meet you—I need to pick your brains—what's the news from Brody?

FIRST From Brody?—Why, what's happening at Brody?

JOURNALIST I mean, what about the battle at Brody?

FIRST So there's been a battle at Brody? You don't say!

SECOND Holy Mary!

FIRST A battle. Well I never! So you want to know—*(after some thought)* Y'know what? We'll pull it off.

JOURNALIST *(in haste)* So I can report: At Brody we're still holding on—? No wait, y'know what I'll write? I'll write: "Brody no longer scarified!"

(Change of scene.)

Scene 23

Headquarters.

ARCHDUKE FRIEDRICH (reading)—And so—I conclude with the words: His Majesty, our Supreme Commander, hip-hip, hip-hip—*(turning the page)* hooray! *(Cheers. After an interval during which, his teeth bared in a smirk, he surveys a line of young officers, his gaze coming to rest on one of them)* Ah—that's—Buquoy, I see! He—already has—a medal! *(After an interval during which his gaze continues the inspection and comes to rest on another*) And—him there—that's a Buquoy as well! He's—got—a medal, too! (*A pause while he ponders*) Now—two Buquoys—have a medal!

ADJUTANT (*approaches the army commander in chief and reports*) Your Imperial Highness, the Vice Chancellor of the University of Vienna along with the Dean and Pro-Dean of the Philosophical Faculty are in attendance and most humbly beg permission to present Your Imperial Highness with the Honorary Doctorate of the Philosophical Faculty.
(*Change of scene.*)

Scene 24

Enter two devotees of the Reichspost.

FIRST DEVOTEE OF THE *REICHSPOST* Have you read *Our Dynasty in the Field*? Hats off, that's some book! It shows the members of our Imperial House are directly involved in the war, and a sequence of charming photographs depicts all the princely warriors who stand shoulder to shoulder with the common soldier in the field, sharing his trials and tribulations. It begins with the Supreme Commander.

SECOND DEVOTEE OF THE *REICHSPOST* What, you mean His Majesty, our noble—?

FIRST You didn't let me finish. It's true that considerations of age and health prevent him from tarrying with his Field Greys astride his charger, as he loved to do in years gone by—

SECOND Get away!—When was that?

FIRST You didn't let me finish. As he loved to do in years gone by on manoeuvres. But no one could be more intimately involved with the war than this supreme soldier, the head of our imperial forces, whose love and concern, day and night, is for the army out in the field—his army, which is essentially his creation, in all its glory and fighting power. But all his soldiers, too, his brave men, are ever conscious of this, in the midst of raging battles they sense the blessed presence of his loving fatherly care. So y'see, it's true he does feel a shared comradeship with the common soldier out in the field, with all his trials and tribulations. You really must be a fool, if you can't see that!

SECOND And what about his successor, the next in line? What has the author got to say about His Highness, Archduke Karl?

FIRST The most charming episodes. His nonchalance while standing on a hillock under enemy artillery fire, smiling and talking to the men as he studies the map.

SECOND His humour and high spirits have an electrifying effect on all around.

FIRST It boosts the fighting spirit of the firing line tenfold. What a surge—no further stimulants necessary!

SECOND What about our generalissimo, Archduke Friedrich?

FIRST The mastermind? The brains behind the battle, sitting bent over maps night after night with the Chief of the General Staff, Baron Conrad? The troops' faith in him is limitless. "He can handle it, our Field Marshal", that's what they say.

SECOND Of course he can handle it.

FIRST Y'know what they call him?

SECOND Quite simply "the Father of the Forces", what else?

FIRST Exactly. The author of *Our Dynasty in the Field*—I tell you, the things he's experienced! I happened to be standing nearby, he says, in a small group under cover of a hill, and in the company of this unkempt veteran, a seasoned campaigner, he says, one of that almost extinct breed—weather-beaten, hard as nails, y'know the type? He was looking at the generalissimo in the distance as well. I saw in his gnarled face—

SECOND Hold on, how's that possible?

FIRST No, he was the one saw it, not me—

SECOND But who had a gnarled face, then?

FIRST The old campaigner, of course!

SECOND Ah, the old campaigner, that's a different kettle of fish.

FIRST So, the author of *Our Dynasty in the Field* spotted the gnarled face of the old campaigner twitching, and him obviously trying to suppress it. Then he passed his weathered cavalryman's gauntlet over his eyes, and they were glistening with what looked suspiciously like—

SECOND Aha, signalling, was he? Politically suspect—!

FIRST You didn't let me finish—suspiciously like tears! And said with more feeling than he'd ever betrayed before: "The Father of the Forces . . ." (*He sobs.*)

SECOND (*also moved*) Just so. And what about Josef Ferdinand?

FIRST His heart belongs to his soldiers, every one, and every soldier's heart is his. A military commander of incomparable renown and a simple, faithful comrade, worshipped by his men to the point of idolatry. Thus shall he be remembered in the immortal annals of this war.

SECOND Nice one! And Peter Ferdinand?

FIRST Ah—quite phenomenal! Chasing the enemy from the high ground, steadfastly on guard, undaunted by the snowstorm—those episodes made an enormously stirring impact.

SECOND Of course, but what about Archduke Josef?

FIRST A hero! The soldiers say he's invulnerable.

SECOND Get away!—I suppose that'll be why he thinks his soldiers are invulnerable too, and thought a bit of machine-gun fire from behind would—

FIRST Wash your mouth out! They all idolize him, Hungarians and Swabians, Romanians and Serbs—every one of them.

SECOND What, the Serbs too?

FIRST You can say that again! There were heartrending scenes, they say. But you can hardly even hint at that.

SECOND And what about Eugen?

FIRST The noble Teuton knight!

SECOND And Max?

FIRST A dashing young man!

SECOND And Albrecht?

FIRST Young as he is, he's already sharing all the soldiers' hardships—the mud and filth of the roads, the sodden clothes, dire lodgings, rotten bread—he shares it all with them.

SECOND Those are our action heroes. What of our angels of mercy?

FIRST There's a description here of the imperishable glory Archduke Franz Salvator has earned with his stupendous organizational efforts for the Red Cross; then there's a depiction of the sublime example of public welfare set by the Archduchesses Zita, Marie Valerie, Isabella, Blanka, Maria Josefa, Maria Theresa, Maria Annunziata, and many other members of the Imperial House. Admiration is bestowed in glowing terms on the blessed, self-denying, heroic activities of Archduchess Isabella Maria.

SECOND What about Leopold Salvator, then?

FIRST He's done his bit.

SECOND You've left out a few.

FIRST Archduke Karl Stephan displays ceaseless endeavour, Archduke Heinrich Ferdinand carries out onerous missions as a mounted messenger, Archduke Maximilian has entered military service and, like Archdukes Leo and Wilhelm, Franz Karl Salvator, and Hubert Salvator, has been made a lieutenant, and they are all undaunted.

SECOND Truly a rich laurel crown!

FIRST This book, which can lay no claim to completeness, will hold a place of honour in the literature of this war.

SECOND (*sobs.*)

FIRST What's up?

SECOND I'm thinking of the hospital for amputees.

FIRST Come on, that's no reason to cry, old chap, war is war y'know—

SECOND I do know that—and that's not the reason, it's because—

FIRST What is it, then? What's the matter?

SECOND (*crying*) It's because you don't let me finish. I'm thinking the whole time about Archduchess Zita in the hospital for amputees! For the casualties, the 8th of May was a day of joy, one to make up for many an hour of pain. I often heard the words ringing in my ear: "If only Archduchess Zita would pay us a visit!"—"If only I could see Archduchess Zita!" At last the longed-for day arrived. The great bright building was all in a quiver with joyful expectation. The imperial motorcar drew up at a quarter to 10 in the morning, and the Archduchess got out. A new convoy of casualties had arrived that very minute (*he sobs*).

FIRST Yes, but that's no reason to—war is war y'know, old chap—

SECOND I know—it's only because of Zita—Well—with incomparable charm the young Archduchess addressed each of the new arrivals. The weather-beaten faces, which pain and suffering had marked with many a furrow, lit up and beamed. Germans and Hungarians, Poles and Czechs, Romanians and Ukrainians, all felt a new unifying bond binding them more intimately together once more.

FIRST Ah yes, it's a nice story, all those artificial limbs—

SECOND A shared joy made their hearts beat faster. The great lady, in whom they recognized their Empress-to-be, took a lively interest in each and every one, and when patients were brought forward who had had both feet replaced with artificial ones on which they moved briskly—(*he cries.*)

FIRST Enough, enough, war is war!

SECOND Oh, I know that—it's on account of Zita! Well, as they moved forward briskly, the Archduchess's gaze followed them, and there was a glimmer of joy in her eyes. And they all forgot their sufferings, their pain, feeling nothing but springtime, hope and joy. When Zita left the hospital around one o'clock, the glowing and smiling expression remained on their faces, with delighted pride in their hearts.

FIRST I see what you're getting at. A war like this one is a passion. If someone has the good fortune to end up in a hospital for amputees, and it so happens that Her Imperial Highness bestows on him—

SECOND Yes, he can talk of his good fortune—but y'know, that's only a half-way house! Not everyone has the privilege of dying for the Imperial Dynasty—!

FIRST No, my friend, not everyone can be so lucky! One mustn't hope for too much. We shouldn't have ideas above our station.

(Change of scene.)

Scene 25

In front of the War Ministry.

FIRST YOUNG MAN Hi! Where are you going?

SECOND YOUNG MAN Up there.

FIRST What for?

SECOND To wangle my exemption. What about you?

FIRST Me too.

SECOND We may as well go together. (*Exeunt.*)

(Change of scene.)

Scene 26

Ringstrasse.

FIFTY DRAFT DODGERS (*enter, all pointing at each other*) They should take *him*!

Scene 27

In front of the War Ministry.

FIRST YOUNG MAN Hi! Where are you going?

SECOND YOUNG MAN Up there.

FIRST What for?

SECOND Import. What about you?

FIRST Export.

SECOND We may as well go together. (*Exeunt.*)

(*Change of scene.*)

Scene 28

Ministry of Defence. A captain is sitting at a table, in front of him a civilian, standing.

CAPTAIN Look, as to whether you can be exempted or not, the simplest thing is to consult the statutory regulation. Then you can convince yourself, I'll do you a favour, so listen: "The Austro-Hungarian Ministry of Defence ruled by the decree of 12 July 1915, no. 863/XIV, acting in concurrence with the Austro-Hungarian Ministry of War, that in consideration of the war situation at that time—as similarly decreed by the directive of the said Austro-Hungarian Ministry of 13 January 1915, Section XIV, no. 1596, modifying that of 1914, finalized by the decree of 18 January 1915, code number 1068, as promulgated on the subject of preferential treatment (as family provider) according to articles 31 and 32 of the Conscription Act—the certificate of proof, in accordance with Article 109, Section I, Paragraph 1, and Article 121, Section I of the *Military Code*, Book I, June 1915, relating to the continued existence of the conditions justifying preferential treatment, in accordance with Articles 30, 32 (applicable to farmers) and 82 of the Conscription Act (Article 32 from *Military Code* of 1889), is hereby abrogated with immediate effect, whereby the above-mentioned preferential treatment—in accordance with Article 30 and Article 32, and coming into effect, according to Article 108, Section I, Paragraph 2 of the *Military Code*, Book I, when proof of the continued existence of the said conditions has been produced within the prescribed time limit—are for the time being to be considered still applicable." So there you are—but now you must excuse me, others are waiting, OK? So, good-bye—

(*The civilian bows and leaves.*)

(*Change of scene.*)

Scene 29

Innsbruck. A restaurant. At one table, three ladies speaking Swedish. From a table nearby a colonel storms over to them, his face flushed with anger.

COLONEL I forbid you to speak English here! (*His wife tries to pull him back to his seat.*) Permit me—as the brother-in-law of the Chief of the General Staff—

COLONEL'S WIFE But they're only speaking Swedish!

COLONEL Aha—(*he sits down.*)

Scene 30

Market square in Grodno, Belarus. The population has gathered, at the front a group of young girls.

TOWN HALL OFFICIAL (*makes an announcement*) In accordance with a request made by the head of the German administration in response to the wish of the Commander in Chief of the XII Army and with regard to the latter's decree of 29th April 1916, no. 6106, the captain of the town militia hereby issues the order that young girls be instructed to greet the German officers as well as the dignitaries of the town by curtseying. (*The girls curtsey. Dignitaries pass by.*) Curtsey! (*The girls curtsey. German officials pass by.*) Curtsey lower! (*The girls curtsey lower. German officers appear.*) Now curtsey as low as you can! (*The girls curtsey as low as they can.*)
(*Change of scene.*)

Scene 31

Censorship at a German front unit.

OFFICER IN CHARGE OF CENSORSHIP Phew, talk about busy today! Since nine o'clock I've censored 1,286 postcards and 519 letters, and most of them were to Otto Ernst. Whoever else is on reading duty today can spare me the addressee and signature. My poor eyes have just about had it. (*They read out excerpts from fan mail to the folksy author, which receives the censor's stamp of approval.*)

A CAPTAIN Your work is a real God-given gift, an inestimable blessing for us Germans in these hard times. For me it signifies the confirmation, indeed the incarnation, of faith in our German manliness today. That's why I can't help myself, I simply must pour out my heart to you and you alone.

AN AIRMAN I don't want to indulge in mere platitudes, but your book was the most beautiful, the most profound, and the most inspiring that I've read in years.

A SENIOR NCO Heartfelt thanks for *The Blessed Storm*, which reinvigorated and revived me. To hell with all defeatists and moaning minnies! That book expressed my innermost thoughts, and those of all the Boys in Grey!

A SERGEANT Today is Easter Sunday. This afternoon, comrades from the next dugout are to pay us a visit, and to mark the occasion there will be a reading of "A German Sunday." Your work will replace the most beautiful Easter festivities!

A TERRITORIAL RESERVE In off-duty hours we read as if we're competing with each other. Everyone wants to be first to read one or other of your books, and since we've only received three of them so far, there's quite a waiting time till a comrade has finished the book.

GUN CREW OF 9-CM CANNON, NAMED "ASSAULT COLUMN" (*in unison*) Our job doesn't always allow us to work together, so we prefer reading your novel individually.

SIXTEEN DRIVERS Sixteen drivers of the 10th Army read your "Open Letter to d'Annunzio" with rapture. It put in words just how we feel!

A LIEUTENANT Every one of your audacious lines bursts on the ear like a grenade exploding right on time.

A RECONNAISSANCE AIRMAN As someone who embodies all that is life-affirming, you are our redeemer from the tedium of our humdrum existence.

A SECOND-LIEUTENANT Once again your humour has given me heartfelt pleasure, and I hope its effect will continue unabated under shellfire.

A MILITARY BANDSMAN Your wonderfully healing and consoling works shall help sustain my poor, dear, unhappy fiancée through the time we are apart.

A LANCE-CORPORAL Wielding your divinely inspired pen, you are of more use to the Fatherland than with a bayonet.

A SOLDIER Your poems which stir all loyal hearts shall last as long as the world can distinguish German loyalty from English duplicity.

A CAPTAIN IN THE MEDICAL CORPS I read your open letter to d'Annunzio. That's just how I feel! I fight with the scalpel, you with the pen, each of us to the best of our ability. The main thing is that we win through. *Gott strafe England!*

A GUNNER I've racked my brains over how I might thank you with deeds.

A JUNIOR COMPANY COMMANDER Your splendid humour often helped us through times of trouble and stimulated a spirit of enterprise.

AN ACTING OFFICER We were in a trench. Whether or not another attack was expected, no one knew, but we were keeping a sharp lookout. Our nerves had been put through the mill yet again, and to calm them we crept into the dugout, where I was obliged to read something aloud as a distraction. I chose your sketch "On Time-Twisters", which went down very well. I was just about to start on "Anna Menzel" when we were recalled to our platoons on the news that enemy riflemen had been spotted at the edge of the wood. Talk about an Introduction to the Waltz! More and more attackers emerge from the wood. And now our machine gun, situated between the first platoon and mine, joins in too. Our artillery was likewise on alert and began bombarding the enemy with clusters of shrapnel shells. I noticed my men were uneasy, some of the enemy had already reached the barbed-wire entanglements. A lot of my chaps were very young, and this was their baptism of fire. As platoon leader, what else could I do but give them the order to stay calm and fire? That was the moment I remembered those warning words of yours from "On Time-Twisters": "Caaalm-ly, now, caaalm-ly does it!" Ducking from man to man, from group to group, I repeated this injunction. You could soon see the effect it had. The enemy, about to break through our barbed wire, were picked off by our riflemen, who were plainly now taking aim and firing calmly. The attack was easily beaten off; we had only a handful of casualties. So once again we managed to give the enemy a bloody nose, thanks to our alertness and the calm firing of our riflemen, for which your story can claim most of the credit. It had an unimaginable effect!

A SAPPER From the battlefield I offer you, great maestro and friend of the young, my most heartfelt greetings! May we soon be privileged to see the enemy, already bleeding from multiple wounds, under our heel. Hail the artist whose fiery spirit fights for the honour of his people!

A VOLUNTEER In the telephone cabin there is a book by Otto Ernst. Sunshine dapples its pages. I got such pleasure from reading you, indeed all morning I felt such a joyful glow that I need an outlet for all the exuberance of spring coursing through my veins. Run off somewhere, run into the forest, run into the world, that's what I would like to do! Damn it all! That's what I would like to do if I weren't bound to my post! So, what to do? Sing! Perfect, that always helps! Can't think right off what best to holler, though. Then in a flash—inspiration!—lickety-spit, there's a message-pad! Pencil at the ready—Otto Ernst shall hear from me, a salutation! Good morning, Otto Ernst! Do you know you are an old, old acquaintance of mine? Yes, indeed, young-at-heart as you shall ever be! *(A major-general appears.)*

OFFICER IN CHARGE OF CENSORSHIP Ah, you too, General?

MAJOR-GENERAL *(reads)* Yesterday I was uplifted by your "Christmas Celebration." Unfortunately I was unable to find out from your books whether—when you need to refresh yourself for your writing—you do so with red wine or white? *(Laughter.)* Given your splendid traits of character and your humour, I'd guess (as a Mecklenburger!!) red wine! But one thing I do know: If there are sofas in heaven, there's a seat there reserved for you!
(More and more officers and soldiers from all branches of service appear.)

OFFICER IN CHARGE OF CENSORSHIP OK, that's it for now, chaps. Tomorrow's another day!

(Change of scene.)

Scene 32

A quiet poet's retreat in the Styrian Woods.

FIRST ADMIRER OF KERNSTOCK Ssh—quiet—there he is, sitting lost in thought—

SECOND ADMIRER OF KERNSTOCK It's from here he sends forth his songs throughout the land, songs uniquely powerful yet also sensuous and often indescribably tender, songs—

FIRST Y'know, I shouldn't be at all surprised if he wasn't about to—

SECOND That's my impression, too. Hush! All who sit at his feet, kindled by his flame, shall become keepers of that flame, and in times to come spread it a thousandfold into the hearts of a new generation for them to absorb the mysteries that this one man has fathomed, working decade after decade in the isolation of his castle amidst the murmurs of the forest.

FIRST Truly, Festenburg's parish priest is a man with the gift of a fiery tongue who knows how to celebrate God's world in all its living beauty. Shush!

SECOND Pst—something seems to have come over him. A poem? A prayer?

KERNSTOCK *(murmurs)*

Thy people, Lord, are sore afraid,
The haughty foreign horde
Harasses them with wanton wiles,
Brings death by fire and sword.

FIRST Oh, I recognize that. It's the "Prayer Before Battle with the Huns", isn't it?

KERNSTOCK *(murmurs)*

Who once didst sacrifice Thy son,
Oh Lord, now save us from the Hun!
Kyrie eleison!

SECOND No wonder he accepted when he was summoned to Vienna. His priestly calling is true nobility, it's inevitable he shall also make the most profound and lasting impression on those of his young followers who hear him speak in person.

KERNSTOCK (*murmurs*)

The heavenly host provides our shield,
St. Michael leads us in the field.

FIRST Festenburg's parish priest will surely have hesitated for an instant before exchanging the tranquility of his dreamy poetic seclusion in the Styrian Woods for the din of the metropolis. Just for an instant—

KERNSTOCK (*murmurs*)

God gave a sign—Th'avenger came
And drew his sword of wrath,
Who fled its bite fared just the same,
The swamps choked them to death.

SECOND But then he must have come to understand the lofty mission opening up to him here, the new ethical and artistic possibilities Vienna offers him to be active in the promotion of culture. And this recognition must soon have prevailed over the enticing murmurs of the pinewoods around the Festenburg.

BOTH Hush!

KERNSTOCK (*like a man possessed*)

With rifle butts hewn out of Styrian wood
Let lumberjacks cut down the Serbian brood.
Styrian hunters, take aim with care
And shoot down that grizzly Russian bear!
Styrian vintners, cut grapes from the vine
And crush full-bodied Wogs into blood-red wine!

FIRST Not exactly innovative, but it still carries you away every time. The sacred moment has arrived. If we take him at his word and hold out our albums as if we were impressionable young autograph hunters, wouldn't that be something to treasure for life?!

SECOND Struth! Let's do it!

(Change of scene.)

Scene 33

At a sector control post.

ALICE SCHALEK When we left the War Press quarters and got up to the lines yesterday, I had an odd experience. Night after night the old men working to bring supplies to the front positions have to cross the field of fire with their pack

mules. I was just contemplating the sight when the C.O. interrupted my rapt admiration with a robust exhortation: "You goddamned herd of bullocks! Why can't you spread out! D'you want a single shell to wipe you all out?" That was not directed at us from the War Press Bureau, of course, but at the old workers, and he apologized at once, for he greeted us with a laugh and the words: "Forgive the lively reception!" However much sympathy one feels for those poor, antiquated heroes, I can only say how dashing and engaging I found the officers. We were met with an unforgettable sight. All the gentlemen were gathered to receive us. Normally, each of them would have hunkered down under cover or be asleep, in any case he would take good care not to go walking around in the open. But because the first war reporter is expected, the gentlemen are all sitting cosily together as if in their favourite tavern, waiting for us. And not only that. They'd waited until we arrived before starting the bombardment, otherwise the retaliatory fire could have made the way up pretty unpleasant for us. That was a welcome course of action, not only for us journalists, but also for the officers who finally had a chance to show themselves in the open, and ultimately for the poor old workers too, who could have undertaken their trek confident that it held no danger—if, that is, they had kept up with the press corps and hadn't arrived with supplies later than us. Couldn't one conclude that, with proper planning, all concerned would benefit from a daily visit of the press to front-line positions? The dangers of warfare would be appreciably reduced for officers, for members of the press, and last but not least, for the simple soldier.
(Change of scene.)

Scene 34

Berlin, Tiergarten.
Enter an Exchange Professor and a National-Liberal Reichstag Deputy.

EXCHANGE PROFESSOR We are waging a defensive war. Our Chief of Staff Helmuth von Moltke told an American interviewer that our High Command had never entertained any plans for the predatory military conquest our enemies are always blathering about. How could we have been so irresponsible, he said, as to have sought a war with such superior forces as those of our most powerful military and maritime neighbours!

NATIONAL-LIBERAL DEPUTY Exactly, and we are firmly resolved to extract from this war everything our armies and our Boys in Blue can get out of it, and not to rest until England's global arrogance has been totally crushed. The moment has now arrived when the result of the war can only be a peace based on the expansion of our borders to the east, to the west, and overseas, with Germany as a world power setting the agenda.

EXCHANGE PROFESSOR Exactly, England's global arrogance must be smashed, and whoever doubts our peaceable intentions will soon see the other side of the coin! The German's sole desire is to stay at home, sustained by the honest products of his colonies. After all, in exchange we give the world the benefit of our erudition!

NATIONAL-LIBERAL DEPUTY Yes, up to now the world has shown too little appreciation for our unique culture, so let us now really knock it into their heads.

EXCHANGE PROFESSOR That will take time, unfortunately, and America alone has to bear the blame. Moltke told that American that the war will go on until America stops supplying weapons and munitions to our enemies. Moltke does admit that such shipments are the work of a private trust, but he is astonished that so many Americans are infringing neutrality for material advantage, and that the government doesn't put a stop to it. The fact that German arms factories themselves supplied our enemies in peacetime is something quite different. The armaments industry does that everywhere. Consequently, we were in the same boat as our opponents, the only difference being, according to Moltke, that we were forced to help ourselves, while our enemies, in addition to being supplied by German arms factories, could count on the support of American industry as well.

NATIONAL-LIBERAL DEPUTY Yes, I read that. The same issue of the paper takes note of the "revelation" in the *New York World* that we ourselves made attempts to get munitions from America. And they call that a revelation—how naive can you get! Priceless! As if it wasn't a perfectly natural thing to do.

EXCHANGE PROFESSOR Absolutely, and since we didn't obtain any, we've surely a perfect right to complain about their breach of neutrality at least!

NATIONAL-LIBERAL DEPUTY Absolutely, and all the more so since there was no breach. For look, the United States specifically states that its definition of neutrality permits it to sell weapons and munitions just as freely to us as to our enemies. And why shouldn't we make use of this neutrality if the factories were willing to supply us? That's also the line taken by the *Frankfurter Zeitung* in its discussion of the *New York World*'s amazing "revelation." The only drawback is that we are unfortunately unable to obtain the munitions we would like from the German factories in America—neither from the German-American ones nor the Reichs-German ones, both of which supply our enemies.

EXCHANGE PROFESSOR What? You mean German, Reichs-German firms? Not English ones?

NATIONAL-LIBERAL DEPUTY No, no. Some of the British-owned firms in America apparently refused to supply England. Oh well, they would probably have refused to supply us, too. That's just our bad luck, the enemy firms won't supply us, and the German ones are already committed to supplying the enemy. Well, there you are, a factory as such is under no obligation to uphold the principle of neutrality. It's certainly not being violated by the German factory owners when they supply arms to the enemy!

EXCHANGE PROFESSOR But surely—wait a minute—yes, surely—oh, it's so confusing! These concepts all seem to have exchanged their meaning in this war. If only it were peacetime again, then I could at least arrange another academic exchange and everything would be back to normal.

NATIONAL-LIBERAL DEPUTY Come on, put your mind at rest. We mustn't make a mountain out of a molehill. The debate should soon be redundant anyhow. Fortunately, America is sure to enter the war, and then the German Americans will have no choice but to think again and instead of supplying weapons to our European enemies, supply them to the American army.

EXCHANGE PROFESSOR That's the way of the world!

(Change of scene.)

Scene 35

Lecture hall in Berlin.

POET

. . . Step by step we thread our way through
Spent shells, barbed wire, flesh in tatters.
We must reach the line on cue,
Obey our orders, naught else matters!
Don't call for heroes in a crisis—
We do our duty, that suffices.

(Shouts of "How true!")

. . . With stirring battle orders ever ringing in our ears,
The thunder of the guns is like the music of the spheres.

(Shouts of "That's how it is!")

. . . March on, cries God, protect your land,
And save your children's Fatherland!

(Lively applause.)

. . . Steely grey our German fleet,
Each gun flashes a white incisor

To rip apart, destroy, defeat,
The scum who steam against our Kaiser,
Under the German sky.

(Stormy applause and bravos.)

. . . The Kaiser did create the fleet,
God saw that it was good (*Shouts of: "It is!"*)
The sons of Satan to defeat
In Germany's global feud.
The red tongues of our boys in blue
From hissing cannons' mouths do spew
Their tongues of fire, and so propel
The enemy through the gates of Hell,
Under the German sky.

(Tumultuous applause.)

. . . Up and at 'em, through enemy fire,
Rat-a-tat-tat in the rolls of barbed wire,
While larks sing for joy in the heavens above!
Hurrah! Hurrah! Put an end to that screaming,
Enemy flesh stabbed by bayonets gleaming,
While larks sing for joy in the heavens above!

(Thunderous applause.)

. . . Sing, comrades, our faith expressing:
This earthly horror has our blessing!

(Endless applause. Shouts of "Long live Dehmel!")

Scene 36

Lecture hall in Vienna.

GRUMBLER
"With Watch in Hand"
"On the 17th September one of our U-boats in the Mediterranean sank a packed enemy troop transport. The ship sank within 43 seconds."

So death is now reduced to a mechanical device.
Once bravery meant power—shall that no more suffice?
For here the clock is ticking towards the hour of doom,
Can the valiant god of battles save us from the tomb?

Once clumsy stage effects produced a god from the machine,
But precision engineering now dominates the scene!
There it stands, its legs apart and iron arms akimbo,
A proud machine but soulless, for its soul is lost in limbo.

A mortar there, the man beside lies in a trench, protected,
The gun was man's invention but the link's been disconnected.
Since dwarfs confounded giants, there is now a new device,
A clock that halts the march of time, and one that's quite precise!

Go, fall asleep, sleep through it all, have peaceful dreams and fair,
For otherwise you'll find one day a cripple in your chair,
In your office, at your keyboard: London disappears in smoke,
There's speculative profit for you, millions at a stroke!

And has the time not come when this might really come about?
Eyes stung with poison gases find it hard to make things out,
But the bell has tolled at midnight and the ear's as sharp as ever,
The glass is falling hour by hour—you can't hold up the weather.

Such motley jokes the people love, the papers too that feed them,
But God forbid that God himself should ever have to read them!
When progress creates amputees as well as profiteers,
Holding a watch in hand inspires their patriotic cheers.

LISTENER (*to his wife*) Say what you like about him—he sure can write! (*Change of scene.*)

Scene 37

Subscriber to the Neue Freie Presse *and Patriot in conversation.*

PATRIOT No bathroom in Downing Street! What d'you say to that!

SUBSCRIBER What can I say, the edifice is crumbling.

PATRIOT No bathroom in Downing Street!

SUBSCRIBER Yes, and to whom do we owe this disconcerting discovery? To Him!

PATRIOT Certainly, though you have to admit it was in fact Mrs. Lloyd George who made the disconcerting discovery.

SUBSCRIBER Yes, all right, but our editor in chief broke the news!

PATRIOT Yes, and y'know what follows from that with compelling logic?

SUBSCRIBER He's made no secret of it: British prime ministers, who have lived in Downing Street for a hundred years or more, have either done without the luxury of a bath or had to use public baths.

PATRIOT Serves them right, filthy beasts, I'm glad to hear it.

SUBSCRIBER And mark you, not like here in Austria, because of the war—no, they put up with the filth for over a hundred years!

PATRIOT Asquith lived there with his family for nine years.

SUBSCRIBER So he didn't take a bath for nine years, him and his whole family.

PATRIOT Well, you can't quite say that. Perhaps they went to the public baths.

SUBSCRIBER But that was never reported! Or did you ever read—

PATRIOT Not that I remember.

SUBSCRIBER There you are, then!

PATRIOT But y'know what might have been the case? OK, there's no bathroom in Downing Street. OK, it's been established they never went to the public baths either—but it doesn't follow from that that they never bathed at all for a hundred years.

SUBSCRIBER Why not? It seems to me you're something of a sceptic!

PATRIOT Look, He's written that the Lloyd George woman discovered it, when they moved in. Well, if she discovers something like that—what will she do in the future?

SUBSCRIBER How do I know? No business of mine!

PATRIOT She'll presumably do what the Asquith woman most probably did as well—

SUBSCRIBER And what did she do?

PATRIOT What did she do? She probably did what everyone did who has lived there for a hundred years.

SUBSCRIBER So what did they do?

PATRIOT What did they do? Well, is there a bathroom in Schönbrunn?

SUBSCRIBER So what's there, then?!

PATRIOT Well—from what they tell me—though I'm not saying for sure—but let's suppose—has the Emperor not had a bath for a hundred years, or do you think he goes to the central baths?

SUBSCRIBER A fine patriot you are! But why talk about that, I'd sooner you told me what they did in Downing Street.

PATRIOT What they did? Any fool can tell you that—they sent the maid to fetch water, and she made the tub ready and splish-splash they plunged in.

SUBSCRIBER (*puts his hands over his ears*) All the soap bubbles are bursting! You're taking away any illusions I had left!

PATRIOT Well, that's only a guess. In fact, I rather suspect myself that the Editor's right—they either never bathed at all or were forced to use the public baths.

SUBSCRIBER And what I say to you is: they never bathed at all! End of story! Poincaré is shocked and Lloyd George humiliated. The English and the Germans are to meet in Stockholm.

PATRIOT What's that got to do with it? What's the connection? You're getting to sound like Old Biach.

SUBSCRIBER And you, you should recognize that's how editorials always finish!

PATRIOT Of course—I know that! Y'know what I think? The edifice is crumbling.

SUBSCRIBER You don't need to tell me! But it's not because of the water pipes! There's not a single bathroom throughout the Entente, is what I hear.

PATRIOT Hmm, that's an exaggeration, didn't you read about the Tsarina in the bath?

SUBSCRIBER Yes, but it's common knowledge she had to share it with Rasputin!

PATRIOT Y'know what I'm dying to find out?

SUBSCRIBER What? I'm dying to know.

PATRIOT Whether there's a lavatory in Downing Street! Or were they forced to do without the luxury for a hundred years, or to go to a public convenience? *Gott strafe England!*

SUBSCRIBER You ain't seen nothing yet! (*Exeunt.*)

(*Change of scene.*)

Scene 38

In a railway compartment.

FIRST SALES REP Isn't the new operetta delightful: *I Had a Loyal Comrade*?

SECOND SALES REP Seen it. I'm an agent for "Hindenburg" honey flycatchers, motto: "You won't find any better." What's your line?

FIRST War chocolate "Diana." Pictures of our army commanders on the wrapper. Try some—(*Opens his case of samples.*) Before that I was a big gun in various sales branches.

SECOND Don't mind if I do (*he eats.*) Extraordinarily delicious. Incidentally, I also do patent foods. For instance, Hygiama—

FIRST Go on, you do Hygiama? My hearty compliments!

SECOND (*opens his case of samples*) Try some—

FIRST I will. Ah, it comes with instructions. (*He eats and reads*):

If the fleeing French you're tracking,
Catch and give 'em a good whacking.
A kicking's what the Brits deserve,
They pay their soldiers, what a nerve!
And if you spot the Russian bear,
Take a potshot at its lair.
(But keep your distance, if you please,
The ugly brute just swarms with fleas.)

Fantastic!

To do such deeds, in scale Byronic,
We recommend a healthy tonic.
These iron rations please do buy,
For food supplies may soon run dry.
Our pills are not for recreation,
But they will save you from starvation.
So keep them for emergencies,
Since pills like these don't grow on trees!
You suck them slowly, but don't chew,
Then fire your rifle as you do.
They'll still your hunger, slake your thirst,
In place of meat and bread and wurst.
So savour every one in turn,
The victors' health is our concern.
Then kindly send us a report
Saying how valiantly you fought.

Dr. Theinhardt's Nutrient Laboratory
Stuttgart-Cannstadt

The verses are as wholesome as the product. Marvellous packaging! Aren't we Germans a poetic people, say what you like, there's no denying it.

SECOND Aren't we just! They can't compete, those Brits, just a nation of shopkeepers! It's *made in Germany* all over, even if not in so many words—a surefire hit. For the Fatherland and for business, and when everything's at stake, the poets give the salesman a break. Y'see, I can even get it to rhyme.

FIRST Are these delightful verses your own, then?

SECOND No, no, my firm only uses first-class poets. I'm not even sure who, in this case.

FIRST At a guess Presber, or perhaps Bewer?

SECOND I really don't know. At any rate, our Field Greys will be amused. When the German seriously puts his mind to it, humour can really come into its own. Helps you fire your gun and keeps you healthy. Anyone from your firm among the fallen?

FIRST Certainly, the boss's son paid the ultimate price for the Fatherland. Here's the obituary.

SECOND *(reads)* "—With his far-ranging commercial vision he was quick to recognize the great objectives of the struggle, and it was with joy he took to the field for the glory of the Fatherland. The Fates have now blocked the way so lovingly paved for him with faithful toil." *Donnerwetter!* Fantastic packaging! *(Change of scene.)*

Scene 39

Optimist and Grumbler in conversation.

OPTIMIST What's on your mind? Some linguistic problem?

GRUMBLER Yes, indeed. I read today that the Germans have taken the enemy's advanced positions. It just occurred to me that the most advanced intellectual positions have also been taken over and made untenable. The damage is as great as that on the battlefield.

OPTIMIST How do you mean? In a physical sense or figuratively?

GRUMBLER Both the one and the other, so—figuratively. I'm sure Schopenhauer would have redefined *The World as Will to Power* as a premature German advance.

OPTIMIST Yes, but what about Nietzsche?

GRUMBLER Would have regretfully abandoned *The Will to Power* as an untenable position.
(Change of scene.)

Scene 40

The German spa Gross-Salze. In the foreground a children's playground. View along a tree-lined walk, at its entrance on the right, a sign "Free up soldiers!", on the left a sign "No admittance to the wounded."

On the left, Villa Wahnschaffe, a building adorned with parapets, embrasures, and turrets, with flags fluttering on the gable end—one black-red-yellow and one black-white-red. Below the gable, in a niche, a bust of Wilhelm II. Above the entrance, the inscription "Whole-hearted and ever at hand for God, Kaiser, and Fatherland!" A modest front garden with figurines of deer and gnomes, in the middle an ancient suit of armour. In front of the entrance, right and left, two dummy mortar shells, one bearing the inscription "Let 'em Have It!", the other "See It Through!" Medieval bull's-eye panes in Gothic arched windows on façade. Commercial Counsellor Ottomar Wilhelm Wahnschaffe emerges from the villa and sings the following vaudeville song; the last line of every verse is accompanied by an unseen choir, representing laughter at its reception abroad.

They're surely villains who don't care
for war at sea or in the air.
But since I'm used to durance vile,
and front-line service ain't my style,
I'll use my wits, as is my wont,
and fight right here on the home front.
To see it through, I'll slog away,

whatever all those villains say.
So let'em have it! For I'm a German!

While peace, for me, was really slavery,
I now can call it wartime bravery,
working my fingers to the bone,
now war sustains me, war alone.
Prewar I had to bear the brunt,
so now I'm grateful for the front.
A drudge's life's the life for me,
employed in heavy industry.
Heil Krupp! Hail war! Yes, I'm a German!

The work can never be too tough,
the days are never long enough.
I'll just keep at it, rain or shine,
to back the Watch kept on the Rhine.
My prewar fervour every day
led to the war, now we're OK
to boldly face the coalition
and see off any competition.
Unto the death! For I'm a German!

One thing we never should ignore:
it's vital that we export more.
A place in the sun is ours by right,
that's why we're in the trenches and fight.
Though life in a trench is not so grand,
it's there we'll win the right to expand.
But, for the moment, let's be stoic,
New Germans are nothing if not heroic.
The New Germans are true Germans!

War means weapons, as I've explained,
nothing ventured, nothing gained.
We used to make a cult of food,
so what we now eat may seem crude.
Prayers with profits, that's our device,
art in the service of merchandise.
The Faerie World's beyond recall,
Valhalla's turned into a shopping mall.
Yes, the Germans live for their ideals!

A vegetable salad is healthy eating,
if a bit of a drag from constant repeating.
When that has gone too, the pickings are thin,
well, life may go on, but you eat from a tin.
Such hand-to-mouth eating, with nothing between,
that won't see us through—so change the routine.
We shut our mouth and take a hand
in defence, to the death, of the Fatherland!
The Germans live from their ideals!

This principle rules, it's a good one at that,
no matter how gory our new habitat
on a planet that's bleeding, humanity's pain
the result of exchange rates and trading for gain.
Give gold up for iron, take poison for bread,
to the god of the Germans we bow down our head!
Blood-money, so long as we hold our nerves,
Is the best way to boost our financial reserves!
So the Germans hope to profit!

If things are going only so-so,
the truth comes through the Wolff Bureau.
But "what is truth?"—the age-old question!
Home truths give us indigestion.
A foreign word like "surrogate"
we're told we must eradicate—
but we've a substitute, and that's
the good old German word *ersatz.*
To put it plainly: I'm a German!

Since we possess the will to power,
their plan to starve us is bizarre.
And that is why we just pooh-pooh it,
our U-boats captains smirk: let's do it!
Just a nod, to save time, and we're down and away—
navigational skills we learned on the Spree.
And are we afraid of enemy ops?
We're not, for we'll eat any old slops.
The German's not worn down by war!

Each devilish banner against us unfurled
will raise our esteem in the eyes of the world,

we'll disregard the barbs of their malice
and triumph with *Deutschland über alles*!
It's because we're so very resolute
that the whole world's envy is so acute.
God knows alone how great is our bravery,
we hope he punishes England's knavery.
By the god of the Germans, I'm a German!

And so to God our praises rise,
raised (like our prices) to the skies.
Our God is just, to him we hearken,
and fight those who this world would darken.
A life of constant sunshine would
lead to sloth and lassitude.
Shooting is the only cure,
so *gaudeamus igitur.*
A merry fellow is your German!

Of one thing only I am sure,
we Germans have the best *kultur.*
Endowed with gifts—to generalize—
kultur (with a "k") still wins first prize.
We may admire the military,
but adulate philosophy.
We're proud of Schiller, make quite a fuss,
and Goethe, too, was one of us.
Kultur embellishes each German home!

In every German heart and mind:
God, Krupp, and Fatherland entwined!
While Hindenburg fends off our foes,
my inner resolution grows.
We Germans have had too much luck,
so modestly let's pass the buck,
pull back in triumph from time to time,
back to our very own Siegfried Line.
Sieg heil! is then the German's cry!

Our proud boast is that, with each foe,
our honour, if not our rations, grow.
We've got no butter for our bread,

the cannon's mouth is filled instead.
And German science, with God's blessing,
will teach the Brits a bitter lesson.
It was the aim of his creation
to make the Germans the top nation.
Only the German's made in God's own image!

So hammer away at those foes who fight us,
but even more at these words that unite us.
For the truth of the matter is: we intend
"to see it through to the bitter end!"
The iron and steelworks of Briey-Longwy
we must retain, for they're ours now, you see.
And as for peace, that concept's hexed
Till the whole world has been annexed!
That's the least the Germans deserve!

It's a question of honour and honour alone.
No, giving back Belgium we cannot condone!
The code of honour's kept intact,
our hands are clean, and that's a fact!
Our victory proves that might is right.
with world encirclement in sight.
We'll triumph over all our cares
so we can sell our shoddy wares.
Yes, the German is *made in Germany*!

A place in the sun was our delight,
now we've plunged the world into hideous night.
With poison and gases and fumes and more smoke,
we'll fight to the final thunderstroke,
till the voice of God shall summon the dead—
but till then our thunder will serve in its stead.
The song we sang so oft before,
We'll sing it now: "A thund'rous roar . . ."
Practical, your German, eh?

The world's ablaze, now who's to blame?
Our press bureau has fanned the flame.
While other peoples still exist,
we're the one they've always hissed,

and if, to boot, they're pacifist,
then we come bottom of their list.
Our feats of arms the world deplores,
our ructions, rumpus, thund'rous roars.
So everyone will hear the Germans!

Postwar there'll be more work again,
then another war and yet more pain.
Already I'm rubbing my hands with glee,
for my love of war lasts eternally!
If only peace broke out once more,
then I could grumble: what a bore!
Advanced technology's a must,
just take the U-boat: in thee we trust!
The Germans really do love progress!

The age of conscription we must lower,
and teach kids to use a flamethrower.
We'll still need veterans in the line,
so they'll continue to do their time.
To show we've learnt what war has taught us
we'll build barracks, make Europe a fortress!
To liberate the world from peace,
the Watch on the Rhine must never cease!
A history lesson for the Germans!

If the world full of devils, of which Luther spoke,
were turned to a wasteland, and one day we woke
to a world where our enemies all were defeated,
our glorious mission at long last completed,
and the future were bright, with no repercussions,
for then there'd be nothing, yes nothing but Prussians—
We'll *still* tell our troops to beware of the swine,
as they maintain their Watch on the Rhine!
And still the Germans celebrate their triumph! (*Exit.*)

(*After he has left, his wife, Frau Kommerzienrat* Auguste Wahnschaffe, *appears with her children, who immediately disappear into the playground to play a war game.*)

FRAU KOMMERZIENRAT WAHNSCHAFFE I've only two children, neither of them fit for active service, alas, one of them—to our eternal regret—even less so, since she's a girl. So I have to resort to a subterfuge and pretend my boy was at the front, though also, of course, that he's already died a hero's death, otherwise I'd be mortified if, say, he were to return home uninjured. Under no circumstances would I want to see him confined to base, though naturally the odd shell may land there, too. This fantasy is one of my greatest consolations, one that enables me freely to dismiss any doubts that may beset me, and which sustains me when my dear Ottomar is busy working. So in fact I'm continuously occupied except for the half-hour my hubby, who's just gone off to work, allows himself for lunch. As for the meal itself, able housewife that I am, I use my imagination there too. Today turned out well in that respect. We had hotchpotch: a wholesome broth of *Exzelsior* Hindenburg-cocoa-powder-cream-soup cubes, tasty imitation stuffed beef rolls with surrogate swedes, potato fritters made with paraffin and a homemade mash, all prepared in a special *Obu Fat-Free* frying pan, of course, and to round it off simulated puffed pastry cones filled with *ersatz* whipped cream à la Schiller, which really tickled our palate. A German housewife knows how to give her husband his due in this grave but grandiose age. It's true, hubby got into a huff when he didn't get his delicious homemade egg noodles. No chance! He just had to make do. What we really missed at first was the substitute margarine, but since we've had our *Obu Fat-Free* pan, we no longer lack for anything. We recently decided unanimously in the Housewives' Association that mineral nutritive yeast, whose protein content is mostly obtained by using urine, has a nutritive value equal to brewer's yeast, and therefore should not be distributed exclusively to the communal kitchens. The done thing these days is to cater for the general public. We must put a stop to such arbitrary favoritism. The middle classes also need to keep the wolf from the door. Those moaning minnies who object even to that, point out that the thing smells of herring and tastes of petrol, and consequently can cause nausea. But we German housewives know what's what, and we trust these peculiarities will disappear entirely after cooking, indeed we are convinced that mineral nutritive yeast lends a distinctive relish to the dishes. After lunch, it's time to start worrying about dinner again. Today, as ever, that will be a stew, but for a change with liver sausage made from starch paste and red-dyed vegetables, and Berlin quark with mock paprika as an alternative to real cheese. And today we're also going to try out *Gotitall*—it's on everyone's lips—*Yolkfix* egg substitute, made from ground gourmet chalk with baking powder and a little instant *Saladfix* vinaigrette, a delicious ingredient which I much prefer to either *Saladin* or *Saladoil*. Only the best is good enough for the German dinner table, and unlike poor folk, we have everything. Yesterday for afternoon tea we tried Deutscher's *Teafix with Rumaroma* and were pleasantly surprised. To be sure, the kiddies kicked up a fuss since they didn't get their *bombes glacées*, spiced with *Only the Best for Our Warriors* rum. Hubby got his acorn brew, which tastes almost as good as *Trench* brand *Tutti-Gusti* coffee, which they've run out of now. Unfortunately we had to make do without *ersatz* saccharin-water, so the dispenser stood empty on the table. Prompted by a sudden inspiration, I was going to fill it with liquid hydrogen substitute, so hubby wouldn't be disillusioned; but that would have meant deceiving one's husband, and one step from the straight and narrow is soon followed by a second. So I didn't. I'm afraid the good times are past when we still had it easy and with a mere squirt could sweeten our *ersatz* war coffee. But as we otherwise would have had no inkling that it's now a question of holding out to the bitter end, such petty privations are a price we gladly pay. All the more willingly, in fact, since there is nothing else we can pay for these days, so we can simply put aside the pots of money that hubby earns. The morale-sapping peace will come soon enough, and with it all the baubles we can start spending it on again. But let us hope the war lasts long enough to see a turn for the better in that respect, too. At the last conference of the Fatherland Party, my hubby proposed that the war, forced upon us by British envy, French revanchism, and Russian rapacity, should be taken up again after the conclusion of a peace treaty, a proposal approved by an overwhelming majority. Now it's a matter of holding out, the longer the better. We'll make it. Not a day goes by without some news that makes the heart beat faster. What is it Emmi Lewald says? "Three thousand dead Englishmen at the front!—At this moment, no symphony could sound more ravishing to my ears! How pleasantly, how joyfully it sets all my nerves atingle, a harbinger of hope. Three thousand dead Englishmen at the front!—it even echoes in our dreams and hums around our heads like a beguiling melody." As published by Velhagen & Klasing. My sentiments entirely. And the wonderful Anny Wothe, how I love her when she has the splendid soldier's wife announce the birth of a healthy boy to her husband: "Another soldier, praise be to God! The boy shall be called Wilhelm, may he turn out as tough as our Kaiser and hammer 'em till the sparks fly. But the other boys are all praying, day in, day out, for you to massacre lots of the French. I pray too, but not for your life. That lies in the hands of God. I pray that you may do your duty, well and truly, stand up to shells and bullets without flinching, and die calmly, if die you must, for our Fatherland, for our Kaiser, without thinking of us. And if you can die for your captain, don't think of us then, either. The five all send their greetings, as do I. At Wilhelm's baptism they want to sing *Hail to Thee in Laurels Crowned*, and I remain your faithful wife!"—O, God knows the only reason I can't write like that to my husband is because, alas, he is not in the field, since he is fortunately indispensable, and moreover because I only have one son, the younger child being, as I said, unfortunately a girl. Business success must compensate for the sacrifice of not being able to make a sacrifice for the Fatherland. Wahnschaffe has just created a really interesting wartime innovation: in Germany and in Austria-Hungary, which is fighting with us shoulder to shoulder, it has been patented and marketing rights awarded to efficient salesmen who give us a good cut. It's a *Hero's Grave for the House,* combining a reliquary and a photo frame, so it provides both an ornament for the home and religious edification. How sad I am that we ourselves have unfortunately no need for such a topical domestic death cult. My children, not old enough to die for the Kaiser or to be able to make some other sacrifice for the Fatherland, bear the additional misfortune of not having been born after the war broke out. Otherwise my boy would have been called Warsaw and the girl Vilnia, or else he would be Hindenburg and she would be Zeppelina! For calling the boy Wilhelm went without saying before the war, I can't see it as a particular patriotic homage. Ah, there they come running, the two little rascals! What's up? Why aren't you playing "World War"?

LITTLE WILLY *(in tears)* Mama, Marie doesn't want to be dead!

LITTLE MARIE We were playing at encirclement, then world war, and now—

LITTLE WILLY *(in tears)* But all I wanted was a place in the sun, since—

LITTLE MARIE He's lying!

LITTLE WILLY I managed to bomb her position, and now she doesn't want to be dead!

LITTLE MARIE *(in tears)* No, it's not true, it's a lie spread by the enemy, it's just like Reuter's News Agency! First he takes my advanced position, and now he's coming at me from the flank! I repulsed the attack easily, and now he says—

LITTLE WILLY Marie's lying! Her counterattack collapsed under our fire. The last English nests have all been cleaned up. Five of ours didn't make it back.

LITTLE MARIE A fresh outbreak of fighting at Smorgon in Poland.

LITTLE WILLY We took prisoners.

LITTLE MARIE We took a certain number of prisoners. The waves of attack broken up by our fire had to stream back in disorder, leaving many corpses behind on the ground we held.

LITTLE WILLY That's the ruthless Russian tactic, driving their hordes forward in mass offensives. We maintained our positions. We scored direct hits.

LITTLE MARIE I went on the attack.

LITTLE WILLY I'm preparing for a third winter campaign.

LITTLE MARIE For God's sake! Big head!

LITTLE WILLY Just you wait, I'll fight to the last drop of blood!

LITTLE MARIE You black-faced Brit and Frog!

LITTLE WILLY The Russians managed to gain a foothold in our front-line trenches, but our counterattack at dawn—

LITTLE MARIE —drove them out again.

LITTLE WILLY Several counterattacks attempted by the enemy in the course of the afternoon—

LITTLE MARIE —were thwarted by a bold surprise attack.(*She hits him.*)

LITTLE WILLY She's lying! Anyway, those initial successes are normal at the start of every offensive. (*He hits her.*)

LITTLE MARIE Guard against exaggerating the optimistic prospects of the offensive.

LITTLE WILLY At the last air attack on Fortress London—

LITTLE MARIE I retaliated at once! Karlsruhe—

LITTLE WILLY Yes, three civilians dead, one of them a child. The military damage is insignificant. End of story.

LITTLE MARIE And what about you? Two civilians and a woman! The military damage is insignificant. End of story.

LITTLE WILLY She didn't respect the flag of the Red Cross. End of story.

LITTLE MARIE He didn't either! End of story.

LITTLE WILLY Who started it?

LITTLE MARIE It wasn't me!

FRAU KOMMERZIENRAT WAHNSCHAFFE (*who until now has been listening, eyes sparkling*) You watch your step, Mariekins. Papa says you're allowed to play "World War", but you must respect the bounds of humanity. Willikins wouldn't hurt a fly, he's protecting what's his as best he can. He's waging a sacred defensive war.

LITTLE WILLY War was not my intention.

LITTLE MARIE Then who's to blame?

LITTLE WILLY Let 'er have it! (*He hits her.*) A direct hit!

LITTLE MARIE (*hits him*) Just wait till you come up against my blocking position!

FRAU KOMMERZIENRAT WAHNSCHAFFE O do stop, sweetie!

LITTLE WILLY Just wait, I'll bring up my flamethrower!

FRAU KOMMERZIENRAT WAHNSCHAFFE Play on, children, but keep to the rules! If Willikins is a good boy, Papa will bring him an Iron Cross from the office.

LITTLE WILLY Hurrah! Then I'll strike another blow against Belgium! (*He hurls himself at Marie and thrashes her. Marie in tears.*)

FRAU KOMMERZIENRAT WAHNSCHAFFE Willikins, Willikins, be humane! Don't forget your good upbringing! (*She goes to Marie with a handkerchief.*)

Back to your posts, now, each little fighter.
But here, wipe your nose first, my lass.

LITTLE MARIE (*in tears*)

He's shelling my candy shop, cheeky blighter!
And he's using poisonous gas!

(*She gets up and puts Willy to flight.*)

LITTLE WILLY A strategic withdrawal, no more. (*Running*) In expectation of this attack, the evacuation of the arc threatened by a two-sided pincer movement had been envisaged for years and has been under way now for days. That's why we didn't fight to the bitter end, but implemented the planned manoeuvres. The enemy could not prevent them. (*From a distance*) Hurrah, I've reached our Siegfried Line!

(*Two wounded soldiers limp past in the direction of the tree-lined walk.*)

FRAU KOMMERZIENRAT WAHNSCHAFFE But now I must see that everything's in order. We're using the new-formula *ersatz* soap *Child of War* for scouring today. (*She spots the wounded soldiers.*) Not again! That really is tiresome! If they don't see the sign, I'm going to report them to the chairman of the local council.

(*The two stop at the sign, then turn round.*)

FIRST WOUNDED SOLDIER So where now?

SECOND WOUNDED SOLDIER Back into battle. That's still allowed. (*They limp off.*)

(*Enter a nursemaid with a three-year-old boy, who's picking his nose.*)

NURSEMAID Master Fritz, aren't you ashamed of yourself! Just wait, I'll tell Hindenburg!

(*Fritz, terrified, removes his finger.*)

(*Hänschen meets Trudchen.*)

HÄNSCHEN *Gott strafe England!*

TRUDCHEN *(looking him right in the eye)* Amen to that!

(They go off, shoulder to shoulder, striking up Lissauer's Song of Hate.)

(Hans Adalbert, three years old, meets Annemarie, aged two and a half.)

HANS ADALBERT I hear you've signed up to the War Loan.

ANNEMARIE Certainly, I thought it my duty. From the conversations of grown-ups I gathered just how very significant the War Loan was, so I put my foot down (*she stamps her foot and gesticulates forcefully*) that I would not just play "Sign the War Loan", but do it in good earnest. Since I had set my mind on it, my parents withdrew everything in my savings account, 657 Reichsmarks, and—

HANS ADALBERT with collateral, or without?

ANNEMARIE With collateral, of course!

HANS ADALBERT Blimey!

ANNEMARIE That should be a lesson to you all.

HANS ADALBERT Only a scoundrel would deny it!

(Enter August and Guste.)

GUSTE England will be forced to its knees within two months.

AUGUST You think so? I'm no defeatist, but what about America?

GUSTE Shady customers, as we know!

AUGUST Our mood is solemn, but—

GUSTE —sanguine! (*Exeunt.*)

(Enter a nursemaid with a three-year-old girl, who is picking her nose.)

NURSEMAID Mieze—look out, if the General Staff see you doing that!

(Mieze, terrified, removes her finger.)

(Klaus meets Dolly.)

KLAUS We were encircled, any child knows that by now.

DOLLY British envy, French revanchism, and Russian rapacity—yes, we know. The question of war guilt is self-evident. Germany wanted a place in the sun.

KLAUS Europe was a powder keg.

DOLLY The Belgian treaty—a scrap of paper. (*Exeunt.*)

(Walter meets Marga.)

MARGA My father signed the protest of leading intellectuals justifying the invasion—the *Manifesto of the Ninety-Three.* But he said he hadn't read it, just signed it blind. What about your father?

WALTER My father did read it.

MARGA And what did he say?

WALTER That he would still sign it. (*Exeunt.*)
(*Little Paul meets little Pauline.*)

LITTLE PAUL Bethmann Hollweg is clearly open to the idea of a compromise peace.

LITTLE PAULINE Tirpitz would give that the thumbs-down.

LITTLE PAUL Me too. What about you?

LITTLE PAUL Impossible! I'd shoot that idea down right away! (*Exeunt.*)
(*Enter Jochen and Suse.*)

JOCHEN What we need above all is colonials. I'll tell you this, if we don't improve our overseas trade, Germany will have lost out from the war.

SUSE Hard cheese! What we've got to do is to annex some of mainland Europe. We need Belgium as an air base and, say, the Briey basin for ore mining, otherwise—

JOCHEN What you're talking about is the bare minimum! (*Exeunt.*)
(*Mother between little daughter and a gentleman.*)

MOTHER Well, Elsbeth, don't you want to play?

LITTLE DAUGHTER Naw.

MOTHER Go on, dear, go and play.

LITTLE DAUGHTER Naw.

MOTHER What a strange mentality for a child! Why ever not?

LITTLE DAUGHTER This gives us an advantage over the English, and that's why they envy us.

MOTHER Oh, do listen to this—tell us why, sweetie. Why do the English envy us? Tell Uncle, Lizzikins!

LITTLE DAUGHTER The English envy us because we're racing ahead while they're falling behind. That's because the Germans go on working after work, while the English enjoy games and sport.

MOTHER Golden words, Elsbeth. No, nobody's going to force you to play any more, Elsbeth. A child like that puts one to shame.

GENTLEMAN Out of the mouths of babes and . . .

MOTHER I'm going to write and tell the *Berliner Zeitung.*

GENTLEMAN No, it would make a better contribution to *The Child and War* anthology—children's sayings, essays, descriptions, and drawings. (*Exeunt.*)
(*Father and little son.*)

SON Papa, there's a report in the *Berliner Zeitung* from the Wolff Agency that the war has brought about a very welcome decline in infant mortality, at least in urban Germany; statistics for rural areas are not yet available, they say, but one can well imagine that conditions there are even more favourable. The war has actually become a source of rejuvenation. But Papa, I can understand that infants are not being killed by the war—after all, they haven't yet reached an age at which they can serve the Fatherland—but can you please explain, Papa, why the war has actually reduced infant mortality?

FATHER The fall in the birthrate caused by the war—

SON Oh don't talk nonsense, then surely there would be fewer infants, not more—

FATHER Now just pipe down! In any case, the fall in the birthrate caused by the war has been offset, at least partially, by the healthier diet infants now enjoy.

SON Oh rubbish—in wartime the diet's lousy! How can infants lead healthier lives now than in peacetime? Where would you get the milk from?

FATHER That's enough, now, I don't want to hear another squeak out of you, you pint-size little runt!

SON Heh! You can't still call me that—

FATHER Hold on—why not?

SON Pint-sized! For heaven's sake—I'm old enough to have forgotten what a pint of milk looks like!

(The father gives him a clip round the ear. Exeunt.)

(Another father with his little son.)

FATHER That's it, my boy—how is it Schiller puts it in *Wilhelm Tell*: Hold fast your Fatherland in firm embrace, your dear Fatherland!

SON Papa—

FATHER Well?

SON Has the Fatherland got dearer now, too?

FATHER Prohibitively so, my boy, prohibitively!

(Change of scene.)

Scene 41

Optimist and Grumbler in conversation.

OPTIMIST The *Neue Freie Presse* is right to praise Count Berchtold for doing the decent thing, now he's no longer in office, and setting off for the Italian front, sabre in hand, to face the sworn enemy who frustrated his policies.

GRUMBLER You mean the treacherous ally that General Conrad has been wanting to attack for years now? As for Berchtold, his action is right and proper and may well work out to our advantage, although, as you know, I'm pessimistic about the potential of sabres in this war. But if, unexpectedly, Berchtold should not find an opportunity to meet the sworn enemy face to face, since the latter is not invited to the staff binges of the Austro-Hungarian Army, our former Foreign Minister will at least have done his duty; for volunteering is his way of wangling it.

OPTIMIST I see you're still sticking to your habit of denigrating everything, even with heroic examplars of our military epoch before your eyes. Here it is in *Die Woche*, Count Berchtold in combat uniform. This image—

GRUMBLER —is the cause of the war.

OPTIMIST How could that be? The photograph was taken later than the ultimatum—

GRUMBLER Certainly. "One face before the deed is done, but after—a very different one"; yet in Austria, if not Schiller's Messina, they are identical. The Serbs rejected the ultimatum because they had a sense of this fatuous photograph. Austria's fear that they might accept it after all was completely groundless. Nor was there any prospect of "localizing" the war as Austria wished, so it could give Serbia a thrashing undisturbed by the rest of the world, for the world was haunted by this face.

OPTIMIST Again, I don't follow you.

GRUMBLER You're right in your own terms. But the battle of the Doberdo plateau, where 100,000 men have perished, was planned on the playing fields of Freudenau, Berchtold's favourite race course.

OPTIMIST I still don't get it. You mean, this photograph tells you—

GRUMBLER —that a betting man drove the world to its doom!

OPTIMIST Now I'm beginning get your drift. But he surely wasn't fully aware of what he did!

GRUMBLER No, otherwise he would have hedged his bets and not done it. The staggering thing is that he wasn't fully aware of what he was doing. *And* that this argument is an extenuating factor for statesmen, and for heads of state who in any case cannot be held legally responsible for their actions. They knew not what they did, none of them. Austria can't help it! It merely allowed itself to be encouraged by Germany to drag Germany into the war. And Germany drove Austria into a war which it did not want. The Germans are the innocent instigators, the Austrians the fleecy lambs. Neither can help it.

OPTIMIST This face is the image of conscience without guilt.

GRUMBLER One that could serve as a feather quilt, if staff quarters didn't already supply them. But at the sight of this simple uniform, one is convinced he would be equally at home in the trenches. A plain though courageous platoon sergeant, a swaggering Viennese braggart, winking, hands on hips, at the sworn enemy, as if to say "Look me straight in the eye, and come and get me, if you dare!" The simple statesman at the front, a wristwatch but no earrings, a swagger stick perhaps replacing the sabre, not smoking the imperial Virginia but sporting the Order of the Golden Fleece—derived as we know from fleecy lambs. Don't take him too seriously, but he'll stand his ground if necessary, and as we know his own decision of August 1914 makes it necessary. All in all, far removed from being high-handed or fainthearted, and even further from the front; man about town, not malingerer.

OPTIMIST This photograph—

GRUMBLER —is taken from the rogues' gallery of world history and at the Final Judgment will help to identify those responsible for causing the war. The original, of course, will be acquitted on the basis of diminished responsibility or nonresponsibility.

OPTIMIST How can that be proved?

GRUMBLER Among other things it shall be established that a harmless racehorse owner took Grey's offer to the Austro-Hungarian monarchy, namely to meet its alleged desire for satisfaction by occupying Belgrade and some other Serb localities, and stuck it between the pages of his racecard. For England really did want the "localization" that Austria hoped to achieve in a different way. That's why they called the only man of honour in this war "that liar, Grey." The photograph will help clear the actual culprit, but convict all of his compatriots. In its total shamelessness it justifies the aggressive intentions of our enemies in the eventuality that we really were waging a sacred defensive war, as claimed. For even if it were shown that we were justified in attacking Serbia because the Hungarian pig breeders had closed the market to Serbian pigs, this document would still stand up and bear witness against us.

OPTIMIST But I ask you—a photograph! A random snapshot! To think of all the other photos we got to see during the war, quite different ones.

GRUMBLER You mean all the others of people smiling during the World War. The soothing smile of the army commanders standing with their wounded troops. Alas, such smiles in war were more profoundly disturbing than the tears. The photographer didn't even need to ask them to smile for the camera, they already believed all was right with the world. Archduke Friedrich, innocent as a child unable to count—one gallows, two gallows, three gallows; Karl Franz Josef, the front-line smiler, unable to feel grief for those killed in action, while the glorious days fly past like some dreamy operetta waltz; the beloved German Crown Prince, known far and wide as the "Smiling Mosquito", and all the other smilers. My tables—meet it is that I should set it down that one may smile, and smile, and be a general! Then there are the ladies at this masked field ball! For instance, the Archduchess Augusta, Mother to the Troops, who, after their Father has used machine guns to galvanize his sons' advance, puts in a brief appearance before their heroic death as—in their mind's eye—a symbol of sacrificial patriotism. There is no defence against this aggravation of the duty to die for the Hungarian cause, and it is a spectacle from which the genius of mankind, if such a one still exists, certainly turns away, but from which the postcard industry profits.

OPTIMIST The self-sacrificing work of the Red Cross nurses is surely first and foremost, when one of the seriously wounded is about to undergo an operation—

GRUMBLER —to have their picture taken with him.

OPTIMIST Those photographs have been staged!

GRUMBLER The contempt comes across even better that way. Even Berchtold's photograph is merely posed, in order to bring out the unfathomable void of his visage—the void into which we have all plunged and which has swallowed us up.

OPTIMIST You exaggerate. I admit this photograph may not flatter us—

GRUMBLER Set against the fields of corpses, a background provided by our congenial subject in person, it catches us with deadly accuracy. I think of it as the only luminous image amid unspeakable darkness, and am consoled by the conviction that an Austrian face with such features will be seen no more. Should we not confront this image with that of those untold martyrs held in Siberia or slaving in French munitions factories, incarcerated on Asinara or rotting by the roadside after the death march from a Serbian to an Italian prison camp. One of those photographed is already a skeleton, standing upright, mouth agape like a starving bird. It's an image seen by some human eye that captures my eye. Should we not present it to the smiling Berchtold, along with all the horrors of an evacuation, all those buried alive and burnt alive, the rape of half-massacred women, whom the more tenderhearted of the murderers finish off by shooting! Was none of that photographed for consumption at home or abroad? Yet here someone took a snapshot of Berchtold, smiling, just as he was about to take a shot at the enemy!

OPTIMIST But surely he is not responsible—

GRUMBLER No, only we are, we who made it possible for such rogues to play a game for which they are not held responsible. We are, for we were prepared to live and breathe in a world which wages wars for which it can make no one responsible. Responsible for the only thing that absolutely calls for responsibility, namely control over life, over health, freedom, honour, property, and the happiness of one's fellow men. Greater cretins than our statesmen—

OPTIMIST —are those of our enemies?

GRUMBLER No, we ourselves. With our enemies we share only the stupidity of making one and the same god responsible for the outcome of the war, instead of ourselves for the decision to wage it. As far as the statesmen of our enemies are concerned, they can be no more stupid than ours, for that would defy nature.

OPTIMIST Of ours it can at least be asserted—

GRUMBLER —that we would save ourselves from fighting wars if we were to send them to the front, for that is somewhere you will never find Berchtold and his ilk. But far from the front as they are, we are even further from a state system like that of the Spartans, also known for seeing things through to the bitter end. They exposed their cretins on a mountaintop in the Taygetus, while we put ours at the summit of the state and in the responsible diplomatic posts.

OPTIMIST Though there, in many cases, they are—

GRUMBLER —not responsible!

(Change of scene.)

Scene 42

During the Battle of the Somme. Gateway to a park in front of a villa. A company marches past into the first line of trenches as if in knowledge that they are marching to their death.

CROWN PRINCE *(at gateway to park, dressed for tennis, waves to them with his racquet)* Give 'em hell!

(Change of scene.)

Scene 43

War Ministry. A room facing the Ringstrasse. A captain sits at his desk; before him stands a civilian in deep mourning.

CAPTAIN Well, what else do you want? It's simply impossible to keep records in such cases. How can we know if someone is dead, or wounded, or taken prisoner? Go and enquire in the Italian War Ministry, my dear fellow! Well then! What else do you want us to do? It's really quite incredible, the things people expect of us!

CIVILIAN Yes—but—

CAPTAIN My dear man, that's all I can tell you. Anyhow, it's almost three, we're surely entitled to a little consideration, office hours are over. It really is the giddy limit.—Well, what else?—Look, just between ourselves, what I will say is: you haven't heard from your son in six weeks, so you can safely assume he's dead.

CIVILIAN Yes—but—

CAPTAIN There's no but about it! Where would we be if in every such case—this sort of thing happens thousands of times, as you can well imagine. There's a war on, my good man! Civilians have to do their bit as well! Look at us sitting here! We're standing up to be counted, each of us at our post! And besides, my good man—you must know anyway, but I'll tell you again in confidence, and don't quote me—for a soldier there can be no higher ambition and no richer reward than to die for your country. So, good-bye, honoured, I'm sure—

(The civilian bows and leaves.)

(Change of scene.)

Scene 44

Kastelruth, South Tyrol. Nighttime, after a farewell party for officers of a machine gun detachment. Some are lying under the table.

SECOND-LIEUTENANT HELWIG More—more—more food! And wine!

WAITRESS It's almost two, Lieutenant, the kitchen—

SECOND-LIEUTENANT HELWIG More wine, I say!

WAITRESS We've closed, Lieutenant—there is no more!

SECOND-LIEUTENANT HELWIG Hey—you—cornet—! *(He seizes the duty officer's service pistol and shoots the waitress dead.)*

WAITRESS Jesus, Mary, and Joseph! *(She collapses.)*

ANOTHER SECOND-LIEUTENANT But Helwig—what have you done? Don't be so careless! They can confine you to barracks for that!

(Change of scene.)

Scene 45

A Viennese night spot. The night after the second seizure of Czernowitz by the Russians. Officers, barmaids, night owls, Red Cross officials, Polish legiona-

ries, waiters, performers. The little Nechwatal salon orchestra and the Miskolczy Jancsi gypsy band.

ROLF ROLF, IMPROMPTU POET *(is composing a poem, half-singing, and extemporizing with well-known quotations and homages to the military types present)*

The legionaries have done their stuff,
That's only natural when you're tough.

(Shouts of "Bravo! Bravo!")

D'you know—come to think about it—
My heart's at ease once more—
That lady there—must be delighted—
She's diamonds and pearls galore!

Our German soldier here, now let me see:
Two grenadiers heading for France.
But today—you'll agree—in all honesty,
We're hard up—with holes in our pants!

(Laughter, shouts of "Aha!" "Bravo! Bravo!" As two officers enter, the little orchestra strikes up: "Hoch and Deutschmeister Are We, the Emperor's Fourth Infantry." Everyone sings along.)

FRIEDA MORELLI *(the chanteuse appears and sings, alternately clasping her hands to her bosom and reaching out to the audience)*

Ah, Vienna, my heart is thine!
Berlin, too, is very fine!
A lieutenant there—a real charmer—

(runs a finger across her upper lip)

Could woo a girl, and then disarm her,
He's one I might have invited . . .
But best not get overexcited,
Or even adventuresome—
It's too easy to succumb!
So Vienna, my heart is still thine,
Though Berlin is also so fine!

(Shouts of "Bravo! Bravo!")

A VOICE Rosa, we're off to Lodz!

(The music strikes up this tune, later switching to "The Dear Old Gentleman in Schönbrunn.")

HUNGARIAN CATTLE DEALER *(to proprietor)* Fantastic, what you have on offer here!

PROPRIETOR Yes, I pride myself that we've a first-rate ensemble. Anyone who visits my establishment must admit that the notice advertising a *42-cm Mortar Review* delivers what it promises.

HUNGARIAN CATTLE DEALER It certainly does, a 42-cm mortar is child's play compared with your programme!

PROPRIETOR Even the enemy would have to admit it's gone down a bomb.

HUNGARIAN CATTLE DEALER A bomb! Bombs are mere tiddlers compared with such smash hits!

PROPRIETOR Well, Commercial Counsellor, sir, by way of thanks for such flattering recognition, let me straightaway offer you a special homage.

(The orchestra strikes up the "Rakoczy March", then, after the cattle dealer has smashed a champagne bottle, the "Radetzky March", during which one of the officers smashes a champagne bottle, upon which the "Prince Eugene March" strikes up, followed by the "National Anthem." All the clients and the bar girls stand up and remain standing during "Hail to Thee in Laurels Crowned", which follows, and, finally, "The Watch on the Rhine." The cloakroom and washroom attendants have appeared in the hall and join in the homage.)

GRAIN MERCHANT *(shouts across the hall)* Long live the Special Relationship!

ALL Hurrah! Hurrah! Hurrah!

PROPRIETOR *(to one of his regulars)* Do you know the gentleman who just shouted?

REGULAR Of course, Commercial Counsellor Knöpfelmacher—from the Chamber of Commerce.

(Proprietor rushes over to gypsy band, which strikes up "I Had a Loyal Comrade.")

DRUNKEN RED CROSS OFFICIAL You there—bring me another whisky and soda and a—dripped Tap—tipped Trab—Trabucco cigar. Hey, you. *(He belches.)*

COLLEAGUE Hey, what's up with you?

OFFICIAL Look, there's one of our walking wounded—it's off to the Neuhaus garrison with him tomorrow—for a medical—

COLLEAGUE Oh, leave him be!

OFFICIAL Excuse me, but—that's not on—I'm sending him to the—(*belches*) front!

OFFICER (*to another*) What did it say in the communiqué today?

SECOND OFFICER Nothing new.

FIRST OFFICER What about the loss of Czernowitz!

SECOND OFFICER But that's nothing new, is it?

ARMY DOCTOR (*to another*) Oi veh, look at him there in the second booth. I gave him a C-rating yesterday—light clerical duties only. Now he's out on the binge. Damned draft dodger! Still, I wouldn't mind being as loaded as his old man.

COLLEAGUE I don't understand you, I'm just the opposite. None of mine ever gets as far as the Appeals Board. You can make the odd exception. But in general, it's just a gut reaction when you see the perishers trembling in front of you. As soon as one of them starts to shake, I just call out: "Fit for service!" He can bet his life on that! All the more so since we're not allowed to pass less than 50 percent as fit now, that in itself makes exceptions more difficult. Especially with the new Draft Board.

ARMY DOCTOR Oh, I must tell you. There was quite a stir at the hospital yesterday. I still scare the living daylights out of that nurse, Adele, so she goes and drops the bedpan of some Bosniak who'd been shot in the pelvis. The others were in fits, you should have seen it. Talk about giggles! Until I intervened! Well, you've got to show those women who's boss. All in all, it was quite a day yesterday—

COLLEAGUE We're the same. I don't understand how those high-born women can take on so much. The others do the laundry or serve meals and things like that. But they're literally falling over themselves to do the bedpans.

ARMY DOCTOR I must admit, at first it tickled me to see such swanky wenches actually doing it—but the attraction of even that eventually wears off. I've been thinking about it—why do they do it? Well, they want to be fulfilled—patriotic, and all that. I read somewhere that it's up to us doctors to oppose it, on account of the shock to the female nervous system, and because it ruins their marriage prospects! Some problem, that! You'd be meshugga to take any notice of such problems in wartime. We practitioners—

COLLEAGUE What I was going to say—yesterday was the sort of day you'd have thought you weren't in a hospital but in a lunatic asylum. Fast work! I sent five cases of shell shock to the front.

ARMY DOCTOR With me it was five intestinal adhesions and three syphilitics. I say to each of them straight out: you're faking it! No answer to that, so it as good as proves the point—they're shirkers. (*The little orchestra strikes up the "Prince Eugene March."*)

COLLEAGUE I'm catching others out too now, especially ones with the typical shot wound in the left hand—I really don't see how you could do it any other way, what with the major in the Medical Corps always breathing down your neck and trying to get Teisinger from the Recruiting Board off his back.

ARMY DOCTOR Yes, it's a cross we have to bear. Yesterday I gave a wonderful kidney inflammation with acute cardiac insufficiency an A-rating—fully fit for service—after all, I haven't seen much sign yet of anyone going off to war singing. Very lively here tonight, eh?—

COLLEAGUE It's picking up. It's incredible how callous we've become. You simply don't have the opportunity to be humane.

ARMY DOCTOR A good doctor—as anyone who sat at Professor Nothnagel's feet always quoted—has first and foremost to be a good person. That's certainly something that gets completely forgotten, as I'd be the first to admit, and it's the first thing one does forget in war. On the contrary, a good military doctor can't be a good person, otherwise he'd better look out, or his next position will be at the front. Anyhow, Teisinger can't complain about me this month. I deliver before he sends in his orders. So what, if that's what it takes!

COLLEAGUE Listen, when one morning up north you've seen a couple of hundred Ukrainians strung up and swinging in the air, and down south a couple of hundred Serbs—and I have—then you get used to anything. What's an individual life worth? You know the case, don't you, where someone writes to his parents not to worry, in case of emergencies he always carries a white handkerchief in his pocket—the letter arrives, marked—

ARMY DOCTOR I know: "Sender executed by order of a court-martial." Worse things have happened here.

COLLEAGUE And what about with us? I don't look to the right, I don't look to the left, I look straight ahead! It's enough to make you suicidal. But you want to stay alive.

(*Everyone has stood up. The little orchestra plays "O You, My Austria", then switches to "There, Take My Last Cent."*)

ARMY DOCTOR Very lively here tonight, eh?

COLLEAGUE Yes, probably on account of Czernowitz.

ARMY DOCTOR What do you mean? Because the Russians—

COLLEAGUE Well—no—or rather, yes. Or—I don't really understand—Look at Paula there, with the lieutenant from the Deutschmeister. I'd accept her for service any time.

ARMY DOCTOR Fancy her, then?

(Shouts of "Tango!" Others of "Boo! Down with the tango! Waltz! This is a German establishment!" Someone shouts "Foxtrot!" Response: "Idiot!")

DRUNK No English music here, by God—We're in Vienna, play a waltz, you sod!

PROPRIETOR *(buttonholes his regular)* Know who the cornet is that's just come in? Y'see, you don't know. That's the one you read about in the papers, Russian soldiers saved him from a swamp using rope ladders. Now he comes here to us every night!

(Change of scene.)

Scene 46

Night. The Graben in Vienna. It is raining. Deserted. In front of the Plague Column. With a view down a side street.

GRUMBLER *(enters)*

Rain again, I see, rain rising from below,
a soporific sludge, the same old sloppiness,
torpid of tongue, mumbling the formless drawl
of old Vienna—mishmash of goy and Jew.
The city's heart is here and in Vienna's heart
a monument commemorates the plague.

(He stops in front of the Plague Column.)

This heart of old Vienna is made of purest gold,
that's why I'd gladly trade it in for iron!
O barren, lifeless world, the night has come,
which naught can follow except Judgment Day.
The din of slaughter will be swallowed up
by the eternal harmony of the spheres.
Rhythmically gurgling, the last Viennese
seeks for his soul some physical relief,

sprays it through the last rainfall of this world
so that it splashes on wet paving stones.

(He looks down the side street and spots a drunkard answering the call of nature in the middle of the street.)

So here he stands, a column to himself,
an indestructible hulking beast!
He cannot perish, he exemplifies
falsehood made flesh, shaped out of sludge,
the nadir of Creation, knowing he'll survive
when every living thing returns to dust.
He couldn't care a fig about the slaughter,
for he must satisfy his deepest need,
leaving a trace of his immortal mission
as words of wisdom far too good to miss.
So harken to the man's exalted vision,
and let the cosmos hear his Faustian creed—

DRUNKARD *(rooted to the spot, his words accentuated by rhythmical body language)*

Make me immortal with—a piss!—like this!—sheer bliss!

ACT IV

Scene 1

Vienna on the eve of the American declaration of war. At the corner where the Kärntnerstrasse meets the Ring. Masked figures and spectral apparitions, arm in arm, in groups of five. Hollow mirth alternates with deep, brooding silence. A gaggle of young bucks stand glaring eyeball to eyeball at one another as if linked together by some secret. The crowd moves, when it moves at all, between rows of civilians, cripples, disabled veterans, their heads and limbs constantly twitching, all kinds of wrecks and freaks, male and female beggars of all ages, the blind and the sighted, who stare vacantly at the empty show. Here and there bent figures searching for cigar butts on the pavement.

FIRST NEWSPAPER VENDOR Ex-tra-aa edi-shun—! Eye-talians annoyilated!

SECOND NEWSPAPER VENDOR Ex-tra-aa edi-shun—! Note from President Woolson!

FIRST OFFICER (*to three others*) Evening Nowotny, evening Pokorny, evening Powolny—the very man! You know all about politics. Come on, tell us, what do you think about America?

SECOND OFFICER (*with walking stick*) All bluff!

THIRD OFFICER Yep—spot-on.

FOURTH OFFICER Absolutely—I was at a bash in the mess last night—! Did you see the latest Schönpflug cartoon? Fantabulous!

FIRST OFFICER Y'know, I think it's just an American publicity stunt—that kind of thing.

FOURTH OFFICER Business is all they want—so it said in the paper. *Bizniz!*

THIRD OFFICER Y'know, when they do arm, it'll be against China.

SECOND OFFICER What are you talking about? Against Japan!

THIRD OFFICER Or Japan, of course, same thing—I always get them mixed up.

SECOND OFFICER Bluff, I say. In the first place they can't, because of the U-boats—

FOURTH OFFICER Of course, especially now we've intensified the attacks on their merchant shipping.

SECOND OFFICER And y'know, if they do come across—one regiment of ours will easily take out their divisions—child's play, my friend! Rat-a-tat-tat and that's that!

THIRD OFFICER High time we had some peace and quiet.

SECOND OFFICER What's that you're saying!

THIRD OFFICER I mean, so we can go for supper in the Gartenbau again.

SECOND OFFICER Ah, that's different.

FIRST OFFICER Come on, you know all about politics, I keep reading that they're going to make a blockade—what's a blockade?

SECOND OFFICER It's—y'know—look, think of us and the Germans, we're a block they can't defeat, so instead they cut off our food supplies and things.

FIRST OFFICER Ah, so that's what it is—but is it true the Socialists are to blame for the Czechs deserting to the Russkies?—Hey—isn't that—I know that broad, look over there—say, what are legitimate interests?

SECOND OFFICER Reporting for duty—she's the one from last night—tasty dish!—hang on a minute, I'll just—(*exit.*)

THE OTHERS (*calling after him*) See you later in Hopfner's then!

THIRD NEWSPAPER VENDOR *Tagblatt!* No one can stop our boys' advances!

A COUNTESS (*noticing one of the officers, to her lady companion*) Look at all his decorations, I bet he put up a good fight. I adore it when they're good fighters. (*A blind soldier in a wheelchair appears, his uniform in tatters.*) When I was still working at the Palffy Hospital—

INTELLECTUAL (*to his companion*) I assure you, as long as the enemy's mentality is so frivolous—(*exeunt.*)

A car draws up in front of the Hotel Bristol. Inside, reclining, Baby Fanto.

POLDI FESCH (*appears at the car door*) *Noblesse oblige.* Can you hang on a moment? I have my reasons.

BABY FANTO How many place settings? Is she coming?

POLDI FESCH *Que sera sera.* I'm raring to go today, though I lost a packet yesterday—in the Chapeau Rouge—so stupid—something that hasn't happened to me since I was cleaned out down on the south-west front.

BABY FANTO I really don't understand you, why you consort with such types—they're not top-drawer!

POLDI FESCH Very sorry, I'm sure—but then, tomorrow I'm out partying with the Sascha Film people again—and in any case—before you start lecturing me—how old are you?

BABY FANTO Twenty-two.

POLDI FESCH So you can just pipe down—a first-class joint, I tell you! As long as I'm stuck here, I'm under orders. But you can bet your life—the moment the peace is signed, and of course it'll be a stalemate—one way or the other, whatever the outcome, I'll be the first on the Orient Express to Paris!—So, now we can go in, laddie!—*(He beckons. The black hotel porter opens the car door.)*

BABY FANTO Listen, I'm really crazy about Lona, think I've got a chance?

POLDI FESCH *Que sera sera. (Exeunt.)*

(Old men march by. Strains of the song "In der Heimat, in der Heimat da gibt's ein Wiedersehn"—)

BERLIN EXPORTER *(smoking an imported cigar, to his companion)* No sweat, our boys have the fighting spirit. One of our most eminent professors has established that the psychic readjustment happens when they're still in the barracks. Your morale here in Vienna is lousier than ours at the front! No, no, my fine friends, not much sign here of a victorious peace—no Siegfried, eh! Dreadful mood in this dear old Vienna of yours! Loyal allies? You can tell that to the marines! No, not what I imagined at all. Some friends you are, making such a ballyhoo about peace as if you can't wait for it—! *(Exeunt.)*

(One passerby approaches another, hands raised, pointing to what's left of the cigarette in the other's mouth.)

OFFICER'S WIFE *(to her male companion)* There they are already queueing for tomorrow morning. I wouldn't mind if the war lasted another ten years, my husband sends me everything I need—*(exeunt.)*

FIRST WALKER If you don't obey the regulations, they fine you. If you do obey the regulations, they condemn you to death.

SECOND WALKER How so?

FIRST WALKER Didn't you read about it today? Interesting case, a professor starves to death.

SECOND WALKER Why a professor?

FIRST WALKER Middle class. Didn't manage to procure anything on the black market, he was just living on the prescribed rations.

SECOND WALKER Sheer lunacy. *(Exeunt.)*

FIRST DEVOTEE OF THE *REICHSPOST* And now the offensive is about to be launched, just you wait—rat-a-tat-tat, and that's that!

SECOND DEVOTEE OF THE *REICHSPOST* And after that, it's the Jews' turn—a clean sweep! (*Exeunt.*)

ODDBALL Look, yesterday I had a splendid meal here in the grill room. But when will they finally stop calling it the "Bristol"? We must cleanse our language of these outlandish French and Italian expressions. In the old days I used to take 10 percent commission, now, when we use the phrase "out of a hundred", it has to be 40, on principle!

HIS COMPANION You're right. Hey, look at that girl there—

ODDBALL Well, *chacun à son goût*, no sorry, *de gustibus* . . . , no sorry, each to his own—go on after her, maybe she'll give you her address. (*Exeunt.*)

(*A corpulent lady in Red Cross uniform with lorgnette gets out of an electric car.*)

LENZER V. LENZBRUCK (*in uniform of a captain of horse*) Humble respects, my dear Baroness—So you haven't left for your estates yet? It's the talk of all Vienna! And how splendid you look in your uniform, I'm quite speechless!

FRAU BACK V. BRÜNNERHERZ Well, you too! Are you going into the restaurant over here for breakfast? My husband's waiting.

LENZER V. LENZBRUCK Your noble spouse, the commercial counsellor? How absolutely charming! But your decision to become a nurse, that's the biggest sensation imaginable in Vienna!

FRAU BACK V. BRÜNNERHERZ I can't complain, this way we can keep the car, my husband's been fighting over that for two years, so I finally decided to join the Red Cross. Between ourselves, it's only a gesture, because it's the done thing. I'm actually looking after—

LENZER V. LENZBRUCK So you really are looking after—!

FRAU BACK V. BRÜNNERHERZ —my reputation. I only go in when I feel like it. Now that the war's almost over anyway, it's not worth the trouble. Yesterday Annunziata stopped me and said—

LENZER V. LENZBRUCK (*clasps his hands together*) The Archduchess! Oh, *do* tell, *do* tell, Baroness—

FRAU BACK V. BRÜNNERHERZ I don't like to boast, let my husband tell you. *Apropos*, I read that you'd been made Captain of Horse, my congratulations. You know you cut more of a dash now than as a civilian? That's probably why you're going round in uniform! Am I right? You men!

LENZER V. LENZBRUCK (*flattered*) You think so?

FRAU BACK V. BRÜNNERHERZ And the Distinguished Service Cross! Praise the Lord! Just look at that!

LENZER V. LENZBRUCK *(waving this aside)* Not worth mentioning.

FRAU BACK V. BRÜNNERHERZ The next thing will be—I wouldn't put it past you—you'll be off to the front! Have you ever been?

LENZER V. LENZBRUCK How could I possibly go?

FRAU BACK V. BRÜNNERHERZ Why not?

WOMAN SELLING FLOWERS Yellow! Yellow flowers!

LENZER V. LENZBRUCK The Executive Committee won't let me, will it?! God knows I've tried—*(both leave.)*

FIRST GENTLEMAN Oh yes, do tell me, what's your friend signed up to do, the painter? Having an easy time of it?

SECOND GENTLEMAN I suppose so. He started by drawing crosses for gravestones—

FIRST GENTLEMAN Well, there you are!

SECOND GENTLEMAN But one fine day this glorious state of affairs came to an abrupt end, he was meant to join a battalion with marching orders for the front—

FIRST GENTLEMAN Oi vey, and then what—?

SECOND GENTLEMAN Well, then there was a fortunate turn-up for the book. It so happened that the captain was an art lover.

FIRST GENTLEMAN So?

SECOND GENTLEMAN So now he's drawing naked women for the captain.

FIRST GENTLEMAN Ah, there you are!

(Enter Storm, the popular actor.)

FRÄULEIN LÖWENSTAMM Look, here comes Storm!

FRÄULEIN KÖRMENDY And in uniform, too!

(A gentleman gets out of a cab.)

CABBY *(holding out his hand)* Is that all you're giving me, guv? *(Turning his hand over)* Just look at them scars!

(Change of scene.)

Scene 2

Optimist and Grumbler in conversation.

OPTIMIST Are you off to Switzerland again soon?

GRUMBLER I'd dearly like to, though I'd be sure to run into the same people there that I'm trying to escape from here. Well, at least I wouldn't completely lose sight of the cast of the doomsday drama I'm writing. Being in Berne is like being in Vienna, with the Austrian state in meltdown exporting the products of its corruption, its crooks and diplomats, black-marketeers, and hack writers. Their travel arrangements are taken for granted, and they make propaganda in Switzerland for our loathsome body politic which has incensed the whole world. But for someone like me, travel is not so easy, and all the red tape prevents me from getting away.

OPTIMIST Ah yes, the same old story about passports. One department doesn't know what the other one requires. But after all, war is—

GRUMBLER —war, I know. But even more of a nuisance than being officially prohibited from doing something, is for it to be officially permitted. And then you have to give a "valid reason."

OPTIMIST Don't you have one?

GRUMBLER Lots. Not counting the prospect of getting hold of a proper sandwich in Switzerland. I'd rather put forward what all my reasons for wanting to leave have in common: being all too aware of living in Austria. The authorities would save themselves a lot of paperwork if you had to put forward a valid reason why you wanted to stay at home. But their asking whether you have a valid reason is in itself a valid reason to be up and away. Granted, it's not merely a valid reason for applying for an exit visa for a visit abroad—

OPTIMIST But rather?

GRUMBLER For emigrating.

OPTIMIST So you'll have no difficulty in finding a reason. Is there anything for which your dialectical method could not find a valid reason?

GRUMBLER Yes, for coming back.

(Change of scene.)

Scene 3

A railway station near Vienna.

A sheepish crowd, some 500 strong, has been waiting at the closed ticket window for two hours.

FIRST VIENNESE It'll be here in 10 minutes.

SECOND VIENNESE *(to porter)* Can you tell me when the train will arrive, please?

PORTER 'E loiks t'arroive round sevun.

THIRD VIENNESE But it's already a quarter to eight.

PORTER True, but look 'ere. 'E's goin t'be two-n-u-arf 'ars late today. It sez so on the board.

GRUMBLER Is that definite?

PORTER (*annoyed*) Well, what'm I gonna say? Them knows shit-all, and they ain't gonna give the public a sniff of wot they does know, are they?

GRUMBLER Aha, and why not?

PORTER 'Cos them still knows shit-all!

GRUMBLER But it's announced on the board.

PORTER Yea, announced, denounced, but arroive later 'e sortainly wull all the same.

GRUMBLER As a general rule?

PORTER Nat as a rule, zaktly, but a late arroival on toim wud be a bloody mirakul.

GRUMBLER Then why do they announce the time it's going to be late?

PORTER 'Cos it's beyond yuman 'telligence, that's why. Them out there at other stayshuns doan tell us, and us in 'ere sez nothin.

FOURTH VIENNESE I think I hear it coming!

PORTER Y'see? Mirakuls never cease!

GRUMBLER Yes, but how is that possible?

PORTER Let me tell you, Mister, grumbling'll get you nowhere. Go an arsk yer Aunt Fanny. Trains run late, an that's a fact! Us in 'ere doant get no news and them out there sez nothin—with orl the traffic these days, our 'ands are tied—there's a war on!

FIFTH VIENNESE Here's the train!

SIXTH VIENNESE The fellow in the ticket office is asleep!

CRIES What's keeping you?!—Open up!—(*The Grumbler knocks on the counter with his cane.*) That's the way!

(The ticket window opens. The Austrian Face appears. It is extraordinarily undernourished, but bloated with diabolic self-satisfaction. A spindly forefinger, wagging from side to side, appears to extinguish all hope.)

THE AUSTRIAN FACE Ain't na tuckets f'sayle todaye! Ain't na tuckets f'sayle todaye!

(Murmurs, rising to a tumult. Groups form.)

SOMEONE IN THE KNOW Come on, I'll show you how to sneak through a side door! No need fer na tuckets there! (*All leave through the side door.*) *(Change of scene.)*

Scene 4

Vienna, Kohlmarkt. In front of the window display of a picture gallery.

MARGOSCHES One of our most distinguished businesses for art and such like.

WOLFFSOHN Superb! (*He studies the display.*) What strikes me as so touching in this wonderful Vienna of yours is that, even after three years of war you're still so fond of symbols of the Special Relationship. Everywhere you look you see your good old Emperor standing shoulder to shoulder with ours, not wanting to detach himself, for he can't—they're inseparable. And look, that's His Majesty the Kaiser in the Reichstag, the historic sitting when he draws his sword. Well y'know, Commercial Counsellor, that was some day!—Who's our fat friend there?

MARGOSCHES Don't you know? That's Archduke Friedrich.

WOLFFSOHN Fine figure of a man!

MARGOSCHES And behold all the archdukes and archduchesses!

WOLFFSOHN Well, well, real character studies, every one! Ah, you've even got that beautiful picture of our Kaiser crying.

MARGOSCHES *And* the picture of *our* Emperor crying! Over there!

WOLFFSOHN Ah no, that's only a genre painting, he could just as well be praying. But ours is at the front, with his troops, and the painter has painted in real teardrops.

MARGOSCHES That one there is one of the greatest pictures, *This Age of Grandeur*, by Ludwig Koch. That's our Emperor again, right at the heart of the battle!

WOLFFSOHN Yes, that's the way it looks. All of them galloping into the breach together, your old Emperor and our Kaiser, our Hindenburg and your Hötzendorf—there's a lesson for your shirkers!

MARGOSCHES Do you know this one, Commercial Counsellor? I'm told it's by Theodor Körner.

WOLFFSOHN Yes, I do. It's famous! A picture full of genuine feeling, a fine young man. (*Reading*) "Father, hear my cry, we're not fighting for worldly gain!"

(*Leaving*) Yes, but what I say is, we must win, we must win! Then the value of our currency will shoot up spontaneously.
(*Change of scene.*)

Scene 5

Two poets in conversation.

THE POET STROBL —With moonlight threading through the greenery and pouring out into the far, far distance of houses glinting white and sombre mountains, as in Eichendorff's bewitching poem to a summer night . . . (*sinks into a reverie*) And as I step out from the dark hall on to the terrace, the officer cadet, his great clasp-knife in hand, cuts off a piece of smoked pork and says quite casually "With this knife I cut a few of the throats of them dirty Wogs." (*After a pause, pensively*) He was a good lad!

THE POET ERTL What an experience! I envy you. (*He ponders.*) I have a project in mind. I'll suggest that the seventh war loan should be called the "Truth Loan."

THE POET STROBL Truly an ingenious thought. But why?

THE POET ERTL Because our victory will finally ensure that Truth shall prevail, as it must! Because the precondition of successful peace negotiations must be the Truth, namely the official rectification of all the lies and libels with which the malicious politicians and hack journalists of the *Entente* countries deceived, poisoned, and misled their own peoples and the world. (*Strobl silently clasps his hand. They proceed on their way.*)
(*Change of scene.*)

Scene 6

Student drinking fraternity. Celebration in honour of Hindenburg.

AN ALUMNUS —Honourable members and thirsty souls, imbibers of the amber nectar! Mark well what the *German Fraternities' Journal* urges you to take to heart. (*He reads out*) Another essential requirement is to provide scope for drinking to excess and of making others do likewise. If we were to prohibit the obligation laid on all new recruits to down their glass in one, then any youngster who can hold his drink could always drink a less solid senior fraternity member under the table, and that would subvert authority. Alternatively, we abolish our initiation ceremony and with it the basis of all convivial carousing. If we ban tanking up, we deprive ourselves of an educational tool. (*Cries of "Quite right!" "Respect the Rules of Procedure!"*) I beg you not to take these comments out of context. After all, life within our fraternity, its *esprit de corps*, consists of a whole chain of experiments of an educational nature. And every corps student will confirm that never again in his life did he hear the unvarnished truth proclaimed so clearly, and at times so incredibly crudely, as within the corps. And why did he put up with it? Ludicrous as it may sound, because of the beer-drinking ritual! The ritual is, for us, what the much-maligned parade ground drill and march-past is for the soldier. (*Cries of "Hurrah!"*) Just as the hundredfold command "Knees bend!" eliminates laziness, indifference, defiance, rage, inertia, and exhaustion, and transforms a feeling of helpless impotence, and total lack of willpower in the face of one's superior, into military discipline (*Cries of "Hurrah"!*)—so, too, the command "Down in one!" always provides our senior member with a chance to demonstrate his absolute superiority over a recruit, to punish, to keep his distance, to maintain that atmosphere which is absolutely essential for the continuing educational function of the corps, if it is not to degenerate into a mere club. (*Cries of "On no account!"*) "Down in one!" is of course not always appropriate, and not for everyone, but it must hang over our revels just as the "Knees bend!" does over the barrack square!

ALL Hurrah! Hurrah! Hurrah! (*They clink glasses.*) Down in one!

RECRUIT (*brandishes the special Hindenburg number of the Munich magazine* Jugend, *singing to the tune of Scheffel's song celebrating Hermann's rout of the Roman legions, "When the Romans Had the Nerve"*):

No sooner is he in the train,
He's mapping out the whole campaign,
And says, after a moment's thought,
"Lake Narew"—the main onslaught!
Soon after Hindenburg arrived,
Into the lake the Russians dived,
Joining the fish that smell so vile—
Yes, that's our commander's style!

Attacks three times, and with each swoop
They're back with frogs and toads in the soup.
Russian blood fills swamp and pond,
Making waves throughout the land!

ALL Hindenburg Hurrah! Hurrah! Hurrah! Down in one!

(*Change of scene.*)

Scene 7

Medical convention in Berlin.

PSYCHIATRIST —Gentlemen! You see before you the most remarkable case I've ever come across. By good fortune, the man was released from protective custody into my care. Since it would be clearly impossible to serve as many years' hard labour as he could have expected for his crimes, there was no alternative but to turn to psychiatry. In this case, it is irrelevant to ask if the criminal is subjectively responsible for his deed, rather, the deed is itself objective proof that he is not responsible for his actions. Let me straightaway give you a full picture of the patient's insanity, gentlemen, by pointing out that the man openly declared that the food situation in Germany is precarious! (*Agitation.*) More than that, the man has called Germany's eventual victory into question! (*Commotion.*) But to crown it all, the man maintains that the intensified U-boat war, and indeed U-boat warfare in general, is inappropriate—for I established straightaway that he rejects the U-boat as a weapon not only because he thinks it inappropriate, but because he considers it downright immoral! (*Heated exclamations.*) Gentlemen, we as men of science have a duty to keep a cool head, and to confront the object of our outrage only as the object of our research, controlling our anger, of course, so as to maintain impartiality.(*Laughter.*) Gentlemen, it is now my sad duty to sketch for you a complete picture of the patient's unbalanced mental state, and I must ask you to hold neither this unfortunate creature responsible, nor myself, whose lot it is to demonstrate this repugnant case of insanity. His accountability has been ruled out by his affliction, mine by science. (*Cries of "Quite right!"*) Gentlemen, the man is suffering from the fixed idea that Germany is being driven towards her destruction by a "criminal ideology", as he calls the noble idealism of those in authority over us. He claims that we are lost if we do not capitulate at the very height of our triumphant progress, that our government, our military leaders—but never the English! (*Cries of "Oho!"*)—are to blame for the deaths of our children! (*Cries of "Shame!"*) He maintains that our children are dying because of the precarious food situation—this alone is clear proof of his mental confusion. (*Cries of "Quite right!"*) I have now laid out the case, esteemed colleagues in internal medicine, so you can attempt to exert an influence on the patient by conveying firsthand information about the wartime health of the German people. From his reaction I hope to round off the clinical diagnosis, perhaps to correct it as far as criminal responsibility can be ascertained after all, since no pathway must be left unexplored—that is to say, I hope the patient may be so carried away by your authoritative disclosures as to express opinions that will make it easier for us to come to a decision, one way or the other. (*Cries of "Leave it to us!"*)

PSYCHIATRIC PATIENT If any of the 93 who signed the *Manifesto of the Intellectuals of Germany* against "the lies and calumnies" of the Allies is present, I shall leave the room. (*Cries of "Oho!"*)

PSYCHIATRIST I hope, gentlemen, you will evaluate this outburst as a symptom rather than an insult. I myself, as you all know, signed that protest, which will live on in the annals as a landmark of this age of grandeur, and I am proud of it. May I now ask our esteemed colleague Boas to probe the mind of the patient.

PROFESSOR BOAS (*comes forward*) As I have declared time and again, let me repeat: the food restrictions have had no deleterious effect whatsoever on the nation's health. (*Cries of "Hear, hear!"*) It has been shown that half of the previous protein ration in our food suffices, without energy or work levels being affected; the fact is: our weight and physical well-being have even been enhanced.

PSYCHIATRIC PATIENT Presumably the black market keeps you supplied! (*Heated protests.*)

PSYCHIATRIST Gentlemen, please, in view of his mental state—Professor, please tell us what the situation is concerning infant mortality, a topic which repeatedly stirs the patient's imagination.

PROFESSOR BOAS We have found no evidence of food supplies having a negative effect on infant mortality.

PSYCHIATRIC PATIENT My dear sir, you've been obliged to find no evidence—! (*Cries of "Hold your tongue!"*)

PSYCHIATRIST What do you hope can be achieved by a continuation of the war, Professor?

PROFESSOR BOAS Rising affluence and the increased consumption of luxury foods have played havoc with our health. Now, however, under the pressure of current privations, millions of people have found their way back to nature and the simple life. Let us ensure that the next generation does not forget the lessons of this war. (*Cries of "Bravo!"*)

PSYCHIATRIC PATIENT The man's right—the rich on the Kurfürstendamm stuffed themselves before the war. But they still do. So there's really been no deterioration of their nutritional situation. But as far as the next generation of the rest of the population is concerned—those circles who do not consult Boas about their obesity—as for Germany's next generation, then, I see it being born with rickets! A generation of child invalids! Happy are those who died in the war—those born in the war will have artificial limbs! The insanity of seeing it through to the bitter end combined with the gloating about enemy losses so typical of German men will, I predict, leave Germany itself crippled. The passion with which fanatical German women celebrate the heroic death of their sons, nurtured by an atmosphere of orchestrated euphoria and self-deception, forms part of the same perverse social outlook and will have the same crippling effect! (*Cries of "Disgraceful!"*) As for Boas, I challenge him to deny that some 800,000 civilians have died of starvation so far, in the year 1917 alone 50,000 children and 127,000 old people more than in 1913; and that the estimated figure for deaths from tuberculosis for the first half of 1918 is higher—70 percent higher—than in the whole of 1913! (*Cries of "Enough! Enough!" "Scandalous!"*)

PSYCHIATRIST You see what we are faced with here, gentlemen. I thank our esteemed colleague Boas and now ask Professor Zuntz to pursue our enquiry further. If our esteemed colleague would be so kind as to address the question of whether the priceless national asset of German efficiency has suffered in the least through nutritional factors.

PROFESSOR ZUNTZ There can be no question of a reduction of efficiency given the current diet. Admittedly, malnutrition has occurred in a few instances where people are reluctant to eat *ersatz* vegetables with reduced calorific content in sufficient quantities.

PSYCHIATRIST If I understand my esteemed colleague correctly, the population has only itself to blame. For there is no objective reason for malnutrition.

PROFESSOR ZUNTZ Correct.

PSYCHIATRIST But malnutrition, when it occurs, or rather, if it occurs at all, it has no deleterious consequences?

PROFESSOR ZUNTZ Correct.

PSYCHIATRIST (*to the Patient*) I take it there is nothing you can say to refute this?

PSYCHIATRIC PATIENT Nothing.

PSYCHIATRIST His big mouth has an insolent answer to everything, but now he's reduced to a stunned silence! I thank my esteemed colleague Zuntz, and now call upon Professor Rosenfeld from Breslau, whom we are honoured to welcome as a guest of the Berlin Faculty, to continue our enquiry.

PROFESSOR ROSENFELD (BRESLAU) Though undernourished, our population has become healthier, and the great anxiety about malnutrition has proved to be unfounded. On the contrary, overindulgence in peacetime represents a greater threat to life than wartime food shortages. According to statistics, almost all wartime illnesses in the female population have produced fewer deaths than in peacetime. To summarize: at all events, the wartime diet has not reduced the resistance of the population in any demonstrable measure—neither to the vast majority of diseases, nor to illness in general, nor to physical overexertion.

PSYCHIATRIC PATIENT It has only reduced resistance to the dishonesty of professors! (*Loud cries of indignation.*)

FIRST VOICE Troublemaker!

SECOND VOICE Throw him out!

THIRD VOICE Call the police!

PRESIDENT OF THE MEDICAL BOARD OF GREATER BERLIN This outrage provides me with an opportunity to raise my voice in an urgent appeal. Esteemed colleagues! You are father confessors to your patients, it is your patriotic duty to encourage them, by word of mouth or in any other explanatory or instructive way, to hold on to the bitter end! You must take the most resolute stand against the fainthearted! Reject any unfounded, adverse rumours, such as are often spread maliciously or by careless talk! We on the Home Front can hold on to the bitter end, we must and shall see it through! Esteemed colleagues! The simple life and simple fare, a moderate intake of protein and fat, have been to the benefit to many!

PSYCHIATRIC PATIENT To the benefit of black-marketeers and doctors! (*Cries of "Disgraceful!" and "Throw him out!"*)

PRESIDENT OF THE MEDICAL BOARD OF GREATER BERLIN School doctors have proved conclusively—

PSYCHIATRIC PATIENT —that Germany has been successfully fed lies! (*Boos.*)

PRESIDENT OF THE MEDICAL BOARD OF GREATER BERLIN —that the health of the very young today is no worse than before.

PSYCHIATRIC PATIENT Infant mortality has only increased by 37 percent! (*Cries of "Shut your trap!" and "Unpatriotic rascal!"*)

PRESIDENT OF THE MEDICAL BOARD OF GREATER BERLIN Infant mortality has fallen. An eminent expert recently established that our infants have never had it so good. (*Cries of "Hear, hear!"*) Hospitals are less crowded than before.

PSYCHIATRIC PATIENT Because they're all dead! (*Commotion.*)

FIRST VOICE Prove it, you bastard!

PSYCHIATRIC PATIENT Doctors' reports from many hospitals sound desperate when they describe starving inmates trying to allay their hunger pangs by forcing down discarded cabbage stalks and all sorts of indigestible stuff. When a hospital for incurables had to submit a report, it stated laconically: "All our inmates have died."—But you, who are alive and gathered here today for your expert opinions, are under orders, and will pluck up courage to tell the truth only after the unavoidable collapse of the Lie which is the German Reich! But that will be too late, and no amount of confessing will save you from contempt in the eyes of the world. For German science has prostituted itself, and German scientists are its pimps! Those gathered here under orders from the General Staff, to serve the Great Lie by disputing infant mortality figures and arguing black is white, have more blood on their hands than those who stained the battlefield red! The 93 who signed the *Manifesto*, chanting "It's not true!" and "We protest!"—whose protest opened the emotional floodgates of the Lie and stained the honour of Germany—these people have led German culture even further astray from the legacy of a Goethe, a Kant, and all its other luminaries than even those who compel them to lie—the romantic arsonists and murderers. In the hands of such physicians the world, fearful of being infected by Teutonism, will certainly not recover its health. Add professors to aggressors—as the poet says—and the Fatherland is lost! (*A tumultuous outcry. Shouts of "It's not true!" and "We protest!" Some of the professors want to lay hands on the Patient, others restrain them.*)

PSYCHIATRIST Gentlemen! We have just witnessed the most savage outburst of hatred of our Fatherland, a hatred that cannot possibly have its roots in German soil. The reaction of the patient to the experiments of our esteemed colleagues Boas, Zuntz, and Rosenfeld from Breslau, and especially to the profound and illuminating exposition of our revered President of the Medical Board of Greater Berlin, for which I owe him a heartfelt collegiate debt of gratitude—the patient's reaction, I say, has made it crystal clear that the man is not of unsound mind, but in the pay of the Entente! We are dealing here with an acute case of Northcliffe propaganda, and medical practitioners in Greater Berlin in particular are duty-bound to stop it spreading. The poison of pacifism has already found its pernicious way even into healthy minds, and the exaggerated idealism of opponents of the war encourages wimps and shirkers in behaviour as dire as any afflicting the German body politic. Add to that the criminal propaganda of our enemies, and the resulting state of the nation will soon tend to paralyse our great enterprise on the very threshold of final victory. It is this spirit of defeatism which bolsters the backbone of our enemies and clips our wings in this defensive war, forced upon us by British envy (*Heckler: "A nation of shopkeepers!"*), French revanchism (*Cries of "And Russian rapacity!"*)—and Russian rapacity. Here we have a typical case. I can only stress that I thought from the start that he was a dubious character, and I am now convinced we are dealing with a hardened criminal. Those were not the words of a mentally sick person, gentlemen, those were the words of a traitor! Further, gentlemen, I can reveal that while in protective custody the man's unrepentant behaviour, his continued outrageous attacks against everything we Germans hold sacred, even extended to a derogatory remark about the official German News Agency (*Agitation*) which attracted attention in the highest circles, and that a personality whom we all revere (*Those assembled rise*)—our Crown Prince—even declared that someone should knock the living daylights out of him. (*Cries of "Hurrah!"*) The decision whether such a remedy might be implemented, perhaps as a way of increasing the penalty, lies with the highest authority in these matters. Our role, gentlemen, is to declare that the case clearly lies outside our competence, since it is of no concern to medical science, and to transfer custody to the appropriate criminal authorities. (*He opens the door and shouts*) Constable!

CONSTABLE BUDDICKE (*enters*) In the name of the Law—quick march off to the clink!

(*Exit with the Patient. The assembly rises and strikes up "The Watch on the Rhine."*)

(*Change of scene.*)

Scene 8

Weimar. Gynaecological clinic.

PROFESSOR HENKEL No one else needs operating on, then? His Highness will be here in a minute, and I promised him—I wanted to give him a chance to witness an operation at first hand. Well?

PROFESSOR BUSSE There's no one.

HENKEL But we have to operate on someone.

PROFESSOR BUSSE There isn't anyone.

HENKEL But you do have another patient. Bring her in.

BUSSE But—she's just had her breakfast.

HENKEL No matter. (*The patient is brought in. To an assistant*) Prepare her for surgery and pump out her stomach.

PATIENT (*resists, in a state of great agitation*) No—no—I—don't want to—

HENKEL Stop making a fuss. She'll disgrace me in front of His Highness! (*Enter the Prince of Lippe with entourage. Welcoming ceremony. The operation begins.*) It's going very nicely, Highness—there—that's it—

NURSE (*tugs sleeve of assistant*) Oh—my God—

HENKEL What's up? (*The assistant administers a camphor injection.*)

ASSISTANT Professor, sir—

HENKEL (*dismissively*) Shush—

PRINCE OF LIPPE (*to Henkel*) You operated quite splendidly, I'll inform my sister at once.

(*Change of scene.*)

Scene 9

A German Reserve Division.

COLONEL (*dictates*) At the obstacle, grid square 4674, two members of a French fatigue detail were shot dead with three shots by trench sentry Lance-corporal Bitter of 7 Company of the Imperial Infantry Regiment 271. I congratulate Lance-corporal Bitter on his achievement.

(*Change of scene.*)

Scene 10

The Isonzo front. Brigade headquarters. After dinner.

ALICE SCHALEK (*standing, surrounded by officers*) I have now covered the whole of the Gorizia sector of the front on the Isonzo, every step of the way. They showed me everything! The things I experienced there! Those sitting back home simply can't imagine. After repeated requests I finally got permission to accompany them. I sensed that the fact that I was going of my own free will made it harder for them. Being under no compulsion to go creates an inner conflict. At the appointed time, five o'clock in the afternoon, I present myself to the general as ready to march off. I ask permission to accompany a gentleman who would be going back to his post in any case. No one shall be endangered on my account, beyond what duty dictates!

A very young second-lieutenant, utterly delighted at the prospect of doing something different, takes me on a diversion round the foot of the mountain, which we then tackle from the flank. My previous orders are to be back punctually to where we started by nine o'clock. Whee, whee, wheeee!—it comes whistling in at us from the flank. And so, chatting away, we strolled on through the moonlight to our destination. But then! I was sitting beside the artillery observer up on the Podgora plateau, waiting breathless to see what would happen in his sector. Well, instinct began to take over, personality was coming to the fore—something previously out of bounds. I was being fired at from over the wall surrounding the castle grounds. We stand where we are, motionless. If the enemy sees us, so what! We haven't exchanged a single word yet. I look at him. He's thin and pale. Can't be much more than 20. I have a funny feeling. I look at the lieutenant; he's a primary schoolteacher in some Hungarian village. And like a blinding light, a sudden intuition strikes me. During the heavy barrage on the crest of San Michele, a new understanding illuminates every convolution of my brain. The lieutenant has no notion of the impact his whole bearing is having on me. He looks at me and smiles. He feels my thoughts are in tune with his, that our nerves vibrate in unison during the barrage. It sounds like an orchestral solo . . . Tikka, tikka, tikka—rings out . . . It's the first sound at daybreak, when I get up at half past three to go to my post. Whee, whee, whee—tikka, tikka, tikka—kaboom! But neither of us imagines for a moment that we could be disobedient and not comply with orders. The immense driving force behind an order—I can feel it now in my very bones. The lieutenant is still standing there. A nightingale is calling and the fragrance of the acacias is intoxicating. But now it's coming from the other side, the noise; no longer an urgent whip crack but a slow roar, almost singing in mockery. The lieutenant presses me against the wall. Voo—voo—phut—a dud, fizzled out . . . No question of staying where we were, or looking for cover. The order was: Report back by nine o'clock. For the first time, I know exactly what the men must be feeling. What a relief an order is! How amazingly easy it is to go through fire, if that's what you've been ordered to do. Happy the nation that can live under orders, trusting, believing that the order must be correct, since it emanates from on high. The same applies to the order here on the Isonzo—to push forward, cutting off all possibility of retreat, in order to protect our birthright! Wounded soldiers catch up with us . . . One has been struck deaf and dumb. He gestures to indicate what happened to him . . .

The motor cars are waiting and soon we're back at headquarters. The table is laid, and the meal is served up in steaming bowls. The reflected glory of a decisive experience lingers in every eye. But we eat like troopers and sleep like logs, and at lunchtime next day the military band strikes up outside the officers' mess. After all, we've captured the trench we wanted. So we can dine in the open air, the asparagus tastes quite superb and sweet waltz melodies compete with the cuckoo and the woodpecker . . . All Salandra will hear about in Rome is that he lost a trench today. Well, the barrage on Monte San Michele was by now just a memory. But the next day it was off again to the front. The columns of the wounded are interesting. Those with light wounds can still straighten up and salute, others look up wearily and try to raise a hand to their cap, but many are lying motionless, their coat drawn over their face, and see and hear nothing

. . . The exchange of fire is over. So we can go. The next day I tell myself: "Oh well, time to move on from Monte San Michele."

Today I'm off to the next division, the Army's Hungarian troops. The stench of corpses wafts across the road. There are more people on this shell-scarred road than you'll ever see on any bustling cosmopolitan boulevard. For some eight to ten months now, corpses, riddled with holes and completely mummified, have been lying between the lines. The trenches are narrow, seldom more than the width of a man, and the soldiers lie there stretched out to sleep. Others clamber over them, but they don't wake up . . . We count the impact of six shells and manage to take a quick camera shot . . . I'm allowed to observe through the armour plate and am amazed at the crater . . . At the battalion commander's I'm given a glass of eggnog. Very soothing, since my nerves are still tingling from the relentless, thunderous noise all around! "Lay out a fresh sheet of newspaper", this hospitable officer cries. (Evidently that's meant as a compliment.) Six artillery rounds—six direct hits . . . I take pictures for the future, fill one plate after another . . . And then back to here. Breakfast awaits us at the Brigadier's; I accept gratefully. And what a breakfast—! Since Cadorna spared me again today, since the shell once again arrived that crucial quarter of an hour too late, we cracked a bottle of champagne—the real thing—and, as a special reward, a tin of genuine caviar. Crisp croissants and brightly coloured flowers, radishes and damask linen table settings—such contrasts you'll only find here at the front!

THE OFFICERS Cadorna couldn't determine her fate, since the shell arrived just a little too late—

> Cadorna couldn't determine her fate,
> since the shell arrived just a little too late.
>
> There were croissants and caviar and flowers,
> that's how it should be in this army of ours.
>
> We're the staff at headquarters, an awesome elite,
> and do ourselves proud in our cosy retreat.
>
> The trenches, however, are not our affair,
> the cannon fodder have no shampers there.
>
> Nor caviar blinis, that's not their style—
> it's a hero's death for the rank and file.
>
> We do the eating, while they only pay
> with their lives, for the Fatherland, hooray!

Andante
rit.
p
f
a tempo
rit.
mf a tempo
f
Im Walzertempo
p
ff

To fall for one's country is fine, we're assured,
but we only fall when we're drunk as a lord.

Cadorna has spared us their fate. To be blunt,
such contrasts you'll only find here at the front!

(Change of scene.)

Scene 11

Divisional headquarters.

A COMMANDING OFFICER This venture was doomed from the start, Your Excellency, for lack of artillery support. The enemy simply started shooting practice at the pontoons we had put in place, and at those manning them. Hundreds of bodies disappeared into the River San that day, and we finally had to give up trying to force a crossing. The situation now is unchanged.

KAISERJÄGERTOD You must hold on at all costs.

COMMANDING OFFICER Excellency, the troops are freezing to death in the icy groundwater that has seeped into the foxholes.

KAISERJÄGERTOD How many eventual casualties do you estimate?

COMMANDING OFFICER Four thousand.

KAISERJÄGERTOD Orders are, the troops must be sacrificed.

COMMANDING OFFICER When they come out of their holes they're up to their knees in snow, and then they're expected to attack a raised enemy position.

KAISERJÄGERTOD Don't you have any padre who could put some fire in their bellies? Under no circumstances can the offensive be delayed!

COMMANDING OFFICER Excellency, the snow's deep enough to wipe out a whole regiment.

KAISERJÄGERTOD A regiment? What do I care about a regiment?

COMMANDING OFFICER The men are standing in water, half-starved. They're putting up a desperate fight against unremittingly powerful Russian attacks.
(Kaiserjägertod is called to the telephone.)

KAISERJÄGERTOD What? Relief or reinforcement? Colonel, your orders are to hold on to the last man, I have no troops available, and with me there is no such word as "retreat", whatever the price! What? You want a day's respite to dry clothes? What's that you're saying? Your poor brave Tyroleans are lying out there, shot to pieces, their bodies floating in the water? (*Bawling.*) That's what they're there for, to be shot to pieces! End of story!—And as for you, huh, the same applies. The troops stay in position, come what may. It's my reputation that's at stake! (*Exit.*)

A MAJOR (*to the Commanding Officer*) There is no alternative. His Excellency always commits his crack troops to the most difficult missions, simply because of their outstanding qualities. His Excellency is a general endowed with immense energy; he's single-minded and impulsive and personally courageous, while demanding strict adherence to duty and absolute self-sacrifice from his subordinates.

(*Change of scene.*)

Scene 12

Regiment on the retreat. In a village.

KAISERJÄGERTOD (*to a colonel*) No one to break ranks, and no buying provisions! (*A starving soldier holding a piece of bread emerges from a shop. Kaiserjägertod lashes him with his riding whip.*) What a bunch of greedy swine you've got here, Colonel! Anyone breaking ranks is to be bound hand and foot for three hours! Give the order that anyone trying to buy bread and milk off the peasants during an advance or a retreat will be shot! (*He rides off. Here and there soldiers leave the unit. Officers shoot at those walking away. Panic. Shrieks of terror: "The Russians are coming!"*)

LIEUTENANT GERL (*strikes a pose*) You lot can starve to death for all I care, I'll always have enough to eat!

(*Change of scene.*)

Scene 13

Hospital near a divisional headquarters. The regimental band can be heard playing jaunty tunes.

SERIOUSLY WOUNDED PATIENT (*whimpers*) No music—no music!

WARDEN Pack it in! That's the dinner-table entertainment His Excellency, Field Marshal von Fabini, always has performed at dessert! If you think he's going to stop it on your account, you've another think coming!

(*The door opens. One can hear the song: "I'd Rather Be Sozzled, I Swear, Than Smashed Up in Intensive Care."*)

(*Change of scene.*)

Scene 14

A German Reserve Division.

A COLONEL (*dictates*)—Now the last item on the order of the day. Note! The Masurian laundry in Lötzen has delivered to General von Schmettwitz three stand-up collars—white, make: Maingau, size: 42 cm., no name tag—which don't belong to him. However, he is missing three stand-up collars—white, size: 43 cm., two with the name tag v.Sch., and all three with grey thread around the back buttonhole. Please arrange for exchange.

(Change of scene.)

Scene 15

Optimist and Grumbler in conversation.

OPTIMIST One thing I would warn you against: you shouldn't generalize.

GRUMBLER You mean I should avoid thinking every scoundrel must be a general?

OPTIMIST No, you shouldn't overlook the profusion of examples of those who have fulfilled their duty and acted without regard to their own life—and that includes officers.

GRUMBLER One shouldn't generalize. But since that profusion of examples is evidently beyond my grasp, it's better to focus on the exceptions. Were one, instead, to draw attention to those who retained their honour in the war, it would emphasize what should be self-evident and impugn the officer class by implying that honour is something exceptional. It is precisely by pointing to the scoundrels that one avoids generalizing—it's only the scoundrels that would object. I have no desire to impugn any particular individual, but rather a whole institution which hardly deserves my praise for allowing honest men to remain honest, but certainly deserves my censure for changing weaklings into scoundrels. Don't imagine that I regard these cowardly ignoramuses as conscious tyrants, simply because they are using the power structure to revenge themselves on their men for their own lack of manliness. They spill blood only because they can't stand the sight of it, nor have they ever seen it. They act in a state of intoxication at suddenly being their own superior officers and allowed to do things for which the indispensable "cover" is provided by circumstances alone—not by personal integrity. And most of these scoundrels won't even be held to account, since their actions were covered by a code of honour that permits and indeed requires them to commit all those actions which the Criminal Code had hitherto forbidden: namely by Military Regulations. Such was the Age of Grandeur that those who committed rape, pillage, and murder walked away with the Distinguished Service Cross, while the Maria Theresa Order was awarded to those who authorized their crimes!

OPTIMIST One shouldn't generalize. I was reading only today that spilling their fresh young blood for the Fatherland creates a spirit of amicable comradeship that binds the men to their officers—

GRUMBLER —hand and foot!

(Change of scene.)

Scene 16

Goods station in Debrecen, Hungary. A goods waggon, guarded by sentries. Inscription in chalk: 40 men, 6 horses. Curious bystanders.

SENTRY *(to local inhabitants)* Clear orff!

LIEUTENANT BEINSTELLER How long have they been cooped up in there now?

SECOND-LIEUTENANT SEKIRA Only an hour and a half.

BEINSTELLER Another half-hour then! How many are there?

SEKIRA Twenty.

BEINSTELLER So, room for another 20! Cannon fodder, living like pigs in clover—

SEKIRA I had them already dry-shaved in any case, then smacked their faces. Since we can't bind them hand and foot, I know what I'll do. Put each in a sentry box and wind barbed wire round him, so he has to stand to attention!

(Change of scene.)

Scene 17

Vienna. Town Hall.

OFFICIAL *(to an applicant standing before him)* So you want to go into the country—let's see now, here we are—all you have to do is adhere to the following regulation, listen *(he reads aloud, emphasizing one word with particular animation, but at the same time continuously wagging his right index finger in a way that seems to preclude all hope)*: "Persons wishing to change their domicile in the year 1917, either temporarily to a health resort or for a period of at least four weeks to a spa or summer holiday resort, must, by 1 June at the latest, give notification of change of address to the district authority of their permanent domicile on the official form which can be obtained from that authority, stating name, permanent domicile, location of summer residence, prospective day of arrival, number of accompanying persons and intended length of sojourn; a second, identical copy of this notification of change of domicile to be forwarded to the district authority of the location chosen for the summer residence. Before departure, the persons in question must collect a *Food Ration Book Change of Address Certificate* from their ration book issuing office, to enable them to cancel the purchase of those foodstuffs which are officially sanctioned for sale at the relevant retail outlet, as confirmed by the *Food Ration Book Change of Address Certificate*. The retailer of officially sanctioned foodstuffs must keep a list on which are entered the name, domicile, day of departure and number of persons accompanying the person giving notification of change of address, in addition to the quantity of foodstuffs no longer provided; such a list to be presented to the office controlling the allocation of sanctioned foodstuffs at the end of each week. In the health resort, spa, or summer holiday resort, both on arrival and before departure from such locations, the persons in question (*the applicant disappears*) must present their *Food Ration Book Change of Address Certificate* to the bread ration book issuing office. The issue of food ration books, both at the summer holiday resort and after the permanent domicile has been resumed, can only be authorized on presentation of the *Food Ration Book Change of Address Certificate* containing the appropriate official stamps. The regional political authorities are authorized to monitor the purchase of foodstuffs by visitors, and also to regulate the provision of food in the restaurants of the health resorts, spas, or summer holiday resorts. In general, restaurants may claim increased allocations of foodstuffs to supply food to health resorts, spas, or summer holiday resorts only if they submit coupons detached from the ration books of the consumers as proof of increased need. No special food provision can be made for tourists making only short visits to health resorts, spas, or summer holiday resorts. In order to prevent the hoarding of foodstuffs, the regional political authorities are further empowered to forbid the direct purchase of foodstuffs from producers by visitors to health resorts, spas, or summer holiday resorts." — So, there you are, now you know, now you can — (*he looks up*) Where the devil has he gone? (*He searches on the floor.*) Hey, wait for your *Food Ration Book Change of Address Certificate* form! (*Shaking his head*) Odd customer. The liberties some people take! (*He continues searching, then gets up.*) Couldn't wait. He's probably in the country already!

(*Change of scene.*)

Scene 18

The Durchhalter family apartment.

MOTHER Take you sandals off in the house, I can't hear myself think!

CHILD Ain't we got nothing to eat again today, Ma?

MOTHER Cheeky pup! I'll learn you—(*she's about to have a go at him. The doorbell rings.*) That's your Dad! He's been queueing for swedes, let's hope—(*Sandals clatter. The father, in a cheap suit made of wood pulp yarn, appears in the doorway.*)

CHILDREN Bread, father!

FATHER Children, Russia is starving!
(*Change of scene.*)

Scene 19

Subscriber to the Neue Freie Presse *and Patriot in conversation.*

SUBSCRIBER We'll soon have wheat from the Ukraine now, you'll see.

PATRIOT More power to Czernin's elbow! Brest-Litovsk means "peace with bread"! Let them try to starve us out now!
(*Change of scene.*)

Scene 20

Sofia. A banquet of German and Bulgarian newspaper editors.

COUNT OBERNDORFF, GERMAN AMBASSADOR (*rises*) Esteemed guests! It gives me great pleasure every time I have the privilege of bringing together German and Bulgarian friends for a congenial exchange of views under one roof and the fluttering black-white-red banner. But today it is a very special pleasure. For I welcome you, esteemed gentlemen of the German and Bulgarian press, as—if I may so put it—colleagues.

CRIES OF Bravo! Cheers, dear colleague!

GERMAN AMBASSADOR Even if we have a bone to pick with each other now and again, as can happen between those in the same line of business, diplomacy and the press are closely entwined with one another.

CRIES OF Bravo! Bravo!

GERMAN AMBASSADOR No good journalist lacks that diplomatic sixth sense, no capable diplomat ever made the grade in his profession without a good dash of printer's ink in his veins.

CRIES OF Stout fellow!

GERMAN AMBASSADOR I say profession, but the word is inadequate. What we practise is an art, an exalted art, and the instrument on which we play is the noblest imaginable, the very soul of the peoples!

CRIES OF Quite right!

GERMAN AMBASSADOR What diplomacy and the press united can achieve, this World War has demonstrated.

CRIES OF Absolutely!

GERMAN AMBASSADOR We should learn from our enemies. If we turn our thoughts to all the diplomatic powers-that-be in the Entente, and evoke such names as *The Times* and *Le Matin*, *Reuter's* and *Havas* news agencies, *Novoje Vremja* in St. Petersburg, not to mention the minor satellites in Rome, Bucharest, Belgrade, then we must admit that this was an alliance that can boast of its successes. Successful lies, success in pulling the wool over people's eyes—

CRIES OF And how!

GERMAN AMBASSADOR —rage and hatred, the like of which the world has never seen. It is indeed a powerful alliance, one fearful to behold, yet it is but an artificially inflated colossus which will one day implode and collapse. For it lacks the spirit which animates and sustains life—the truth. And the truth is on our side in this fight.

CRIES OF Hear! Hear!

GERMAN AMBASSADOR You are fighting with it, gentlemen of the German and Bulgarian press, and you are fighting for it, in the proud knowledge that every success won by the truth is also a success for our communal cause. On the day the scales finally fall from the eyes of the peoples who are being incited to a futile war against us, the day when they realize what we're really made of—

CRIES OF Hurrah!

GERMAN AMBASSADOR —our invincible armies and our unconquerable souls—on that day the World War ends! (*Sits down. Toasts all round.*)

CRIES OF Hurrah—Cheers, dear colleague!—Mud in your eye, Count!

KLEINECKE (BERLIN) I get the feeling, my friend, that the Balkan crew are running scared. Haven't you noticed, not a peep—!

STEINECKE (HANOVER) That hadn't escaped my notice. But anyway, what the hell! Oberndorff was wonderful.

KLEINECKE (BERLIN) One good point after the other. The man really does have a good dash of printer's ink in his veins.

STEINECKE (HANOVER) He's just about the best speaker we have right now. The truth is on our side in this fight—a simple statement, yet at the same time, how true!

KLEINECKE (BERLIN) Yes, since the day we were able to announce that French planes dropped bombs on Nuremberg. That's what started the war.

STEINECKE (HANOVER) Yes, ever since then we've been fighting against enemy lies.

KLEINECKE (BERLIN) What diplomacy and the press united can achieve, this World War has demonstrated, a war forced upon us by British envy, French revanchism, and inordinate Russian greed. Golden words!

STEINECKE (HANOVER) It reminds you of that very apt formulation of a famous colleague of ours. What was it Ernst Posse said in the *Kölnische Zeitung*? The war has revealed what power the modern journalist wields. Just try, if you can, to imagine, says Ernst Posse, if there were no newspapers in this international turmoil of minds and hearts. Would war have been possible at all without their reporting the factors which caused it and the ways it is being waged?

KLEINECKE (BERLIN) How very true! Ernst Posse even omits the role of diplomacy.

STEINECKE (HANOVER) That's the journalist speaking. Oberndorff is a diplomat, that's why he's giving the press its due.

KLEINECKE (BERLIN) But tell me this, friend, those good-for-nothings in the Balkans—

STEINECKE (HANOVER) Oh, let's not get depressed about them. Look, Oberndorff is toasting us—

BOTH Mud in your eye, Count!

(Change of scene.)

Scene 21

Foreign Ministry.

HAYMERLE *(to a newspaper editor)* If only His Excellency, God rest his soul, had lived long enough to see me writing an article commemorating the anniversary of his death for the *Neue Freie Presse*—how pleased he would have been! I'm at the front right now and came in specially—out there you don't get a minute's peace to write. But since I'm here, I prefer dictating it anyhow. Yes—I remember it as if it were yesterday. So—I'd be grateful if you would be so kind as to publish the following few lines in your esteemed journal.

From the end of January 1914, I had the honour of serving His Excellency Count Szögyeny-Marich as Austro-Hungarian Ambassadorial Attaché in Berlin.

It is not my intention to discuss in detail the time shortly before the outbreak of the World War, nor am I entitled to do so; I only wish to mention an episode which is characteristic of the great statesman, and which does him credit.

It was on the evening of the declaration of war between Serbia and the Austro-Hungarian Monarchy.

It was just half past eight in the evening when I came down from my office to ask for a signature from His Excellency.

The Ambassador was about to return from the dining room to his bedroom.

When he saw me, following his custom of always first asking his visitors or officials if there was anything new to report, even when he himself had important news to communicate, he asked me: Anything new to report? At my answer that I knew of nothing important, the old gentleman looked at me with a half-proud, half-melancholy look, which was quite characteristic of him—you know, very firm—and stretching out his hand to me, deeply moved, said: We've just declared war on Serbia.

EDITOR So you still didn't know that by half past eight, sir? Though the population seems to have had the information already?

HAYMERLE Wait a minute. Literally at the same moment you could hear coming from Moltkestrasse, which runs between the Ambassadorial Residence and the Prussian War Ministry, thunderous cheering, hurrah after hurrah, and a moment later our beloved National Anthem—hundreds of people of all classes—officers, gentlemen in top hats, ladies in evening gowns—had begun to—

EDITOR Interesting. So the crowd was already massing.

HAYMERLE Ordinary women, workers, soldiers, and children—

EDITOR What, children too?

HAYMERLE Naturally. Oh, children are often wise beyond their years! The ambassador was particularly fond of children! So, where were we—they had begun to sing, and everyone was shouting with a single voice for the ambassador: "Come to the window, come to the window", "Show yourself!", "We want to see you!"

EDITOR It seems the crowd wasn't acting on information, but on instinct.

HAYMERLE That goes without saying. The German people, with that instinct typical of the psychology of the masses, already sensed how intimately bound to one another our two empires were destined to be in the hour of need.

His Excellency was so deeply moved, it was only with difficulty that I could persuade him to go to the window of his study.

The ambassador was so overcome that it was all he could do to wave his thanks to the rapturous crowd. But tears ran down his cheeks. And I'm not ashamed to admit that I, too,—(*his voice choking with emotion*) standing in the background and permitted to witness this exalted moment—gave way to copious tears.

For the ambassador, however, it must certainly have been the greatest and most beautiful moment of a momentous life when this distinguished statesman, shortly before departing from the office he had held for 22 years, lived to see the inestimable fruits bestowed on our beloved Fatherland—(*he is too moved to continue.*)

EDITOR (*deeply moved*) Compose yourself, sir, we of the press feel just as strongly! I'll finish it off back at the office. I gather from your moving depiction that tears were shed even before the World War began. Even if they were happily only tears of joy, the diplomats intuitively anticipated the burden of grief subsequently imposed upon their peoples. But believe me, sir—journalism was not indifferent in this matter. On the contrary, as a naturally liberal profession it did everything in its power to increase the flow of tears from that great moment on.

HAYMERLE (*deeply moved*) How can we thank you enough!

(*Change of scene.*)

Scene 22

In the Wahnschaffes' sitting room.

FRAU POGATSCHNIGG Well, I must say, *Hero's Grave for the Home* is selling like hotcakes back in Austria and everyone is wild about it.

FRAU WAHNSCHAFFE (*modestly disclaiming credit*) Oh, that only benefitted the dead. But my hubby has now invented *Hero's Pillow,* the ultimate present for our returning warriors to rest their heads on after all their exploits. It comprises: 1. A fitting dedication: Victorious warriors. 2. The Iron Cross. 3. The warrior's name, encircled by oak leaves as a symbol of German strength. 4. Little German and Austrian flags as a sign of the Special Relationship—

FRAU POGATSCHNIGG Aha, splendid!

FRAU WAHNSCHAFFE —and 5. Welcome home! Price: 3 marks 50.

FRAU POGATSCHNIGG Very reasonable. What about children's books and children's games? Anything new in the Reich?

FRAU WAHNSCHAFFE "Let's Play World War".

FRAU POGATSCHNIGG Pardon me?

FRAU WAHNSCHAFFE "Let's Play World War", a topical picture book for our little ones. And as for fully functioning toys—there's the 42 cm Mortar, though that's actually one of yours—wait a minute—oh yes, do you know "Divide the Spoils"?

FRAU POGATSCHNIGG Yes, but that hasn't gone down well with us, I don't know why.

FRAU WAHNSCHAFFE Oh, it's a charming game. My kids just love it. Yes, indeed, for us Germans only the best—

FRAU POGATSCHNIGG —is good enough. On the other hand, we've now got "Death to the Russians", that's first-rate.

FRAU WAHNSCHAFFE Sounds great.

FRAU POGATSCHNIGG "Death to the Russians", Countess Taaffe's ingenious invention, an interesting game of patience for big and small alike, produced by the injured patients of the Red Cross Military Hospital on the Kleinseite in Prague, where the Countess is a first-aid volunteer and matron. Inside a very tastefully constructed Easter egg there's a minifortress with barbed-wire entanglements and a swamp, along with our soldiers fighting Russians. You shake the egg and try to get our troops into the fortress and the Russians into the swamp.

FRAU WAHNSCHAFFE Awesome!

FRAU POGATSCHNIGG "Death to the Russians" is a suitable Easter present, not only for young people, but also for soldiers in the hospitals: a pleasant diversion and an exciting entertainment. The "Death to the Russians" Easter egg, very tastefully finished in black and yellow silk, costs 3 crowns 60 and is available from the central retail outlet of the War Welfare Bureau in Prague.

FRAU WAHNSCHAFFE How delicate! And how sensitively the high-born volunteer has taken the taste of the wounded soldiers into consideration! That's the Austrian nobility for you! They may be languid, but they do have more grace than ours, even I must give them that. So, my dear Mrs. Pogátschnigg, how does it work? You shake the egg and have to get our brave boys into the fortress, but the Russians into the swamp—awesome! It's like Columbus having to make his egg stand on its end without cutting it!

FRAU POGATSCHNIGG Ever since her invention, all of society has been paying homage to the countess. You in the Reich, now—don't you have anything comparable?

FRAU WAHNSCHAFFE Well, I shouldn't really be promoting what Wahnschaffe has created—blowing one's own trumpet, and all that—but I can't help singing the praises of the new "War Spinning Top". This new game is a must in every German household and provides an exciting entertainment for old and young alike in every family, at every social gathering and on every occasion. First, each player deposits a stake in the pot. Then the top is set spinning by the fingers of each player in turn. The letters and numbers have the following meanings: R.w.o: Russia—wins nothing. E.l.1/1: England—loses everything. F.l.½: France—loses half stake. T.w.⅓: Turkey—wins a third of the pot. A.w.½: Austria—wins half of the pot. G.w.e.: Germany *über alles!*—wins everything—the whole pot.

FRAU POGATSCHNIGG Bravo! But if Austria has won half of the pot, how can Germany get the lot? Does Germany then take our share?

FRAU WAHNSCHAFFE There you go again, you bone-idle Austrians, never satisfied!—That's all the thanks we get for doing your dirty work and saving your skins time and again! You made a nice mess of the last offensive!

FRAU POGATSCHNIGG (*grasps her hand and squeezes it*) You've convinced me. Austria may only win half of the pot, but—I am a German housewife! (*They leave, shoulder to shoulder, singing "Deutschland, Deutschland Über Alles."*)
(*Change of scene.*)

Scene 23

Three fashionable German ladies looking at a German fashion magazine.

FIRST FASHIONABLE GERMAN LADY Look at item number 4393: The latest hit! Bluebell fancy-dress costume, in light mauve silk, bell-shaped flared skirt with pinked edging, chimes well with cloche hat—just the thing for the Carnival season!

SECOND FASHIONABLE GERMAN LADY No, no, what about this little number? 4389: Mortar ensemble in glossy satin, appliquéd mortar-motif trimmings; large mortar-shaped headdress—that's what I want. Anyway, the Carnival is in full swing!

THIRD FASHIONABLE GERMAN LADY I'll go a step further and make a sacrifice. I'll turn the Bluebell into a Mortar.
(*Change of scene.*)

Scene 24

Subscriber to the Neue Freie Presse *and Patriot in conversation.*

PATRIOT What do you say about the exaggerated way the enemy press covered the attempted mutiny by three—I ask you, three!—German sailors?

SUBSCRIBER There's only one response: Huge Mutiny in the English Fleet.

PATRIOT Where? How come?

SUBSCRIBER At Spithead in the Nore.

PATRIOT You don't say!—There was a mutiny there?

SUBSCRIBER I should say so! Mutiny's too weak a word! Almost all of Admiral Duncan's fleet mutinied. The mutineers blocked the Thames with 26 warships.

PATRIOT Come off it! Where did it say that, what mutiny was that?

SUBSCRIBER A mutiny that seemed to be a prelude to revolution.

PATRIOT You don't say! What revolution, what mutiny?

SUBSCRIBER What mutiny? The mutiny recalled by the esteemed reader in his letter to the *Neue Freie Presse.*

PATRIOT All right—but when was that?

SUBSCRIBER In the last few years.

PATRIOT But I never read anything about that. It's just appeared, has it? Do tell me, when?

SUBSCRIBER 1797.

PATRIOT Yes, but—that's hardly in the last few years—

SUBSCRIBER —of the eighteenth century!

PATRIOT Yes, but—what good does that do us?

SUBSCRIBER Well—word gets around.

PATRIOT Yes, especially if it's true! Y'know, if it affects the morale of the Entente, that would please me, especially if, for example, in France—

SUBSCRIBER Well, what more do you want—in France the French Revolution broke out!

PATRIOT Come off it!—Where did it say that?!

(Change of scene.)

Scene 25

Hindenburg and Ludendorff at lunch.

HINDENBURG (*shakes hands with Paul Goldmann, foreign correspondent of the* Neue Freie Presse) Ah, there you are.

PAUL GOLDMANN (*aside*) The grip of a lion. He greets me with the heart-warming magnanimity characteristic of the man.

LUDENDORFF (*shakes hands with Paul Goldmann*) Ah, there you are.

PAUL GOLDMANN (*aside*) He looks just the same as a year ago, two years ago, three years ago, except that the distinctive features of his noble head have taken on an even more spiritual quality.

HINDENBURG AND LUDENDORFF (*aside*) He hasn't changed.

(*They sit. Paul Goldmann sits between them. They speak at him alternately from right and left.*)

HINDENBURG (*sighing*) Now it's a question of holding out to the end.

LUDENDORFF (*sighing*) It's hard, but success is assured.

HINDENBURG Everything is going well.

LUDENDORFF Given the situation, we can be fully confident.

HINDENBURG It's true we have the winter before us.

LUDENDORFF The date set for peace is naturally not for us to decide.

(*Goldmann nods to both sides and makes notes.*)

PAUL GOLDMANN (*to himself*) It is naturally impossible to give a definite indication of *when* peace will come. But perhaps about *how* it will—? I shall put a question which must surely lie close to everyone's heart back home. (*Aloud*) What are the surest means of securing peace?

HINDENBURG Peace will be the more readily brought about

LUDENDORFF the more favourable our military situation. It's still a question of deeds prevailing

HINDENBURG over words.

LUDENDORFF That's why we should not at present

HINDENBURG talk about peace. It's the Russians

LUDENDORFF who apparently want to take the first step.

(*Pause, while Goldmann makes notes.*)

PAUL GOLDMANN (*to himself*) Details of what followed in the discussion about peace are not for publication. Perhaps all that can be stated is that Hindenburg and Ludendorff are desirous of a peace which will produce maximum safety and stability, a peace which will secure our borders and global free trade by land and sea.

LUDENDORFF What's next?

PAUL GOLDMANN If I may just—

LUDENDORFF Ah, understood—Hindenburg, what's next?

HINDENBURG AND LUDENDORFF We are of the opinion that views about peace cannot be immutable since they depend on the current military situation.

HINDENBURG And the situation on the Western Front is one I can also

LUDENDORFF describe with absolute equanimity.

PAUL GOLDMANN What may we expect from the Supreme War Council that the Entente is in the process of creating? (*To himself*) Hindenburg laughs. (*He notes this and turns to the question of Alsace-Lorraine.*)

LUDENDORFF A question mark over Alsace-Lorraine may exist for the French

HINDENBURG but not for Germany.

PAUL GOLDMANN What about America, then?

HINDENBURG The way America has been trumpeting

LUDENDORFF what it will achieve in the war

HINDENBURG is impressive, and worthy of the country that produced

LUDENDORFF the Barnum and Bailey Circus. So let us wait and see

HINDENBURG if the achievements themselves are as impressive.

LUDENDORFF And if they are, well—in the first place, America has lined up its army against Japan—

HINDENBURG secondly, they lack the tonnage—

LUDENDORFF and thirdly, we have the U-boats.

HINDENBURG AND LUDENDORFF In short, the great American army is still a long way off, shrouded in mist.

PAUL GOLDMANN One question is of great concern to me, and that concerns submarine warfare.

LUDENDORFF Well, Hindenburg, do you want to field that one?

HINDENBURG No.

LUDENDORFF We never envisaged that our U-boats would starve England into submission within a few months. Our objective was not to starve England, but to make it more inclined to peace.

PAUL GOLDMANN Fine, let's talk a bit about the operations in Italy now.

HINDENBURG Vying with us Germans, the Austro-Hungarian soldiers fought
LUDENDORFF valiantly.

PAUL GOLDMANN We've already discussed all the other theatres of war, the Balkans are the only one still outstanding.

HINDENBURG (*reassuring him*) The situation there is

LUDENDORFF unchanged.

PAUL GOLDMANN (*to himself*) That's reassuring. Lunch was a simple military affair, though the coffee was made with real beans.
(Hindenburg and Ludendorff rise. Paul Goldmann remains seated.)

HINDENBURG (*taking leave of his visitor, half turned to Ludendorff*) If our strength and our patience hold out for a time, it'll come right in the end. (*Turning to Goldmann*) Tell that to Austria-Hungary, with my compliments!
(Goldmann has risen and waits, hesitating.)

LUDENDORFF (*going up to him, laying stress on every word*) Today was perhaps the last time you will visit us.

GOLDMANN (*aside*) The quartermaster general's parting words allude to the fact that, for as long as the war has lasted, I have had the honour of being invited to the field marshal's table every autumn—as long as the war lasts.
(Change of scene.)

Scene 26

Semmering, mountain pass and health resort. Ridgeway walk.

HONORARY COUNSELLOR —Well, what can I say, the 10 freight trucks simply landed in my lap. In Marienbad, how shall I put it, everything is available, but naturally at a price, but what does it matter if it costs 15 times as much? Good, solid stuff—when I get to the Southern Railway Station, everything's jammed full to bursting, nothing but soldiers and so on, jostling and shoving. The noise, my dear fellow, and the people! You've never seen the like of it—well, if they think they can keep me from bagging a seat—I tell you, I simply cleared a way through, straight off round to the back and the conductor says leave it to him, he'll see to it, I offload my luggage onto a soldier, and believe it or not, a compartment all to myself, right up to Semmering, the people all standing jam-packed like herrings in the corridor—phew, the heat!—(*takes out a small paper bag*) Cheap—! from the Sweetie King! Two crowns each, fantastic value. What do say about the communiqué today?

OLD BIACH That cannot but have repercussions on the morale of the Entente.

HONORARY COUNSELLOR I'm not so sure—I can't help thinking—the report today—well, what do you say about the Austrian defeat at the Battle of Lutsk?

OLD BIACH A growing sense of weakness in the Entente.

HONORARY COUNSELLOR How come?

OLD BIACH The Entente is still hiding behind strong language, but it's already feeling its weakness.

HONORARY COUNSELLOR Yes, but what about Lutsk?

OLD BIACH The peace secures us a breakfast without Russia.

HONORARY COUNSELLOR Explain—

OLD BIACH We can't calculate it in thousands of millions. But there are untold thousands of millions.

HONORARY COUNSELLOR All is possible, given the will.

OLD BIACH A hundred thousand million marks a year is a monstrous amount—a financial Leviathan, however you look at it.

HONORARY COUNSELLOR Where are you going to get your hundreds of thousands of million marks? In this day and age?

OLD BIACH These are hard times.

HONORARY COUNSELLOR So the upshot is—what?

OLD BIACH Kerenski said Russia is exhausted.

HONORARY COUNSELLOR That may be. But Lutsk—?

OLD BIACH The battle on the Upper Isonzo only began early this morning, we mustn't jump the gun as to its outcome.

HONORARY COUNSELLOR But I'm talking about Lutsk—!

OLD BIACH We mustn't revel in dreams of the future, but it would be worth the risk if we could prove our superiority.

HONORARY COUNSELLOR Lutsk—!

OLD BIACH We sense in the words of the War Press Bureau that History is looking over our shoulder. Now they are crying out for American assistance, that will-o'-the-wisp leading the Entente on ever faster and deeper into the swamp, defeat and disaster.

HONORARY COUNSELLOR Yes, of course, but—

OLD BIACH But already we can sense the Spirit of Victory—

HONORARY COUNSELLOR That goes without saying, but—down south! What about up north?!

OLD BIACH (*erupts*) Today's top priority: the commercial traveller must put out feelers and sound out the market.

HONORARY COUNSELLOR I can see that, but—

OLD BIACH When we take stock, we're still some 40,000 men to the good.

HONORARY COUNSELLOR Down south! But up north—??

OLD BIACH One hears the thunder of the cannon and knows how many of the dead, the wounded, and the prisoners must be entered in the debit column.

HONORARY COUNSELLOR So you do assume—

OLD BIACH London and Paris must be pretty disheartened today. Government securities are at an all-time low.

HONORARY COUNSELLOR Yes, well, the war—

OLD BIACH War has a threefold impact on all peoples: bad money, shortages, and exorbitant prices.

HONORARY COUNSELLOR Talking of which—whoever—

OLD BIACH Whoever puts themselves in the Italians' shoes—

HONORARY COUNSELLOR Well?

OLD BIACH The population will be panicking already, I imagine.

HONORARY COUNSELLOR I very much fear so.

OLD BIACH Without yet being in a position to give a detailed, point by point account of the possibilities, before the task has been completed—

HONORARY COUNSELLOR What do you think of the conferences in Rome?

OLD BIACH Coolly received in Paris.

HONORARY COUNSELLOR Do you remember—back then—the *Lusitania* affair—

OLD BIACH (*shaking his head indignantly*) The whole thing was exaggerated.

HONORARY COUNSELLOR Y'know what would do us good? Like when you used to be able to read—and by God, those were the days!—Russian troops encircled by German army—

OLD BIACH (*enraptured by the rhetoric of the* Neue Freie Presse)—and driven into the Masurian swamps!

HONORARY COUNSELLOR And what about Romania?

OLD BIACH Women got up in their finery were sitting at the tables in the brightly lit salons of the hotels in Bucharest. We can imagine—

HONORARY COUNSELLOR Why, what was going on?

OLD BIACH The painted women of Bucharest turn pale.

HONORARY COUNSELLOR That's all malicious gossip.

OLD BIACH The city is panic-stricken, the windows shaking in their frames.

HONORARY COUNSELLOR Of course they were. But what can *we* expect?

OLD BIACH The advent of a golden age. The eyes of the peoples turn towards the West.

HONORARY COUNSELLOR Hearing you say that, you'd think it was the headline of one of Benedikt's editorials, with a subheading in the Evening Edition. But—

OLD BIACH The women in Paris have their ears turned towards the East.

HONORARY COUNSELLOR How come?

OLD BIACH In the streets of Paris the eyes of the women are red with weeping.

HONORARY COUNSELLOR Oh, really! That's nothing to laugh about—we're no better off.

OLD BIACH (*with gusto*) Hymns resound in our hearts. The philosopher Fichte joined the Territorial Reserve.

HONORARY COUNSELLOR Wherever did you read that?

OLD BIACH (*carried away by the story*) He did his military exercises alongside the philologist Buttmann, the historian Rühs, and the theologian Schleiermacher. Buttmann and Rühs couldn't ever distinguish between right and left. That era, which is so similar to our own, excites our curiosity, and perhaps the past can answer the question of how economic crises caused by a war evolve? The comparison leads to striking similarities, right down to the details. Are we not experiencing right now the miraculous birth of the nitrogen industry?

HONORARY COUNSELLOR I get the message. But do you know what we could do with?

OLD BIACH (*vehemently*) Strong characters, men who make a total break with the past and give themselves up to the instinctive urgings of the present, like a bride to her bridegroom.

HONORARY COUNSELLOR That depends.

OLD BIACH Sales sometimes decline in wartime, in peacetime too. Market factors are variable and need to be regulated by the state, which is attuned to the voice of the people and follows its lead, and which in these anxious moments of change calculates levels of need and of production as its supreme duty. The year of destiny is at hand.

HONORARY COUNSELLOR That's pitching it a bit high, don't you think—?

OLD BIACH (*triumphantly*)—How gloriously everything has turned out, the land free, our enemies repulsed, the Serbian troops eradicated, the Russian fortresses destroyed.

HONORARY COUNSELLOR Hang on!—What about the Austrian losses at Lutsk?

OLD BIACH (*startled but composed*) Flags at half mast! But why bother with such empty gestures?

HONORARY COUNSELLOR Now you're talking as if we'd been completely victorious—

OLD BIACH (*drawing breath*) Russia in submission, Serbia crushed, Italy humiliated! Mankind's burden has been lifted for decades to come, no longer shall one's nerves be continually on edge, and that must spread a sense of well-being and usher in periods of amazing economic expansion that capture our imagination.

HONORARY COUNSELLOR Talking of being captured, at Lutsk—

OLD BIACH The historian will investigate reports on how news of the victory in eastern Galicia was received, and whether celebratory bonfires were lit on mountaintops and burning candles placed in the windows of houses—

HONORARY COUNSELLOR If you'll forgive me asking—since I'm in the dark—where do you get your candles?

OLD BIACH —and ravishing music reflected the mood—

HONORARY COUNSELLOR All that stuff about Tarnopol is rubbish. Stick to the facts about Lutsk!

OLD BIACH (*pensively*) The late general secretary of the Austro-Hungarian Bank, Wilhelm v. Lucam, has been all but forgotten.

HONORARY COUNSELLOR How sad.

OLD BIACH The present governor, Herr v. Popovics, has a past which promises well for the future.

HONORARY COUNSELLOR Fine. But why do you bring that up?

OLD BIACH Can't you just visualize the officer, the soldier, starting out from Cattaro in Montenegro to climb Mount Lovcen, up through scree and boulders, higher up through ice and snow, constantly threatened by enemy fire. He must have emerged transformed.

HONORARY COUNSELLOR I can well believe that. But what really impresses me is your lively imagination.

OLD BIACH The imagination revels in conjectures—

HONORARY COUNSELLOR Hang on a minute. You switch to the Austro-Hungarian bank, then jump from that to the summit of Mount Lovcen. But I'm interested in what you think about Lutsk—

OLD BIACH *(timidly)* We don't want to awaken memories of Tyrtaeus and his Spartan war cries.

HONORARY COUNSELLOR But why not? Feel free.

OLD BIACH *(snidely)* Clemenceau will be astonished.

HONORARY COUNSELLOR Serve him right!

OLD BIACH *(whimsically)* The Russian poet Pushkin married a young girl of good family. Natalia Goncharova was flirtatious and Pushkin was jealous. The son of the ambassador of the Netherlands in St. Petersburg, Baron Georges Heeckeren, through trying to gain the affections of the beautiful woman, aroused the poet's suspicions—

HONORARY COUNSELLOR I remember. That idiot Pushkin was killed in the duel. But what are you getting at?

OLD BIACH *(musing)* Posterity has not forgotten him, and at the inauguration of his monument Dostoevsky was invited to give the commemorative address. He said, the deepest conviction of the Russian people is: suffering must be endured! The communiqué from the German High Command reports that the enemy losses at Postov—

HONORARY COUNSELLOR Yes, all right, but at Lutsk, by my estimation, we lost—

OLD BIACH People walking in the streets exchange glances, trying to read in each other's eyes their thoughts about Durazzo, Verdun, and the Champagne.

HONORARY COUNSELLOR And about Stanislau too, surely! What do you say about Stanislau?

OLD BIACH *(with conviction)* Stanislau is a dramatic warning that will curb General Brusilov's arrogance and remind him how transitory the local Russian conquests are.

HONORARY COUNSELLOR And what do you say about Brody?

OLD BIACH *(subdued)* Brody is a sore point.

HONORARY COUNSELLOR And Gorlice?

OLD BIACH (*casually*) Gorlice is just a scratch.

HONORARY COUNSELLOR Take my word for it, things never turn out the way you imagine.

OLD BIACH In reality, lines and surfaces are inseparable from the body, yet our mental faculty operates with them and constructs sentences which are absolutely true, while neglecting breadth and depth. The battles on the Somme are among the bitterest disappointments.

HONORARY COUNSELLOR But all things considered, people must surely know what they want.

OLD BIACH Perhaps one day people will realize that there are no straight lines in the lives of different nations, but everywhere intersections and convergences.

HONORARY COUNSELLOR Hang on. The diplomats of the Entente—

OLD BIACH (*heatedly*) The diplomats of the Entente are like the sons of Noah, who covered the nakedness of their drunken father.

HONORARY COUNSELLOR Well put. But since Romania—

OLD BIACH (*in a frenzy*) When they decided to declare war in Bucharest, the leaders of the Entente behaved as if they'd been inhaling Indian hemp.

HONORARY COUNSELLOR They're crazy. But what do you expect from Bratianu these days?

OLD BIACH Bratianu will be having sleepless nights right now.

HONORARY COUNSELLOR Why do you think that?

OLD BIACH If the dial is set for the offensive and has to be switched round to defensive, it can easily break.

HONORARY COUNSELLOR I think so, too. Surely in Vienna they'll also be thinking again—!

OLD BIACH There'll be many in the streets of Bucharest today with doubt in their hearts.

HONORARY COUNSELLOR Excuse me! We can—

OLD BIACH We can imagine the effect it has on the Romanian people.

HONORARY COUNSELLOR But that's surely all in the past—there are other things to worry about right now—!

OLD BIACH (*despondently*) It's time to worry again.

HONORARY COUNSELLOR Now listen here—

OLD BIACH Yes, in the streets of Bucharest they are already listening to the thunder of the cannon from Tutrakan and Silistria.

HONORARY COUNSELLOR But that's all over and done with—!

OLD BIACH So endeth the first phase of a war wildly disproportionate in its origins and manifestations.

HONORARY COUNSELLOR Let me tell you, those developments you envisage—

OLD BIACH (*firmly*) Those developments cannot fail to have an impact in England.

HONORARY COUNSELLOR That's the editor's opinion! But there really are other things to worry about right now other than Tutrakan! The Bulgarian victory was a sensation at the time—

OLD BIACH (*vehemently*)—because it was achieved so effortlessly, with a single sweep of the arm!

HONORARY COUNSELLOR What matters now—is how can we recapture Lutsk?

OLD BIACH (*teasing*) As she milks her cow, Anzengruber's Vroni thinks how nice it would be—

HONORARY COUNSELLOR Oh, spare me that one!

OLD BIACH (*sunk in thought*) Alix of Hesse is the maiden name of the Empress Maria Feodorovna. Of all the saplings in the plantation of life, her bark had already been notched.

HONORARY COUNSELLOR Biach, are you feeling all right?

OLD BIACH (*wistfully*) Whatever happened to poor little Alix, who could not even say the German prayers her late mother had taught her, after she had been confined to gloomy solitude beside the throne of a Tsar?

HONORARY COUNSELLOR Who cares! Why are you interested?

OLD BIACH The question arises because of the strange announcement that the Empress had gone right up to the firing line on the Russian Front, where the German positions were already visible.

HONORARY COUNSELLOR So what?

OLD BIACH (*muses*) Maybe there were men from Hesse in the trenches that Maria Feodorovna saw on her visit to the battlefield; young men, old men, friends from her youth perhaps, as fate decreed, the sons or husbands of her playmates, her neighbours' children—

HONORARY COUNSELLOR Perhaps. But that would have been quite a coincidence!

OLD BIACH —but whatever else, compatriots, Germans.

HONORARY COUNSELLOR Germans in any case, certainly. But, of all people, the sons and husbands of her playmates? You surely don't imagine they would be the ones heading into the frontline trenches—and she probably didn't even know any neighbours' children, and even if there were any, and if by chance they really were in the frontline trenches, how's she going to recognize them after so many years and at that distance, tell me that?! But—why does it affect you so deeply?

OLD BIACH (*plaintively*) Alix stood right up against the Russian barbed-wire entanglement and looked across at meadows and fields only yards away—

HONORARY COUNSELLOR Meadows and fields! Think they'd let her go that close?! And where are these meadows and fields at the front, what do you imagine it's like there? Where—

OLD BIACH (*dreamily*)—where a puff of wind could waft across sounds, accents she must still remember well, in spite of all the changes in her circumstances.

HONORARY COUNSELLOR Biach, you are living in a fantasy world!

OLD BIACH (*persists*) Alix lives on in the Empress Maria Feodorovna.

HONORARY COUNSELLOR Come on, tell me—I know you're a sensible chap—of what concern is Alix to you?

OLD BIACH (*with compassion*) She is an unhappy, broken woman, her mind constantly tortured by a gnawing grief.

HONORARY COUNSELLOR For the love of God, just tell me—why does that matter to *you*?!

OLD BIACH Wringing her hands, she implored Heaven.

HONORARY COUNSELLOR Why, what happened to her?

OLD BIACH (*distressed, but with restrained vehemence*) The Russians could strip her of her name, like the clothes off her back. They could force their prayer book into her hands, but they could not divest her of her German spirit. There must still be a trace of the real Alix.

HONORARY COUNSELLOR Well, think that if you like. But how do you know what Alix is thinking or feeling?

OLD BIACH (*lost in thought*) She looked across towards the Germans—

precious blood flowed in their veins, too—and perhaps thought of her grandmother.

HONORARY COUNSELLOR Perhaps. But then why didn't she say they should stop the war?

OLD BIACH (*bitterly*) Because, as Empress, Maria Feodorovna cannot be seen to give in to Alix too much. She looked across, and the word "peace" may well have played around her sealed lips.

HONORARY COUNSELLOR But do you really think they'll have led her right into the battle. Perhaps—

OLD BIACH (*pensively*) Perhaps they staged part of a mock battle for her benefit. After all the frenzy of success, perhaps they haven't yet realized in St. Petersburg that the crisis is slowly on the wane. The tsar listens to her, and Alix the convert means more to him than Maria Feodorovna.

HONORARY COUNSELLOR And why did she convert? All right, let's suppose—if it makes you happy, imagine it did happen.

OLD BIACH (*resolutely*) Let us imagine the tsar's headquarters when the news arrives.

HONORARY COUNSELLOR And where does that get you?! But as for Alix, let me point out one thing—Maria Feodorovna is not her name!

OLD BIACH (*peeved*) You're needling me!

HONORARY COUNSELLOR As truth is my witness, her name is—let me see now, what is it?—her name is Alexandra Feodorovna!

OLD BIACH (*morosely*) A printer's error.

HONORARY COUNSELLOR That reminds me, what do you say about Grand Duke Nicholas? He's pretty miserable, too.

OLD BIACH (*with malicious glee*) First, stabbing liver pains, then bilious attacks, shows his gallbladder's ruined.

HONORARY COUNSELLOR That's needling him. But what good is all that to us—General Brusilov is healthy!

OLD BIACH (*transfigured*) The capture of Bucharest presents us with one of those rare moments when man is convinced he can hear the wings of talent whirring overhead.

HONORARY COUNSELLOR What do you mean, talent—it was a stroke of genius! But still—Brusilov is no paper tiger! What wouldn't we give today for someone—! If the news—

OLD BIACH (*ecstatic*) When the news comes through that our victories in Romania have driven the enemy troops back to the palace gates of Bucharest, we shall bow down in awe before the human spirit.

HONORARY COUNSELLOR Yes, they certainly managed to bring ruin on themselves that time, the Romanian king and his consort!

OLD BIACH (*fantasizing*) No one speaks of the dear departed—perhaps the perfume from the wall facings wafting through the rooms is the only trace they left behind of their former wanton luxury.

HONORARY COUNSELLOR Well, it's no skin off my nose. The victory—

OLD BIACH (*resolutely*) The victory satisfied a need.

HONORARY COUNSELLOR Let's leave it at that. What we want today—

OLD BIACH Today we want to talk to the powerful gentlemen in the Big Four.

HONORARY COUNSELLOR And you'll persuade them, eh? You're dreaming!

OLD BIACH (*in an ingratiating tone*) We do not want—

HONORARY COUNSELLOR You can talk till you're blue in the face if you want, and it'll just be hot air for the Big Four.

OLD BIACH (*zealously*) Because they paid no attention to people's illusions and moods, and poisoned the very air we breathe with such provocations. That said, there's greed behind such calculations—

HONORARY COUNSELLOR Just you watch, they'll end up reaching Constantinople.

OLD BIACH (*passionately*) Hagia Sophia is the mirage driving Russia's expansionist policy. The promise to make this mirror image come true is the political nose ring the English used, and still use, to manipulate the Russian bear.

HONORARY COUNSELLOR Y'know, it seems to me you've something of a grudge against England.

OLD BIACH (*unequivocally*) England is not under threat. Schiller's William Tell says: Every man's intent on his own business—mine is murder.

HONORARY COUNSELLOR Yours?

OLD BIACH His!

HONORARY COUNSELLOR His?

OLD BIACH Tell's!

HONORARY COUNSELLOR Why Tell's?

OLD BIACH England's!

HONORARY COUNSELLOR So England is Tell? On the contrary, surely England is the tyrant Gessler and Germany is the idealistic William Tell! Tell says: Quiet and harmless was the life I led.

OLD BIACH You?

HONORARY COUNSELLOR Him!

OLD BIACH Him?!

HONORARY COUNSELLOR Tell!

OLD BIACH Why Tell?

HONORARY COUNSELLOR Germany, of course! Tell says: The milk of human kindness thou hast turned to rankling poison in my breast.

OLD BIACH (*bitterly*) How perverse!

HONORARY COUNSELLOR You're right there.

OLD BIACH (*gloomily*) We can imagine him as one of the Italian leaders sitting there on the government bench in the palace on Monte Citorio, a gloomy, taciturn figure.

HONORARY COUNSELLOR Who? There's absolutely no sign of that!

OLD BIACH There are recognizable signs of dejection. The neutral countries are beginning to speculate.

HONORARY COUNSELLOR That may be. But perhaps—

OLD BIACH Perhaps it's already being whispered in English society that the war no longer pays. The policy of encirclement is bankrupt.

HONORARY COUNSELLOR I'm convinced of that. But Lloyd George—

OLD BIACH But that policy was the one Lloyd George—

HONORARY COUNSELLOR He needs some good advice. What do you say about Russia?

OLD BIACH (*weightily*) Their wings are made of lead.

HONORARY COUNSELLOR And where does that take us?

OLD BIACH (*more to himself*) To an age of terror!

HONORARY COUNSELLOR Think I don't know?

OLD BIACH You can imagine the bombs thundering down.

HONORARY COUNSELLOR Quite. But what good is that to us?

OLD BIACH (*satisfied*) The Entente is losing heart.

HONORARY COUNSELLOR You're alluding to the fact that Lloyd George is getting mad at Clemenceau. If Germany pulls it off—fine. But—

OLD BIACH (*with some aplomb*) We can imagine Lloyd George getting up from his seat in church and beginning to preach because, as the Good Book says, the spirit of the Lord has come upon him. But Clemenceau? That would be unthinkable.

HONORARY COUNSELLOR Look at the facts—

OLD BIACH President Wilson once said: The ear of the leader must ring with the voices of the people, so I put my ear to the ground.

HONORARY COUNSELLOR You? Ah, you mean Wilson! And what good did it do him?

OLD BIACH (*shrugging*) Wilson is surely a traveller who has missed the train.

HONORARY COUNSELLOR Bad for business.

OLD BIACH (*forcefully*) But Lloyd George has one political motive which is no less important.

HONORARY COUNSELLOR I can imagine.

OLD BIACH We can imagine the impression it would create in Vienna if news came of a major battle taking place nearby—in Gloggnitz, say, or Neunkirchen.

HONORARY COUNSELLOR God forbid! But what do you think about—

OLD BIACH (*mysteriously*) The edifice is crumbling.

HONORARY COUNSELLOR Tell me another. But I ask you, what do you think about Lutsk?

OLD BIACH (*consternated*) You've got to put yourself in Russia's place.

HONORARY COUNSELLOR And where does that get you? Look, Lutsk—

OLD BIACH (*ardently*) In a major offensive, psychology is vital.

HONORARY COUNSELLOR Where does it say that?

OLD BIACH (*slyly*) A soldier stands on guard in the mountains above Asiago.

HONORARY COUNSELLOR So—?

OLD BIACH (*morosely*) That's degenerate.

HONORARY COUNSELLOR How do you mean? The Entente—

OLD BIACH (*angrily*) The Entente wants to inflict humiliation.

HONORARY COUNSELLOR How am I to understand that?

OLD BIACH (*moans*) What did the Austro-Hungarian monarchy do to Wilson to make him—

HONORARY COUNSELLOR Just a minute—

OLD BIACH (*groans*) What did our monarchy do to England to make it—

HONORARY COUNSELLOR But now it's a question of—

OLD BIACH (*cries out*) What did our monarchy do to Serbia to make it—

HONORARY COUNSELLOR Now, now, calm yourself!

OLD BIACH The Entente knows it can't defeat us with weapons, but (*winks*) they are needling us.

HONORARY COUNSELLOR But that'll get them nowhere. D'you know what we *can* say today, however?

OLD BIACH (*resolutely*) Heroes' death likely for garrison at Kiautschou.

HONORARY COUNSELLOR That's all history now! What's interesting is what's in today's *Neue Freie Presse*: Resolution of crisis imminent.

OLD BIACH Probably tomorrow.

HONORARY COUNSELLOR And did you see: Count Czernin leaves for Bucharest?

OLD BIACH Saturday, the day after tomorrow.

HONORARY COUNSELLOR D'you know what that means? Peace in sight. And how did that come about?

OLD BIACH Thanks to today's communiqué.

HONORARY COUNSELLOR Which read: Slight easing of crisis.

OLD BIACH In yesterday's London papers.

HONORARY COUNSELLOR Stirring times.

OLD BIACH As illustrated by the news on hand.

HONORARY COUNSELLOR I've just been reading the article: The Evacuation of Asiago. D'you know who by?

OLD BIACH By the civil population.

HONORARY COUNSELLOR The subtitle is crucial—that says it all. But sometimes a sentence is enough—

OLD BIACH (*with tongue in cheek*) Sibyl was the daughter of a labourer.

HONORARY COUNSELLOR If only you knew how wretched I feel.

OLD BIACH (*irritably*) You keep scratching at the same open wound.

HONORARY COUNSELLOR Just wait, I tell you, you'll see, the situation—

OLD BIACH (*harshly*) That's tantamount to running up the white flag—bankruptcy!

HONORARY COUNSELLOR Well how do you explain the fact that we were repulsed?

OLD BIACH The British are just playing at war.

HONORARY COUNSELLOR On the contrary, it seems they're in deadly earnest—if you consider our present positions—we're far from—

OLD BIACH Far from being either high-handed or fainthearted.

HONORARY COUNSELLOR But that was way back at the start! Those were the days, by God, best not think about it—!

OLD BIACH (*firmly*) A suit of clothes costs 2,000 roubles, a locomotive 60,000.

HONORARY COUNSELLOR What, here in Austria—? That would be cheap! But just tell me, who needs a locomotive now? We need freight trucks!

OLD BIACH Ask a silly question—

HONORARY COUNSELLOR Please don't remind me!

OLD BIACH (*implacable*) Once the separate peace treaty with Russia has been signed, Lloyd George is a goner and maybe Clemenceau, too.

HONORARY COUNSELLOR And what about us?

OLD BIACH (*relenting*) We should put ourselves in the Entente's shoes.

HONORARY COUNSELLOR Isn't that pretty far-fetched? Let us imagine—

OLD BIACH (*self-satisfied*) Let us imagine that the prisoners of war return, a million, perhaps more—

HONORARY COUNSELLOR By my reckoning it can't be more than 15,000 all told, at most!

OLD BIACH (*complacently*)—mostly young fellows, hardened by the Siberian climate.

HONORARY COUNSELLOR And how! But if we stick to Lutsk for the moment—today's report—can't we talk straight for a change—?

OLD BIACH (*feeling his way*) The first thing that strikes us in the report is the little word "still"—we're "still holding on"—it literally hits you in the eye, and you can imagine—

HONORARY COUNSELLOR As true as I'm standing here, that was the first thing I said to her this morning, she was still in bed, and she said: talk to Biach about it! You see, you've become a pessimist now, too. The way I see it—how can I put it—the losses at Lutsk—after all—well, what do you think?

OLD BIACH (*simply*) The Brodskys are one of the richest families in Kiev. (*Erupts*) That's what I believe and I'll never recant!

HONORARY COUNSELLOR Hang on a minute. I can't see the connection?

OLD BIACH (*agitated*) You can't see? You can't see? The way the editor launched today's editorial about panic in Russia, haven't you—

HONORARY COUNSELLOR Oh, good Lord, yes, of course—it's just—I didn't quite recognize it, taken out of context—me, who knows every word by heart!—the way he captures the prevailing mood—he really goes for them, needling Wilson and flirting with Czernin. But to tell you the truth—I don't like the news about Lutsk.

OLD BIACH (*effusively*) Cleopatra's nose was one of her most beautiful features.

HONORARY COUNSELLOR I don't see how—

OLD BIACH You can't see? You can't see? The way He launched yesterday's editorial—

HONORARY COUNSELLOR Oh, good Lord, yes, of course, really fascinating—but—I don't like the news about Lutsk! A brilliant strategic withdrawal, of course—but—

OLD BIACH (*tersely*) People must eat.

HONORARY COUNSELLOR Naturally, but I can't see the connection—

OLD BIACH (*heatedly*) You can't see? You can't see? The way He finished today's—

HONORARY COUNSELLOR Oh, good Lord, yes, of course—

OLD BIACH (*bitterly, but with noble dignity*) It has repeatedly been the fate of the *Neue Freie Presse* that the personalities who are attached to it, the contributors and correspondents, are directly and personally affected by the repercussions of world affairs.

HONORARY COUNSELLOR Though, of course, that always adds to the paper's prestige. But if you look at the current situation, d'y'know what the man in the street can't help thinking? A Bismarck is what we need!

OLD BIACH (*unequivocally*) We'd need a Demosthenes to bring clarity into the international situation. We hope our Foreign Ministry will protect the interests of all the peoples of the Austro-Hungarian monarchy.

HONORARY COUNSELLOR Hang on a minute. If there was still—

OLD BIACH If there was still space for a diplomat as cunning as Gentz in our present, so very altered, society, he would grin maliciously.

HONORARY COUNSELLOR Interesting. But why wouldn't there be space?

OLD BIACH (*resolutely*) Talent will always create space for itself. Beethoven participated in the Congress of Vienna, too, with his Cantata—our moment of glory is no more.

HONORARY COUNSELLOR But what good is all that to us, we're already so depressed as it is!

OLD BIACH (*raising his eyes heavenward*) Where is there a Fichte today, someone who could give new courage to these stricken souls, who could be both a mentor and a guide to the German people!?

HONORARY COUNSELLOR How true, how true! (*Looks at his watch.*) Oh my God, half past seven!

OLD BIACH (*taking his leave, in a hollow tone*) The Russian defences at Ivangorod are already crumbling.
(*Change of Scene.*)

Scene 27

Berlin, Tiergarten.

PADDE The battle—on film! The majesty of dying and death—on film! We already knew the English were an ignorant, uncultured lot; but the present case shows the extent to which envy and deceit lead to outright callousness as well.

KLADDE Shouldn't *we* be screening such lifelike images of the latest events, too—for Germans on the home front? There is surely no shortage of opportunities to film suitable images. The exploits of our soldiers, projected in images, would certainly provide material for more than one film, and the people, often more attached to images than to words, would be mightily interested in such projections, even if we would happily do without the embellishments to which the English and French resort in the interest of national self-glorification.

PADDE Let's do it. What do you say about *Hias*? Last night saw a performance at the Berliner Theater of *Der Hias*, a Field Grey play in three acts, amidst the din made by all sorts of firearms and the whoops of charging soldiers. It was advertised without mention of the author, but this is thought to be a Field Grey, and it was performed by Field Greys (officers and men from Berlin and Bavarian reserve units, among whom there were certainly some professional actors). Ladies of the aristocracy offered their services in the female roles.

KLADDE Good for them!

PADDE The play was able to present an amazingly naturalistic view of life in camp and bloody battles. The genuine soldiers on the stage acted as if they were at the front. When martial events defied the technical resources of the stage—

KLADDE —film stepped into the breach.

PADDE There, you see, we can do that too! And the projector interpolated (in the last act) a series of fitting battle scenes as a backdrop. The impression was enhanced by the noise of machine guns and hand grenades and by the wailing and groaning of the fallen.

KLADDE A first-rate cultural scandal—

PADDE What'ya'mean?

KLADDE —the English medal commemorating the Battle of Jutland.

PADDE Oh, that.

KLADDE After the English had gradually rewritten their heavy defeat at Jutland as a victory, they crowned this mendacious fabrication by striking a medal commemorating the naval battle. "To the glorious memory of those who perished on that day."

PADDE Yes, that's a bit thick! We Germans don't need any commemorative medals!

KLADDE Compared with recent German commemorative medals, this English one can be described as poorly conceived and lacking artistic merit. The text, which says nothing about victory, is rather modest by English standards. The commemorative medals are intended for sale—the gold one for 230 marks, the total proceeds to benefit the surviving dependants of the sailors who have perished. Abhorrent as this English hypocrisy is, one cannot deny that there's method to it, and it will undoubtedly be successful, for there can be no doubt that once again many individuals in neutral vassal states will fall for this deception.

PADDE Trademark: Liar-Grey. There's an opportunity for *us* right now to strike a commemorative medal! Kaiser Wilhelm as an agricultural labourer! As we know, the Kaiser undertook a trip to the Eastern Front. His Majesty delighted his Silesian troops by assuring them of his personal recognition and gratitude for their bravery. All of Silesia rejoiced. But all of Silesia rejoiced at something else as well.

KLADDE I know. Let me tell it. Why are the people running, why are the crowds streaming out into the mown fields? To see the Kaiser. It's between five and seven in the afternoon. Happy people bring the precious sheaves of corn to hay wains standing by. Suddenly all hands are still, silence reigns, caps are doffed, everyone is lost in wonder: the Kaiser is coming!

PADDE He's there already, takes his coat off and—you can hardly believe your eyes—in shirtsleeves the supreme head of the German Reich starts to lend a hand, working in the field. On the furrows of our beloved Fatherland, strewn with sheaves of golden corn, a happy smile lights up His Majesty's countenance, itself deeply furrowed by the worries of the war years.

KLADDE How to describe it?! At any rate, an uplifting, heart-warming moment.

PADDE There he is, in person, helping his people gather in the blessing bestowed "from above."

KLADDE Like master, like man. His attendants, distinguished gentlemen and officers, follow the Kaiser's lead. "Isn't that our Reich Chancellor there, working in the field?"—"Indeed, it really is."

PADDE Let me take it from there. Hot from his brow, the sweat is running now—it's real work. The people watch in astonishment as His Majesty wipes the beads of sweat from his brow with his shirtsleeve, time after time; for stacking sheaves onto the hay wain with a pitchfork, under a sweltering sun, makes you sweat, even with your shirtsleeves rolled up, and it's thirsty work.

KLADDE God knows!

PADDE And there we have another lovely image: His Majesty sitting in the midst of his loyal Upper Silesian subjects on—

KLADDE On what?

PADDE —on whom he can rely, sitting on—

KLADDE On what?

PADDE —on a ridge at the edge of the field, drinking fresh water from a simple jug—Well? The mind boggles! What a subject for a commemorative medal!

KLADDE —which the English could copy for us—no, I mean, copy from us! *If* they could!

PADDE Forget your commemorative medals! It should be filmed!

KLADDE Yes, you're right. Listen, a highly interesting film will be opening in the cinemas in the next few days: *The Battle of the Somme*, the greatest event in this war.

PADDE You may well call the film the greatest event in this war. It is the first and at the same time the most recent documentary footage that the Archive of the General Staff released for public consumption. The film was made during the utmost turmoil of the battle. Four cameramen were killed during the shooting, but one after another they were replaced, until they had finally completed the whole work, which shall convey to future generations the glory of our heroic warriors. We hold our breath as a blockhouse is blown up, stormed, and taken after a heavy barrage of nerve-wracking intensity. We're right there in the midst of the enormous showers of earth caused by exploding mines and the impact of huge, heavy-calibre shells, and in the vapours of white smoke from hand grenades, and almost more than the death-defying courage of the troops, we marvel at the man or the men who, in the hail of missiles and the rain of steel and in the very front line, are also cool enough, with an iron sense of duty, to obey the command to keep the handle of the camera turning. On all sides we see the utmost exertion of every resource, the exploitation, but also the extinction, of human energy—we see death triumphant!

KLADDE This film will doubtless go down very well with cinema audiences throughout Germany. How was it that recent official report from the War Press Bureau of our fraternal Austrian allies put it so strikingly? Our assault troops advance—

PADDE —and on their heels, our film troops. That's the way! Death triumphant! Let our cousins on the other side of the water match us if they can! The mind—

KLADDE —boggles!

(Change of scene.)

Scene 28

Cinema.

Showing: Oh, Amalia, What Have You Done? *and the hit detective film* No One Escapes Me. *The music is playing "My Little Poppet, Apple of My Eye."*

CINEMA MANAGER *(steps forward)* There now follows the first showing of the great film of the Somme. You will see the heroes of the battle, the bloom of youth and grizzled veterans, both equally weather-beaten and hardened in combat, pouring forward, surmounting obstacles, charging and engaging the enemy, between a rain of fire and a hail of shells, over loose earth pulverized by mines, pummeled and pounded in the forge of a deafening, invisible war. In three parts there unfold scenes from the terrible battle of autumn 1916, which buried the enemies' greatest hopes. Columns of German reserves as far as the eye can see, and the impressive echo of tramping boots. Under fire from their own compatriots, German soldiers gently usher French women, children, and the aged to safety. Where once flourishing villages stretched out far and wide, and the historical beauty of picturesque old towns pleased the eye—Bapaume and Peronne and all the rest—all has been razed by Allied batteries to debris and dust, and there now remain only heaps of rubble. Next, thanks to the unique courage of valiant cameramen, four of whom met a hero's death while filming in loyal pursuit of duty, there flicker up jerky images, a sublime example of accurate timing and resolve: "Divisional Headquarters orders bombardment and attack for 8.30 am!"—Everything is ready.—The assault troops are itching to go.—The modern machines of war, monsters that open their jaws and spew fire, the most terrible weapons of our technical age show what they're capable of—but behind them are human bodies breathing life into dead machines. Through minefields and over obstacles, running the gauntlet of death alleys heavy with explosives, only to plunge into fierce hand-to-hand combat!—hand grenades cut a swathe! . . . From trench to trench, and on into the main enemy position! Our artillery gives them a breathing space and spreads terror among the enemy reserves, one trench after another is taken. This film belongs among the most beautiful and impressive of the present World War.

A FEMALE VOICE Emil, keep your hands to yourself!

(Change of scene.)

Scene 29

Optimist and Grumbler in conversation.

OPTIMIST So, the harmless parodies of the most beautiful Romantic poems that are so much in vogue here and in Germany—their play on U-boats, and ours on vanilla kipfel—even they make you blow your top?

GRUMBLER They do. War poetry is something we can live with if we have to. The monsters of modernity cheerfully manipulate not only the machinery of death, but also the verse that glorifies it. Everything cobbled together in this most vacuous and soulless age would amount to some million tons of intellect sunk daily, for which one day the injured genius of mankind will need to be compensated. That includes not only the guilt of the many opportunist scribblers who have pinned their colours to this bestiality, but also the few real poets who got carried away by it. But let me tell you this: if nothing more were to be said in Germany's favour than that there originated on its soil the most sublime lyrical ballads—with Goethe fully the equal of Wordsworth—then her true prestige, which is ultimately more important than those passing prejudices which wars are waged to reinforce, would emerge unscathed. There is only one fact the prosecutor might reveal that could endanger our case on Judgment Day. Namely the fact that this epoch—which should be exposed as toxic and simply erased from evolution in order to restore the German language to favour in God's sight—that this epoch has not been content to produce literature influenced by the technology of death, it has even desecrated the sacred treasures of its defunct culture by parodying its crowning achievements, in order to celebrate the triumph of its inhumanity with a grotesquely derisive sneer. What haunt of humanity, whose mouth everywhere proclaims abhorrence of the barbarities its hand is committing, could possibly be so satanic as to take the most sacred poem of the nation and expose it to the vulgar herd! Goethe's "Wanderer's Night Song", like Wordsworth's "I Wandered Lonely as a Cloud", is a national jewel whose sublime six lines cry out for protection against the slightest whiff of life's vulgarity. Who in the world would be capable of mustering so little reverence for a poet's most profound and lingering cadences as to subvert it into an abominable mocking jingle? The wickedness of such a brainwave, marking the triumph of a trend that began with classical quotations reproduced on toilet paper, surpasses any other atrocity that those keeping the home fires burning have perpetrated during this war. To enlist our greatest poet! The time has come to turn a parody into an epitaph.

OPTIMIST Believe me, two meatless days a week are a greater pain, yet they, too, must be endured.

GRUMBLER Certainly. But seven mindless days—that I cannot endure! And I see no escape from this undernourishment. The dumbing down of mankind through war, the pressure which drives grown-ups back to the nursery, where, to their horror, they no longer find any children—these developments leave us no escape from this experimental laboratory for the end of the world!

OPTIMIST As long as the conflict lasts, all intellectual energies have to focus on the war effort.

GRUMBLER Which just about enables us to grasp such concepts as "human raw material", "holding on to the bitter end", "doing one's bit", "hoarding", "medicals for recruits", "reconscripted veterans", "shirkers", "compulsorily enlisted"—in short, the whole ABC of social and medical classifications in all its unfathomable profundity, without our being able to gauge the total futility of the activity to which we allowed ourselves to be condemned as cogs in the machine. But the cowardly white-collar assassins who betrayed our future to their primitive ideals—

OPTIMIST So you actually believe the World War was instigated by a handful of evil men?

GRUMBLER No, they were merely the tools of the demon that has led us to our ruin, and through us, Christian civilization. But we can only point to them, since we cannot grasp the demon that has left his mark on our brow.

OPTIMIST So what would we look like if we bear the mark of a demon?!

GRUMBLER Like a Schönpflug caricature.

OPTIMIST Very lacking in talent!

GRUMBLER Exactly. But his lack of talent has a deeper significance. We are left hanging in the air when we think we have our feet on the ground, and rooted to the spot when we think we are moving forward. The frivolity of the dashing, hail-fellow-well-met lifestyle, which is now as popular in Vienna as the figures drawn by that diabolical dauber; the fundamental inability to occupy one's own space, which makes the lowest forms of both life and art perfectly coincide; the corpse-like rigidity of what is alive—these turn our doomed lives into a simulacrum of that crassly colourful humour. I see a direct connection between a botched life, an evolutionary stage in which we are bombarded by the sounds of Lehár and the colours of Schönpflug, and an ultimatum by which the most abysmal cretinism invites the world to clean out the Austro-Augean stables, having launched a war to uphold their prestige. And I thirst for the hour when all shall be accomplished—even if the world conscience ranged against us should at the moment of victory wear the same grotesque mask of power as that of the deluded would-be victors who have destroyed our lives. It's possible the crime perpetrated by Central Europe was so great that it corrupted the world that set out to punish it. Whatever happens—belonging to Habsburg Austria was intolerable!

OPTIMIST The Austro-Hungarian monarchy is a historical necessity.

GRUMBLER Perhaps, since the whole national mishmash that landed us in cultural disgrace and material misery has to be dumped in some godforsaken corner of the world. But all the revolutions and wars aimed at removing this necessity will weaken it, and if at first they don't succeed, if the Austro-Hungarian Idea proves initially ineradicable, then there will be new wars. To preserve its prestige, the monarchy should have committed suicide long ago.

OPTIMIST If Emperor Franz Joseph had been granted a longer life, our unity would—

GRUMBLER My spirit shudders and my mind recoils from the implications of that idea, even before you've finished thinking it. But you overlook the fact that the gentleman has indeed been granted a long life, in spite of which—

OPTIMIST But the Emperor died last year—?

GRUMBLER How do you know?

OPTIMIST I don't understand you—surely his life came to an end—

GRUMBLER How do you know?

OPTIMIST You're perhaps alluding to those jokes the Allies like telling about there being a whole brood of emperors in Austria-Hungary, and since one looks like the other—

GRUMBLER There might be some truth in that. You know, even if I could persuade myself that Franz Joseph is dead, I could never believe he was ever truly alive.

OPTIMIST I'm sorry, but surely the last 70 years cannot be denied?

GRUMBLER Absolutely not. They are a nightmare, as if some harpy, not content with our life blood, had also sucked out all we have and hold dear, then shown her gratitude by turning us into complete idiots in our worship of the Emperor's whiskers. Never before in the history of the world has such a formidable nonentity left his formal stamp on all things. That was what we saw behind every desperate situation, every obstacle that blocked our path, and running through all our misfortunes: the imperial whiskers. This nonperson embodied "muddling through", the hereditary principle of his ancestors, having chosen not Justice, but "Just so as it suits us" as his ruling maxim, as he eked out the decades towards his still shrouded doom, like a chronic catarrh. A demon of mediocrity decided our fate. He alone insisted on creating global instability through our lethal national hassles, stemming from the chaos ordained by God under Habsburg's sceptre, whose apparent mission is to hang over world peace like the sword of Damocles. He made this conglomeration possible, its budget forever provisional, its eternal ethnic conflicts only capable of resolution "according to protocol" by means of the arcane, exclusive argot of officialdom, and with mutual understanding attempted only in a linguistic mishmash, the like of which a sceptical epoch had never heard before and which it met with derision. Seventy years of softening of the brain and weakening of character was the price to be paid for unifying these peoples, though even that was not enough! Day after day, it was a reign marked by intellectual decline, casual neglect, and corruption of the noblest national characteristics, unparalleled in world history. Unparalleled, above all, in the mendacity with which the era's only progressive development, new technologies of communication, endowed a nonentity with an aura and papered over the lethal void with the legend of relaxed conviviality. The fact that the signal for bloodshed was hoisted on both the accession and the demise of this merry monarch surely provides confirmation—as well as a radical critique—of a mind-set midway between the nursery rhyme and the press release!

OPTIMIST What?! The most peace-loving emperor of all time, the champion of the young with his proverbial affability, the chivalrous monarch, the kind old gentleman in Schönbrunn who was spared nothing—is that any way to speak of him, especially now he's dead?

GRUMBLER He's dead? Well, aside from the fact that I wouldn't believe it, even if I knew it to be true, I have to say that this won't save his bacon at the

Last Judgment. For once he won't be able to claim favours or plead piety: no more wangling it! Above all, death will count less as a means of exoneration from punishment than as a prerequisite for judgment. I'd also like to think that it is more pleasing to God to honour the awful majesty of death at the graves of ten million men and boys, of hundreds of thousands of mothers and infants who starved to death—than before a single tomb in the Capuchin Crypt containing the old man who had weighed everything in the balance and, with a stroke of the pen, brought it to pass; and that the tortured visage of the human survivors will bear implacable witness before that supreme tribunal against this same dead individual. For this embodiment of homely congeniality who was spared nothing—which was why he spared the world nothing, let them say what they like and be damned!—one day passed a death sentence on the world.

OPTIMIST But surely you don't believe the Emperor wanted this war? After all, he's supposed to have said he was tricked into it!

GRUMBLER Absolutely. That's what happens. I don't mean him as an individual being tricked into it. I mean the lunacy of these monarchical systems that made it possible to trick both him and us. I'm thinking of the bloodthirsty demon of his accursed dynasty, whose workings were made manifest in just those imperial whiskers and in a conviviality that shed precisely the blood it could not see. I do not know who, I only know what governed us; and that for seven decades this spectral state presented the world with the spectacle of a commode disguised as a throne, on which the inveterate absentee of legend squatted manfully at his ease. Of him as a person I know only that he was mediocre and stiffly formal. But precisely these attributes, in conjunction with the lethal poisons of the times and of this country's tangled nationalities, meant we were inevitably heading for disaster. Franz Ferdinand, he of the grim visage, who could have avoided this by sheer willpower—for it is not what one wills, but simply the fact of willing, that could stem the chaos—Franz Ferdinand was destined, by his death, only to cause gleefully malicious flames to shoot up from the witch's cauldron of the monarchy. If this Franz Joseph, who was spared nothing except a personality, had not been tricked into world war, he would have died rejoicing in the calamitous but well-preserved Austro-Hungarian world. As his successor, Franz Ferdinand might well have put things right without bloodshed. But Franz Joseph was spared that possibility—thanks to the safety measures provided for touring heirs to the throne. He preferred to prepare its final eclipse by world war and inevitable defeat.

OPTIMIST Franz Joseph was in a helpless situation.

GRUMBLER Certainly, he'd been tricked into it, while Germany, the more active partner in the Special Relationship, obliged him to hurl us into the breach.

OPTIMIST What are you insinuating by safety measures provided for touring heirs to the throne?

GRUMBLER That one could safely predict the result of the trip to Sarajevo.

OPTIMIST That's merely a conspiracy theory. Though it's certainly amazing that the most powerful man in the monarchy couldn't arrange greater security for the trip, but—

GRUMBLER —it's understandable. For when he tried to arrange it, he was no longer a living force. Deprived of that, a powerful man no longer has any influence.

OPTIMIST But surely he was only assassinated after—

GRUMBLER —his attempts were unsuccessful, quite so. All right, then, if you insist on the chronology: a powerful man can do anything except prevent his own assassination.

OPTIMIST You surely aren't suggesting that Franz Joseph, who was spared nothing, had his nephew done away with! That would be easy to disprove, for when he received news of the assassination—

GRUMBLER —one eye wept and the other shone. His Majesty's need of rest meant that the funeral service was curtailed and the World War initiated. It was mankind that was awarded a first-class funeral.

OPTIMIST The assassination of an heir to the throne surely provides—

GRUMBLER —a welcome pretext for a purposeful strategy. The fact that the speculation came unstuck and Austria suffered heavy losses in her search for lost prestige—that's another story. Malice aforethought and criminal intent will still count at the Last Judgment.

OPTIMIST But surely you won't blame the monarch's personal characteristics for—

GRUMBLER They're of little interest to me. Doubtless he was merely a pedant, not a tyrant, cold but not cruel. If he *had* been, then perhaps he would have retained enough mental vigour into old age not to allow himself to be tricked. He would have known his limits. All he did was count the buttons on his uniform—so the uniform had to prove its mettle. He was a tireless worker, and one day, among the execution warrants he signed, there was a document that condemned mankind to death. It wasn't what they intended, none of them. But since the rest of us most definitely didn't want it, all we can do is blame them.

The imperial calling just happens to require that whoever wants to be left in peace, and then starts a world war to achieve it, is saddled with total responsibility on Doomsday. Just as the uniform of a retired country postman would provide no alibi if he turns out to be a vampire. A Christian on his deathbed should not regard the danger of losing his benefice as a greater evil than if he were to endanger all his fellow men, nor purchase the salvation of his soul by calamitously encumbering everyone else. And so I believe, at the very least, that the evil genius of his house was involved in the decision, and I believe most definitely in the possibility that a few villains, lacking in imagination, were able to make him sign his famous manifesto, passing the buck for their bloodthirsty senile dementia on to the peace-loving old man who sees no option but to sign the stylistically perfect document. He had weighed everything in the balance—then he was tricked into it. It's typically Austrian bad luck that the ogre who provoked the catastrophe should have the features of a kindly old gentleman. He has weighed everything in the balance, but he can't do anything about it: that, finally, is the most cruel tragedy of all, one that he was not spared. I've composed a song about it, as long as his life, a never-ending melody which I put in his mouth when he appears in my drama of the World War. I wrote this tragico-satirical song, like a large part of the play, in 1915—that is, when he was still alive—in case you want to insist, dreamer that you are, that we're now governed by a Karl and no longer by a Franz Joseph.

OPTIMIST Will you not at least do justice to him as a chivalrous monarch and as a friend of young people?

GRUMBLER No, for the scene when, for the first time, he has to tolerate Franz Ferdinand's wife sitting beside him at the imperial table, and turns his back on her; and then, having been urged by his daughter for the sake of appearances to turn occasionally to his left, he makes it all too obvious by the abruptness of this gesture—that scene doesn't appear in the drama. Nor does the scene in Weissenbach, near his holiday resort of Bad Ischl, where he listens to a dear little four-year-old nipper saying his piece in greeting, and then—

OPTIMIST —in best grandfatherly fashion, but with a spring in his step, goes over to the little chappy and fondly gives his cheek a gentle pinch?

GRUMBLER —er, no, he salutes, yes really, salutes, and does an about-turn: this scene is missing, too. There's only the satirical song. But let me reassure you. If he had been a private citizen with the most demonstrably unpleasant characteristics, perhaps one whose wife had been driven to hysteria by the lifelong cross of the conjugal bond she had to bear—then death would settle all scores and the rest would be silence. But in world history there is no statute of limitations, and so even the kindest of kindly old gentlemen, even after his death, must appear in the form to which he was condemned by the curse on his house. It's not Franz Joseph in person that I put on stage, but the embodiment of the Habsburg demon. A spectre appears to us, and it appears to him too in his sleep. Seventy years sing their Funeral Dirge, and that includes all his predecessors, each "villainous Franz"—like Schiller's Franz Moor, or the jailer of Spielberg fortress at Brno—right back through the gallery of ancestral portraits as far as their original castle, from which the whole clan should never have been allowed to enter Austria.

OPTIMIST When will your drama appear?

GRUMBLER When the enemy has been defeated.

OPTIMIST What?! So you do believe that—

GRUMBLER —Austria will no longer exist a year from now! I had taken the manuscript to the ancestral land of the Habsburgs, Switzerland—

OPTIMIST To keep it safe?

GRUMBLER No, to put the finishing touches to it. I brought it back again, for I'm not afraid of the enemy. So careless has he become in the management of his bloody affairs that I've already brought the manuscript over the border and back—twice. Still, publication is impossible right now. That would certainly cost the author his freedom, and if the army big shots develop a taste for dictatorship before they ring down the curtain, even his head, which he has managed to keep through all the offensives, wave after idiotic wave, in four years of war. It will be published when this techno-romantic adventure, launched as a power play against mankind, has been suppressed by a superior power. When the glorified devilry, which, as we speak, is turning thousands of living bodies into corpses or cripples—and all for nothing!—comes to an end and we are liberated from the infantilizing surveillance of the military censorship. In short, when Alice Schalek has said the last word.

OPTIMIST What have you against Frau Schalek?

GRUMBLER Only that the World War has forced me to overrate her. That's why I can only think of her as the most singular phenomenon of this apocalypse. But when the tragic carnival lurches to a befuddled halt, and I run into her back home as it sobers up from the communal hangover, then I shall acknowledge her as a woman.

OPTIMIST You really do have an incorrigible knack of taking the smallest detail—

GRUMBLER Yes, I really do.

OPTIMIST And that must be the source of this whole drama. Your unfortunate tendency to link trivial phenomena to major events.

GRUMBLER In exactly the same way our infernal fate led from trivial events to the major phenomena of the actual tragedy. My tragic drama synchronizes our sufferings with the forms and sounds of a world bent on destruction. You surely won't fail to ask me what I have against Benedikt?

OPTIMIST Nor will you fail to answer.

GRUMBLER He is merely the leader writer responsible for the World War. He is only a newspaper publisher, yet he triumphs over our intellectual and moral honour. He has called the tune that claimed more victims than the war it provoked and enflamed. The shrill tones of a man banking on victory, threatening both our pockets and our throats, provide the ground bass accompanying the bloodshed. Even readers remote in time and space will feel that in Vienna we have suffered special torments. In my play a veteran subscriber to the *Neue Freie Presse* succumbs to its lethal language—a language that convulsively expresses the ancient Jewish significance of the modern German scenario. That language overwhelms life until inflammation of the brain brings merciful release.

OPTIMIST To understand that, I'll have to wait until your tragedy is published. So it will appear—

GRUMBLER —when this one is over. It can't be done any sooner. It isn't finished anyhow, and after all, I need to keep my head in order to complete it.

OPTIMIST I think only your freedom would be threatened.

GRUMBLER As long as Vienna lies in the hinterland. But what about high treason, crimes against the military establishment, insulting the royal family, defaming dried vegetable speculators and other big cheeses who can only be aggrieved victims, never criminal perpetrators, and who in pursuance of their profiteering are protected by the law governing respect of person—don't forget, the highest majesty of all in Austria is the gallows! Nor is this just a fixture of Spanish ceremonial, it is also an integral part of the design of my play. Remember, under the command of Archduke Friedrich alone—someone I see as a spectre with more potential than Frau Schalek—11,400 or, according to another version, 36,000, gallows were erected. Someone who couldn't count up to three! That Archduke is a warrior whose exploits make Napoleon seem a mere defeatist, a man in the same martial and erotic mould as his ally, the monstrous and barbaric German Kaiser, emperor of the intellectual potato people, who couldn't keep his fingers off any flesh and blood, while slapping his own thigh and emitting his raucous wolfish laugh: the laugh of the Fenris wolf in the saga when the world went up in flames. Amidst his beloved archeological collection of Assyrian bricks and the maps of his General Staff, torturing an entourage obliged to stand for hours, he flaunts his pseudo-science, constantly making obscene jokes about people's physical appearance. Revelling in the embarrassment of any companion when out hunting or at some official function, he surprises him with a slap on the bottom, a kick in the leg, or a question about his sexual preferences. Those were our blue-blooded lords and masters. The one who started it, as devoid of intelligence as the global slaughter he caused; the other, splashing about with mindless relish in a sea of blood. Our Austrian hero, who would shout "Kerbang!" in the cinema when he saw soldiers shot down, this honorary Doctor of Philosophy, this cretin was the marshal of our doom. However different, they were still bosom friends, greeting each other with knowing smiles like gourmets swapping impressions, and when it came to the shapely figures of Germania and Austria, sharing a sigh about the changes wrought by time. There's no mistaking the way such wartime fashions promptly rub off on our whole culture, the sheer scale of our current joys and sorrows; our consciousness of being governed by such nonentities is a constant torture, and we are complicit in our awareness of the low life of those living it up in high places, making a mockery of suffering humanity. Madames and mistresses would certainly have tales to tell of their influence on people's private lives: when defenceless manhood found itself dragged towards despair, when the consecrated union of pure hearts was bloodily reft asunder, and when innocent men facing the gallows desperately searched for a sign of clemency. Do you know what it is we're now paying for? It's the respect such figures exacted from us!

OPTIMIST But the Austrian face is surely different from the Prussian face.

GRUMBLER The Austrian face comes in all varieties. It looks out slyly from the ticket counter of life's railway. It smiles, or it grumbles, depending on the weather. Yet this Gorgon's head had the power to transform what it saw into blood or excrement. Is there anywhere it didn't pop up? Was this not the face you saw if you went into an office for advice—and instead got an earful of abuse? I could track it down, if you insist, to the toilets of Vienna's police stations, the lice-infested, germ-ridden cells of Vienna's garrison prisons, the squalid hospital beds where military police graduates and their medically qualified henchmen put soldiers with shattered nerves through electric shock treatment, to clear themselves of trying to avoid front-line service by shifting suspicion of being shirkers on to their victims. Was it not the face of every humiliating, loathsome act of officialdom, above all the summary justice of those drumhead courts, one of which, over and above judicial murder, immorally demanded that the attitude of Austrian citizens towards the authorities—those selfsame authorities—should be "reverential and loving"?! The harshness is aggravated by the certainty that we're not dealing with naivety here, but with that villainous shrug, signifying "so long as it suits us", and the diabolical glee of testing our patience one last time. The Italian government has long banned that tourist attraction of exposing dogs to natural gas in a grotto, but the Austrian government has imposed the same experiment on millions of its citizens daily, and the Austrian face winks at this great joke, breaking into a blissful beam when people start to suffocate. The Austrian face, its left eye twinkling, has been seen so often in shop windows these last four years, shoulder to shoulder with its more martial partner, that it will take all of 40 years of peace to expunge the memory. No, it is not like the Prussian face, although it has a multitude of other traits—with the exception of that golden heart which the feature writers sing and write about. Above all, it is the face of the hangman. The Viennese hangman, on a picture postcard of the dead Battisti, holding his paws over the head of the man he has just executed, standing there like a stuffed dummy in smug triumph and "just look at us" geniality. Grinning faces, both civilians and officers proud of their honour, crowding around the corpse to make sure they all get their picture on the postcard.

OPTIMIST What? Is there really such a picture postcard?

GRUMBLER It was produced on official instructions, circulated at the scene of the crime, "those in a position of trust" showed it to their confidants, and now it's on display in the shop windows of all enemy cities as a group portrait of Austro-Hungarian humanity, a monument to our executioners' black humour, transformed into the scalp of Austrian culture. It was perhaps the first time since the world began that if you cried "the Devil take you!"—the Devil would refuse!

OPTIMIST But those who witnessed the execution surely didn't volunteer to have their photographs taken?

GRUMBLER They all wanted to be part of the action. Not only to be present at one of the most bestial executions, but to stay there afterwards; and they all wore a happy smile on their face. This Austrian face is on another picture postcard, too, one deserving no less cultural-historical significance among many more of the same, the faces of numerous soldiers craning their necks, shoulder to shoulder, between two Ukrainian women strung up between them, to be immortalized in the picture at all costs. God knows what puffed-up devil of a general, crying blue murder at the interruption of some swinish regimental feast, signed the order for "summary execution" that cost the two unfortunate women their lives.

OPTIMIST You don't give up, do you! No wonder you'll be denounced one day as a bird fouling its own nest—

GRUMBLER —and tearing it to bits instead of building a new one, I know. That accusation would certainly kill one bird with two stones. How unjust when he's actually fulfilling the moral precept of cleaning his own backyard. This dirty world accuses whoever clears away its dirt of being the one who brought it. My patriotism—unlike that of the patriots—could not bear to leave the job to an enemy satirist. That is what determined my position during the war. I would advise any English satirist who rightly found us impossible to turn his satirical attention to the affairs of his own country. Though of course there is no English satirist.

OPTIMIST Bernard Shaw.

GRUMBLER That proves my point. Yet even he practises the genuine patriotism that prefers to censure his fellow countrymen rather than deceive them. But whoever puts universal interests above those of his country must use the examples nearest at hand to demonstrate the vileness of the situation and the abominations of a world at war. The testimony of someone who has breathed the same air as those he satirizes cannot be refuted.

OPTIMIST But as counsel for the prosecution, you are truly implacable.

GRUMBLER Against such countries as these, yes.

OPTIMIST If you had your way, Austria would have been condemned to death long ago.

GRUMBLER Unfortunately that will only happen after it has condemned the Austrians to death. I'm thinking here of those surviving Austrians who, by virtue of their sense of belonging to the monarchy, face a fate which, as a people, they didn't deserve. Austria itself carried out the death sentence on the others while they were still alive, those who resisted this sense of belonging or in most cases did not even resist.

OPTIMIST And do you believe similar things didn't happen among the enemy? The English also executed their traitors. Think of Casement.

GRUMBLER I possess no picture postcard about that case. Apart from the fact that Casement was condemned to death by a court of law and then executed, while not much time was wasted on Battisti, who was captured and simply strung up, though the death sentence was indeed aggravated by making him first stand and listen to the Habsburg national anthem—it is unlikely that official photographs were taken of Casement's execution, which England did not celebrate as if it were some country fair. Pictures that record for posterity not only the gallows procedure but also the bestial participants—as if it were a triumph! Even in the homeland of coloured Englishmen you would be hard put to find pictures of a beaming hangman encircled by officers, some in high spirits, others with an ecstatic look on their face. But I would like to offer a special prize to whoever identifies the wretched oaf of an Austro-Hungarian lieutenant who has positioned himself directly in front of the suspended corpse and presented his fatuous visage to the photographer; also those loathsome dandies, gathering as if for a cheery stroll on the Ringstrasse or hurrying with their Kodaks to get into the picture—not only as spectators but as photographers—a picture that would not be complete without a so-called saviour of souls, surrounded by a hundred expectant participants. For while some were being hanged, others were posing for the camera; and photos were taken not only of executions, but also of the spectators, and even of the photographers. The consequence of our bestiality is that enemy propaganda has no need to photograph our deeds, since instead of lying it now simply reproduces our truths, having to its surprise discovered our own photos of our deeds at the scene of the crime. Thus it has a comprehensive picture of us, utterly lacking in self-awareness. For we failed to recognize that no crime could expose us to the world more starkly than our triumphant confession, the pride of the criminal who even has himself photographed, smiling, at his deed, because he's tickled to death to be caught in the act. For it is not the fact that he is a killer, nor that he photographed his crime, but that he photographed himself as well, and that he photographed himself photographing it—that's what makes this type an imperishable snapshot of our civilization. As if what we have done did not speak for itself! The infernal military judges, whose exploits have exempted them from the need to die a hero's death—an exemption comparable only to that of the war poets—have truly done a good job. But after the hangman, it was the photographer's turn next! The group photos taken for the Imperial and Royal Military Archives are a mark of national disgrace for Habsburg Austria that will not be erased for centuries!

OPTIMIST Emperor Franz Joseph certainly knew nothing of all that.

GRUMBLER All he ever knew was that his hangman was the sole indispensable and ultimate bastion of central power. There he stands, its radiant laughing symbol, endowed with all the dignity of a Viennese coffeehouse proprietor genially presiding over the Day of Judgment, far from being either high-handed or fainthearted, for who needs a judge when we have such an executioner?

OPTIMIST As a chivalrous monarch—

GRUMBLER —Franz Joseph was still a young man when he rejected the appeal by the procession of mothers, wives, and daughters, dressed in mourning, who flocked from Mantua in an attempt to avert the death by hanging of their sons, husbands, and fathers. Afterwards, they still had to pay the hangman's fee themselves. To this day, memories of Austria are ineradicable in those parts, and "Italian treachery" as a theme with world-historical significance may perhaps be explained by the fact that people there still shudder with horror when talking of what happened then, and by the diplomatic tradition according to which "la corde savonnée"—that speciality, the hangman's slippery rope—was Austria's sole export. In this sign—unlike the Cross of Constantine—thou shalt not conquer! Austria itself will pay its hangman's final fee.

OPTIMIST How so? When?

GRUMBLER After its execution!

(Change of scene.)

Scene 30

Court-martial.

CAPTAIN-ADVOCATE STANISLAUS V. ZAGORSKI (*passes sentence. The following extracts, given special emphasis, are audible.*)

—In view of the fact that the accused Hryb, 26 years old and unable to read or write, is consequently illiterate, and in further consideration of the fact that the accused Hryb, in the judgment of the Court, is guilty to a lesser extent than his fellow defendants, the Court has resolved that the said accused should be the first on whom the pronounced sentence of death, in accordance with Section 444 of the Military Penal Code, be carried out.

... The sentence of death pronounced on the accused Struk shall be the second to be carried out because his guilt is more blatant than that of the first defendant.

... In view of the fact that the accused Maeyjiczyn was in lengthy contact with the Russians, it was resolved that he will be the third on whom the death sentence is carried out.

... It was unanimously resolved that, in consideration of the crime with which he was charged, this defendant shall be the fourth to be put to death.

... The accused Dzus shall be the fifth on whom the sentence pronounced upon him in accordance with Section 444 of the Military Penal Code shall be carried out, because his lying defence indicated that he had completely succumbed to Russian influence.

... shall be the sixth on whom sentence passed on account of his actions is carried out.

... The accused Kowal shall be the seventh on whom sentence of death is carried out.

. . . Because Fedynyczyn has been found guilty on two charges, he shall be the eighth on whom sentence of death is carried out.

. . . Taking into account the seriousness of the charge on which Fedor Budz has been found guilty, he shall be the ninth on whom sentence of death is carried out.

. . . Petro Dzus shall be the tenth on whom sentence of death is carried out on account of his high level of culpability.

. . . the Court has resolved that he is the most guilty, and that he therefore be the last on whom the sentence of death passed against him is carried out. Case concluded.

(The prisoners are led away.)

FIRST OFFICER Congratulations. Very juicy! One can see right away that you're a lawyer. Tell me, how many death sentences have you under your belt so far?

ZAGORSKI That's exactly the hundredth—or rather, 110 now.

OFFICERS Congratulations! That calls for a celebration. Why didn't you say so before?

ZAGORSKI Thank you, thank you. And I've personally witnessed every single execution, and proud of it! Without counting the ones pronounced by others!

SECOND OFFICER Get away! You drive yourself too hard. You're too conscientious.

ZAGORSKI Yes, it's an exhausting business.

FIRST OFFICER Don't forget he's a trained lawyer, it's not as if—

ZAGORSKI Yes, well, with a death sentence you have to make sure to give proper grounds—it's not child's play.

SECOND OFFICER Oh God, yes, the trouble we had with the colonel, the last one before you! He was dead set against court-martials. He said it was just irrelevant legal quibbling. Just shoot 'em, he always said.

FIRST OFFICER But that's nothing compared with old Ljubicic, you know, when I was with the Eleventh Corps. He had that fellow Wild, I remember Wild had 12 political suspects strung up between Christmas and New Year 1914, six in one day alone. Used to say, as an intelligence officer he didn't need any court verdicts. And a lot he just had bayoneted.

SECOND OFFICER And what about Lütgendorf! He's another always used to say he didn't need a court, "I prefer the short sharp shock", he would say. Once he had a corporal bayonet three men because they were drunk. That was in

Schabatz, on the Emperor's birthday, I remember it like it was yesterday. And people got a good thrashing and were driven out of their homes, that was really something. And then the house burnings, brilliant! In Syrmia, remember, they burned down every other house! Once he wanted to set an example and they selected a whole village for destruction, and he marched them all off including heavily pregnant women to Peterwardein. Whether they eventually shot all of them, I don't know. But I do know the ones who escaped killing straight away were made to stay all night with the bodies of those who had been killed, their relatives and so on. The Hungarian gendarmes in charge of patrols also preferred the short sharp procedure, all the corpses just left lying—teachers, ministers, local notaries, foresters, and the like.

FIRST OFFICER Yes, but it was even more rewarding when we interned them!

SECOND OFFICER That came later, with full-scale extermination, as planned. The Hungarian camps were well equipped for it. Starvation, floggings, typhoid fever—that soon settled their hash, them Serbs!

THIRD OFFICER Yes, but if truth be told, that really isn't a judicial procedure any more.

SECOND OFFICER Granted. Well, sure, it's more an administrative measure. But don't think—look, I can tell you, under Lütgendorf every single case was properly certified: "Execution ordered!" But for a real court case like this one here, Lütgendorf just had too short a fuse. He gave the judges a real bollocking, and how! Scribblers! Nitpickers! Bunglers! If it was left to him, it would be: String 'em up straightaway, of course only when there were extenuating circumstances, otherwise it was mainly the bayonet.

FIRST OFFICER Ever had a Jehovah's Witness?

SECOND OFFICER What's that? Surely they're all extinct!

FIRST OFFICER No, Jehovah's Witnesses, y'know, conscies, those fellows who object to bearing arms for religious reasons, it's common knowledge. I'd one once, he was a farmer and we used him as a driver. His previous conduct was good, he'd a spotless record, so there was actually nothing against him except that he wouldn't carry no rifle when ordered to fall in. But the way he stood before us, he made a very unfavourable impression on me. For when he already knew he was going to be sentenced to death, he simply declared—without showing the slightest remorse, mind you—that he wouldn't bear arms, even if he were shot for it. Such stubbornness naturally meant there could be no grounds for clemency. So the Minister of War, Stöger-Steiner, naturally confirmed the verdict, on account of the very unfavourable impression the man had made. But what happened next—that was a ticklish situation. For the head of the tribunal, y'know Colonel Barta, later reported to the Supreme Military Court that the verdict was based on an unfortunate oversight. It appears the death penalty can only be imposed for an act of violent insubordination, and that as early as 1914 the War Ministry had arranged for Jehovah's Witnesses to be detailed for duty at the front as noncombatants, and for them not to be court-martialed until after the war. But this decree only reached us after the execution, in 1916, so there was nothing to be done. Barta got three weeks' military detention.

SECOND OFFICER That wouldn't have happened under Lütgendorf. Under him a Jehovah's Witness would have been strung up and—rrrtsch (*gesture of strangling*) rubbed out, my friend!

ZAGORSKI Yes, but you see, us lawyers, we don't have such a free hand. I take my time—yet I've still been more productive than even Wild.

SECOND OFFICER You certainly have!

ZAGORSKI The most interesting case I had was in Munkacs, in the autumn of 1916—when we were all still committed heart and soul to the campaign. There were three Galician refugees, a priest by the name of Roman Beresowszkyi, one Leo Koblanski, and Ssemen Zhabjak, I sentenced them all to death, of course, and had the sentence carried out—

SECOND OFFICER And the same nice arrangement—one after the other—?

ZAGORSKI Good heavens no, they could all read and write, and besides, they were all equally guilty—or to be more exact, all equally innocent.

FIRST OFFICER They were—innocent? How come?

ZAGORSKI That's what makes the case so interesting. The investigation was later reopened by the military court in Stryi, and it turns out they were innocent.

OFFICERS Tough luck for you.

ZAGORSKI (*laughing*) That's what you think! When the Ukrainian national assembly go and complain about me to High Command, you can imagine what happens!

FIRST OFFICER I get the message! And what rank were you then?

ZAGORSKI Lieutenant.

FIRST OFFICER And when did they make you captain?

ZAGORSKI When it turned out they'd been innocent.

SECOND OFFICER So do you think there was a direct connection—that they wanted to make it up to you, as it were?

ZAGORSKI I wouldn't go so far as that, they aren't exactly that sensitive at High Command—but the complaint drew their attention to me, they realized I was a hard worker, and of course, if the complaint against us comes from a politically suspect nation—! You see, a Ukrainian can't do us any damage by a complaint. The most damaging thing about him is still being alive.

THIRD OFFICER If it comes to that—do you think the 11 we sentenced today are innocent as well? Strictly speaking, the only thing that was proved was—

ZAGORSKI —that they were Ukrainians. Guilty as charged! One o'clock! Time for lunch.
(Change of scene.)

Scene 31

Schönbrunn. The Emperor's study. Franz Joseph sits at his desk, asleep. On each side stands a valet.

VALET ON RIGHT Working again, he never tires.

VALET ON LEFT It's a quarter to nine, the audiences start at 9.23. It's a heavy cross for him to bear, that it is.

VALET ON RIGHT Sssh—listen—that's Himself saying something—

EMPEROR (*speaking in his sleep*) Absolutely not—Out of the question—I won't make peace with those Italian rogues—I just want to be left in peace and quiet—They tricked me into it—Charmed, I'm sure—Leave us!—The second buttonhole is a millimetre too high—What's that? Franz Ferdinand's back?—turf 'im out!—A pleasure. Have you come far?—Rudolph shouldn't be fraternizing with his coachmen—that's no way to behave!—am I to be spared nothing?—let them wait, the audiences don't start until two minutes past the half hour—what do you say, Kathy—clever you, can't stand the Prussians—a real mess—they tricked me into it—so it goes, there's simply nothing I can do—(*He wakes up.*) What—what is it?—All right, I was just about to sign. (*The valet on his left hands him the pen. The Emperor signs several documents.*) Tell me, who's scheduled for today?

VALET ON RIGHT Emanuel Edler von Singer is to be enobled, Your Majesty—

EMPEROR Ah yes, Mendl, a good choice.

VALET ON LEFT Then there's Ludwig Riedl, for the Order of Franz Josef.

EMPEROR Ah yes, Riedl, I am pleased—how's he doing, Riedl?

VALET ON RIGHT He's not the man he was. It seems he was in bed ill last week. He may not make it today.

EMPEROR That would be a shame—a young man like him!

VALET ON LEFT Yes, Your Majesty, 30 years younger than Your Majesty, but as for vigour—

EMPEROR Yes, true enough—but tell me, Ketterl, how's Count Beck?

VALET ON RIGHT Oh dear, oh dear, Majesty! (*He mimics an old dodderer.*)

EMPEROR What, and him only 84, the rascal ought to be ashamed of himself—(*he laughs and has a coughing fit. The valets support him.*) It's all right. (*The valet on his left leaves the room.*) Where are you going?

VALET ON RIGHT He's only getting a powder.

EMPEROR I don't need any powders, absolutely not—

VALET ON LEFT (*returns with the powder and makes him take it*) I've just heard—

EMPEROR (*takes the powder*) They tricked me into it.

VALET ON LEFT I've just heard, your Majesty, that Riedl is too ill to come today.

EMPEROR Don't go on. Am I to be spared nothing?

VALET ON RIGHT (*to valet on left*) Oh no, here comes that same song again about his long life.
(*The Emperor falls asleep again. Both valets leave on tiptoe.*)

EMPEROR (*sings in his sleep*)

When first I saw the light of day
the world was out of joint.
So, what to do? All I could say
was: what on earth's the point?
Vienna was chaotic,
as only it can be,
expectations were demotic,
I'm spared nothing, as you'll see.

When but a lad, life still was fun,
I was the cat's pyjamas,
and played—it fits!—in *Chaos*, one
of Kotzebue's melodramas.
From barricades they cheered me—
all unwhiskered as I was—
soon, as Emperor, they feared me:
I'm spared nothing, save applause.

All I want is peace and quiet,
so my head can cease its spinning,
and play a hand of Sixty-six
without the Prussians winning.
Fate certainly was most unkind,
you cannot but agree.
The Empire's preyed upon my mind,
I'm spared nothing—pray for me!

My life was one of toil and stress,
a personal Gehenna.
My memories are of duress
abroad—and in Vienna.
Think of my relatives, my wife—

through to my jubilee.
If words can capture so much strife:
Nothing but woe for me!

My relatives brought me no joy,
I barely persevered,
then one fine day I said: ahoy,
when Kathi Schratt appeared.
The actress is my only friend,
though somewhat past her prime.
Her spending I must reprehend,
She hasn't saved a dime.

But Austria, and Kathi too,
could be quite delightful,
so let's hope we'll muddle through,
though finances are frightful.
A gift of gold's a welcome sight,
but honour says: beware!
And still I dub the Jew a knight—
he's plenty, and to spare.

Often my rage keeps me awake,
there's so much dismal news.
At Ischl on my summer break
I'm cheered up by some Jews
who're making money near and far,
their profits nice and fat,
not least out of this splendid war—
Why didn't I think of that!

The only time that I recall
a cause for celebration
was my nephew's final curtain call—
it was the land's salvation! (*He wakes up.*)
They broke the news with bated breath
and due commiseration.
I chuckled at the Archduke's death:
Thank God, He's spared the nation!

Welcome! I said, and meant it too,
As mourners stood in line,

and laughed and cried, as people do,
and said: The pleasure's mine!
It serves him right, he's paid the price
for wishing me in my grave.
A skinflint—that was his great vice—
I'm spared, him none could save!

A happy day it was for me,
for me and the whole land,
when with formal Spanish rites we
disposed of Ferdinand.
My nephew's cortège—small, alas,
as if we really cared!
His funeral was just third class—
so some expense was spared!

That story's done, now here's the gloss:
his death was welcome, for
to compensate us for our loss
I started off the war
If Princip hadn't seized his chance,
say, if he hadn't dared,
we'd still be in our sleepy trance,
that deadlock we were spared!

So let us all now praise the Lord!
My cross has turned blood-red.
The people, of their own accord,
give gold for iron, not bread! (*He falls asleep.*)
My pain was almost infinite—
see how my Empire fared.
The common people did their bit,
they too were nothing spared!

Do I regret it? Not at all!
Our special new alliance
means I continue to walk tall
and bid our foes defiance.
Wilhelm's a dashing soldier,
but blood-brotherhood?—pure fiction!
They're leaning on my shoulder—
oh please spare me the affliction!

For his support brings me no hope,
just makes me short of breath.
I really cannot see the joke
of staging Siegfried's Death.
To master fate I'll always try,
but it's a bitter pill.
The Prussians simply bleed us dry,
and make me foot the bill!

It's not a real relationship,
I hate the whole caboodle!—
so "special" it gives me the pip,
I'm just their bloody poodle!
And when we swore blood-brotherhood
with caviar and schnapps,
I call it shabby gratitude
to spare us only scraps.

If I'm the horse, he sits on top,
I follow his direction,
a crazy rider we can't stop—
a high price for protection!
The people thought at first: hooray,
we love good fellowship,
but look at where we are today—
he didn't spare the whip!

I fear I gambled like a goof—
he gets right up my nose.
Though people's cheers might raise the roof,
our prices are what rose!
A horse cannot work out where we
have planned our journey's end.
That Prussian, though, oh spare me
for he drives me round the bend!

With bloody flanks I twist and turn
in vain!—I took the bait.
Triumphant when he jerks a rein,
I must capitulate!
I've got that Prussian on my back,
I'm mute—I dare not groan.

He tramples all things underfoot—
nor does he spare my throne!

There is no limit to my strife
and anger with those brutes!
To think that at my stage in life
I lick the Prussian's boots!
Why ever did I take the plunge
with that man into war?
That blot, alas, I can't expunge,
so spare me, speak no more!

And why is everything askew?
Am I not my own master?
Yet there is nothing I can do—
he'd drop me, then disaster!
When King Edward came to Ischl,
our friendship unimpaired,
if I'd made *that* link official,
the war I'd have been spared!

Berlin papers cry "by jingo!",
yes, even *Kladderadatsch*,
but in Vienna's lingo
that's shambolic *pallawatsch*.
They keep reporting victories
which I'm meant to extol,
but none to put me at my ease—
spare me this wretched role!

It's history now, those 70 years
of Empire in decline.
The *History*, when it once appears,
will all my deeds combine.
But muddle is my watchword,
and when all is said and done,
I led my peoples unperturbed,
nor spared them all their fun.

My song, alas, has one defect—
it's endless, as you see—
since each new strophe must reflect

each new catastrophe.
Tribunals now would be a joke,
our revels now are ended.
At least when only ruins smoke
we save tobacco—splendid!

Yes, history will still record
whatever comes my way,
and it will have the final word
when we reach Judgment Day.
Titles I showered on every man,
my whiskers all could see,
but when this bloody war began
the rod was spared—for me!

The moral as a child I drew:
all effort was deluded.
Now I delight in muddling through—
both mud and blood included
I'm sprightly still as ever,
for release still unprepared,
for there's much I still must suffer
to redeem you—if I'm spared!

I'm wiser now, I dare say,
than all those years ago,
for *Chaos* then was just a play—
now I want blood to flow.
I still play the father figure
and wear a laurel wreath.
May God preserve my vigour,
although I've caused Him grief!

Lord, it's surely hard to measure,
for the time is not yet come
for me to say "What a pleasure",
"Quite delightful", "Are we done?"
So graciously I now will wait
until the world's despaired.
The sentries at the Devil's gate
Will ask: should he be spared?

To live in peace was his main task:
eternal peace he's got!
But there's one thing he wants to ask
before the coffin's shut.
"So young? And after so much toil?
I'm really not prepared
to shuffle off this mortal coil—
Surely I should be spared?"

(Both valets appear on tiptoe.)
(Change of scene.)

Scene 32

Kragujevac. Court-martial.

LIEUTENANT-ADVOCATE *(shouts angrily)* Let 'em go hang! *(to clerk of court)* Have you made fair copies of the three death sentences? Those three fellows from Karlova who had guns, I mean.

CLERK Yes, but *(he hesitates)*—I should point out—I've just discovered—they're only 18—

LIEUTENANT-ADVOCATE So what? What are you getting at?

CLERK Well—according to the Military Penal Code—they can't be executed—the sentence needs to be changed—to hard labour—

LIEUTENANT-ADVOCATE Let's have a look *(He reads.)* Hmm. We won't change the sentence, we'll change their age. In any case, they're strapping lads. *(He dips his pen in the inkwell.)* So instead of 18, we'll just put 21. *(He writes.)* There, no problem—now we can hang 'em.
(Change of scene.)

Scene 33

Promenade in Bad Ischl. A group of sympathizers surrounds Julius Korngold.

KORNGOLD *(wringing his hands)* But my son Wolfgang, he's a sick boy! He's a sick boy! *(The group leads him away.)*

FIRST VISITOR TO SPA *(addresses another)* You'll know the answer, I'm sure. After all, you're well in with those theatre people. So tell me, is it true what you hear, or is it only a rumour?

SECOND VISITOR Old Biach?

FIRST VISITOR No, no, young Korngold!

SECOND VISITOR (*solemnly*) It's true.

FIRST VISITOR Get away!—the son—young Korngold—they've enlisted him?

SECOND VISITOR That's what I'm telling you! What about Biach, though? (*Exeunt.*)

THIRD VISITOR (*shaking his head; to his companion*) Wolfgang's another Mozart! And they've conscripted him even though his dad writes for the *Neue Freie Presse*!

FOURTH VISITOR (*glancing over his shoulder*) The army's revenge! (*Exeunt.*) (*Enter Fräulein Löwenstamm and Fräulein Körmendy, both wearing Dirndl costumes.*)

FRÄULEIN LÖWENSTAMM The rain's stopped!

FRÄULEIN KÖRMENDY So what's the plan? Are you going to the lake this afternoon?

FRÄULEIN LÖWENSTAMM Yes, if it stays fine, otherwise tea at Zauner's, of course. What about this evening? Are you going to the show? We've got seats already, Franz Schalk from the Opera is conducting. (*Another girl in a Dirndl passes by.*) Psst—look at her in her finery—!

FRÄULEIN KÖRMENDY Who does she think she is, going around got up like that!

FRÄULEIN LÖWENSTAMM Well, her brother's a great admirer of Else Wohlgemuth of the Burgtheater.

FRÄULEIN KÖRMENDY Look, there's Franz Lehár with the librettist Julius Bauer. (*Exeunt.*)

BOB SCHLESINGER (*in loden jacket, with bare knees*) The fuss he's making! Bet Korngold's exempted by next week! Only needs a word from me to Hans Müller!

BABY FANTO (*dressed for tennis*) A word from papa, more like! The whole of the General Staff is in and out of our house in Baden, as everyone knows. General Arz is in fits every time Thury tells a joke, and I do a takeoff of Leopoldine Konstantin acting.

(*An automobile with the Habsburg crest drives past. They bow.*)

BOB SCHLESINGER Empty, I think.

BABY FANTO Salvator, I think. (*Exeunt.*)

REGULAR SUBSCRIBER TO *NEUE FREIE PRESSE* D'ya read about young Korngold—what d'ya think?

THE OLDEST SUBSCRIBER Can't fail to make an impact in England.
(Exeunt.)
(The lamentations of Julius Korngold can be heard at some considerable distance.)
(Change of scene.)

Scene 34

Police station.

INSPECTOR Aha, another syphilitic slut! Lice-ridden, too!

POLICEMAN I know this one already. She's got previous for theft and was put away for vagrancy. Checked for VD, too.

INSPECTOR What age are you? Who do you belong to?

17-YEAR-OLD Father's in the field. Mother's dead.

INSPECTOR And how long have you been leading this life?

17-YEAR-OLD Since 1914.
(Change of scene.)

Scene 35

Berlin all-night bar.

RAUCOUS VOICE *(at the back)*

What a brew—I'm feeling queasy—
This diluted beer's disgusting—
but I'll sick it up dead easy
when my gut is full to busting.

Bring some bubbly, you cheeky puppies! Don't go, Friedekins, my precious little moppet—park your little bottom down there again!—Hey you, you treacherous traitors!—what?—come on, come on, once more into the breach, into the Somme!—

FRIEDE GUTZKE *(spits on the top of his bald head)* Oops! Didn't see that, pops, eh—*(comes forward.)*
(Solly Katzenellenbogen, export, Frankfurt on the Oder, taps his neighbour, Krotoschiner II, lawyer, on the shoulder.)

KATZENELLENBOGEN How does Nietzsche put it in *Zarathustra*? "When you go to women, don't forget your whip"!

KROTOSCHINER II Now listen, just don't mention that man, he cuts no ice with me, *and* he came to a sticky end, as we know—Rotten to the core, I'm telling you. D'ya know Dolorosa?

KATZENELLENBOGEN No. Isn't that Hertha Lücke from the Palais de Dance?—15 Kantstrasse, first floor, telephone 854757?

KROTOSCHINER II Rubbish, it's Gerda Mücke from the Casino Unter den Linden, 59 Leibnizstrasse, second floor, telephone 957853, with hot water, internal lift, bathroom in each apartment, tip-top! She can really turn you on!

KATZENELLENBOGEN Sure can! One of Berlin's finest, right now—and d'ya know who that is beside her? Motty Mannheimer—no wonder, when he showers them all with 100-mark notes.

(The band plays the song "Wotsa Matter, Honeybaby?")

FRIEDA GUTZKE *(to Katzenellenbogen, in passing)* You heard—wotsa matter?—sitting there so cheesed off, the two of you? What ho, tallyho!—*(to Krotoschiner II)* well, sweetie? Old man with monocle!

KROTOSCHINER II Hi, gorgeous!—come and join us!

FRIEDA GUTZKE Nothing doing, early closing time—see the lord of the manor back there, that big Pommeranian stallion with his ugly red mug—some other time—for a grand you can drive your nail into Hindenburg for me. *(She goes to the back.)*

RAUCOUS VOICE

> Your clothing ration for the year—
> all right, I heard your snickers—

(Frieda Gutzke joins in)

> it barely covers up your rear:
> a single pair of knickers!

(Change of scene.)

Scene 36

Optimist and Grumbler in conversation.

GRUMBLER Now that's what I call propaganda for a good and just cause!

OPTIMIST What is?

GRUMBLER A proclamation in the press: "End of war bond subscriptions!" Very welcome and very opportune.

OPTIMIST I'm pleased you're thinking so clearly. All this talk of a negotiated peace was futile, as it turned out.

GRUMBLER Just as you say. And it's become ever clearer that Germany was right: the war will be decided by force of arms.

OPTIMIST So even you see that now! For once we're—

GRUMBLER in complete agreement.

OPTIMIST And I'm hoping to win you over to my views on the patriotic education of the young, too. As to that, there's no end to what needs to be done, since it's a question of focusing all our thoughts on final victory. To convince you that pupils are in no way compelled to immerse themselves in military topics, I've brought you the annual report of the Technical School named after our peace-loving new Emperor, Kaiser Karl. Rather, pupils are presented with an alternative—at any rate in most cases. For example, in form 5B: "A holiday hike" or "The most modern armaments." In 6A: "Why is Lessing's *Minna von Barnhelm* an archetypal German comedy?" or "Holding on to the end!" What would you choose?

GRUMBLER Holding on to the end!

OPTIMIST Then, for instance, there's either: "Reflections on the eighth battle of Isonzo" or "An autumn ramble." Or again: "To what extent can climate affect the intellectual development of mankind?" or "Our struggle against Romania."

GRUMBLER For that one, I'd make things easier for myself and choose both topics at once.

OPTIMIST "The main characters in Goethe's *Egmont*" or "The escalation of submarine warfare."

GRUMBLER I'd say that if the Germans hadn't escalated submarine warfare, they would have called on the hero of Goethe's play to force England to its knees.

OPTIMIST That's what I call optimism! Here's another exam topic: "The fate of man, how like the wind!"—from Goethe's "Song of the Spirits over the Waters"—or "The Turks and us—then and now."

GRUMBLER Here I'd definitely take both—it seems to me the link between those two couldn't fail to inspire a snappy essay.

OPTIMIST And how would you react to the alternatives: "My thoughts on beholding Radetzky's statue" or, to adapt Schiller on the new century: "His tentacles stretch far and wide, his merchant fleets are mighty, his greedy aim to subjugate the realm of Aphrodite."

GRUMBLER As for the second topic, I'd throw it back at the German teacher's head and advise him to quote Lissauer's "Song of Hate Against England" for his pedagogical purposes instead, and I'd prove to him that I know the first verse of Schiller's poem as well: "Noble friend! Where is the haven, where peace and freedom get their due? One century bows out in havoc, murder ushers in the new."

OPTIMIST And the first topic, "My thoughts on beholding Radetzky's statue"?

GRUMBLER I could easily handle that one, for I already have thoughts when beholding Radetzky's heroic statue opposite the War Ministry. For instance, that the gains made by black-marketeers are putting those of the commander in chief into the shade.

OPTIMIST I've just noticed—in that annual report: "Countess Bienerth-Schmerling presented two copies of Alice Schalek's *Tyrol Under Arms* to the school library, while the author herself presented one copy to the teachers' staff room library." Well intended, I'm sure, but—

GRUMBLER Now you're the grumbler! The rising generation cannot learn soon enough how to clean out enemy trenches. Isn't there any essay topic that takes up Schalek's ideas directly?

OPTIMIST (*leafing through*) Perhaps this one, for Form 6B: "Which of our enemies seems to me the most despicable?"

GRUMBLER This is such an appealing topic that no alternative is needed. But it suggests another line of thought, admittedly a problematic one.

OPTIMIST And what would you have chosen?

GRUMBLER (*ponders*) Wait a moment—no, I'd have to leave the question open.

OPTIMIST If you were to keep strictly to the essay topic set for the first years of the Kaiser Karl Technical School—

GRUMBLER —then I'd say: the most despicable is Habsburg Austria! But now I look more closely at this press announcement, the militarization of the school curriculum seems child's play compared to the shining example set by adults.

OPTIMIST (*reads out*) "High-calibre salesman, Christian, exempted from military service, presentable yet discreet, strong record selling advertising space throughout Germany, excellent references, seeks sole agency of solidly capitalized concern with scope for international expansion—" Well?

GRUMBLER You've answered the question for me. *Now* I know, as a patriot, which of our enemies seems to me most despicable!

(Change of scene.)

Scene 37

German headquarters.

WILHELM II (*to his entourage*) Morning, gentlemen.

THE GENERALS Morning, Your Majesty.

WILHELM II (*taking up a stance, eyes raised skyward*) The Lord on High certainly has ambitious plans for His chosen German people. We have preserved our ideals so it is our duty to bring about a better world. We must fight for justice, loyalty, and morality. Our wish is to live in friendship with our neighbours, but first they must acknowledge the victory of German arms. The year 1917, with its great battles, has proved that the German people has the staunchest of allies: the Lord of Hosts! An ally whose armour-plated support provides us with our essential foundation. What lies before us, we know not. But in these last four years we have all seen the hand of God manifestly in command, punishing treachery and rewarding courage and tenacity, from which we can be quite confident, now and in the future, that the Lord of Hosts is with us! If the enemy spurns our offer of peace, then we must bring peace to the world with an iron fist and a gleaming sword, to smash down the gates of those who do not want peace. Divine judgment has struck down our enemies! Our total victory in the East fills my heart with profound gratitude. It affords us another of those glorious moments when we can marvel, awestruck, at God's historical power. (*Raising his voice*) Once again a victorious Germany can say: What a miraculous transformation at God's behest! The heroic deeds of our troops, the victories of our magnificent commanders in the field, the admirable achievements on the home front—ultimately everything stems from the moral strength our people have had ingrained into them, from the categorical imperative! If the enemy still haven't had enough, then we'll screw 'em—(*the Kaiser makes a military gesture which evokes grim smiles on the faces of his vassals.*) The spectacular collapse of the enemy was an act of divine judgment. For our victory we are indebted not least to the moral and spiritual values bestowed on our people by Immanuel Kant, the sage of Königsberg. May God sustain us through to final victory!
(*The Kaiser extends his right hand, the generals and officers each kiss it in turn. In what follows, whether roused or amused, he emits a sound like a wolf howling. When agitated his face turns red, his expression resembles that of a boar, his cheeks are puffed out, making the ends of his moustache stand up vertically.*)

FIRST GENERAL Your Majesty is no longer God's instrument—

WILHELM II (*snorting and puffing*) Ha—

FIRST GENERAL —but God is Your Majesty's instrument!

WILHELM II (*beaming*) Very good, very good! Ha—!

SECOND GENERAL When we make our breakthrough, with the help of God and poison gas, we owe it exclusively to Your Majesty's brilliant strategic planning.

WILHELM II (*goes to the General Staff's map*) Ha—From here to here it's 15 kilometres. I'll throw in 50 divisions! Stupendous, eh?! (*He looks around. Murmurs of approval.*)

THIRD GENERAL Your Majesty's farsighted strategy is one of the wonders of the world!

FOURTH GENERAL Your Majesty is not only the greatest orator, painter, composer, huntsman, statesman, sculptor, admiral, poet, sportsman, Assyriologist, business expert, astronomer, and theatre director of all time, but also—but also—(*he begins to stutter*)

WILHELM II Go on, go on!

FOURTH GENERAL Your Majesty, I feel incapable of listing all the fields in which Your Majesty is a world leader.

WILHELM II (*nods in satisfaction*) Well, what about the rest of you? (*They smile in embarrassment.*) What, you damned rascals, laughing at your—ha!—supreme commander? I'll show—Seckendorff!

(*He goes to an adjutant and stamps several times on his foot.*)

ADJUTANT (*hops in embarrassment.*) Your Majesty—Your Majesty—

WILHELM II Ha!—Click your heels! It's all right, Seckendorff, I was just chivvying you. Champagne!

AN OFFICER Yes, sir! (*Exit.*)

WILHELM II Caviar! (*A second officer makes to leave.*) Ha—wait! Germans shouldn't overindulge, it's unworthy!—Just caviar! (*The officer leaves.*)

FOURTH GENERAL Your Majesty—

WILHELM II Well, what is it?

FOURTH GENERAL Your Majesty is also the most discerning gourmand of all time!

WILHELM II (*beaming*) Very good, very good. (*Champagne and caviar on toast arrive. He drinks.*) French champagne! Ugh, disgusting!

FOURTH OFFICER (*sticks a German label on the bottle*) No, Your Majesty, it's sparkling German wine.

WILHELM II Ah yes, German sparkling wine, one of the best, too!—Ha!—

Hahnke, like a drop of bubbly as well—? Hey ho!—(*He sprays the contents of his glass over the others and gives a raucous laugh.*)

GENERALS (*bowing deeply*) Too kind, Your Majesty!

WILHELM II (*scrapes the caviar and butter off a piece of toast with the forefinger of his right hand, and smears it into his mouth*) Ha!—Hahnke, like some caviar, too—? (*He tosses the plain piece of toast to the generals and roars with laughter, slapping his thigh with his right hand.*)

GENERALS (*bowing deeply*) Too kind, Your Majesty!

WILHELM II (*turning to an adjutant*) Ha!—Duncker, tell me now, what type of women do you fancy? Fat or skinny? (*The adjutant smiles in embarrassment. Wilhelm to the others*) He adores the fat ones. A nice soft pillow.

GENERALS Very droll, Your Majesty! (*The Kaiser laughs like a wolf.*)

WILHELM II Ha!—Krickwitz! (*Punches him in the belly.*) What sound does a rooster make?

KRICKWITZ (*crows*) Cock-a-doodle-doo—cock-a-doodle-doo!

FOURTH GENERAL (*to his neighbour*) His Majesty is a god.

WILHELM II Ha!—Flottwitz—look, what's happening over there?—(*The admiral turns. The Kaiser sneaks up and gives him a mighty slap on his behind. The admiral doubles up in pain.*)

WILHELM II Have you gone mad? Why do you keep pissing over my boots? (*To the Surgeon General Martius*) Ha!—Martius, look, what's happening over there? (*The surgeon general turns. The Kaiser sneaks up and pounces, grabbing him between the legs with his right hand. The surgeon general staggers in dreadful pain and grabs a chair for support. He is white as chalk. The Kaiser gives a crazy laugh, then turns away in anger when he registers the effect of his action. With a red face and puffed-out cheeks, snorting and puffing*) You blokes are so boring—ha!—no sense of humour!

GENERALS Very droll, Your Majesty, very droll!

FIRST GENERAL (*in an ironic aside*) An object of "love and delight to the human race", as the Roman historian said of Emperor Titus.

(*Change of scene.*)

Scene 38

Winter in the Carpathians. A man tied to a tree.

COMPANY COMMANDER HILLER How cold is it, do you reckon?

FIRST SOLDIER About minus 30 centigrade.

HILLER OK, you can untie him then. (*The soldiers do so. The man—fusilier Helmhake—collapses, unconscious. Hiller gives him several slaps in the face.*) Now into that dugout with him! (*The soldiers throw him into the dugout.*) You're sure it's really wet and stinking?

FIRST SOLDIER Yes, sir.

HILLER A nice high fever, has he—shivering fits?

FIRST SOLDIER Yes, sir.

HILLER Double the guard—jump to it!—the swine gets nothing to eat or drink. No taking a leak or a crap either, day or night. (*Laughing.*) Not that he'll need to, anyway. So, same drill as yesterday. Anyone who objects I'll tear to shreds. (*He goes off with his men. Two soldiers stay behind at the dugout. Whimpering can be heard.*)

SECOND SOLDIER D'y'a not think it would be more Christian if—instead of this one—we were to see to—*him?*

FIRST SOLDIER Sure do.

SECOND SOLDIER Two are dead already. Thomas he made strip naked when it was just as cold, and Müller had to go on watch when he was sick. There were five others he—(*A groan can be heard. It sounds like "Water!"*) Damn, I can't take any more of this! I'll give 'im a snowball to suck. (*He crawls into the dugout and returns in tears.*) Not even 20 yet—and signed up as a volunteer—! (*Hiller returns with his men.*)

HILLER I've had another idea. I want to see if—get 'im 'ere, the louse!—On the double!

SECOND SOLDIER He—I don't think he can, Lieutenant.

HILLER Why not? Get the son of a bitch out here! (*Several soldiers pull Helmhake out and drag him along, inert, like a lump of meat.*) What a sight! He's only play-acting, the skunk, give 'im a kick in the arse. (*He stamps on him with the heel of his boot.*) On yer feet, scum! Hasn't he kicked the bucket yet, the stinking swine?!

SECOND SOLDIER (*bends down over the brutalized victim, touches him, then stretches his hands towards Hiller as if in self-defence.*) He has—just now. (*Change of scene.*)

Scene 39

Same location. Hiller's dugout.

JUNIOR DOCTOR MÜLLER Death from hypothermia. Attempted resuscitation to no avail. The tricky bit is that he got no food.

HILLER We just have to wangle it so no one can pin it on us.

MÜLLER No doubt about it, the human resources are exhausted and sick. Nothing but tinned soup, and that's bad for their health. There's direct evidence of delirium due to exhaustion. The men are grubbing in the snow and jumping around like madmen.

HILLER I freely admit that starvation, beatings, chaining them up—none of that is enough to revive their fighting spirit. What can y'do? As far as Helmhake is concerned, I can say I took every conceivable measure. Here's what I'll write to his father:

> Dear Mr. Helmhake,
>
> It is my painful duty to notify you herewith of the sudden demise of your son, Fusilier Carl Helmhake. The doctor diagnosed dysentery of the small intestine. During his brief illness your son received the best possible physical and medical care. We mourn the departed as an able soldier and a good comrade, whose passing is a grievous loss. His remains lie in the cemetery in Dolzki.

(Change of scene.)

Scene 40

Optimist and Grumbler in conversation.

OPTIMIST Here, read the uplifting declaration that opened the Congress of German and Austrian Military Physicians: Let us all share the warm glow, the uplifting and truly fraternal thought that at this moment, while battles still rage on all our fronts, we here have been sanctioned by His Majesty to deliberate how best and most effectively to make provision for our triumphant warriors, to make good with appropriate care any damage caused to their health, and to consider how to endow ailing heroes with a renewed capacity for work and zest for life—

GRUMBLER —for death!

(Change of scene.)

Scene 41

Austrian military hospital. Convalescents, wounded soldiers of all ranks and men on their deathbed.

GENERAL STAFF PHYSICIAN *(opens the door)* Aha, there they are, nicely assembled, all the shirkers. *(Some of the patients suffer serious fits of nerves.)* Come on, come on, no need for drama. We'll soon fix that—just wait a moment! *(To a doctor)* Well, what's keeping you? Where the hell's the electric shock apparatus? Quick, I want to sort out the shirkers and fakers. (*The doctors approach various beds with the relevant equipment. The patients get convulsions.*) Him over there, bed number five, a particularly suspicious case! (*The patient begins to scream.*) There's only one remedy for that, one we prescribe in the very worst cases. Exposure to a heavy barrage! Yes sirree, the best way would be to shove everyone with shattered nerves into one container and expose them to a brisk burst of gunfire. Then they would soon forget their sufferings and be fit for front-line duty again! That would put an end to their shakes! (*He bangs the door behind him. A patient dies. Enter the commandant, Lieutenant-Colonel Vincenz Demmer, Baron von Drahtverhau.*)

DEMMER VON DRAHTVERHAU Aha, sloppy saluting again, for a change! You gents here in the hinterland are making yourselves nice and comfortable in your beds. And that's exactly why you see me here today. You, Medical Officer, buck your patients up so they hear what I have to say—an announcement of exemplary importance. I'm talking about the new saluting regulations—I don't mean saluting here in the hospital, but for when you're back on your feet, so you can get used to them before you've been compulsorily reenlisted. So, pay attention! (*He reads out*)

Directives concerning saluting:

The salute must always be carried out when fully at attention, as prescribed; the prescribed salute must be given to any superior or person of higher rank at no more than 30 paces distance from the subordinate or person of lower rank. The salute consists of spontaneously raising the right arm towards the head, with the palm of the hand to the side of the right eye and turned towards the face, so that the tips of the closed fingers touch the peak of the headgear (with caps without a peak, the border of the cap). On encountering the person to be saluted, or if the person to be saluted walks past the person saluting, the salute is to be carried out at a distance of three paces from the person to be saluted, and ends as soon as the person to be saluted has passed by a distance of three paces. If the soldier is carrying something in his right hand, he salutes with his left hand, if he has something in both hands, he salutes by a smart turn of the head. This latter also applies to saluting on all occasions. On encountering a superior or someone of higher rank, the soldier must avoid passing the other at a distance of less than one pace. Other unfortunately entrenched forms of salute are strictly forbidden, *viz.* raising the right hand with the palm pointing outward to the right, fingers spread and touching the peak of the cap with the forefinger possibly even in front of the nose; saluting with a cigarette or cigar (or short pipe—the so-called nose warmer) in the hand raised in salute or even in the mouth; saluting outdoors when uncovered, and bowing with cap in hand. Military personnel who fail to salute according to regulations or who—for whatever reason—fail to salute at all, are liable to severe punishment; those on leave, besides being reported to their commanding officer, will be compulsorily reenlisted.—

So, get that into your heads, whoever does not spontaneously raise his right hand, with the palm of the hand to the side of the right eye and turned towards the face, so that the tips of the closed fingers touch the peak of the headgear (with caps without a peak, the border of the cap), can be forced to do so! Get that into your heads! That's the example to follow! As far as the other regulations concerning saluting are concerned, namely those in force here in the hospital, as long as you're lying around here you must set a good example, too, and I don't need to impress upon you that, irrespective of your accredited ailments, you each must salute as per regulations when a superior appears. You've no caps at the moment, but each of you has a forehead, so you'll have no problem raising your hand—if you have a hand—to your forehead, got it? So—eyes right! Hey, what's that—him in bed five—seems he can't wait to rejoin a battalion with its marching orders for the front—(*the Medical Officer gives him some information.*) Ah—all right, then—if you say so—but as a general rule—see to it that everything is in order next time!

Just make sure you get these people back out there, Medical Officer! There's a black mark against your name already—don't stir up more trouble by being too humane! A patriotic doctor is one who supplies the front! Follow the example of Dr. Zwangler, he just stuffed a bit of cloth in the mouth of a fellow with the shakes, and after two electric shocks rated him Category B and fit for nonarmed service. Or Dr. Zwickler! There's ambition for you! He's the one, you remember, who had the idea of applying electric shocks to the genitals—wants to get results, as quickly and as many as possible—which he does! Let him be an example to you! We need to buck up a bit! The Germans are using alternating current that trigger muscle spasms—while we're as pure as the driven snow! All that blather about being humane, but how can you reconcile it with patriotism? War is war, and a doctor's prime duty is to set a good example and replenish human resources. The surgeon general is complaining that you're putting medical considerations first. He's tried to make you understand, as one colleague to another, that a Category C is fit for more than just clerical duties, he should be in the trenches, but he says he always has his work cut out with you.

So I ask you—how d'ya fancy getting sent to some typhus hospital in Albania? Well then! For all I know you may be right from a medical point of view—like when you dug your heels in recently over that fellow who was haemorrhaging from the lungs, because he was a family man and so on—but the sole consideration here is the military one! We accept responsibility! Or that fellow with renal failure—what a laugh—why get worked up over him?—first he has to fire his 50 shots, then he can die! Serving His Majesty means that anyone who can walk is not left lying around here a minute longer than is necessary—keep your scruples for peacetime!

For as long as our country is in danger, everyone must be at his post, on guard! Me too, I'm no different, by jingo!—Over to the sergeants now, they'll take you through the saluting exercises, and I don't want to hear any complaints—no one's ever had any complaints against me—if you had Medinger von Minenfeld in charge here instead, or Gruber von Grünkreuz, oh boy, oh boy! What more do you want? You've got food, you've got soup, nice dried vegetables, and a nice cup of tea to wash it down, I've never had any complaints. All right, I suppose you've got time on your hands before you get back out to fight the good fight. But the saluting exercises will take care of that! And if it's not granted to some of you to get back out into the good fight for your country, your country is looking after you in the most exemplary way. Six hellers a day, without having to do a stroke, isn't that quite something? And if you behave you'll even get an artificial limb, and if you set an example you'll be reincorporated into the reserves. We're pure as the driven snow!—thank your lucky stars we're not with the Germans, otherwise I'd have you standing to attention—lying down! A bit of saluting before you get back out never finished anyone off. So—that's it for today! (*Exit.*)

(At one bed the sergeant conducts saluting exercises. At another a padre is administering the sacraments.)

(Change of scene.)

Scene 42

Optimist and Grumbler in conversation.

OPTIMIST Everyone is asking: "What have we achieved in Albania?"—

GRUMBLER —I can answer that: an epidemic of malaria.

OPTIMIST Is there nothing else in Albania for us?

GRUMBLER Oh yes there is: typhus.

OPTIMIST But down there—

GRUMBLER —conditions are terrible.

OPTIMIST But Albania served us mainly as—

GRUMBLER —a penal colony. "Send 'em to Albania!" was an aggravated form of the honour of dying for one's country.

OPTIMIST The invasion of Albania makes one thing certain—

GRUMBLER Death.

OPTIMIST Among our troops in Albania—the name Pflanzer-Baltin says it all—

GRUMBLER —since soldiers died in vast numbers.

OPTIMIST It's well known we had major political interests in Albania, and apart from that—

GRUMBLER —bug-ridden huts as barracks.

OPTIMIST But our officers in Scutari had very good billets, apparently, and they were known for—

GRUMBLER —whoring.

OPTIMIST As for hygiene in Albania, of which you paint such a black picture, I'm told that, on the contrary, the field hospitals were empty.

GRUMBLER Because those with malaria were left to die without treatment.

OPTIMIST On the contrary, the chief medical officer of Army Group Albania protested strongly against—

GRUMBLER —having his patients evacuated for the summer.

OPTIMIST But he was known for having healthy soldiers—

GRUMBLER —shot out of hand for stealing tins of preserved food.

OPTIMIST At any rate, arrangements were made—

GRUMBLER —for a field cinema, for officers.

OPTIMIST The evacuation of patients you mentioned did actually take place, though only—

GRUMBLER —when we were forced to flee.

OPTIMIST You mean the strategic withdrawal. As for the means of transport employed, it was admittedly difficult, given the huge numbers of the sick—

GRUMBLER —to make provision for them, though they hadn't existed before.

OPTIMIST But since the few hospital ships were inadequate for the evacuation, by requisitioning automobiles we managed—

GRUMBLER —to transport the baggage of the officers in the High Command.

OPTIMIST How do you mean?

GRUMBLER I mean the stolen furniture.

OPTIMIST Ah, yes. But the sick troops—

GRUMBLER —had to march through the mud and dirt.

OPTIMIST But they were permitted—

GRUMBLER —to remain lying by the roadside, for a prolonged rest.

OPTIMIST That was the exception, unless—

GRUMBLER —unless it marked the Emperor's birthday or an anniversary of his coming to power. For otherwise the retreat of an Austrian army, specifically an Albanian nightmare with thousands of horrific deaths from starvation or in the mud, tends to be linked with a certain dynastic date—as if it weren't one such date itself.

OPTIMIST How so?

GRUMBLER Since the siege of Belgrade, Austrian generals have felt the need to lay at the Emperor's feet not only their own criminal stupidity, but also some town they've captured, only to vacate it again the following morning.

OPTIMIST You don't seem to be aware that such red-letter days in our national history provide both incentives and compensations for the front-line soldier's sacrificial courage. If, as events unfold, shortages of transport facilities, refreshment posts, board, and lodgings should occur—well, war is war!—and still you can't deny—

GRUMBLER —that the personal baggage train of the army commander consisted of 25 truckloads, under the supervision of a captain.

OPTIMIST How do we know that?

GRUMBLER From the diary of a doctor who returned from Albania after finding that no sick men arrived at his hospital, even though everyone was ill.

OPTIMIST It can't have been so bad if he got out himself. How did he get back?

GRUMBLER With high fever, in a truck, on top of the crate containing the piano from the officers' mess, stolen from a certain—

OPTIMIST Well, even I may sadly have to admit that events have provided a discouraging answer to the question "What have we achieved in Albania?" But we undoubtedly have major political interests there, and you should surely never forget: What the staff officer retains to the very last is—

GRUMBLER His piano!

(Change of scene.)

Scene 43

War press quarters.

A CAPTAIN (*to one of the journalists*) Now laddie, I want no beating about the bush, today you're going to write an article, a real humdinger—Observations on the State of Hygiene. So here are some guidelines. (*He reads out*) "The victorious campaign in Galicia, with the capture of Lemberg, contributed to the continuing improvement of hygiene in our army." What are you gawking at?!

JOURNALIST So in Lemberg we're still holding on—again?

CAPTAIN How you spin it is your affair. "While the hectic struggle was being waged in the Carpathians, there was naturally less scope for an organized hygienic effort focusing on detail. Given the heavy pressure exerted by the general situation, the individual soldier could not receive as much attention as we might have wished. 'Hold out to the end!' was the watchword—without regard for the individual soldier, who matters at the front only as long as he's fighting. That was how it had to be in those difficult times. They were all lice-ridden! Now that we've our heads above water, we can turn to hygiene and set an example in how to implement it. In those hard times the seed was sown, the fruits of which, on a vast scale, will help sustain the vigorous manhood of all who had fought so hard and suffered so deeply. That seed came to fruition in the uninhibited, sunlit days after Lemberg had been retaken. The feeling of infinite gratitude for our valiant warriors, our consciousness of the absolute need to be sparing of individual life after such heavy losses, prompted us to employ all powers and means at our disposal to maintain the health and fighting capability of each individual soldier." At this point you must write about how we got rid of cholera.

"Consequently, across the board, hygienic deliberations and measures were intimately bound up with medical procedures." Listen to this, now! "The new service offered was delousing! Roughly every four weeks every man was given a bath, or let's say, every two weeks. This was applied systematically, across the board. Disinfecting was a precautionary measure against infectious diseases transmitted by personal contact." Brilliant, eh? That's from a colonel in the medical corps! He knows what's what! "The regular bath, often spiced up with film shows, had a most salutary moral influence on the troops, raised their fighting capacity and military zeal: an important step forward in maintaining vigorous manhood." I'm only giving you the guidelines, the rest is up to you. But things didn't stop there. "Over time the front has been developed into a virtual holiday camp. Often the men found themselves in sunny, wooded countryside, they could swim and sun themselves, and there were plans to add educational instruction and music, a library, sport, and theatre—all of which would have presented an opportunity to familiarize the still sensitive and receptive soldier's soul with important hygienic problems as a preparation for the social tasks of the future. The project still awaits implementation! When the times become calmer, that will be our priority." You've got to really bring that out! It's obvious that these measures are partly intended to create a feeling of home for the man at the front. The constantly caring, comradely contact between officers, doctors, and men creates a favourable climate in which all can flourish.

JOURNALIST What about the infectious diseases, Captain?

CAPTAIN Are you joking?! "Close cooperation between officers, doctors, and men is certainly not a problem awaiting implementation. The doctor is no longer only a physician, it is his role, over and above his purely medical activities, to maintain that physical and psychological balance in the men which constantly underpins the winning of battles and the ability to endure suffering. For months now, new admissions with infectious diseases have been few and far between. Venereal diseases are the only thing that still cause us concern." (*Giggling.*) "At all events, how they can be successfully treated is the most important problem we've encountered so far. Still, in the apparently hopeless battle against venereal diseases, we must not simply lay down tools." (*Merriment.*) "Bear in mind that a not inconsiderable number of soldiers have become venereally infected during this campaign, bear in mind further that, as a direct consequence of the war, the population has already suffered the loss of many soldiers in their prime—it is consequently clear that we must counter the damage due to venereal diseases with all means in our power. Even though what we have already achieved in maintaining the vigorous manhood of the individual is of benefit to the people, the battle against venereal diseases is an essential precondition if we are to sustain the health of our race. The gravity of the situation demands intervention, it demands that as far as possible we should work towards the same goal with unflagging energy. Among the measures to sustain the vigorous manhood of individual lives and, more broadly, of the people—measures taken under the auspices of our army commander, His Excellency Colonel General von Böhm-Erbolli, and which also bear the personal stamp of both the chief of the Army Medical Corps and the Quartermaster-General—along with the prophylactic units and the central hospital with its first-rate staff and therapeutic equipment, there is an institution which enables us to uphold—stalwart and true—the individual soldier's vigorous manhood and ensure the regeneration of our race, an institution in which those sunny days after the retaking of Lemberg brought forth fruit on a vast scale. We have established"—and you can take

this down exactly as I got it, direct from head of the Medical Corps: "We have established brothels with impeccable human resources and under the strictest military control."
(Change of scene.)

Scene 44

Army training unit. Vladimir-Volinski, Ukraine.

A CAPTAIN (*dictates to a clerk*) The following order is to be read out to all men in the troop on three consecutive days: Cases of venereal disease are to be treated as self-inflicted and subject to court-martial. To lend force to this decree, soldiers thus infected are in every case to report to the head of the Army Training Unit. Recent cases proved to have been contracted by artificial means or deliberately self-inflicted will be subject to corporal punishment. The flogging will begin with five strokes of the birch, to be increased by one stroke daily, and continue until symptoms of the disease disappear.

The first flogging is to be administered today at 2 pm to the following—

That's it, copy it out.

Punishment to be administered by the provost marshal. Two strong men from the technical company are to be put at his disposal.
(Change of scene.)

Scene 45

Count Dohna-Schlodien at home. He is surrounded by 12 press reporters.

A PRESS REPORTER We consider ourselves extremely privileged, Captain, to receive from the mouth of one of our immortal heroes in person an authentic account of the glorious naval exploits of the cruiser *Möwe*, which our children and our children's children will relate to their grandchildren, and which shall live on in the annals of our nation. (*They prepare to write.*)

DOHNA Gentlemen, I am a man of action and few words. You may note the following essentials. On the basis of information received from reconnaissance I drew up a fairly precise plan. On day one I was lucky enough to spot a large steamer. As you know, it was the French battleship *Voltaire.* I waited through the night before approaching the *Voltaire.*

A VOICE IN THE GROUP Bravo!

DOHNA Later I was able to put the *Voltaire* out of action. Then I cruised the North Atlantic without spotting any further ships for the first three days; later, however, I managed to eliminate a steamer almost every day. All the ships were carrying valuable cargo, partly war material; one of them had a cargo of 1,200 horses.

PRESS REPORTER Fully functioning horses? 1,200 horses, Captain?

DOHNA 1,200—! (*Gesture of sinking.*)

PRESS REPORTERS (*all speaking at once*) By thunder!—Fully functioning horses!—Bravo!—Military precision! Breaks all records!—What panache!

ACT V

Scene 1

A cold, wet evening at the corner where the Kärntnerstrasse meets the Ring. Rain is falling upwards. A pack of pigheaded diehards gawking in silence. The street is lined by the wounded and the dead.

VOICE OF A NEWS VENDOR Evening paper—eight o'clock edition!

FIRST OFFICER (*to three others*) Evening Nowotny, evening Pokorny, evening Powolny—the very man! You know all about politics. Come on, tell us, what d'ya think about Bulgaria?

SECOND OFFICER (*with walking stick*) You know what I think—a complete no-brainer!

THIRD OFFICER Y'know—that's spot-on.

FOURTH OFFICER Absolutely—I was at a bash in the mess last night—! Did you see the latest Schönpflug cartoon? Fantabulous!

VOICE OF A NEWS VENDOR Entente angling for peace!

THIRD OFFICER Dismal tonight, isn't it?

FIRST Y'know what Schlepitschka von Schlachtentreu in the War Ministry said today: giants would be a peaceful step—no, hang on—peace would be a giant step for mankind, that's it. Think that's true? Optimistic, isn't it?

SECOND OFFICER It's pessimistic.

FIRST OFFICER Pessimistic, is it? Y'know, he said there's a sick man in Turkey, then it's our turn—what's that mean, d'y'think?

SECOND OFFICER He means the situation, and all that.

FIRST OFFICER Ah.

THIRD OFFICER No tarts about today.

SECOND OFFICER But Fallota's back.

Some old men pass by. Strains of "In der Heimat, in der Heimat da gibt's ein Wiedersehn"—

POLDI FESCH (*to his companion*) I'll be out partying with the Sascha Film people tomorrow—(*exit.*)

(*A cabby's voice can be heard: There's a war on—fare's 50 times that!*)

FOURTH OFFICER Know what they call old Fallota in the War Ministry? A hero, that's what.

FIRST OFFICER Why?

FOURTH OFFICER Y'don't know? Because he was at the front! Says he preferred it there.

FIRST OFFICER They shouldn't detain him here, then. Live and let live! Well, it's true, isn't it?

(*Enter Turi and Ludi.*)

TURI Hey Ludi, d'y'know if Rudi Nyári's playing at the Lurion tonight? (*Exit.*)

FALLOTA (*enters*) Hi there!

ALL Hi there, hero!

FALLOTA What'd'ya mean, hero? You having me on?!

FLOWER SELLER Yellow, lovely yellow flowers!

FOURTH OFFICER Hey, how was it? Feeling great? Tell us at Hopfner's.

FIRST OFFICER Yes, come on, you dashing young devil—

SECOND OFFICER So, what was it like at the front?

FALLOTA A lot of dashing, certainly.

THIRD OFFICER (*absorbed in his own thoughts*) Not a single bit of skirt—it's dismal.

FIRST OFFICER So, how was it then?

FALLOTA I'm still alive.

(*Two leg stumps in a ragged uniform cross their path.*)

SECOND OFFICER Let's be off, nothing but shirkers here! (*Exeunt.*)

VOICE OF A NEWS VENDOR Ex-tra-aa edi-shun—! Losses in millions for the Een-teent!

A WHISPERING VOICE C'm over here, I've got news for you.

(*Silence. Suddenly an enormous roar, like the thunder of patriotic gunfire: "Here he comes!" Then: "Slezak! Leo Slezak!" The clamour appears to come from the Opera House. A car door slams shut. Then silence.*)

(*Change of scene.*)

Scene 2

Optimist and Grumbler in conversation.

GRUMBLER

O gods! Who is't can say "It is at the worst?"
It is worse than e'er it was.
And worse it may be yet; the worst is not,
So long as we can say, "This is the worst."

Children with faces that suggest they've been starving for a generation, and still no end in sight! But the worst is contained in this report on a clinic for nervous diseases. One man is sitting in a blue-striped gown, incurably melancholic, atoning for the glory of Asiago where he was buried when a shell exploded. Another has a bullet lodged in his head—addicted to morphine as the only escape from the agonizing pain. In the evening he screams in despair for the nurse, and everyone is overwhelmed by tears. A mentally disturbed child is crying, born two months after its expectant mother received the news that her husband had died a "hero's death." For one whose sons made it back unscathed, it was too late—she went out of her mind. But who can say: this is the worst?

OPTIMIST Yes, it's undeniable, the war is leaving its mark on everyone's life. How much longer do you think it will last?

GRUMBLER At all events, we shall continue to keep telling lies until the last breath of man and mount. Whether we shall also keep fighting is a different matter. It seems we're trying to escape German pressure by betraying the Special Relationship. A little treachery will be our revenge on Germany for their not having prevented us from provoking them to declare war. But who would not prefer one's own country to suffer any disgrace rather than humanity as a whole, whose burden of shame increases every minute this war continues. Fortunately, it is now being shortened by our defeats rather than prolonged by our victories. Did I not once predict that the breakthrough at Gorlice, which we have to thank for delaying the inevitable collapse, would cost millions of human lives? What would Hamlet have said? This was sometime a paradox, but now the grandeur of the age gives it proof.

OPTIMIST Well, as for the age of grandeur, I have to admit myself that it hasn't grown appreciably since the ultimatum to Serbia. You're right about that, it's probably shrunk in every respect, just as you always predicted. Or perhaps it would be more accurate to say that an age of grandeur was inhabited by a race of pigmies.

GRUMBLER Rotten luck! But what have you seen that supports your view?

OPTIMIST I didn't want to tell you, but I came across a notice in the personal column of the paper today that makes you think, even though the front pages are carrying such momentous reports from the General Staff.

GRUMBLER At a time when the front pages of the papers are carrying such momentous reports from the General Staff, what possible significance can a notice in the personal column have?

OPTIMIST Judge for yourself.

GRUMBLER *(reads)*

> My little chickadee!
> Do you love me? Love me lots? Love me to bits?
> Shall wait, sweetheart, till you write or come.
> Mitzi.

You see, there's still time for love. There was I thinking only hatred had grown and hunger to go with it. But as for stupidity, its dimensions are obviously expanding as I always thought they would. You want to see the Austrian face? It may be undernourished, for which it has only itself to blame, but it is reflected spiritually in the dumpling depicted on this picture-postcard, the romantic ideal of the Viennese imagination. It's my turn now—the text must surely be by that little chickadee.

OPTIMIST *(reads)*

> If I could have my greatest wish,
> Let me describe my favourite dish!
> It must be a dumpling, fine and white,
> Freshly made for my delight!

GRUMBLER Published by Treuland Press! It conveys people's deepest feeling better than Mignon's song "Knowst Thou the Heart's Desire." In 1914 the population condemned itself to the ideal of the dumpling, and I could prove by the standards of the Last Judgment the linkage between dumplings depicted on postcards and bombs dropped from aeroplanes, both marking the last resort of the same materialistic epoch. If the powers-that-be, who are so godforsaken as to possess nothing but power, were capable of grasping such connections, the war would never have started or would have ended long ago.

OPTIMIST There's not much prospect of that now that they're conscripting the next age group.

GRUMBLER Otherwise man might forget why God created him.

OPTIMIST And why was that?

GRUMBLER So that he could appear before the recruiting board. They were naked and were not ashamed.

(Change of scene.)

Scene 3

In front of the Parliament building.

Some members of the Upper House have just left the building and are engaged in debate under the statue of Pallas Athena. A tram has stopped, with limbs hanging out on both sides. Amidst an indescribable tumult of screamed abuse, curses, and inarticulate noises, through a tangled pile of kitbags and knapsacks and squashed bodies in the second car, full of undernourished, unwashed, and ragged people crammed together like sardines—a woman who has just collapsed from hunger is dragged out.

PATTAI THE PATRIOT I won't retract an iota from my riposte to that damned pacifist Lammasch—he can have it framed! We are the victors and we demand the spoils!

(Change of scene.)

Scene 4

Foreign Ministry.

COUNT LEOPOLD FRANZ RUDOLF ERNEST VINCENZ INNOCENZ MARIA *(looks in his pocket mirror)* Another fine mess we've got ourselves into. If I'd had an inkling of the difficulties it would cause, I'd have spoken out against the ultimatum!

BARON EDUARD ALOIS JOSEF OTTOKAR IGNAZIUS EUSABIUS MARIA What's up?

COUNT Another fine mess. If you're going to wage war, you've got to anticipate such difficulties!

BARON I can't make you out. What more d'you want? I've just read that the krauts have sunk another 4,000 tons, and we haven't been idle either. Five.

COUNT Five thousand?

BARON Five tons!

COUNT You're kidding! If the Swiss don't get us out of this—

BARON What! You're still hoping the neutrals will—?

COUNT I've never been so on edge, waiting for the courier. I'm dying of impatience.

BARON So what's going on?

COUNT We sit here twiddling our thumbs—you just can't depend on our people in Berne! By God, if I weren't indispensable here, I'd be in the saddle and off; I'd soon get things sorted! I know exactly what I want, but you're handicapped whatever way you turn. A charming affair, this war! But this I guarantee, we're going to see some changes now!

BARON You always were madly optimistic. What d'you imagine they can do in Berne?

COUNT What I wrote down for them, black on white! But no, they would play bridge all day long—and at night, you know as well as I do what they get up to. During the day, too, for that matter—they've got time on their hands.

BARON Oh come on, what's got into you—Look, let me say it again, if you will send out people who aren't from the top drawer, then they don't even put on a good show.

COUNT Oh, stop it—having to go and pester the War Ministry every week for an unrestricted visa for some Jew, so they can find suckers to fleece at bridge in Berne—that's all they need us for! And all the flappers I have to pull strings for to get out of the country! I'll tell you this, since Bubi became a counsellor at the Embassy, he's no damn use at all. Just wait till Bubi and Affi get back to Vienna, I'll soon show them the game's up. I'll tell them to their face: You fellows, I'll say, you're full of charm, but when the going gets tough, you're not dependable. It's ridiculous. This war was the last straw! Y'know, I feel sorely tempted right now to chuck the whole thing in!

BARON But I thought you were pinning your hopes on the neutrals!

COUNT I'm telling you, the neutrals are the greatest disappointment. The Netherlands have left us totally in the lurch—

BARON I really don't know what to make of you. You've become so prickly you make me laugh! You were the confident one—more than any of us. From the very start. When Berchtold told us: Now the army can have its way!—your eyes lit up even more than his, you almost threw yourself round his neck. The ultimatum is terrific—that's what you said—absolutely spot-on—You can't say don't you remember!?

COUNT Oh, don't remind me! The ultimatum was a pig's breakfast. We can't go on like this. If Switzerland lets us down this time, I really don't know—I'm desperate! Anyhow, tomorrow—I've never been so on edge, waiting for that courier! (*Looks in pocket mirror.*) Another fine mess.

BARON Holy Moses! What are you waiting for that's so special?

COUNT Dimwit—my Colgate shaving cream, of course—!!
(*Change of scene.*)

Scene 5

Near Udine.
Two generals, each in an automobile piled high with baggage, arrive from opposite directions.

FIRST GENERAL That's my last trip. We've got all we can.

SECOND GENERAL We've got all we can.

FIRST Pity. Such a rich country.

SECOND Yes. Those Germans!

FIRST Beat us to it again!

SECOND Those Germans!

FIRST They're efficient, you may envy them, but you've got to give them that. They've got special looting officers, it's all organized. Centralized collections. Whereas we have to pick up bits and pieces by ourselves.

SECOND Organization, that's what they have. As soon as they got to Udine, they immediately divided it into Udine North and Udine South. Udine S had the silk, so that naturally belongs to the Germans.

FIRST Udine N had zilch. So, of course, that's ours.

SECOND And, of course, we're not allowed across the demarcation line.

FIRST Bad show.

SECOND Bad show.

FIRST The German silk merchants had got there before our advance units.

SECOND And the German looting officers are quicker off the mark than our galloping consumption. Gotta hand it to them!

FIRST Yes, though our chaps got hold of some wine. Not all of it's been drunk yet!

SECOND But our chaps were sloshed. Like in that "Death to the Russians" game!

FIRST D'you get anything? Some abandoned property maybe?

SECOND Nothing much, only the odd memento from the front, anything that wasn't nailed down.

FIRST Today I requisitioned three carpets, 30 kilos of rice, some meat, two bags of coffee, three door panels, and four pictures of saints, beautifully painted, very naturalistic!

SECOND Today I got a gramophone, 20 kilos of macaroni, some copper, five kilos of cheese, two dozen tins of sardines, and a couple of pictures, in oils! So long. (*He drives off.*)

FIRST So long.—What's that I see? One of our infantrymen, pinching a cob of maize! Hold on, you rascal, that's robbery! (*He gets out of the car and slaps him.*)
(*Change of scene.*)

Scene 6

The base at Fourmies, near the Ardennes.

TERRITORIAL RESERVIST LÜDECKE Let those moaning minnies come, from the front or from back home, we won't let them spoil our war here at the base. The boozing and whoring is just fine, there's no sign of a peace without annexations here. The Crown Prince has a fully functioning harem on the go, with a terrific addition the other day—when the parents objected, he simply had them deported. Here in the west we're just mopping up. After all, what do they expect back home? We send back all we can. I'm told the loot from Lille is already being sold at Wertheim's in Berlin. I must drop a line home and say how well out of it we are here. (*He writes.*) May the 8th. My dear friend, I've been posted to the requisition unit of the base at Fourmies. We relieve the French population of all their lead, brass, copper, cork, oil, etc., chandeliers, cooking ranges; everything collected from far and wide makes its way to Germany. It's often very unpleasant taking wedding presents from the young women, but the necessity of war compels us to do it. With one of my comrades I recently made a rich haul. In a walled-up room we found 15 musical instruments made of copper, a whole orchestra, a brand new bicycle, 150 bed sheets and towels, and six copper chandeliers, which alone weighed 25 kilos; also a lot of other valuable objects. You can imagine how mad the old witch who owned them was; I couldn't stop laughing. Everything together was worth over 10,000 marks. A few bales of sheep's wool and a lot of other stuff. The commandant was more than delighted and we're even going to get a reward. Maybe the Iron Cross as well. And then there are the young girls, it's fun deflowering them. All good wishes—
(*Change of scene.*)

Scene 7

Circus Busch. Mass rally for "Peace on German Terms."

PASTOR BRÜSTLEIN (*arm outstretched*)—In the west: the iron and steel centres of Longwy and Briey! And we'll never return the Flemish coast! (*Deafening applause.*) In the east, the notorious line of fortifications—by hook or by crook they must remain in our hands and never again threaten East Prussia! (*Lively applause.*) In the Baltic, we'll never return Courland and occupied Lithuania! (*Deafening applause.*) And linked to Courland: Livonia and Estonia. (*Right arm outstretched.*) They've sounded the alarm. We must come to their aid!
(Shouts of "Hurrah! Hurrah! Hurrah!" The speaker stands down. The crowd strikes up Luther's hymn "A Mighty Fortress Is Our God.")

EDITOR IN CHIEF MASCHKE My beloved comrades! I shall be brief. I demand one thing only, one thing which inspires us all: Down with the conscience of the world community! (*Shouts of "Hurrah!"*) Down with the spirit of universal brotherhood! (*Shouts of "Hurrah!"*) The only voice of conscience that we hear and obey is the imperative of German power! And its watchword is "More power! More power to Germany!" Anyone who talks or writes as his global conscience dictates, or his feeling of responsibility towards mankind, rather than the power of the German sword, is a political dreamer with his head in the clouds. (*Deafening applause.*)

A DISSENTING VOICE Let me remind this august gathering of just one thing. The Minister of Finance recently tried to gloss over the harm inflicted on public morality by the war when he pointed to the brilliant victories of our troops. But the Bible tells us: "What shall it profit a man if he should gain the whole world and lose his own soul?" Our modern civilization takes the same view as the Bible: the moral corruption of society by fraud, theft, and deceit can never be glossed over by military glory. Great national institutions such as the Post Office have been turned into dens of thieves, whole classes of people have been hurled into the bottomless pit, all because of the insatiable greed for profit—(*shouts of "Throw 'im out!" The speaker is ejected.*)

PROFESSOR PUPPE Ladies and gentlemen, I'll be brief, since the guidelines for a peace on German terms lie so clearly before our eyes that we can stretch out and touch them. (*He does so.*) A friendly reconciliation with France is impossible. (*Shouts of "Impossible!"*) We must render France so powerless that they can never attack us again! (*Deafening applause.*) For that, we must push forward our western border; the iron ore mines of northern France must be ours! (*Lively applause.*) We must never lose control of what used to be known as Belgium—militarily, politically, or economically! In addition, we need a large colonial empire in Africa! (*Deafening applause.*) To secure this, we need naval bases! It is imperative that England be expelled from the Mediterranean, from Gibraltar, Malta, Cyprus, Egypt, and her recent conquests there! (*Shouts of* "Gott strafe England!") Naturally, we shall also demand reparations! (*Tumultuous applause.*) – This to be achieved by forcing the enemy to put a substantial part of their merchant fleet at our disposal to supply us with gold, foodstuffs, and raw materials. (*Shouts of "Hurrah!"*) Further –

(*Change of scene.*)

Scene 8

Optimist and Grumbler in conversation.

OPTIMIST What's that you're reading?

GRUMBLER Listen to this: "Madman Takes Control of Cab Horse. An alarming incident last night at the junction of Alserstrasse and Landesgerichtsstrasse created a protracted sensation among the many passersby. Around half past seven a one-horse carriage with two lady passengers and their luggage stacked up on the driver's seat was travelling down the Universitätsstrasse towards the Alserstrasse. As the carriage drove slowly towards the junction of Alserstrasse and Landesgerichtsstrasse, a young man in infantry uniform suddenly ran into the street and lunged at the cab horse. He grabbed the reins and tried to stop the horse. The cabby was startled, the two passengers shocked. The cabby whipped the horse to get it to go faster and elude the young man; the horse did speed up, at which the young man launched himself forward again and jumped on its back. With his bare hands he got the poor beast to go even faster by repeatedly shouting 'Hurrah!' By now the cabby had totally lost control of the horse, and the strange rider made the horse turn right around. At a gallop it made for the crossing with the carriage pitching and tossing behind. The escapade could have ended in disaster if a policeman at the crossing hadn't seized the horse's reins and brought it to a halt. The policeman hauled the rider to the ground. Cabby and passengers breathed a sigh of relief. A large crowd immediately gathered around the carriage. The young man, evidently deranged, was taken to a psychiatric hospital."

OPTIMIST So what? A trivial local incident. Why do you bother with such things? Surely there are matters of greater moment now. The big question, according to Harden in Berlin –

GRUMBLER The most urgent question is surely: how long do *we* have to wait for a policeman? When you really need one, he's naturally never there!

OPTIMIST Yes, but why do you get worked up about that? A trivial local incident!

GRUMBLER I'll tell you this, nothing can protect us from such local incidents! The strange rider won't dismount—until a policeman appears!

OPTIMIST I don't understand. You're a typical Viennese grouse. International politics are surely more important.

GRUMBLER But mine is a roundabout way of getting at the heart of the matter. World affairs are too remote for my taste. With the possible exception of Japan, that does interest me.

OPTIMIST It's revealing what you come up with. Why Japan?

GRUMBLER There—listen to this—"The Sino-Japanese Military Convention. Japan Totally Dominant in China. According to the *Shanghai Gazette*, the content of secret agreements in the military convention just signed between Japan and China is as follows: The Chinese police force will be reorganized by Japan. Japan takes control of all Chinese arsenals and naval dockyards. Japan is empowered to extract iron and coal in all regions of China. Japan has privileged status in all matters in Outer and Inner Mongolia, also in Manchuria. Finally, a number of measures have been taken which subject Chinese finance and food production to Japanese influence."—Oh, I really do take an interest in international politics!

OPTIMIST Yes, but of what interest is Japan to us? The relationship between Japan and China seems, in your eyes, to have been—

GRUMBLER —expanded and intensified!

(Change of scene.)

Scene 9

The esplanade at Bad Ischl. Subscriber to the Neue Freie Presse *and Patriot in conversation.*

PATRIOT Full agreement was reached and the decision taken to expand and intensify the Special Relationship.

SUBSCRIBER In a word, then, expansion and intensification of the alliance.

PATRIOT There was full agreement reached on all issues and the decision taken to expand and intensify the existing alliance.

SUBSCRIBER In a word, then, expansion and intensification of the existing alliance.

PATRIOT As of today, the form which the expansion and intensification of the alliance will take, has not yet been revealed.

SUBSCRIBER However, the war has made the expansion and intensification of the alliance necessary.

PATRIOT The direction in which the expansion and intensification of the alliance will proceed, is not indicated in the official communiqué.

SUBSCRIBER It will certainly be what both General Staffs want—to expand and intensify the advantage the Monarchy and Germany gained from the resolution "to stand shoulder to shoulder", as they say in wartime.

PATRIOT Have you any reliable inside information?

SUBSCRIBER All I can tell you is that we must hold fast to this defensive alliance and simply create further preconditions for an expansion and intensification of the alliance.

PATRIOT (*after a pause*) What do you think about the expansion and intensification of the alliance with Germany?

SUBSCRIBER The factual situation created by the Central Powers should be established as our guideline for future expansion and intensification.

PATRIOT We only need to follow the events of the war to understand why the expansion and intensification of the alliance have become inevitable.

SUBSCRIBER For the Central Powers, the united front is sufficient cause for the military intensification of the alliance.

PATRIOT And what about its expansion?

SUBSCRIBER The plan to continue depriving the Central Powers of raw materials after the war is countered by news of the economic expansion of the alliance. The expansion of the alliance with Germany from an economic point of view—

PATRIOT The expansion and intensification of the alliance between the Monarchy and Germany are connected with the Polish Question. But one reads news of fake German overtures of peace. What's the truth of the matter?

SUBSCRIBER The truth is the expansion and intensification of the alliance between the Monarchy and Germany. I'm telling you!

PATRIOT Here's hoping! You seem to be referring to the official announcement that, when the Emperors met at German Supreme Headquarters, the expansion and intensification of the existing alliance between Germany and Austria-Hungary was finally agreed upon.

SUBSCRIBER Do you know what the consequences will be? The world will have to reckon on the British Empire, with its four hundred million inhabitants, expanding and intensifying its relationship with the United States to put it even further ahead in the supply of raw materials. They copy everything we do.

PATRIOT Of course they do. What influence could news of the expansion and intensification of the alliance have on the politics of the Entente? The effects could well be long-lasting.

SUBSCRIBER One might conclude with some justification that the public has correctly recognized the essential purpose of the expansion and intensification.

PATRIOT You don't say! My definite impression is that everyone who witnessed the historic meeting between the monarchs felt at its culmination that the alliance between the two Central Powers was intensified in the truest meaning of the word. Namely, the foundations of an essential intensification—

SUBSCRIBER That reminds me, the expansion of the Technical University—

PATRIOT The effect of the expansion of the alliance on the Polish Question—

SUBSCRIBER The effect of the expansion of the alliance on the Entente—

PATRIOT In the circumstances, the expansion and intensification of the alliance can only surprise the Entente.

SUBSCRIBER No wonder! The great significance of the political and military expansion of the alliance was subjected to close examination on the Stock Exchange. Particular emphasis was laid on the intensification—

PATRIOT It is to be expected that discussions on the arrangements to be made for expanding and intensifying the alliance will now commence. As far as the expansion of the economic alliance with Germany in particular is concerned, it has, however, just been—

SUBSCRIBER That is why it is especially interesting to hear what Herr Wekerle, as a prominent cabinet minister, has to say about the resolutions concerning the expansion of the economic alliance with Germany.

PATRIOT Wekerle? But he's always been angling for an intensification of the economic relationship!

SUBSCRIBER The world was apprised of the announcement that the decision to expand and intensify the alliance had been taken.

PATRIOT After the war, the Monarchy and Germany will see that it is imperative to intensify the alliance.

SUBSCRIBER Say what you will, security can only be achieved by the expansion and intensification of the alliance.

PATRIOT Yes, but—the budget, government bonds and taxes cannot be put off until after the alliance with Germany has been expanded politically, militarily, and economically.

SUBSCRIBER In discussing the intensification of the alliance between the Central Powers, did he not explain—?

PATRIOT You mean Friedjung. But on the contrary, Friedjung's conclusion was a hearty three cheers for expanding the alliance of the two Central Powers with Turkey!

SUBSCRIBER And what about its intensification? The question was initially about the intensification of the alliance of the Central Powers.

PATRIOT But that's something completely different! It was a question of the expansion of the Austro-Hungarian-German alliance in a military sense.

SUBSCRIBER That may be, but the intensification of the alliance is imperative in a military sense, too.

PATRIOT All I know is what Wekerle and Tisza said on the subject of the intensification of the alliance—

SUBSCRIBER Comments were made by one side which indicated reservations about an intensification of the alliance.

PATRIOT That reminds me, what do you think about the way we expanded the victory at Noyon?

SUBSCRIBER And did you read what Burian said about the intensification of the alliance?

PATRIOT And did you read about the consultations in Salzburg on expanding the alliance?

SUBSCRIBER Hang on, it was only the prevailing views about the economic intensification they were discussing!

PATRIOT But the German Kaiser was singing the praises of the Hetman for having begun to expand the new state system in Ukraine.

SUBSCRIBER Yes, but the Hetman immediately expressed the hope that relations between the powerful German Reich and Ukraine would be increasingly intensified!

PATRIOT That's what he says! But you know, intensification is a risky business. Didn't you read the communiqué from Berlin on information from The Hague that London has reported Turin's announcement that the Italian Stock Exchange is in the doldrums since the meeting of the German and Austrian Emperors, and that it's thought the Italians are very disappointed by the intensity of the alliance?

SUBSCRIBER And how intense is that?! Still, since you mention The Hague, I'm convinced the institution of international courts of arbitration will be greatly expanded after the war.

PATRIOT That's possible. For the moment they're only negotiations and still ongoing, the general idea being to intensify the alliance.

SUBSCRIBER On the other hand, the preventive measures are being constantly expanded.

PATRIOT Preventive measures against theft of articles in the post? Don't I know! But what good is that? It's theft on trains that has really become rampant, in this era of expansion and intensification.

SUBSCRIBER It's all the more vital now that we expand regulations covering the insurance of luggage, since—

(Old Biach arrives, out of breath.)

BIACH Have you heard? Expanded and intensified!

PATRIOT So what's new?

BIACH But I tell you, the alliance has been expanded and intensified! Though—

PATRIOT So what? Get a grip on yourself!

BIACH That's all we needed—

PATRIOT What's bothering you?

BIACH Heavens above—it's not that simple—listen—it's been construed in different ways! D'you know how the Viennese version differs from the Berlin version? (*Beside himself.*) A close examination of the text of the communiqué released in Vienna and Berlin reveals a difference that leaps into your eyes.

PATRIOT How d'you mean?

BIACH Look, both communiqués are identical—same sentences, same expressions, same sparseness of detail—

PATRIOT Well, there you are!

BIACH —with one exception. (*Panting.*) Vienna and Berlin announce—Vienna and Berlin state—Vienna and Berlin report—Identical in content and in form—will be received with great satisfaction. For nothing can be more important than our rock-solid alliance—nothing can give us a greater sense of security—

PATRIOT Well, what more can you ask?

SUBSCRIBER Where's there any difference, then?—What are you worried about?

BIACH (*ever more deranged*) What good is all that? The communiqué released in Vienna says the meeting of the two Emperors confirmed "that the illustrious monarchs abide by the decision made in May to *intensify* the alliance." The communiqué released in Berlin says the meeting "confirmed the *identical and most faithful interpretation* of the terms of the alliance." If you compare the sentence in the Viennese communiqué about abiding by the decision made in May to *intensify* the alliance, with the sentence in the Berlin communiqué about the *identical and most faithful interpretation* of the terms of the alliance, there is no contradiction, but simply the fact that each of the communiqués refers to something different.

SUBSCRIBER So what more do you want?

BIACH The *identical and most faithful interpretation* of the terms of the alliance cannot stand in contradiction to the decision in May to *intensify* the alliance, and the latter would be unthinkable without the identical and most faithful interpretation of the *current* terms of the alliance.

PATRIOT Of course.

BIACH But the German public is being told something that is not in the Viennese communiqué, and vice versa. These are two explanations which, were they to appear one beside the other, in one and the same communiqué, would not strike you as odd. They only seem so because one communiqué contains nothing about abiding by the *intensification* of the alliance, and the other nothing about the *identical and most faithful interpretation* of the *current* terms of the alliance. Announcements regarding the meeting of the Emperors are normally formulated and made available to the public by mutual agreement. So Count Burian will have agreed to the *identical and most faithful interpretation* of the terms of the alliance, and Count Hertling will have consented to the confirmation that both Emperors abide by the decisions made in May to *intensify* the alliance. It is the voice of both statesmen that is heard in both communiqués, and neither can make comments on the meeting of which the other does not approve.

SUBSCRIBER That goes without saying.

BIACH Yet the dissimilarity of the versions may not be without significance. There is a perceptible hint that with the *intensification* of the alliance after the decision made in May, the Monarchy wants to achieve a solution to the Polish Question. Count Burian already made the connection in June. That's why the *intensification* of the alliance is underlined in the Viennese communiqué. The Berlin communiqué talks of the *identical and most faithful interpretation* of the current terms of the alliance. He does not want to make its continuance and effectiveness in any way dependent on the unsettled questions about its *expansion*, nor on a solution to the Austro-Polish Question.

SUBSCRIBER That's surely obvious, the intensification can be expanded, but the expansion is meant quantitatively—it cannot be intensified. So I don't see what you're getting worked up about—

BIACH Even the *most faithful interpretation* of the terms of the alliance is identical in the Monarchy and in Germany, as the Berlin communiqué states. Count Burian wants to intensify the alliance, as does Count Hertling. (*He starts to stamp his foot.*) But the German Chancellor wants the alliance on *current* terms, even if they *cannot be intensified.* The Monarchy agrees. These fundamental positions on cooperation are born of necessity. (*Already flagging.*) The *most faithful interpretation* of the alliance is mutual support on all fronts against the enemy. That's how the Allies operate, and so should the Central Powers. (*Exhausted, he begins to stagger. The subscriber and the patriot support him.*)

PATRIOT But they do—get a grip on yourself—it will all work out—calm down—just wait and see—

BIACH There is a difference—there is a difference—You may think there's no difference, but I tell you there is a difference—(*he sobs.*)

PATRIOT Of course there's a difference—just, please, don't get so worked up—anyone can see there's a difference!

SUBSCRIBER Why are you getting him even more upset? There's *no* difference!

PATRIOT There's no difference?

BIACH (*groaning*) There's—no—difference—?

SUBSCRIBER Haven't you heard? Listen. Latest report from Berlin. Contrary to certain interpretations in the press, informed sources here stress that, up to this moment in time, no official statement has been released concerning details of the discussions at Supreme Headquarters. There can be *no question* of any difference between the official German and Austrian reports of the meeting. (*Biach collapses.*)

SUBSCRIBER Heavens—there really is something up with him—

VISITORS AND SPA PATIENTS (*gathering*) What's happened?—Biach's been taken ill—

PATRIOT It's nothing. He got worked up—

BIACH (*groaning*) All—for—nothing—. There's—no—difference. All—my—efforts—

SUBSCRIBER Heavens—if I'd thought for a moment that we would—terrible!

PATRIOT That he would take it so personally!

SUBSCRIBER Yes, but after all, it's no trifling matter.
(Everyone wants to be part of the action.)

VISITORS AND SPA PATIENTS I don't like the look of him—someone should call a doctor—someone ought to inform his wife—yesterday he was still—I remember him when he was—

PATRIOT Y'know what I think? (*Looking around cautiously.*) Those inflammatory editorials are to blame!

SUBSCRIBER That's blasphemy!—Listen, he's saying something—

BIACH (*groaning*) Expanded—and—intensified—

SUBSCRIBER Please listen—

BIACH (*transfigured*) Cleopatra's nose—was one of her most beautiful features.

SUBSCRIBER He's hallucinating.

BIACH (*sitting up straight*) The—edifice—is—crumbling!

PATRIOT Prophetic!

BIACH (*collapses*) So—ends—the—editorial!

SUBSCRIBER (*sobbing*) Biach—!
(He dies. Subscriber and Patriot remain, transfixed. Silent groups of visitors and spa patients.)

SUBSCRIBER He'll be sadly missed.

PATRIOT Rest in peace.
(Change of scene.)

Scene 10

Berlin. A wine restaurant in Kaiserpassage. A mechanical barrel-organ is playing, alternately, the waltz "Emil, You're a True Berliner" and "I Hear, My Dear, You're a Racketeer." The public passing by outside consists mainly of aging rent-boys with hands like paws. A newspaper vendor is hawking the magazine Lonely Hearts. *A barker advertises Kastan's* Waxworks.
Two liberal politicians, Zulauf and Ablauf, are sitting at a table. Each has a low stand-up collar with crossover ends, a ready-made bowtie and horn pince-nez.

ABLASS (*raises his glass*) To the constitutional reform! Mud in your eye!

ZULAUF (*raises his glass*) Skin off your nose!

ABLASS Listen, Zulauf, I'm not at all happy with this word "reorientation."

ZULAUF No?

ABLASS I'd propose "repackaging."

ZULAUF Marvellous! Mud in your eye!

ABLASS Skin off your nose!

ZULAUF Tell me, Ablass, did you read the *Roter Tag* today?

ABLASS Yes.

ZULAUF And tell me, Ablass, did you read the *Berliner Tageblatt* today? Look, there's a report from the Press Bureau—(*produces the paper.*)

ABLASS No.

ZULAUF But it's a real corker. Listen: Brussels, 23 July (Wolff Bureau). In accordance with age-old custom, one also followed in the history of Flanders by princes and their representatives, the governor-general seized the opportunity offered by the national day of remembrance of the Flemish people on the 11th of July to imprint it on the memory of present and future generations through a special act of grace: he acceded to the request of 3,000 Flemings assembled in Antwerp for the Festival of the Golden Spurs.

ABLASS Great news!

ZULAUF Given that the commemoration of the Flemish struggle for freedom in 1302 was occurring for the first time since he assumed office, the governor-general wanted to imbue it this year with particular significance through measures for the implementation of the rights of the Flemish people.

ABLASS Great!

ZULAUF Accordingly, the governor-general commuted the death penalty imposed on five Flemings by the Antwerp government's court-martial into hard labour for life.—Now what do you say about that!

ABLASS Fantastic!

ZULAUF Isn't it! Now that's the wind of change. Three thousand Flemings reprieved at the request of five!

ABLASS What? Nonsense!

ZULAUF No it's not—oh, well—yes—anyway, it's all the same. At any rate, a reprieve is a reprieve. At least they got life imprisonment. So, the rights of the people are certainly being rigorously applied.

ABLASS No doubt about it, they'll be imprinted on the memory of present and future generations.

ZULAUF A fine act. And it'll remind them it's the first day commemorating the struggle for Flemish freedom under German domination!

ABLASS Tremendous!

ZULAUF Isn't it! Hey—Mud in your eye! To German freedom!

ABLASS As you say. German freedom! Skin off your nose!

ZULAUF *(after a pause)* So, tomorrow we've an appointment with Hindenburg and Ludendorff.

ABLASS Tomorrow? Tomorrow we're surely at Schneider-Duncker's cabaret!

ZULAUF At Schneider-Duncker's before lunch?

ABLASS No, in the evening. In the morning we're with Hindenburg and Ludendorff.

ZULAUF That's it. And we've been allotted 15 minutes each. We have to report for duty by 11 on the dot.

ABLASS Ordinary clothes?

ZULAUF No, evening dress!

(Change of scene.)

Scene 11

General meeting of the Social Democratic wartime election campaign for the mega-constituency of Teltow-Beskow-Storkow-Charlottenburg.

COMRADE SCHLIEFKE (TELTOW) —As Speaker of the general meeting of the Social Democratic wartime election campaign for the mega-constituency of Greater Berlin covering Teltow-Beskow-Storkow-Charlottenburg, let me therefore summarize: If Prussian Social Democrats accept the invitation of the Reichsminister of the Interior and if the Kaiser participates in this discussion, this does not run counter to Social Democratic principles. Comrade David also acted quite correctly when he accepted the Crown Prince's invitation. Social Democracy is a revolutionary party *(Cries of "Oho!")*—so when altered conditions require, it must also break with old traditions—

HECKLER By rubbing shoulders with the Kaiser?

SCHLIEFKE —I mean its own traditions! It must be revolutionary in its own ranks. For it is a thoroughly revolutionary party! *(Cries of support.)*

(Change of scene.)

Scene 12

Bad Gastein. Subscriber and Patriot in conversation.

SUBSCRIBER I'm convinced that the expansion of the alliance would—

PATRIOT I have no doubt that the reduction of hatred would then—

SUBSCRIBER I guess the intensification of the alliance would—

PATRIOT I'd say that this would lead to a cost inflation—

SUBSCRIBER Doubtless a cost reduction could—

PATRIOT It seems to me, on the other hand, that an inflation of hatred—

SUBSCRIBER —But I think a price expansion—

PATRIOT —I think that, in its wake, an intensification of hatred—

SUBSCRIBER I reckon an inflation of the alliance—

PATRIOT I'd say that, in its wake, an expansion of hatred—

SUBSCRIBER On the other hand, I'm convinced that by a reduction of the alliance—

PATRIOT —we could easily achieve a deflation of prices.

(Change of scene.)

Scene 13

Office in a command post.

GENERAL STAFF OFFICER *(on the telephone)*—hello—no—it's me, Kobatsch—Peham is on leave—Now listen—of course, mass slaughter—thanks, I'm surviving—About those preposterous numbers of prisoners the Russians are claiming—look, all you have to write is: how can they know exactly, there's no way you can count them!—What's that?—Look, I know it's hard to make people believe it. Look, all you have to say is: as long as the numbers claimed stayed within reason—say, 10,000 a day—fair enough, that's acceptable, but now it's suddenly got to over a 100,000, that's no go!—What's that?—Look, all you have to say is: one really can't count that many etc., it's simply too many!—What's that?—We always count the prisoners? Yes *we* do, *we* do—but the enemy? That's a different kettle of fish!—What's that?—What'll they say? The enemy can't count fast enough when they stream across to him, but it's easier for us to count our losses—? Now hang on, take it easy, we did count, and after careful calculation we came up with a much smaller figure, got it? The main thing is, you keep repeating: the number of prisoners they claim is preposterous—you must keep saying that, that's the main thing. Go on, you'll manage it—once it says "official", that's half the truth already, and the other half you just make up and add on, clever chap like you. So long, then—end of story!

(Change of scene.)

Scene 14

Battlefield near Saarburg.

CAPTAIN NIEDERMACHER Our boys keep holding back. Every man jack of them knows by now that when General Ruhmleben was describing the current situation, he categorically ordered prisoners of war, whether wounded or not, to be finished off with rifle butts or revolvers, and to shoot the wounded in the field, just as the lying propaganda of the enemy claim we do.

MAJOR METZLER Ruhmleben is faithfully following the instruction of our Supreme Commander: Give no quarter, take no prisoners! His Majesty has also ordered the sinking of hospital ships, and we landlubbers must not lag behind!

NIEDERMACHER I had the order about finishing off the prisoners of war passed on from Brigade to the Company by word of mouth. But still the men hesitate.

METZLER We'll soon see about that, look, here's an opportunity. (*He kicks the inert body of a French* NCO.) Ah, he can still open his eyes. (*He beckons to two soldiers. They hesitate.*) Don't you know the orders from Brigade? (*The soldiers shoot.*) There's one crouching over there—drinking coffee, I do believe! (*He beckons to a soldier.*) Listen, Niedermacher, I'll leave that one to you, I must check on my own lot. (*Exit. The wounded man falls to his knees before Niedermacher and raises his hands in supplication.*)

NIEDERMACHER (*to the soldier, who is hesitating*) No prisoners!

SOLDIER But Captain, a moment ago I was dressing his wounds and giving him something to drink—!

NIEDERMACHER And he'll thank you by stabbing your eyes out and slitting your throat. (*In a rage, as the soldier hesitates.*) They lie in wait and snipe at you from behind and from above. Shoot 'em down from the trees like sparrows, that's what the general said. Shoot the lot of 'em, the general said. Do I have to make it a direct order, you bastard? We've killed 20 today already, and you're still shilly-shallying, you bastard? Call yourself a German?! You'll pay for this! Do I have to do everything for you, you pathetic wankers?—Look—here's how it's done! (*He shoots the wounded man kneeling before him.*)

(*Change of scene.*)

Scene 15

Near Verdun. German prisoners are lined up. They are being punched, horse-whipped and hit with rifle butts by French NCOs, and driven forward. Some of the wounded sink to the ground, exhausted. One has blood spurting from his mouth and nose. After the column has passed, General Gloirefaisant enters. He gestures, and captured officers are paraded past him. A French officer strikes one of them across the thighs with his horsewhip.

GENERAL GLOIREFAISANT *(to a captain)* Too many prisoners! We've been slacking instead of finishing them off. That American manual on hand-to-hand combat—it vividly demonstrates how to use the bayonet. It shows young bloods how to attack, how to cut and thrust into the liver, eyes, and kidneys of the enemy! What was it the book said? "You might come up against a German who'll plead 'Spare me, I have 10 children!'—Kill 'im, or he'll have 10 more." Our blacks are the only ones we can depend on. Their knapsacks are full of incontrovertible trophies—ears and heads they've cut off, just like the lying Boches reported. We've mustn't let our colonial auxiliaries put us to shame. *(Exit.)*

CAPTAIN DE MASSACRÉ There's no pleasing him.

COLONEL MEURTRIER What? How come you've so few prisoners? Twenty? I thought you had a whole company!

CAPTAIN DE MASSACRÉ I did have. But the others copped it in the trenches. I gave my men the order to finish off 180 of them with their bayonets. It's true they hesitated, brave lads though they are, but when I told them what would happen to them double quick, they went to work with a will, cutting throats and slitting open bellies.

COLONEL MEURTRIER *(annoyed)* A hundred and eighty? That's too many! Even for the general! I advise you not to mention anything about it, or you'll risk having your name struck from the Legion of Honour.

CAPTAIN MASSACRÉ *(self-assured)* On the contrary, Colonel, I believe I shall be wearing the cross of the Legion of Honour a few days from now! And then I'll get command of the Corsican regiment. What I have achieved here opens up the path to glory—that's my ambition!
(Change of scene.)

Scene 16

War Press Bureau in Rodaun.

ALICE SCHALEK *(to a fellow reporter)* The 208 photographs of corpses are certainly proof enough: posterity can have no doubts that I was present at the very heart of the heroic action. But so you can follow my example, so you can see what a depiction of battle really is, I'm going to read you the key sentences from my next article. My starting point is the 70 batteries divided into four groups:

one is bombarding the infantry, a second the artillery, the third the reserve positions, and the fourth is blocking the access routes, got that? So listen:
The main question is: How and where and when can the position be sealed off? Everything unfolds almost as if in a well-rehearsed play.
Fighting in forested areas is the horror of horrors.
You think you're surrounded, but in the meantime reinforcements have arrived elsewhere and already "mopped up."

REPORTER Mopped up?

ALICE SCHALEK Listen—the dead are dead, only the survivors get the glory.

REPORTER Brilliant!

ALICE SCHALEK A munitions waggon drawn by six horses takes a direct hit.

REPORTER Kaboom—!

ALICE SCHALEK Bits and pieces of soldiers, lots of bits and pieces, end up in the treetops.
The enemy hurl hand grenades and a furious hand-to-hand brawl ensues; they fight with daggers, rifle butts, knives, their teeth.
If the grenades overshoot, they wave their caps at the missiles and make a bow.

REPORTER A genre painting.

ALICE SCHALEK "Delighted to meet you", they shout as the grenades sail over their heads. Between times they curse and swear at the Russians for launching their offensive on payday, of all days!

REPORTER Of all days.

ALICE SCHALEK "D'they want to save our paymaster from paying out? Our wages were due today!"

REPORTER Humour on the battlefield.

ALICE SCHALEK What's wrong with that? Listen.
Lieutenant Radoschewitz is completely calm at present. His inner crisis has passed.

REPORTER You give his name?

ALICE SCHALEK Why not, if he's achieved something. Listen.
How delightful! There's a crate of German eggs—

REPORTER Expect me to believe that?!

ALICE SCHALEK Let me finish.
How delightful! There's a crate of German egg-shaped hand grenades. They're the little bombs you can throw like stones.

REPORTER Oh, I see.

ALICE SCHALEK One of the platoon caught it in the arm, another had his eardrum perforated. The lieutenant is as good as deaf. He's staggering. The one beside him is a nervous wreck. Sergeant Janoszi is ranting.

REPORTER You give his name?

ALICE SCHALEK Why not, the quiet heroism of the common man—? Listen. Singing, they head off. "Wrench 'em from the trench"—that's the beginning of the merry ditty that ends so plaintively.

REPORTER I like it!

ALICE SCHALEK Now they all stream over the third line of trenches, the storm troops advance on either side and "mop up." Methods are always changing, and the very latest involve "storm troops" and "cleaning out trenches."

(*Her eyes aglow.*) Once you've seen a storm troop marching out at night, you'll never think anything else is as romantic, as adventurous, as audacious. And if you've ever been part of it, you'll never want to leave, not for all the tea in China.

REPORTER I know exactly how you must feel!

ALICE SCHALEK Young lads, each and every one, must be unmarried and under 24. Clean-limbed, agile, intrepid, and up for any crazy caper.

REPORTER Ah yes, the young—!

ALICE SCHALEK They're laying out a training ground behind the lines but modelled exactly on the real front, for practising mopping up—under genuine fire!

If some special mission is to be carried out on enemy territory, it's rehearsed in every detail, just like a play. Simple cleaning out is easiest, of course.

REPORTER Of course.

ALICE SCHALEK Two grenadiers take the lead.

Once the grenades have been thrown, the group runs round the traverse. Then the following infantry occupy the trenches that have been cleaned out—that means, they've been taken.

The storm troops in Lysonia in central Poland, under the command of Lieutenant Tanka, Second-lieutenant Kovacs, and Officer-cadet Sipos, are working as if they're on an exercise. They are aglow with fervour and an awareness of their importance.

The precision of their movements, the effective way they interconnect, is amazing, deeply moving, overpowering.

The cleaning out goes on until 10 in the evening.

REPORTER It surely must be all clean by now?!

ALICE SCHALEK You think? Far from it!
Second-lieutenant Pintér and Lance-corporals Juhasz and Baranyi carry out their tasks with particular care and totally by the book.
But it takes another three days to clean out the first line of trenches. On the third day, they come across a wounded soldier, saved by the fact that the "cleaning out" lasted for three days. He'd been shot in the stomach, and was only saved by having to lie for three terrible days without food or drink.

REPORTER It just shows you how healthy cleaning up is.

ALICE SCHALEK Obviously.
When the storm troops then smoke them out of their dugouts with hand grenades, they beg for mercy.

REPORTER Do tell me, did you see all that with your own eyes?

ALICE SCHALEK I could tell you a lot of other things, too! Don't keep interrupting.
During the three days they're mopping up at the front, the commandant of 318, Colonel Söld, is cleaning out the wood with the troops he had left.

REPORTER Where were the rest?

ALICE SCHALEK He'd never seen so many corpses. They work day and night to get them all buried.
A few silly geese escape when their cage is destroyed, and are happily strolling around during the barrage.
What d'you say to that?

REPORTER I'm thrilled! If it wasn't for the bit about cleaning up, not a soul would realize it was written by a woman!

ALICE SCHALEK How do you mean?

REPORTER I mean, the way you describe the cleaning up—attaching so much importance to cleanliness in the trenches—

ALICE SCHALEK What?

REPORTER I mean—the cleaning up—the way you praise it!

ALICE SCHALEK (*casting a contemptuous glance at him*) What a greenhorn! Cleaning up means massacring!

REPORTER (*reels back, stares at her*) Y'know—

ALICE SCHALEK You didn't know that? You men, call yourselves reporters!

REPORTER But—

ALICE SCHALEK Get a grip!—All's fair in love and war.

REPORTER I must admit—the rest of us—

ALICE SCHALEK Well?

REPORTER I take off my hat to you! (*After a pause during which he regards her silently, in ecstasy.*) It could only happen in Russia. Or in France, as with Joan of Arc! Do you recall how Salten evokes the scene? When the men had almost lost all hope, such a girl arose, awakened and inspired, whom the impact of the calamity had wrenched from the life to which she had been born, and stepped forth to rouse the men. It is on such individual figures that we bestow our admiration; they are trailing clouds of glory, they are invested with the fascination of great bravery and poetic exploits, and it is precisely because of the exceptional status they enjoy that we so readily idealize them, to the point that sober reason is simply incapable of recalling all the many terrible, hateful, brutal things they must without doubt have done themselves or seen done.

ALICE SCHALEK What must be must be!

REPORTER No, that didn't appear in the "So-must-it-be" article, but in the one about the Russian death battalion. Where women are transformed into hyenas, as Schiller says.

ALICE SCHALEK What are you trying to say—?

REPORTER Don't interrupt me. We can't simply ignore such perversions of female nature, for they clarify certain aspects of our experience of war. The repulsive lack of femininity, the openly exhibited heartlessness—these are signs of serious degeneracy—

ALICE SCHALEK I beg your pardon—what you've just said is—is very inconsiderate towards one of one's colleagues—where does it come from?

REPORTER From the editorial, from Himself, let me finish—And as is usually the case when woman abandons the characteristics of her sex—discarding her gentleness and becoming disfigured, a virago—she tends towards a strange cruelty—as the English experience has also reflected.

ALICE SCHALEK Aha!

REPORTER That's where women become hyenas! The spinsters—

ALICE SCHALEK Who are you saying's a spinster? I'll lodge a complaint with Colonel Eisner von Bubna of the War Press Bureau!

REPORTER Listen, there's no comparison between an English spinster and her European sister. The latter is a sweet, good-natured, modest creature.

ALICE SCHALEK (*flattered*) There's no one else these days can write an editorial like Him!

REPORTER Thank heavens the preferred place of an Austrian woman in this war is caring for the sick, restoring spirits, and consoling the oppressed.

ALICE SCHALEK What's he mean? Is that what it says? Y'know—sometimes he gets carried away by his temperament. One shouldn't generalize. Everything has its place. You can't just sit around back home. Everyone knows I was the one who initiated the Black-and-Yellow Cross charity, together with Countess Anke Bienerth!

REPORTER We know, don't get worked up—

ALICE SCHALEK (*fighting back her tears, with determination*) I'll send Him my article straight away!

REPORTER Of course you should. But I'd advise you to leave out the last sentence.

ALICE SCHALEK The last sentence? (*She looks at her draft.*) "A few silly geese escape when their cage is destroyed, and are happily strolling around during the barrage"—should I take that out?

REPORTER Yes.

ALICE SCHALEK Why?

REPORTER Just do it.

ALICE SCHALEK But tell me—

REPORTER (*hesitates*) Well, haven't you heard—

ALICE SCHALEK Heard what?

REPORTER —that the War Press Bureau has decided—

ALICE SCHALEK What?

REPORTER —from now on to accredit a few more female war reporters, apart from you!

ALICE SCHALEK (*taken aback, then tragically, with a bitter laugh*) Such is the gratitude the House of Habsburg—showers on its loyal servants! (*She is too stunned to move.*)

(*Change of scene.*)

Scene 17

Subscriber and Patriot in conversation.

SUBSCRIBER What do you say about the rumours?

PATRIOT I'm worried.

SUBSCRIBER In Vienna it's rumoured that there are rumours circulating in Austria. They're even being passed by word of mouth, but no one can tell you—

PATRIOT Nothing's known for certain, they're only rumours, but there must be something in it if even the government has let it be known that rumours are circulating.

SUBSCRIBER The government warns explicitly against believing or spreading rumours, and calls upon everyone to do the utmost to help suppress them. Well, I'm doing what I can; wherever I go I say "Who believes in rumours?"

PATRIOT The Hungarian government also says that it's rumoured in Budapest that rumours are circulating in Hungary, and it's also issued a caution.

SUBSCRIBER In a word, it seems very likely that rumours are circulating throughout the whole Monarchy.

PATRIOT I think so, too. Y'know, if it were only something you heard as a rumour—but the Austrian government is quite explicit, and the Hungarian, too.

SUBSCRIBER There must be something in it. But who believes in rumours?

PATRIOT Exactly. If I bump into any of my acquaintances, the first thing I ask him is whether he's heard the rumours, and if he says no, I tell him not to believe them but to do his utmost to deny there's any truth in them, as we're called upon to do. It's the least we can do—our prime duty as loyal citizens.

SUBSCRIBER There must be something in them, otherwise those three Members of Parliament—y'know, the ones who always hang out together—surely wouldn't have gone to see Prime Minister Seidler and drawn his attention to the rumours circulating.

PATRIOT Exactly! But the prime minister said he knew all about the rumours in question—and in circulation.

SUBSCRIBER Exactly! Y'know what I think? Just between the two of us—the rumours have something to do with the House of—(*drops his voice, holding the paper over his mouth.*)

PATRIOT You don't say! But I'll tell you something else. Whoever's spreading the rumours wants to undermine the people's faith in the House of—!

SUBSCRIBER You said it! And they even say that the rumours always start spreading at the same time in completely different places, and that's why—

PATRIOT —one is justified in concluding that we're dealing with an organized conspiracy!

SUBSCRIBER So they say. But after all, they're only rumours—who could have worked that out so exactly, I ask you—at the same time in completely different places!

PATRIOT Don't say that. The government could! Y'know what people are saying? They say spreading rumours is fresh evidence of attempts by the enemy to cause confusion. But their efforts are all in vain!

SUBSCRIBER So I heard. They even say rumours are one of the enemy's secret weapons, and that they'll stop at nothing to shake the very foundations of the Monarchy and loosen the ties of love and respect we feel towards the House of—(*drops his voice, holding the paper over his mouth.*)

PATRIOT You don't say! Well—in that case they'll hit a brick wall!

SUBSCRIBER Y'know what?

PATRIOT What—?

SUBSCRIBER I'd like to know if there's anything in the rumours.

PATRIOT That I can tell you—nothing at all, and the best proof of that is that nobody knows what they're about. But y'know what?

SUBSCRIBER What—?

PATRIOT I'd like to know if there is any truth in those rumours.

SUBSCRIBER Well, what truth could there be in them? Brilliant rumours they must be, when no one can say what they're about. The rumour mill is spinning—

PATRIOT —and we don't have a grain of truth!

(Change of scene.)

Scene 18

Optimist and Grumbler in conversation.

OPTIMIST What do you say about the rumours?

GRUMBLER I haven't heard them, but I believe them.

OPTIMIST Oh come on, they're lies put out by the Allies—!

GRUMBLER —but not nearly as dubious as our truths.

OPTIMIST If the worst comes to the worst, the one thing that could feed these rumours would be—

GRUMBLER —if we couldn't feed our people.

(Change of scene.)

Scene 19

Vienna. Michaelerplatz. Military band from the Hofburg Palace marches past. Behind it, the riffraff. Drum roll.

CHOIR OF THE RIFFRAFF (*to the tune of the "Radetzky March"*)

Nama bread, nama flour, nama baccy to smoke—
Nama bread, nama flour, nama baccy to smoke—
We've gone bust, we've gone bust.
Where oh where has my Austria gone?

(*The music grows fainter.*)
(*Change of scene.*)

Scene 20

Military command post.

CAPTAIN (*dictates from a text*) Strictly confidential!—Prisoners of war who have absconded from their work for no good reason and who have been apprehended and returned, are to be punished by being bound and fettered for at least two hours—(*the telephone rings*) What is it?—Aha—yes, of course—20 kilos of flour, extra fine—well, I'll see what can be done—bye—So, where were we?

CLERK —punished by being bound and fettered for at least two hours—

CAPTAIN —and on completion of punishment—if this seems appropriate in view of special cases—are as a matter of principle to be returned forthwith to their previous place of work. Those in command of prisoner-of-war camps must use all permitted punitive measures, followed by employment in the most arduous tasks in the prisoner-of-war camp, in order as far as is possible to inflict maximum discomfort on those prisoners who have absconded, been apprehended and then returned to the prisoner-of-war camp.—(*The telephone rings.*) What is it now?—Aha—yes, of course—unfit for active military service—five kilos of lard—tell him, I'll see what can be done—keep a note of everything—Hang on a second, don't forget to remind the editor about the tickets for *Blood of the Hussars*, give him a call at the paper, d'you hear—Say I'll be a bit late—bye, old girl!—So, where were we?

CLERK —the period spent there—

CAPTAIN —as far as is feasible—

CLERK —no, as far as is possible—

CAPTAIN Your attention is drawn to the fact that detention generally seems ineffective as a punishment for reducing the number of attempts to abscond, except when implemented on officially regulated days of rest or on such as qualify as public holidays, through application of the approved form of enhanced punishment. — Right — it's almost four. Bye, gentlemen, enjoy your evenings! *(Change of scene.)*

Scene 21

War Ministry.

CAPTAIN *(dictates from a text)* Strictly confidential! — In view of the fact that almost a million Russian prisoners of war will leave the Austro-Hungarian Monarchy and return to their homeland in the course of the next few months, what these prisoners of war feel when they think back on the time spent in our country is of crucial importance. It therefore seems highly desirable that we should aim to ensure that those few unfavourable impressions experienced should be weakened, the innumerable pleasant and favourable ones, on the other hand, encouraged and strengthened. Then the Russians returning to their homeland will not think back on us with blunt indifference or even vengeful hatred, but will knowingly become fully committed and active ambassadors for Austro-Hungarian culture in their own country. The way such a favourable outcome can be achieved is by developing political, social, and economic propaganda which speaks to the Russian soul, and which is open-handed and honest in intention. The plan is, shortly before expulsion —

CLERK Expulsion?!

CAPTAIN — expulsion of the Russian prisoners of war, to evoke by means of propaganda lectures on political, social, and economic issues a pro-Austrian spirit among the Russian prisoners of war. Quite apart from all the important consequences — for instance, for our economy — such a realignment of the Russian soul can help demolish the lying propaganda disseminated by the enemy worldwide. To make a lasting impact on the Russian prisoners of war, the propaganda cannot of course be limited to lecturing the Russian prisoners of war, rather the time up to their final deportation must be used to make as good an impression in all respects on the Russian prisoners of war as is feasible. — New paragraph.

As matters stand, however, it is evident that such propaganda, if implemented exclusively by members of the military administration, would doubtless lose much of its original value — aha, a true word for once! — and it would seem advantageous, given the goal, to involve as far as is feasible people suited to the task who are also interested both idealistically and practically, in order that the impact may be raised to a level as far removed from the military perspective as possible. — Hmm, that's a bit over the top! — This essential consideration in turn requires, for reasons of military discipline, that such propaganda can only commence shortly before the deportation of the Russian prisoners of war—that's self-evident!—though it is to be hoped that they return to their homeland with the full force of what they have learnt fresh in their minds.—New paragraph.

Political considerations: It is with the deepest and most sincere conviction, here in Austria-Hungary of all countries, that a candid assurance can be given to the Russians about to be repatriated that we never wanted the war, but had ardently sought peace—that's what he'd do well to emphasize, we're as pure as the driven snow—

CLERK Pardon me? We're pure as—

CAPTAIN No, no, don't write that!—ardently sought peace, and how emphatically and sincerely we regretted the undoubted hardships that the fate of imprisonment inflicts on prisoners of war, and how any trials and tribulations possibly suffered by the prisoners of war—steady on!—in no way sprang from dislike or a low opinion or even hatred of the Russian people, but solely from the accumulation of difficulties caused by the long duration of the war.—New paragraph.

Social considerations: Without in any way touching on current social conditions in Russia, those Russians returning home can be suitably enlightened as to the merits and characteristic features of our social structures, their attention drawn in particular to the ways in which prosperity and progress are continually rising, to the lasting benefit of both the community and individuals—and individuals . . . Well, at least that bit's true!—New paragraph. Now comes the all-important bit.

Economic considerations: Since facts prove that the great difficulties caused on all sides by the long duration of the war and its disturbances can be surmounted only by maximum deployment of all available labour, aligned with the swift implementation of the exchange of goods organized on liberal, supranational lines, returning Russians will readily understand that trade relations with the Monarchy must be established rapidly and without restraint as an absolute necessity. From this perspective it should prove simple to demonstrate to the peasants in a convincing manner that those who hoard their produce, and by so doing prevent it being utilized in free trade, only harm themselves, since they will not, or only belatedly, come into possession of those articles for daily use which they desire, since our own population, which is employed in the manufacture of such goods, would lack adequate nourishment to develop their commercial energies fully, energies which in peacetime, with proper nourishment, are required for a flourishing export trade.—Well, surely they'll see the point of that.—New paragraph.

Gangs of agricultural workers, however, especially prisoners of war in farming communities, have no need of such propaganda, except perhaps to influence the behaviour of Russian prisoners of war working on the land by suggesting that food supplies to the urban population leave much to be desired, and that imported food is urgently needed. — They must see that. — New paragraph.

However, Russian prisoners of war working in factories, on building sites, and in administration are a different matter. It would very useful if employers in such cases were to take upon themselves the patriotic duty of lightening the load of the Russian prisoners of war as much as is feasible during the final days of their labour here. — New paragraph.

All military directors of firms operating under the Industrial War Service Act, and of military mining enterprises and their commandants, are accordingly instructed to visit and inspect forthwith all places of work where Russian prisoners of war are employed, and similarly to bring their influence to bear on the prisoners of war, as already required of camp commandants — see below (and under heading Ministerial Decree no.14169/18). — New paragraph.

The camp commandant must visit dormitories, officers' quarters, and camp hospitals in turn, and enter into personal contact with the Russian prisoners of war. (*In warm tones.*) He will ask how they are, enquire after their parents, after the food, postal service, clothing. Any complaints he must deal with at the time and in public, in the presence of all the prisoners of war, investigating all the details. He must convince them that he personally will leave no stone unturned to get to the truth, and thus dispense justice. Any complaints about food and clothing he will use to prove to the Russians that it is not our fault but that of our Western enemies, and that we would be especially delighted to give the Russian prisoners of war more if we had it. For they, the Russians, are after all no longer our enemies. (*In even warmer tones.*) We never did think of them as our enemies, as is proven by the many earlier wars in which Russians and Austria-Hungary fought bravely shoulder to shoulder. The camp commandant must visit the kitchens now and again, when the meat or fish is being distributed. He must seize two or three prisoners of war just as they're —

CLERK Pardon?

CAPTAIN — must seize them just as they're taking their ration back to their bunk. (*Fervently.*) Put down the mess tin, fetch the scales, weigh the meat or fish. The more people watching, the better. Then produce the rations book, how much meat bought today altogether? Subtract 25 percent for bones, 20 percent during cooking, divide the rest by the number of individual portions and (*threateningly*) if even 10 grams are missing per portion, then, if there are, say, 200 portions, two kilos of meat or fish have been stolen. (*Sounding stern.*) Who did it? Food ration tribunal, summon the cooks, the officers in charge of rations! Hold court in front of all the prisoners of war in the unit—law must be strictly observed. Outcome: Cooks, officers in charge of rations, and everyone else working in the kitchen subjected to punishment, if culprit not found.—New punishment!—I mean, new paragraph.

If the commandant should find any Russian in possession of tobacco, cigarettes, bread bought outside, sausage, etc., he must enquire as to the price the prisoner of war in question paid for it. It will soon become clear that there are many black-marketeers among the prisoners of war. These shady traders are not always Jews. They have sources outside the camp from whom they can buy when they get the opportunity, and sell to their comrades in the camp, the prisoners of war, for three or four times as much. If the camp commandant manages to catch one of these shady traders—(*in a rage*) strip him, body search, and go through his belongings. He'll often find 500 crowns or more. Confiscate it and distribute to the other prisoners of war everything in excess of what he can't legally account for.—New paragraph.

At the present time, the Russian prisoners of war will listen to the commandant for hours if he is able to tell them something about exchange of prisoners. How long will it be until it's our turn? If he's in a position to prove to them in words of one syllable that it's not our fault the exchange is taking so long, then the prisoners of war will be happy to shoulder their shovels again, only he mustn't denigrate Russia in the process. That would be a big mistake.—New paragraph.

(*With feeling.*) Russian hearts will swell if the colonel can pass on the latest news from Russia, which he's just read in the *Morgenblatt.* (*Adopts a stance.*) Standing to attention, they'll salute obediently, there's no chance of discipline breaking down when he addresses them. He must set a good example here as elsewhere, and salute standing to attention, insofar as his age and infirmity permit. (*He salutes.*) A visit of the camp commandant to the camp hospital—

AN OFFICER CADET (*enters*) Beg to report, Captain, the colonel wants the report on the Russian prisoners of war.

CAPTAIN The propaganda edict? I'm working on it.

OFFICER CADET Not the propaganda one, but the one about those who died of starvation.

CAPTAIN —who died of starvation? What, are they still dying of starvation? Gimme the dossier!

OFFICER CADET It's the case of a Russian who was asleep with two others on a plank bed and died of starvation. He was already in a state of decomposition when the inspector came into the dormitory, and the two others were too weak to get up or even to call for help.

CAPTAIN Just a mo!—you can tell the colonel I'll look in the pending tray right away, but I'm dealing with the propaganda at the moment, y'know, trying to reduce the unfavourable impressions among the prisoners of war so we can reestablish trade relations and they can send us foodstuffs, the Russians, once they're safely home, or whatever.
(Change of scene.)

Scene 22

Provincial government in Brno.

GOVERNOR I've an idea! *(To clerk)* Take this down: Among the most important lessons we can draw from the murderous World War and the sacrifices it demands from the whole population is undoubtedly that of how important it is to inculcate the patriotic spirit in our children starting from their schooldays, to indoctrinate them with knowledge and love of their Fatherland in both the narrower and the broader sense. We must implant in their childish hearts all those seeds from which grow the glorious virile qualities that enable the young man, as an ardent patriot inspired by love and a sense of duty towards the Imperial House and the Fatherland, to fulfil his civic duties gladly and conscientiously, and moreover, if called upon, to sacrifice even life and health for those ideals.

Unfortunately, in Habsburg Austria there has been little preparation in this regard, and it seems to me to be incumbent on all the leading personalities in the Empire to make good this omission, and to take responsibility for the further development of the patriotic and dynastic sentiments of the coming generation, which—praise be!—are already omnipresent in embryo.

A little Czech monthly entitled *Mladé Rakousko*, or Young Austria, written in a popular style and adapted to the spirit of our schoolchildren, should be distributed to our primary and secondary schools, as also to our vocational colleges. I consider it the sacred duty of all persons of like station and mind, and a noble obligation for the landowning classes, to promote the circulation of this journal in those schools from which it can radiate economic influence, by subscribing a number of copies for each school, thereby enabling the journal to be distributed free to pupils without means, and beyond the pupils themselves, in justified expectation of exerting influence on the older members of every family.

The journal, costing 2 crowns 40 for an annual subscription, can be ordered from No. 18, Kaiser Franz Joseph-Platz, Brno.

May this appeal—
(Change of scene.)

Scene 23

In a primary school.
Some benches are empty. The surviving children are undernourished. All are wearing cheap suits made of wood pulp yarn.

TEACHER ZEHETBAUER —Beware of the rumours circulating and resist them wherever feasible. The enemy's insidious plan is to confuse you, but they shall not succeed. Close your ears to allegations that we cannot hold out until victory is assured, and that we are at the point of starvation. Whose fault is that, after all, if not the enemy's? Now they are even beginning to poison the very wellsprings of our—(*a boy raises his hand.*) What is it, Gasselseder?

GASSELSEDER Please, sir, can't we drink water anymore either?

TEACHER Sit down, stupid boy. I didn't mean it figuratively, of course, but literally. The enemy can't defeat us in the field, so he's trying to wear us down on the home front. That's why you must beware of rumours! And suppress them with all the energy you can muster. They're part of the enemy's arsenal—(*a boy raises his hand.*) What is it, Anderle?

ANDERLE Please, sir, have the enemy got an arsenal, too?

TEACHER They do indeed, but it only contains rumours, and they don't shrink from using every means to undermine the foundations of the Monarchy, and even loosen our ties of love and veneration towards our hereditary rulers. Kotzlik, you're interrupting, repeat what I said.

KOTZLIK The enemy—the enemy have—undermined the arsenal—and—and we don't shrink from loosening our ties—and—spreading rumours about—about—our hereditary rulers—

TEACHER You little wretch! You'll stay in after school and write out the sentence I'll give you 10 times. Sit down, you good-for-nothing! As for the rest of you, remain steadfast! Let the Iron Warrior be an example to you all. There he stands, a symbolic landmark built for eternity, for as long as the Habsburg double-headed eagle soars above our heads. See for yourselves—with your parents' or guardians' permission, of course—go and hammer in a nail, if there's any room left for another nail. Close your ears to any rumours you hear on the way, for they're even saying the days of the Iron Warrior are numbered and a hot-dog stand will take his place. We haven't sunk to that yet, thank God, and we gladly accept the privations imposed upon us by the Fatherland for as long as the battle has not yet been decided once and for all, but still fluctuates, now one way, now the other. Nevertheless! If we—(*a boy raises his hand.*) What do you want, Zitterer?

ZITTERER Please, sir, I want peace!

TEACHER You little wretch! Sit down, you good-for-nothing! I can see it now, you'll end up on the gallows before you're done! Shame on you! And you, there, in the third row, what's going on? Merores! What are you whispering?

MERORES Papa says he doesn't understand all this agitation for peace—he doesn't mind waiting, he says, on the contrary I think he'd rather peace didn't break out since he's been making good money and the peace would put an end to that.

TEACHER It's good to hear your father is holding out so manfully and setting such a good example, Merores, but you were talking out of turn, and that's a sign that discipline's breaking down, thanks to the enemy stirring things up. I'm not saying you're in the service of enemy propaganda exactly, though it has its tentacles everywhere, but I must say I take a serious view of such behaviour, now our hour of destiny is at hand. I can only repeat, over and over: remain steadfast, to the end! Can you imagine what would happen if you began to waver, too? The enemy would come among us, then woe unto you, woe unto your sisters and your brides-to-be, woe unto your parents or guardians! (*A boy raises his hand.*) What do you want, Sukfüll?

SUKFÜLL Please, sir, the foreigners! Father said he can't wait any longer, he can't stand it, it's high time for the foreigners to come among us, he says.

CLASS Yes, Promote our tourist trade!

TEACHER No! That's not what was meant! The tourist trade is a tender plant that needs proper loving care. Do you want an invasion of spaghetti eaters?

CLASS Yes! Anything, so long as we get something to eat!

TEACHER Shame on you, you good-for-nothings! What must our erstwhile illustrious monarch be thinking, God rest his soul, as he looks down on you from his portrait? He could never have imagined it would lead to such degeneration when he unsheathed his sword against the superior force of the enemy in the deliberately provoked defensive war he was compelled to declare. Woe unto us, if the enemy come among us. They would occupy our best hotels, it would be no laughing matter, and our women, guardians of hearth and home, would pay the price! Have you forgotten everything I ever told you? I do hope not!

CLASS The wild storm clouds of war are sweeping over our lands since our illustrious monarch called thousands and tens of thousands of our sons and brothers to arms, yet there are already signs that tourism is on the increase. So never let us lose sight of this ideal, but let us today strike up the old song that we learned in days of yore when peace reigned: "Promote Our Tourist Trade!" (*They sing.*)

A a, Ha ha! Here come tourists, hallelujah!
We're not broke, we're up and running,
Now we see the tourists coming,
A a, Ha ha! Here come tourists, hallelujah!

(Change of scene.)

Scene 24

National Tourist Association.

REPORTER —to ask you for comments on the development of tourism after the war, insofar as any such measures are already under consideration.

OFFICIAL Of course. As you know, in addition to the Congress of Military Physicians, there has been a recent exchange of ideas between representatives of the Federation of Comrades-in-Arms specialising in the promotion of tourism in Germany, Hungary, and Austria.

REPORTER So we can expect that the problem of tourism will be examined from quite new perspectives after the war?

OFFICIAL Indubitably.

REPORTER Perhaps you would kindly give me a pointer about the angle our comrades-in-arms might develop in regard to tourism. I suppose we can assume that the enemy will also suffer losses in this respect?

OFFICIAL In all probability, Germans will naturally not visit the French and Belgian tourist resorts.

REPORTER Do you mean the Germans won't be able to visit these resorts, or won't want to?

OFFICIAL I mean, the Germans won't be able to—want to—visit these resorts.

REPORTER So the Germans will look for some alternative, then? I mean, some alternative in their own country?

OFFICIAL The German coast offers sufficient alternatives to the cosmopolitan North Sea resorts.

REPORTER But where will the Germans find alternatives to the French Riviera? Surely here?

OFFICIAL The Austrian Adriatic coast certainly offers an excellent alternative to the French Riviera with its climatic advantages for spring and autumn visits, so it can expect a great influx of foreign visitors.

REPORTER When you talk of the Austrian Adriatic coast, you mean: as distinct from the Italian, do you not, or at any rate you mean: The Adriatic remains—

OFFICIAL —in our hands. Certainly, for otherwise the Germans would have to find an alternative to the Adriatic as well.

REPORTER So if I understand you correctly, you think it is principally the German public that our tourist trade will attract?

OFFICIAL Certainly.

REPORTER Turning now to the main issue. What attractions will we be able to offer our visitors after the war, or rather, what alternative attractions to those sights that may have been destroyed in the war? Quite rightly, your forecast for the Adriatic was a favourable one. But what else will we be able to offer?

OFFICIAL The Alpine lands, with their outstanding memories of the war, will offer an additional attraction to visitors from central Europe.

REPORTER What kind of memories of the war do you have in mind?

OFFICIAL We are hopeful that pious visits to the graves of heroes and war cemeteries will result in a lively tourist trade. It's a question of setting our house in order once more. And in this respect we call above all upon the understanding and collaboration of the press, since it is our task to make the best of the attractions inherent in every epoch. What could be more ideally suited for promoting tourism than the Graves of the Fallen!
(Change of scene.)

Scene 25

Café on the Ring. Afternoon. Various fauna, sitting or standing, involved in heated debates. Conversation on the most diverse subjects: rice, sugar, leather, even bets being laid on trotting races; one person unpacks an oil painting, another shows a diamond ring for valuation by a group of excited bystanders. Among the dealers there are also those in uniform, a diminutive lieutenant giving "tips" to a gigantic commercial agent. In the midst of all this, on benches to the side, girls in insectlike costumes. Waiters and waitresses bring drinks. Someone is selling race cards. Armadillos amble past. The air is thick with price quotations.
Anyone coming in is met by a cacophony of sounds—at first unintelligible, then in all registers—gasps, yells, whistles, croaks, mainly reinforcing points made. Straining his ears, he can eventually distinguish one from the other.

CACOPHONY —Sez he!—me own words!—off the record!—lemme tell ya!—gimme yer word!—watch me lips!—getta loada this!—watch yer langwidge!—on his say-so!—him's my witness!—lemme tell ya a secret!—what more can I tell ya?—You can say that again!—

MAMMUT Hey—pst—got any of them spicey pancakes?

WAITER Banned since last week.

MAMMUT You can't get a damn thing! Nothing doing—zilch? Okay, but ain't there anything? (*To his neighbour.*) But as I was tellin ya, wot it cost me to dodge the draft today!

ZIESELMAUS Ya can say yer prayers for that.

WALROSS (*studying his race card*)—Leave off! I wouldn't back Hindenburg, I wouldn't back Primadonna, I'll tell you which one I would back, I'd put my shirt on Doberdo!—

HAMSTER —He's got it made now—self-supply! I've got a hot line to Kornfeld from Central Supplies, so I ups tracks down to Dairy Products and sez to them: here I am, Solly Hamster—

NASHORN —Who gives a toss for rumours? I'm not going to tear me hair out 'cos of rumours! Just 'cos there's supposed to be summat in the papers about peace feelers. Perish the thought! I tell ya, bizniz is booming—like a bomb!—

TAPIR —What do you want from me, think I'm Hindenburg?—

SCHAKAL —Ya can't count on Siegfried Hirschl, I wouldn't give a dime for someone on desk duties only! Ya should've seen how they kowtowed to me at the War Ministry, what a riot! Nuff said!—

LEGUAN —Lira, lira, unlimited supplies!—

KAIMAN —Without an export licence, nothing doing—Julius Kaiman knows, y'know!—

PAVIAN —Albania? You're wasting yer breath, a gorilla war!—

KONDOR —Couldn't give a cuss for a brat like you! I was coining it before you was even thought of! Five minutes ago, if you'd been listening on the blower—eight tons and 50,000 credit on my word alone! From Vienna, pronto—buyer collects! Go for sugar, you won't make a dime flogging bandages!

LÖW —Get a life—if only I could!

HIRSCH —And me kvetching at my old woman, day and night—

WOLF —There'll be a riot when the evening paper comes out! I just can't believe it!—

POSAMENTIER —How'd I know? They say Burian put out some kinda peace feelers!—

SPITZBAUCH Pst—a hot chocolate—no, wait, I know, bring me a—

SCHLECHTIGKEIT —That sparkler, between you, me, and the lamppost, wasn't worth—

VOICES OF PEOPLE RUSHING IN I'm telling you, it ain't true!—As I live and breathe, from the most impeccable source, it's true!—And what if I tell ya it ain't true!?—And I'm tellin ya, it's the fuckin truth, we're done for!—Wanna bet it's not true, then?!

(A fur coat is stolen. A hubbub ensues.)

GOLLERSTEPPER But I know him, he's always snooping and sniffing around here, the miserable hack!

TUGENDHAT What use is a fur coat to anyone now?

GOLLERSTEPPER What a question—! Ask Mundi Rosenberg from the rag trade!

MAMMUT (*wheezes*) I could do with two more truckloads—

MASTODON —of cooking fat? How can I get my paws on cooking fat? Think I'd risk—?

RAUBITSCHEK —Crazy, prices have gone through the roof. I'll let you in on a secret—if ya really wanna get yer dirty paws on summat, go up and schmooze 'em in uniform!—

VORTREFFLICH —Y'know summat? To hit the jackpot?—Soap's the thing! Thread's wearing thin, nowadays.—

GUTWILLIG —He's a big cheese in groceries right now! *Teenovin* imitation tea and *Punchnovin* punch substitute, basta! And now he's good for two million on credit. Top-grade merchandise, what a sensation!—

AUFRICHTIG —As I live and breathe, cross my heart, word of honour, he pointed to Titian's signature on the picture and said: a dead snip! When I prove to him later that it's not a genuine Titian, all he says is: I weren't there when Titian painted it, woz I? I ask ya, is that kosher?

BESTÄNDIG Well, if he didn't guarantee it wasn't a genuine Titian—?

BRAUCHBAR It makes me head spin, now he turns round and explains he swapped the Titian for four racehorses, that beggars belief!

TOILET ATTENDANT (*calls in*) Telephone call for Herr Pollatschek! *(Pollatschek rushes out.)*

LUSTIG Y'see—? Chase after him—

(A disabled ex-serviceman appears, trembling. His head is shaking continuously. He is led away.)

(In the background, an elderly war profiteer sits huddled up, evidently a broken man. Friends try to help him. A woman keeps a hand on his shoulder. A girl talks to him. Others who are curious or solicitous join in.)

FIRST FRIEND But surely—! It doesn't have to be true!

SECOND FRIEND Just look at you!—I don't know what to think—throwing in the towel without—you're a queer'un—!

ELDERLY WAR PROFITEER (*groaning*) Leave me be—leave me be—yes, I know—I'm a lame duck—my God—my God—you get one big chance in life, and—there's no—my Skoda Works shares—my Skoda armaments shares—

WOMAN Bernie—pull yourself together—who says it's true—the war's strained your nerves—

DAUGHTER Don't upset him any more—look, everyone's coming over to look—!

WOMAN Oh, my God—his heart!

ELDERLY WAR PROFITEER Leave me in peace—leave me in peace—my heart—the evening paper—my Skoda shares—

DAUGHTER Look at him rubbing his hands there, Weitzner—gloating away—! Uncle, tell him to go away—The mere sight of him gets on Papa's nerves!

UNCLE Sorry—but you can't stop customers—in a public restaurant—

WOMAN You're all we needed!

FIRST FRIEND Moldauer—listen—I thought—look, you've got your head screwed on—I'm at a loss to understand the man I once knew—

ELDERLY WAR PROFITEER But if it's—true—and I know it is—God—God—my Skoda shares—

SECOND FRIEND What d'you bet it's not true—come on, what d'you bet?—I'm on a winner—boy oh boy, won't you be happy to pay up—!

(*The elderly war profiteer sobs convulsively. Everyone tries to help, their faces contorted with anxiety.*)

A RELATIVELY YOUNG PROFITEER (*pushes forward*) Has he got any truckloads—? How many trucks has he got? Cross my heart and hope to die, I'm willing—

UNCLE Get away, you cheeky monkey!

ELDERLY WAR PROFITEER (*now merely whimpering*)—Skoda shares—

RESTAURANT MANAGER (*appears*) What's happened—? What's up with Herr von Moldauer—?

FIRST FRIEND Nothing—Rappaport comes rushing in and tells him—tells him he knows—that he, Rappaport of all people, knows!

RESTAURANT MANAGER Knows what? Good God, he's passed out! Whatever happened—?

FIRST FRIEND Nothing—it was just gossip—but he took it all to heart.

RESTAURANT MANAGER Yes, but—gossip about what?

FRIEND What d'ya think? About the threat of peace!

(Change of scene.)

Scene 26

Berlin. Friedrichstrasse. A procession of hoodlums, middlemen, operetta singers, Bohemians, faith healers, pimps, rent boys, floozies, con men, procurers, profiteers, and prostitutes.

CHORUS OF VOICES (*Shouting slogans in Berlin slang*)—Stunning victory at Caporetto!—Ready for the push on the Piave!—*Lonely Hearts Weekly*!—*Simplicissimus*, latest issue!—*Berliner Zeitung*, midday edition! The neutral countries opt out—Wax vestas, wax vestas!—*Tageblatt*, evening edition, no German ships requisitioned!—*Lokalanzeiger*!—*Grosse Glocke*! Sensational revelations, scandal at Wertheims!—*Welt am Montag*! Temple of Venus for men in Kochstrasse closed by police!—For our little ones! Lifelike imitation of our biggest guns firing!—First heralds of spring in bloom! Fifteen pfennigs!—*Lonely Hearts Weekly*!—Sexy stories from Moabit Prison!—*Berliner Zeitung*, midday edition, *B.Z.*!—Laugh with *Die Woche*!—Wax vestas, wax vestas!—The Rosenkavalier for wine and the snuggest place to dine!—Lifelike imitation of our biggest guns firing!—*Vossische Zeitung*, evening edition: we'll never surrender Alsace, declares Foreign Minister Kühlmann!—For our little ones: model of Big Bertha! The latest hit, 10 pfennigs! The rattling and droning when manoeuvring the cannon into place sounds like real shells howling through the air!—*B.Z.*, midday edition! The neutral countries opt out—*Tageblatt*, evening edition, no German ships requisitioned!—*Die Wahrheit*, latest issue! The secrets of the Kurfürstendamm! Sensational revelations!—Kühlmann will never surrender Alsace!—Provocative language in *Vorwärts*!—*Lokalanzeiger*!—Ready for the push on the Piave!—Like real shells howling through the air!—*Lonely Hearts Weekly*!—*Simplicissimus*!—*Grosse Glocke*! scandal at Wertheims—First heralds of spring in bloom—*Berliner Zeitung*, midday edition, *B.Z.*!—Frau von Knesebeck and the secrets of the boudoir: fragrant!—For our little ones! Lifelike imitation of our biggest guns firing!—Ready for the push on the Piave!—

A YOUTH (*to a passing girl*) Floozywoozy!

GIRL Toy boy!

A YOUTH What d'you say? Hooker! (*Passersby gather.*)

GIRL What? Ponce!

POLICEMAN Come on, move along now! (*The procession re-forms.*)
(*Enter a Berlin profiteer and a Viennese profiteer, shoulder to shoulder.*)

BERLIN PROFITEER What's keeping you? When's the launch?

VIENNESE PROFITEER I've three truckloads in reserve, but I'm holding them back.

BERLIN PROFITEER For God's sake, kiddo, I mean launch the offensive! Pull yer finger out!

VIENNESE PROFITEER Ain't gotta clue—!

BERLIN PROFITEER You Austrians—what pathetic wankers! It's time you got stuck in! Aren't you ever going to let rip? (*The Viennese profiteer is at a loss for words.*) Well? Yes?

VIENNESE PROFITEER (*plucking up courage*) Yes, well—

NEWSPAPER VENDOR Eight o'clock evening edition, Count Burian's peace offer—20 tons of high explosive fired into the fortress of Paris!
(*Change of scene.*)

Scene 27

High Command garrison. A cabaret. General Staff officers, war profiteers, hostesses. The band plays the "Prince Eugene March", "When the Last Tram's Gone, the Gentleman Drinks on to Dawn", and "The Watch on the Rhine." At a table, right, Kohn, a Viennese trafficker, with a girl on his knee, behind them a group of waiters dancing attendance. At a table, left, Fettköter, a Berlin trafficker, with a girl on his knee, behind them a group of waiters dancing attendance. In the middle, a table with General Staff officers and girls.
The scene roughly follows the melody from Offenbach's "La Vie parisienne":

DRUNKEN GENERAL STAFF OFFICER (*propped up by his comrades, beats time on the table*)

The front is crumbling? God forbid!
When I hear that, I flip my lid!
Of food and drink there is no dearth,
we Austrians know just what that's worth.
Out here we have no qualms or fears,
Austria will last a thousand years!
A thousand years on Habsburg's throne—

CHORUS OF WAITERS

Quick, more champagne for Herr von Kohn!

GIRL ON RIGHT

What's up with you? My grumpy lover!

KOHN

Don't laugh—the war is almost over!

DRUNKEN GENERAL STAFF OFFICER

Don't make a fuss, no need to squeal—

FRITZI-SPRITZI *(slaps the wandering hand of the General Staff officer)*

Don't touch!—A sack of flour's the deal!

PROPRIETOR *(to waiters on right)*

It's time those soldiers paid their bill!
They're honour-bound—you know the drill.

(to the waiters on left)

They may be broke, but one thing's clear,
they're officers, you've naught to fear.
The suckers, they won't do a bunk!

DRUNKEN GENERAL STAFF OFFICER

Habsburg for ever!—else we're sunk—

(He falls under the table.)

TOILET ATTENDANT AND CLOAKROOM STAFF

Habsburg for ever!—else we're sunk—

FETTKÖTER *(to the girl on his knee)*

If Hindenburg could see you now—
the things you Viennese allow!
I'll tell him it's the giddy limit

GIRL ON LEFT

It's just a bit of fun, now, innit?

GENERAL STAFF OFFICERS

"Prince Eugene's March"—stand up—three cheers!

DRUNKEN GENERAL STAFF OFFICER (*under table*)

Austria will last a thousand years—

TOILET ATTENDANT AND CLOAKROOM STAFF

Yes, Austria will last a thousand years.

FETTKÖTER

You've got it wrong, you're on the slide,
you're run-down, tired, self-satisfied.
So what you need's a Prussian scheme—
a fully functioning regime!

GIRL ON LEFT

Oh Putzi, don't be such a stickler!

FETTKÖTER

Oh yes? Well you're not too particular!
Back home, today, for one and all:
Sober but Confident's the trumpet call.
Hey, waiter! waiter! What's the score?

GIRL ON LEFT

O stop it, you are such a bore!

GIRL ON RIGHT

Upon my soul, if I could choose,
some caviar I'd not refuse.
I'm picky, though, depends who's buying—

KOHN

That's news to me, but edifying!

FETTKÖTER (*prepares to leave*)

A whole day in this charming land,
I've still not seen the High Command.
I'll leg it now, it's time for me

to book a new delivery!
Must get a deal in place *before*,
not *after*, we have won the war!

(He starts to smooch.)

But first a pretty Viennese,
and this one here's a classy squeeze!

GIRL ON LEFT *(giving the waiters a sign)*

You're rich then, Putzi, promise me?

CHORUS OF WAITERS

Some more champagne? Yes, certainly!

PROPRIETOR AND WAITERS

He's not from here—and we've the knack
to have the shirt right off his back!

KOHN

I won't have that, let's make it clear—
why ogle them? I'm paying here!

GIRL ON RIGHT

It's not my fault, look, can't you see
it's them that's staring back at me!

KOHN

You think that this is just a laugh,
flirting with the General Staff!

GENERAL STAFF OFFICER

And if we lose, it's no big deal,
our honour's safe, that they can't steal.
See, war is war—and win or lose—
there's Fritzi here to chase the blues.

CHORUS OF GENERAL STAFF OFFICERS

Out here we have no qualms or fears,
Austria will last a thousand years!

And even if we faced a rout,
our German friends will pull us out.
More champers, waiter, while there's time!

FETTKÖTER

Staunch stands and true the Watch on the Rhine!

(Change of scene)

Scene 28

Viennese lecture hall.

GRUMBLER (*recites* "Prayer")

Almighty God, we've reached the end of time,
so close my eyes to scenes my spirits dread.
Let me not witness how they swill their wine
to compensate for all the blood they've shed.

Almighty God, banish this age I hate
and help me to become a child again.
Eternity's a realm we all await.
Let sovereign blindness mitigate the pain.

Almighty God, help me to hold my breath!
I will not speak a language so uncouth.
Their hatred brings stupidity and death,
taking revenge on those who tell the truth.

Almighty God, the gift of thought you gave,
but they adapt it to their vulgar needs.
The words they speak send values to the grave,
negating death and nullifying deeds.

Almighty God, if only you could quell
the crude cacophony that fills the sky!
The Devil, once condemned to freeze in hell,
feels really cosy as the bullets fly.

Almighty God, you lit the lamp of science,
infused it with your breath, but now, alas,
we render thanks by placing our reliance
on suffocating clouds of poison gas.

Almighty God, why ever was I born
into this godless age—it's hard to take!
The starving population's left to mourn,
while profiteers are feasting at the wake.

Almighty God, why at this hour of strife
was I compelled to live in Habsburg lands,
where all of those who still cling on to life
feast at the funeral with bloodstained hands?

Almighty God, this realm of poster boys
carousing as they eat and drink their fill
is stained blood-red. Their callous song destroys
all empathy and death must foot the bill.

Almighty God, was it at your decree
that vampires haunt us with a cheery face?
Surely the time has come to set me free
from laughing hangmen who defile our race.

Almighty God, please lead us to the land
where money does not poison people's health
and earthly goods, passing from hand to hand,
perpetuate the shame of unearned wealth!

Almighty God, can't you devise some means
of passing laws that ban warlike parades
and switching off those programmed man-machines
that churn out dividends and hand grenades.

Almighty God, please spare me from the sight
of bloodstained battlefields. Grant peace, I pray!
Let gentler feelings guide me through the night
and dreams find their reward on Judgment Day!

(Applause, in which the front rows also join.)

MEMBER OF AUDIENCE *(to his wife)*—There's something you should know—he wanted to be a journalist once—

(Change of scene.)

Scene 29

Subscriber to the Neue Freie Presse *and Patriot in conversation.*

SUBSCRIBER Old Biach said up in Kolberg—

PATRIOT Eh? How could he—?

SUBSCRIBER I mean, old Hindenburg—he's saying in today's paper what he said in Kolberg: I'll go to my grave hoping for a better future for the German people.

PATRIOT You'll go to your grave?

SUBSCRIBER What d'you mean, me? Him!

PATRIOT Ah, the Editor Himself?

SUBSCRIBER No, no—just him! Hindenburg!

PATRIOT If only old Biach could have lived to hear that!
(Long pause, during which they gaze at each other.)

SUBSCRIBER Since Biach died, I keep picking up the wrong vibrations.

PATRIOT Instead of vibrations, we've got rumours now—a bad sign!

SUBSCRIBER I've a strong hunch—we're weakening.

PATRIOT *(raises his eyes to the heavens in distress)* We ain't seen nothing yet.
(Change of scene.)

Scene 30

Two commercial counsellors emerge from the Imperial Hotel. A one-armed beggar woman with a wooden leg stands in front of them.

FIRST COMMERCIAL COUNSELLOR *(looking around)* Ain't there any cabs? Wotta scandal!

BOTH *(waving their walking sticks at a passing car)* Taxi—!

FIRST *(calling after a cabby)* Hey, there—are you free?

CABBY *(shrugging)* I'm booked.

SECOND *(as they are surrounded by beggars of every description)* At least you can still get summat to eat, that's the only thing we've got left. *(A woman collapses from hunger and is carried off)*—Wotta scandal!—and on the Ringstrasse, too!—Even young Rothschild's getting grey hairs—

FIRST No wonder, these days.

SECOND He can only be, at most—wait a minute, how long ago was it that he took over—

FIRST But what's the use? There's a weird mood in Vienna—Y'know, since old Biach died—

SECOND The exchange rate's on the slide—

FIRST If we'd managed to get our money out last week—

SECOND I'd planned to go to the foreign currency exchange tomorrow—but why bother to wangle it when there's an easier way out.

FIRST (*throws down his cigar butt and a 20-heller note in front of a beggar*) Summat else has gone up—at New Year, a box at the Tabarin nightclub cost me all of 600—my wife wouldn't let up—if it goes on like this, it'll be 1,000 next New Year.

SECOND And why not?

(*The Grumbler passes by.*)

FIRST (*spits*) Bad cess to him!

SECOND Hey, if I tell my youngest you said that—

FIRST Why?

SECOND Thinks he's great. Can't wait for the next public reading. He's one of the Grumbler's greatest fans.

FIRST If it were me, I'd give the boy a clip round the ear.

SECOND Watch out, the way things are now! The boy might even get him to make fun of you in that red rag of his, *Die Fackel*.

FIRST Y'know, it's scarcely credible the censor tolerates it, anywhere else they'd have strung him up long ago! Stirring up trouble all the time—against the war, even against the papers! Yelling that the war should stop!—well, the war's still going on, so he should pipe down.

SECOND A pretty sight, I'd say, peace-mongering in wartime!

FIRST Recently, so they say, at one of his readings he called quite openly for people to refuse to fight and stop buying the papers! If he's not in the pay of the Entente, then I'm a Dutchman. Hey, look, Baron Wassilko's coming thisaway with the lovely Gerda Walde. On foot!

SECOND Whichaway?

FIRST (*pointing*) Thataway.

SECOND The Grumbler's turned my lad's head. But I really lost it recently and gave him a piece of my mind, told him there's no point grousing about the war, but for the war there'd be no war profits, end of story. Well, he got the message. But so what? He still goes to the readings. What about your youngest? Making progress?

FIRST *(proudly)* I'll say! He's out partying with the Sascha Film people!

SECOND Mmm! Quite right too, make the most of it while you're young. Funny, when I read *Die Fackel*, I can't help laughing—what do you say to that piece today about Hirschfeld?

FIRST Brilliant! And the Schalek woman? He even attacks her!

SECOND But say what you like, she's courageous. Let him try planting himself down in the firing line and writing about it! We got seats to hear Piccaver at the Opera—

FIRST I had to sort my wife out recently, she's always going on about it—if only the war was over, she feels sorry for the soldiers in the trenches. I keeps tellin 'er, they'll still get their payoff, their fame in the history books! And watta we get? War-profiteering taxes! That's what people forget.

SECOND Yes, and the risk of peace—?!

FIRST Don't even think about it. Y'know—when one of them comes back from the front and starts to tell all—it's always the same—they've had a rough time of it, fair nuff, we knows that! I've 'ad an earful, it's such a bore.

SECOND We've had enough of them 'orrors.

(A disabled war veteran limps past.)

BOTH *(waving their walking sticks at a passing car)* Taxi—!

(Change of scene.)

Scene 31

Optimist and Grumbler in conversation.

GRUMBLER The veterinary clinic was not able to save this horse. It was martyred and had to be put down. It bore the mark of this age of grandeur on its back, a veritable stigma. On both sides, the same fairly regular distinguishing pattern. On its spine you could see the yellow of the bones; also on its haunches. A grazing shot had taken its tail off. Its girth had bitten right into the flesh. The wound had turned green with pus, and looked like a first-degree burn. Diagnosis: a portable artillery piece, strapped on for weeks on end. The load had not been lifted off its back either by day or night.

OPTIMIST Yes, animals have to endure war, too, there's no escaping it.

GRUMBLER And the sufferings of animals will testify against those who butcher and desecrate the created world even more eloquently than those of human beings, for animals cannot speak. The stricken horse, with the form of a heavy gun engraved in its back, the burden of human death—these are nightmare images whose horror will haunt, until their dying day, those who have lain down to rest on their laurels.

OPTIMIST While we're on the subject of animals—I cut out an odious advertisement for you: "Dogs required for slaughter, good money offered." There ought to be a law against it! What conclusions would the enemy draw about the state of Austrian nutrition if they heard—

GRUMBLER The conclusions they would draw about the state of Austrian culture seems even more dangerous to me.

OPTIMIST Why so? If a man needs food, he won't spurn even dog meat, so he kills his dog.

GRUMBLER Unlike the dog, who refuses food if its master dies.

OPTIMIST I've never heard of such a case.

GRUMBLER There's one you can read about here—in *The Animal Lover* magazine: "A faithful dog. A member writes that Hermine Pfeiffer, a casual worker for whom our association several times provided a reduced-price dog identity disc, died some weeks ago. Since the day of the woman's death, her female poodle refused all food, and died a few days later. The faithful animal was found in the morning with its head on a pillow that its mistress had formerly used. Curiously, its late mistress had once said that, should anything happen to her, she would be happy for her dog to pass away too, lest it fall into the wrong hands and suffer maltreatment. And the dog, deeply attached to her benefactress, did indeed die from grief very soon after her." After reading this report one can only say: lucky dog!

OPTIMIST Why so?

GRUMBLER Otherwise it would have been eaten. Provided it wasn't already too thin from malnutrition. If dogs didn't love their owners, they would be tempted, before heading for freedom, to affirm their moral superiority.

OPTIMIST But there surely must be deeper reasons why "doggon it" is a swear-word and "like a dog" such a term of abuse.

GRUMBLER You're dead right. It designates the character of those who will pay good money for dogs to slaughter. Or those described in this theatre review: "The Deutsches Volkstheater has demonstrated that it also supports authors who do not slavishly follow the taste of the well-off paying public with doglike devotion."

OPTIMIST The taste of the well-off paying public at the Volkstheater and the taste of those paying good money for dogs to slaughter—you're surely not implying—

GRUMBLER Why not? Those paying good money for dogs to slaughter are already sitting in the best boxes. But whatever can be said about dogs, not a single one has ever been accused of trying to follow the taste of the well-off paying public with devotion. Nor do I believe that a dog would die from grief at the death of one of the Volkstheater regulars. The loving creature would draw a line at that. No dog would want to be seen alive in such a dismal place.

OPTIMIST You speak more highly of dogs than of human beings, it seems.

GRUMBLER Without exception. Come rain or shine, night or day, war or peace. In this war the animals, too, saw it through to the bitter end—though they were even more vulnerable. And every war-dog sent to the front could show the five-star gang who dubbed the common soldiers "front-line schweinhunds" that being a dog is a badge of honour compared with those inhuman monsters. Tear off their medals and award them to the dogs serving at the front! In contrast to the General Staff they are models of poverty and dignity.
(Change of scene.)

Scene 32

Reporting to battalion.

MAJOR What were you?

SOLDIER Beg to report, sir, a saddler.

MAJOR Look at me when I'm talking to you, did they teach you nothing?! You dog! Dogs, the lot of you! Son of a bitch! (*To another*) You wrote to your wife, complaining about how you were treated.

SOLDIER (*terrified*) Beg to report—Major—sir—please—

MAJOR (*brandishing the letter*) Here's the letter! What you staring at?! Didn't you know I was the censor? You dog! Dogs, the lot of you! Son of a bitch! The biggest swine in all the barracks! Twenty-one days solitary, three days a week without food, then compulsorily enlisted in the front line. You'll soon see what's what, you schweinhund! You won't know what's hit you! (*To another soldier.*) Ah, this is the one with the bellyache! So mama sent you a nice food parcel, eh? Hope it chokes you! (*He lands three blows with his cane to head and back. The soldier staggers off, in tears.*) Just so you know, the four infantrymen who refused their four-ounce bread ration are up in front of the divisional court-martial and will be shot. Czechs, of course! If any soldier fails in his duty to protect his fatherland, it's always a Czech! Deserters, every man jack of them! A German soldier always does his duty. I'm Czech myself, but I'm ashamed of belonging to that nation. (*To a lance-corporal.*) You there, you'll do the shopping for me tomorrow, that'll give me an opportunity to lock you up. You won't find anything at the regulation price, and you mustn't bring back anything above that price. If you bring nothing, you'll get short shrift, it's straight off to the cooler. Well—what else?

LANCE-CORPORAL Beg to report, Major, sir, Second-Lieutenant Ederl bought sliced cheese in the Zillertal on the sly at 10 crowns the kilo, and wanted to sell it to the officers' mess for 24 crowns.

MAJOR What's that you're saying?—That's outrageous!

LANCE-CORPORAL The quartermaster turned the offer down for the mess—said it was poor quality. But so the second-lieutenant shouldn't lose out, the cheese was bought for the men, and their meat ration cut accordingly. I think, Major, in the interests of the men, and since this action was against regulations, that I should—

MAJOR This is outrageous! It's not your place to criticize anything officers may or may not do! Six hours in irons! (*To another.*) You put in a complaint about poor food and not enough of it?

SOLDIER Beg to report, Major, sir, yes sir!

MAJOR (*cuffs him*) It's not the quartermaster who's at fault, it's your appetite! Think yourself lucky there's a war on! In peacetime you'd get even less! I'll put you on exercise drill till your tongue's hanging out down to your navel—that'll put a stop to complaints about food all right! You dog! Dogs, the lot of you! Son of a bitch!

(*Change of scene.*)

Scene 33

Optimist and Grumbler in conversation.

OPTIMIST To get some idea of what a soldier at the front really feels, all you need do is—

GRUMBLER —read a letter home. Especially one where the writer managed to bypass the censor so that it reached its destination.

OPTIMIST Still, such letters would show you that every soldier's highest ambition is to fight well, and that he even puts devotion to duty above his longing for his wife and children.

GRUMBLER Alternatively, you would be filled with horror at the incalculable crime of those scoundrels who caused, or prolonged, the war: the crime of disrupting millions of individual destinies, tearing them apart and trampling underfoot all individual happiness; the dread of imminent disaster for years on end, both at home and in the trenches; people in both cases trembling in anguish when there is no word, or else fearful that any communication is a herald of death. A wife gives birth, a mother dies—and the person most concerned is lying somewhere out there in the mud—for the Fatherland. Now the scoundrels have come up with the ingenious idea of periodically suspending correspondence to and from the front entirely—this accursed though longed-for invention of the devil. The unfortunates then know more than enough, for the silence is the silence before the storm. How unimaginable the mechanism that subordinates the existential parameters of life—birth and death—to the inscrutable dictates of the General Staff! Only love eludes those dictates. What is love to the General Staff! (*He reads out a letter from an Austrian officer to his pregnant wife.*)

> —it seems that, in general, the reason for the postal delay from here to back home is that the letters are no longer censored, but simply held back until events make them redundant.
>
> I am resorting to every conceivable way to make these trying and terrible times easier to bear—all to no avail. If I think of you a lot, I only get sadder, and if I try to take my mind off things, I only feel sadder afterwards. It's best just to live for the moment, then time goes quicker. For every day that passes brings us closer together, we mustn't forget that!
>
> I'm still totally dejected, worrying about you today, but I intend to shake it off and cling only to the hope of receiving good news from you tomorrow. To think that I could be with you right now, see your beloved face, talk to you about the days ahead, which will surely put the finishing touch to our happiness—yet here I am, far away, and you all alone! Truly, it is so cruel, this war, so unnatural, and we are not the only ones to suffer, so many others, an innumerable number, are made unhappy by the arbitrary actions of the unscrupulous few. But what do I care about others, my heart is breaking when I think of what we two now have to go through. It's too terrible, hardly endurable! And I still have to carry out my difficult, responsible, dangerous duties, and set an example of bravery, devotion to duty, and all the rest of these virtues *which I hate*, while every step I take fills me with disgust and revulsion and goes against my innermost conviction. They demand that you lose all your better feelings, and whoever is too good to do that suffers unspeakably, and does whatever is demanded of him with disgust. And we were so happy, so bound up in each other, we are so united that one is quite lost without the other. Without you I am so diminished, so impoverished, there are times you would not recognize me. Often, when I give free rein to my thoughts, even when they don't instantly take wing to you, time and again I want to ask you something, to know what you think, to hear your opinion, but

I'm alone! I don't need anyone else's advice, it's you I want to hear, all my thoughts and feelings are for you, whatever they are, and without you I'm not me, only half of me, diminished. Your love, even from a distance, sheds light on my gloom, it alone sustains the joy of living. Why say more, why keep twisting the knife in wounds already throbbing?! You know that you are all in all to me—or rather, you are the cause of my pain, for without you it would none of it feel so terrible! Sometimes I think of the future. The two of us lying in each other's arms, drained of life to the point of utter exhaustion—from love, from love!

Oh why can I not be there! I would not have stirred from your side throughout the difficult hours that lie before you, and all would have been made so very much easier for you.

Don't worry about me. If I could transport you here by magic, I would quite naturally take you into the trenches with me.

Oh, why can I not be there with you! I belong there, after all, yet cannot be there! God grant that you did not suffer too much, that nothing happened to you, that you're in good health and you will recover and get stronger day by day. Grant God that I may receive a handwritten card from you today. By the time you get these lines—God willing—you will be well again. Did you feel my presence, that I suffered everything you suffered? Oh, the time will come, the time must come, when we shall make up for all the suffering we have gone through.

So far away, so far from you at this time! Oh why, why can I not sit with you, warm you and strengthen you with my infinite love! I can't help it, I can hardly see what I'm writing for the tears constantly in my eyes.

Oh God, that I cannot be with you! And no hope! They no longer send you home or to a base unit, but to some hospital or other.

I've got so many grey hairs, I can no longer count how many. But I love you, whether far away or by your side, I love you, love you, love you, beyond words, insanely.—

OPTIMIST So what's the fuss? He goes home, and finds wife and child well.

GRUMBLER No, his country needed him! At home, a human being comes into the world, at the front another departs. I've never read anything sadder, anything truer, than this letter by a soldier who becomes a father at the moment of his death. I'd give the whole of our country, bag and General Staff baggage, for a single one of these millions of martyrs for love!

(Change of scene.)

Scene 34

In the Bohemian village Postabitz.

A WOMAN (*sitting at a table, writing*)

Derest husband,

This is to inform you I have gone astray. I couldnt help it, dere husband. I know youll forgive everything I tell you. Im in the family way by another. I know your a good man and that youll forgive me everything. He talked me into it and said you wouldn't be coming back from the war anyway and thats when I had my weak moment. You know how weak women are, and its best you forgive me, its already happened. I was already thinking something must have happened to you for you hadnt written for three months. I was quite shocked to get your letter and you were still alive. Im glad for you but forgive me dere Franz, maybe the child will die and then all will be well again. I dont like this bloke any more for I know your still alive. Everything here costs the earth, its good you are away, at least you don't have to pay for food in the field. The money you sent me will be very useful. Your unforgettable wife sends you her love once more

Anna

(*Change of scene.*)

Scene 35

Hospital in Leitmeritz in northern Bohemia.

DISABLED PRISONER OF WAR ON RED CROSS EXCHANGE (*to neighbour in next bed, breathing heavily*) You must never—lose—patience. There's only—one more stop to go. First they'll send us to Prague—or Vienna—but then soon—I'll be in Postabitz. (*Letters are distributed.*) It may be—from my Anna—(*He stretches out his left hand towards the letter.*) Oh God—yes, it is! (*He tries to raise himself. He holds the letter clenched between his teeth, opens it with his left hand and reads. He sinks back, thunderstruck.*)

(*Change of scene.*)

Scene 36

Transit camp in Galicia for repatriated prisoners of war.

THE FRIEND (*writing a letter*)—Especially since they died in the field, it no longer seemed fitting to complain in the least about one's own relatively tolerable fate. But I'm nearing 40, with wife and children and one or two other troubles that threaten to engulf me, and now it's the fourth year (and who knows how many more to come!) that I have to stand impotently to attention, as it were, at the mercy of this most desperate of wars, in the ludicrous reflected glory of feats of arms which render you the most defenceless creature on God's earth. My nerves are frayed, my spirits dejected. I ask you to make allowances for that and to forgive me if, even now that fortune has undoubtedly turned somewhat in my favour, I cannot pass mutely over all my little troubles, although my respect for the silence of those to whom your moving lament was addressed is profound, and my recognition of all that you have done for me—for me, who is still alive!—deep and indelible.

Certainly, I have every reason to thank a benevolent fate which has long kept me far from the front. But I don't know if I'm not perhaps too dazed to be fully conscious of it as a blessing; and sometimes—imagine!—I feel as if I might occasionally have breathed more freely out there, in danger, than here in safety. In that I may be deluding myself, or if not, that may be because, at the front, the will to live strangely stirs the blood, while here I am paralysed by the fear that my weariness of life could become second nature to me. As far as that is concerned, I can only say that the horrors of the war machine—at least, in a figurative sense—never affected me as deeply as my current torment, relegated as I am to a circle of officers—mainly Hungarian Jews—who on closer inspection reveal themselves to be a consortium of black-marketeers in uniform. Add to that the desolate look of the camp—a veritable symbol of our misery—which puts our own repatriated prisoners of war on show behind a rusty barbed-wire fence as if they were some barbaric tribes, while wretched figures with fixed bayonets guard the entrances and especially the main gate, which, adorned with fluttering flags and garlands, bears the heart-warming inscription "Welcome home!" Good God, the embarrassment is painful and almost touching, as in so many other instances, but it is understandable, as the result of the whole-scale ruin into which the nations of Europe have been plunged by the war, our own to the fore. If you were standing on the outside—outside the gates—you could, at a pinch, see the humour of the situation (especially now that the returnees opt to do a quick about-turn at the border and flee back to the chaos of Russia). But if you are, so to speak, a forced labourer in the bustling funfair which is our Administration, and if, penetrating to the core of the enterprise, you come across a cartel of wheeler-dealers taking foodstuffs, laboriously acquired by hand and intended to alleviate the hunger of some poor devils, and making them disappear into a shadowy hinterland that knows no hunger—except hunger for money; and if, further, you are under orders from some export clerk, from whose lips, when he recently surprised me reading your *Fackel*, burst the cry of astonishment: "You don't mean to tell me he's still trying to set the world alight?!"—then you get in a cold sweat, and now and then you want to escape, not just from this cage, but from the universal monkey cage of these times and *this* world!

And now imagine that an exclamation like the one just mentioned is spat out in front of you, on the off chance, while you are reading "On Eternal Peace" and other poems! Perhaps at a moment when I was starting to think what I can only dare suggest with an image here: Never before was your heart so laid bare and so hallowed! How its tempest subsides in the roar of the deep, in the song of the heavens! Like some distant shining shore it rises into view through the veil of your verses: the dawn of childhood—the dawn of humanity! And suddenly, today appears like all our yesterdays. God's world, young and old!

That, in some measure, was how the face of your creation appeared to me, before the brute defiled it. Only in writing to you do I now feel once more suffused with the will to live. Those of us denied immortality through our own intellect must make do with the satisfaction of our earthly desires and destiny; even if the birth of a son in the natural course of things immortalizes only our fated mortality. Perhaps my love for my son (who sends me the most touching drawings and letters—he recently wrote "we're doing fine, so far")—perhaps it is so painful and profound for that reason alone. For just as in your sonnet "Half Asleep", one way or another, the unborn son is everywhere at hand.

But for now, farewell! Wait, one thing more: you quote Goethe writing that letter to Frau von Stein about his affection for ordinary people! How true I found his words in my dealings with the returnees! In my last posting, for instance, I had a company consisting of people from every imaginable nationality. The only service I could render them was to take it upon myself to improve their food rations, and instead of exercising with them, I took them out to a meadow and had them tell me of their life in captivity and, when they needed it, helped them a bit with their letters to their relatives. And how touchingly they paid me back! When the company was ready to move off, two men of each nationality—Germans, Ukrainians, Poles, Czechs, Italians, Bosnians—stepped forward and thanked me in the name of their compatriots. After a few words of farewell on my part, they gave me three cheers, a Viennese compositor quickly stepped out from his column and asked if he might send me a card from Vienna, and waving their caps, the company marched off into the beautiful spring evening to the railway station. Our lieutenant-colonel, who had been watching from a distance, then said: "They gave three cheers for the Emperor, of course", which I naturally confirmed.—

(Change of scene.)

Scene 37

In freezing conditions after the winter offensive in the Sette Communi on the Italian Front. A parade ground at the rear. The remnants of a regiment, each man emaciated to a skeleton. With their uniforms in tatters, their boots torn apart, their filthy underclothes, they look at first sight like a pack of sick, bedraggled beggars. They drag themselves to their feet, practise arms drill and saluting.

FIRST WAR CORRESPONDENT How their eyes will light up when they hear their commander in chief, currently visiting his gallant troops at the front, has deigned to inspect the victorious regiment.

SECOND WAR CORRESPONDENT He's still at the front, at Gries near Bolzano, but will be here any minute. I'd say they sense it.

FIRST SOLDIER *(to another)* Now he's coming, that pathetic wimp!

SECOND SOLDIER Never shows his nose where the action is!

FIRST WAR CORRESPONDENT The young Emperor enjoys the blind confidence of his men.

SECOND WAR CORRESPONDENT All he has to do is smile at them, and they're happy, the gallant lads.

CAPTAIN Snakes alive, get a move on, His Majesty will be here any second! Thought you would get some leave while the regiment is re-forming? Hard shit! His Majesty is coming to inspect his glorious regiment, so it's every man present and correct, you rotten rabble!

FIRST WAR CORRESPONDENT Oh look! That's interesting—what's happening now! They're changing clothes—getting fitted out with new uniforms, head to toe.

SECOND WAR CORRESPONDENT What'll they do with the old rags?

FIRST They'll get them back after the Emperor has left.

SECOND The companies are reduced to between 15 and 60 men, they're going to have to top up numbers, of course—?

FIRST What d'you mean: "going to"? They're at it already. Think they'd show the Emperor losses of 2,500 men?! Not a chance!

SECOND Where'll they get the human raw material from?

FIRST Oh, cobblers, tailors, orderlies, cooks, mule drivers, grooms, whoever's on the sick list, and so on—they've all got their rifles already and have been doing drill. I wish he'd show up soon! I'm perished with cold!

SECOND Look what they're doing now—what is it?

FIRST That's obvious, those with decorations and the better looking ones are being put in front, they're changing places.

SECOND I can see that, but what are they doing to their faces?

FIRST What they're doing to their faces? Don't you know? What an ignoramus! They're rubbing snow in so that everyone, including the sick ones, turns a healthy colour.

SECOND Brilliant idea! Look, they're already glowing! But what's happening now? Something's being handed around.

FIRST Postcards with the Emperor's picture. That'll cost them half their bread ration.

SECOND Some of them will be happy enough with the exchange, gallant lads!—For God's sake, that's the motorcade now—Can't you hear?

Motorcars arrive. Plump figures get out, among them a weedier-looking one, wrapped in heavy furs and with large earmuffs. Little more than two blubbery lips are visible.

FIRST There you are, see it with your own eyes: the commander in chief at the front, inspecting troops just returned victorious from battle, engages in conversation with the humblest of his men.

SECOND He has a charming manner. Just look how their hearts fly out to him.

FIRST He's having an electrifying effect!

SECOND If only I could hear what he's saying. What's he saying?

FIRST Nothing. But he's smiling.

(There can now be heard, as the Emperor passes from man to man, from one platoon to the next, at regular intervals of five seconds, either "Aha! Very nice!" or "Aha! Very good!" or "Aha! Very fine!" or "Aha! Carry on!" It continues for two hours. The officers then say goodbye. The cars depart.)

COLONEL *(to major)* The following order is to be announced this evening: "His Majesty was full of praise for the regiment. Both the spirit and the appearance of the troops are excellent, the courage mirrored in the eyes of each and every man is incomparable. His Majesty was particularly pleased that the losses suffered by the regiment were small. His Majesty's concluding words were: 'So, Colonel, this regiment can truly be counted, as in the past, among the troops most loyal to their Emperor and their Fatherland, and in the battles ahead, which will be hard but which we shall win, will gallantly stand its ground to the last and so add laurel upon laurel to its banner.' To which I replied: 'Yes indeed, Your Majesty, that I promise.'"

CAPTAIN (*to the soldiers*) What you experienced here today, you can tell to your children and your children's children—if you so desire! But first, the watchword is: into battle and victory! And above all—off with those new uniforms at once!

FIRST WAR CORRESPONDENT Well, was that worth the trouble? At minus 28 degrees centigrade, it's no picnic!

SECOND WAR CORRESPONDENT You're telling me! I don't like these missions! The theatre's my thing—as General Hoehn very well knows! I'll just have to speak to divisional headquarters about a theatre at the front. The general really took to the idea.

FIRST WAR CORRESPONDENT A theatre at the front? But they're already taking off their makeup!
(*Change of scene.*)

Scene 38

Hofburg Palace. Press office.

CAPTAIN WERKMANN (*dictating*) Esteemed editor! I would deem it a great kindness if you would publish in full, if feasible, today's reports of His Majesty's inspections of the troops and the visit by Empress Zita to the army kitchens at Ottakring. As it is, the reports are by no means overlong. I'd wish to stress the depiction of the homage paid to Their Majesties. I was myself a witness to these truly overwhelming tributes, and certainly did not exaggerate them in my report. Allow me to convey to you my sincerest thanks in advance. Most respectfully yours—
So, and now this:
Esteemed editor!
I am very anxious that the report of the attack led by His Imperial Highness Archduke Max, as carried by the *Österreichisch-ungarische Kriegskorrespondenz* on the 27th of this month, should be given the widest possible distribution. Accordingly, I would ask you to ensure reliable publication of this report in your esteemed journal. Allow me to convey to you my sincerest thanks in advance. Most respectfully yours—
(*Change of scene.*)

Scene 39

Kärntnerstrasse. Passersby surround an operetta star. A car from the Hofburg stops, greeted by passersby. A lackey opens the car door.

ARCHDUKE MAX *(calling out from the car)* Hi there, Werner—Fritzl, my dear boy! Coming along to Sacher's with me?

OPERETTA STAR No can do, Your Highness—I've got a date with a pretty girl! *(Both are cheered.)*

ARCHDUKE MAX Ah! Well, so long, old boy!

(The lackey closes the door. The car drives off.)

NEWSPAPER VENDOR —Austrian advances on the Piave!

(Change of scene.)

Scene 40

A side street. In a doorway, a soldier with two medals on his chest. His cap is pulled down low over his face. At his side, his little daughter, who has been guiding him, and who now stoops to pick up a cigarette butt from the pavement, which she puts in his pocket. In the courtyard of the house, a disabled soldier with a hurdy-gurdy.

SOLDIER That's enough now. *(He pulls out a wooden pipe, into which the girl stuffs the tobacco from the cigarette butts.)*

LIEUTENANT *(who has passed by, turns round, infuriated at not being saluted)* Are you blind?

SOLDIER Yes.

LIEUTENANT What?—Oh, I see—

(He turns away. The soldier, guided by the girl, leaves in the opposite direction. The hurdy-gurdy plays the "Long Live Habsburg" march.)

(Change of scene.)

Scene 41

Army High Command.

MAJOR *(to another)* There's really nothing, nothing but hassles from the fronts. Devilishly depressing reports yet again, I don't have a clue what to do. If I pass them on to Waldstätten, he gets mad at me, if I don't pass them on, he still gets mad. What can you do? Look at this:

"Some regiments are in urgent need of an improvement in rations, to keep the men's energy levels up. In one division the average soldier's weight is 50 kilos." There you have it!—And this one:

"Every deserter in the rear, even if he has to live hiding in the woods, can sustain himself better than a soldier at the front." Deserter! How can you even write the word! "As for clothing, a full outfit is often no longer present, since shirt or underpants or both are missing. Some have no longer any sleeves in their shirts, some are missing the back, and others have only half their underpants or bits of rags for their feet. Those with malarial fever are made to wait, naked, until their rags have been washed and dried." Rags! What insolence! The liberties they take when they report to us from the front! Almost implying that we're responsible—as if! "In one regiment every third soldier has no coat. There are sentries with helmets and coats, but no trousers." Well, that's a sight for sore eyes! "It's no longer a question of a soldier's self-respect or sense of honour, it's simply an affront to human dignity." Come on, cool it, fellows! The sheer insolence! Those guys at the front understand neither the exigencies of war nor the appropriate way to communicate with High Command. It's as if we started the war! And the things they dream up! Listen to this:

"To raise morale, it would be advisable to allocate the younger members of the Royal and Imperial House to fighting units and to the particularly difficult sectors of the front." Well, I ask you—surely that's an insult to members of the Imperial House! No, no, my friend, that's over the top, laying on royals to raise the soldiers' spirits—there are other ways we can put fire in their bellies! It's pure defeatism—sending members of the Imperial House to the front! Make things worse!

SECOND MAJOR Why get so worked up? Think we could ever chivvy 'em into going?

(Change of scene.)

Scene 42

Optimist and Grumbler in conversation.

OPTIMIST Believe me, the young Emperor really looks like a man who has groomed himself thoroughly for his role as ruler.

GRUMBLER I can easily believe that. After all, when he was Crown Prince he had the walls of his study lined with military cartoons from *Die Muskete*.

OPTIMIST You wouldn't believe how serious he's become.

GRUMBLER No wonder—he's stopped attending operettas since the run of *Walzertraum* ended.

OPTIMIST Yes, but look, seeing *Walzertraum* 50 times—

GRUMBLER —would make anyone feel in low spirits, that's true.

OPTIMIST Much else about him has changed, too. His youthful enthusiasm—

GRUMBLER —for the *Parrot* cabaret—

OPTIMIST —the good times whooping it up in barracks at Brandeis in Bohemia.

GRUMBLER —the cinema in Bad Reichenau—

OPTIMIST He doesn't go there now anymore either.

GRUMBLER After his hundredth visit he's supposed to have said it was getting to be a bore.

OPTIMIST No, believe me, you underestimate his intellectual qualities.

GRUMBLER I'm convinced his face gives an exaggerated impression of them. Recently, someone who knows him assured me that he's quick on the uptake. That's the highest praise monarchists can adduce for the object of their veneration, whenever they want to convince a sceptic. But for a ruler, the prerequisite is actually that he should be quicker on the uptake than his subjects.

OPTIMIST Doesn't the fact that he wants peace speak highly in his favour?

GRUMBLER That, too, is hardly a quality that raises him above most of his subjects. I, for instance, am even keener on peace; moreover, I've never told lies in order to obstruct it when I could have brought it about by telling the truth. And the likes of us never even had the opportunity to renounce a throne if we didn't want to wage a war or continue fighting one.

OPTIMIST That's the only thing he can be reproached for: he's fickle and thinks whoever talked to him last is in the right.

GRUMBLER The diversity of his views is astonishing. For he looks such a simple soul.

OPTIMIST But all in all, you've got to admit, the way he's turned out is surprising. He was always promising, and all his promise has been fulfilled.

GRUMBLER True, but not his promises.

OPTIMIST His fickleness—saying one thing one day and something else the next—

GRUMBLER —apparently comes from the Saxon branch of the Habsburgs, and that quirk in their lower lip.

OPTIMIST But all in all, he's surely a good-natured fellow? You can say what you like—

GRUMBLER That's just it, you can't say what you like.

OPTIMIST What is it you can't say?

GRUMBLER That I don't want to be ruled by an operetta star—to have a matinee idol like Marischka or Fritz Werner perched on the throne. That it's far more gruesome having to feel respect for a dashing young man about town than for a bewhiskered old freak of an Emperor. That I find it intolerable to be ruled by a cartoon character who might have been created by Schönpflug. By someone who can smile and smile and be—not a villain but a jaw-dropping cretin. Someone frozen in the stance of continuously greeting others.

OPTIMIST And he does the jokey caption for each picture as well. The other day at a court banquet he's supposed to have cracked this one: "What's the opposite of Apponyi?—A horse!"

GRUMBLER I can just hear the braying laughter of those who can send us to our deaths. No, it's no good. I refuse to take part in the winter campaign.

OPTIMIST But look, you can't seriously blame him for his humour. He's simply inherited the proverbial affability of the Habsburgs—Franz Ferdinand being the only exception—and even Harden, surely a principal witness, held out high hopes for him. That was the time after the assassination in Sarajevo when he appeared smiling to greet the crowds, arm in arm with Franz Joseph, the greater figure—

GRUMBLER —the greeter figure! A monarch whose cheerfulness gave the lie to the official bulletin which reported that he lunched alone to signal his profound grief at Franz Ferdinand's death. The predecessor and the successor to the assassinated Heir to the Throne took their leave, greeting the honourable public as they went. The successor promptly justified the hopes placed in him with a historic utterance along the lines of: "Home, James, and don't spare the horses!"

OPTIMIST Don't overlook the symbolic significance inherent in such utterances.

GRUMBLER How could I? With his utterance "Let the ancient bastions fall" in 1888, Franz Joseph made a first breach in the ramparts of old Vienna.

OPTIMIST And Crown Prince Rudolf famously expressed the hope that "a sea of light" would stream forth—

GRUMBLER —at the opening of the Electricity Exhibition in 1883. But if Goethe on his deathbed had not called out "More light", as the legend goes, but merely "Open the other shutter and let more light in", it would still be more enlightening than all the maxims of the Habsburgs, though such endorsements were indeed valued at a right royal rate imposed on the exhibiting firms, while their mind-numbing impact was the last straw for peoples afflicted by the deeds of the Habsburgs. Nevertheless, Archduke Rudolf—in the intimate company of his coachmen Bratfisch and Mistviecherl, a shining light to later generations of revellers—slaked his thirst for culture through his journalist friends Szeps and

Frischauer. For all that, these Habsburgs and Hasbeens have pathetically failed to blaze a trail for progress; under their lamentable aegis the arts and sciences had no option but to bloom. One would be hard-pressed, I'd say, to imagine more than one or two of them with a book in their hands, even one of the primers by Leo Smolle about the military virtues of the double-headed eagle. Their mark of intellectual nobility was "to be quick on the uptake" of what they were slow to understand. But of all Franz Joseph's utterances, the most authentic seems to me to be one he made when contemplating an aquarium at a cooking exhibition: "Aha, goldfish, their swimming looks so natural!" The keenest intellects among the Habsburgs, and also the most reliable, are probably the homosexual ones. But if, like Ludwig Salvator, you are credited with human impulses, you will certainly be lying buried on Majorca, not in the Capuchin Crypt. The others—those who were able to fulfil their historic destiny and increase the power of their House through marriage, and those who, on the contrary, diminished Austria's happiness through wars—they would not have enjoyed their Indian summer if their peoples had had more sense. Otherwise the unremitting misfortune of being ruled by individuals, about whom the best that could be said was that you couldn't offend them, would have long been unendurable; and the dire situation that in the twentieth century there were not only archdukes, but also compulsive adulterers dignified by royal titles, would have been eradicated before the war was lost.

The brain fog generated by these characters will be fully felt in all its destructive force only after its dispersal, which now seems imminent. God's patience must be running out, after listening for so long to appeals by a submissive population to "preserve and protect" the Habsburgs, in the words of the national anthem. I hope to celebrate the next Imperial anniversary without the festive bowing and scraping of the arse-lickers who have made their way to the spas for this great day; and also without the resounding cries "All present and correct!" of those disreputable journalists who, in the midst of a world war, still dared ignore the suffering of our blood-soaked front to puff up these cliques of devotees in the rear, and drown out the curses of millions of mothers with the cheers of loyal lackeys. Anachronistic Austria, deferential to every Imperial Highness, will only come to its senses when it finally recognizes the trail of destruction left by those majestically striding past; when it decides to create republics rather than guards of honour, and firmly and incisively slams the door of the imperial carriage shut in the face of all the Salvators and Annunziatas.

OPTIMIST But that still seems to lie some way off. I had the impression just recently that Archduchess Blanka's car drew the most respectful attention, and when the traffic comes to a standstill on the Graben, it can only be Archduke Eugen's stately appearance that has drawn the crowd.

GRUMBLER Archduke Max in particular is undoubtedly popular. He inherited his cheerful disposition from his father and could even gallop over coffins if need be, something the World War would provide plenty of opportunity to do.

OPTIMIST Only a grumbler could take it amiss that he—

GRUMBLER —organized a sausage supper at the Polo Club during the seventh battle of the Isonzo, and used official court motorcars to transport the guests and musicians. One is deeply ashamed at being forced to stand up or doff one's hat whenever the gullible, infatuated mob takes it into its head to pay homage to one of these feudal bloodsucking leeches, to raise three cheers for one of these parasitical buffoons, who can't even do without their orgies and idiotic revels while a military offensive is under way; just as the memory of the connections between the Capuchin Crypt and all-night bars, doubtless a reflection of the times, fills one with nausea. What price imperial loyalty when dynastic nausea has become indissolubly linked with a smoke-filled nightclub, suddenly the scene of a right royal rave-up where patriotism is blended with sentimental love songs, now that the sacred melodies of a faded glory have been dishonoured by modern militarism! Only in such a place can we envisage the shameful spectacle of profiteers, barmaids, thieves, and suckers of every stripe rising deferentially to their feet, flanked by waiters bearing drinks, cloakroom personnel, and last but not least the lavatory attendant. This was the milieu in which love for the House of Habsburg was most deeply rooted. Monarchists, who are not in short supply, whom a war cannot kill off, and who will survive even this war, disregard those self-defeating characteristics of a ruling family, as if they were the heritage of all dynasties. But they can't possibly deny that such displays, blatant excesses in permissive times compounded by the scandalous, even criminal complicity of those in high places, far from setting an example to a world they themselves have bled white, undermines the monarchic idea; and that this idea might have been damaged by the sad recognition that a world war has been fought for an imperial family that was not worth a charge of buckshot. When an Imperial Highness is not only Inspector General of Artillery, but also an army contractor in cahoots with a profiteer on a deal worth millions, one that in no small measure contributes to the starvation at the front, then the national anthem is in urgent need of a new text, or else laurels would inevitably be confused with dried vegetables. Spectral figures who wanted only peace and quiet, which is why they waged war, and dashing devils who spent it carousing and profiteering—they shall rule us no more!

OPTIMIST In truth, what rules us all is—

GRUMBLER —Wolf in Gersthof's face on that nightclub poster! Look, there it is! Do you remember my prophecy? Four years ago—and how the face has grown! The bloodshot eyes are still there, yet this Austrian visage claims a golden heart.

OPTIMIST You exaggerate. You're saying he's turned into a symbol of our national character, like the head of Hindenburg has for Prussia's?

GRUMBLER Hindenburg is head and shoulders above us. We're fine fellows, but we don't look so serious or confident! Just as old Radetzky once surveyed us from his pedestal, so now the head of this folksy hero serenely contemplates the chaos into which we are plunged.

OPTIMIST But my God, it's just a poster—all it signifies is—

GRUMBLER —that millions had to die; but he survives, he is larger than life! How the enemy will stare when they arrive, a year from now.

OPTIMIST But I don't think you'll be able to extend the link between a poster and the World War any further.

GRUMBLER Right to the bitter end! If the posters had been shot, the people would have survived.

OPTIMIST I don't follow your train of thought.

GRUMBLER Don't worry, just stay as you are. The monologue I'm conducting with you has tired you out. The realities that you don't see are my visions, and where nothing has changed for you, for me it's a prophecy come true. Between my prediction that the World War would transform the world into a vast hinterland of fraud, degeneracy, and the most inhuman betrayal of the divine, and my assertion that it has already happened, there lies only the World War. If you harbour the same doubts about the connection, all you need do is ignore the state of the world. Are you not the one grumbling against the ideal which you grant has been dishonoured by the world? While I, an optimist, must acknowledge that my most pious hope remains unfulfilled, since my prophecies have come true. At the outset of this calamity I prayed that God might make the misbegotten feel that it is finished! But it was not their blood that was shed to expiate the deed that was in the beginning, the blood of the fraudsters, degenerates, and betrayers of the divine. He permitted them, instead, to sacrifice the blood of others, and to survive the destruction of the world unscathed. Truly, were the ways of the Lord not unfathomable, they would be inexplicable! Why did he allow the war to blind us!? Behold, the halt and the lame, tap-tapping their way through life, trembling beggars, pallid, prematurely aged children, mothers

deranged by the trauma of military offensives, heroic sons, their eyes wavering with mortal fear, and all strangers to daylight and to sleep, mere ruins of a shattered creation. Meanwhile, the laughter rings out of those who have presumed to defy the judge enthroned on high—too high above the stars for his arm to reach out and smite them. It is finished—is it not? *Their* soul retains no scar, for it was never wounded by what they did, what they knew, what they allowed to happen. It is the fate of mankind to have a bullet go in through one ear and out through the other. Let us turn our backs on this laughing monstrosity, the Austrian face with its infinitely bloodstained smugness!
(Change of scene.)

Scene 43

Vienna, Stadtpark. An enormous crowd surrounds the terrace of the Kursalon restaurant and dance hall.

NEWSPAPER VENDOR Midday News! The Battle of the Piave! Austrians storm into attack!

FIRST LADY My God, I'm so excited—

SECOND LADY So you're going to subscribe to the war loan?

FIRST LADY Me? Are you mad, I'm just curious—
(The public becomes restless.)

GENTLEMAN No pushing, please, ladies and gentlemen—!

HUSBAND It's all a hoax, you'll see.

WIFE But I'm telling you, it was in the paper this morning—

HUSBAND Here's *Die Zeit*—show me where.

WIFE Are you blind? There, at the top, even before the editorial—

HUSBAND Upon my soul! I never thought to look there—*(he reads)* Today, Thursday, 23 May at 12.30 pm, on the terrace of the Kursalon in the Stadtpark, Herr Hubert Marischka of the Theater an der Wien will bestow a kiss on the lady who makes the greatest sacrifice for the Eighth War Loan.—Well, I can tell you right now, you won't be making any sacrifice for the Eighth War Loan, d'you hear?!

WIFE Don't get all worked up, I only want to watch! D'you think everyone's turned up just to subscribe to the War Loan? All they want to do is watch!

HUSBAND You ain't seen nothing yet—you'll soon see it's a hoax. Come out of the crush! You know what it'll be—I'll tell you, a film, that's what it'll be!

WIFE You always want to put a damper on things! Even if it is a film—you'll still see Marischka giving a kiss.

HUSBAND And that's a pleasure, even if it's all a sham?!

A FAT BLACK-MARKETEER *(arm in arm with a girl, warbling)* "Kissing is no sin—a pretty maid—".

GIRL Give over, that's one of Girardi's, I never could stand him!

BLACK-MARKETEER COMPANION I never could stand him! Give me Thaller any day.

VOICE OF A SCEPTIC You think Treumann's a dead duck, then—?

FRÄULEIN KÖRMENDY God, Marischka, I'm so excited!

FRÄULEIN LÖWENSTAMM I'll only subscribe to the War Loan if Storm is giving a kiss!

FRÄULEIN KÖRMENDY God, there's—

FRÄULEIN LÖWENSTAMM —Nästelberger!

MAN ABOUT TOWN *(to snooty lady)* Morning, my dear lady—without your esteemed spouse—? Aha, I've a special reserved seat for your ladyship—just wait a moment!—

(People start to mutter.)

CRIES It's only a film!—A hoax!—Where's Marischka?—Long live Marischka!—But it's a Sascha film!—A hoax—They've had us on!

NEWSPAPER VENDOR Midday Journal! Preparations on the Piave!

SPEAKER Ladies and gentlemen, let us be patient and you will see—

VOICE IN THE CROWD If it's only a Sascha film, they should have said so right away! There are many ladies here who have made a sacrifice for the War Loan, and they're waiting!

CRIES Boo!—Wotta scandal!—Where's Marischka!

SECOND VOICE IN THE CROWD They say Marischka cried off!

A GROUP They're having us on!—We've been standing here a good hour—! We're exhausted!—Our wives—!

ANOTHER GROUP Bravo! Quite right!—Where's the committee?—Boo!

SOMEONE *(arrives panting)* Know what they're saying—Marischka's cried off!

ANOTHER GROUP Of course—I thought as much from the start—he won't be doing the kissing himself!

ELDERLY GENTLEMAN (*humming to himself*) "Call me—your teddy—your teddy bear—"

YOUNG MAN IN BELTED COAT AND WHITE SPATS (*warbles while performing dancelike movements*) "Star-gazer—stargazer—beware and take care—"

HIS FRIEND Look at you, it's really true, you're getting more and more like him.

STEFFI Marischka, the spitting image! Come and let me kiss you!

YOUNG MAN I'm quite capable of standing in for him.

STEFFI Some cheek!

YOUNG MAN Think I'd swap with Marischka—? (*Melody as above*) "I've sold off—18—truckloads" (*Laughter.*)
(*Growing unrest in the crowd.*)

CRIES What's going on?—Committee!—Why were we lured here?—Boo!

AGITATOR It could only happen in Vienna! They think time's no object!

REPRESENTATIVE OF THE FILM COMPANY (*appears*) Ladies and gentlemen, may I most respectfully ask you to calm down! You haven't been deceived! This is a publicity film for the War Loan, commissioned by the Austro-Hungarian War Press Bureau. The announcement, of which the Sascha Film Company had absolutely no prior knowledge, was obviously motivated by some patriotic feeling. We ourselves wanted the filming to take place without any public participation whatsoever, but now that you have appeared—

CRIES Bravo!—We've been had!—Long live Marischka!—Where's Marischka?—We want to see Marischka!!
(*Amidst fervent cries of "Hooray!" and "Boo!" the public presses forward and storms the terrace, numerous chairs and tables are upset, the terrace balustrade is destroyed, and considerable damage is wrought on the other fittings.*)

RESTAURANT PROPRIETOR (*wrings his hands despairingly, but plucks up courage and calls out to the film producer*) You, there—you'll pay for this—I hope!

CROWD Marischka! Marischka! Marischka!

REPRESENTATIVE OF FILM COMPANY (*greatly agitated*) In the circumstances—the filming is cancelled!

CRIES What a nerve!—Think they can get away with anything!—Boo!!—Where's the police?—Scandalous, in the middle of a war!—Everything's falling apart!

(Groups form and heatedly discuss what has happened.)

WIFE So he's not coming! The War Loan can go—

HUSBAND Good God—!

WIFE At least cancel the subscription to *Die Zeit*!

HUSBAND Calm down. So, you see—what did I tell you?!

WIFE Of course—! Now you're happy—! Just like you—! Get out of my sight, I can't stand the sight of you anymore! Putting a damper on everything!—

HUSBAND (*warbling*) "Honey, honey, don't be so hard—"

(The crowd disperses.)

FAT BLACK-MARKETEER Let's buzz off—nothing doing!

NEWSPAPER VENDOR Midday News! The Battle of the Piave! Austrians storm into attack!

(Change of scene.)

Scene 44

Grumbler and Optimist in conversation.

OPTIMIST So what is heroic glory, then?

GRUMBLER This theatre review will tell you. I would like to hear it read out in your voice. If there is a theatre at the front, the theatre here is a front, too. Or vice versa. The switch from one to the other is terrifying.

OPTIMIST (*reads, occasionally raising his voice*)

> Bürgertheater. This evening's performance in the Bürgertheater was dedicated to the widows and orphans of the heroes of Uszieczko. The Reserve Squadron of the Austro-Hungarian Dragoon Regiment *Kaiser Nr. 11* (Lieutenant-colonel Baron Rohn) organized a gala performance for widows and orphans of their comrades who fell at Uszieczko. No one can forget the glorious heroism of the Imperial Dragoons at the bridgehead on the Dniestr. They held the advance post against countless attacks, defied enemy forces many times greater, before their massed forces, after months of bitter fighting, were eventually able to take the bridgehead, which had been reduced to a ruin. *The handful of surviving dragoons*, led by their commander Colonel Planckh, nonetheless *forced their way through the enemy lines to reach our troops. The Viennese public received these gallant survivors of Uszieczko today on the stage of the Bürgertheater and gave them a stirring ovation.* The *splendid idea* to celebrate the heroes of Uszieczko was the basis of the scenic prologue composed for the

occasion by that subtle writer, our own Irma v. Höfer. The scene she chose was where the bitter fighting had taken place, and the painter Ferdinand Moser *magically re-created the landscape of the Dniestr for the stage.* In front of the bridgehead, behind which the Dniestr winds away like a silver thread in the moonlit twilight, is *the encampment of the Imperial Dragoons,* and *those dragoons who peopled the stage today were involved in the terrible fighting on the Dniestr only a short time ago.* Most of them *wore their well-deserved decorations.*

Karl Skoda, a member of the *Royal and Imperial Hofburgtheater,* gave his interpretation of Irma v. Höfer's rich and gripping prologue *in the uniform* of a dragoon officer. It tells of the glory of the Imperial Dragoons, the heroic deeds of the "Eleven", their holding out against all attacks, it is filled with *explosive* enthusiasm and profound empathy. *While he awaits the enemy attack at dawn, an Imperial dragoon thinks of his home, of mother, wife and children, he caresses and kisses the last postcard from his dear ones, before going out to confront the enemy.* Irma v. Höfer's prologue is a poetic and aesthetically pleasing depiction of the Imperial Dragoons' final heroic action, and retraces in broad outline the history of the glorious regiment. After the glowing address of the officer, its rhetorical pulse and mounting emotional impact ravishingly rendered by Karl Skoda, the new regimental song was sung—a composition by Captain of Cavalry Zamorsky, a hero of Uszieczko, *to a rousing text by the wife of Captain of Cavalry Perovic.* Then figures portraying those who raised and led the famous regiment passed before us: Colonel Heissler, Prince Eugene, Radetzky, and, finally, our own Emperor. The regimental bugler sounded the Call to Prayer! *The soldiers on the stage knelt and struck up the national anthem, joined by the public, among whom could be seen, besides the top military brass, also the leading figures in the civilian administration and the most distinguished members of high society.* Tumultuous applause followed this prelude by Frau v. Höfer, who had brought recent events to the stage in such *a palpably vivid* form. Inevitably, there were many curtain calls, and *the packed house cheered the heroes to the rafters, which they gratefully acknowledged, standing to attention and saluting.* Frau v. Höfer received *tumultuous ovations,* and many expressed the wish that further performances might make the poetic work accessible to greater numbers. After the scenic prologue there followed a performance of Eysler's *The Lady Killer,* with Fritz Werner and Betty Myrain in their most brilliant roles.

—No! That can't be true!

GRUMBLER Why ever not?

OPTIMIST *(casts another glance at the paper and says)* The public cheered the heroes to the rafters—which they gratefully acknowledged, standing to attention and saluting. *(Pause. He stares at the Grumbler.)* That can't be true! What—is heroic glory, then?

GRUMBLER A piece of theatre, a play. Or again: a mouldering hill with weeds shooting up like red fire—as a Chinese war poet says. A German door-to-door salesman has much less defeatist thoughts.

OPTIMIST How do you mean? You shouldn't talk about these things like that. Heroic glory is not something hawked door to door.

GRUMBLER Yes, it is. Just read this extract from a specialist journal someone sent me.

OPTIMIST *(reads)*

> *Important announcement for door-to-door salesmen!* If you are interested in a splendid article, selling at 1 Mark, we recommend our patriotic commemorative print: *He died a hero's death for the Fatherland.* The picture measures 44 cm × 60 cm. It takes the form of a highly artistic, imitation copperplate engraving, a fitting wall decoration for any family that has lost one of its dear ones on the field of honour. Beside gripping battle scenes with all kinds of armaments, it depicts a peaceful soldier's grave, with space underneath for the name of the dead and where he fell to be entered. His photograph, framed by a garland of oak leaves, is attached to the centre of the print and glorified by the rays of the Iron Cross above it, while the Goddess of Peace bestows on him the laurel crown of victory. His Majesty the Kaiser can be seen, uttering the memorable words to representatives of the people: "I no longer recognize political parties, I recognize only Germans", and from the clouds shine forth the faces, transfigured, of the founders of the German Reich—Kaiser Wilhelm I., Bismarck, and Moltke. A commemorative print so noble and gripping that rich and poor alike will want it. It far surpasses all that has appeared so far in the genre! Special price for agencies—

—That can't be true!—Tell me, it's—your invention—that it's all your fantasy!

GRUMBLER *(presses his hand)* Thanks for the compliment, but don't you remember? My most lurid fantasies are quotations!

(Change of scene.)

Scene 45

Innsbruck. Maria Theresienstrasse. Midnight. Deserted. Enter a girl holding a sabre in her right hand and waving it about. From the other side, a butcher's boy.

BUTCHER'S BOY Wot's that? (*He recognizes her.*) Oi—(*he grabs the sabre.*)

GIRL WITH SABRE Lego—lego, I'm tell'n'ya—!

BUTCHER'S BOY You're a protestute! You were trying to soilisit me last week! You've no right to have no sabre! (*He wrenches the sabre from her.*) How did someone like you get hold of a sabre with a war going on—

(*Three officers appear running, one without a sabre.*)

OFFICER WITHOUT SABRE (*staggering*) Ah! Who's that with my sabre, then? Give it here, at once! (*He tries to wrench the sabre from the butcher's boy.*)

BUTCHER'S BOY Sorry, Lieutenant, but this lady is well known to me—she's a—she's a protestute—so I'm duty-bound—I've got to bring the sabre to the police station—isn't that right? How did someone like her get hold of a sabre?

OFFICER WITHOUT SABRE (*becoming more forceful*) You, fellow, give it here, or—(*he makes to draw out his sabre from where it normally is.*)

BUTCHER'S BOY There's no way someone like her should have a sabre. I have to report it!

SECOND OFFICER (*draws his sabre*) We don't want any commotion! You rascal, give it back this minute—

THIRD OFFICER (*holding him back*) No commotion! Weber, be sensible! They're all drunk!

BUTCHER'S BOY (*waves the sabre around*) Wot? Drunk? Look at this, Lieutenant, I've got a sabre too!

OFFICER WITHOUT SABRE (*grabs his arm*) Scoundrel!

GIRL WITHOUT SABRE C'm'on, Pipsi, leave 'im alone—he's only a syphilian!

BUTCHER'S BOY Police! Police! We'll see about that!

(*Two policemen appear. Everyone talks to them at once.*)

FIRST POLICEMAN Please! Calm down, please! No bloodshed, Lieutenant—now there's a war on!

THIRD OFFICER Y'hear, no bloodshed, be sensible!

SECOND POLICEMAN Let's all go down to the main police station in the City Hall, we'll get to the bottom of it there.

(*A military inspector appears. Everyone talks to him at once.*)

INSPECTOR What's up? Every night there's something. Aha, her I recognize. Run off with your sabre, eh? You're not the first. Take it! (*He takes the sabre from the butcher's boy and hands it to the lieutenant, who drops it. His comrades come to his aid.*) So what's up with this girl?

BUTCHER'S BOY She tried to soilisit me last week! She's a protestute—she is!

BOTH POLICEMEN (*to girl without sabre*) It seems to me you're not registered!

INSPECTOR (*to lieutenant*) Say, Pöffl, how far did you go with her?

BOTH POLICEMEN (*to girl without sabre*) You're leading a disorderly life, without authorization!

FIRST POLICEMAN On suspicion of venereal disease—

SECOND POLICEMAN —and unregistered prostitution—

BOTH —you'll come with us down to the station!

INSPECTOR Larking about with a sabre when there's a war on—you'll pay dearly for that, my girl. And the third time, too, that I'm aware of.

GIRL WITHOUT SABRE (*pointing to lieutenant*) Oh please, he's my friend. Aren't you, Pipsi, aren't you my friend?

OFFICER WITH SABRE (*pointing to butcher's boy*) Take him, too. He touched my sabre!

BUTCHER'S BOY Oh please, I'm innocent—!

INSPECTOR And did you pay her the wages of sin, Pöffl?

GIRL WITHOUT SABRE (*calling back as she is led away*) I'm not one of them—! I was just looking for a bit of fun!—He owes me 20 crowns—! Twenty crowns—! Swindled me, the rotten devil—

BUTCHER'S BOY What a trollop! The lieutenant surely won't be having anything to do with the likes of her!

OFFICER WITH SABRE He touched my sabre! (*Makes to draw his sabre.*) Front-line rookies! Motherfuckers! Whoever touches me—not so fast—fondles my noodle—for king and cuntry—ooaah—(*He pukes up. The others drag him away. The street is deserted.*)

(*Change of scene.*)

Scene 46

Two devotees of the Reichspost, *asleep.*

FIRST DEVOTEE OF THE *REICHSPOST* (*speaking in his sleep*)—and asked for the homage of his loyal people to be laid on steps of the imperial throne.

Mayor Weiskirchner responded: My beloved Viennese, we are all living through an age of grandeur, in unswerving loyalty we pay homage to our venerable and beloved Emperor, tumultuous cheering, we also remember and honour our ally in shining armour, thunderous applause, and today—

SECOND DEVOTEE OF THE *REICHSPOST* (*speaking in his sleep*)—and today the Italian ambassador visited our minister to deliver the solemn declaration that loyal Italy stands side by side with Austria, delirious storm of ovation—Dagoes!—

FIRST In Prague, Brno, and Budweis—everywhere they are rejoicing at the Emperor's decisions.

SECOND At the Emperor's summer residence in Bad Ischl!

FIRST In Sarajevo they sang God Preserve our Gracious Emperor.

SECOND Prince Alfred Windischgrätz has volunteered for military service.

FIRST His Majesty has been straining every nerve and sinew all day long.

SECOND The Father of the Army.

FIRST On 27 July 1914, between 12 noon and 1 pm, the financial arrangements for the war were finalized at the Post Office Savings Bank.

SECOND The supply of provisions to Vienna for the duration of the war was settled by the Mayor in collaboration with the prime minister and the minister of agriculture.

FIRST No price rises because of the war.

SECOND Nothing but enhanced virtues.

FIRST What a treasure trove of enhanced virtues has already been bestowed upon us by this war!

SECOND War is a harsh taskmaster for the nations.

FIRST A Promethean bringer of light and clarity.

SECOND Light-bringing—life-giving—Dagoes!

FIRST Wars are processes that reform people's character and purify them, they're seedbeds of virtue and inspiration for heroes.

SECOND A renaissance of Austrian thought and action.

FIRST A clean sweep!

SECOND Rat-a-tat-tat—and that's that!

FIRST We are for peace, though not for peace at—

SECOND —at all costs!

FIRST In Lemberg we are still—

SECOND —holding on.

FIRST First take Belgrade, then take a second breakfast—intimate family affair—then a relaxing stroll—

SECOND —with a spring in our steps and a song in our hearts—

FIRST Confound their politics—

SECOND —Frustrate their knavish tricks—

BOTH —Long to reign over us, God save the Emperor!
(Change of scene.)

Scene 47

First-class compartment. In the unlit corridor a pile of luggage and bodies.

LIEUTENANT-COLONEL MADERER VON MULLATSCHAK OF THE GENERAL STAFF *(lies drunk in the compartment, mumbling)* Nice bit o' fluff—for blindman's buff—my popsy wopsy!—Woops!—Ups-a-daisy—drives me crazy—can't get enough! D'you get that half ton of dried veg.?—What? What? No, no, no!—Y'don't mean it? 100,000 crowns a truckload, you've clinched it?!—I haven't yet—you little rascal! little rascal!—I—I've—a co—loss—al deal in pork bellies—up my—sleeve—no, not thieves, sleeves!—Kinkering Congs their titles take—he can kiss my arse—What? That idiotic point of honour—Le—Leleopold—he can take his Lleopold Order and st—I'll bang out the "Radetzky March" on yr backside today—point of honour!—scum!—let'm tell his mother-in-law if he wants—she knows how to cut a deal—or his aunt—good luck t'em!—if I cd make 'em an Arch-duch-ess-timate—I'd clean out the Treasury—and that Sal—Salvator!—ye gods, what a laugh!—what, my pet?—what a load of tripe!—I'm covered—what—Mariska darling—hee hee, ho, ho!—I'm—top-notch—with a nice savings account—that's *my* point of honour!—Woops!—Ups-a-daisy—my popsy wopsy!—all I say is—I'm very pleased with this war!—Five thousand crowns con—com—commission on every truckload—all registered as military con—consignments—the Jew—pays on the nail—but don't 'magine—don't 'magine I haven't turned a trick or two myself—oh, those pork bellies—those pork bellies—you'll see—who're you starin' at? profeshnal misconduct?—civilian scum—Woops!—I had all the others thrown out of the compartment—you know the rest—my popsy wopsy—hope they drop dead—let'em go hang—no wait, let us string 'em up—kick the bucket—for the Fatherland, if they're—beyond the pale—Attent—shun!—that drunk—hic!—I had 'im shot—I'm covered—popsy wopsy—I'll bring you—guess, guess!—tasty, eh?—pork bellies—50 kilos!—*(Starts, looks at his watch.)* What—11 already?

We're almost there—in Steinbrück—woops!—oh!—now—now—if they just do what they were told—I sent instructions—by telephone—that what's-his-name should—keep the express train waiting—little does he know, the idiot—that it's—all for you, my tasty little piece of tail—Christ alive, I've got a letch for you right now—why isn't he here yet—my batman, that lazy cow—we're almost in Styria—Steinbrück—the bridge—Horatius stood—upon the bridge—brr!—who're you *starin'* at?—Stein—Steinbrück—if he hasn't messed things up—That was (*yawn*)—some sleep!—Oh, it's all—a load of—tripe—

(Change of scene.)

Scene 48

At 3,000 metres.

OFFICER CADET (*half asleep*) Four years—God, oh God, what's—it—all—for—Helene—oh—where—are—you—

(Alice Schalek appears.)

ALICE SCHALEK So, what are you feeling right now, what are you thinking about, you must be thinking of something—(*Artillery salvo.*)

(Change of scene.)

Scene 49

Optimist and Grumbler in conversation.

OPTIMIST If only it were over! What do you say about the English and French desecrating the graves and corpses? German propaganda maintains that the bones of the fallen are being processed and fat extracted from the corpses.

GRUMBLER I can't check if that's true, but as a metaphor it seems to authenticate a higher reality: it corresponds to how things generally happen in the world, and it perfectly depicts the use those left alive make of heroic death and glory for their aspirations and interests.

OPTIMIST To hear you talk, you'd really think the spiritual uplift that everyone expects hasn't actually occurred.

GRUMBLER I almost believe that myself. But I also believe that this bloodbath, which those responsible wanted to tempt people to accept because of such uplift, will end as the greatest bankruptcy the planet has ever endured. Above all in the empires of this misconceived central Europe. For we spread murder and rape and pillage with the Bible in one hand and fairy tales in the other. We wanted to conquer the global market like knights in shining armour, but we'll have to make do with selling everything off in the flea market—at bargain basement prices.

OPTIMIST (*tries to light a cigarette*) Funny, the match won't light.

GRUMBLER That's because of the ultimatum to Serbia.

OPTIMIST I said, the match won't light!

GRUMBLER And I say, that's because we managed to set the world alight!

OPTIMIST Is there a connection here, too?

GRUMBLER The closest of all! There is nothing in our daily lives that has remained unchanged, neither our inner nor our outer lives, neither here nor abroad, neither values nor prices. If a statesman alive in 1914 had had enough imagination to know that a match would not light in 1918, he would not have set the world on fire! He would have visualized the war he was about to declare, and the peace as well, with all the growing misery it would, and will, bring.

OPTIMIST But when peace finally comes—

GRUMBLER —then the war begins!

OPTIMIST But every war so far has been concluded by a peace.

GRUMBLER Not this one. It didn't play out on the surface of life, but in its very core. The fighting front has expanded back into the hinterland. There it will stay. And our same old mental attitudes will be applied to an altered life—if there still is life. Like the sun, the world will set, and we won't notice. All our yesterdays will be forgotten; we will not see what today means; nor fear for the future. We will have forgotten that we lost the war, forgotten that we started it, forgotten that we waged it. That is why it will never cease.

OPTIMIST But when peace has finally come—

GRUMBLER —we won't be able to get enough of war!

OPTIMIST You even grumble about the future. I am and will remain an optimist. The nations will bite the bullet—

GRUMBLER —and make it even more destructive! So dumb! Dumdum!

(Change of scene.)

Scene 50

Swiss mountain railway.

Two enormous blobs of fat, whose indescribable proportions defy all human criteria, occupy the whole of one bench. The winter sports breeches and long woollen socks of the one reveal two distinct masses of flesh; the creature has massive cheeks with bluish shadows, a tufted moustache gleams under saucer eyes like a black shrub, exposing two blubbery lips. The other—a recently arrived business partner on a visit—is encased in a shabby winter overcoat. No neck, only a quadruple chin mediates between the spherical body and the spherical head, the whole completely undifferentiated and resembling a globefish. Both have alpenstocks. The former's wife is sitting on the bench opposite, wearing a brooch inscribed "Gott strafe England!" They are the giants Gog & Magog. Through the window can be seen a landscape of glittering snow under a deep blue sky.

GOG Luverly pictures—that's what I want next. They doan 'ave ter be Rembrandts or Böcklins—

MAGOG I've got masses of 'em already.

GOG A luverly picture is really luverly, Trudchen, don'tya think? Giv'us a nice big smacker, then. (*He kisses her.*)

MAGOG (*after a pause*) If you doan get rich in this war, you doan deserve to live through it.

GOG Sure thing.

MAGOG I'm goan for miniatures now, sixteenth century are best, tapestries too, snuffboxes, albums of coats of arms, stuff like that—gives me a kick. Cultural knickknacks, the older the better—that's what I'm after.

GOG And what about your books, then? That lad of yours is one of the best in the German rare-book business right now—

MAGOG Yeah, we buy up all the numbered editions on handmade paper that come on the market. Soon there woan be nothin left. Before I left Berlin, I bought 60,000 marks worth of books, all bound in leather—gotta be leather. My taste is for Dutch-printed uncut books—Enschedé en Zonen—on handmade van Geldern paper. Gotta be handmade. Next comes imperial Japanese vellum, parchment-backed, and at a pinch Old Stratford half-linen.

GOG (*glances at the newspaper*) Hey, what d'ya think about this, then: (Wolff News Agency)—"60,000 kilos of bombs dropped in 24 hours!—All of Dunkirk in flames! An extraordinary achievement for our bomber squadrons. Their indubitable effectiveness in bombing Fortress London also confirmed."

MAGOG We're wiping 'em out on the Western Front.

GOG Must be over the moon, those fighter pilots of ours! You've gotta read von Richthofen's book—the one Ullstein published—to get a sense of it! The way he blitzed those Russki railway stations—you can really feel the thrill of bombing! Great story, the way he worked his way up from a boring backroom job to undisputed ace fighter pilot! Must feel over the moon to have it all spread out beneath you, and you can smash everything—like a king, loaded with bombs, like a god!

MAGOG Our U-boats aren't exactly paper tigers, either.

GOG No, certainly not. (*Glances in the paper.*) Getta load of this: (Wolff News Agency)—"Few people can fully appreciate what a magnificent achievement it was yet again for our U-boats to have sunk 16 steamers yesterday and today, as reported, while the steamer that was shot at, but which unfortunately escaped, will certainly be out of action for several months at least."

MAGOG Yes, our boys in blue are on the ball.

GOG And listen to this, the 42-cm cannon will teach those rogues a lesson good and proper. That shot into the church the other day, slap bang into their festivities—boy oh boy, that'll learn 'em!

MAGOG Another two months at most, and England will be on its knees. Maybe three. Sorted. Defeatism is in the air. You can tell that from all that humanitarian bleating we're hearing again.

GOG Total humbug. What d'ya think of their protest against the use of poison gas?

MAGOG Probably shows our gases are more effective.

GOG Exactly! We Germans welcome all attempts to make international law and humanity prevail, but we refuse to be taken for a ride.

MAGOG We shall observe further developments on this issue calmly and with a clear conscience.

GOG Getta load of this—the same old story! The old chestnut about negotiations! Reuters accuses us of dodging the issue by not "clearly and honestly subscribing to the principles of a future system of international law." D'y'ever hear such claptrap!

MAGOG International law? We've got poison gas!

TRUDCHEN (*pointing out of the window*) Oh hubby darling, just *look* at that—!

GOG Yes, luverly. But until we have broken the destructive will of the enemy—

MAGOG Oh, do spare me the lousy lies of the Allies. Always blathering about their negotiated peace!

GOG Bunkum! Those guys can't fool us. What we need is a peace on German terms, and a peace on German terms is no soft touch—understand that, Lloyd George, my fine friend!

MAGOG Spot-on! We'll soon put that lot to bed, make no mistake! Sorted! A lousy bunch of gangsters, I'm telling you. They're trying to make out that America wouldn't have got involved if we hadn't intensified the U-boat war. But the U-boat war can't be intensified enough! That Wilson—an arch-hypocrite and a no-brainer, don'tya think?

GOG I've had it up to here with him!

MAGOG He's a nonstarter!

GOG Sheer bluff! Scheming nonstop! Here's how things stand: thanks to our towering triumph at Brest-Litovsk, we freed up an enormous number of troops. Once the Russkies have been finished off, *then* everything else follows. *Then* our little friends will start feeling the heat. *Then* let Uncle Sam come across the Pond!

MAGOG At all events, we've got Belgium as security. We need a solid naval base, we need a robust air base, we need colonies, and, of course, we need that iron-ore basin. Not to mention all the *other* things we need. Everyone can see our heavy industry needs to be fully operational—except our idiotic enemies. If there's to be any talk of peace, under no circumstances must we enter into negotiations about Alsace-Lorraine!

GOG Absolutely. The enemy's double-talk is a clear sign they doan want peace.

MAGOG They're just stuck in a rigid mentality and can't get out.

GOG At least we now know who's procastinating the war. As to who started it—we've known that all along.

MAGOG All we Germans can do is see it through to the bitter end.

GOG If those League of Nations twits maintain they're fighting for a moral idea, we have to answer with brute force. Just let that clown on the other side of the Pond try it on with his "humanity."

MAGOG I always say—patience and keep your powder dry. They won't believe their eyes when they find us Berliners—whoosh!—in Baghdad. By express train!

GOG (*looking out of the window*) Still not there?—Run out of steam, have we?—Surely not!—What d'ya think of our guys interned in Switzerland—sturdy fellows, eh?

MAGOG Oh, you mean the Hindenburg pageant on the Rütli Meadow?

GOG And the Rütli Oath—they've even compared that to our Oath of Allegiance!

MAGOG Splendid, I'd like to have been there, too! When *our* confederates come marching in, that'll put new wind in their sails, oh yes! What d'ya say to our plucky compatriots in Lugano? They really made it so uncomfortable for the enemy consuls, they were obliged to leave the hotel, the manager had to give in.

GOG There's not enough action. Switzerland needs ethnic cleansing! There was someone speaking French in the tram in Zurich the other day! I kicked up a shindy at once, told the fellow to his face that that was a breach of neutrality.

You should've been there! The scoundrel was too flabbergasted to speak! Then in Berne, Trudchen was in a cake shop and insisted the assistant say cream, not *crème*. They'd run out of cream, but still Trudchen stuck to her guns. Didn't you, Trudikins? Giv'us a nice big smacker, then. (*He kisses her.*)

TRUDCHEN Yes, my darling doodle.

MAGOG Sadly, those are just isolated incidents. Our embassy should take a much tougher line. We're not doing half enough to win the sympathy of the neutrals.

GOG Our propaganda isn't working. Sure, now and again the odd bomb gets dropped, but it all turns sour.

MAGOG And it'll get worse—there'll be a heavy price to pay. It's true they'll be afraid of us after we've won the war, but we should be putting out feelers already and making 'em love us to bits.

GOG Oh, things won't change much here, one way or the other. Back home—yes; but—

MAGOG So what d'ya think'll be the difference between the time before the war and, y'know, the time after the war—in general?

GOG Very simple. Before the war we worked from eight to seven, after the war we'll work from seven to eight.

MAGOG Absolutely. British envy—

GOG French revanchism and

MAGOG —Russian rapacity

GOG —forced this war upon us.

MAGOG But I'll tell ya this—foreigners are still a factor we mustn't ignore! Even when they're beaten, we have to make ourselves respected and loved! That's vital, believe you me. Defusing hatred—that's what real propaganda should be aiming at. Even if they've been bled white, those jerks must never be allowed to forget that we are the Nation of Poets and Thinkers!
(*From the next compartment comes the sound of a French song.*)

GOG What a nerve! In a neutral country! Let's show 'em who's in charge! (*He strikes up "Deutschland, Deutschschland über alles." Magog joins in, also Trudchen. The song from the next compartment breaks off.*)

MAGOG Aha—here we are! (*They waddle out of the compartment.*)

GOG (*outside*) Well, just look at *that* sunshine, and *that* sky!

MAGOG Big business! And that snow is worth every cent!

GOG And the glacier—they doan make 'em like that every day!

MAGOG And the air—!

GOG You can forget about your gas mask here! Ahh—the Fountain of Youth! At last Germany has its place in the sun!—boy, oh boy! (*half singing*) No froggy officers cross the Rhine, parlez-vous! Well, Trudikins? Aren't you pleased your hubby doesn't have to fight-for-'is-Fatherland, eh?

TRUDCHEN Yes, Siegfried darling.

(As the group moves off, it is as if their giant black silhouette momentarily blots out the glittering white and blue of the whole universe.)

(Change of scene.)

Scene 51

A barracks in Siberia. Undernourished men, their hair turned grey, barefoot, in tattered uniforms, crouch on the ground, vacantly staring out into the distance. A few are asleep, a few are writing.

AN AUSTRIAN CAPTAIN (*enters and shouts*) You filthy swine!

(They rise and perform a salute. While some stand to attention, the others practise rifle drill with shovels.)

(Change of scene.)

Scene 52

Northern Railway Station, Vienna. The platform bathed in pale morning light. Refreshments for the troops. Officials, dignitaries. A prisoner-of-war exchange train has just arrived carrying wounded soldiers. Bodies writhing in convulsions are unloaded from the carriages on stretchers. The stretchers are lined up.

A VOICE Make sure the relatives don't push to the front.

(Members of the association Laurels for Our Heroes and officials in formal dress take up position in front of the waiting crowd. A military band arrives.)

A SECOND VOICE Two hours late it was, now it's 'ere and we've been standin 'ere for two hours and still them as oughta be 'ere ain't 'ere.

A THIRD VOICE So what—eight days from Sweden, can't complain!

(Ten gentlemen in frockcoats arrive and position themselves in such a way that they can observe what's happening, but almost completely block off the view to others. From the moment they arrive, the stretchers are no longer visible. While each of the 10 takes out a notebook, two officials approach the group and exchange introductions.)

ZAWADIL Spielvogel.

SPIELVOGEL Zawadil.

BOTH (*speaking together*) A dismal morning. We've been here since six to make the arrangements.

ANGELO EISNER V. EISENHOF (*joins them and speaks intently with one of the 10. They all begin to write. He points to various figures who crane their necks and try to push forward through the rows of people. He motions to each in reassurance, gesturing towards the 10 and miming the act of writing, as if to signal that their presence has been duly noted. Meanwhile Hofrat Schwarz-Gelber and his wife have managed to get close to those writing and to tap one of them on the shoulder.*)

HOFRAT SCHWARZ-GELBER & HOFRÄTIN SCHWARZ-GELBER No power on earth could have kept us from being here in person.

SECTION HEAD WILHELM EXNER I am here as a pioneer in the field of artificial limbs.

DOBNER V. DOBENAU As Lord High Steward I should rightly be in there with the pillars of society.

RIEDL At the Adria Exhibition I had dealings with His Imperial Highness, as chairman of the committee striving to ensure we continue undaunted along the path on which we had already embarked.

STUKART My presence is required as a matter of course.

SIEGHART Today I am Chief Executive.

ANGLOBANK PRESIDENT LANDESBERGER They call me a financial tycoon.

A VOICE Come and stand here, you'll see them better, the returning warriors.

ANOTHER VOICE They say it took them eight weeks to cross Siberia. There are so many train delays these days—

A MOTHER Don't go too close, you never know what diseases they might be spreading. Look at that one writhing around.

HER DAUGHTER No wonder, if he's been shot in the stomach.

DR. CHARAS Under my direction the First Aid service has also turned out for this occasion, though there have not yet been many opportunities to assist. (*Meanwhile a lady in deepest mourning has entered. Everyone makes way for her.*)

FRAU SCHWARZ-GELBER (*thunderstruck, elbows her husband in the ribs and says)* What did I tell you! She turns up everywhere she isn't wanted. Can't one ever be among one's own kind!

FLORA DUB How peaceful they look, lying there!

NEWSPAPER EDITOR *(to his neighbour)* Write how the eyes of the returning warriors are shining.

TWO CONSULS *(exchange introductions)* Stiassny. We have hastened to get here.

THREE HONORARY COUNSELLORS *(appear side by side)* We come as delegates of the Laurels for Our Heroes campaign, to pay tribute to the returning representatives of our glorious army.

SUKFÜLL As a delegate commissioned by the committee, let me take this opportunity to respond wholeheartedly to the joy of our valiant warriors, who, though in distant parts, have invariably demonstrated their concern for our interests, and can now rest assured of the success of their efforts. Though it cannot be denied that the hotel industry has suffered because of the war, and though tourism was also handicapped by difficulties with food supplies, we cannot close our eyes to the glorious fighters who have bled for the honour of the House of Habsburg.

BIRINSKI & GLÜCKSMANN The fine arts have sent us here today as their representatives.

HANS MÜLLER Let it be! Those contemplating these frail creatures, who are now received into hospital care at the end of their journey home, will be shaken to the very core of their being, as if vouchsafed a sudden glimpse through a crack at life's dying embers.

(People appear, men and women, who have made helpful suggestions, led by Honorary Counsellor Moriz Putzker.)

PUTZKER At my suggestion, in order to calculate exactly the duration of their captivity, our prisoners of war in Siberia kept a record of the hours up to their arrival.

(The "Prince Eugene March" strikes up. Some of the disabled soldiers faint.)

THE MOTHER Don't get too close, I've told you why.

THE DAUGHTER Oh God, I've given refreshment to so many sufferers already!

(A commotion arises. One of the ones who had fainted has died.)

A VOICE Look at the expression on his face. Like he's in bliss to be at journey's end.

ANOTHER VOICE What's keeping Hugo Heller?

A THIRD VOICE He will live on in the annals of history.

DOBNER V. DOBENAU As Lord High Steward I should rightly be—

HUGO HELLER, BOOKSELLER (*has forced his way through*) Thanks to my extensive cultural contacts it would surely have been easy for me to have established an attachment to those who are now beyond the world of culture, had it not been for the fact already noted that death intervened.

HANS MÜLLER Let it be!

(*While officials distribute war medals among the disabled, the "Radetzky March" strikes up.*)

NEWSPAPER EDITOR (*to his neighbour*) Describe how they listen entranced!

(*Change of scene.*)

Scene 53

A deserted street. Nightfall. Suddenly figures rush in from all sides, each with a bundle of newspapers, breathless, corybants and maenads; they tear madly up and down the street, yelling as if to announce a murder. Their cries are unintelligible. Some seem to groan as they announce their news. It sounds as if the woes of all mankind were being drawn up from a deep well.

Ex-tra-aa edi-shun—!—stradishun—!—xtradishun—! Both muniqués—! Cmuniqués—! Stradishun—! Extraa—!—dishun—! shun—Late Night Ex-tra-aa—!

(*They disappear. The street is deserted.*)

(*Change of scene*)

Scene 54

Grumbler at his desk.

He is reading.

> Wishing to determine the exact time a tree growing in a forest requires to become transformed into a newspaper, the proprietor of a paper mill in the Harz Mountains conducted an interesting experiment. At 7.35 am he had three trees felled in the nearby forest, and after the bark was removed, had them transported to his pulp mill. The conversion of the three trunks into pulp was so swift that the first roll of newsprint emerged from the machine by 9.39 am. This was promptly delivered by motor car to the printers of a daily paper four kilometres away, and by 11 o'clock the newspaper was for sale on the street. Accordingly, it took no more than

3 hours 25 minutes for the public to be reading the latest news on material produced from trees on whose branches, that very morning, the birds had still been chirping.

(From outside, the very distant cry: "—Ex—traaa!")

So, it's five minutes before midnight. The answer has come. The echo of my bloodstained insanity, and this is the only sound I hear reverberating from the ruins of creation, the sound from which ten million dying men accuse me of still being alive, of having had eyes to see and a vision so precise that this world became what I saw. If such carnage was heaven's idea of justice, it was surely unjust not to have destroyed me first! Did I deserve to see my fear of a living death fulfilled? What is it that haunts my nights? Why was I chosen only to vindicate the prophetic railing of Thersites, not to forestall the heroic posturing of Achilles? Why was I not granted the physical strength to free this planet from its sinfulness with a single blow of the axe? Why was I not granted the intellectual power to compel suffering humanity to cry for help? Why is my cry of protest not stronger than the hollow words of command that held dominion over the souls of the whole created world?

I have preserved documents for an epoch that will no longer comprehend them or will say that I forged them, so remote will they be from today. But that day will never come for there will be no survivors. I have written a tragedy whose doomed hero is mankind; whose tragic conflict, that of the world with nature, ends in extinction. Because this drama has no hero other than mankind, it will sadly have no audience. But what caused the death of my tragic hero? Was the world order stronger than the hero's personality? No, the laws of nature were stronger than the world order. We are torn apart by a fundamental falsehood: the hollowness displacing traditional humanity has been projected into anachronistic life-forms. The merchant masquerading as hero, compelled to fight heroically so as to succeed commercially! He is destroyed by a toxic mix of compulsion and euphoria. Who are the guilty men? There are none, otherwise there would be retribution, otherwise mankind, my hero, would have resisted the curse of being enslaved by the means at his disposal and martyred by what he took to be necessity. For if the means of subsistence erode the purpose of existence, they enslave us to the instruments of death and even poison the survivors.

If there were guilty men, mankind would have resisted the compulsion to fight heroically for such a shallow cause! There would have been a concerted reaction against those who ordered it. But those men are not tyrants. Their mindset is cut from the same cloth as that of the masses. We are all isolated. We each suffer our own pain and it doesn't flare up in others. And we don't flare up at the contrast between our daily sacrifice and the profit—the cruel profit—others gain from it. Tyrants would yield to insurrection. But time after time we would have replaced them with new tyrants from within ourselves. For we all submit to the petty tyranny—not of the autocrat but of the machine. The revolver is powerless against mechanized warfare. Unlike William Tell's crossbow, which slew the tyrant Gessler, the bullet simply bounces back. We're trapped by our own inventions, and what threatens our backs is not the machine gun, but the unholy miracle that such a thing exists. Our enterprise loses the name of action because of threats of our own creation.

No single person can reverse the process by commanding us to destroy our weapons! Can I speak in a European forum? Thus you will be forced to go on dying for something to which you attach the name of honour or Bukovina without knowing what is at stake, for the weaponry itself is in command! What did you die for? If your minds had grasped the contrasts, your bodies would have been spared the torments. Contempt for death? Why should you despise what you don't know? One may well feel contempt for the life one doesn't know, that's true. You will only get to know it when a piece of shrapnel fortuitously doesn't quite kill you, or when the beast in charge, foaming at the mouth, formerly a human being like yourself, comes down on you like a ton of bricks and you are momentarily conscious of standing on the edge of an abyss. And the beast in charge has the nerve to report that you defied death? And that you didn't use that moment to shout at your superior that he wasn't superior to God, and couldn't order Him to unmake His creation. No, you let him drive you out—claiming God on his side—into that breach where mysteries begin beyond the ken of earthly kingdoms! To which each nation sends its heroes, from which no spy returns! If only you had known, at the moment of your sacrifice, about the war profits accumulating in spite of—no, *because of*—your sacrifice, growing fat on it! For until this still inconclusive war of machines there have never been such ungodly profits, and you, win or lose, will have lost the war from which your murderers will have profited. Your craven, technically sophisticated murderers who can kill, and live, only at a distance from the scene of their crimes.

From my own circle, Franz Grüner, you pure-hearted friend who followed my writings with eyes raised to the heaven of art, softly and studiously listening to its heartbeat. Why, dear Franz, did you too have to die? I saw you on the day you left. Rain and the dirt of our Austrian Fatherland with its strident music marked your departure as they crammed you into the cattle truck! I see your pale face amid the orgy of filth and lies as we parted so painfully at the freight depot used for "human raw materials", following the cruel command that mobilizes bodies while paralysing minds, transforming condemned men into the hapless victims of cattle drivers. You looked so out of place, you might have died from the shock of this initiation, compared with which *Wallenstein's Camp* seemed like the foyer of a Grand Hotel! For the victims of machines become grimy before they are gory. So began that legendary Italian Journey for you, a student of fine art!

And you, Franz Janowitz, with your noble poet's heart? Amidst the shrieks of mortars and murderers you devoted yourself to the mysterious music of words. As you spent four years of your springtime underground, were you trying out your future abode? What were you looking for? Lice for the Fatherland? Waiting for the shrapnel to arrive? To prove that, faced with the firepower of the Schneider-Creusot factories, your body was more resistant than that of some soldier from Turin faced with the power of Skoda? Are we merely travelling salesmen for arms factories, compelled to advertise their products not by word of mouth, but by using our bodies to demonstrate the inferiority of the competition? When travellers set out, cripples return! It was bad enough to turn export markets into battlefields. But compelling noble spirits to serve as drudges—the Devil himself would never have dared imagine such a consolidation of his domain. For the Devil would have supported a compromise peace, instead of urging childlike nations more fervently to do his bidding—if one had whispered to him that, in the first year of the war alone, a petroleum refinery would achieve a net profit of 137 percent on its total share-capital and David Fanto 73 percent, the Creditanstalt 19.9 million crowns net profit; and that profiteers would be compensated a hundredfold for the losses of other people's blood by speculating in meat and sugar and alcohol and fruit and potatoes and butter and leather and rubber and coal and iron and wool and soap and oil and ink and weapons. And that is why you lay in mud and slime for four years, that is why letters from home took so long to arrive, and why books sent to comfort you were delayed. They wanted you still alive, for they had not yet stolen enough on their stock markets, lied enough in their newspapers, or chivvied people enough in government offices; they had not yet whipped mankind into utter frenzy, not yet finished using the war as an excuse for the incompetence and sadism of all their doings, hoping the magnitude of their crimes would exonerate them. They had not danced the last dance and begun their fast at the end of this whole tragic carnival, in which men died before the eyes of a female war correspondent and bloodthirsty generals became honorary doctors of philosophy! And so you lay for weeks on end under mortar fire; were threatened by avalanches; suspended from a rope at 3,000 metres between the enemy barrage and equally devastating "friendly fire"—the treachery of that phrase!—exposed a hundred times to the prolonged torments of the condemned man, often enough without the condemned man's last meal; forced to experience the deadly clash of man and machine in all its guises—high-explosive mines, barbed-wire entanglements, spiked obstacles, dumdum bullets, bombs, flames, and gases and the seven hells of artillery bombardment—and all because those idiots and profiteers had not yet lost their appetite for war! Exposed to such terrors, you were still expected to remain "fit for service", assuming that mankind had not been inoculated with enough syphilis to compensate for the death of the imagination?

How much longer are you people at the front, like us at home, expected to keep staring into the graves that we had to dig for ourselves on orders from above? Graves like those the old men in Serbia were forced to dig, for the sole reason that they were Serbs and still alive, and hence suspect! Supposing that our bodies were unscathed, though careworn, impoverished, and aged by this adventure—supposing by the magic of divine retribution we could call them individually to account, those irrepressible conspirators of global crimes: then we would lock them in their churches and, just as they did to the old men in Serbia, have every tenth man draw his death sentence by lot! But then not kill them—no, merely slap their faces! And then address them thus: So, you wretches, you didn't know, didn't suspect, that among the millions of horrific and ignominious consequences of a declaration of war would be children without milk, horses without oats, and men blinded by methyl alcohol even though far from the front, if it so suited the strategy of the war profiteers? So, you didn't ever fathom the misery of even one hour for a man held captive for years on end? Of one sigh of longing for a love which has been defiled, torn asunder, and annihilated. Were you not even able to imagine the glimpse of gaping hell as a mother listens, day and night, waiting for years on end for news—of a hero's death?

Did you not sense how tragedy turned into farce, an operetta fusing innovative trash with anachronistic conventions, one of those repulsive modern operettas whose libretto is an insult and orchestration sheer torture? And did you not sense how the most insignificant of your orders, even the most trivial consequence of your most insignificant order—say, the idiocy that made it difficult to register a change of address, unleashed the various war surveillance departments against one another, causing intense confusion? Your passport offices, passport directive offices, passport modification offices, border crossing permit offices, registration authorities, border protection agencies—did you not sense that the most insignificant measure resulting from those crazy controls would stamp an indelible mark of infamy on human dignity? And you overlooked the fact that when you had dressed everyone up in uniform, they would all have to salute each other continuously. And you didn't notice that one day, all of a sudden, this gesture was no more than the tapping of one's forehead to signify doubts as to the other's sanity. And that the disabled were twitching and shaking their heads at you, and you alone? And still you continued your pursuit of the doomed glory that was bleeding the world dry!

And you there who were slaughtered, why did you not rise from the grave to protest against this regime? Against this murderous system, this war economy that condemned all future life to "holding out to the bitter end", blocking all prospects and sacrificing the pursuit of even the slightest happiness to the hatred of nations. Guilty of the absurd ravages of war, and of senseless ravages against each and everyone under the pretext of war! This system spread monstrous poverty, starvation, and ignominy among refugees and natives alike, confining and constricting one and all, wherever they may be. Was it not the duty of statesmen, in times of precipitous decline, to restrain man's bestial urges? Yet it was those statesmen who unleashed them! Contempt for life, tolerating peacetime violence against animals and children, has cravenly seized upon the war machine to lay waste all that grows. Hysteria, under the mantle of technology, overwhelms nature, newsprint mobilizes weapons. The rotary press made cripples of us all before we succumbed to cannon fire.

Were not all the realms of imagination evacuated when that famous manifesto declared war on all the peoples of the world? At the end was—the Word. Having killed the spirit, the printed word had no alternative but to bring forth the Deed. Weaklings gained the strength to crush us under the wheels of progress. It was the newspaper press that achieved this, the press above all—the harlot that corrupted the world! Not that the press set the engines of death in motion—but that it hollowed out our heart and made us incapable of imagining what it would be like: that is its war guilt! From the wine of her fornication all nations have drunk, and the kings of the earth have committed fornication with her. And the apocalyptic rider found favour with her, the apocalyptic rider whom I once saw, long before it came to pass, storm through the German Reich. A decade has passed since I saw his task fulfilled. "There he goes, charging full tilt! His moustache stretches from the rising to the setting of the sun, from north to south. 'And power was given unto him who sat thereon to take peace from the earth, so that they should slay one another.'" And I pictured the Kaiser as the beast with 10 horns and seven heads and his mouth as the mouth of a lion. "And they worshipped the beast, saying Who is like unto the beast? And who is able to make war with him? And there was given unto him a mouth speaking great things." And through him we fell, and through the Whore of Babylon, who in the tongues of all the peoples persuaded us we were enemies and must wage war!

And you, the victims, why did you not rise up against that strategy—against the compulsion to die with the option of becoming murderous fire-raisers? Against the diabolical plan that clothed the conquest of the textile market in the sacrificial colours of a moral crusade! Manipulating reverence for God in order to obtain approval for profits sealed in blood! All sovereign rights and essential values traded away for a single Idea—materialism. The child in its mother's womb subjected to the imperative of hate, and the image of fighting manhood, and even of caring womanhood, swathed in armour and gas masks, a horde of mythical creatures created to make posterity's flesh creep. Shooting at the faithful with shells recast from church bells and unrepentant before altars made of shrapnel! So that was what constituted Glory and Fatherland! Oh yes, you discovered what Fatherland meant even before you died for it! Fatherland began the moment you had to wait in death's departure hall, naked amid the stench of sweat and beer, while they examined men's bodies and extorted from their souls a godless oath of loyalty. Naked you were, as before God and your beloved, facing a draft board of swinish tormentors. Shame, shame for your body, shame for your soul should have compelled you to reject the call of patriotism. We have all seen it, this Fatherland, and the final glimpse of it for those fortunate enough to have escaped was the insolent border guard. We saw it in the protean lust for power of the liberated slave and the affable blackmailer greedy for his perks. Except that we noncombatants did not experience it in the shape of the enemy—the real enemy, who used friendly fire to make you face the foe's machine guns.

Truly, we would have wished to call time on this bloodstained bordello even if we'd only seen it in the portraits of those monstrous generals, profiled like high-class prostitutes in the theatrical scandal sheets as symbols of a world where fornication was outstripped by slaughter! How could you, poor mangled dupes, not rise again to denounce their perfidy? How could you tolerate the freedom and the frolics of those press strategists, parasites, and buffoons, while enduring your own misery under orders? You knew that they were awarded medals for what you suffered. Why did you not spit their glory in their face? You lay in hospital trains which those scoundrels were permitted to portray. Why did you not break out, desert, and join the holy war to liberate us at home from our mortal enemy, who bombarded our brains day after day with their lies? And you died for this business? You lived out the horror and thereby prolonged the agony for those of us struggling for breath, caught between loan sharks and penury, tortured by the contrast between well-fed insolence and consumptive silence. Alas, you felt less for us than we for you, for we strove to reclaim a hundredfold each hour of those long years that they tore from your lives, with a single question on our lips: What will you look like if you survive such torments? If you avoid the crowning glory: that the hyenas become tourist guides and your graves tourist attractions! Stricken, impoverished, demoralized, lice-infested, starving, snuffed out, sacrificed for the tourist industry—must this be our shared destiny?

They sold your skins on the world market, while their cunning created wallets out of ours. You had weapons—yet you did not invade this hinterland? You did not turn from the field of shame to launch the most just of wars, to save both us and yourselves. And you do not rise from your final foxholes to call the whole base breed to account, to haunt their sleep with your distorted grimace as you breathed your last, your eyes clouded in heroic anticipation, the unforgettable expression of doomed youth—doomed by orchestrated insanity! Arise and confront them with your heroic death, so that those cowards who lay down life's laws face the truth at last, their gaze transfixed forever by your death! Jolt them from sleep with your agonized death rattle! Spoil their sensual pleasures with the vision of your suffering! That they were capable of enjoying women's embraces during the night after the day they had you strangled! Save us from them, save us from a peace that brings us near to their pestilential presence! Spare us the pain of having to shake hands with those who once handed out death sentences in military tribunals, or meeting hangmen on their return to civilian life. For the conscience of those inflicting such uninhibited vile cruelty—their imagination having been stultified simply by sheer mechanistic repetitiveness rather than any particular passion—will adapt to the daily grind just as quickly as it once resorted to murder to escape the banality of the past.

Help me, you who have been done to death! Help me, so that I don't have to live among those who, for ambition's sake or to save their skins, gave orders for beating hearts to be terminated and mothers' hair to turn white! Forasmuch as there is surely a living God, only a miracle can redeem their fate! Come back to life! Ask them what they did to you! What they were doing while you suffered for them, before you died for them! What they were doing while you spent your winters in Galicia! What they were doing that night when commanders phoning your forward position received no answer. All was Quiet on the Eastern Front. Only later did they see you standing there, resolute, shoulder to shoulder, rifles at the ready. For you were not among those who deserted to the enemy, nor those who retreated, nor among those freezing troops a fatherly commander in chief felt the need to heat up with machine-gun fire. You held your positions and did not fall back a single step into the murderous clutches of your Fatherland. The enemy in front, your own country behind, and above you the everlasting stars! You didn't take refuge in suicide. You didn't die for your country, you didn't die because of your country; you died neither through enemy armaments nor your own—you stood there and died from natural causes—you froze to death! What perseverance! What a Habsburg Crypt!

Corpses ready for the fight, protagonists of the Habsburg death-in-life: close ranks and haunt their sleep! Wake from your frozen state! Step forward, you dear friend and kindred spirit, step forward and demand that they give back your life! You died in a field hospital—where are you now? The last letter I sent you was returned, stamped "Deported. Address unknown." Step forward and tell them where you are and what it's like, and that you will never again permit them to use you for such a purpose! And you, too, condemned in your last moment to have death written in your face when the beast in charge burst into your trench, formerly perhaps a creature like yourself, now foaming at the mouth—step forward! Not that you had to die, no, but that *this* was what you had to live through—this makes all future sleep and dying in bed a sin. It is not your death, but what you lived through that I will avenge on those who forced you to die!

I have cast them as the shadows that they are—hollow men putting on an empty show! I have stripped them of their flesh! But I have given shape to the thoughts behind their stupidity and the impulses behind their depravity, making them act out the disjointed rhythms of their nonexistence. If the voice of this epoch had been recorded, the outer truth would have belied the inner, and the ear would have recognized neither. So time renders reality unrecognizable and would grant an amnesty even to the greatest crime ever committed under the heavens. But I have preserved the essence of their actions, and my ear has uncovered the sound of what was done, my eye the gestures of what was spoken, and my voice, even when merely quoting, has caught the keynote of the era for all time.

And let me speak to the yet unknowing world
How these things came about: so shall ye hear
Of carnal, bloody, and unnatural acts,
Of accidental judgments, casual slaughters;
Of deaths put on by cunning and forc'd cause,
And, in this upshot, purposes mistook
Fall'n on the inventors' heads; all this can I
Truly deliver.

And if the times no longer hear, surely an ear above shall hear. I have done no more than condense the scale of mass murder, taking the measure of the amorphous alliance between the age of journalism and the journalism of the age. Its blood was merely ink—now the writing will be in blood! This is the World War. This is my manifesto. *I have weighed everything in the balance.* The tragedy, fractured into scenes reflecting mankind's fallen state, I have taken upon myself, so that it may be heard by a spirit that takes pity on the victims, even if it had renounced forever all connection to a human ear. Let it hear the keynote of these times, the echo of my bloodthirsty obsession, which makes me complicit with these cries. Let it be an act of redemption!

(From outside, at a great distance, the cry:—"Ex—traaa!")

(Change of scene.)

Scene 55

Ceremonial banquet at the headquarters of an army corps. A colossal painting, In This Age of Grandeur, *takes up the whole of the wall facing the audience. A collation of pork dishes known as Sow Dance is being served. The band is playing "Our old friend Noah knew what's best,/The softest boa won't warm your breast" to the music of Kálmán. The feast is almost over. Officers from the armies of the Central Powers are toasting each other. Distant rumbling of cannons. A lieutenant of Hussars hurls a champagne glass against the wall.*

PRUSSIAN COLONEL (*beside the general, humming and nodding*) Our old friend Noah knew what's best, eh?—Down the hatch!

AUSTRIAN GENERAL (*rises to cheers, taps his glass for silence*) Gentlemen—well, now—now that our officer corps has—come through—four years of unparalleled struggle—against the vastly superior strength of the whole world—let me just say—given the faith I place in my staff—I'm totally convinced—we shall continue—undaunted—if at all feasible—to take it on the chin! Our heroic warriors—brave lads!—hardened in battle—are marching towards new victories—we shall stand firm!—the enemy are shattered and sundered—and we'll shatter 'em wherever we find 'em—and this day—this day, gentlemen—will be a millstone—I mean a milestone in the annals of our glorious army for evermore! (*Cheering.*)—Up and at 'em! But from you, gentlemen, on whom the most difficult task in this unparalleled struggle is—incumbent—just as it is—encumbered—by our faithful troops, faithful unto death and duty-bound to the—utmost flogging—to the most unflagging—efforts—I expect you one and all to do your duty putting aside personal interests to the last breath of man and mount! The time has come for the final flourish, it will be hot work, but we know—the stakes are high. Indeed! That's why we are assembled here, each of us at his post—and each of us will stand our ground, hold out to the last—in this very place—where our duty has posted us as soldiers—where service to His Majesty has sent us—as loyal officers! (*Cheering*)

At this time we think fondly of our loved ones back home—who are far away and thinking of us with faithful devotion. Especially the mothers who have set us an example—joyfully sacrificing their sons on the altar of the Fatherland, as if it were the most natural thing in the world! Truly, it is not easy to collect one's thoughts at such a time as this—for they are perforce all directed towards the one goal. It is time—and I'm aware of the full import of what I'm saying—it is time for victory! Victory, gentlemen—do you know what that means? It is the choice a soldier has—if he doesn't want to die covered with glory! To this end, I shall turn a blind eye to the expectation—namely with respect to achieving a more intimate, more heartfelt contact with your, ah, men—the expectation that you, gentlemen, should have sacrificed yourselves to achieve maximum reduction of personal danger all round. (*Cheering.*) For as we all know, gentlemen, the heart and soul of an officer—especially a staff officer—is (*Cries of "His honour!"*)—Just so, gentlemen—his honour! And our honour, gentlemen, we shall *not*—oh, I know only too well—subversive elements exist—and they go right to the top, to the front line—but—gentlemen—we'll still keep our heads above water! Oh yes! Our human raw material can still put up a fight! (*Cries of "Bravo!"*)—And we who are blood of their blood and kindred spirits—no, a thousand times, no!—an officer feels at one with the rank and file, the simple soldier, who in this day and age is our bulwark, and the enemy will just be beating his head against a brick wall and getting a bloody nose!

Let them say what they like, those scribbling hacks—you can't generalize! (*He thumps the table*)—Do they have the right? (*Cries of "No!"*) Those damn muckrakers—I don't of course mean the two gentlemen war correspondents who have honoured us with their presence here this evening—we know only too well what the army owes to a well uniformed coverage of the war—and the press that fulfils its highly patriotic duty by undermining—er—underlining people's courage at home, can always count on our support! (*Cries of "Bravo!"*) I am not speaking of these gentlemen, and I hope you gentlemen do not think I was speaking of these gentlemen—for as far as feasible we recognize their beneficial activities to the hilt. (*Cries of "Bravo!" The war correspondents bow.*) I'm speaking of those—those anarchists, those defeatists—who are sowing discord and helping to propagate it by scattering rumours! Those are the mischief-makers I mean! Those are the agitators who stir things up and then foment trouble. So I ask you, gentlemen: Do we have to put up with that? (*Cries of "No!"*) In my corps—with all nationalities in peaceful coexistence with one another—there are German gentlemen on our staff, there are Czech-speaking gentlemen, there are Poles and Croats and Romanian gentlemen, and we've got some of the Mosaic persuasion, too. And have we not also representatives of our splendid Honvéd? (*Cries in Hungarian: "Hoorah!"*)—And no one has complained yet! All they ever say is: Nationality?—who cares! So I ask you, gentlemen—did you ever hear anything different? Well then—that's why I always say—the frying pan is cooler than the fire. That's how we handle things, at any rate! So please show our esteemed allies, whom we are proud to see at this table here today—(*Cries of "Hurrah!"*)—just how unified we are! Everyone has his role to play—putting aside personal interests—for we all know that we must hold out to the bitter end, and why we must hold out to the bitter end, and that goes for every nationality here without exception, in this defensive war that has been forced upon us, between the Germanic and the Slav races! (*Cries of "Hurrah!" and cheering.*)

Our weapons in this unparalleled struggle are confidence and discipline! (*Cries of "Bravo!"*) Oh yes! I'm all for discipline, with an iron fist! And we all of us know—how to sing that tune! At the last inspection I was obliged to recognize certain failings in this respect, and I unfortunately had to voice the criticism that too few gentlemen had died in the field. I don't want to name names, but it is essential that we set a good example. Instead of looking after your own carcass! (*"Bravo bravo!"*) I take as my model His Excellency Pflanzer-Baltin (*cheering*), who coined the phrase "I'll soon teach my men how to die!" I hold to that! What do people expect? Do those dogs want to live forever? This is not the moment for such selfish sentiments, gentlemen—now that the Fatherland is in danger, but, God willing, it will arise like a phoenix from the steel bath of the World War! Self before service is what we need—I mean service before self! I won't put up with mollycoddling. What a privilege it was when His Imperial Highness, the Most Serene Archduke Friedrich—(*deeply moved*)—the Father of his Men (*cheering*)—made his way through to the front-line trenches to convey gracious greetings from His Majesty, the Commander in Chief, to the troops (*cheering*)—sheer delight for one and all, naturally enough. What more can they possibly want, those people? It was still pretty quiet in the field that day, not like today when they have to brave one storm after another. But no, they're forever niggling, and there are some mischief-makers that finally managed to get the men up in arms—complaining about dried vegetables and the like—they'd doubtless like one of Sacher's little suppers, as in peacetime (*general mirth*), and a cream puff three times a day! Right now we must simply hold out to the bitter end! (*"Bravo, bravo!"*) Gentlemen, grumbling is something I loathe, and if I see any sign of it, I shall be merciless! Discipline, gentlemen—d'you know what that means? Discipline means knocking men into shape! It means authority—the soldiers' daily bread! If you undermine that, you can kiss goodnight to peace and quiet! These scribblers—wasn't it Bismarck—though it's true he was once—at any rate, now our great ally—wasn't it Bismarck who said it all: "What we won by the sword—we lose again by the pen!"—Gentlemen, let us not lose sight of that! Remember it!—But I'm amazed how long our esteemed War Minister has put up with it. If it was left to me, the censor should set an example and string 'em up, the lot o'them! (*Cries of "Bravo!"*) Counsel for the defence? Overruled! I've fought against the dagoes in my time, before those mischief-makers had seen the light of day! (*Cries of "Bravo!"*)—and I'm proud of it! But gentlemen—if concessions are made around the table, well—we surely can't be held responsible for that! People shouldn't believe all the lies the enemy are peddling about us. There would be no shortage of the spirit of self-sacrifice in our dear Fatherland; what we lack is commitment, and it is precisely commitment that counts! So—we mustn't allow such subversive currents to develop—for they could undermine us! If each of us here remains steadfast, then we shall confront the enemy in the final reckoning it forces upon us—according to plan and with our honour untarnished! Which of us is not mindful of the well-nigh unparalleled, death-defying deeds of our men, who have repeatedly proved their mettle, faithfully following our orders up front—into the valley of death! And it is certainly true—our staff officers have again and again put their heads on the line, accepting responsibility and carrying it through in unprecedented fashion.

Have we not often achieved success? Success that will live on in the annals of our army, while we ourselves may lie among the fallen, covered in glory. Have we not achieved successes that make our allies—our enemies—so green with envy that they want to belittle them? They didn't make things easy for us, gentlemen, oh no. Are we not encirculated by enemies on all sides, and yet we boldly face up to their superior numbers! One victory after another, gentlemen! Who would have thought that, when we set off into the unknown to trample Serbia underfoot—according to plan and with the "Prince Eugene March" on our lips. (*Cheering.*)—And were we not successful? *Did* we not trample Serbia underfoot, gentlemen? We *did*! (*Cheering.*)—They told us: Stop right there, not an inch further! So—we had to clean up—with the iron fist! One final step, gentlemen, and victory is ours! It becomes ever clearer that Russia is a colossus with feet of clay! It's as good as finished! And as for the dagoes—well, which of us can doubt any longer that we will triumph in the end? A soldier's duty, gentlemen, is to fight the good fight, and we have certainly fought it! Those brave warriors of ours, who risked their lives up front creating mayhem! They live on in our memory—for they have held their regimental banner aloft, a covenant sealed where feasible with their blood.

Gentlemen—we live in an age of grandeur and its priceless fruits for our Fatherland are still ripening—its prestige in the world—and, above all, what we owe to this steel bath is the indescribable spiritual uplift we have experienced. Is that of no account? Only one more step and we have won invincible laurels! That is why I say—and this goes for the officer corps as well as the rank and file—trust in God and keep your powder dry, gentlemen! You're the last line of defence, so, never forget, it's down to you! You know who has called us to the colours! His Majesty! (*cheering*)—our most gracious Emperor! (*cheering*)—each of us to the best of our ability, whatever our plight, yet will we fight—unto death!—through storm and stress, however perilous and exacting the strategy, as befits a doughty warrior! (*Cheering*)—May God comfort and sustain us! I raise my glass to our indomitable allies—whom we see here as a reminder of our Special Relationship, who are tried and tested in the heat of battle, standing shoulder to shoulder with us for better or for worse! (*Cheering and cries of "Hurrah!"*) His Majesty the German Kaiser and His Majesty, our Commander-in-Chief, our most gracious Emperor and King, and the whole Imperial House—Hurrah! Hurrah! Hurrah! (*Thunderous cheering and cries of "Hurrah!" General clinking of glasses. He sits down.*)—What's that you're serving?

ORDERLY Beg to report, Excellency, sir—hand grenades.

GENERAL (*roars with laughter*) They're *bombes glacées,* but here we call them hand grenades! All right, then—fire away with the hand grenades!

PRUSSIAN COLONEL Hand grenades, bring 'em on!—By Jove! Aren't you Austrians the little devils! Well, we've been making mincemeat of the pigs we slaughtered—cold cuts with blood sausage (*laughter*)—and for just desserts: whipped cream torpedoes. (*He sings*)

> Our customers, I guarantee,
> are sorry to depart.
> They get blown up and sunk maybe,
> but we do it from the heart!

(*Cheering and cries of "Hurrah!" Laughter.*)

GENERAL To the German U-boat! (*Cheering and cries of "Hurrah!" Clinking of glasses.*)

PRUSSIAN COLONEL I'm not one for speeches, Excellency, and as for making a toast—that's beyond me at the moment. Your good Hungarian wine has seen to that. (*Laughter.*) But this much I can say—your words went straight to my German heart! Where there's a lack of discipline, the end is nigh. The doom and gloom that's taken hold of you Austrians back home would soon have the front teetering, too—no two ways about it—(*a captain has collapsed under the table, provoking general agitation.*)

GENERAL It's those scribblers' fault! What are they after—we're as pure as the driven snow!

PRUSSIAN COLONEL Hold on. Your whining for peace really was unseemly. You shot yourselves in the foot there. And that's the spirit that threatens to infect your front.

GENERAL Hear that? Discipline is essential, no two ways about it!

PRUSSIAN COLONEL Ludendorff has every confidence in you, Excellency.

GENERAL Too kind. Oh yes, it's true, I look at the human raw material I'm sent—but I look at these gentlemen, too! Time to fill in a few gaps again—especially the cavalry training units—the antiaircraft crews aren't too bad—and our medics are in general doing a great job—they do what they can, passing the latest bodies of men as fit for service. They've all been grafted already. Y'know, the replacements—

PRUSSIAN COLONEL Replacements?—Grafted?—Artificial limbs?—Oh, you mean—.

GENERAL I meant drafted, not grafted!

PRUSSIAN COLONEL (*distant artillery fire*) Say—things are warming up today.

GENERAL (*wiping his brow*) Hellish hot in here.

(*A telephone officer appears, goes to the General Staff duty officer, and hands him a dispatch. The duty officer opens it, rises, staggers over to the general, and whispers in his ear.*)

GENERAL The idiots!

PRUSSIAN COLONEL What's up?

GENERAL Advance position taken. Withdraw to second line. That's Wottawa's fault!

PRUSSIAN COLONEL What a pain! Well, caught on the wrong foot again with your celebration, eh? (*The band strikes up a Viennese song.*) Ah, delightful! (*He sings along*) Let's crack another bottle o' wine—hollodrioh—Let's crack another bottle o' wine—hollodrioh—Is this your shout, or is it mine?—(*Looking around*) But wait, I don't know some of these gentlemen—(*he points to a group of officers.*)

GENERAL (*beckons*) You, there! (*The officers rise.*)

LIEUTENANT OF HUSSARS Géza von Lakkati de Némesfalva et Kutjafeleg-faluszég.

PRUSSIAN COLONEL Funny name. Cheerful fellow.

GENERAL He's one of the red devils.

PRUSSIAN COLONEL Red devils—gung-ho! The splendid Honved militia!

CAPTAIN Romuald Kurzbauer.

PRUSSIAN COLONEL Viennese?

GENERAL No, from Salzburg.

LIEUTENANT Stanislaus v. Zakrychiewicz.

PRUSSIAN COLONEL Croat?

GENERAL A Pole, a Pole.

PRUSSIAN COLONEL Ah, a noble Pole!

SECOND-LIEUTENANT Petričič.

PRUSSIAN COLONEL Romanian?

GENERAL No, a Croat.

LIEUTENANT Iwaschko.

PRUSSIAN COLONEL Czech?

GENERAL Romanian.

CAPTAIN Koudjela.

PRUSSIAN COLONEL Italian?

GENERAL Just a Czech!

CAPTAIN OF HORSE Felix Bellak, Baggage officer.

PRUSSIAN COLONEL Aha. (*Those who were introduced sit down. The senior medical officer clinks glasses with the senior military prosecutor. The field rabbi with the army chaplain.*) Our Holy-water-sprinklers, eh? Chin up! Look lively, look lively! That's it!

CAPTAIN That's our valiant anti-temptation weapon!

(*Peals of laughter, in which the army chaplain joins.*)

ARMY CHAPLAIN Truly, truly—I can put a damper on lusty spirits!

PRUSSIAN COLONEL A damper? Charming expression! Presumably for damage limitation? He's from the provinces, I guess?

ARMY CHAPLAIN No, colonel, from Linz.

PRUSSIAN COLONEL Ah, lovely Linz, amidst the greenery of Styria!

GENERAL Let's have something from one of my talented younger gentlemen now!

CHIEF SUPPLY OFFICER Wowes!

GENERAL Wowes! To the piano! At the double!

WOWES (*sits at the piano, plays and sings along*)

> When I see you—at your window—
> How my heart—misses a beat.
> How I long—to be back with you.
> For you make—my life complete.

(*Cries of: "Bravo Wowes!"*)

WOWES It's not finished yet!

PRUSSIAN COLONEL (*humming and nodding*) You make—my life complete. Very nice!

WOWES *(continuing)*

When I'm with you—in your bed—
I lie happy—all day long.
I don't want—ever to leave it.
For it is—where I belong.

(Laughter. Cries of: "Bravo Wowes!")

PRUSSIAN COLONEL *(humming and nodding)* For it is—where I belong. Splendid chap! *(Raises his glass to him.)*

GENERAL He composes them himself! *And* he does conjuring tricks as well. Prestige actor! He could entertain the whole company!

PRUSSIAN COLONEL Y'don't say.

GENERAL Yes, he's a cheeky young blighter! But I won't have him sent to the front line. I've just put him up for the Silver Medal first class. *(Rumbling of guns.)*

GERMAN GENERAL STAFF OFFICER Long live Austrian hospitality! *(Cheering and cries of "Hurrah!" Clinking of glasses.)*

SENIOR MEDICAL OFFICER Long live German organization! *(Cheering and cries of "Hurrah!" Clinking of glasses.)*

GENERAL Oho! And ours—gentlemen!—We're orgy-nized too!—O yes! Don't think we're—always feeling—so muddled—*(The band strikes up "Tonight I'm Feeling Fuddled." Laughter and singing at the end of the table.)* What'r'you laughing at?

CAPTAIN OF HORSE *(singing)* Tonight I'm—feeling—

CHIEF SUPPLY OFFICER Who's that just tootled in—? *(Laughter.)*

(A telephone officer rushes in, goes to the General Staff duty officer, and hands him a dispatch. The duty officer opens it, rises, staggers over to the general, and whispers in his ear.)

GENERAL What imbeciles!

PRUSSIAN COLONEL What's up?

GENERAL *(reads)* Position—knocked out. Lines of approach under—under heavy annihilating fire—Those squinty idiots—go and ruin everything when we were sitting pretty. *(Drops the dispatch.)* What the hell—complete no-brainer!

PRUSSIAN COLONEL *(lifting the dispatch)* Reserves deployed. Sector reserves totally exhausted. Batteries must be withdrawn to fallback position—Good God! *(Louder rumbling of guns.)*

GENERAL STAFF DUTY OFFICER *(to orderly)* Don't keep filling my glass.

I need a—clear head—today. How many boots and caps we lost he doesn't say, of course. Numskull!

GERMAN GENERAL STAFF OFFICER Boots and caps?

GENERAL STAFF DUTY OFFICER Y'know—men and officers.

PRUSSIAN COLONEL You Austrian fellows seem to have had more success with your peace offensives. Let's hope Hindenburg will sort things out. Another fine mess you've got us into, we'll have to get you off the hook again!

GENERAL Gentlemen—we are proud—proud—to stand shoulder to shoulder with—our battle-hardened allies—in shining armour—gentlemen, I raise my glass to the Special Relationship—in this alliance—that has now been expanded—(*Cries of "Bravo!"*)—and—and—

PRUSSIAN COLONEL Intensified! (*Cheering and cries of "Hurrah!" The band plays "The Watch on the Rhine", followed by "Hail to Thee in Laurels Crowned."*) Thank you, gentlemen—thank you! Skipping the pomp and circumstance, and without further ado—let's keep the "happy and glorious" until the final victory! For now, let's have another of your delightful Austrian songs—one by that splendid Lehár, who gave us such pleasure on the Western Front. (*Cries of: "Bravo!"*)

GENERAL Play "Call me Cuddle Bunny"!

PRUSSIAN COLONEL Cuddle—what's that then? Ah, Cuddle Bunny, capital! (*The band strikes up the melody.*)

GENERAL But what's up with those who plump up the pillows in the field hospitals? The girls are off-colour today. Why aren't you singing along?

CAPTAIN OF HORSE (*calling out across the table*) Sister Paula—what a lovely rump—spotless—! Sister Ludmilla tails along behind!

SISTER PAULA (*screeches*) Oi!—Hold your tongue—you dreadful man!

CAPTAIN OF HORSE What's wrong with that? What's wrong with that? Can't a man pay a compliment any more?

SISTER LUDMILLA He's forever making lewd remarks.

LIEUTENANT He's longing for those fun-boobies!

PRUSSIAN COLONEL Fun-boobies? The names you people come up with—what's that supposed to mean—? (*The general explains.*)

CHIEF SUPPLY OFFICER Let the girls sing a duet! (*Cries of "A duet!"*)

LIEUTENANT The field rabbi should sing one with the army chaplain, too! (*Cries of "A duet!"*)

ANOTHER LIEUTENANT The field rabbi can yodel from alp to alp—and the army chaplain can—er—do it the other way round—(*Peals of laughter.*)

PRUSSIAN CAPTAIN Wonderful!

THIRD LIEUTENANT That's fantabulous! (*Loud rumbling of guns.*)

ARTILLERY OFFICER They're really laying it on today—listen, you guys—! They've got rhythm!

FIELD CHAPLAIN (*singing*) Macaroni's off the menu, the battlefield's our only venue! So there they lie, those dirty rats—had their noses all squashed flat! (*Laughter; others join in singing.*)

SEVERAL Cheers, Reverend! (*Clinking of glasses.*)

PRUSSIAN COLONEL I fear it's hotting up today!

GENERAL (*wiping his brow*) The dog days. (*The band plays "On the Banks of the Manzanares."*)

(*The telephone officer rushes in, goes directly to the general, and whispers in his ear.*)

GENERAL What! Those miserable—pathetic front-line fogies—!

PRUSSIAN COLONEL What's up?

GENERAL I—don't—understand. I—explicitly—said—

PRUSSIAN COLONEL Come on, you guys, don't start cracking up, just as we have victory in the bag!

GENERAL Gentlemen—we're up shit creek!

PRUSSIAN COLONEL (*to telephone officer*) What's happened?

TELEPHONE OFFICER (*extremely agitated, stammering*) The first of the divisions in full retreat are already at corps headquarters—the artillery has all been abandoned—the roads are totally blocked by the baggage train—the troops are demoralized—the enemy cavalry is on their heels. (*Exit. The colonel speaks forcefully to the general. The others are in desultory conversation.*)

CAPTAIN Say—Koudjela—

KOUDJELA Uh huh.

CAPTAIN That upside-down cake! Pretty good pudding—Really was!

KOUDJELA Uh huh.

CAPTAIN Say—Koudjela—

KOUDJELA Uh huh.

CAPTAIN A good wine! Really good!

KOUDJELA Uh huh.

LIEUTENANT-COLONEL (*to a sleeping colonel*) Hey, Colonel!

AUSTRIAN COLONEL (*wakes up*) What's up—

LIEUTENANT-COLONEL Nothing! (*Laughter.*)

SECOND-LIEUTENANT (*shouting across the table*) Hey, Windischgraetz—what were you playing with Schlesinger today—bridge or baccarat?

CAPTAIN OF HORSE —Oh give over, the press coverage was in its heyday at the start, when they still had a Roda Roda—now there's nothing.

LIEUTENANT-COLONEL (*prods him*) Shush, but look at those two Jew-boys! (*Aloud.*) Y'know, I think Schalek's stuff is first-rate—very instructive!—she's coming out to us next week—above all, isn't she courageous—even the enemy would concede that!

CAPTAIN OF HORSE (*prods him*) Shush, that'll annoy 'em even more! (*Aloud.*) Y'know, that Roda Roda, he knew how to capture a military situation in a sentence—for example—I'll never forget—when he wrote: "You'll hardly need your overcoat any more", said the lieutenant, as he had the Serbian Orthodox priest tied to the Uhlan's stirrup. End of story.

LIEUTENANT Very good, but why did that make such an impression?

CAPTAIN OF HORSE Idiot—can't you guess who the lieutenant was? Me!

LIEUTENANT Really!—What had he done, then?

CAPTAIN OF HORSE Oh, subversive activities or whatever. Had a red nose—a sure sign! He was certainly one of them!

LIEUTENANT (*to another who is sitting in a daze*) Hey—what'r'you thinking about? You thinker!

ANOTHER LIEUTENANT Y'know, I was just thinking—at this very moment, if only we were back home on the Ring—. Here you just sit around—

LIEUTENANT Yep—me too.

PRUSSIAN LIEUTENANT —No, no, you people shouldn't bother me with that, you'll get your victorious peace without my help—I've got to go to Berlin next week. For the Heroes Memorial Horse Races.

SECOND PRUSSIAN LIEUTENANT Why think of tomorrow at a time like this? What we need is a few bottles more, so we have enough ballast to collapse into bed. Back home those idle bastards have mucked everything up—

CAPTAIN OF HORSE I don't fancy home leave either, thanks very much! Oh, no—into a land flowing with swedes and stale bread! (*Laughter*)—No, thank you!

CAPTAIN Hold on, Reischl, you've no appetite for the front either! (*Laughter.*)

CAPTAIN OF HORSE You're one to talk, shirker-in-chief!

SECOND PRUSSIAN LIEUTENANT One of the worst things at the front is the jam, day after day.

FIRST PRUSSIAN LIEUTENANT And the heroes' butter is all gone, too. In Russia our boys are really up against it now. In one sector they've got cholera—no joke. All because the men drank from a pond that had Russian corpses in it.

CAPTAIN OF HORSE That's not my poison, I need champagne! (*Peals of laughter.*)

SECOND PRUSSIAN LIEUTENANT —Sure, you Austrians know how to cook, but compare that with what we had for lunch in Bad Homburg—the Kaiser's favourite watering hole, look (*he produces the menu*): beef broth—chicken vol-au-vent—fried Rhine fish with remoulade sauce—casserole of pheasant—saddle of spring lamb with home-made Halberstädt sausages—leg of mutton with haricot beans and artichoke bottoms—asparagus with cream dip—Niersteiner Auflanger from the mess in Duisburg—sparkling Kupferberg-Gold—bombe glacée—fruit compote—cheese straws! Yes indeed! No comparison! (*Cries of "Oho!"*)

PRUSSIAN COLONEL —Say, boys, that famous Royal and Imperial Court Ballet of yours—did you get a visit from them?

GENERAL Yes—and next week there'll be a cabaret—really hot stuff!

FIRST WAR CORRESPONDENT That's my work, Colonel!

SECOND WAR CORRESPONDENT What'd'you mean? I was the one suggested it!

LIEUTENANT —No, no, it was at the seventh Battle of Isonzo, remember, when Sascha was out here—

ANOTHER LIEUTENANT —The colonel's getting worked up about the noise from the guns. He can't get to sleep at night. The previous quarters were better. I always said this was a bad location. It'll be another one of those nights tonight! Nothing will happen, but the noise at night is intolerable. (*Loud detonation.*)

ARTILLERY OFFICER That was a big bazooka!

LIEUTENANT —Scharinger of the Eleventh? Lucky sod! They've put him up for—

CAPTAIN OF HORSE Talk about fun-boobies (*gestures*) out—standing!

LIEUTENANT Yes, but y'know who I have lined up—! a real knockout—!

CAPTAIN OF HORSE Champion skirt chaser that you are! In the last *Muskete*—

MAJOR Here's to our quartermaster! (*Cheering. Clinking of glasses.*)

MAJOR-GENERAL Ah yes, the good old purser! Doing a good job! Twelve courses—you have to take your hat off to that! (*Toasts him.*)

SENIOR MILITARY PROSECUTOR Well, I've let the law take its course before, but 12 courses! (*Laughter.*) I can only say—your health, Quartermaster!

MAJOR Say, heard anything of Haschka?

SENIOR MILITARY PROSECUTOR Haschka! The same as ever. Hard at it—!

MAJOR But he can't still be working for Stöger-Steiner at the Ministry? There surely can't be that much that needs doing anymore!

SENIOR MILITARY PROSECUTOR Yes, time marches on. But Haschka is one hell of a character. Still has the same fixation. He puts off the death sentence until the soup course is finished. He looks at the time, jumps up, says they should put the roast on hold—then, boom-boom, they're in the billiard room for the verdict. His most memorable case was with the march formation units of the Fifteenth Corps, y'know, at Wocheiner-Feistritz. There were a couple of those human rights wimps, holding up progress—saying "simply not acceptable"—just because Stöger-Steiner ordered it—well, they had to be made an example of.

MAJOR Politically unreliable?

SENIOR MILITARY PROSECUTOR No, no—it's a famous case. A fellow stole a wallet, and in the guard room they put the wind up him—that he'd get shot for it. The fellow does a bunk—in a funk! Well, says Haschka, even if it's not clear-cut desertion, since he only did it because he was afraid—still, he has to be made an example of. Because Stöger-Steiner is all for that, naturally.—Well, the human rights wimps get on their high horse! And after that, they don't convict him! What d'you say to that! Scandalous! Regulars, too!

MAJOR (*perplexed*) Regulars—?

SENIOR MILITARY PROSECUTOR Yes, that too! But look—I've had cases myself where, even with self-inflicted injuries, they've tried to extricate the bugger. I ask you—regulars! Who've voluntarily donned the Emperor's uniform! Should be kicked out! These subversive ideas have even started to penetrate our own circles.

MAJOR What d'you expect, even in the front line they're already stirring up trouble among the troops. Well—lips sealed, mustn't generalize, fortunately spirits are still intact.—Anyway, what happened then?

SENIOR MILITARY PROSECUTOR Well, he had to promise them—Haschka, on record—that the fellow gets pardoned, provided they find him guilty. But Haschka, the sly bastard, when it comes to the bit, doesn't let on what's on record—so, naturally, the sentence is carried out on the spot. Y'know, we've set many an example, too—but an execution like that—all you can say is: hat's off! Yes, Haschka is something special.

MAJOR Y'know, those human rights wimps—I've had a bellyful of them. I see red if I so much as get a whiff of one. Rebel against Stöger-Steiner! In one case General Tersztszyansky applied rough justice. Or rather, no justice at all!

SENIOR MILITARY PROSECUTOR What d'you mean?

MAJOR Well, another of those human rights wimps—one of your peers—

SENIOR MILITARY PROSECUTOR Hey, don't go casting aspersions on me!

MAJOR Oh go on, only pulling your leg. Anyhow, listen—he refuses to treat this fellow summarily according to martial law. Says it's a simple disciplinary case, no names no pack drill. Well, in comes Tersztszyansky, into the mess, starts on his soup—and I've never seen Tersztszyansky so quiet before!—and says, Captain, he says to the prosecutor, no further need of any trial for your delinquent. Why's that, the other asks. There he is out in the garden, have a look—there he lies. Tersztszyansky had simply told the sergeant to take him out, with his bayonet, and—squelch! Just because he was mad at him for being so obstinate.

SENIOR MILITARY PROSECUTOR Mad at the fellow?

MAJOR No, no—mad at the prosecutor!

SENIOR MILITARY PROSECUTOR Oh, of course. Tell me—I was in an argument the other day—Tersztszyansky's an honorary Doctor of Philosophy—isn't he?

MAJOR I think you're right. Incidentally, what about Stanzl in the Telegraph Regiment, what's he up to? Still in Albania? I heard they want to send him to Feldkirch to do something a bit more elevated.

SENIOR MILITARY PROSECUTOR Some chance! He's up to his eyes in things in Albania! But that Hungarian judge, Balogh—y'know, in Kossovo-Mitrovica—

MAJOR Oh yes, right, there was some story I heard about an execution with teeth being extracted or something—

SENIOR MILITARY PROSECUTOR That's just gossip. It's unbelievable the way that fellow gets slandered—I was just about to tell you. It's the most harmless story imaginable. It's all because he had to hang a 16-year-old for being a Macedonian rebel. So he says to the doctor, see if the lad's got a wisdom tooth yet. Yes, says the doctor. So he just wrote "20 years old"—and strung 'im up. After going to the trouble of checking with the doctor. That was his mistake—that's how it came out. And after, when he got a reprimand from Supreme Headquarters, that's when all the gossip began. Well—between ourselves—in cases involving experienced officers, Headquarters didn't use to dish out reprimands! Simply add a year or two to the age, no one would say a thing.

MAJOR It's a mystery to me, too. In our division—great God, weren't those the days!—when Peter Ferdinand had more of a free hand—they once bet—y'know, His Imperial Highness and Prince von Parma, the chief of staff—whether when 14-year-olds were executed there would be a—what was it the doctor called it—some funny word—

REGIMENTAL DOCTOR Aha, *ejaculatio seminis*—a spontaneous ejaculation! (*Laughter.*)

MAJOR That's it, of course! Oh that was interesting. It all was—in those days!

CHIEF SUPPLY OFFICER Executing 14-year-olds—do they have a right to do that? (*Laughter.*)

MAJOR My dear Chief Commissary, it *is* wartime, *comprendez-vous*? No names no pack drill! Eh? In the 92nd, guys who took conserves from the iron rations used to be tied to the barbed wire outside, so the Russians could shoot 'em—

CHIEF SUPPLY OFFICER Well, if they'd taken iron rations—

MAJOR My motto is: war is not just against the enemy, your own side should feel its effects as well! My, oh my! Once we were all made to turn out for an execution. Well, this woman who was supplying butter to the staff mess had to wait a bit—so, they told her just to line up with the others—well, she got strung up as well! (*Peals of laughter*). But—no, wait—it's no laughing matter—everyone makes mistakes—it can easily happen—among the lower ranks! She simply joined the wrong bloody line. And that was that. Still—happy days! When Weiskirchner came to visit us and the Deutschmeister, they ordered a lively salute from the cannons in his honour—ah, yes! And they had the 30.5-cm mortar shoot at some peasants out ploughing—ah, yes! And—

CHIEF SUPPLY OFFICER But why—?

MAJOR Because an archduke was visiting, of course!—but my dear judge, even if you twist my arm, I can't remember which one it was—I imagine so he could convince himself of the accuracy of their fire. And he did say he was impressed! In the most affable way—ah, so it must have been Josef Ferdinand, yes!—But y'know, I've always wanted to ask you—you had that case in Kragujevac with the 44th. Didn't you have a spot of bother there—(*the band strikes up*

"Let's Crack Another Bottle o' Wine, Hollodrioh!" The officers sing "and then one more for auld lang syne, hollodrioh!" Lieutenant of Hussars Lakkati throws a champagne glass against the wall.)

CHIEF PROSECUTOR And how! That was a binge and a half! It's really incredible the amount they can knock back. Y'know, I could've had 300 executed! We simply can't tolerate such excesses of drunkenness. I made an exception and granted them an honourable death—the firing squad.

INTELLIGENCE OFFICER (*butts in on the conversation*) That rabble is always drunk. But at least that's when they give away what they're really thinking. There's not as much needs doing now as in 1914, though. Y'know, judge, once I accompanied a transport of the 28th from Prague to Serbia. I had a funny feeling right from the start! Sure enough—just past Marchegg it flares up. The men dig their heels in, start to complain to the NCOs because they're being sent against the Serbs, those bandits! But again they landed on the wrong bloody side! Nice an' easy, we got them all unloaded, took 25 of them and stuck them in a special railway truck. Room for 40—so, every comfort! Then, every hour or so we stopped in open country, then an NCO patrol extracted three men each time and stuck them in the truck at the back of the train. Then—off we go again! Two minutes later—rrrtsch (*gesture of mowing down*) rubbed out! Every time three new ones were pulled out, y'should have seen their faces. Always in threes—one lot after the other. The last one all by himself. The brute! By the time we reached the terminal in Budapest, all 25 had been neatly finished off. That last truck—when they uncoupled it—what a sight! Great guns! A clean sweep! Riddled with bullets, like a sieve—spot-on!—and buckets of blood—

CHIEF PROSECUTOR Should have taken a photo. Good job y'did there!

INTELLIGENCE OFFICER I was only doing my duty. The colonel had said: set an example. But compared with Captain Wild, it was nothing.

MAJOR Ah, Wild!

INTELLIGENCE OFFICER It's Ukrainians he has it in for. He sent me his picture postcards yesterday—of four strung up and him in the middle. What a dashing devil!

CHIEF PROSECUTOR Ah, Wild!

INTELLIGENCE OFFICER But compared with Captain Prasch, even Wild is nothing! There's your perfect front-line officer! The things he's done with his own bare hands—

PRUSSIAN COLONEL —What was that dish called again? Sow Dance? What a song and dance you make with words! To die for, the weird names you give to things! You Austrians—! But unfortunately there's no escaping the fact you don't take life seriously enough. Which is essential—for war is a steel bath! Since your old Emperor passed away, chivalrous gentleman that he was, things have rather gone to pot. Not so disciplined any more, no backbone, more's the pity! So, what's the red devil going on about over there?

GÉZA VON LAKKATI DE NÉMESFALVA ET KUTJAFELEGFALUSZÉG (*speaking with a Hungarian lilt to a group*)—Well—I see straight away, dung on hoof. Blighter says, hooves were clean, must happen on way from stable! No! I take my sabre—scrape dung off hoof—and smear it over swine's mouth. (*Laughter. Cries of: "Bravo!"*) Yes, is a—is a—a reservist puppy standing there—butts in—I say damned dog, he go before tribunal! He soon see what what! (*Cries of "Bravo!"*)

CAPTAIN OF HORSE And did he say anything, the fellow?

GÉZA VON LAKKATI DE NÉMESFALVA ET KUTJAFELEGFALUSZÉG But—not able—had dung in mouth! (*Peals of laughter. Loud explosion.*)

ARTILLERY OFFICER Hey! Take it easy!—They'll end up giving us a thrashing soon!

PRUSSIAN COLONEL —No, no, no ifs or buts—your retreat in Galicia wasn't very glorious. Your archduke—

GENERAL Excuse me, but there was no alternative. His Imperial Highness did all that was humanly possible—but the poor combat fitness of the troops—and another thing I just happen to know—something His Excellency Field Marshal Boroevic expressly acknowledged—His Imperial Highness was not lacking in energy—not at all—but the men were committing suicide! How d'you stop that? Individually with a machine gun, or the normal decimation—it was simply a terribly weak corps. That's just the way it is sometimes on our side. The men didn't get enough sleep, and so on.

PRUSSIAN COLONEL Aha?

GENERAL Yes—look—Excellency Boroevic had to admit it himself—those who froze to death while asleep—as he wrote to the top brass—it makes people afraid to go to sleep.

PRUSSIAN COLONEL Aha! If that's the case, then clearly it's not Archduke Josef's fault. Anyway, it's not important. Just make sure that everything's in order now. You did the right thing adapting this present offensive to the season. The time of year is not unfavourable. The setback in your sector of the front—

GENERAL Well, it probably won't be much better in the other sectors—

PRUSSIAN COLONEL Let's hope for the best. Though it's certainly ominous that the enemy appear to have gone over to the offensive on this part of the front. But that means there's a better chance of encircling him. We've tried that a dozen times on the Western Front. In that respect, I'm optimistic. We Germans are concentrating all our efforts on final victory—so all I can say is: let's get it sorted!

GENERAL Yes, sure, we'll manage it. (*Lakkati hurls a champagne glass against the wall.*)

LIEUTENANT —Hey—I dumped that little typist today—she was getting uppity—well, I settled her hash!

SECOND-LIEUTENANT So what'd'ya do to her?

LIEUTENANT Ruined her, that's all! (*Laughter.*)—Well, what d'ya think?—cretin—! Go get your head deloused!

CAPTAIN OF HORSE —My dear fellow, say what you like—the Honveds will stand firm!

GERMAN CAPTAIN Yes, but the Bavarians will bite your throat out! That's something I might wish on you, you—!

CAPTAIN OF HORSE What d'ya mean by that—! (*Laughter. The sound of Austrian artillery fire decreases.*)

ARTILLERY OFFICER —Oh, give over—I've seen some real bonanzas in my time, my friend—in the seventh and eighth battles of the Isonzo!

CAPTAIN OF HORSE Call that a bonanza, where the girls aren't up for it! (*Calls out*) Music!

LIEUTENANT I was at a bonanza in Russia—!

ANOTHER LIEUTENANT Y'remember, at Rawa-Ruska—when Fallota was still—

PRUSSIAN SECOND-LIEUTENANT Hey—the music-chappie's asleep!

PRUSSIAN CAPTAIN Play "In the Graveyard at La Bassée"!

MAJOR No—on my command—play "Mitzi, Mitzi, Be Nice to Your Fritzi"!

PRUSSIAN CAPTAIN Ah—Mitzilein! Wonderful!

DUTY GENERAL STAFF OFFICER They were always singing that at the Gartenbau—Varady and Rollé—

CHIEF SUPPLY OFFICER Ah, the good old Gartenbau! When Schenk was still performing there—(*sings*) "Mother-in-law—mother-in-law—that would be the final straw"—Play "Shampers Calms Our Tempers" (*Cries of: "Shampers, champers!" "Bravo!"*)

CAPTAIN OF HORSE Play "The End of the World Is Nigh, So More Champagne, I'm Dry"! *(Cries of "Bravo!" The band plays. The officers sing along.)*

CHIEF SUPPLY OFFICER Play "That Lovely Dance of Yore, They Won't Play It Anymore"!

CHIEF PROSECUTOR *(repeating)*—they won't play it anymore!

(The telephone officer rushes in, white as a sheet, goes directly to the general, and whispers in his ear.)

GENERAL What—?! A mutiny?! Decimate them—the whole damn lot o' them! Send in new regiments—time for some fresh blood. Get going, get going—at the double!

PRUSSIAN COLONEL What's up?

(The telephone officer whispers something else in the general's ear.)

GENERAL What?! The poison gas shells aren't working either?! What a shambles!!

PRUSSIAN COLONEL Oh, come *on!* That surely can't be allowed to—! *We* would never tolerate such—!

GENERAL What—bunglers! What rotten luck!—What can you do—?

PRUSSIAN COLONEL Another fine mess you've got us into! A bit too sloppy, our dear Austrians, a bit too sloppy!

FIRST WAR CORRESPONDENT Look at the general, what did I tell you—!?

SECOND WAR CORRESPONDENT Major, sir, perhaps you could tell me how the battle is going—?

MAJOR An enemy offensive has begun.

FIRST WAR CORRESPONDENT Oh dear!

MAJOR The enemy has made a breach in the front-line positions—

SECOND WAR CORRESPONDENT A breach—in our positions?

MAJOR We hope we can successfully thwart this stratagem. But please don't mention my name.

FIRST WAR CORRESPONDENT Our superior artillery—

SECOND WAR CORRESPONDENT As long as it's not a flank attack!

SISTER PAULA —Ow!—cheeky blighter!

CAPTAIN OF HORSE Oh, go on—flank attacks are still permitted, eh?

SISTER LUDMILLA Enough! It's always the same, him and his—!

CAPTAIN Jacko, don't you dare!

PRUSSIAN CAPTAIN Ah yes, "Jacko, Jacko, don't you dare"!

LIEUTENANT —D'you mean Madler or Madlé, fellow who was with Hausenblas at Sabac? Madler, I can tell you, is the greatest shirker in the whole army. The little squirt is mad because I was put up for a medal.

ANOTHER LIEUTENANT Where is he now?

LIEUTENANT Where d'you think? Back at base! While we work ourselves to the bone—Say, how's your little doll?

(The band strikes up a czárdás. Lakkati and a female ancillary worker dance. Lively cries of "Bravo!")

PRUSSIAN COLONEL Ah, wonderful! Marvellous! A proper red devil!

GERMAN GENERAL STAFF OFFICER —Oh, why can't you leave me in peace with your damned gas! We have mustard gas—yellow-cross blister gas, green-cross choking gas, blue-cross poison gas—the French have tasted all the colours of the rainbow!

DUTY GENERAL STAFF OFFICER Pardon me, but our gas was pretty effective at Tolmino, too. They were falling over like ninepins.

CHIEF SUPPLY OFFICER Play "My Brown Isonzo Lassie"! (*Cries of "My Brown Isonzo Lassie!" "Bravo!" The band strikes up.*)

THE OFFICERS *(sing along)*

My brown—Isonzo—lassie—
Your eyes set me on fire,
My brown—Isonzo—lassie—
You are—my heart's—desire.
Another kiss—just one more,
So take me—in your arms,
Sweet brown Isonzo lassie,
I'm captured by your charms.

PRUSSIAN COLONEL *(humming and nodding)* I'm captured by your charms. How sweet!

CHIEF SUPPLY OFFICER *(singing)*

Nor did she fear—the raging war—

But even that doesn't compare with the third verse when a year later the little bambino appears, with peepers as black as its mama's and curls just like its dad once had. A chubby wee bairn!

PRUSSIAN COLONEL A bairn? Charming! And who was the father, eh?

CHIEF SUPPLY OFFICER A lieutenant in our elite Kaiserjägers—a natty dashing devil! A bit like Wowes. Let's have another song from Wowes!

PRUSSIAN COLONEL Say—who's that wonderful song by?

CHIEF SUPPLY OFFICER It's one of Egon Schubert's.

PRUSSIAN COLONEL Ah, of course—should have known. Your immortal Schubert! That's one thing you Viennese beat us in, no question. And Vienna in general—glorious city! Oh, yes! Your Viennese cabby, what a character, and his cab with rubber tyres, whisking you out to a tavern among the vineyards in the Prater for the latest vintage—nothing to beat it! And your Viennese laundresses—oh, yes—we know all about them! Done that! Kept singing the whole time—(*he sings and claps his hands*) "I'm up all night carousing"—or something like that. That was Papa Strauss's heyday, with his—what d'you call it?—Schwammerl—Schrammel quartet. Good old Johann! Probably seen some changes there, though! (*The noise from the artillery grows weaker.*)

DUTY GENERAL STAFF OFFICER Pardon me, but at Tolmino—

GERMAN GENERAL STAFF OFFICER But that was ages ago. We've gassed far more in a single day than you have in a whole year! Smoking out the last pockets of French resistance, the white and coloured Englishmen and so on. Oh, yes—our famous gas grenade mark B! The poison sprays out everywhere and produces suppurating wounds with secretions exactly like a fully functioning dose of clap. (*Laughter.*) Well, so what? It's undeniable—been scientifically proved! The buggers don't kick the bucket until the next day.

THE BAND (*plays and sings along*)

We're happy
As the day is long!
It's in our blood!
So sing this song!

(*The officers repeat.*)

GENERAL (*mumbling*) It's in our blood! So sing—

(*The noise of gunfire falls silent.*)

VARIOUS VOICES Hey! What's happening? What's happening?

WAR CORRESPONDENTS What does that mean?

GENERAL (*face ablaze, jumps to his feet, bangs on the table*) Jesus Christ! I specifically ordered—! It could only happen here—What—did I tell that rabble? (*Roaring.*) If anyone fails to fire, I'll eat 'em alive! Why aren't you cheering and hurling yourselves at the enemy?—get up close, let one off under his nose, then bayonet straight in the ribs!—Anyone hesitates, cut 'em down without pity! Hand grenades—machine guns—for all that, your rifle's still the infantryman's best friend!—Officers must be ruthless and get the best out of everyone! And what did they do—those front-line swine, those gutless bitches, those—those (*wailing*) they screw it all up—Wottawa!—those scribblers—"It was not the enemy, it was starvation!"—starvation—that's where it all started—(*clenching his fists*) the undermining, the sapping—string 'em up!—I was the one—I always predicted—the misfortune of our army—will drag down even my men!—This crass, wanton frivolity—ineradicable—they think of nothing but feasting and whoring—total demoralis—(*he breaks down.*)

DUTY GENERAL STAFF OFFICER (*jumps up*) It's all those shirkers' fault—out there—those front-line swine—

AUSTRIAN COLONEL (*awakening*) What's happened?

LIEUTENANT Nothing! Shooting is reported from the suburbs of Vienna!

GENERAL Where—where were the machine-guns to drive them back?—What about our superior artillery?!—Villains!!—After an unparalleled struggle for four long years—against—exemplary superior numbers—our exemplary—our glor—(*he falls into his seat, whimpering*)—and at the end of it all—they'll come—marching in—

PRUSSIAN COLONEL No, no, Excellency, chin up! Gentlemen—we must not, we cannot let our spirits sink—now, before our final victory—we can and we may hold our head up high—rest assured, gentlemen, what we are seeing is merely the typical initial success of every enemy offensive—it's bluff, that's all! Nothing to fear! Now we undertake a strategic withdrawal—a strategic withdrawal always succeeds! (*A few cries of "Hurrah!" and scattered cheering.*) And I have been certain from the start that the enemy will not prevent the manoeuvres we have envisaged for years and now been implementing for days. Our operations are being carried out according to plan. We have simply disengaged from the enemy and now we are drawing him after us! Then we'll give 'em a kicking! The men's morale is sky-high! Gentlemen, we shall be as firm as a rock and we shall never yield! The more opportunity we give the enemy to push forward, the more chance we have to wear him out! That is the tactic we put to the test on the Somme. That is the tactic which will also succeed on the Piave. So, let's have no defeatist talk! God is on our side! We'd pull it off—against a world full of devils! The enemy—be assured, gentlemen—the enemy will shatter against us as against a bronze wall of flame—

The horizon is a wall of flame. Panic-stricken sounds. Many of those present are lying under the table. Many are rushing or staggering towards the exit, some come back, their faces distorted with terror.

CRIES What's happened?—What's—what's—

GENERAL (*mumbling*) They've—broken—through—! Go on—playing!

All the lights have gone out. Tumult outside. Bombs dropped from aeroplanes can be heard exploding. Then silence reigns. Those present are asleep, lie in a somnolent stupor or stare blankly at the wall on which the painting In This Age of Grandeur *hangs, and on which the following apparitions rise up, one after the other.*

Narrow mountain path leading to Mitrovica. Driving snow. Between thousands of carts an enormous mass of humanity, old people and women, children, half-naked, holding the hands of mothers, many also holding a baby. A little boy at the side of a peasant woman from the Morava valley raises his little hand and says:
Tschitscha, daj mi hleba—Mama, give me bread—

The scene is supplanted by another tableau. The Balkan Express is racing through the countryside. It slows down. The two war correspondents are leaning out of the windows of the dining car; they appear to be toasting their mirror images in the banqueting hall. One calls out:
There's something splendid about war, all the same—

The first tableau returns. The exhausted refugees, now almost dead from the cold, are lying on stones that are covered with ice. The morning light falls on pale, sunken faces which still bear traces of the horrors of the previous night. A cry: a horse plunges over a precipice. Another cry, even more piercing: its driver has plunged down after it. At the edge of the path a horse, almost dead from exhaustion, a little further off an ox, its intestines hanging out, a person with a crushed skull. The straggling procession begins to move off. Enfeebled animals at the end of their tether are left behind. They stand motionless. Their gaze of deathly sadness follows the procession. A peasant woman, her face deathly pale, sits leaning against a fir tree—it is the woman from the Morava valley—in her arms a tiny lifeless body, by its head the flickering light of a little candle.
(The apparition vanishes.)

A garrison. The following scenes are played out in jerky sequence. Slovak peasants, returned home from Russian captivity, some in peasants' clothes, some in Russian uniforms, are asking for an extension of their leave to catch up on harvesting. The company commander orders the petitioners to be attached at once to the next company bound for the front. Two young returnees, 19 and 21 years old, are seen asleep. They are wakened by the noise of what is going on outside.

The sergeant is distributing uniforms. The men are refusing to take them and demand they be allowed to report to battalion headquarters. The sergeant hits some of them, and is himself struck in the face. The barracks guard is alerted, guns are loaded, the mutineers driven into the barrack square and surrounded. The captain appears, everyone obeys his order to line up in rank and file. The two young soldiers are now part of this. The captain is informed about the incident. No one knows who struck the blow. The captain has every tenth man seized and led off to the guardhouse. There they are beaten, their ankles shackled, and they are taken to the garrison prison. Martial law is imposed. Then come the hearings. Six are court-martialed. The prison courtyard at dawn next morning. The judges, the battalion commander, the military prosecutor, and two priests appear. A table and a crucifix are brought. The tribunal is grouped around the table, a priest on each side. At the sight, one of the six has a seizure, howling and foaming at the mouth he collapses, others tear their hair, rage, rip their clothes. The guards try to calm them with the assurance that only two would be sentenced to death. A judge reads out the charge. The 19-year-old and the 21-year-old are sentenced to death by firing squad, the others to many years' imprisonment. The 19-year-old falls on his knees before the head of the tribunal and, racked with sobbing, begs for mercy. He shows a locket with the picture of his old mother. She won't survive his death, let them send him to the front, he would show that he is a brave soldier, he had been asleep during the incident, he is totally innocent. The judge has him taken away. The other accused is deathly pale, but stands upright. He speaks the words:
God knows that I die an innocent man!
He lets himself be taken away, while the others weep over their comrades. The judges go off to the mess. There one of them says:
It's quite clear that only that married one can be the culprit. But can you shoot a father of six children? The state would have to pay for his surviving dependants! This way, he's got six years, as many as he has children, and the state provision for military convicts can be withdrawn anyhow.
A second says:
Three others were married, too—so that only left the two young ones to be shot. In any case, they'll certainly have done something wrong. And if not today, then tomorrow! Innocent or not—one has to set an example.
At night in the prison. The younger one is standing with a rosary, praying, behind the barred window. The priests appear in order to give the last sacrament to the offenders. The younger one howls and asks to see his mother one last time. They pray together. He asks for paper and pencil to write to his mother. He writes. It is already a quarter past eight. He gets up.
Mother!

He collapses. The other one:
Is that why I fought, is that why I returned from Russia, to be led like an ox to the slaughter?—Let them tie me up and carry me!—Is that why I lived for 21 years—to be shot?—Quick, get it over with!
On the way to the place of execution. He takes his leave from the radiant August sun. He pulls off a green leaf from a tree and kisses it passionately. The younger one weeps incessantly for his mother. At the place of execution. The courtyard of an old castle. Entrance confined to those producing the correct papers. Among those present are the top officials, senior officers, and dignitaries with their ladies. There are representatives of the best social circles. The judges, the battalion commander, and those officers not on duty take up their positions in the middle of the hollow square. The prisoners are brought in. The judgment is read out. The elder one:
If the sergeant gave that evidence, he deserves to stand here and be shot.
They refuse blindfolds.
I no longer fear bullets.
They are blindfolded. They kneel.
Fire!
The sabre falls. Two corpses lie in the grass. The commander orders prayers. All salute. One of the priests, in officer's cap and with gold braid on his sleeve, makes a speech, points with his raised right arm to a standard, and, with an ecstatic expression on his face, raises his eyes heavenward to the Habsburg coat of arms above the gate.
(The apparition vanishes.)

Kragujevac. Two parallel rows, each with 22 open graves. In front of them kneel 44 returnees, veterans with all grades of medals for bravery. Bosnians shoot at a distance of two paces. Their hands tremble. The first line writhe on the ground. None is dead. Gun barrels are put to their heads. Officers' mess. The chief supply officer raises his glass and, toasting his mirror image in the banqueting hall, speaks the words:
Y'know, I'd have had 300 executed. Excessive drunkenness cannot be tolerated. I made an exception and granted them an honourable death by firing squad.
(The apparition vanishes.)

Captain Prasch is standing in front of his shelter, completely covered in blood, holding above his head a head that he has impaled on a pole. He speaks:
That's my first Italian prisoner, I did it with my own sabre. My first Russian prisoner I had tortured first. Czechs are my favourites for that. I'm from Graz by

birth. Anyone I encountered in Serbia, I shot 'em down on the spot. I killed 20 people, civilians and prisoners among them, with my own hand, at least a 150 I had shot. Any soldier who held back in an attack or hid during a barrage, I shot down with my own hand. I always hit my subordinates in the face, either with my cane or with my fist. But I did a lot for them, too. In Serbia I raped a Serb girl, but then left her to the soldiers, and the next day had her and her mother hanged from the railings of a bridge. The rope broke, and the girl was still alive when she fell into the water. I drew my revolver and shot away at her until she disappeared under the water. I always did my duty, to the last breath of man and mount. I was decorated and promoted. I always kept my wits about me. War makes strict demands—you must concentrate all your energies. You mustn't let your spirits sink. Head held high! (*He raises the pole higher.*)
(The apparition vanishes.)

A lieutenant of the lancers has an Orthodox priest tied to a lancer's stirrup. He is stripped of his overcoat.
You'll hardly need your coat anymore.
The rider departs at a brisk trot.
(The apparition vanishes.)

Winter in the Carpathians. A man tied to a tree. He is untied and collapses, unconscious. The company commander digs him with the heel of his boot, then points to a hole in the ground to which the soldiers carry him.
(The apparition vanishes.)

Troops on the retreat. It is raining. The general from the banquet is sitting in an automobile. He gives instructions to take the tarpaulin from a wounded man's stretcher and to spread it over his car. He waves to his mirror image and drives off.
(The apparition vanishes.)

A turnip field in Bohemia. Two children carry a child's coffin to the graveyard. They drop the coffin. They drag the body, which is lying in the field, back to the coffin and continue on their way.
(The apparition vanishes.)

Beside a large bakery a pile of rubble, slag, and industrial waste. Half-starved children hunt for bits of bread. They find an unexploded shell. They play with it. It explodes.
(The apparition vanishes.)

Line of hanged men in Nowy Sacz. Children push and twist the corpses.
(The apparition vanishes.)

A woman who has bought potatoes is killed by other people who didn't get any. They stamp on the corpse.
(The apparition vanishes.)

A goods train on a railway track: the living quarters of a mass of bedraggled humanity; they are refugees, including pregnant women, old men dying, sick children.
(The apparition vanishes.)

In front of a hut in Volhynia. A peasant with his sheepdog. A soldier passes by and stabs the dog with his bayonet, wounding it.
(The apparition vanishes.)

Officers' drinking bout. A lieutenant shoots a waitress.
(The apparition vanishes.)

Lull in the fighting on the Drina. A Serb peasant fetches water. A lieutenant on the other bank takes aim. He shoots the peasant dead.
(The apparition vanishes.)

Good Friday in a Parisian church. It is hit by a shell from the 120-kilometre cannon.
(The apparition vanishes.)

Easter Sunday. Russian prisoners of war, who have refused to carry out trench work under enemy fire, say their final prayers.
(The apparition vanishes.)

Soldiers in their death throes on the barbed-wire entanglements before Przemysl.
(The apparition vanishes.)

Hand-to-hand fighting and mopping up in a trench.
(The apparition vanishes.)

A schoolroom, hit by a bomb dropped from an aeroplane.
(The apparition vanishes.)

A soldier is dragged out of a mound of earth. His face is covered with blood. He spreads his arms like a cross. His eyes are lifeless.
(The apparition vanishes.)

A bomb falls from an aeroplane on a field dressing station.
(The apparition vanishes.)

A mine explodes. A soldier stretches his bloody arm stumps out towards the banqueting hall.
(The apparition vanishes.)

Double tableau. A German officer shoots a French prisoner who is begging for his life. A French officer shoots a German prisoner who is begging for his life.
(The apparition vanishes.)

Desolation on the Somme. Clouds of smoke like gigantic flags of mourning. Buildings collapse. Wells are blown up by sappers and filled with earth. Evacuation. Old people are chased out of their houses. People shivering with cold at the assembly points. Women fall to their knees before officers. Deportation to forced labour.
(The apparition vanishes.)

The Sorel dairy farm at Loison is reduced to ashes and 250 of the wounded housed there burned alive.
(The apparition vanishes.)

A hospital ship is sunk.
(The apparition vanishes.)

Longuyon set alight with barrels of petroleum, the houses and the church plundered. The wounded and small children burned alive.
(The apparition vanishes.)

Flanders. A gas mask sits before a cooking pot in a hut that has been plundered. On her lap a smaller gas mask.
(The apparition vanishes.)

A horse appears, the outline of the artillery piece it was made to carry marked in blood on its back.

(The apparition vanishes.)

Winter on the island of Asinara. Prisoners strip the clothes off comrades who have died of cholera. The starving eat the flesh of those who have starved to death.
(The apparition vanishes.)

Barracks in Siberia. Men crouch on the ground, their hair turned ashen, undernourished, in tattered uniforms, barefoot, staring blankly ahead, their eyes seeming hollows. Some sleep, some write, some exercise with shovels and practise rifle drill.
(The apparition vanishes.)

Thousands of crosses in a snowfield.
(The apparition vanishes.)

A battlefield. Craters and caverns. Paths through those barbed-wire entanglements still standing. Luxury automobiles arrive. Tourists disperse in groups, photograph each other in heroic poses, parody salvoes of gunfire, laugh, and shout. One of them has found a skull, puts it on the end of his walking stick and returns triumphant. A grief-stricken man interrupts, takes the find and buries the skull.
(Groans of the sleeping. The apparition vanishes.)

A procession of gas masks appears; they form up facing those present in the banqueting hall and appear to approach the table.

THE GAS-MASKS

> Can masks still filter wondrous smells?
> Our curiosity compels,
> though we no more can swallow.
> Alas, our plates contained today
> dried veg, prepared the German way,
> Green-cross grenades to follow.

(The apparition vanishes.)

In the very front line in the Carpathians. All is quiet. Standing corpses in the trenches. Men shoulder to shoulder, guns in the aiming position.

THE SOLDIERS WHO HAVE FROZEN TO DEATH

A night to freeze your breath.
Oh, who thought up this death?
While you sleep, undisturbed,
cold stars stare, unperturbed.
We died, without exemption,
but you're beyond redemption!

(The apparition vanishes.)

An old Serb peasant digs his grave.

THE OLD SERB PEASANT

We stood around the family chest,
soldiers shouting: Where's the rest?
They wanted more than what I gave,
that's why I now must dig my grave.
We had no more, we stood there naked
with nothing more, that they could take it.
They put my children against the wall.
They'll meet me at the trumpet call.
Burnt is my crop, burnt is my home,
so now I dig my grave alone.
My children are calling—yes, I'm coming!
Help me, Lord, enter the kingdom of heaven!

(The apparition vanishes.)

Crown Prince Wilhelm with the flamethrowers of the Fifth Army. As a greeting to the Crown Prince, the flames form a "W."

THE FLAMES

We are the flames! The shape we form
has roasted in infernal fire
so many men, of women born,
who suffered for their heart's desire.
"W" for Woe—scourge of our time,
devoid of sanity,
the Crown Prince plays his crazy game,
mowing down humanity

in the Devil's name.
A Death's Head blazons his crime!

(The apparition vanishes.)

Twelve hundred horses emerge from the sea, come ashore, and set off at a trot. Water streams from their eyes.

THE TWELVE HUNDRED HORSES

Here we are, here we are, here we are, here we are—
here we are, we're the twelve hundred horses!
Dohna's horses are here—Dohna, now do you hear—
for we've risen right up to the surface!

Oh, we'll come, Dohna, now we will haunt your worst dream,
those regions below heard our sighs.
Without light, we were blind, though the water would stream,
too much water, from hundreds of eyes.

Count Dohna, surrounded by 12 members of the press. Suddenly they are replaced by 12 horses. They attack him and kill him.
(The apparition vanishes.)

An inventor's antiquated workshop.

LEONARDO DA VINCI —how and why I do not describe my method for remaining under water as long as is possible; and this I do not publish or explain on account of the evil nature of man, for they would use it to commit murder on the sea bed by breaking up ships' hulls and sinking the same, together with all on board—
(The apparition vanishes.)

A sweet sound. Dead calm after the sinking of the Lusitania. *On a piece of floating wood, two children's corpses.*

THE *LUSITANIA* CHILDREN

We pitch and toss upon the brine,
who knows where now we dwell—
and yet how bright this life doth shine
and children's cares dispel—!

(The apparition vanishes.)

Two dogs of war, harnessed to a machine gun.

THE DOGS OF WAR

Our burden is evil, and yet we bear it,
faithful to death, though the price be paid.
How lovely God's sun, inviting to share it!
But the Devil called, and we obeyed.

(The apparition vanishes.)

A dying forest. Everything has been shot to pieces, cut down, and sawn up. Earth stripped bare, with only a few sickly trees protruding. The felled trunks still lie around in the hundreds, their branches cut off and their bark already decaying on the ground. A dilapidated narrow-gauge railway runs through it.

THE DYING FOREST

Once I was green, now I am grey.
This is your crime, your mad power play.
Behold me now, after your feud.
I was a wood! I was a wood!

My treetop canopy's the soul's true home.
Hark, you believers in eternal Rome!
Wrapped in my silence was the eternal Word.
You've put the whole creation to the sword.
A curse on those who violated me,
defiling heaven's communion with the tree!
No more green glory in full plenitude—
I was a wood! I was a wood!

(The apparition vanishes.)

A colonel has a Dalmatian woman with her 12-year-old blond-haired boy arrested. As the woman is dragged off, he gives the order to shoot the boy in the head. He stands smoking while soldiers kneel on the boy's hands and the execution is carried out.

THE MOTHER

Through all the days that you defile
may this sight haunt you all the while!
And when your hellish journey's done,

may it remain, the final one.
Let splinters from this noble brow
pierce through your heart and brain somehow!
May you live long and each night dream,
your ears filled with a mother's scream!

(The apparition vanishes.)

Viennese wine-tavern music, feverishly distorted. The execution of Battisti. Laughing soldiers surround the corpse. The curious stretch their necks. The jolly executioner with his hands above the dead man's head.

THE AUSTRIAN FACE

Death becomes a dancer
and hatred turns to fun.
Hard times?—a joke's the answer.
It's funny, that—how come?
We know we're the greatest,
although our life seems mean.
To enjoy the latest
we must join the scene.
A Christian good and true
tells his children how to pray,
and if he's a hangman, too—
just for laughs, he'll say.

(The apparition vanishes.)

During the following phantasmagoria the sounds escalate to become horrifying music. On Monte Gabriele on the Isonzo. Unburied, half-decayed corpses piled high in a heap. A flock of ravens circle their pickings.

THE RAVENS

Those whom honour killed in war
feed us in the fields of anguish.
Generals, scenes your hearts adore
mean that ravens never languish!

It was not us had to apply
for nourishment to fill our maws.
It is not you nor us who die,
but soldiers slaughtered for our cause.

Our victories we celebrate
with piles of victims growing higher.
Those fools at home failed to abate
the orgies in which we conspire.

The generals as birds of prey
will screech their slogans through the land.
Out there unburied soldiers lay,
while ravens seized the high command!

What matter if the battle's lost,
for you like us need have no fears.
We do not have to count the cost,
for war makes us both profiteers!

We're species that survived the war,
the general as the raven's friend.
There is one duty we adore:
to hold out to the bitter end.

When officers enjoy their feast,
we ravens won't be going short.
We've never hungered in the least
while on the trail where armies fought.

For hunger never was our taste.
The very thought—we'd die of shame!
You've made the hinterland a waste,
but here we'll stay and share your game.

The starving children's fate is sealed
and old men find their final rest,
while out here on the battlefield
the soldiers die at our behest!

Your slaughterhouse you'll always fill
with raw recruits lined up for war.
When shall we cease to claim our kill?
Croaked the ravens: nevermore!

(The apparition vanishes.)

The music, completely muffled, accompanies the pageant now commencing, before gradually falling silent. An interminable procession of ashen-faced women marches past, flanked by soldiers with fixed bayonets.

THE FEMALE AUXILIARIES

The army put us on parade
as whores to give the men a thrill,
but now our whole haggard brigade
must leave, for we have had our fill.
Sacrificed to heroes' urges,
infected by your courage, too,
upon our cheeks a rose-bloom surges—
syphilis, if you but knew.

Blood and tears and wine and sperm
fuelled your hectic bacchanal.
Now that through you we're all infirm,
our homeland is the hospital.

And so, today, by all despised,
in shapeless smock, barely discreet,
our spoils of war but ill-disguised,
our scourge we'll bear in some retreat.

Yet we shall grow through future ages!
A human storm will shake the land,
a thousand years and more it rages,
a constant challenge to mankind!

(The apparition vanishes.)

A phosphorescent glow fills the banqueting hall.

THE UNBORN SON

Lest we witness this transgression,
we ask you to abort our birth.
For shame! Expect no intercession,
for such heroes have no worth.
Sons to fathers such as thee—
unborn may we ever be!

And so it goes, pain follows pleasure,
my father's lust bequeathed to me
his syphilis, his earthly treasure,
I shun the villain's company!
For this base world I will not share
with living dead to breathe foul air.

(The glow dies out.)

Total darkness. Then on the horizon a wall of flame rises towards the heavens. Distant cries of the dying.

EPILOGUE

The Final Night

Battlefield. Craters. Smoke clouds. Starless night. The horizon is a wall of flames. Corpses. Dying soldiers. Men and women in gas masks appear.

A DYING SOLDIER (*crying out*)

Captain, call out the firing squad!
No one can make me shed my blood
for King and Country. Go ahead, shoot!
Once I'm dead, you can't make me salute!

When I'm up there with the Lord on High,
Kings and Emperors I'll defy
and scorn their Orders of the Day!
Where is my home? Is my son at play?

While in the arms of our Lord I sleep,
a letter scribbled on paper cheap
will be read by a woman who starts to weep,
aware of a love so deep, so deep!

Captain, you must have lost your mind,
you've sent me to face a dreadful end
and turned my heart to a firebrand.
I'll not fight for any Fatherland!

What you've destroyed with your iron rod
are the bonds that kept me from my God.
It's Death that should face the firing squad!
Not for no Kaiser I'll shed my blood!

FEMALE GAS MASK (*approaches*)

This man, I guess, has died at God's behest,
but on this battlefield there is no rest,
for duty calls us all in this momentous age,

both men and women dressed for some mad masquerade.
Blood, sweat, and toil and tears all claim an equal right,
seeking new honours when both genders fight.

MALE GAS MASK (*prepares to join her*)

If only your face
got accustomed to mine,
we then might embrace,
for your mask is so fine.

But no features are shown
when such horrors appal.
We must stay unknown
and obey duty's call.

While we shoulder our rifle,
we dread a reprisal
from fumes that could stifle
our will for survival.

But while flames fill the air
we still feel hale and hearty,
so let's form a pair
and be off to the party.

Distant gunfire.

FEMALE GAS MASK

Distinguishing features
we have to surrender,
for we're merely creatures
without face or gender.

Our life is a fight
between spectres and drones,
so we revel at night
to the sound of trombones.

BOTH (*arm in arm*)

Distinguishing features
we have to surrender,

for we're merely creatures
without face or gender.

(They vanish.)

(Two generals, fleeing in a motorcar.)

GENERAL *(Speech-song)*

Our transport can't save us,
the earth's full of shell holes,
barbed wire, and barriers
plus deeper hell holes.
The fortunes of war
mean we're facing defeat.
So we've begun our
strategic retreat.

Men of our years
soon run out of breath,
and nightmarish fears
scare us to death.

The troops give no quarter
while we do a bunk.
Drive on through the slaughter,
or else we are sunk!

There's a corpse dead as mutton
and a man moans he's hurt.
Goddammit, a button
has come off his shirt!

I'm such a stickler,
this makes me see red.
"Sew it on quick, there!
Else you are dead!"

Don't dare make me frown,
or I'll blow a fuse,
won't take things lying down!
The war's no excuse!

“Stand to attention!
Report to the Sarge!
Even if deaf and dumb,
you’re on a charge!”

It’s a scandal, such squaddies
mean all hope is lost!
Drive over the bodies
and don’t count the cost!

The generals drive off. Dawn is breaking.

Two war correspondents alight from a motorcar, wearing military-style breeches and carrying binoculars and camera.

FIRST WAR CORRESPONDENT

This place looks good
for us to pause,
capture the mood
of vibrant wars.

SECOND WAR CORRESPONDENT

Yes, I feel you’re right,
we could see an exchange,
for we may be in sight
of enemy range.

FIRST

Our soldiers fight,
the foe engage,
and what we write
will make front page.

SECOND

With words and pics
reports are filled,
a surefire mix
when men are killed.

FIRST

We love to quote
from briefing sessions
and always note
firsthand impressions.

(He approaches a dying soldier.)

SECOND

Meeting your death
should feel like rapture!
Your final breath
we wish to capture.

FIRST

While you're alive,
the scene's appealing,
so please describe
just what you're feeling.

SECOND

Share your impressions,
your final thought.
Can one draw lessons
from how you fought?

FIRST

Thrills for our readers:
"His Final Breath"!
Details you feed us
give flavour to death.

SECOND

They spice our writing,
the boss applauds,
make news exciting,
earn us awards.

DYING SOLDIER

I'm barely surviving—
see how I'm writhing—
I need a helping hand—
else I'll be dying!

I have lain here all night—
my wound's a dreadful sight—
lacking medical care—
to set it right.

There is no time to spare—
Bleeding—I gasp for air—
give me a helping hand—
why are you standing there?

My breath—as you can see—
leaves me—gasping for air—
give me—a helping hand—
show that you really care!

FIRST WAR CORRESPONDENT

Has this guy had a drink?
He seems a dead loss.
Why should he think
I'm from the Red Cross?

SECOND

War is war—hear me cough!
Our work's hard to bear!
If a man's head's shot off,
I'd just say "c'est la guerre."

FIRST

I've never been taught
how to offer First Aid.
We just write a report,
and for that we're well paid.

SECOND

Evoking a climate
is what earns our crust.
If a hero is silent,
then he's dead as dust.

(They turn away, preparing to leave.)

DYING SOLDIER

My wife—I'm not strong—
think of my situation—
and take me along—
to the—medical station!

FIRST WAR CORRESPONDENT

What a brazen request!
This man's a real pain!
"You must take a good rest
and stay where you've lain."

SECOND

We've honoured a creature
who serves at the front
with a picture feature!
"What more do you want?"

FIRST

We beat death to your bedside,
your photo's on file.
"Have you no pride?
Just give us a smile!"

SECOND

The man remains silent,
so lest we forget,
once more . . . (*takes photo*) Our client
ain't seen nothing yet!

FIRST

There's no need to moan,
when wonders are happening.
You're all on your own,
so where is the chaplain?

SECOND

We'd ask him to kneel
by the man who must perish.
Our readers would feel
this a scene they could relish.

FIRST

He would do it for me,
for priests are so docile,
and all would agree
that it raises their profile.

SECOND

"Where the devil's the priest?"
you ask as a joke.
He's missing the feast
and the odd puff of smoke.

FIRST

A shell? Time to go,
get the hell out of here.
At the Press Bureau
we'll have nothing to fear.

SECOND

Think that gave me a fright?
No, those bangs make me laugh,
but there's not enough light
for a photograph.

FIRST

You're only too right.
It's time for a change!

We may be in sight
of enemy range.

SECOND

Not born for fighting,
we'll swiftly withdraw
and call what we're writing
"Impressions of War"!

(They drive off.)

A corporal with a revolver drives a platoon into action.

CORPORAL

Quick march! I'm gonna teach ya, you lily-livered lot!
You're dying for the Fatherland, or else you'll all be shot!
Doan imagine for a second I'm gonna let ya skive!
You'll bombard the enemy if you wanna stay alive!

(They disappear.)

BLINDED SOLDIER *(groping forward on all fours)*

Thanks, Mother Earth! It's good to feel your hand,
feel freed from dreadful night and Fatherland!
I breathe the forest and the joys of home.
You guide me back towards your primal womb.
At last the thunderclaps of night have passed.
I'm still not sure quite what it was they asked.
Dear Mother Earth, I now await your dawn.
Soon in the sight of God I'll be reborn.

(He dies.)

FEMALE WAR CORRESPONDENT *(appears)*

At last I've reached the end of my long hunt,
I've found the common man here at the front!

A WOUNDED SOLDIER *(groping forward on all fours)*

My curses on the Kaiser, I feel his heavy hand
has poisoned and polluted our German Fatherland!
His reign has brought disaster, destroying every hope,
his visage is a gallows, his beard the hangman's rope.

His laughter taught us falsehood, his pride was full of hate,
his anger signified a vain attempt to compensate
for the limitless ambition that tore the world apart,
defying inhibitions that constrain the human heart.
From India to the Rhineland and across to the Atlantics
the whole earth was disrupted by his mock-heroic antics.
Instead of mounting a defence of our rich heritage,
he piled it high with bric-a-brac from an archaic age.
Powers of imagination were swiftly put to flight
by a slimy global salesman who dressed up as a knight.
Over land and over sea he spouted out a flood
of malicious verbal venom that curdled up our blood.
He commercialized the values of the whole created world,
so its essential meaning to the depths of hell was hurled.
An Emperor's insanity causes lamentation,
as sales of cheap and shoddy goods disfigure the Creation.
Not ruling by the grace of God, the power in which we trust,
that man's reduced the universe to ashes and to dust.
Wearing the armour of the Lord! By God, our hearts will leap
when history throws such useless junk onto the rubbish heap.
The crazy world that's then revealed is ruled by dynamite,
of all created planets—the most appalling sight!
If only all those statesmen, those diplomats and peers
were now compelled to wallow in this sea of blood and tears!
So curses on the Emperor and all of royal blood,
for those who've caused such carnage should perish in the Flood!
Though born of German parents, when I sit at God's right hand,
I shall denounce the Kaiser who's defiled our motherland!

(The wounded soldier dies.)
(Enter Crown Prince Wilhelm, the Death's Head Hussar, with his entourage.)

DEATH'S HEAD HUSSAR

Into action, you filthy swine!
The scent of battle's just divine.
We shall fight on till our final breath,
for we are the regiment of death.
Proud as we are of our slim figure,
we still attack the foe with vigour.

We may look weird to other eyes,
but those who resist will have a surprise.
Yes, the Hussars have long eyelashes,
but we enjoy heroic clashes.
It's time the boys launched their assault,
each one courageous to a fault.
Victories are won by those with flair,
so into battle if you dare!
While on the Marne the air turned foul,
I did my best to boost morale,
and at Verdun we'll hold the line.
So into action, you filthy swine!

Into action, you filthy swine!
The cut of my tunic's superfine.
My father's simply a paper tiger,
in that respect I'm a real fighter.
I strike as swiftly as a snake,
my country's future is at stake.
My moustache is in fine condition.
If only we had more ammunition!
Though based in France our life is hard,
but we won't retreat a single yard.
Attrition warfare is scarcely fun
for one so young, for one so young.
So before our sacrifice ends in defeat,
we shall arrange a sumptuous treat.
We can still launch our attack in time,
in German a bard can make anything rhyme,
for if duty is harsh, art is sublime.
So into action, you filthy swine!

(The group disappears.)
(A marching song is heard. Enter Nowotny von Eichensieg.)

NOWOTNY VON EICHENSIEG

To counter our flak
they're deploying ack-ack,
so we're fighting back with every man-jack.

The Homeland reserve
are all forced to serve.
They'll be put on a charge if they lose their nerve.

The ordinary blokes
we just treat as jokes.
God only knows why they fights till they croaks.

Those soldiers who skive
have no chance to survive.
Once put inside, they won't come out alive.

I've got a sharp eye
for deserters who try
to sneak off on the sly—they too will die.

If one starts to whine
that he's wounded, the swine
will get his comeuppance back on the front line.

For here I'm the boss!
If a man's a dead loss,
over his dust we'll erect a neat cross.

Army doctors don't bother
to check men's disorders.
Those who recover are just cannon fodder.

They all join the forces,
we can't allow choices,
for all of our boys is—just human resources.

(Exit.)
(Engineer Dr. Abendrot from Berlin appears.)

ENGINEER DR. ABENDROT

If we are to gain final victory at last,
and finally break the constraints of the past,
the decisive campaign has still to be fought,
so we'll call upon science for moral support.
What is the use of the bomb or grenade,
or the most lethal gasses that we have yet made?
The gasses blow back and destroy our own force,

and the enemy gasses affect us far worse.
The arms race should not be a matter of chance.
Science must make the decisive advance.
We face men of iron from legends of old,
who tempt us with offers that glisten like gold,
but such worthless metals we'll just cast away,
for our new inventions will carry the day.
We still dream of fighting with daggers drawn
in an era when flamethrowers define the norm,
but why wield the sword when explosive devices
like mortars and landmines prove far more decisive?
High-flying metaphors cover for crimes
that were not even thought of in earlier times,
but war's not a tournament for the victorious
when the methods employed are actually chlorious!
Who rides into battle like a chivalrous knight
when chemical weapons determine the fight?
Inspired by the legends of German folklore,
we deploy ultramodern weapons of war,
and to prove we're not Huns, if all else fails,
we echo motifs from Grimms' fairytales.
As narrator-inventor it's my impression
that naughty children should be taught a lesson.
If they think we're barbarians, they'll have a surprise:
our electro-technology will open their eyes.
Poets may sing of "red sky in the morning",
But "Evening Red" is the ultimate warning!
Abendrot, Siegfried – my name's dark as sin,
For Death is a master that hails from Berlin.
"There once was a maiden" – that's a good start
for stories that tug at the listener's heart,
There once was a made-in-Germany plague
so toxic the record provokes helpless rage.
That virus our doctors sought to contain,
but where is it now, when we need it again?
Scientists rapidly sense the demand,
and we have the ear of the High Command.
For all your needs we can fake an Ersatz:
cookies and coffee and meat in choice cuts.

To cook up a substitute death I'd be willing,
and market it under my name—what a killing!
The gasses that we have deployed in the past
affected our own men—that method can't last.
From now on we'll slaughter whoever we please
by means of our substitute lung disease!
No need any longer to make any sound,
as we turn the whole earth to a burial ground.
It's easy to strengthen our front if we try.
Whole armies will perish without knowing why.
One press on the button's enough to expunge
hundreds of thousands of enemy lungs.
We don't need to shout now, we just hold our breath,
and our victims will silently go to their death.
We scientists follow the military's bidding,
the proof of our weapons will be in the pudding!
Defeatists may try to stab us in the back,
but our miracle weapons will counterattack.
Our methods will take even Death by surprise,
as we engineer one last throw of the dice,
and—whoopee!—the enemy's out of the hunt,
while we settle accounts on the Western Front.
The huge piles of corpses will prove that we've won,
and we shall have conquered our place in the sun.
I imagine already a sunset crowned red,
as Abendrot's howitzers heap up the dead.
Both the army and navy must concede defeat,
for with the new science no God could compete.

(He releases chemical weapons with the touch of a button. Three brigades succumb without a sound.)

Children, my children—the news you have heard:
you'll not find salvation in the arms of the Lord!
The Watch on the Rhine need no longer be sung
after this Götterdämmerung.
There'll be no more restrictions on how wars are fought.
Global destruction's the final resort!

(He disappears.)

(Darkness is falling. Hyenas with human faces appear. Their spokesmen Fressack and Naschkatz take up position to the left and the right. They crouch over the corpses and speak into their ears.)

FRESSACK

Should you need something, you just have to ask.
Don't be deterred though my face is a mask.
First you faced the enemy, now you have—seen us!
Don't be afraid for we're merely—hyenas!
What we are doing here let me explain:
we'll ensure your sacrifice wasn't in vain.
Cash you don't need now but we'd like to save.
Why take your valuables into the grave?

NASCHKATZ

Count yourselves lucky that you've been slain!
Military losses bring financial gain.
You risked your lives willingly out in the field,
While we assessed what investments would yield.
While our aim was profit, to fight was your task,
now there's just one more thing we'd like to ask.
For why shed your blood without any reward,
when on the meat market the prices have soared?

FRESSACK

You can trust us to get everything right,
soon the Kaiser's army won't force you to fight.
What do we care about grenades and mortars?
Making a profit is what war has taught us.
You no longer need to feel hunger or cold.
The sleep of the dead is a joy to behold.
Please listen carefully—this is God's truth:
Food and fuel prices have gone through the roof.

NASCHKATZ

Let us tell you in whispers: you owe us your thanks,
for death during battle brings wealth to the banks.
As our capital grows we spend money like water,
we're making a bid for the business of slaughter.

Count yourselves lucky that you're lying there,
while banknotes and bullets just fly through the air.
Of your heroic actions such tales will be told!
While you're soaked in blood we're just swimming in gold.

FRESSACK

In the Annals your fame will last till judgment day!
Easy death achieves nothing, and someone must pay.
It wasn't us, the money men, that provoked the war,
but as you marched away we already knew the score.
Of the profits we have earned no poet will be singing,
but the ears of fallen soldiers with praise are always ringing.
In years to come your children will have wondrous tales to tell,
while our kids must be contented with stocks and shares to sell.

NASCHKATZ

How narrowly my children missed conscription in the war!
As luck would have it none was drafted by the army corps.
Though the first was far too honest to ask for intercession,
his line of work is classified as a reserved profession.
For the next I used my contacts, for his pride was simply daft.
In return for a down payment he too has dodged the draft.
Now if they call up my youngest, I pull some other string.
Of course you all were young once—and youth must have its fling!

FRESSACK

My oldest boy has wangled the whole business on his own,
the next one was exempted when he wrote a victory poem.
So when his country called him, he knew how to stay alive:
his talents earned admission to the cushy War Archive.
But back there in Vienna you know what's all the rage:
he chats up a director and is writing for the stage,
though of course he's got to churn out some trash about the war.
And my youngest, oh, dear boy! His health is far too poor.

NASCHKATZ

By enlisting in the army, you bagged a better deal.
You chose the softer option, while we need nerves of steel.
For seven days a week our anxious lives are filled with toil,

stocking up with leather goods and soap and cooking oil.
We guarantee delivery, but sometimes by bad luck
a deal to sell a trainload completely comes unstuck.
We'll get by, but in peacetime? Oh God, I hope you'll grant
that someone will create a brand-new weapons-making plant.

FRESSACK

From that may God preserve us, for no one talks of peace,
the aches and pains of wartime we don't want to increase.
We produce and deliver, making our contribution,
but peace might bring disaster, exacting retribution.
A plant to make new weapons? But I'm happy with Skoda!
Their devastating impact's been praised by Roda Roda.
You chaps when you're buried won't be needing any kit,
but my better half—the fur she wants must be the latest fit.

NASCHKATZ

It's for us you dead soldiers should go into mourning.
Times are getting tough and those rumours are a warning.
Should we have to acknowledge that we toiled in vain,
the hazards of peacetime will bring us further pain.
So what's left? For my son I'll buy an estate,
and one of my friends has been made a magnate.
Thus each to his own: to the heroes a grave,
but we're the hyenas—and know how to save!

CHORUS OF THE HYENAS

That's life! That's life!
Don't talk too loud!
The warlike strife
has done us proud.
We've raised the price,
knowing God's ways.
Three trucks of rice
and three of maize
wait on the track.
We'll seize our chance
and the whole pack
can join the dance!

(Tango of the Hyenas around the corpses. The wall of flames in the background has disappeared, and a sulphurous yellow glow covers the horizon. The gigantic silhouette of the Lord of the Hyenas appears. The Hyenas stop dancing and cluster around.)

(A dark, greying, woolly, closely trimmed beard, growing out of a similar head of hair, encloses his face like the hide of an animal; dynamically curved nose; large, bulging eyes with whites very prominent and tiny piercing pupils. The hunched physique is reminiscent of a tapir. Smart suit with embroidered waistcoat. The right foot seems to be striding boldly forwards. The left hand, clenched into a fist, rests on the trouser pocket, the right hand, on which a diamond ring sparkles, gestures towards the Hyenas.)

THE LORD OF THE HYENAS

Fall in and stand up straight!
We've lots to celebrate,
So—On parade!
You've beaten every foe
and now it's time to show
you've made the grade.

You needn't waste your breath
begging for loot from Death.
No cause to be afraid!
God knows we've got the right
to put such fears to flight,
we've got it made!

The Son of Man who suffered,
and on the cross was offered,
deserves to be despised.
In place of life eternal
I've kindled fires infernal.
I am the Anti-Christ.

To heaven we give thanks.
The crooks who run the banks
have made His realm redundant.
His blood He may have shed
but as He bows his head,
our power remains abundant.

His love could not prevent
our rise. His power is spent.
We've nothing more to fear.
We are the true believers,
redeemers and deceivers.
The Anti-Christ is near.

While you sharpen your claws
to further our great cause,
myself I lead the fight.
Against their feeble sword
I wield the printed word.
Our might is right.

While others do their duty
we carry off our booty,
far stronger than before.
Archaic powers advance,
complete the circle dance.
The Cross has lost the war!

So those who crucified Him
now openly deride Him.
Judas has his reward!
And from this vale of tears
completely disappears
the servant of the Lord.

A world that needs redeeming
succumbed to evil scheming.
The Saviour's cause is lost.
We continue on our course
without the least remorse,
scorning the cost.

Now we inaugurate
a realm of endless hate
from which all love is banned.
Global destruction means
the laughter of the Fiend
echoes throughout the land.

Mankind must walk on crutches
when all that Progress touches
is up for tender.
The Devil may be lame,
but his triumph, just the same,
makes God surrender.

He hobbles everyday
to the Stock Exchange to play
with market trends.
For him there's nothing sacred,
for the world has been stripped naked,
his power never ends.

His realm cannot stagnate
when a newspaper magnate
marks the end of time.
For souls are in my grasp
and just watch how I kick ass
of anything sublime!

Their minds I cauterize,
so I deserve first prize,
as hero of the hour.
My sovereign powers arise
from those who advertise
and boost my power.

Hyenas are my mates,
and everyone who hates
takes my advice.
So where bodies are buried,
for the future we are readied,
and we control the price.

To beat the competition
you build up your position.
Don't cut things fine!
History is soaked in blood,
but the market we can flood.
Watch the bottom line!

The old guard must take the blame,
for Moriz is my name,
and all boxes I have ticked.
Teachings of the Christian shepherd
with errors full are peppered!
My name is Benedikt!

The Christian world may hope
for salvation from a Pope,
to whom I'm not related.
I have my own believers,
the swindlers and deceivers,
whose gains have escalated.

Before my profane throne
the insolent lie prone,
adoring filthy lucre.
I trust that Mammon's lure
for ever will endure.
To us belongs the future!

Merchants of death grow rich,
for they control the pitch
with a clenched fist.
Although the world is tragic,
the press has the black magic
none can resist.

We've formed a vital link,
forged out of printer's ink,
technology, and death.
So with thanks you should assess
how we squeeze blood from the press,
and stifle every breath.

With newsprint's satanic art
I've pierced the Saviour's heart.
Now the way is clear,
and like Judas we'll betray
our neighbours every day.
The Anti-Christ is here!

(Waltz of the Hyenas around the corpses.)

THE HYENAS

That's right! That's right!
With sharpened claw
we join the fight
and guzzle gore.

We slake our thirst,
our fists are tight,
so do your worst!
The price is right.

Guzzle, muzzle,
stir the pot.
Prices bubble,
drink it hot!

That's life! That's life!
With eager paw
we plunge the knife
and bathe in gore.

Just join the dance,
keep up the fight
as if in trance.
The price is right.

Guzzle, muzzle,
stir the pot.
Prices bubble,
drink it hot!

Our thirst we slake
by drinking gore,
squeezed by our paw.

With sharpened claw
we bathe in gore.
The price is right.

Sleep tight, sleep tight!
You've lost the fight.

Abracadabra!
That's right! That's right!

(The Hyenas cluster around the corpses.)
(Three gossip columnists appear.)

FIRST GOSSIP COLUMNIST

A silver lining illumines the skies.
The waltz, not the tango, has won the first prize.

SECOND GOSSIP COLUMNIST

No need any longer for asking what ails one.
We greet the arrival of travelling salesmen.

THIRD GOSSIP COLUMNIST

Life's become easier, so we can give thanks
to the captains of industry who run our banks.

FIRST

No longer a loner, I make a good fist
of adding more names to the attendance list.

SECOND

The race is no longer just for the few.
I'm proud to be granted an interview.

THIRD

Now Mars no longer reigns supreme,
men about town shape the social scene.

FIRST

Those who've survived can keep hale and hearty.
Methinks I scent the morning air, so let us join the party!

SECOND

Fashion designers are launching new angles.
Frau Fanto's dress simply sparkles with spangles.

THIRD

The upper circle won't be empty for long,
as new arrivals join the merry throng.

FIRST

If the crush is too great, there'd be a sensation,
for all are engaged in polite conversation.

SECOND

The usual suspects announce their arrival.
Where would we be without their survival?

THIRD

Prince Salvator walks with elastic stride.
Three Honorary Counsellors come for the ride.

FIRST

Two Consul Generals don't want to be missed
from our overflowing attendance list.

SECOND

Check the list of the fallen? That would be a waste!
Those present include all men of good taste.

THIRD

Such a grand occasion—and so "déjà vu":
It's 'im 'n me 'n 'er 'n us 'n you!

FIRST

So many stars, the smartest set!
The world just ain't seen nothing yet!

SECOND

Field Marshal Höfer's here, but not the General Staff.
The news from the front gives us no cause to laugh.

THIRD

World history has reached its carnival night.
Now we see what made the nations fight.

FIRST

The response of the enemy's only a rumour,
but we'll never lose our unique sense of humour.

SECOND

All classes are present, the show's reached its height,
and the kids will be dancing throughout the long night.

THIRD

Will it still feel so good when the carnival closes?
The Devil's new partner is tuberculosis!

(They make their escape.)

(Now the whole horizon is covered with clouds of smoke. A moon flecked with scarlet emerges from black-and-yellow clouds which are fringed with colourful shreds. On the battlefield military units are retreating in chaotic disorder. Three armoured vehicles appear. Men and animals in panic-stricken flight. A babble of voices.)

FIRST VOICE

Our firepower's repelled the latest attack,
but shivers of panic run right down my back.

SECOND VOICE

To capture their trench was a daring feat,
but I fear we'll soon be forced to retreat.

THIRD VOICE

We've forced the enemy to fall back,
but what the devil's the point of that?

FOURTH VOICE

Such a short-term victory is hardly God's gift.
Two of our comrades are sadly missed.

FIRST

I fear that our losses may be many more,
and now we are burdened with prisoners of war.

SECOND

The enemy threatens from every side.
An infant and two civilians have died.

THIRD

Our long-range cannon have hit the mark,
but where are the children who played in the park?

FOURTH

The military damage could be far worse,
but we've suffered casualties, both foot and horse.

FIRST

Our mates over there who are throwing a party
must be the Bavarians, hale and hearty.

SECOND

And those who are raising the cheers that disturb us
must be those doughty Wurttembergers.

THIRD

So many brave men, risking their life,
hail from all parts of the German Reich.

FOURTH

And others whose exploits show hair-raising daring
are hot-blooded warriors speaking Hungarian.

FIRST

Our Bulgarian allies are on the retreat,
but we drive them forward to stave off defeat.

SECOND

And those who manoeuvre in spasms and jerks?
They're our Islamic allies, the Ottoman Turks.

THIRD

Those cracking their whips to give others a thrashing
can only be German—and probably Prussian!

FOURTH

And who's losing heart now the rain's caused a flood?
An Austrian army, stuck in the mud!

THIS VOICE

Our forces undoubtedly are in the soup,
the counterattack's coming cock-a-hoop.

THAT VOICE

With fierce battle cries the proud German shouts:
"You must be the Frogs, but we are the Krauts!"

DIFFERENT VOICES

Can we still be allies when anything goes?
Do the foes shoot their friends or the friends shoot their foes?

OTHER VOICES

The claims of true brotherhood hardly require
casualties caused by our guns' friendly fire.

ALL TOGETHER

The crisis has reached its acutest extreme!
We're repelling the danger as if in a dream.

AUSTRIAN VOICE

Salvation at last for us band of brothers:
the sky is transformed into Austrian colours!

GERMAN VOICE

Dead wrong, old boy! Don't make me laugh:
the German colours run up the flag-staff!

AUSTRIAN VOICE

Don't talk such tripe! Just look here, young feller:
on your side it's black, on ours it's bright yellow.

GERMAN VOICE

Heavens alive! We won't throw in the spanner:
dead Germans salute the Imperial banner.

BOTH TOGETHER

The stars in the heavens make us all feel bolder.
We're proud to be fighting shoulder to shoulder.

AUSTRIAN VOICE

The verdict of history will be on our side—

GERMAN VOICE

because our Krupp cannons are turning the tide.
We're thrashing the enemy with an iron rod—

AUSTRIAN VOICE

thanks to Skoda munitions and the grace of God.

BOTH TOGETHER

As a last resort we can still win the day
with the most modern howitzers blasting away.

(Flashes of lightning.)

ALL VOICES *(in confusion)*

We fight in a frenzy
with bullets and knives!
The enemy's envy
won't save their lives!

(Snakes of fire in the sky, red and green lights.)

Alas, alack! Alas, alack!

VOICES FROM ABOVE

The heavens above are fighting back!

VOICES FROM BELOW

The powers of darkness making gains!
Look up—those are our fighter planes!

VOICES FROM ABOVE

Yes, fighters, but with another mission:
to crush your military position.

VOICES FROM BELOW

Their strategy is far too wild:
they'd even kill an unborn child!

(Flaming stars, crosses, and swords in the skies.)

Look, shining swords!
With decorations
this night rewards
our conflagrations.

(Shining spheres, swathes of fire.)

Those our brothers
mark your defeat
with blazing colours
and seething heat.

(Three comets appear.)

VOICES FROM ABOVE

Three fiery horsemen on flaming steeds!
The End is approaching—prepare for your fate!

VOICES FROM BELOW

Our cannonballs answer at far higher speeds,
with gun carriages made out of armour plate!

VOICES FROM ABOVE

Our forces are unimpressed by your pranks,
with weapons forged out of far finer steels!

VOICES FROM BELOW

Don't try to bluff us—you can't stop our tanks,
apocalyptical automobiles!

(Two messengers arrive.)

FIRST MESSENGER

Let's sing hosannas and ring the church bells:
They've bombarded the Mount of Olives with shells.

SECOND MESSENGER

For true believers there can be no question:
The holy Mount was a fortified position.

FIRST

Now let us praise the brave and the wise,
those who have launched this audacious attack,
but it's also our duty to praise to the skies
the cunning defenders who've thrown it right back.

SECOND

We scarcely care who emerge as the winners
and harvest their laurels where thorns once grew.
Whatever their strategy, those dreadful sinners
we cannot forgive for they know what they do.

BOTH

If the bombardment has shattered the cross,
its splinters so numerous that we've lost count,
our pundits will play down the military loss,
hoping it proves but a trivial amount.

(A large bloodstained cross appears.)

VOICES FROM ABOVE

Show due respect, fear where you tread:
Our cross is stained the deepest red.

VOICES FROM BELOW

We'll not be fooled nor change our minds,
we scorn both prayer and augury!
Astronomers may read the signs,
Satan commands our loyalty.

(Blood rains down.)

VOICES FROM ABOVE

Retreat to dry land and be on your guard:
it's raining blood and it's raining hard.

VOICES FROM BELOW

Surely you've grasped our latest trick:
we're shooting to pieces the forces of love.
There's war in heaven and the air is thick
with blood that comes pouring from above.
No one can shake the morale of our chaps—

VOICES FROM ABOVE

as long as your battlefronts don't collapse!

VOICES FROM BELOW

Headquarters report we're more powerful than ever.
We're strong in the air, in the field undefeated.

VOICES FROM ABOVE

But you must beware of a change in the weather!
The sky's turning black and your ranks are depleted.

(Ashes rain down.)

VOICES FROM BELOW

That must be a blessing, that's a good sign:
we've created a blanket of ashes so fine.

(Stones rain down.)

Stones hurled from heaven? The same old trick!
Hand grenades are what one really fears.
Hardened by battle, we've been in the thick
of hailstorms of fire that lasted for years.

VOICES FROM ABOVE

Yes, it's true that our tactics may seem rather slow.
We've got lots to learn, but we'll catch up with time.
Wandering stars are still planets that shine,
forming a contrast with bandits below.

VOICES FROM BELOW

Don't forget our firepower has backing from Berlin!
Your attack is faltering, you've got no chance to win.

(Sparks rain down.)

A VOICE FROM BELOW

This apparition
dazzles my eyes.
In my submission
we're caught by surprise.

SECOND VOICE FROM BELOW

What is that thundering?
Whence comes that spark?
It seems we are wandering
all in the dark.

(Total darkness.)

FILM CAMERAMEN

How the hell can we film without any light?
Our thrillers supply what the audience wants.
We're trying to shoot *How the Armies Fight*
as a sequel to *Willy Loses His Pants.*
If we can't meet our contract, we'll all feel so vexed.
We do need a hit, can't afford any duds.
Isonzo had customers weeping in floods,
Judgment Day aims at more dazzling effects!

A VOICE FROM ABOVE

Your ceaseless struggle for military gains
we watch while you're splitting each other's brains.
At last, here on Mars, our position's defined:
we'll break off relations with humankind.
You've been weighed in the balance and found wanting:
it's a war of defence that we are mounting.
Now we're determined to settle the score
with planet earth and its frontiers of war
and with all the miserable earthly species
that are trying to storm the heavenly reaches.
The planets rotate from station to station,
but earthlings defile the whole Creation.
You torture animals, enslave kith and kin,
reprimand dignity and reward sin.

Good men are massacred, villains grow fat,
for the concept of honour you don't give a jot.
Virtue just serves as a means to grow rich,
while articulate discourse is dumped in the ditch,
along with spirit and senses, language and thought,
while the afterworld's packaged and sold for export.
No longer is evil redeemed by God's promise:
creation is placed in the service of commerce.
Consumption becomes the sole purpose of life,
and shopping obsesses the world and his wife.
You've all become slaves of practical needs,
losing spiritual life to material creeds.
For increased production you'd sell your own skin,
battling for raw materials like copper and tin.
You complete cash transactions and buy real estate,
and poison the eyes of the world with your hate.
You forfeit all claim to eternal light,
for ruthless ambition has blinded your sight.
Who cares for the stars and the warmth of the sun?
Your only concern is the battles you've won,
the killing fields spreading from pole unto pole,
with minds set on murder as primary goal.
From the West you may conquer the Orient,
but pollute the whole natural environment.
When you pray, it's to beg an increase in your kill,
unblushing about all the blood that you spill.
God the creator and his natural world
into the chasm of darkness are hurled.
Cursing the heavens till you're blue in the face,
you plaster the landscape with emblems of race.
You may play it tough, but we're not surprised
that the victories you claim are a packet of lies.
About brotherly love you're continually boasting,
while giving your neighbours a terrible roasting,
stealing the food from strangers in need
to satisfy your own insatiable greed,
piling their heads with coals of fire,
hoping to gain the warmth you desire,
for a cosy feeling make others work hard

while greasing your palms with expensive lard,
you blackmail and plunder, you lie through your teeth,
regurgitate madness as if true belief.
Invalids churn out the anthems of glory,
TB and syphilis tell the opposite story.
You're hunters of men, heroes and traders,
spreaders of infection, hand-grenaders,
you plunder the treasures of fantasy
and bankrupt the world's economy,
using ideals as a tactical screen
to spring an ambush on victims who scream.
Bolstered by culture, skills, and belief,
your bellies are empty but you're armed to the teeth.
Pagans who worship the power of machines,
and proudly devise the most devious schemes;
underlings boasting the power of your brain,
constructing a journey to Baghdad by train.
High-flying swindlers, plumbing new depths,
hyenas that creep with cadaverous steps,
airmen impelled by destructive intentions,
slaves of the latest cunning inventions,
technicians who transform wrong into right,
barbarians armed with electric light,
ingenious experts equipping with pride
the journey to death as a comfortable ride,
so Death shares your vision of military strife
as a desperate flight from the Sources of Life!

We might have accepted a peaceful solution,
but your cosmic offences require retribution.
We Martians have no aggressive intentions,
but what we've begun we'll do with a vengeance.
We're hoping our strategy redeems
the whole universe by using your schemes,
for our pious researchers will mobilize
earthly techniques for wiping out lives.
Viewed from a distance your world we'd ignore,
if you Lilliputians weren't addicted to war.
It's not your frontiers that we'll be storming,
but you are to suffer severe global warming.

The challenge was tough, the results worth a wait:
you are to endure an exceptional fate.
It's not that we're planning to conquer the earth.
That would reduce our own sense of worth.
The peace of the cosmos will be protected
provided our boundaries are still respected.
Territorial conquest has had its day:
we'll settle accounts in a different way.
For the costs of the war you'll still carry the rap,
since we're planning to wipe you right off the map,
so for all eternity nobody fears
your threat to the harmony of the spheres.
No inventive thinker, no aggressive race
shall launch an attack on the realms of space;
no thunder of battle, no crude calculations
disrupt the planets' silent gyrations.
For too long you earthlings have wanted your say,
from now on Eternity carries the day.
It's been a long wait for all those concerned:
with patience we waited while ambitions burned.
So all aspirations of planet earth,
all dreams of victory, hopes of rebirth
will now be erased with no right of appeal.
Let's start the bombardment and see how you feel!

(Hail of meteors begins.)

VOICE FROM BELOW

With flags unfurled
we'll still make gains
throughout a world—

DISTANT ECHO

consumed by flames!

(Incandescent flames.)

VOICE FROM BELOW

Give them a clout!
Surprise attacks!
And raise a shout—

DISTANT ECHO

like thunderclaps!

(Cosmic thunder.)

VOICE FROM BELOW

Who dares to break
our battle line?
No power can shake—

DISTANT ECHO

Watch on the Rhine!

(Total destruction.)

VOICE FROM BELOW

Now we are damned!
Pains never cease!
The Fatherland—

DISTANT ECHO

can rest in peace.

(Eternal peace.)

VOICE FROM ABOVE

The tempest worked, although the night was wild.
Behold God's image shattered and defiled!

(Great silence.)

VOICE OF GOD

THIS IS NOT WHAT I INTENDED.

Wayside Crucifix on the Western Front

TRANSLATORS' AFTERWORD AND ACKNOWLEDGMENTS

As retired British university teachers of German we are aware that our combined efforts to do justice to Kraus's cornucopian text will fall short, but we hope to have shown that it is not untranslatable, given a blend of perseverance and ingenuity. We approach the task from complementary angles. Fred Bridgham's publications include *The Friendly German-English Dictionary*, a study of lexical idiosyncrasies that explores the divergences between the two languages. He is also the editor of *The First World War as a Clash of Cultures*. Edward Timms is best known as author of the two-volume study *Karl Kraus—Apocalyptic Satirist*, while his memoirs, *Taking Up the Torch*, review fifty years of involvement with Kraus research. Over a period of eighteen months we have read and refined each other's work, with Bridgham producing the original drafts of the bulk of the play, together with the Glossary, while Timms gave priority to the poetry. Each draft has been fine-tuned and doubtful passages debated and amended until an integrated text emerged.

Our contract with Yale University Press specifies that the translation should "neither omit anything from the play nor add anything other than such slight verbal changes as are necessary." But imaginative writing has to be adjusted to the rhythms of the target language and the expectations of a new audience. Elucidation, enhancement, and equivalence are among the techniques we use: making verbal changes to elucidate obscure conceptual or historical allusions; enhancing the impact of slogans and punch lines; and finding modern equivalents for antiquated phrasing. Thus our version, taking account of cutting-edge research (particularly the Lexicon by Agnes Pistorius), brings out the implications of Kraus's monumental period piece for a modern audience.

Concepts such as "Nibelungentreue"—the "Troth of the Nibelungs"—would be baffling without explanatory footnotes, for only Wagnerians might surmise what the phrase means. They too would be on the wrong track, for Kraus's target is not operatic pathos but political propaganda: the claim that Austria and Germany have from time immemorial been linked by an indissoluble alliance. In March 1909, when war with Russia threatened during the Bosnian annexation crisis, Chancellor Bernhard von Bülow used this phrase to express Germany's unconditional support for Austria-Hungary—a pledge that was to have fateful consequences five years later. How is this to be conveyed without another weighty footnote? Our solution is to use the modern equivalent: the claim that Britain and United States are bound together by an indissoluble alliance. Thus "Nibelungentreue" becomes the "Special Relationship"—and no footnote is needed. This idea is echoed at other points where Austrian-Prussian tensions are indicated by contrasts between British and American English. Such semantic shifts accentuate the paradigmatic value of Kraus's antiwar satire, media criticism, and critique of globalization.

Kraus peoples his play with a multitude of identifiable historical characters, ranging from statesmen led by Emperor Franz Joseph and Kaiser Wilhelm II to patriotic authors such as Hans Müller and Ludwig Ganghofer. For further information, readers may turn to our Glossary and Index. Just as important as who they were is what they represent. In the Prologue one passerby boasts about socializing with a celebrity: "Gestern hab ich mit dem Sascha Kolowrat gedraht." In our version this becomes: "Last night I was out partying with the Sascha Film people", foreshadowing the impact of cinema in the play as both satirical motif and dramatic technique—a theme highlighted in a pioneering article by the American scholar Leo Lensing. Our Glossary also elucidates historical references, names of places, authors and composers, popular and patriotic songs, and other significant motifs featured in the dialogue. With a few exceptions, characters with fictional or symbolic names are not listed, since many of them are merely platitudes on two legs.

This medley of authentic detail and imaginative fantasy may remind readers of Joyce's *Ulysses*; and there are anticipations of Orwell's critique of doublespeak in the recurrent duologues between the naively patriotic Optimist and Kraus's raisonneur, the sceptical Grumbler. Their discussions provide a commentary on fundamental issues raised by the play, including the question of responsibility. It would be tempting to blame diplomats like Count Berchtold, the Austrian Foreign Minister who drafted the ultimatum to Serbia that provoked the outbreak of war. But equally significant for Kraus, as the Grumbler explains (in Act III, Scene 41), is the failure of citizens like himself to exercise democratic control over the political, military, and financial elites that are running—and ruining—the country.

Further challenges for the translator arise from the musical motifs that permeate the play, from patriotic marches to the tinkling tunes of Viennese operettas and Berlin nightclubs. Kraus orchestrates this medley of sounds and voices into the death knell of a doomed civilization. Sources are identified in the Glossary so that the original scores can be used in stage productions. The spirit of the most celebrated songs is not hard to recapture: "Staunch stands and true/The

Watch on the Rhine" or "Prince Eugene made a bridge, a bridge he made,/So they crossed the river and took Belgrade." But it is difficult to convey in English the resonance of "In der Heimat, in der Heimat da gibt's ein Wiedersehn" (an equivalent would be "Keep the home fires burning/Till the boys come home", as we indicate in a stage direction). The haunting German words recur in each Act as the men marching away grow increasingly grey and the prospects of their returning home more remote.

The play is enriched by literary allusions that are difficult to convey in translation, and purists may find some turns-of-phrase too free. We debated at length how to convey the allusions to "Wanderers Nachtlied" (Wanderer's Night Song), one of Goethe's most delicate early poems. The Grumbler indicts the vogue for crude parodies that equated peace on the mountaintops with the silent threat of submarine warfare. This sense of desecration is hard to recapture, since there is no canonical English translation of verses described by Kraus as the nation's most sacred poem. Is an actor to interrupt the dialogue and read out a scholarly footnote? Our solution, recalling the affinities between Goethe and Wordsworth, is to borrow lines about a solitary wanderer that will resonate with English audiences. Goethe's mountaintops are transmuted into Wordsworth's vales and hills.

We have also debated how to convey the ethical underpinning derived from the Kantian distinction between "Lebensmittel" (the means of life) and "Lebenszweck" (the ends of life). Drawing on secondary associations—"Lebensmittel" in the sense of "food and drink"—the Grumbler uses this contrast to mock mindless self-indulgence and the impact of consumerism. War (he claims) is being waged to expand export markets, regardless of the loss of life. Thus in his final diatribe the Grumbler warns: "Und zehrt das Lebensmittel vom Lebenszweck, so verlangt es den Dienst am Todesmittel." Our translation highlights the existential risk: "And if the means of subsistence erode the purpose of existence, they enslave us to the instruments of death" (V, 54).

Flexibility is also needed in rendering verses that modulate from staccato mockery into plangent lament, sustaining rhymes and rhythms that blend pathos with humour. When the "Lebensmittel/Lebenszweck" motif recurs in one of the couplets of the Epilogue, we translate: "Consumption becomes the whole purpose of life/and shopping obsesses the world and his wife." Further ingenuity is required in rendering the Freudian slips and associated tongue twisters that permeate the play. The Holy War, proclaimed by a tub-thumping demagogue at the outbreak of hostilities, comes out as a "lowly whore" (I, 1). In scenes where the satirical effect depends on a vivid use of the vernacular, we have done our best to find colloquial equivalents—without attempting to distinguish between Austrian, Bavarian, and even Swabian dialects, as Kraus does with such versatility.

Perhaps the greatest challenge arises from the pervasive wordplay, designed to deconstruct received opinions. Nineteenth-century Germans liked to identify themselves as the "nation of poets and thinkers"—"das Volk der Dichter und Denker." Responding to atrocities, Kraus's Grumbler inverts this into "das Volk der Richter und Henker"—"the nation of judges and hangmen" (I, 29). Put into plain English, the verbal felicity of this dictum is lost. Translators sleep more peacefully when such patterns can be reproduced. Thus the proverb "Ein gutes Gewissen/ist ein sanftes Ruhekissen" finds its way into English as "A conscience without guilt/is like a feather quilt." The wordplay becomes more complex in a reference to army chaplains as "Heiligenscheinwerfer" ("Heiligenschein" = "saintly halo"; "Scheinwerfer" = "searchlight"). In our version this becomes "Holy Water Sprinklers" (V, 55).

A more contentious issue arises from speech patterns that reflect tensions between Christians and Jews. Kraus's satirical panorama includes a range of characters whose German betrays traces of Yiddish. Sometimes a comparable English-Yiddish or American-Yiddish phrase can be used, but more often the Jewish-inflected nuances are barely detectable beyond the original cultural matrix. At the outbreak of war European Jews attempting to assimilate to gentile society often felt themselves to be outsiders. Their aim was to become fully accepted citizens of their chosen nation. What Kraus recognizes—and sardonically dramatizes—is that their efforts are self-defeating, not least because of the resistance they encounter. His play shows them composing patriotic songs or newspaper articles that are even more pro-German (or pro-Austrian) than those by German or Austrian gentiles. The gap between these exalted aspirations and the increasingly problematic fortunes of war generates a tragicomedy abounding in satirical ironies.

Should we consistently attempt to recapture those Jewish undertones, for example, by rendering "meschugge" as "meshugga", rather than "crazy"? This can be clarified by posing a parallel question: When translating scenes that satirize mainstream German militarism, should we always translate "Vaterland" as "Fatherland"? To do this would restrict the meaning of Kraus's play by implying he is only satirizing German (or Austrian) militarism. But the tragedy of mankind has implications for the superpatriots of all belligerent nations, so we sometimes anglicize the phrasing to show that "Vaterland" signifies "my country, right or wrong." Even "Kaiser" is not always "the Kaiser." This broader perspective is epitomized by the verses of the Dying Soldier with which the Epilogue begins, freely translated as follows:

Hauptmann, hol her das Standgericht!	Captain, call out the firing squad!
Ich sterb' für keinen Kaiser nicht!	No one can make me shed my blood
Hauptmann, du bist des Kaisers Wicht!	for King and Country. Go ahead, shoot!
Bin tot ich, salutier' ich nicht!	Once I'm dead, you can't make me salute!

Kraus based these verses on an antiwar poem from the Chinese.

A more formidable challenge is how to render such a complex play performable. Kraus's Preface may claim that it is not intended for an earthly audience, but there have been numerous German adaptations, and as early as 1982 there was a landmark Edinburgh Festival production of selected scenes translated by Robert David MacDonald, later broadcast by BBC Radio. Taking our cue from MacDonald's pioneering achievement we have done our best to attune the dialogue to the stage. Kraus's primary aim was to dramatize the propaganda that sustained the slaughter, and a play thus burdened with history cannot avoid longueurs—passages that are best read as book drama. His documentary technique exposes the pronouncements of political and military leaders, from the German Kaiser to the Viennese editor in chief, as "unspeakable"—in every sense of the word. But there are innumerable more dramatic and imaginative scenes that cry out for performance.

The sprawling play gains an inner coherence from networks of recurrent imagery, which we have done our best to sustain. The dialogues are dense with metaphors from a multiplicity of semantic fields: animal life, food and drink, parts of the body, clothing, costume and uniform, health and sickness, theatre and performance, hunting and shooting, location and landscape, buying and selling, mopping up trenches and cleansing ethnic minorities—the range is inexhaustible. Dualisms such as "up" and "down" and "inside" and "outside" create further contrapuntal patterns. Streets and buildings become symbolic spaces, alerting us to the military-industrial complex taking shape as profiteers besiege the Ministry of War. Some verbal patterns evolve into leitmotifs, associated with a particular catchphrase such as "I went up there and wangled it" (our rendering of "Ich bin hinaufgegangen und hab es mir gerichtet"). Dodging the draft becomes linked with landing lucrative contracts.

Patterns of metaphor form an ironic counterpoint to the harsh realities of war. Thus a pervasive preoccupation with food and drink spills over into vernacular phrasing such as "das hab ich gefressen"—a metaphor for "I'm losing patience." Our version sustains the metaphor, so that "I've had a bellyful" becomes the phrase used by the irate Viennese grocer who throws starving customers out of his shop (III, 30). Ironic forms of body language permeate the play, as smugly obese members of the ruling class patronize severely wounded veterans. Meanwhile, spokesmen for the Austro-German alliance proclaim the need to stand staunchly "shoulder to shoulder", a Homeric image utterly out of place in a war conducted with machine guns and poison gas.

Rendering animal imagery, which reaches its climax in the verse Epilogue, requires a similar sensitivity to nuances. Boasting of his courage, the Death's Head Hussar declares: "Ich bin ein junger Jaguar,/das Vaterland ist in Gefahr." In our version this becomes: "I strike as swiftly as a snake,/my country's future is at stake." Rhyme and rhythm are sustained, but the bestiality of war is differently embodied. War as pictured by Kraus reduces human beings to scavengers and predators, but these motifs are balanced by scenes portraying God's creatures as helpless victims, notably the 1,200 horses drowned when a transporter is sunk by a warship (IV, 45). The metaphorical patterning becomes more highly charged when animal images acquire Jewish connotations. In a coffeehouse scene (V, 25), semiassimilated speculators with names like Hamster and Mastodon chew over the latest commodity prices in a veritable feeding frenzy, while impending losses leave an elderly investor feeling he's a "Pechvogel"—a "lame duck."

In his use of animal imagery Kraus is both heir to Aristophanes and a contemporary of Kafka. Such scenes may have attractions for costume designers, but the horizon darkens as Ravens appear on the battlefield. These motifs culminate in the Epilogue with the identification of Moriz Benedikt, the Jewish-born editor in chief of the *Neue Freie Presse*, as Lord of the Hyenas. Like his star reporter Alice Schalek, Benedikt is an identifiable contemporary who has been "reimagined"—as the big beast of Austrian journalism. Kraus clips key phrases from the press and restages them as dialogue in order to reveal their pernicious implications. The essential point is not that such writings are "Jewish" but that they are "journalistic"—in the worst sense: churning out patriotic rhetoric to justify the horrors of war.

There is a passage in *Die Fackel* of January 1917 where Kraus juxtaposes a photo of Moriz Benedikt against a bust of Lord Northcliffe, the chauvinistic British press magnate who controlled *The Times* and the *Daily Mail*. The heading identifies Northcliffe as the "English Benedikt" and Benedikt as the "Austrian Northcliffe." There is a clear implication that if there had been any English satirist worth his salt, the proprietor of *The Times* would have been targeted for his jingoism as fiercely as Kraus mocks the rhetoric of the *Neue Freie Presse*. There is indeed an English writer whose memoir of the First World War neatly encapsulates Kraus's findings: the poet Robert Graves, author of *Goodbye to All That*. While serving with the British army on the Western Front, he describes how he felt when returning home on leave: "England was strange to the returned soldier. He could not understand the war madness that ran about everywhere, looking for a pseudo-military outlet. Everyone talked a foreign language; it was newspaper language." This takes us to the heart of the issues dramatized in Kraus's play. The interconnections between pseudo-militarism, war madness, and newspaper language—and their impact on the destinies of mankind: these are themes likely to resonate with modern readers.

Kraus places war-torn Vienna within a cosmic framework, as foreshadowed by the Preface: "Even what occurs at the corner where Kärntnerstrasse meets the Ring is controlled from some point in the cosmos." This metaphysical perspective is signaled in the Prologue by the Grumbler's response to the ominous implications of the funeral of Franz Ferdinand (in words addressed to Almighty God):

War dies die Absicht, als Du Tod und Leben
Zu seligem Unterschied erfunden hast?
Stürzt in die Bresche der Unendlichkeit
der irdische Feind, ein tollgewordener Haufe?

Was this Your purpose when You first devised
the blissful counterpoint of life and death?
And can the mortal foe, that rabid mob,
now storm the uplands of eternity?

By the time these questions are resolved in the Epilogue, we have indeed reached the End of Time. The mortal foe is ultimately identified as an unholy alliance between "printer's ink, technology, and death" ("Tinte, Technik, Tod"), represented by the journalistic Anti-Christ (Moriz Benedikt), the fanatical scientist Dr. Abendrot (alluding to Fritz Haber, pioneer of chemical warfare), and the Death's Head Hussar (the German Crown Prince). Thus Kraus's documentary drama culminates in apocalyptic allegory, sealed by the destruction of planet Earth by meteors from Mars. A symbolic coda is provided by the photograph placed at the end: the figure of the crucified Christ from a wayside shrine situated near the Western Front. The wooden cross has been shot away but the figure remains intact, arms uplifted as if in supplication.

Acknowledgments

We are grateful to our friend Nicholas Jacobs, publisher of Libris, for encouraging our collaboration. Thanks are also due to Robert Baldock, Managing Director of Yale University Press in London, for guiding us towards the Margellos World Republic of Letters. The path towards publication has been smoothed by Elina Bloch, Margellos World Republic of Letters coordinator, and special gratitude is due to our Editor, John Donatich, for his constructive suggestions and expert guidance; and to Danielle D'Orlando as Publishing Coordinator.

Although our aim is to produce a completely fresh version, we have consulted previously published excerpts from *The Last Days of Mankind*, as translated by Alexander Gode and Sue Ellen Wright, and by Max Knight and Joseph Fabry. When the Gode-Wright edition, abridged and edited by Frederick Ungar, was published in New York, an anonymous review in the *Times Literary Supplement* of 6 December 1974 complained that the play had been so radically pruned that much of the complexity was lost. Looking back forty years later the author of that review, Edward Timms, wishes he had been more appreciative of a pioneering effort. Over the years he has found it helpful to exchange ideas with other experienced colleagues and translators, including Harry Zohn, Michael Rogers, Gilbert Carr, Christiane Reitter, Ritchie Robertson, and Patrick Healy. More recently, the journalist Jennifer Bligh has made spirited contributions to the fine-tuning of our text, while Julia Winckler produced high-resolution illustrations, Bill Nelson drew the map, and our manuscript editor Jeffrey Schier guided us so expertly through the copyediting process.

Our task as translators has been facilitated by reference to *Les Derniers jours de l'humanité*, the complete French translation by Jean-Louis Besson and Henri Christophe. Their version elucidates passages from Kraus's original that might otherwise remain obscure, also providing a model for the Glossary that concludes our book. Further guidance has been derived from information incorporated in the excellent German editions of *Die letzten Tage der Menschheit* produced by Kurt Krolop and Christian Wagenknecht.

Anton Hölzer's study of documentary photos from the First World War has enhanced our understanding of Kraus's indictment of war crimes, especially those committed against ethnic minorities. Even more helpful have been the explanations in the *Lexikon zu Karl Kraus, "Die letzten Tage der Menschheit"*, by Agnes Pistorius, a model of precise scholarship that identifies not only obscure historical references but also a wealth of literary allusions. Following her lead, our Glossary entries on Goethe, Schiller, and Shakespeare elucidate a dazzling array of ironic effects. Long before the word "intertextuality" was coined, Kraus had evolved his own method of creative interpolation, which he designated "Einschöpfung." As a tribute to this innovative technique we introduce an echo of Edgar Allan Poe into the play's most haunting poem, "The Ravens" (V, 55).

References

Karl Kraus (editor), *Die Fackel*, Vienna, April 1899 to June 1936 (for the images of Benedikt and Northcliffe, see F 445–53, January 1917, p. 33; for the concept of "Einschöpfung", see F 572–6, June 1921, page 62)

Karl Kraus, *Die letztenTage der Menschheit*, Vienna: Verlag Die Fackel, 1922

Robert Graves, *Goodbye to All That: An Autobiography*, London: Jonathan Cape, 1929 (quotation from page 283)

Karl Kraus, *The Last Days of Mankind*, abridged and edited by Frederick Ungar, tr. Alexander Gode and Sue Ellen Wright, New York: Frederick Ungar Publishing, 1974

Karl Kraus, *In These Great Times: A Karl Kraus Reader*, Montreal: Engendra Press, 1976; contains "'The Last Days of Mankind': Selections arranged and translated by Max Knight and Joseph Fabry" (pages 157–258)

Karl Kraus, *Die letztenTage der Menschheit*, ed. Kurt Krolop, 2 vols., Berlin: Verlag Volk und Welt, 1978

Karl Kraus, "The Last Days of Mankind", unpublished translation by Robert David MacDonald of selected scenes for the Edinburgh Festival production of 1982 (with Giles Havergal in the role of Kraus the Grouse)

Leo A. Lensing, "'Kinodramatisch': Cinema in Karl Kraus's *Die Fackel* and *Die letztenTage der Menschheit*", in *German Quarterly*, Vol. 55, No. 4 (Nov. 1982), pages 480–98.

Karl Kraus, *Die letztenTage der Menschheit*, ed. Christian Wagenknecht, Frankfurt: Suhrkamp, 1986

Edward Timms, *Karl Kraus—Apocalyptic Satirist: Culture and Catastrophe in Habsburg Vienna*, New Haven and London: Yale University Press, 1986

Fred Bridgham, *The Friendly German-English Dictionary*, London: Libris, 1996

Karl Kraus, *Les Derniers jours de l'humanité: Version intégrale*, tr. Jean-Louis Besson and Henri Christophe, Marseilles: Agone, 2005

Edward Timms, *Karl Kraus—Apocalyptic Satirist: The Post-War Crisis and the Rise of the Swastika*, New Haven and London: Yale University Press, 2005

Fred Bridgham (editor), *The First World War as a Clash of Cultures*, Rochester, NY: Camden House, 2006

Anton Hölzer, *Das Lächeln der Henker: Der unbekannte Krieg gegen die Zivilbevölkerung* 1914–1918, Darmstadt: Primus, 2006

Agnes Pistorius, *"kolossal montiert": Ein Lexikon zu Karl Kraus, "Die letzten Tage der Menschheit"*, Vienna: Ibera Verlag, 2011

Edward Timms, *Taking Up the Torch: English Institutions, German Dialectics and Multicultural Commitments*, Brighton and Portland, Ont.: Sussex Academic Press, 2011

GLOSSARY AND INDEX

Unless otherwise specified, military, political, and diplomatic positions are Austrian or Austro-Hungarian, the location Vienna, and the war the First World War. An arrow indicates a separate entry. Significant examples from the play are denoted by act and scene in parentheses, while page references are given wherever possible. To identify locations, grid references in the form, for example, Plan B2 or Map C3 relate respectively to the Vienna City Plan (page vi) and the Map of European War Zones (page 646). The abbreviation F + issue number refers to Kraus's revue *Die Fackel.*

ADRIATIC (Map D4/E6), branch of the Mediterranean giving the Austro-Hungarian Empire access to the sea, celebrated in 1913 by an exhibition in Vienna (→Prater); The Habsburg crown land of Trieste (1382–1919) and adjacent coastal villages had developed into the Austrian Riviera, linked by rail to Vienna in 1857. After 1915 control over the Adriatic was hotly disputed in naval engagements with the Italians: 42f, 62, 87, 142, 227ff, 456f.

AEHRENTHAL, Count Alois Lexa von (1854–1912), foreign minister (1906–12) who pursued a more aggressive policy towards South Slav separatism, including the annexation of →Bosnia-Herzegovina: 124.

AERIAL BOMBARDMENT, pioneered in January 1915 by Zeppelin attacks on English coastal towns; denounced by the Grumbler (I, 29): 159f, 164, 227f, 240f, 264, 421, 501, 504, 539, 543f, 580f, 587f.

AGE OF GRANDEUR, leitmotif taken from the colossal painting by Ludwig Koch (1866–1934) entitled *Die große Zeit*, which transforms the nineteenth-century slogan into a depiction of troops led by →Emperor Franz Joseph, →Conrad von Hötzendorf, and →Kaiser Wilhelm II on horseback, and which presides over the play's apocalyptic climax (V, 55): xv, xvi, 61, 73, 74, 95, 104, 127, 132, 162, 164, 165, 169f, 212, 255, 299, 325, 329, 340, 420, 470, 497, 517, 520, 539.

ALBANIA (Map F5), occupied by Austro-Hungarian army in 1915 against the wishes of the German High Command: 411ff, 458, 530.

ALBRECHT, Archduke (1897–1955), →Archduke Friedrich's only son: 275.

ALEXANDRA, Tsarina Feodorovna (1872–1918), m. →Tsar Nicholas II (1894): 360ff.

ALIX OF HESSE →Alexandra Feodorovna.

ALLMER, Anton (1881–1946), "secular" RC priest in →Galicia (1914–15) and Italy (1916–17): 179f.

ALSACE-LORRAINE (Map B3/C3), French provinces annexed by the German Reich in 1871: 352, 503.

ALSERSTRASSE (Plan A1): 427.
AMALFI, Italian battle cruiser, sunk in →Adriatic by German U-boat (July 1915): 142.
AM I TO BE SPARED NOTHING? (Mir bleibt doch nichts erspart), leitmotif, Franz Joseph's recurrent "lamentatio" (IV, 31): 376, 378f, 390ff.
ANDRIAN ZU WERBURG, Baron Leopold ("Poldi") von (1875–1951), a member of →Hermann Bahr's modernist circle in the 1890s, mocked by Kraus for the decadence of his writings; later an influential diplomat and advocate of territorial expansion, ambassador in German-occupied →Warsaw (1915–17), and participant in negotiations at →Brest-Litovsk: 108f, 123.
d'ANNUNZIO, Gabriele (1863–1938), patriotic Italian author who became an aviator during war, dropping propaganda leaflets over Vienna in August 1918: 245, 280.
ANTON GRÜSSER, fictional restaurant, its proprietor an early exponent of irritating interruptions (F 261, October 1908): 204ff.
ANZENGRUBER, Ludwig (1839–1889), dramatist and novelist; Vreni: main character in moralistic drama of peasant life *Der Meineidbauer* (The Peasant as Perjurer, 1871): 360.
APOLLO, variety and (after 1914) operetta theatre in Gumpendorferstrasse (Plan C4), under →Ben Tibur: 48, 251.
APOSTELGASSE, continuation of Landstrasser Hauptstrasse (Plan F5): 177.
APPONYI, Count Albert Georg von (1846–1933), Hungarian politician, minister of culture and education (1917–18): 485.
ARTSTETTEN (Map E3), village in Lower Austria, site of Hohenberg Castle, residence and final resting place of →Franz Ferdinand and wife →Sophie Chotek: 37, 122.
ARZ VON STRAUSSENBURG (1857–1935), Baron, lieutenant-field marshal, succeeded →Conrad as Chief of Staff (1917): 399.
ASIAGO (Map D4), centre of "Sette comuni" in Vicenza, taken by →Conrad's army group (9 November 1917), totally destroyed during war: 365f, 420, 479.
ASINARA, island off NW Sardinia (Map C5); prisoner-of-war camp where 5,000 Austro-Hungarian prisoners died in cholera epidemic (1916): 309, 545.
ASQUITH, Herbert Henry (1852–1928), prime minister under whom Britain entered the war: 289.
"A THUND'ROUS ROAR" →"Watch on the Rhine".
AUERSPERG, Prince Karl ("Cary", 1859–1927), privy councillor and member of Upper House: 123.
AUFFENBERG VON KOMAROV, Moritz (1852–1928), general, war minister (1911–12), victor at the battle of Komarov (26 August 1914), scapegoat for defeat of Fourth Army at →Lemberg (September 1914): 53, 101ff.
AUGUSTA, Archduchess (1875–1964), m. →Josef August (1893), active in nursing the wounded: 309.
AUSTRIAN FACE, satirical leitmotif symbolized by the Frontispiece Kraus chose for his play, a postcard showing "grinning faces, both civilians and officers proud of their honour, crowding around the corpse of →Caesare Battisti to make sure they get their picture on the postcard" (IV, 29). The leitmotiv ironizes the title of →Felix Salten's *Das*

CAPORETTO (Map D4), Battle of, scene in autumn 1917 of disastrous defeat inflicted on Italian army under →Cadorna by combined German and Austrian forces: xviii, 461.

CAPUCHIN CRYPT, and Habsburg tomb, in Kapuziner Kirche (Plan C4): 37, 377, 486f, 515.

CARNEGIE, Andrew (1835–1919), American industrialist and philanthropist: 191.

CARPATHIANS (Map F3/G3), 1,300-kilometre mountain range in south-east Europe; attempted Russian breakthrough to Hungary partially successful (late 1914–early 1915), but conquest of Galicia thwarted by February 1915 (→Uzsock Pass): 85f, 89f, 246, 406ff, 414, 542, 545.

CASEMENT, Sir Roger (1864–1916), Irish patriot, executed by the British for attempting, with German support, to enlist Irish prisoners of war in fight against Britain: 384.

CASSIAN, supposedly refused to record trial of suspected Christian centurion, Marcellus, in AD 298; both became Christian saints and martyrs. →Hans Müller wrote newspaper features as "Cassian at the Front": 254.

CATTARO/Kotor (Map F5), Austrian navy base in Montenegro until 1918: 357.

CENTRAL POWERS (Zentralmächte), designation for the German Reich, Austria-Hungary, and other nations opposed to the →Entente.

CHABATZ (Schabatz, Šabac, Map F4), disputed Serbian frontier town on →River Save, scene of fierce fighting (August 1914–autumn 1915): 49, 388, 536.

CHAPEAU (Chapeau Rouge) (Plan C4), nightclub in Annagasse: 82, 319.

CHARAS, Heinrich (1860–1940), head of Viennese Voluntary First Aid Service: 43, 506.

CHERUSCAN SOCIETY, Cheruscia was a nationalist German duelling fraternity which became notorious in 1910 for serious injuries (III, 11): 258ff.

CHINESE WAR POET, Chong-fu-tse (c. 551–479 BC), author of "Epitaph for a Warrior", trans. Klabund (1915): 494.

CHOTEK, Sophie (1868–1914), Bohemian countess, later Duchess of Hohenberg, →Franz Ferdinand's morganatic wife: 31, 33, 34, 37, 41, 45, 122.

CLEMENCEAU, Georges Benjamin (1841–1929), French prime minister (1906–9, 1917–20): 358, 365, 367.

CLEOPATRA'S NOSE, satirical leitmotif deriving from a pretentious editorial in the *Neue Freie Presse* of 16 April 1915 containing absurd speculations about the causes of the war.

CONRAD →Hötzendorf.

CONSTANTINE, Roman emperor whose conversion to Christianity after the Battle of the Milvian Bridge (AD 312) is associated with a vision of the Cross and the words "in hoc signo vinces" (In this sign you shall conquer): 386.

CSARDASFÜRSTIN (*The Gipsy Princess*, 1915), operetta, with music by Emmerich Kálmán (1882–1953), libretto by Leo Stein (1861–1921) and Bela Jenbach (1871–1943): 59, 170.

CZERNIN, Count Ottokar von und zu Chudenitz (1872–1932), foreign minister (1916–18) who represented Austria at the Treaty of →Brest-Litovsk, criticized by Kraus for vacilliating between conquest and conciliation: 343, 366, 368.

CZERNOWITZ (Cherniowce, Map G3), capital of Habsburg crown land →Bukovina, occupied by Russian troops (August 1914), retaken by Austrians (October 1914), positional warfare until 1916, taken by Russians during →Brusilov offensive (June 1916), retaken by Central Powers (August 1917): 103, 219, 311, 314, 316.

DALMATIA (Map E4/E5), Austrian crown land: 548.
DANGL, Johann (1870–1944), hotelier and mayor of →Semmering: 182.
DANKL VON KRASNIK, Count Viktor (1854–1941), commander in chief of First Austro-Hungarian Army (1914), regional commander in Tyrol (1915, Map D4): 101ff.
DANZER'S ARMY JOURNAL, military journal (1899ff): 80.
DAVID, Eduard (1863–1930), Social Democrat, German Reichstag deputy (1903–18), first president of Weimar National Assembly (1919): 437.
"DEAR FATHERLAND, SLEEP EASY NOW" (Lieb Vaterland, magst ruhig sein), refrain from →"Watch on the Rhine": 191.
DEBRECEN (Map F3), main Hungarian livestock market: 341.
DEFENSIVE WAR (Verteidigungskrieg), leitmotif for German and Austrian insistence that, "encircled" by enemies, they are fighting a "holy defensive war": 92, 145, 190, 220, 266, 284, 302, 308, 332, 359, 429, 455, 518.
DEFREGGER, Franz von (1835–1921), popular Tyrolean genre painter: 139.
DEHMEL, Richard (1863–1920), popular poet, initially gripped by war fever; Kraus quotes from his *Kriegs-Brevier* (War Anthology, 1917): xix, 184, 286f.
DELBRÜCK, Max (1850–1919), German agricultural chemist: 258.
DEMEL, famous café and confectioner on →Kohlmarkt (Plan B3/C3): 63, 120.
DEUTSCHES VOLKSBLATT, nationalistic, anti-Semitic daily: 243.
"DEUTSCHLAND, DEUTSCHLAND ÜBER ALLES" ("Deutschlandlied"), music by Joseph Haydn (1732–1809) and text by August Heinrich Hoffmann von Fallersleben (1798–1874), patriotic song that became German national anthem from 1922: 296, 349, 504.
DEUTSCHMEISTER (Hoch- und Deutschmeister), celebrated Viennese "house regiment" of the Habsburgs, with barracks in the Rudolf (Rossauer) Kaserne (Plan B1/C1): 106f, 312, 316, 531.
DOBERDO, plateau above Gulf of Trieste (Map D4), scene of fierce battles between Austro-Hungarian and Italian troops in March 1916 (fifth battle of →Isonzo, when it fell to Italian troops) and August 1916 (sixth battle of Isonzo, when Italians captured →Gorizia). The Grumbler's reference (III, 41) to "a hundred thousand men" having perished overstates actual losses, but casualties on the Italian front were indeed exceptionally high. Total Austro-Hungarian military deaths during the First World War are estimated at 1.5 million (almost double the figure for Britain): 307, 458.
DOBNER v. DOBENAU, Friedrich (1852–1925), last Lord High Steward to the Habsburgs. 42f, 506, 508.
DOBRUDJA, →Tutrakan, 270.
DOHNA-SCHLODIEN, Count Nikolaus (1879–1965), commander of German

cruiser *Möwe*, which broke through British North Sea blockade in 1916 and attacked merchant shipping in the Atlantic: 416f, 547.
DÖRMANN, Felix (Felix Biedermann, 1870–1928), author, especially of poetry, film scenarios, and operetta librettos (→*Walzertraum*), also responsible for "Those Serbs and Russian shits,/We'll hack them all to bits!" (I, 1): 185, 254.
"DRAUSSEN IM SCHÖNBRUNNER PARK" (Out there in Schönbrunn Park), song eulogizing the "dear old gentleman" →Franz Joseph from the Singspiel *Anno 14* (1914), music by Ralph Benatzky (1887–1967) and text by Fritz Grünbaum (1880–1941): 219, 313, 376.
DRINA, river marking much of the frontier between Austria-Hungary (Bosnia-Herzegovina) and western →Serbia (Map F4/F5), scene of fierce fighting: 68, 110, 543.
DUB, Flora, prominent Viennese socialite who featured regularly in →*Neue Freie Presse*: 45, 180, 234ff, 507.
DUNCAN, Adam (1731–1804), British naval commander who defeated Dutch at Battle of Camperdown (1797): 350.
DURAZZO (Map F5), capital (1913–21) and main port of Albania, occupied by Italy (late 1914), taken by Austro-Hungarian troops (February 1916): 182, 358.

EDWARD VII (1841–1910), British monarch who initiated the Anglo-French →Entente and made similar overtures to Franz Joseph at →Bad Ischl in 1907 and 1908: 396.
EGGER-LIENZ, Albin (1868–1926), Tyrolean painter specializing in battle scenes: 139.
EISNER v. EISENHOF, Baron Angelo (1857–1938), ubiquitous society figure, conservative publicist, editor of *Die Information*, providing confidential diplomatic and financial news: 42, 43, 121, 180, 235, 506.
EISNER VON BUBNA, Colonel Wilhelm (1875–1926), head of War Archive (1916), commandant of War Press Bureau (1917–18): 444.
"EMIL, YOU'RE A TRUE BERLINER" ("Emil du bist eene Pflanze"), waltz (1908) by Wilhelm Aletter (1867–1934): 435.
ENGELHORN, German magazine specializing in sentimental stories; publisher of a series of popular novels: 110.
ENTENTE, military alliance led by Britain, France, and Russia, later joined by Italy and other nations.
ERNST, Otto (Otto Ernst Schmidt, 1862–1926), German writer of sentimental stories. Allusions to "Brief an Herrn Gabriele →d'Annunzio" (Open Letter to d'Annunzio), in *Gewittersegen* (The Blessed Storm), *Ein Kriegsbuch* (1915); "Sonntag eines Deutschen" (A German Sunday), in *Vom geruhigen Leben, Humoristische Plaudereien* (1908); "An die Zeitknicker" (On Time-Twisters) and "Anna Menzel", in *Vom Strande des Lebens* (1908); "Weihnachtsepistel" (Christmas Celebration), in *Stimmen des Mittags* (1903): 126, 279ff.
ERTL, Emil (1860–1935), author of regional and historical novels: 326.
ESTE →Franz Ferdinand.

FREUDENAU, racecourse in →Prater: 307.
FRIEDJUNG, Heinrich (1851–1920), patriotic historian; accused members of Croatian Diet of treasonable complicity in →Serbian independence movement (1909, →*Slovensky Jug*), sued for defamation in celebrated "Friedjung Case" (I, 6): xi, xii, 65ff, 431.
FRIEDRICH, Archduke von Österreich-Toskana, Duke of →Teschen (1856–1936), field marshal, appointed commander in chief of Austro-Hungarian forces in 1914: 111, 113, 176, 208, 216f, 222, 252, 272ff, 308f, 325, 381f, 519.
FRIEND, The, Ludwig von Ficker (1880–1967), founder of bi-monthly journal for art and culture *Der Brenner* (1910–54), from March 1918 in →Galicia as commandant of company of repatriated →prisoners of war (letter to Kraus dated 17 July 1918, V, 36): 476ff.
FRISCHAUER, Berthold (1851–1924), war correspondent on Bosnian campaign (1878) and companion to →Crown Prince Rudolph on tour through Balkans, later Paris correspondent for the →*Neue Freie Presse*: 74, 486.
FÜRSTENBERG, Prince Maximilian Egon (1863–1941), hereditary member of Austrian and Prussian Upper House, friend of →Kaiser Wilhelm II: 234.
FÜRSTENKIND, Das (1909), operetta, music by →Franz Lehár and libretto by →Viktor Léon, 170.

GALICIA (Map G3), Habsburg province on the frontier with Russia, scene of fierce battles; home to some two-thirds of all Austrian Jews, many of whom became refugees during the war: 85, 96, 120, 161, 168, 206, 357, 389, 414, 476, 515, 533.
GALLOWS, "an integral part of my play" (IV, 29). The Grumbler's claim that "under the command of Archduke Friedrich . . . 11,400, or according to another version 36,000 gallows were erected" may understate the victimization of allegedly disloyal Habsburg minorities, according to the analysis of Anton Holzer, *Das Lächeln der Henker* (pp. 73–77). The figure 11,400 derives from the diary of Liberal politician Joseph Redlich, but higher numbers were cited by Polish, Ukrainian, and South Slav deputies during debates in the Austrian Parliament after its recall in May 1917. For further details, see Alexander Watson, *Ring of Steel: Germany and Austria-Hungary at War, 1914–1918* (London, 2014): 142, 156, 309, 381f, 384, 455, 561.
GANGHOFER, Ludwig (1855–1920), author of popular romantic novels and dramas celebrating Bavaria, wartime reporting, poems, and articles: 93, 115, 117f, 124ff, 131, 592.
GARTENBAU Gesellschaft (Horticultural Society, Plan D4), location of restaurant on Parkring; hospital during war: 29, 68, 113, 171, 235, 319, 534.
GEIRINGER, possibly Leo von, banker: 34, 35.
GENTZ, Friedrich von (1764–1832), anti-Bonapartist publicist, main proponent of conservative-legitimist principle in collaboration with Metternich: 368.
GERL, Lieutenant Heinrich (1891–1954), sapper on →River San: 339.
GERMANIC NAMES. In addition to sonorously Teutonic invented names like von Schmettwitz, Bambula von Feldsturm, and Demmer von Drahtverhau, Kraus intro-

duces the names of real-life German nationalists that sound incongruously Slavonic or Slovenian, such as Homolatsch or →Pogatschnigg. This onomastic satire counterbalances the pervasive allusions to →Jewish names.

GERSTHOF, suburb in north-west of city, adjacent to →Grinzing and Viennese Woods.

GINZKEY, Franz Karl (1871–1963), writer, war correspondent, then Rilke's superior in →War Archive: 172.

GIPSY PRINCESS →*Csardasfürstin.*

GIRARDI, Alexander (1850–1918), popular actor and operetta singer in mainly comic roles, highly regarded by Kraus: 490.

GLAWATSCH, Franz (1871–1928), singer, first Bogdanowitsch in →Franz Lehár's *The Merry Widow*: 31.

GLÜCKSMANN, Heinrich (1864–1946), dramatist and journalist, dramaturg in →Volkstheater (1910): 44, 45, 507.

GOD PRESERVE (*Gott erhalte Franz den Kaiser*), Austro-Hungarian national anthem, music by Joseph Haydn and original text by Lorenz Leopold Haschka (1797), revised by Johann Gabriel Seidl, *Gott erhalte, Gott beschütze/Unsern Kaiser, unser Land!* (1854): 54, 56, 255, 346, 384, 486f, 493, 497.

GOETHE ALLUSIONS: 107f, 149, 158, 296, 332, 478, 485;

> I, 6: "though the juice bubbles madly in fermentation", says Mephistopheles (in *Faust* Part One, line 6813), "it finally does produce a wine", 66;
> I, 6: "Time's humming loom", a further platitudinous reference to *Faust* Part One (lines 508–9), implying that this will create "the living raiment of the divine": "So schaff' ich am sausenden Webstuhl der Zeit/und wirke der Gottheit lebendiges Kleid", 66;
> I, 29: "Goethe's Iphigenie may not yet have escaped into Esperanto": Kraus regarded *Iphigenie auf Tauris* (1786), in which the heroine's "pure humanity" enables her to escape from the barbarians, as the epitome of German classicism: 149;
> II, 13: For reasons explained in the Translators' Afterword, Wordsworth's "To Daffodils" has been substituted as equivalent for what Kraus regarded as "the nation's most sacred poem" (F 454–56, 1): "Über allen Gipfeln/ist Ruh,/In allen Wipfeln/Spürest du/Kaum einen Hauch;/Die Vögelein schweigen im Walde,/Warte nur, balde/Ruhest du auch" ("Wanderers Nachtlied", 1780)—"O'er all the hill-tops/Silence reigns,/In all the tree-tops/There remains/Scarce a breath of air./The woodland birds fall silent, too,/Just wait, 'til peace envelops you,/And sleep without a care" ("Wanderer's Night Song"): 373f, 593.
> II, 18: "Wasn't it Schiller who said: Life's for the living, so plunge right inside": 210. Our rendering does less than justice to Frau Funk-Feigl's garbled words "Wie sagt doch Schiller, bitte greif nur herein ins volle Menschenleben"—. Her quotation actually derives from Goethe: "Greift nur hinein ins volle Menschenleben!" (*Faust* Part One, line 167). Moreover, she substitutes

"herein" for "hinein", a solecism construed by Kraus as a sign of Austro-Jewish insecurity. See the erudite commentary on a passage from *Die Fackel* of June 1913 (F 376–77, 33) in Agnes Pistorius, *Ein Lexikon zu Karl Kraus* (pp. 202–4).
III, 4: Travesties of "Wanderers Nachtlied": "Unter allen Wassern ist—'U'"— "There, in the deep, is lurking—'U'!"; "Über allen Kipfeln ist Ruh"—"No one's baking the croissants today, the bakers are all asleep in the hay" (II, 13): 373f; "Wanderers Schlachtlied", "Wanderer's Battle Song" (also II, 13);
III, 40: "We're proud of Schiller, make quite a fuss, and Goethe, too, was one of us": Goethe's heartfelt eulogy in "Epilog zu →Schillers Glocke", a decade after death robbed him of his collaborator, is here appropriated by a rabid nationalist: 296;
III, 46: "leaving a trace of his immortal mission", adapted from the "Spur von meinen Erdentagen" passage expressing the dying hero's vision of constructive toil amidst a free people in *Faust* Part Two (lines 11583–86): 317;
IV, 36: "The fate of man, how like the wind!"—from "Gesang der Geister über den Wassern" (1779)—"Song of the Spirits over the Waters": 402;
IV, 36: "if the Germans hadn't escalated submarine warfare, they would have called on the hero of Goethe's play to force England to its knees"—an allusion to the ineffectual hero of *Egmont* (1787), set in the Netherlands at the time of the revolt against Spanish tyranny: 402;
V, 2: "Knowst thou the heart's desire" ("Nur wer die Sehnsucht kennt")— "Mignon's Song", set to music by Franz Schubert, from Goethe's novel *Wilhelm Meisters Lehrjahre* (1795–96): 421;
V, 54: "At the end was—the Word. Having killed the spirit, the printed word had no alternative but to bring forth the Deed": In *Faust* Part One (lines 1224–37) the hero attempts to translate Greek *logos* from Saint John's Gospel. Dismissing "the Word" as inadequate, he settles for "the Deed", committing himself to a post-Christian "Faustian" vitalism: 513.

GOLDMANN, Paul (1856–1935), Berlin correspondent of →*Neue Freie Presse*: 351ff.

GOMPERZ, Philipp von (1860–1948), banker, witnessed assassination of his friend, prime minister →Stürgkh: 34.

GORIZIA (German: Görz, Map D4), town on →Isonzo, Austrian since 1814, disputed with Italy (1916–18); scene of fierce fighting, evacuated by Austro-Hungarian army in sixth battle of →Isonzo (August 1916), retaken October 1917: 252, 334.

GORLICE (Map F3) in Polish →Galicia. Battle of Gorlice-Tarnów, a Russian disaster (May 1915), initiated offensive of Central Powers against Russia and reoccupation of Galicia: 129, 252, 359, 420.

GRABEN (Plan C3), site of →Plague Column: 167, 173, 238, 316f, 486.

GREY, Edward (1862–1933), Viscount (1916), British foreign minister (1905–16), instigator of Triple Alliance, failed to reconcile Austria-Hungary and →Serbia in 1914: 80, 87, 220, 308, 370.

GRINZING, beyond →Gersthof, where the north-west fringe of the city meets the

HOFRAT, official title awarded for distinguished public service.
HOHENLOHE, "Mappl", possibly Prince Gottfried zu Hohenlohe-Langenburg (1860–1933), member of Upper House: 122.
"HONEY, HONEY, DON'T BE SO HARD" ("Weibi, Weibi, sei doch nicht so hart"), song, music by Karl Haupt (1876–1934) and text by Edmund Skurawy (1869–1933): 492.
HONORARY COUNSELLOR (Kaiserlicher Rat), title awarded to nonentities for supposed public service.
HOPFNER'S, fashionable restaurant in →Kärntnerstrasse (Plan C4): xii, xvii, 29, 30, 49, 171, 242, 319, 419.
HÖTZENDORF, Franz Conrad von (1853–1925, generally known as Conrad), Chief of Staff of Austro-Hungarian army (1906–11) and advocate of preemptive strike against →Serbia. Reappointed in 1912, he was responsible for Austro-Hungarian reverses that left them dependent on Germany; Supreme Commander on Italian front; dismissed in 1917 after disagreement with Emperor Karl I over war aims. His son, Lieutenant Herbert Conrad von Hötzendorf, died in battle (September 1914): 38, 63, 102, 129, 222f, 226, 271, 274, 278, 307, 325.
HOW THE ARMIES FIGHT (*Mir kommt keiner aus!*), comic detective film (Wiener Kunst-Film, 1917), featuring →Hubert Marischka: 584.
HUBERT SALVATOR, Archduke (1894–1971), son of →Franz Salvator, captain of horse: 276.
HUMORIST, *Der*, magazine dedicated to art and theatre: 102.
HUNGARIAN COMPROMISE (1867), transformed the Austrian Empire into Austria-Hungary (→Royal and Imperial) after defeat by Prussia at Battle of Königgrätz (1866). Control of foreign policy, finance, and the military remained in Vienna, but in other respects Hungary achieved parity: 80.
HUSARENBLUT (*Blood of the Hussars*, 1894), operetta, music by Hugo Felix (1866–1934) and libretto by Ignaz Schnitzer (1839–1921): 30, 54, 170, 448.
HYMN OF HATE →Ernst Lissauer.

"I'D RATHER BE SOZZLED", refrain of Viennese song "Ja so a Räuscherl", music and lyrics by Carl Lorens (1851–1909): 339.
I GAVE GOLD FOR IRON, appeal to support war effort by exchanging valuables for iron ring or brooch; subsequently an operetta →Viktor Léon: 59, 156, 295.
I HAD A LOYAL COMRADE (*Ich hatte einen Kameraden*), first line of "Der gute Kamerad", poem by Ludwig Uhland (1809), set to music by Friedrich Silcher (1789–1862); and title of operetta (1914, →Viktor Léon): 59, 290, 313.
"I HAVE WEIGHED EVERYTHING IN THE BALANCE" ("Ich habe alles reiflich erwogen"), leitmotif, phrase derived from →Franz Joseph's manifesto of 1914 justifying declaration of war, which becomes Grumbler's "manifesto" (V, 54): 164, 165, 377, 379, 516.
"I HEAR, MY DEAR, YOU'RE A RACKETEER" ("Sie sind doch bekannt mein

"JACKO, JACKO, DON'T YOU DARE" ("Schackerl, Schackerl trau di net"), Viennese song, music by Theodor Wollitz (1875–1937) and lyrics by Armin Berg (1875–1956): 535f.

JANOV, small town north of →Lemberg; Kaiser Wilhelm's meeting with →Ganghofer occurred when Lemberg was once again occupied by Central Powers (summer 1915): 124ff.

JANOWITZ, Franz (1892–1917), Austrian poet, close friend of Karl Kraus, killed in battle: 511f.

JEAN PAUL (Johann Paul Friedrich Richter, 1763–1825), German novelist. The balloon ascent is described in *Kampanertal* (1797): 159, 164.

JEWISH NAMES, sometimes offensive, as when allotted in late eighteenth century by military commission under imperial decree in →Galicia and →Bukovina; alternatively, "poetic" during later Jewish emancipation (Abendrot/evening glow, Rosenberg/rose mountain); based on either transposed first names (Hein, Ornstein), professed characteristics (Aufrichtig/honest, Brauchbar/useful; Gutwillig/well-meaning; Vortrefflich/splendid; Lustig/funny), place names (→Polacco/Pollack/Pollak, Mannheimer, Oppenheimer, Katzenellenbogen, Koritschoner, Krotoschiner, Geiringer), or animals (Löw, Wolf, Fuchs, Katz, Fischl, Biach < It. biacco/adder); sometimes parodied by Kraus (Schlechtigkeit/Badness, Schakal/Jackal, Walross/walrus; Kornfeld/Cornfield).

JEWISH REFUGEES. The Jewish refugee selling newspapers (II, 1) has fled from the war-torn eastern provinces. By October 1915 there were at least 137,000 refugees in Vienna, of whom 77,000 were Jews. This scene dramatizes the cynical responses of profiteers such as →Eisig Rubel, exploiting the wartime shortages to make a fast buck: 168.

JOSEF AUGUST, Archduke (1872–1962), field marshal in Honvéd infantry, commanded Seventh Corps on Russian and Hungarian front, led armistice talks: 275, 533.

JOSEF FERDINAND (1872–1942), Archduke; corps commander of Fourth Army in →Galicia (1914–16), relieved of command after Russian victory at →Lutsk: 111, 274, 275, 531.

JOSEFSTADT, central residential district behind City Hall (Rathaus, Plan A2/A3), known especially for →Theater in der Josefstadt: 231.

JUDGMENT DAY (probably *Das jüngste Gericht*), film of catastrophic earthquake (Nordsik-Film, 1916): 584.

JUGEND, Munich weekly which popularised Art Nouveau ("Jugendstil"): 327.

JUTLAND, on north-eastern North Sea (Map C1), only direct encounter between High Seas Fleet under →Reinhard Scheer and British Grand Fleet under Jellicoe (31 May–1 June 1916) with heavy British losses, although its blockade of Germany was not breached: 247, 370.

KAG (Kavallerieausbildungsgruppe), acronym for cavalry training course: 226.

KAISER →Wilhelm II.

KÜHLMANN, Richard von (1873–1948), undersecretary in German Foreign Office (1917–18), negotiated treaties of →Brest-Litovsk and Bucharest: 461.
KULKA, Georg (1897–1929), Expressionist poet: 235.
KUNDMANN, Rudolf (1869–1934), major, adjutant to →Conrad von Hötzendorf: 131.
KURSALON (Plan D4) in →Stadtpark: 489.

LABOUR LEADER (1891–1922) London daily, mouthpiece of Labour movement: 220.
LACHENDE EHEMANN, *Der*, operetta (1913), music by Edmund Eysler (1874–1949), libretto by Julius Brammer (1877–1943) and Alfred Grünwald (1884–1951): 30.
LADY-KILLER, *The* (*Der Frauenfresser*, 1911), operetta, music by →Edmund Eysler (1874–1949), libretto by Leo Stein (1861–1921) and Carl Lindau (1853–1934).
LAMMASCH, Heinrich von (1853–1920), eminent international lawyer, admired by Kraus for outspoken attack in Upper House on war as "immense catastrophe" and for his advocacy of a →negotiated peace; briefly Austrian prime minister (October 1918): 422.
LANDESBERGER, Edler Julius (1858–1912), president of Anglobank: 44, 506.
LANDESGERICHTSSTRASSE (Plan A2/A3): 427.
LANG, Josef (1855–1925), executioner (→Caesare Battisti): 252, 383, 385f, 467, 515, 549.
LAUFF, Josef von (1855–1933), German writer of dramas glorifying House of Hohenzollern, *Der Burggraf* (1897), *Der Eisenzahn* (1899), and *Kriegslieder* (War songs, 1915–16), admired by →Wilhelm II: 126, 128, 257.
LEBER, restaurant on Babenbergerstrasse (Plan B4): 196, 207f.
LEHÁR, Franz (1870–1948), Hungarian composer of operettas, notably *Die lustige Witwe* (*The Merry Widow*, 1905), against which Kraus, a champion of Offenbach, waged a quixotic war, →*Das Fürstenkind*, *Der Sterngucker*: 185, 375, 399, 525.
LEHMANN, gazetteer, commercial directory for the city of Vienna: 104.
LEMBERG (Lviv, Ukraine, Map G3), capital of Austrian →Galicia since first division of Poland (1792–1918), occupied by Russians (September 1914), relieved by Austrians under →Böhm-Ermolli (22 June 1915), retained with German help after Battle of →Gorlice during →Brusilov offensive (summer 1916). "Lemberg ist noch in unserem Besitz" (In Lemberg we are still holding on) was the phrase used in a report from the Eastern Front, dated 2 September 1914 and signed by the then →Generalmajor von Höfer. In reality, the Austro-Hungarian army had already withdrawn from the city on 1 September. By the time this report appeared (on 5 September in →*Streffleur Militärblatt*) Lemberg was firmly in Russian hands—hence Kraus's use of the phrase as an ironic leitmotif: 53, 58, 63, 64f, 69, 77, 78f, 86, 129, 235, 414f, 498.
LEO, Archduke (1893–1939), son of →Karl Stephan: 276.
LÉON, Viktor (Viktor Hirschfeld, 1858–1940), co-librettist of Johann Strauss's *Wiener Blut* (1899), and →Franz Lehár's *Die lustige Witwe* (*The Merry Widow*, 1905); also contributed to *Der gute Kamerad* (1911; music by Emmerich Kálmán, libretto by E. K.

and Viktor Léon), an operetta subsequently reworked as →*I Gave Gold for Iron* (1914): 59.

LEON GAMBETTA, French battle cruiser, sunk by U-boat captain Georg von Trapp in Straits of Otranto (27 April 1915): 142.

LEOPOLD I (d. 994), initiated Austrian Babenberg dynasty: 66.

LEOPOLD SALVATOR, Archduke (1863–1931), husband of →Blanka, colonel-general (1916), oversaw expansion and modernization of artillery: 251, 275.

LESSING, Gotthold Ephraim (1729–1781), leading author of the German Enlightenment, best known for his comedy →*Minna von Barnhelm*: 402.

"LET'S CRACK ANOTHER BOTTLE O' WINE" ("Jetzt trink mr noch a Flascherl Wein"), aka "Holloderoh Marsch", music and lyrics by Carl Lorens (1851–1909): 522, 531.

LEWALD, Emmi (1866–1946), novelist, quotation ("Three thousand dead Englishmen . . .") from "Gedanken", in Velhagen and Klasing's *Monatshefte* (1915): 300.

LIHARZIK, Franz (1847–1915), section head of ministry of transport (railways), privy councillor: 232.

LINSINGEN, Alexander von (1850–1935), German general, significant victories on Eastern Front: 246.

LIPPAY, Berthold Dominik (Berthold Lipschitz, 1864–1920), genre and portrait painter: 43.

LIPPE, Prince Leopold of (1871–1949), ruled Lippe as Leopold IV (1905–18): 333f.

LISSAUER, Ernst (1882–1937), German writer, author of widely disseminated hymn of hate "Hassgesang gegen England": 74f, 304, 402f.

LJUBICIC, Stephan (1855–1935), commander of Eleventh Army Corps in →Galicia (1914), responsible for arbitrary executions: 387.

LLOYD GEORGE, David (1863–1945), charismatic British politician, minister of munitions (1915) and prime minister (1916–22): 251, 288ff, 364f, 367, 502.

LOBKOWITZ, Prince Ferdinand (1850–1926), member of Bohemian nobility and Austrian Upper House: 42, 122.

LOKALANZEIGER, right-wing, high-circulation Berlin daily: 461.

LONELY HEARTS (*Der Heiratsonkel*), Berlin magazine: 435, 461.

"LONG LIVE HABSBURG MARCH" ("Hoch Habsburg"), music by Johann Nepomuk Kral (1839–1896) and text by C. E. Jaritz (b. 1842): 482.

LORZ (Lorx), Victor Lorx von Ruszkin (1873–1922), lieutenant-colonel, aide-de-camp to →Archduke Friedrich: 176.

LOVCEN, mountain above Bay of →Catarro in Montenegro, taken by Austrian militia (11 January 1916): 254, 257, 357f.

LÖWY, Siegfried (1857–1931), co-head with →Alice Schalek of official War Welfare organization, →Schwarzgelbe Kreuz ("Black-and-Yellow Cross"), editor of *Österreichische Volkszeitung*: 236.

"LOYAL AND UPRIGHT IS EVER MY COURSE" ("Üb immer Treu und Redlichkeit"), popular song, based on poem by Ludwig Christoph Heinrich Hölty (1748–

MARIA JOSEFA, Archduchess (1867–1944), mother of future →Emperor Karl, turned her palace into a military hospital and assisted with nursing: 252.
MARIA THERESA, Archduchess (1855–1944), wife of Karl Ludwig, elder brother of →Franz Joseph, stepmother and confidante of →Franz Ferdinand: 275.
MARIE VALERIE, Archduchess (1868–1924), youngest daughter of →Franz Joseph, m. →Franz Salvator (1890): 275.
MARISCHKA, Hubert Josef (1882–1959), popular actor and operetta tenor (star of →*Der Sterngucker*), director of →Theater an der Wien (from 1916), librettist, film actor: 30, 484, 489ff.
MARNE, French river where initial German thrust through Belgium was halted in September 1914: 561.
MARS, Mela (1882–1919), cabaret singer and diseuse: 48.
MARTIUS, Karl (1879–1946), surgeon-general to German supreme command (1914–16): 406.
MASURIAN LAKES ("swamps", Map F1), in East Prussia, where many Russian troops met their death while →Paul von Hindenburg became a national hero after Battle of →Tannenberg (August 1914): 170ff, 340, 355.
MAX, Archduke Maximilian Eugen Ludwig (1895–1952), major, brother of future →Emperor Karl: 253, 275, 481f, 487.
MEANS OF LIFE, ENDS OF LIFE (Lebensmittel, Lebenszweck), a play on →Immanuel Kant's "categorical imperative" that one must treat all rational beings as ends, not as means; also implies that means of subsistence (Lebensmittel, foodstuffs) should not be the purpose of existence (Lebenszweck): 146f, 150, 151f, 157f, 160, 509, 585, 593.
MEDUSA, Italian submarine, sunk 10 June 1915: 142.
MERCHANTS, Werner Sombart's *Händler und Helden: Patriotische Besinnungen* (1915) sets noble military heroes against morally debased merchants—a riposte against the claim that free trade replaces armed struggle in the evolutionary process: 151f, 292, 586.
MESSAGERO, *Der* (*Il Messagero*), conservative Roman daily: 84.
MICHAELERPLATZ (Plan B3), square where patriotic music was played by military bands, adjacent to →Hofburg: 448.
MILLERAND, Alexandre (1869–1943), French minister of war (1914–15): 83.
MINISTER OF THE INTERIOR, Baron Karl →Heinold von Udynski.
MINNA VON BARNHELM (1767), →Gotthold Lessing's evergreen comedy, based on events at the end of the Seven Years War (1756–63). The good sense of the Saxon heiress Minna overcomes the stiff-necked pride of the impoverished Prussian officer Tellheim: 402.
MITROVICA, Kosovo (Map F5), where Austrians annihilated a →Serb division (early September 1914): 539.
MITTAGSZEITUNG, midday issue of *Wiener Allgemeine Zeitung* (1905–21): 196.
"MITZI, MITZI, BE NICE TO YOUR FRITZI" ("Mizzerl, Mizzerl, sei doch netter"), waltz, music by Béla Laszky (1867–1935) and lyrics by Beda (Fritz Löhner, 1883–1942): 534.

MOB, military jargon for period of mobilisation: 226.
MOLENAAR, Heinrich (1870–1965), author of war poems and a pamphlet against smoking entitled *Warum ist der Kampf gegen den Tabakgenuss eine nationale Pflicht?*: 271.
MOLTKE, Count Helmuth von (1848–1916), nephew of his namesake, "the great Moltke", resigned as chief of the German General Staff (14 September 1914), acting chief from January 1915: 284f.
MONTECUCCOLI, Count Rudolf (1843–1922), admiral, commander in chief of Austro-Hungarian navy (1904–13): 77f.
MONTE GABRIELE, mountain north of →Gorizia, scene of mass slaughter during sixth–ninth battles of →Isonzo: 549.
MONTENUOVO, Prince Alfred de (1854–1927), imperial chamberlain: 36ff, 121ff.
MONTE SAN MICHELE, south-west of →Gorizia, fiercely contested mountaintop during battles of →Isonzo: 335f.
MONTSCHI →Sternberg.
MORGEN, *Der*, liberal weekly, organ of "Reichsorganisation der Hausfrauen Österreichs" (Rorö): 211f.
MORSEY, Baron Franz von (1854–1926), chamberlain to →Duchess Sophie von Hohenberg Chotek: 38.
MOSER, Ferdinand (1867–1938), scene painter: 493.
"MOTHER-IN-LAW – MOTHER-IN-LAW – THAT WOULD BE THE FINAL STRAW" ("Wir brauchen – keine – Schwiegermamama", 1888), march, music by Ernst Simon (1850–1916) and lyrics by Max Althans: 534.
MOULIN ROUGE, nightclub in Walfischgasse (Plan C4) behind →Opera: 173.
MÜLLER, Hans (1882–1950), author of patriotic plays (*Könige*, Burgtheater, 1916) and articles, e.g., "Deutschland steht auf" ("Germany awakes") in →*Neue Freie Presse* (25 August 1914); brought unsuccessful case for defamation against Kraus (1918): 93f, 135ff. 186, 254, 399, 507f, 592.
MÜLLER, Robert (1887–1924), journalist, →Serbian correspondent, and reporter for →*Mittagszeitung* in United States (1909–11). Articles on Roosevelt (1912–13) and Austrian Crown Prince (1914): 252.
MUNKACS, town and Habsburg fortress at south-west edge of →Carpathians: 389.
MUSKETE, *Die*, illustrated right-wing humorous weekly, popular with army officers: xii, xiv, 76, 109, 110, 197f, 483, 528.
"MY BROWN ISONZO LASSIE" ("Braunes Isonzomädel"), song, music by René Richard Schmal (b. 1897) and lyrics by Egon Schubert: 536.
"MY LITTLE POPPET, APPLE OF MY EYE" ("Puppchen, du mein Augenstern"), popular Viennese song (1912), music by Jean Gilbert (1879–1942) and lyrics by Alfred Schönfeld (1859–1916): 126, 372.

NAREW, lake, source of River Narew, tributary of the Vistula with line of Russian fortresses defending Congress Poland; →Rozan taken by German forces during summer offensive in 1915 (IV, 6): 327.

NÄSTELBERGER, Robert (1887–1942), operetta tenor and film actor: 490.
"NECHLEDIL MARCH", from →Franz Lehár's first operetta, *Wiener Frauen* (The Women of Vienna, 1902): 185.
NEGOTIATED PEACE, "All this talk of a negotiated peace was futile" (IV, 36). During 1917, after the abdication of Tsar Nicholas II, there were covert peace negotiations endorsed by the German Reichstag, international socialists, and Pope Benedict XV. On territorial issues such as control of Belgium, Alsace-Lorraine, and Poland the rival governments refused to compromise, and secret peace feelers put out by Austria to France after the accession of →Emperor Karl proved equally abortive (stimulating the febrile rumours dramatized in V, 17): 401f, 418, 458, 461f, 502, 511, 519.
NEITHER HIGH-HANDED NOR FAINTHEARTED, "Far removed from being either high-handed or fainthearted" ("Weit entfernt von Hochmut und von Schwäche"), leitmotif coined by →*Neue Freie Presse* at time of ultimatum to →Serbia: 52, 55, 165, 308, 367, 385.
NEPALLECK, Wilhelm Friedrich von (1862–1924), director of court protocol: 36ff, 121.
NEUE FREIE PRESSE, editorial office in Fichtegasse (Plan D4), liberal-leaning but pro-war daily, main target of Kraus's satire: ix, xi, 29, 30, 31, 53, 57f, 59, 77ff, 86f, 91, 96ff, 125, 165, 168, 175ff, 210, 212, 220f, 222, 240f, 251, 256f, 288ff, 306, 343, 345, 350f, 355, 366, 368, 381, 399, 452, 468, 596.
NEVERMORE, in our translation of "The Ravens" (V, 55), may seem like an arbitrary echo of the celebrated poem by Edgar Allan Poe, but we know from comments in *Die Fackel* that Kraus admired Poe's work and was familiar with the poem, whose refrain has a terrifying finality. When Kraus gave his last recital of "The Ravens", recorded on film, the date was 1934 and a new black-shirted scourge of the battlefields had emerged in the shape of Himmler's SS: 550.
NEW YORK WORLD, organ of the Democratic Party (from 1860): 285.
NIBELUNGS, mythical Germanic warriors whose exploits, supposedly linking the Rhine with the Danube in a →special relationship, are celebrated in the *Nibelungenlied*: 66, 107, 138, 174, 259, 591f.
NICHOLAS (Nicholas Nicholaïevitch Romanov, 1856–1929), Grand Duke, head of Russian army (August 1914), relieved of command (September 1915), appointed commander in chief, Army of the Caucasus: 58, 64, 362.
NICHOLAS II, →Tsar.
NIESE, Hansi (1875–1934), popular Viennese actress: 218f.
NIETZSCHE, Friedrich (1844–1900), German philosopher and "good European", whose ideas were, on the one side, traduced (*The Will to Power* [1906], selectively edited by his sister, seeming to advocate the value-free power politics he deplored), and on the other, demonized (decontextualized lurid metaphors such as the "blond beast" and the "superman" attributed to the arrogant Prussian soldier whom Nietzsche considered a contemptible automaton): 161, 292, 295, 400f.
NO ONE ESCAPES ME (*Mir kommt keiner aus*—Wiener Kunst-Film, January 1917), comedy detective film, featuring →Hubert Marischka: 372.

NORDDEUTSCHE ALLGEMEINE ZEITUNG, Berlin daily: 152.
NORTHCLIFFE, Viscount Alfred Charles William Harmsworth (1865–1922), founded *Daily Mail* (1896), acquired *Times* (1906), leading vehicles for anti-German agitation: 332, 596.
NOTHNAGEL, Hermann (1841–1905), professor of medicine, University of Vienna: 315.
NOYON, in northern France, occupied by Germans (September 1914–March 1917): 431.
NUREMBERG (Map D3), German city rumoured to have been targeted by French planes before declaration of war – a classic example of falsehood in wartime: 64, 345.
NYÁRI, Rudi ("the Gipsy count"), famous Roma musician (with brother violinist Joszi) and composer of Gipsy songs: 419.

OBERNDORFF, Count Alfred von (1870–1963), German ambassador to Bulgaria (1916–18): 343ff.
ODELGA, Anna (1863–1944), m. Baron Adolf Odelga (1851–1915), high official in Ministry of Defence (1884–1907): 235.
"OFF WE GO TO FAR-OFF PLACES!" ("Hinaus in die Ferne!") (1814), marching song in Napoleonic wars, music and words by Albert Methfessel (1785–1869): 75.
OH, AMALIA, WHAT HAVE YOU DONE? (*Ach, Amalia, was haste blos gemacht?* – Luxfilm, Berlin, January 1917), hit comedy film: 372.
"ON ETERNAL PEACE" ("Zum ewigen Frieden"), poem by Kraus inspired by →Immanuel Kant's essay of 1795, in →*Die Fackel*, F 474–83, May 1918: 478.
"ON THE BANKS OF THE MANZANARES" ("Am Manzanares"), song, music by Adolf Jensen (1837–1879) and lyrics by Emanuel Geibel (1815–1884): 526.
OPERA (Café De l'Opera), in Operngasse (Plan C4): 102.
OPERA HOUSE (Plan C4): 172f.
OPPENHEIMER, symbolic name for influential financier, probably derived from Jewish court financier and army contractor Samuel Oppenheimer (1630–1703): 120.
ORSINI-ROSENBERG, Count Maximilian (1846–1922), general, privy councillor, and court chamberlain: 41.
ORTELSBURG, town in East Prussia on south-west edge of →Masurian Lakes: 236.
OSTDEUTSCHE POST, probably Viennese *Ostdeutsche Rundschau*, German-nationalist, anti-Semitic daily: 259.
OTTAKRING, suburb west of Vienna, site of army kitchens (V, 38): 481.
"OUR OLD FRIEND NOAH KNEW WHAT'S BEST" ("Der olle Noah hats doch gewusst"), slow march from operetta *Die Faschingsfee* (1917), music by Emmerich Kálmán (1882–1953), libretto by Rudolf Österreicher (1881–1966) and Alfred Maria Willner (1859–1929): 517.
"O YOU, MY AUSTRIA" ("O du mein Österreich"), song (1849), music by Franz von Suppé (1819–1895) and words by Anton von Klesheim (1812–1884): 315.

PALLFY, probably Aline, member of princely family. The Palais Pallfy on Josephsplatz (Plan B3/B4) was used as a hospital during the war: 63, 124, 319.
PARMA, Prince Elias von (1880–1959), half-brother of →Empress Zita, chief of staff of Fifty-seventh Infantry Division (September 1916), participated in →Isonzo battles: 531.
PARROT (Cabaret Nachtlicht, 1906–8, then Bradys Wintergarten), cabaret in Ballgasse (Plan C4), so called after its insignia, also shorthand for its regular clientele of archdukes: 483.
PATTAI, Robert (1864–1920), Christian-Social politician, president of Chamber of Deputies (1909–11), member of Upper House (1911–18): 422.
PETER FERDINAND, Archduke (1874–1948), brother of →Joseph Ferdinand, lieutenant field marshal (1914), general of infantry (1917): 275, 531.
PFLANZER-BALTIN, Baron Karl (1855–1925), commanded right wing of Austrians against Russians (1914–16), disastrously during →Brusilov offensive; commander in Albania (July 1918); nicknamed "Pflanzer Bald-her, Bald-hin", implying his men were dead soon after arrival: 101ff, 111, 412, 519.
PHAEACEANS, a peace-loving people in Greek mythology, term sometimes applied to carefree Austrians: 66.
PHOTOGRAPHS OF EXECUTIONS, "For while some were being hanged, others were posing for the camera; and photos were taken not only of executions, but also of the spectators, and even of the photographers" (IV, 29)—a reference to the execution of →Caesare Battisti in the Citadel in Trento, Trentino (Map D4), watched by several hundred soldiers and a small number of civilians, some of whom can be seen holding cameras in the panoramic photo reproduced by Holzer in *Das Lächeln der Henker* (p. 27).
PIAVE (Map D4), river north of Venice, scene of fierce fighting after Italian defeat at Caporetto in autumn 1917 until end of war: 253, 461, 482, 489, 492, 538.
PICCAVER, Alfred (1883–1958), tenor with Court Opera: 470.
PLACE IN THE SUN, slogan coined in 1897 by Prince von Bülow, Germany's Chancellor (1900–1909), in respect of her colonial ambitions: 294, 301, 304, 505, 566.
PLAGUE COLUMN ("Säule", Plan C3), on →Graben, erected by Emperor Leopold I after plague of 1679: 172f, 316.
POETS AND THINKERS, "Germany, the land of poets and thinkers", coined by Johann Karl August Musäus (1782), popularized by Madame de Staël in *De l'Allemagne* (1813). Kraus plays "Dichter und Denker" against "Richter und Henker" (judges and hangmen): 148f, 158, 504, 594.
POGATSCHNIGG, Paul (1873–1929), leader of Federation of German Post Office Workers whose name is used to highlight the absurdities of German nationalism in III, 11 (see Timms, *Karl Kraus—Apocalyptic Satirist*, vol. 2, pp. 112–13): 258f, 347ff.
POINCARÉ, Raymond (1860–1934), French prime minister and foreign minister (1912–13), president (1913–20), strengthened Triple Alliance with Britain and Russia: 80, 87, 251, 290.
POISON GAS, in the form of chlorine, was first effectively used by the German army

in April 1915 near Ypres; denounced by the Grumbler as a "chlorious offensive": 262, 502, 535ff, 545, 564ff, 596.

POLACCO, wife(?) of Emil Polacco, president of "Heimat" Mission for girls without means: 236.

POLDI →Andrian zu Werbung; →Leopold Kolowrat.

POLISH QUESTION. The Central Powers fighting in Austrian →Galicia from 1914 purportedly sought Poland's independence from Russia as a central war aim. "Congress Poland" including Warsaw, →Brest-Litovsk, →Grodno, and Vilnius were all occupied by Central Powers in 1915 and an independent kingdom of Poland proclaimed in November 1916: 198, 429f, 433.

POLLAK, Soffi, stereotypical boastful *nouveau riche*, butt of Jewish "Pollak-jokes": 67.

POPOVICS, Alexander (1862–1935), governor of Austro-Hungarian Bank, Hungarian finance minister (1918): 357.

POSSE, Ernst (1860–1943), patriotic editor of influential *Kölnische Zeitung*: 345.

POST OFFICE SAVINGS BANK (Postsparkassenamt, Plan D3): 56, 497.

POTIOREK, Oskar (1853–1933), governor of Bosnia-Herzegovina (1911), commander of Army of the Balkans, invited →Franz Ferdinand in 1914 to final military manoeuvres in Bosnia. Captured →Belgrade on 2 December 1914, dismissed after failure to hold it: 63, 102.

PRASCH, Erwin (b. 1879), captain, active in Montenegro and on →River Save in Serbia (1914), on →Isonzo (1915–17); →sabre: 532, 541f.

PRATER (Plan F1), Vienna's large public park. The "Wurstelprater" section contains numerous amusements and restaurants. The →Venedig in Wien theme park staged the →Adriatic Exhibition in 1913: 42f, 180ff, 537.

PRESBER, Rudolf (1868–1935), German journalist, editor of *Lustige Blätter* (from 1898), author of comic novels and plays: 292.

PRIME MINISTER →Count Karl von Stürgkh.

"PRINCE EUGENE MARCH", hugely popular celebration of →Prince Eugene's bridge-building and crossing of Danube to rout Turks from Belgrade (1717), music, using traditional melodies: Josef Strauss (1827–1870); as song, "He Made a Bridge" ("Er liess schlageen eene Bruckn"), with words reputedly by participant in campaign, adapted by Ferdinand Freiligrath (1810–1876), music by Carl Loewe (1796–1869). The destruction of the railway bridge at the same spot in 1914 initiated hostilities at →Zemun: 32, 47, 51, 52, 55, 58, 118, 313, 315, 462, 464, 507, 520, 593.

PRISONERS OF WAR. Their fate, including sufferings in the camps, forced labour, and Austro-Russian prisoner exchanges agreed at →Brest-Litovsk, is highlighted by the play. Over a million Russian prisoners were held by the Habsburg Monarchy (as indicated in V, 21), while a comparable number of Austro-Hungarian prisoners languished in Russia: 84ff, 367, 438ff, 448ff, 476ff, 505ff, 543, 577.

"PROMOTE THE TOURIST TRADE!" ("Pfleget den Fremdenverkehr!"), winning song (1912) by Else John in competition organized by Ministry of Culture: 75, 455.

PRZEMYSL (Map F3) on River San, stronghold in western →Galicia, allocated to

RING (Ringstrasse, each section differently named, e.g., →Schottenring), boulevard around centre of Vienna which replaced city fortifications; site of major public buildings: xii, xvii, 29, 33, 47, 82, 113, 131, 132, 168, 240, 277, 310, 318, 385, 418f, 457ff, 468, 527, 597.

RODA RODA, Alexander (Sandor Friedrich Rosenfeld, 1872–1945), former officer, journalist, and war correspondent for →*Neue Freie Presse* in Balkan wars (1912–13) and in →War Press Bureau (1914): 53, 68, 93, 115, 125, 201ff, 527, 569.

RODAUN, affluent suburb in south-west Vienna, headquarters of →War Press Bureau (1917): 252.

"AUGUSTE RODAUN", sculptor Auguste Rodin (1840–1917): 252.

ROLLÉ, Fritzi Rolly (1886–1964), operetta soubrette at →Gartenbau (1911, 1913): 534.

ROMANIA (Map G4/H4) entered war on side of the →Entente in August 1916 after Central Powers' losses in the east (→Brusilov offensive). German troops under →Mackensen overran Romania, entering Bucharest on 6 December 1916: xvii, 240, 242, 270, 355f, 359f, 362f, 366, 402.

"ROSA, WE'RE OFF TO LODZ!" ("Rosa, wir fahren nach Lodz!"), march, music by Artur Marcell (d. 1931) and words by Fritz Löhner (1883–1942). "Rosa" was the 30.5-cm mortar: 313.

ROTER TAG (*Der Tag*), nationalistic Berlin daily, "red" on account of red-topped headlines and articles, not political affiliation: 436.

ROTHSCHILD, Louis Nathaniel (1882–1955), took over direction of Rothschild and Creditanstalt banks in 1911 after his father's death: 250, 468.

ROYAL AND IMPERIAL, refers to the dynastic union of the Austrian Empire (Kaisertum Österreich) and the Kingdom of Hungary (Königreich Ungarn) after the →Hungarian Compromise, hence "k.und.k." or "k. k." and Robert Musil's memorable coinage, *Kakanien*.

ROZAN (Map F2), Russian fortress north of Warsaw, taken by German troops in July 1915 after crossing →River Narew: 128.

RUBEL, Eisig, trader in beers and spirits, originally from Hungary, implicated in a profiteering syndicate exposed by a Viennese court early in 1917. The uncouth Jewish German spoken by some of those involved, recorded in *Die Fackel* of May 1917 (F 457–61, 1–19), finds its way into several scenes of the play: 168.

RUDOLPH (1858–1889), Crown Prince of Austria-Hungary until suicide at Mayerling with mistress, Baroness Marie Vetsera: 32, 390, 485.

RÜHS, Christian Friedrich (1781–1820), nationalistic German historian: 356.

SAARBURG (Map C3), Lorraine, in German hands (1871–1918); Battle of Saarburg, 20–22 August 1914: 439.

SABRE, the ceremonial sword worn by infantry officers, prominent in →Fritz Schönpflug's militaristic cartoons, was anachronistic even before the deployment of →poison gas, →aerial bombardment, and the →U-boat. As the emblem of arrogance and brutality it evolves into a leitmotif extending from marching boys with wooden sabres (I, 1) through children subject to "sabres as canes for spanking" (I, 29) and the girl who

helps herself to an officer's sabre in lieu of payment (V, 45), to the ultimate horror perpetrated by →Captain Prasch (V, 55): xii, 55, 112, 154, 306ff, 495f, 533, 541.
SACHER, famous hotel and café, proprietress Anna Sacher (1859–1930), behind the →Opera in Philharmoniker Strasse, corner of Kärntnerstrasse (Plan C4): 63, 205, 519.
SALANDRA, Antonio (1853–1931), Italian prime minister (1914–16), declared war on Austria-Hungary (23 May 1915), on Germany (28 August 1916): 335.
SALTEN, Felix (Siegmund Salzmann, 1869–1945), versatile author who wrote polemical articles in →*Neue Freie Presse* about enemy culture and popularized Austrian military history for →War Archive; his collection of essays, *Das österreichische Antlitz* (1910), suggested to Kraus the motif of the →Austrian face: 93, 444.
SALZER, Marcell (Moritz Salzmann, 1873–1930), cabaret artiste, renowned for songs and recitations in various dialects, author of *Kriegsprogramme* (1914): 133, 172.
SAN, river (Map F3), tributary of the Vistula in →Galicia, frequently front line until May 1915: 338.
SARAJEVO (Map E5), capital of Bosnia-Herzegovina, where →Franz Ferdinand and his wife, Sophie, were assassinated on 28 June 1914: xiv, 29, 38, 43, 44, 56, 378, 485, 497.
SASCHA FILM, largest Austrian production company of the silent film era, founded in 1910 by →Kolowrat.
SAVE, river, tributary of the Danube, marking Serbia's northern frontier between →Chabatz and →Belgrade (Map F), crossed by Austrian forces under →Potiorek on 12 August 1914, repelled on 16 August.
SCHAFFGOTSCH, ("Fipsi"), possibly Count Victor (1850–1919), colonel in Reserves: 63.
SCHALEK, Alice (pseudonym: Paul Michaely, 1874–1954), journalist on →*Neue Freie Presse* (from 1903), only female front-line war correspondent, co-head with →Siegfried Löwy of War Welfare organization →Schwarzgelbe Kreuz ("Black-and-Yellow Cross"); author of *Tirol in Waffen* (Tyrol under Arms, 1915), dedicated to →Boroević: 115, 139ff, 214f, 227ff, 235, 242f, 283f, 334ff, 380f, 403, 440ff, 470, 499, 511, 527, 561, 596.
SCHALK, Franz (1863–1931), conductor of Vienna Court Opera under Mahler's directorship (1900), co-director with Richard Strauss (1918): 399.
SCHEER, Reinhard (1863–1928), German vice-admiral, in command of German High Seas Fleet at →Jutland: 247.
SCHEFFEL, Joseph Viktor von (1826–1886), poet (→*Trumpeter of Säckingen*; →"When the Romans Had the Nerve"): 327.
SCHEIDL, Café/tearoom in house "Zum Fenstergucker", Kärntnerstrasse, corner of Walfischgasse (Plan C4); spicy pancakes a specialty: 102.
SCHENK, Martin (1860–1919), comic (from 1899), later director →Gartenbau: 534.
SCHILLER, Friedrich (1759–1805). Kraus's play abounds in allusions to his poems and plays: 1, 107f, 158, 247, 296, 299.
SCHILLERIAN TRAGEDY:

Preface: "I have portrayed the deeds they merely performed" — an inversion of "Ich habe getan, was du — nur maltest", *Fiesco*, Act II, scene 17; a reprise of "An

artist with any sense of conviction would have declared to Fiesco: "What you merely performed, I have portrayed!" (F 259–60, July 1908, p. 45): 1;
I, 1: "let us rise up as one, with banners fleeing, and unite with the Fatherland in its hour of destiny!"—drunkenly garbled version of Attinghausen's plea to Rudenz to defend his Swiss heritage against Austrian oppression (*Wilhelm Tell*, Act II, scene 1): 49;
I, 17: "Here I stand, a lifeless trunk"—where Wallenstein acknowledges he has been deserted by all, like a tree stripped of its leaves: "Da steh' ich, ein entlaubter Stamm" (*Wallensteins Tod*, Act III, scene 13); Riedl's misquotation—"entleibt" for "entlaubt"—suggests he would be committing professional suicide by returning his decorations: 105;
I, 23: "as Emperor and Poet walk side by side, for the heights of mankind they both bestride"—Karl [Charles VII] in *Die Jungfrau von Orleans* (Act I, scene 2): 126;
I, 29: "the word, propagating itself, brings forth yet more evil"—cf. Oktavio in *Die Piccolomini* (Act V, scene 1): "Das eben ist der Fluch der bösen Tat,/Dass sie, fortzeugend, immer Böses muss gebären": 156;
III, 3: "I tell you . . . it's a wonderful life!"—cf. Marquis Posa to Queen in *Don Carlos* (Act IV, scene 21): "O Gott! Das Leben ist doch schön": 247;
III, 8 and IV, 26: "Schiller's Tell says, every man is intent on his own business—and mine is murder"—*Wilhelm Tell* (Act IV, scene 3): 251, 363f, 510;
III, 40: "Hold fast your Fatherland in firm embrace, your dear Fatherland!"—*Wilhelm Tell* (Act II, scene 1): 306;
III, 41: "One face before the deed is done, but after—a very different one"—Chorus in *The Bride of Messina* (Act II, lines 2005–6): 307;
IV, 26: "Tell says: Quiet and harmless was the life I led. . . . The milk of human kindness thou hast turned to rankling poison in my breast" (*Wilhelm Tell*, Act IV, scene 3): 364;
IV, 26: "So England is Tell? On the contrary, surely England is the tyrant Gessler and Germany is the idealistic William Tell!"—anticipates a similar confusion in the Second World War, when Goebbels belatedly banned *Wilhelm Tell* from the school curriculum in 1941: 364;
IV, 29: "each 'villainous Franz'"—like Schiller's Franz Moor, or the jailer of →Spielberg fortress'—the antihero of *Die Räuber* ("Franz heisst die Kanaille?", Act I, scene 2)—here Emperor Franz I, and by extension the Habsburg dynasty as a whole: 380;
V, 16: "Such is the gratitude the House of Habsburg"—Schalek's "Dank vom Haus Österreich!" echoes Colonel Buttler's bitter "Dank vom Haus Österreich!" at his thwarted ambition (*Wallensteins Tod*, Act II, scene 6): 445;
V, 54: "*Wallenstein's Camp*"—first part of *Wallenstein* trilogy depicting his turbulent mercenary army: 511; with Europe's future again at stake in 1798, Schiller's Prologue idealistically proclaims, "Man grows to match his higher

goals", a sentiment the enlisted dwarf (in I, 12) can safely endorse without ducking out of the line of fire: 94. The Prologue's famous conclusion, "Ernst ist das Leben, heiter ist die Kunst", is echoed by →Crown Prince Wilhelm, the Death's Head Hussar, in the Epilogue: "in German a bard can make anything rhyme, for if duty is harsh, art is sublime": 563.

SCHILLER'S VERSE:

II, 10: "After the war they'll toll no more"—with church bells melted down for armaments, a negation of "*Friede* sei ihr erst Geläute", the last line of "Das Lied von der Glocke" (1799), when the newly cast bell shall toll for peace: 190;
III, 41: "This photograph . . . is taken from the rogues' gallery of world history and at the Final Judgment . . ."—cf. "Die Weltgeschichte ist das Weltgericht" in "Resignation" (1786); in his versified autobiography (IV, 31) →Franz Joseph is also granted the insight that the history of the world is the Final Judgment on his reign: 308;
IV, 27: "Why are the people running . . . [The Kaiser is coming]"—"Der Kampf mit dem Drachen" (1798): 370;
IV, 27: "Hot from his brow, the sweat is running now"—cf. first stanza of "Das Lied von der Glocke": 371;
IV, 36: "Noble friend!"—"Der Antritt des neuen Jahrhunderts" (1801)—laments lost "liberty" after Napoleon's victory over Austrians at Marengo and Britain's maritime expansion: 402f;
V, 16: "That's where women become hyenas!"—"Da werden Weiber zu Hyänen!" in "Das Lied von der Glocke"—Schiller, erstwhile enthusiast and honorary French "citoyen", probably had the "tricoteuses" at the guillotine in mind; Kraus's Grumbler targets suffragettes and female war correspondents; only the master forger of the bell in Schiller's ballad knows when to break the mould, otherwise the molten flow causes havoc: 444;
Epilogue: "For Death is a master that hails from Berlin . . . the proof of our weapons will be in the pudding!"—Dr. Abendrot's conversion of church bells into weapons of mass destruction again perverts the expertise of the "Meister" craftsman in "Das Lied von der Glocke" and prefigures (in our version) a haunting line from Paul Celan's "Todesfuge": 565.

SCHLEIERMACHER, Friedrich (1768–1834), German theologian: 356.
SCHLEYER, Baron Leopold di Pontemalghera (1858–1920), general, deputy minister of war (1915): 225.
SCHNEIDER-CREUSOT, largest French armaments factory, situated at Le Creusot in Burgundy: 511.
SCHNEIDER-DUNCKER, Paul (1883–1956), founder (with composer Rudolf Nelson) of the cabaret Roland von Berlin (1904), and Bonbonniere nightclub on Kurfürstendamm (1915–24): 437.

SCHÖNBORN, probably Karl (1869–1932), chamberlain, member of Upper House: 121.

SCHÖNBRUNN, imperial palace and park in →Hietzing, south-west of city centre, associated in the popular imagination with →Franz Joseph: 289, 313, 376, 390ff.

SCHÖNEBERG, district of Berlin with lively nightlife: 174.

SCHÖNPFLUG, Fritz (1873–1951), celebrated caricaturist, founder of →*Muskete*; his facetiously militaristic cartoons featuring army officers form a leitmotif in the play that can be traced back to *Die Fackel* of December 1912, where the "Let's go along to →Hopfner's" dialogue originates (F 363–65, 72). During the war Schönpflug saw active service on the →Serbian and Italian fronts as a territorial army officer in the Tiroler Landsturm Nr. 1, being decorated for bravery and promoted to the rank of captain. In 1918 he was transferred to the →War Press Bureau in Vienna, where his duties included designing modern uniforms and creating posters to warn people about air raids. Military service prevented him from contributing to the *Muskete* during the war, but his popular cartoons continued to circulate as picture postcards: xii, xiv, xvii, 30, 48, 110, 171, 185, 240, 318, 374f, 418, 485.

SCHOPENHAUER, Arthur (1788–1860), anglophile German philosopher (*The World as Will and Representation*, 1819), his thoroughgoing pessimism a major cultural influence in fin-de-siècle Britain and Europe (see, e.g., Allan Janik and Stephen Toulmin, *Wittgenstein's Vienna* [New York: Simon and Schuster, 1973]): 149, 248, 264, 292.

SCHOTTENRING (Plan B2/C1): 209.

SCHRAMMEL QUARTET, popular Viennese ensemble (violins, guitar, clarinet or accordion), originated with Johann Schrammel (1850–1893) and brother Josef (1852–1895) playing at "Heurigen" (new vintage wine taverns). The Prussian colonel who confuses Egon Schubert, author of →"My Brown Isonzo Lassie", with "the immortal Schubert" ("Schwammerl–Schrammel": 537) clearly knew of the 1912 bestseller *Schwammerl* ("Mushroom"—Franz Schubert's nickname) by Rudolf Hans Bartsch and/or the biographical novel's 1915 adaptation as operetta, *Das Dreimäderlhaus*, music by Heinrich Berté, libretto by Heinz Reichert and Alfred Maria Willner: 537.

SCHRATT, Katharina (Kathi) (1855–1940), actress at →Hofburgtheater (1883–1900), →Franz Joseph's close companion: 390, 393.

SCHWAB, Charles Michael (1862–1939), president of Bethlehem Steel Corporation, United States: 191.

SCHWARZGELBE KREUZ, das ("Black-and-Yellow Cross"), buttonhole insignia of War Welfare charity, →Bienerth, →Schalek, →Löwy: 445.

SCHWARZ-GELBER, symbolic name for patriotic Jewish social climber (black and yellow being the colours of the imperial Austrian flag): 42, 45, 180f, 232ff, 506f.

SCUTARI (Kotor, Map F5), in north-western Albania, occupied by Austrians (January 1916), taken by Serbs (October 1918): 412.

SEE IT THROUGH ("hold out to the bitter end"), slogan transformed into satirical leitmotif; cf. directive of the War Press Bureau in Berlin (March 1917) which prohibited questioning of Germany's ability to "see it through economically" (wirtschaftliches Durchhalten): 118, 237, 297, 300, 303, 310, 329, 331, 374, 402, 414, 454f, 472, 488, 503, 513, 517ff, 550.

SEIDLER, Ernst von Feuchtenegg (1862–1931), Austrian prime minister (June 1917–July 1918): 446.

SEMMERING (Map E3), Alpine pass and fashionable thermal spa in Lower Austria, on first mountain railway line, Vienna-Graz: 182f, 352ff.

SEPARATE PEACE. As agreed within the →Entente, no such treaty was negotiated by the tsar even after Russia lost →Galicia, Poland, and Courland in 1915. There were secret negotiations in 1917—Britain and France unsuccessfully tried to separate Austria from Germany; Germany sounded out Russia (armistice in December 1917, →Brest-Litovsk in March 1918)—but Austria, focused on retaining territorial integrity, did not negotiate with Russia independently as predicted by the →*Neue Freie Presse* and regurgitated by Biach (IV, 26): xviii, 367, 429.

SERBIA (Map F5) achieved sovereignty at Congress of Berlin (1878). Its pro-Russian policy under King Peter I (1903–21), aiming to liberate South Slavs of Austro-Hungarian Empire, was exacerbated by Austrian annexation of →Bosnia-Herzegovina (1908) and strengthened by victories over Turkey and Bulgaria in Balkan wars (1912–13). Unacceptable terms of Austrian ultimatum led to war. Initial success (1914–15) until overrun by united Central Powers (1915–16): x, xi, xiv, xvii, 31, 32, 47, 49, 55, 57, 62ff, 67, 69, 87, 214f, 242, 283, 307, 308, 315, 346, 357, 366, 388, 420, 500, 510, 520, 527, 532, 542f, 546, 592.

SETTE COMUNI, →Asiago.

SHAKESPEAREAN ALLUSIONS:

Preface: "Horatio's message to the forces of renewal" from *Hamlet*, Act V, scene 2: 2, 516;

I, 55: "sicklied o'er with the pale cast of thought" from *Hamlet*, Act III, scene 1: 55;

I, 29: "Shakespeare is, after all, an enemy author"; but the Schlegel-Tieck translation had so familiarized Germans with his work that lines from the great plays figured prominently in popular culture: 158;

II, 33: "Caviar for the People": "Kaviar für's Volk", the phrase used in the Schlegel-Tieck version for "caviar to the general", from *Hamlet*, Act II, scene 2: 235;

III, 41: "My tables—meet it is that I should set it down that one may smile, and smile, and be a general", adapted from *Hamlet*, Act I, scene, 5: 309;

IV, 29: "the rest would be silence", echoing Hamlet's final words from Act V, scene 2: 379;

V, 2: "O gods! Who is't can say 'It is at the worst?'/It is worse than e'er it was", from *King Lear*, Act IV, scene, 1: 420;

V, 2: "This was sometime a paradox, but now the grandeur of the age gives it proof", adapted from *Hamlet*, Act III, scene 1: 420;

Epilogue: "Methinks I scent the morning air" from the Ghost's speech in *Hamlet*, Act I, scene 5: 575.

SUKFÜLL, Karl (b. 1862), honorary president of Austro-Hungarian Association of Hoteliers: 44, 507.
SYRMIA (Srem), part of autonomous Croatia-Slavonia, north-east of Belgrade (Map F4) between rivers →Save and Danube, contested by Serbs and Austrians in September 1914: 388.
SZEPS, Moritz (1833–1902), founder and editor of liberal →*Neues Wiener Tagblatt* (1887–1910), father-in-law of →Clemenceau: 124, 485.
SZÖGÝENY-MARÎCH, Count Ladislaus (1841–1916), ambassador in Berlin (1892–1914), friend of →Wilhelm II: 255, 346f.
SZOMORY, Emil (1874–1944), Hungarian war correspondent: 46, 118.

TAAFFE, Countess Maria Magda von (1871–1918), daughter-in-law of former prime minister Count Eduard Taaffe, military hospital matron in Prague, inventor of game "Death to Russians" ("Russentod"): 348.
TABARIN, nightclub in Annagasse (Plan C4): 469.
TAGBLATT, *Neues Wiener*, influential daily with democratic credentials: 31, 49, 74, 77, 124f, 240, 319.
TANNENBERG (Map F1), Battle of, name given to →Paul von Hindenburg's decisive victory over the Russian Second Army in East Prussia (August 1914): 172.
TARNOPOL (Map G3), →Galicia, occupied by Russians (August 1914), retaken by Central Powers (July 1917): 357.
TARNÓW, Polish town north of Gorlice. See Battle of →Gorlice-Tarnów: 129.
TECHNICAL UNIVERSITY (Technische Hochschule, Plan C5): 430.
TEGETTHOFF, Baron Wilhelm von (1827–1871), commander of Austrian navy in Mediterranean (1866–71), victor over Italian fleet at Lissa (1866): 43, 104.
TEISINGER, Joseph Teisinger von Tüllenberg (1856–1920), general notorious for ruthless approach to recruitment for front-line service: 315.
TEMES-KUBIN (Kovin/Kevevara), on frontier with Serbia north-east of Belgrade (Map F4). An alleged exchange of fire on 27 July 1914 provided Austria with a pretext for military intervention: 63.
TERSZTSZYÁNSKY, Karl von Nádas (1854–1921), general, commander of Balkan forces (May 1915), commander in Volhynia (June 1916, Map G2): 530.
TESCHEN (Map F3), Silesia, →headquarters of Austro-Hungarian army (November 1914–January 1917), whose commander in chief, →Archduke Friedrich, was Duke of Teschen: 113.
THALLER, Willi (1854–1941), popular actor: 490.
"THAT LOVELY DANCE OF YORE, THEY WON'T PLAY IT ANYMORE" ("Schön war der Tanz, aber spieln tan s' 'n net"), Viennese song, music by Ludwig Prechtl (1865–1931) and lyrics by Franz Allmeder (1872–1941): 535.
THEATER AN DER WIEN (Plan B5), famous operetta theatre; opened by Mozart's collaborator Emanuel Schikaneder, home to Beethoven while writing *Fidelio*, which was premiered there: 54, 489.

THEATER IN DER JOSEFSTADT, to west of Rathaus (Plan A2), Vienna's second-oldest theatre, opened in 1788; presented drama, folk plays, and operettas during the war: 54, 183.
"THE CALL GOES OUT, A THUND'ROUS ROAR" ("Es braust ein Ruf wie Donnerhall") →"Watch on the Rhine".
"THE DEAR OLD GENTLEMAN" →"Draussen im Schönbrunner Park".
"THE END OF THE WORLD IS NIGH, SO MORE CHAMPAGNE, I'M DRY" ("Nobel geht die Welt zugrunde"), duet (1910) by Franz Allmeder (1872–1941): 535.
"THEY'RE SURELY VILLAINS WHO DON'T CARE" music (probably) by Otto Janowitz (1888–1965)—its nursery rhyme simplicity in sharp contrast to the sentiments expressed (III, 40): 293.
THIS IS NOT WHAT I INTENDED ("Ich habe es nicht gewollt"), utterance attributed to Wilhelm II in 1915 when surveying carnage on the Western Front; transformed by Kraus into an ironic leitmotif: 302, 307, 378, 588.
THURY, Max von Thurybrugg (1841–1919), industrialist: 236, 399.
TIBUR, Ben (1867–1925), proprietor and director of →Apollo variety and operetta theatre; from 1910 also director of Lunapark in →Prater. His employees avoided military service (F 437–42, 1916, 108): 251.
TIRPITZ, Alfred von (1849–1930), German admiral responsible for expansion of the fleet and intensification of →U-boat warfare: 305.
TISZA, István Tisza de Borosjenő et Szeged (1861–1918), Hungarian prime minister (1913–17), initially opposed to the war, subsequently prominent in war party, shot by mutinous soldiers: 38, 431.
TITUS (IV, 37) "Amor et delicatiae humani generis", from Suetonius, "In Praise of [Emperor] Titus": 406.
TOLMINO (Tolmein), Austro-Hungarian bridgehead south-east of →Caporetto (Map D4), where poison gas was used during twelfth battle of Isonzo (24 October 1918): 536f.
"TONIGHT I'M FEELIN FUDDLED" ("Heut hab i schon mei Fahn'l/Heut is ma alles ans,/Da habt's sa's s'letzte Kranl/und spielt's ma no paar Tanz"), song, music by Johann Sioly (1843–1911) and lyrics by Josef Hornig (1861–1911): 315, 524.
TO THE LAST BREATH OF MAN AND HORSE, from the Kaiser's address "To the German People" (6 August 1914): 252, 259, 420, 517, 542.
"TO WANDER IS THE MILLER'S JOY" ("Das Wandern ist des Müllers Lust", 1817), song, music by Karl Friedrich Zöllner (1800–1860) and text by Wilhelm Müller (1794–1827): 75.
TRAUTMANNSDORFF, "Tutu", Count Maximilian von Trautmanndorff-Weinsberg (b. 1880), or possibly his father Count Maximilian (1842–1924), chamberlain: 124.
TREBITSCH, Siegfried (1869–1956), prolific writer, translator of George Bernard Shaw: 238.
TREUMANN, Louis (1872–1943), operetta singer, first Count Danilo in →Franz Lehár's *The Merry Widow*: 30, 131.
"TRUE AND HONEST EVER BE" ("Üb immer Treu und Redlichkeit"), popular song, music by Mozart, lyrics after Ludwig Christoph Heinrich Hölty: 75.

VALHALLA, in Norse mythology and Wagner, home of gods and heroic dead warriors who will rise again to fight final battle; also Leo von Klenze's doric "Temple of German honour" overlooking the Danube near Regensburg (1830–42): 235, 294.
VARADY, Emil, singer, dancer, comic at →Gartenbau: 534.
VENEDIG IN WIEN ("Venice in Vienna"), a pioneering theme park in →Prater with fake palazzos, canals, and gondolas, designed by the architect Oskar Marmorek in 1895: 31, 38, 241.
VENICE (Map D4), bombed by Austrian naval airmen immediately after Italian declaration of war (23 May 1915): 228, 240f, 244.
VERDUN (Map B3), Battle of (February–December 1916), after initial attack under German →Crown Prince Wilhelm, the French recovered and the resulting stalemate led to heavy losses: 182, 358, 439f, 563.
VIENNESE HANGMAN →Josef Lang.
VILLACH, Carinthia, west of Klagenfurt (Map D4) on River Drava/Drau, close to border with Italy: 115, 245.
VLADIMIR-VOLINSKI (Map G2), main town of Volhynia, important railway junction, strongly defended by Russians (August 1914), taken by Central Powers (late summer 1915): 416.
VOLKSGARTEN (Plan A3/B3), restaurant in garden of that name on Franzensring: 32.
VOLKSTHEATER, Deutsches (Plan A4), founded in 1889 as popular counterweight to →Hofburgtheater; staged such theatrical scandals as →Hans Müller's *Die Dirne* (about a prostitute): 32, 211, 471f.
VORWÄRTS, central organ of German Social Democratic party: 461.
VOSSISCHE ZEITUNG ("*Voss*", "*Tante* [Aunt] *Voss*"), influential Liberal Berlin daily (published by Ullstein): 461.

WAHNSCHAFFE, symbolic name for German super-patriot ("creator of mad delusions"): 293ff, 347ff.
WAHRHEIT, nationalistic Berlin weekly (1905–35): 461.
WALDE, Gerda (1882–1928), popular operetta soubrette and actress, m. →Nikolai von Wassilko (1919): 59, 219, 469.
WALDSTÄTTEN, Baron Alfred von (1872–1952), chief of staff of First Army (1914), chief of operations in High Command (March 1917): 482.
WALTERSKIRCHEN zu WOLFSTHAL, Count Hubert (1871–1916), major, killed during fighting in the Dolomites: 118.
WALZERTRAUM, *Ein*, operetta (1907), music by Oscar Straus (1870–1954), libretto by →Felix Dörmann (1870–1928) and Leopold Jacobson (1878–1942); with →Fritz Werner in role of Niki, rivalled *The Merry Widow* in popularity: 483.
WANGLE IT (sich's richten), leitmotif: to escape military service by bribery or "connections": 48, 81, 168, 183, 196, 235, 277, 377, 469, 568.
WAR ARCHIVE (Kriegsarchiv), refuge for many men of letters (→Hans Müller,

Rainer Maria Rilke), their primary task being to assess applications for military honours and celebrate some suitably stirring wartime exploit: 186, 251, 253ff, 385, 568.

WAR MINISTRY, by 1914 no longer in Am Hof (Plan C2/C3), as marked on our 1905 city plan, but a grandiose new building (the "Sündenburg" mocked by Kraus) on Stubenring beside the Zollamtsbrücke (Plan E3): 53, 89f, 111, 119ff, 217, 223ff, 241, 277f, 310f, 403, 418f, 423, 449, 458, 595.

WAR PRESS BUREAU (Kriegspressequartier), founded in July 1914 under the command of Maximilian von Hoen, with a staff of over 500 operating in variable locations; employed writers and artists charged with boosting patriotism and countering enemy propaganda. Military communiqués issued through →Field Marshal Höfer: 68, 85, 114, 116, 117, 120, 140f, 149, 161f, 178, 200, 216f, 227f, 243, 264, 284, 297, 354, 372, 414ff, 444f, 491, 556ff.

WARSAW (Map F2), Russian onslaught and German retreat (9–19 October 1914); city taken by Central Powers in great offensive (1 July 1915); seat of German General Gouvernement (August 1915, →Andrian): 176f, 197.

WASSILKO, Nikolai von (1868–1924), member of parliament representing →Bukovina (Map G3); ambassador for Western Ukrainian Republic (1919); m. →Gerda Walde: 469.

"WATCH ON THE RHINE", The ("Die Wacht am Rhein"), patriotic song vowing defence against French claims to river as frontier, and proclaiming reassurance that the Fatherland can rest in peace; music (1854) by Karl Wilhelm (1815–1873) to text (1840) by Max Schneckenburger (1819–1849); German national anthem after 1870–71: "Es braust ein Ruf wie Donnerhall/Wie Schwertgeklirr und Wogenprall:/Zum Rhein, zum Rhein, zum deutschen Rhein!/Wer will des Stromes Hüter sein? [Refrain:] Lieb' Vaterland magst ruhig sein,/Fest steht und treu die Wacht am Rhein!" 52, 54, 121, 124, 199, 267, 294, 297f, 313, 333, 462, 466, 525, 566, 588, 592f.

WEDDINGEN, Otto (1882–1915), captain of →U-boat that sank three British armoured cruisers in a single day in 1914: 194.

WEIKERSHEIM, Prince Karl Ernst Bronn von (1862–1925), general, intimate of →Franz Ferdinand and his intended Comptroller of Imperial Household: 38, 40, 41.

WEISKIRCHNER, Richard (1861–1926), Christian Social politician, minister of commerce (1909–11), mayor of Vienna (1912–19): 56, 57, 78, 175, 222, 235, 497, 531.

WEKERLE, Alexander (1841–1921), successor to →István Tisza as Hungarian prime minister (August 1917–October 1918): 430f.

WELT AM MONTAG, independent, republican-leaning Berlin weekly for politics and culture: 461.

WERFEL, Franz (1890–1945), Expressionist poet, proclaiming universal brotherhood, later dramatist and novelist; on Eastern Front (1916–17), then in →War Press Bureau (1917); delivered propaganda lectures: 252.

WERNER, Fritz (1871–1927), celebrated operetta singer (star of →*Walzertraum*): 30, 32, 58, 237, 482, 484, 493.

WERTHEIM, Berlin department store: 425, 461.

WINDISCHGRÄTZ, "Bubi", son [?] of →Prince Alfred von Windischgrätz: 122, 527.
WINDISCHGRÄTZ, Prince Alfred von (1851–1927), leading conservative statesman, prime minister (1893–95), president of Austrian Upper House (1897–1918): 56, 497.
WOCHE, *Die* (The Week), Berlin illustrated weekly (from 1899): 126, 130f, 307, 461.
WOCHEINER-FEISTRITZ, on Trieste-Villach railway line along →Isonzo River: 529.
WOHLGEMUTH, Else (1881–1972), Countess Thun, →Hofburgtheater actress (from 1910): 399.
WOHTE, Anny (1858–1919), prolific author of light novels aimed at keeping spirits up during war. Quotation from *Die Vogesenwacht* (Watch on the Vosges, 1915): 126, 300.
WOLFFBÜRO, official German news agency: 258, 295, 306, 333, 436, 501f.
WOLF IN GERSTHOF, wine restaurant in north-western part of city, with musical entertainment, named after proprietor Franz Wolf, providing a symbol for mindless Austrian hedonism: 37, 38, 164ff, 219, 488.
WORDSWORTH, William (1770–1850), English nature poet whose "I Wandered Lonely as a Cloud" appeared in *Poems* (1807): 373f, 593.
"WOTSA MATTER, HONEYBABY?" ("Ach Puppe sei nicht so neutral!"), duet from operetta *Wenn zwei Hochzeit machen* (1915), music by Walter Kollo (1878–1940), libretto by Rudolf Bernauer (1880–1953) and Rudolf Schanzer (1875–1944): 401.
WURMBRAND ("Putzo"), possibly Count Friedrich Karl Eugen (1865–1938), privy councillor, Master of the Household to →Archduchess Maria Annunziata: 63.
WYDENBRUCK, Countess Mysa von (1859–1926), prominent in charity work: 234.

ZAGORSKI, Stanislaus von (b. 1872), military judge (1914–17), authorized the executions recorded in IV, 30, which actually took place on 18 October 1914 in the Ukrainian village of Synowidzka Wyzna (see Holzer, *Das Lächeln der Henker*, pp. 33–35): 386ff.
ZAUNER'S, tearoom in →Bad Ischl: 399.
ZEIT, *Die*, liberal Viennese daily: 489, 492.
ZEMUN (Semlin), on the left bank of the →River Save, opposite →Belgrade. The destruction by Serbian troops of the railway bridge between Zemun and Belgrade on 27 July 1914 marked the onset of hostilities between Austria-Hungary and →Serbia: 57.
ZEPPELIN, Count Ferdinand (1838–1917), German officer and airship pioneer: 164, 301.
ZITA, (1892–1989), Archduchess (1911–16), Empress (1916–18): 275ff.
ZOIS, Baron Michelangelo von Edelstein (1874–1945), writer, editor of *Kriegsjournal* (War Journal) of Tenth Austro-Hungarian Army, its pamphlet anthologies distributed to all fronts: 246.
ZUNTZ, Nathan (1847–1920), professor of physiology, Berlin: 330, 332.

European battle zones of the First World War

E
F
G
H
BALTIC SEA
Memel
Tilsit
Königsberg
Danzig
EAST PRUSSIA
Masurian Lakes
Tannenberg
Vilnius
Minsk
N
Grodno
Bialystok
Rozan
RUSSIAN EMPIRE
Vistula
Posen
Warsaw
Brest-Litovsk
Oder
Lódz
Ivangorod
Lublin
Breslau
Vladimir-Volinsky
Lutsk
Kiev
VOLHYNIA
Brody
Olmütz
Cracow
Przemysl
Lemberg
GALICIA
Teschen
Gorlice
San
Tarnopol
CARPATHIANS
Stanislau
Uszieczko
Dniester
TRO-HUNGARIAN EMPIRE
Czernowitz
BUKOVINA
Bratislava
Danube
Debrecen
Budapest
Kecskemet
Klausenburg
Drava
Hermannstadt
Kronstadt
Galati
Timisoara
ROATIA
ROMANIA
Belgrade
Temes-Kubin
Bucharest
Chabatz
BOSNIA-HERZEGOVINA
Kragujevac
Danube
Sarajevo
LMATIA
SERBIA
Mitrovica
Sofia
BULGARIA
Cetinje
Kotor
Skopje
ATIC SEA
ALBANIA
Constantinople
Durazzo
Monastir

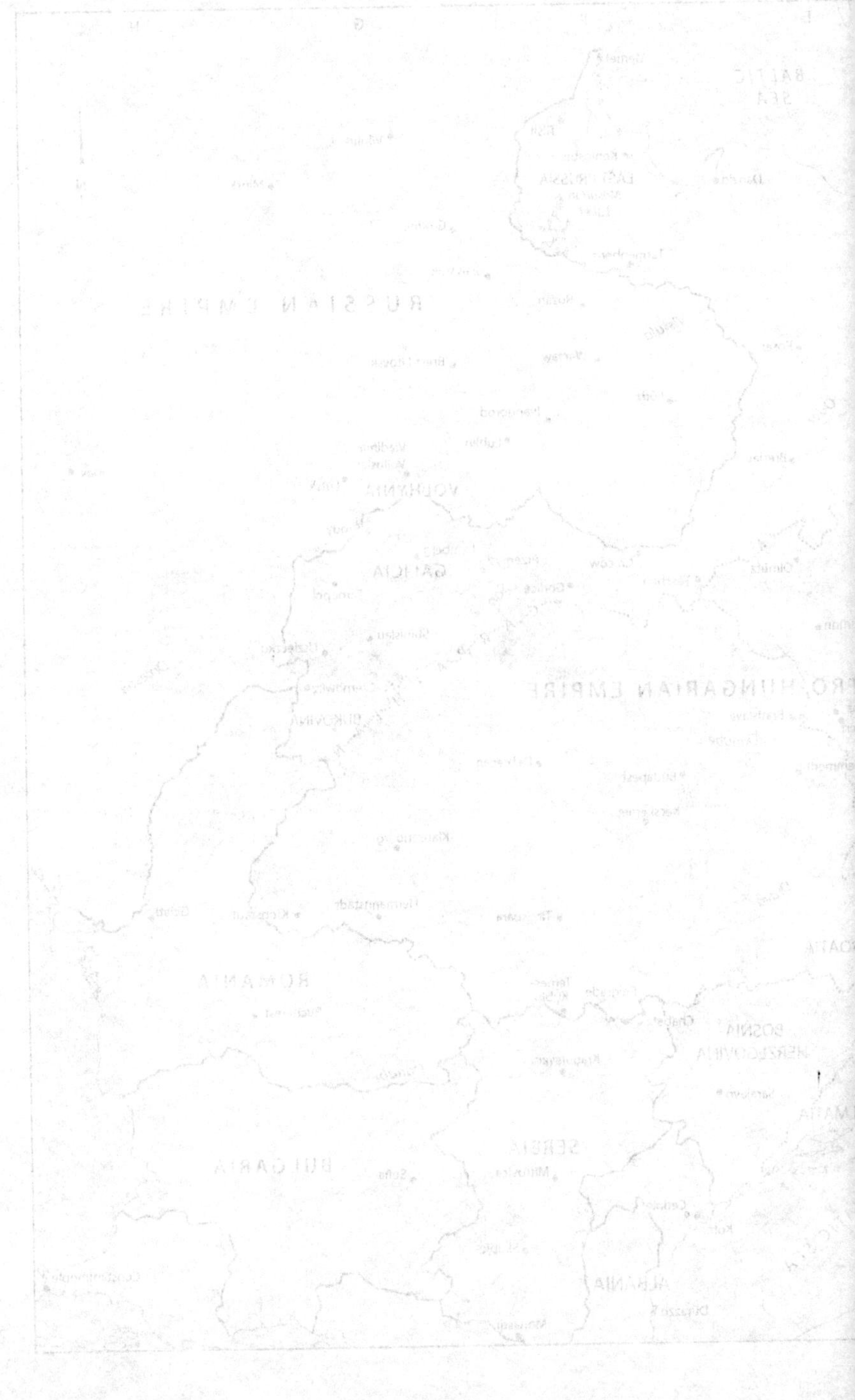

The Austrian Jewish author KARL KRAUS (1874–1936) was the foremost German-language satirist of the twentieth century. As editor of the journal *Die Fackel* (*The Torch*) he conducted a sustained critique of propaganda and the press, expressed through polemical essays, satirical plays, pungent aphorisms, and resonant poems.

EDWARD TIMMS, founding director of the University of Sussex Centre for German-Jewish Studies, is best known for his two-volume study *Karl Kraus—Apocalyptic Satirist*. The title of his memoirs, *Taking Up the Torch*, reflects his long-standing interest in Kraus's journal.

FRED BRIDGHAM is the author of wide-ranging studies in German literature, history, and the history of ideas. His translations of lieder and opera include Hans Werner Henze's *The Prince of Homburg* for performance by English National Opera.